A Novel

Imperfectly Perfect
Vengeance & Mercy

B. Montgomery

ISBN: 978-1-7365667-8-7 (Paperback)
ISBN: (Hardcover)

Cover design by: Author using Canva App
Other Images: Canva App and Microsoft Word
Drawings: Brianne Maijala
Library of Congress Control Number: TXu002254171
Printed in the United States of America

To my beautiful daughters who keep me on this journey...

To all those who have read these books:
you all make writing fun!

"Fear thou not; for I *am* with thee: be not dismayed; for I *am* thy God: I will strengthen thee; yea, I will help thee; yea, I will uphold thee with the right hand of my righteousness." ˜ Isaiah 41:10

"*I need you* to keep your faith! *Please.* I want this woman dead, just as much as the next person, but it needs to fall together like it was meant to, or it could fall apart and Millicent could win!"
˜ David to BriaLynn

Imperfectly Perfect Vengeance & Mercy

INTRODUCTION TO BOOK 3

The Imperfectly Perfect Alternate World

This fictional world takes place mostly in *The United Kingdom of Provinces*, along with fictional duchies. This 'UK' is ruled by a monarchy, but a parliament running the government with the voice of the people *at the leisure of The King*. Which means The King or The Queen can override anything, at any time, passed by The Parliament; a power rarely used.

They manage to convince BriaLynn to become The Queen, and when she is coronated, they hope it will unite her with the people. BriaLynn will need this support, because she will have the biggest and longest trial of her life! Millicent is coming after BriaLynn and BriaLynn has to come to terms with the fact that the only way for her and her family to live peacefully is if Millicent dies. She has an idea of what is awaiting Millicent on the other side, and ultimately for The Duke of Devonridge. While there are souls that aren't as lost as one might think, there are those who can't be helped unless they help themselves.

CHAPTER 1

And So It Begins...

BriaLynn Worthington is on The Royal Jet going to Washington, D.C. with David, Lawrence, Jack, Peter, and Carlotta. Right before they boarded their flight, McMasters and Mitchell discussed increased security measures in the UK and in DC with the family. They needed to build a wall of protection around Natty first and they started by asking DCPD detectives and family friends, Ken Thompson and Bill Barker, who were already at the hospital, to start arranging that piece. Ken and Bill had put some security measures in place earlier, but they will work with McMasters to fortify everything with multiple agencies before Bri and the family arrive in DC.

McMasters and Mitchell knew they couldn't effectively organize all the security measures in flight, so McMasters volunteered to stay behind and sent Mitchell, along with The King's Guard and some of The Royal Guard, to DC with everyone. Mitchell made a few phone calls from the plane to specific Secret Service agents and FBI agents for additional protection within the motorcade and their security detail, once they land in DC. Lawrence asked his father, Phillip, to return to The London Palace with McMasters to help him coordinate everything, then the two of them will fly to DC once it is all in place.

Bri stares out the window replaying Emmie's spirit telling her, '*Mom, you need to get to Natty at Riverside Hospital* right now!' After Emmie disappeared, Henry called and she remembers how emotional he was, but he managed to talk calmly with her. '*All we know is they've been poisoned and the police suspect foul play. They asked if we knew anyone who would want to harm them? I couldn't think of anyone who would want to hurt children!*' Bri didn't have to think about it. '*Millicent.*' She told him. She explained that, if she were evil and wanted to hurt someone she considered an enemy, she would torture them by killing those the enemy cares about the most; usually that is someone's children, then their spouse or significant other, working out to their parents, siblings, and so on.

Bri takes a deep breath, bringing herself back to the present and she begins to fidget in her seat. It feels like the flight to DC is taking longer than usual. Her frustration boils to the surface, and she shoots up out of her seat.

"This is The Royal JET for heaven's sake!" She starts to pace, saying, "*Can't this plane go any faster!*"

"We're going as fast as we can." David stands up and walks over to her. "Come sit and eat a little something. You need to keep up your strength."

"*Don't.*" She steps back, putting her hands up in a stopping motion. "If I eat, I'll throw up!" She looks towards the windows with longing and whispers, "*I just need to get to my Natty!*"

"I know, Love. Herst has arranged an emergency clearance for us to get there sooner than we normally would, but it will still take time." He steps closer to hug her.

"No, David!" She takes another step back. "I have to stay strong, so if you hug me right now, I'll *completely* fall apart!"

"That's okay!" He urges her.

"NO. *IT'S NOT!*" She snaps.

"Yes, it is!" He rebuts.

"*STOP THAT!*" She angrily tells him.

"No, Love!" He gestures to the plane. "*Now is the perfect time to get some of this out!*" He pushes back. "*Get angry, Bri! I'm angry! Hell, we're ALL angry!*" He waves his hand towards the others.

She frowns at him and says with exasperation in her voice, "Then you don't understand, *Mister* Worthington. I'm angry *with you!*"

"No, you're not." He asserts. "You just *need* to be angry with me, because you don't want to face the truth!"

"*Oh?*" She frowns. "Then tell me," she folds her arms asking, "what *truth* am I missing here, because it sure feels like I'm swimming in a whole *nightmare* of truth?!"

"*But you're NOT swimming!*" David pushes more. "*You're holding your breath under that water and if you don't come to the surface to deal with what has already happened to Emmie, you're going to drown!*" She glares at him, but he continues, "*You won't be able to help Natty until you* start *dealing with what has already happened to Emmie!*"

"*LEAVE ME ALONE!*" She snaps.

7

"NO!" He firmly replies. "BRIALYNN!" He takes hold of her upper arms. *"EMMIE IS DEAD!"*

"STOP IT, DAVID!" She slaps her hands against his chest and shoves him away, hard enough that he has to step his foot back, to keep his balance. "WE'RE *NOT* DOING THIS!" She goes to turn away from him, but he doesn't let her.

He keeps hold of her upper arms. *"You have to deal with this!"* She turns her head away, closing her eyes and holds them closed; she knows he is right. He lightly shakes her to get her attention again. "If you keep it all in, it won't be good for Natty, *or the baby!"*

"I CAN'T!" She angrily hits his chest with the sides of her fists. "I DON'T *WANT* TO ACCEPT *ANY OF THIS!"* She inhales sharply as she loses control and her grief overcomes her. She drops her head down and cries, "THIS *CAN'T* BE HAPPENING! *THIS CAN'T BE THE PRICE FOR CHOOSING TO COME BACK?! They would be alive if I hadn't come back!"* Her hands tightly grip David's shirt as she locks her arms straight out. "OH GOD, PLEASE—!" She inhales a gasp, then angrily exhales, *"Millicent!"* Her voice takes an irritated tone, "She threatened Seth's and Abby's lives *all these years*, but never followed through! *Why kill innocent children now?!"* She has a horrified look come over her face and sobs, *"WHAT HAVE I DONE?!"* She tries to push David away again; except he pulls her to him and wraps his arms around her. She halfway collapses in his arms, and he holds her up as she sorrowfully exhales, "OH, EMMIEEE..." she mourns, *"I've lost my Emmie...Oh, God, please don't make me lose my Natty, too!"* She inhales deeply and cries so hard, she is silent. David holds her tighter; his own tears skipping down his cheeks.

Everyone watching and hearing this throughout the plane isn't immune to the heart wrenching cries of a grieving mother's sorrow. Peter and Carlotta are crying as they console each other, while Jack and Lawrence have tears streaming down their own cheeks walking over to hug Bri as she weeps in David's arms.

After a few minutes, Lawrence scoops her up and they take her to the bedroom in back. He lays down with her and hugs her firmly close, the way she likes him to, as she continues to grieve one daughter, and the *looming* reality she will lose her other daughter. Eventually, she cries herself to sleep. David is sitting in a chair at the small desk, while Jack is sitting on the corner of the bed. The three men reeling from Bri's emotional state and feeling powerless to help her.

The plane lands at a military base in the DC area. The door is opened, and everyone makes their way off the plane, except Bri and Lawrence; protocol has them paired up. He walks up to her with an apologetic look.

She shakes her head. "Lawrence, I don't blame you for *any of this*! *Millicent* is responsible for her *own* choices; she did *not* have to do this! If anyone else is to blame, it would be me. *I knew* she would retaliate for revealing her secret, *I just didn't think*—." She chokes up and holds her breath for a moment. She swallows, then whispers, "*Will you take me to my Natty?*" He gives her a loving, compassionate nod as he hands her a tissue to wipe her eyes.

He takes her hand and holds it firmly as he tucks her arm up under his own arm. She always feels safe when he does this, *protected*, and it's comforting now for her. They step off the plane and descend the stairs together, then walk over to the SUV that is for them and climb inside; David and Jack are already sitting in the back seat.

Their motorcade leaves the tarmac with lights and sirens. Bri stares out the window watching the familiar city rush by. She starts to feel lightheaded and nauseous, so she closes her eyes and tips her head back to rest against the headrest. She does this until the feeling goes away, which takes most of the ride to the hospital.

Law enforcement has the streets near, and up to, the hospital blocked, allowing only their motorcade through; all ambulances are temporarily rerouted to nearby hospitals. They have all the doors around the hospital locked and guarded; the sidewalks next to the hospital are blocked; and snipers are on surrounding rooftops. Bri's phone chimes, startling her a bit; it's a text message from Joe.

> Joe: "Your 'other family' has arrived. They are not allowed to go upstairs yet, and we've heard your mother is NOT happy! Maybe you should avoid using the main entrance?"

> Bri: "Thanks for letting me know. I will ask Mitchell about getting us into the hospital a different way."

She takes a screenshot of Joe's message and sends it to Mitchell who is in the front seat. He turns to look at her and tells her it won't take much to change to a different entrance.

"In fact," Mitchell says, "it can be good to have a last-minute change like this. It's unexpected and easy to adjust with the security we already have in place."

When the motorcade pulls up to a side entrance of the hospital, the family gets out of the SUVs and the crowds behind the barriers start yelling. Bri can't make out what they are saying...it could be that they are too far away, or because she is focused on getting to Natty; *maybe both*. Everyone goes inside the hospital where they are met by various staff and introduced to them. Bri can't think about anything other than getting to Natty. She tries not to get annoyed by all the people that keep coming over to meet them and offer their condolences, but all she can feel is precious time slipping away.

When she can't take it anymore, there is a hint of annoyance in her voice asking, "Will someone *please* take me to my daughter?"

"Right." Someone in scrubs replies. "Your—."

"*Your Majesties...*" The Hospital Administrator makes her way through the crowd. Bri is grateful no one takes the time to correct her on the use of 'majesties.' The Administrator takes charge. "This is Dr. Wright and this is Dr. Reeves." She gestures to the man and woman right beside her. "We will take you upstairs." They all walk to the elevators with Bri only half listening as the Administrator explains, "Dr. Reeves treated Natty when they were first brought into the emergency room..." She goes on. Bri thinks she hears somewhere that Dr. Wright is a toxicologist.

Inside the elevator, Bri does notice how small Dr. Reeves looks standing next to a tall Dr. Wright, as he explains what they did for *all of them*; from when they first arrived, up until they figured out, they were all poisoned with crimson powder. This is when Bri realizes *Jeff and Olivia were also poisoned!* The dinging of the elevator interrupts them. They step off the elevator and into a dark hallway that is eerily quiet; the only light coming from the nurses' station. There are no other patients on this floor; it's only Natty.

The Bradshaw family, along with James and Amy, have been waiting for them outside Natty's room. They all hug each other, except Bri; she is walking over to the window of Natty's room. She peers in, placing her hand on the glass and watches her daughter lying in the hospital bed, surrounded by tubes, wires, and monitors.

Bri faintly whispers to herself, "*This can't be happening...*" Her jaw shakes and tears fill her eyes, as the full weight of what has happened starts to take hold again with its suffocating, constricting grip on her heart.

She hears Dr. Wright continue to explain, "As soon as we figured out it was crimson powder poisoning, we administered the antitoxin." Bri's heart sinks knowing what Dr. Wright will say next. "Unfortunately, by the time we figured all that out, Jeff, Olivia, and Emerson, were already in the advanced stages of—." The doctor surprises himself with his own emotions and can't talk until he clears his throat. "Since Natalie didn't have as much in her system, we *had hoped* she might beat the odds..."

The doctors' voices sound like they are in a tunnel. Bri wishes this was all a nightmare she would just wake up from!

Dr. Reeves says, "*Sadly*, the antitoxin wasn't given to Natalie soon enough either."

"We have her stabilized the best we can," Dr. Wright continues, "and we have her *heavily* sedated and medicated to make her as comfortable as we possibly can." He doesn't tell her that it isn't enough for the pain. *Although*, if they were to give her anything more for the pain, they would ironically risk overdosing their already dying patient.

Bri's eyes close, and she holds them closed to brace herself for the answer to the question, "Doctors, are you telling me my daughter is going to die?"

"*Yes.*" Dr. Wright struggles to reply.

Bri turns around, her eyes completely filled with tears, looking at Henry and Maggie, shaking her head. She covers her face and cries at the now definitive, heartbreaking situation: *she will lose* both *of her daughters.* Henry pulls Bri into a fierce hug with Maggie, while the rest of the family consoles each other.

When Bri has stopped crying, she stares at the door of Natty's hospital room. She takes a slow, deep breath, trying to calm herself; only one breath doesn't work, so she takes a couple more... When she is finally able to reach out her hand to open the door, she gets a bit sick to her stomach. She pushes through the feeling and opens the door. She steps into the room and walks over to Natty with tears filling her eyes again. The doctors, along with Jack, David, Lawrence, and the family, follow her inside.

Bri picks up Natty's hand and sits on the bed beside her. "*Oh, Natty...*" Bri whispers, lovingly running her hand through her daughter's soft hair. She turns her head to ask the doctors, "How long do you think she has?"

"It's hard to say." Dr. Reeves says.

Dr. Wright tells Bri, "We weren't able to reverse the effects of the poison, so at this particular stage she might have eight hours, *maybe* twelve hours, but that would be pushing it." They still withhold how bad the pain is, and that Natty will continue suffer through to the *very* bitter end.

She is sadly looking at Natty again, realizing, "The antitoxin is actually *prolonging* her pain..."

There is no way around it now. Dr. Wright simply replies, "It is."

Everyone else has concerned expressions taking that in. They hadn't considered that the antitoxin that was given to try to *save* Natty's life, is now making her suffer in pain *longer*.

"Dr. Wright and I will step out of the room." Dr. Reeves tells Bri and the family. "If you need anything, or have any questions, we'll be right out there." She motions towards the hallway with a soft wave of her arm.

"Thank you." David says.

Jack walks them to the door and holds it open for them, thanking the doctors as they walk out. He closes the door behind them, then goes back over to where he was standing and patiently waits with everyone else.

Bri recalls what she read about crimson powder poisoning and Vivian's death. "Most victims of crimson power poisoning will bleed out internally before anyone knows what's happening to them. That's why the antitoxin is rarely, *if ever*, effective; *it's almost always too late.*" She also remembers that once internal bleeding begins, the organs are in the painful process of liquifying; however, she won't tell them all that. She goes on to say, "Crimson powder poisoning is very painful for the victims and large doses of morphine aren't enough to take the pain away..." She trails off thinking about the *excruciating pain* Natty is in and wishing there is something she could do for her daughter.

Maggie and Carlotta are finding it difficult to hold back their sobs and leave the room. The others go with them to give Bri time alone, leaving David, Lawrence, and Jack there for her support. Jack has Lawrence and David take the chairs, while he sits up on the windowsill; the three sit in silence watching Bri with Natty.

Bri notices a spirit appearing beside her and waits for Emmie to fully appear...she gasps and jumps up when she sees *it's Natty's spirit!* Bri's eyebrows scrunch together in confusion. She looks from Natty's spirit to her body, then the monitors. '*But why aren't the alarms going off?!*' She wonders.

"I-I don't understand..." Bri stumbles to say.

Lawrence, David, and Jack see Bri look from an empty space beside the monitors, then to Natty in the bed. They figure Bri is seeing Emmie's spirit; although, they don't know why she would be confused.

"What's wrong, Darling?" Lawrence asks as the three men walk closer to her.

She holds up her hand and moves the first two fingers around in a small, swift, circular movement for the men to see for themselves, while Bri studies Natty's spirit a bit more closely. She sees that Natty's spirit *mostly* looks like her, yet it is more...*wispy* compared to the other spirits and ghosts she has seen. It's like Natty's spiritual matter is still connected to her mortal body.

Bri recalls something else she had read. "I've read something not too long ago, about a person's theory of coma patients and their spirits." Bri explains, "Their theory is that *some* spirits of coma patients are still *tethered* to their mortal body. It's like their spirit can't *move on* because there is this hold, or grip, the body and spirit still have to each other; the spirit being the body's life force. This tethering could be what we are seeing with Natty's spiritual matter running from her spirit to her body..." She motions the part in between the spirit and body.

She hears one of the guys whisper, "*Incredible.*" And another, "*Amazing.*" When Emmie appears, Bri holds up her hand and moves the first two fingers around in a small, swift, circular movement again so Lawrence, Jack, and David can see her as well.

13

"Mom," Emmie steps closer to her, "this seems awful now, but I promise, it'll get—."

"*It'll get better?*" Bri skeptically asks, finishing her sentence.

Emmie gives her mom an apologetic look replying, "*In time.*"

"Oh, no, Emmie, my life will *never* be as good as it could be without my beautiful girls in it."

"Mom..." Natty points to the bed, "my spirit is still attached to my body." She grimaces in pain. "We were hoping you could help me by setting my spirit free sooner."

Bri's eyebrows come together. "Setting your..." She trails off as she looks at Natty in the bed and all the things helping her live for however long she has left. Bri's mouth falls open as it occurs to her what they mean. "*Do you have any idea what you're asking me to do?!*"

"What is she asking you to do?" Jack asks.

Bri replies looking at Natty's spirit, "Natty wants me to free her spirit, separate it from her body and thus, *end* her mortal life." She pushes down the lump that begins to form in her throat.

"You're not *ending* my mortal life, Mom! *It's already over!*" Natty points to her body. "I'm never waking up again! My physical body is slowly and *painfully* shutting down." She then points towards the door. "The doctors already told you *I'm dy*—." She grabs her abdomen again in severe pain.

Emmie tells her mom, "You can't change what's meant to be, but you *can* help Natty's life end more mercifully!"

Bri sits back down on the bed next to Natty and holds her hand again. "*Mercifully...*" She softly repeats to herself, thinking back to when she said something about that to Lawrence regarding his mother's death. How Vivian's death was very painful and it was an absolutely horrible way to die! She had told him something like, '*A swift death would've been merciful.*' Of course that is *not* what Millicent wanted, nor wants, with anyone's death; she thrives on torturing others.

Natty simply states, "I'm going to die, Mom, because I'm *supposed* to die."

"A mother is supposed to protect her children!" Bri's eyes drip more tears down her cheeks. She says with a bit of frustration, *"This goes against* everything *a mother is supposed to be!"*

"Does it?" Natty asks. "Haven't you felt helpless? Haven't you been wanting to do something to ease my pain?" Bri wipes her cheeks with her hands.

"Mom," Emmie says, and Bri looks at her, "growing up, you always thought that maybe we were so inseparable before we were born, that we just had to come into this mortal life together, and *almost* at the exact same time?" She gives a little grin. *"You were right!"* Bri watches Natty's spirit; she is slightly bent over and tightly gripping her abdomen in pain. "Dad, Olivia, and I didn't suffer as long, because we ingested more of the poison than Natty. *Please don't let Natty suffer any longer like this!"*

Bri steps away from the bed and calls out, "Jessica, will you please come see me right away?!" As Jessica appears, Bri circles her first two fingers again for the guys to see Jessica. Bri asks her, "Is this something I'm *supposed* to be able to do?!"

Jessica walks over to her replying, "Bri, you're looking at death as an ending, but it's really——."

"A continuation, or next step, in our eternal journey?" Bri asks. *"I've had that part down for years!* I just never imagined being in this kind of a situation..."

Just then, Lawrence's memory flashes back to Bri's comment about his mother's death. "Bri," she looks at him, "give Natty what my mother didn't have! *A merciful death!"* She takes in what he said, then she looks at Jack and David. They give her caring looks and nod in sympathetic agreement.

Bri takes a deep breath and holds it as she tips her head back. She stares up at the ceiling for several seconds, then exhales as she brings her head all the way down. She closes her eyes and prays that if she isn't supposed to do what she is about to do, then to have it *not* work! But if it is *His will*, to give her the strength and courage she needs to end her daughter's suffering. *Suddenly*, she feels her body gain that strength and courage. She steps over to the foot of Natty's bed, standing in a position between Natty's spirit and her body.

Bri feels a presence with her as she hears herself say with such commanding conviction, *"Natalie Elizabeth, I command your spirit to release its hold on your body and return to your eternal home.*" David, Lawerence, and Jack feel chills go through their bodies.

The spirit matter, or life force, connecting Natty's spirit with her body disappears. Natty becomes less 'wispy' and looks more like herself in spirit. The family watches through the window and they don't understand what is going on, until they hear the alarms go off and see the doctors rush into the room with the nurse.

They are about to try to revive Natty, but Bri can barely say above a whisper, "Please, don't." She looks at them with a pleading sadness in her eyes.

The doctors solemnly nod, and the nurse turns off the machines. Dr. Reeves calls time of death, which echoes in Bri's ears as she absorbs the finality of the situation. The doctors finish jotting things down, then Dr. Wright tells them that they will have Natty taken downstairs in a little while. Bri is standing there, frozen, but she manages to nod.

Dr. Reeves gives her a sympathetic look; there isn't anything that can be said except, "She isn't suffering anymore." She lightly touches Bri's upper arm and Bri gives her a faint, acknowledging nod. Then the doctors and nurse quietly leave the room.

Bri is shaken by what she was able to do and wrestles with it in her mind and heart. She hears the words in her head, '*Look at your daughters.*' When she looks over at them, she sees how much *joy* they have on their beautiful faces. Both Emmie and Natty are holding each other's hands, excitedly smiling at each other. Then they see their mom, still reeling by what she was able to do.

"Mom, *it's okay!*" Natty tells her. "I'm not in pain anymore and I'm right where I'm supposed to be!"

Bri hears in her mind, '*Where it's always been written.*' Bri grabs another tissue. She wipes her eyes and squeaks, "*I miss you two so much, it hurts to think you two won't be here anymore!*"

Natty tells her mom, "Don't mourn us for too long. Life is meant to be lived by the living and our little brother needs our mom..." She points to her mother's abdomen.

Emmie chimes in with a big smile, "And more siblings to come!" Bri puts her hands on her baby bump and looks at them with red, teary eyes. "Mom,

I know we were difficult to raise without the love and emotional support *you needed.*" She apologetically says to her, "We're sorry for what we put you through growing up."

Natty nods. "If we could take it all back, *we would.*" Emmie agrees.

Bri shakes her head. "It was all necessary for me to learn and grow. At some point, I knew you both would go to college, and I would be able to put the pieces back together and begin again; to find *myself* again."

"Well, it was *you* who went out into the world first." Emmie gives her mom a small grin, then motions to David, Lawrence, and Jack. "*And you had help putting yourself back together.*" She then has a caring expression. "You're nervous about having more kids." Bri has a look that reads, 'I definitely am!' Emmie assures her, "*Don't be!* You will have all the love and support you need! You won't be held back, or pushed down, this time!" Emmie holds her mom's hand. "We may not have said it much, *or shown it much*, but we've *always* been grateful to have you for our mom!" Bri holds a tissue to her mouth to try to hold in her sobs.

Natty teases, "Becoming nobility and royalty were just the cherries on top!"

Bri exhales a small, light, airy laugh. She can barely whisper, "*I've been blessed having you two as my daughters!*"

Jessica walks over to them telling Bri, "I'll go with them."

Bri whispers, "*Thank you.*"

Jack, Lawrence, and David say their goodbyes to Natty and Emmie. The girls ask them to keep taking great care of their mom.

Jack replies with a hint of his signature grin, "*That's easy!*" Lawrence and David agree!

Bri hugs Emmie and Natty one last time, squeaking, "*I love you both, and you are* dearly *missed!*"

Everyone slightly waves goodbye as the light gets brighter and brighter, until the four of them have to look away from it. Those watching from the hallway only see bright white light reflected off of Bri, Jack, Lawrence, and David that gets brighter and brighter. They don't know where the light is coming from, until Bri's gift occurs to them. then they wonder if the four of them are seeing Natty's spirit cross over.

When the light fades, Bri, Jack, David, and Lawrence blink a few times for their eyes to adjust. Bri looks around the room...it feels cold and empty. Bri looks over at Natty's body and notices the blood that is running out of the corner of her mouth, ears, nose, and eyes. It reminds Bri that the pain Natty was in, would have continued to get worse.

CHAPTER 2

A Message to Deliver

Inside Natty's room, there is a cold, emptiness in the air. Lawrence, Jack, and David give Bri some space. She walks over to the decent-sized window and looks outside. All is quiet for several minutes. [1]

Without turning away from the view, Bri says, "Bring Tristan to me." She sees Lawrence's reflection and his eyebrow goes up. She turns to face him. "It's time he knows *you've known* this whole time that he's a traitor. *Plus*, I want him to take a message to Millicent."

Lawrence goes to ask her what kind of message, but when she turns back around to look out the window again, he decides to just go out and have Tristan brought to them. They have Tristan elsewhere to keep him far away from Bri. They didn't want him reporting anything back to Millicent, *least of all* anything about how upset Bri is at the loss of her two daughters.

David and Jack stay in the room with her. David asks, "What can we do for you, Love?"

"Nothing yet." Bri replies going over to the sink.

She puts some water on her face, then dries it off. She happens to see a scalpel on the counter and gets an idea. She opens the package and takes the scalpel out, then throws the package away. She goes to the door and cracks it open; she motions for Mitchell to come over to her.

She whispers so only Mitchell hears her, "*Can I borrow your pocketknife?*" She knows he and McMasters always carry one that is a bit longer than the palm of their hand when it's closed. He pulls it out of his pocket and hands it to her. "*Thank you.*" She whispers, then closes the door.

David and Jack watch her walk back over to the window; they don't see anything in her hands. They wait in silence for Lawrence to return with Tristan. It isn't long before they hear voices in the hallway getting closer to the room. She opens the pocketknife before turning around. She goes over and moves the bed table to be between her and Tristan, so the table will hide the knife and scalpel she is holding. She isn't sure how she will do what she wants to do, but she wants to be ready for the opportunity if he ever rests his hand on the table.

19

The door opens and Bri watches Tristan as he walks confidently into the room. Lawrence is half a step behind Tristan, while David and Jack fall in line behind them; they want to block Tristan's path back to the door, should he decide to leave before Bri is done with him.

Bri rolls her eyes as Tristan starts to say, "My condol–."

"*Cut the crap!*" She snips.

Tristan innocently looks over his shoulder at Lawrence and gives him a shrug. Seeing Tristan's dismissiveness triggers something in Bri to snap. That energy causes the glass in the window behind her to pop and crackle, leaving cracks covering every inch of the glass. Surprisingly, none of the glass falls out! The guys stare in awe at the glass; Tristan is also a little frightened.

"*I* had you brought to me for a couple of reasons." Bri waits for Tristan to look at her again. "First, to inform you that Lawrence, along with David and Jack," she tips her head towards them, "knows of your direct involvement with my assault in The Royal Dungeon *and they've known all along!*" She watches Tristan's face go from surprised, to glaring at her to mask the awkwardness of being there, vulnerable without Millicent there to protect him. Bri says with a ridiculous tone, "*You're a traitor to The King,* and to your country*, and you actually thought* I *was going to be loyal to you and Millicent by keeping a secret from him*?! *From any of them*?!" She scoffs. "The real credit goes to Lawrence, who *somehow* made it all this time never letting on that he knew all about what was done to me, while letting you think everything was fine between the two of you!" Then she explains to him, "I convinced Lawrence not to tip our hand with you, or Millicent, until *we* were ready, *and* it was done on *our terms*. Of course, Lawrence had to let everyone know Millicent was behind my assault in order to strip her of her titles and banish her from all royal residences. That all came *after* I discovered a secret, *a truth*, that she wanted to take to her grave."

Tristan gets an evil grin and says in a tone to match, "*You know she's going to kill you,* after *she's done torturing you.*"

"*OH! I know! That's why I have nothing to lose!* Which is why you're here," she steps up to the bed table, glancing down at his hand resting on it, then tells him, "*you're going to deliver a message to Millicent for me.*"

He scoffs in disgust, "*I'm not your message boy!*" He leans over the bed table and rudely tells her, "*Do it yourself!*"

This time, Bri's anger flows down her arms and she swiftly stabs the pocketknife in, and through, Tristan's hand with enough force that the tip of it sticks into the table. Although the guys are shocked by what she just did, they react quickly! Lawrence twists Tristan's free arm around to his back, while Jack and David help hold Tristan firmly in place to keep him, and his hand with the knife in it, right where they are.

Bri says with stiff anger, "Being disrespectful to me right now is *NOT* in your best interest!" She coldly glares at Tristan as she switches the hand gripping the knife handle, then she starts carving with the scalpel as she talks. "Tell  Millicent I know how her game is played, and the torture she enjoys inflicting on her victims..." Tristan whimpers with the pain. "*She won't survive this either! I WILL bring her down,*" she makes a small 'v' as she enunciates, "*piece.by.piece*" She yanks the pocketknife out of his hand and the guys let go of him. Tristan looks down at the back of his hand and is horrified at the bloody cuts. She tells him, "*I gave you* something to remember *me* by..."

Tristan sneers, "*I never took you to enjoy mutilation.*"

Bri rolls her eyes and tells him, "It's a simple phoenix, Tristan, with half a dozen cuts of lines and arcs. *Don't be such a baby!* What you, Millicent, and Millicent's *other* little minions did to me in The Dungeon was *far worse* than this, and you *never* heard me cry out, *not even once!*"

Bri goes over to the sink and tosses the scalpel into the 'hazardous materials' box. She washes her hands and uses alcohol to clean the pocketknife, then she dries it off as she makes her way over to the door. She opens it and waves Mitchell over to her again. Mitchell comes up to the door and he holds it open, wanting to see what was going on in the room. He sees Lawrence, David, Jack, and Tristan; with Tristan holding his hand and the blood seeping out between his fingers, making its way down his arm. Mitchell looks at his pocketknife Bri is handing back to him and gets a rough idea of what Bri used his pocketknife for.

"If you prefer your pocketknife to be replaced, *we will do that!*" Bri waves her arm out gesturing to Tristan saying, "See to it that Tristan is put on a flight back to the UK *as soon as possible!*" She hands Tristan the paper towel in her hand. "You might as well not drip blood everywhere." She looks at Mitchell. "Would you also see to it that he is bandaged up on your way out?" He nods.

Lawrence tells Tristan. "You are hereby stripped of your titles and your positions within The King's Guard and The Royal Guard. One day, *I will come for you*, and you *will be executed* for *all* your crimes!"

"That's if you can catch me!" Tristan sneers at Lawrence, no longer hiding behind a mask of friendship.

Lawrence tells Mitchell as he pushes Tristan towards him, "Get this *pathetic*, treasonous traitor out of here!" The word pathetic hits a nerve with Tristan, triggering the feelings of hate that will grow and burn into rage towards Lawrence and Bri.

Mitchell calls a couple of guards over to have Tristan taken into custody. The King's Guard have been in on the secret, and they are relieved to *finally* have this traitor out of The Royal Guards *completely*!

Mitchell steps closer to Lawrence. He whispers, *"Are you really going to let him go?!"*

Lawrence looks at Bri replying to Mitchell, "We have him delivering a message to Millicent." She nods. "Besides," Lawrence tells Mitchell, "Tristan has to be lucky *all the time* to evade capture, but *we* only need to be lucky *once!*"

Mitchell raises his eyebrow as he contemplates that, then agrees, "Good point!"

Mitchell, along with Lawrence, Jack, and David, go out into the hallway. Mitchell goes with the guards escorting Tristan and he stays with them until Tristan is on a plane, in the air, and heading back to the UK. Two of the guards volunteer to travel back with Tristan, to make sure the traitor actually lands in the UK and doesn't have the flight diverted to some other US location. Then the guards will come back to the US to take up their protective posts within The Royal Guards once again.

Bri finds herself alone in Natty's room. She looks at her daughter's face and thinks about both of her daughters...how much she loves them and misses them... She wonders how she is supposed to move on with her life without them in it? Then she thinks about seeing Emmie before she leaves the hospital.

When her eyes begin to fill with tears again, she turns to leave. She steps aside when a couple of orderlies come in to take Natty's body down to the morgue. When she goes to join everyone in the hallway, she momentarily gets weak and catches herself with the door frame.

Dr. Reeves sees this and rushes over to her. "Ma'am, you need to sit." She pulls the chair over that is right by the door and helps Bri to sit down.

"Are you alright, Sweetie?" Maggie asks with concern. The family gathers around Bri.

Dr. Reeves runs a light across each of Bri's eyes, explaining, "During times like these it's easy to forget to eat and drink." Dr. Wright waves over the nurse, while Dr. Reeves continues to examine Bri. "If the news is correct and you *are* pregnant," Bri nods, "then it's *imperative* you eat and drink *regularly*. Now, I'd like to run some tests." Dr. Reeves looks at the nurse and tells him, "Draw some blood and start an IV so we can get some fluids going in her." The nurse nods, then leaves to go to get what he needs so he can draw blood and start an IV.

"It's fine. *I'm fine.*" Bri says. "I'll drink some water and eat something when we leave here. There's a lot to do and I still need to go down to the morgue. *I can't just sit here—.*"

"Yes! *You can!*" David firmly states. He kneels down and holds one of her hands. "*This baby* needs you, *their mother*, to eat some food *and get hydrated!*" He isn't mad, but she knows he is serious. "Let's not make this whole nightmare worse." She looks into his eyes and sees the love and pleading in them.

Dr. Wright tells her, "Severe dehydration could cause your body to miscarry." He squats down next to David and explains, "We felt helpless with Jeff, Olivia, and Emerson, *but even more so with Natalie and this poison! Please*, let us help you take care of *this* baby, and we can have *something* go right out of all of this!"

"Love, all we're asking for you to do is pause, *just for a little bit.*" David says.

Bri gives him an apologetic look. "You're right." Then she tells the doctors, "*You all are.*" She looks at David with teary eyes. "I'm sorry, David."

He squeezes her hand. "With everything going on, you just needed help to refocus a bit."

David stands up and helps her up, then they follow the nurse into the next room. Jack and Lawrence follow the three of them, but all three men stay out of the way as the nurse has Bri sit on the bed. He doesn't take long drawing her blood and starting an IV, after which he helps her get comfortable in bed before he leaves the room.

When the comings and goings of the doctors and nurses become less frequent, Henry, Maggie, Carlotta, and Peter come into the room to join the four of them. They see Bri sitting, looking out the window; she is thinking to 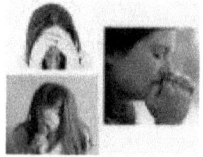 herself... '*My beautiful girls are gone...they will never graduate high school...never go to college...they will never...*' she takes a deep breath and exhales, '*everything...*' She doesn't realize she whispers out loud, "*How am I to move on with my life without them in it?!*"

"Faith, Sweetie." Henry answers. She looks at him and he reminds her, "*Your faith* is a *huge* strength for you!" She hears him, but that will take time to sink into her consciousness.

"What can we do for you, Darling?" Lawrence asks.

There is a couple second delay before she whispers, "*I just want to be left alone...*" Everyone understands and they file out of the room.

She is alone for a bit when she hears angry voices out in the hallway. It's muffled, but she gets a sinking feeling it's her mother. She sees Lawrence, David, and Jack move in front of the door to block anyone from going into her room.

Bri hears the firmness in Lawrence's voice, "You are *not* going in there and upsetting her more!"

Then Bri hears her mother, Martha, angrily tell him, "*You may be in charge in your country, but you do* NOT *get to tell* me *what to do!*"

"The US respects Bri's title as 'The Princess Imperial,' just as they do mine. And, since you took advantage of her position to manipulate people to get you up here without our permission, I could have you arrested!" Lawrence informs her. Martha slightly glares with a *'you wouldn't dare'* look. "She has dealt with a lot today, and *we* refuse to allow anything more to get thrown at her, *especially in her condition!*" David and Jack take half a step to be shoulder-to-shoulder with Lawrence.

Bri cringes when she hears Martha ask with exasperation, "I just want to know *why* she wouldn't let me see MY granddaughter before she died?! *She took those* precious *moments away from me*," she waves her arm at the family with her, "*from all of us!*"

David is *furious* with her. "*THIS ISN'T ABOUT YOU!*" Martha's mouth falls open; David has never spoken to her like this before. The family is about to step in when they hear David say as he points to Bri's room, "*There* is a mother who has just lost *both* of *HER* daughters! You do NOT get to be a narcissistic *monster* and put anything more on *your daughter*, just so *you* can be seen as some sort of *victim!*"

"The focus should be on *the girls* and not on her either!" Martha coldly states. "*My* grandbabies didn't deserve to die like that!"

"*No! They didn't!*" David agrees. "But you sound like she is to blame for their deaths!"

"*Isn't she?!*" Martha jabs back. "Those girls didn't have any enemies, neither did Jeff, or Olivia!"

"*That you know of!*" David shoots back. "You weren't in their marriage, *nor* did you know *all* their personal business!"

Lawrence, wanting to put an end to all of this, tells Mitchell in a flat tone, "Get her, *and anyone else who feels the same way she does*, out of here! *You* will *not* be welcome *anywhere* we are at!"

"I *will* be coming to their funerals!" Martha states and nastily adds, "*You can't stop me!*"

"*Can't I?*" Lawrence fires back at her, with a formidable look that causes Martha to lean back.

Jack has also reached his limit, even for him. He steps right up Martha and tells her sternly, "I will *personally* throw you out in front of all the reporters and make sure *everyone* knows of your *hateful* attitude towards *your own* daughter, *especially* during a time like this!" He knows she is more concerned about what other people will think of her, so she will stand down to continue being seen as a victim of a great loss.

The rest of the family watches Martha storm off, flanked by the two Secret Service Agents Mitchell sends with her to escort her out of the hospital. The rest of the family is mortified and disgusted at Martha's behavior, especially Bri's father, John. The man actually reached his limit with her some time ago; he had been putting more and more distance between him and her.

CHAPTER 3

Why We Should Never Ask Why

In the hospital room, Bri shakes her head, knowing her mother will still do whatever she wants, even if it means making a scene at the funeral, to get her way. '*The funeral...*' She thinks to herself, then she thinks about them being buried in DC...her heart wants them alive *and with her*. Bri pulls her knees up, folds her arms on top of them, and buries her face in her arms to cry again; she keeps thinking about leaving them *physically* behind in DC and her heart aches at that thought.

Some time has passed, and Henry cracks open the door to check on Bri. He sees her still sitting with her knees up, her arms folded on top of them, and her head resting on her arms, staring out the window at nothing in particular.

He asks, "Do you feel up to company, Sweetie?"

"*No.*" She quietly, and bluntly, answers.

He is inspired to ask, "Do you want me to leave?"

She doesn't move, but he hears her squeak, "*No.*"

Henry comes in and shuts the door. The family moves to the window, and the window on the door, to watch them.

"Oh, Sweetie..." he sits on the bed facing her, "there are no words..." He takes a deep breath. "This is a trial I wish you never had to endure..."

"Me, too..." She flatly replies. "I keep thinking if I didn't choose to come back when I was in a coma, they would still be alive..."

"If you didn't come back, your other three children wouldn't be joining our family." He replies.

She wipes her cheeks. "I wrestle with that too..."

"Maggie and I want to know if you would like some help making funeral arrangements?" He clears his throat watching Bri nod. "Do you have any ideas on—."

"Henry," she looks at him with a *deep* sadness in her eyes, "I know it has to be done, and I trust you both to do a *beautiful* job. They've been more your granddaughters than *anyone else's*!" He knows she is referring to her mother. "I know it might be selfish, but I don't want to leave them here; I want—." A lump closes off her throat and she works to push it down. Then she says with frustration, "UGH! *This isn't right! My daughters were killed! WHO DOES THAT?!*" She gets a little loud. David, Jack, and Lawrence come into her room as Bri says, "*This woman is such a coward that she goes after innocent kids instead of facing her real target?! My mother is right! The four of them died because of me! And we all know there is more loss to come!*" She angrily exhales and says, "*I want to ask 'why' but...*"

"And why shouldn't you?" Henry gently guides her.

She furrows her eyebrows a little. "You know why, *you taught us*!"

He motions for the guys to come closer. "Say it for them."

"*You* taught us that asking 'why' when bad things happen can lead us into the dark paths of 'why me,' and feeling sorry for ourselves, which only leads to dead ends and blackholes!" She takes a tissue from the box next to the bed and wipes her eyes. "Because to ask 'why,' or 'why me,' we don't trust that the Lord *does know* what He is doing, even if we don't understand the 'why' behind it. Although, *eventually*, we can understand, *if* we seek to understand *with faith*."

He nods and adds, "We all *chose* to come into our mortal lives. We *trusted Him then, knowing* these mortal lives would be a certain number of years, even days, or mere minutes, but not a moment shorter, or longer, than they are supposed to be. *And* we knew those lives will be full of ups and downs, with good times and bad, and everything in between." He points to her baby bump. "Just as this little one knew when *he* chose to come into mortality, *and come to you*!"

Bri puts her hands on her baby and remembers her eldest son's spirit; how excited he was about coming into their family... Then she thinks of Emmie and Natty, and drops her forehead to her knees asking, "*What have I done?!* I cut sweet Natty's life short—." She holds her breath to stop her emotions from overwhelming her.

"*No*, Sweetie! *You didn't!*" Henry is adamant. "First, didn't I just say that we all chose to come into our lives?" She nods. "Which means that we would have known *before* we came here, what our lives would have entailed." When he sees her nod again, he adds, "*Perhaps*, you should go back and think about what it might have been like for you, when *you* chose to come into mortality." She looks at him with a curious face. "Consider how you might have known that coming into *your* mortal life would include helping Natty with her suffering?" She thinks about what he is saying. He goes on to tell her, "Sweetie, you also need to consider that Natty *wasn't* conscious and she would *never* have regained consciousness again! What you *did, as her mother*, was lovingly, *and mercifully*, stop your daughter's pain and suffering."

"I've thought of that." She replies. "Then I think *I'm her mother*! I should've protected—."

"*BriaLynn!*" Henry gives her a compassionate, fatherly look. "You were, and are, entrusted with an *incredible* gift; a power that I'm sure if you weren't supposed to use in that way, you wouldn't have been able to do what you did *to help* Natty!"

She closes her eyes and tells him, "I *prayed* that if I wasn't supposed to do it, He wouldn't let me."

"*Proving* you *are* being responsible with this *remarkable* gift!"

She looks at him. "I wasn't alone, Henry."

He gives her an understanding nod. "*Think about that for a moment!*" He stresses, "*You prayed*, then you were given Divine help to do what you were being asked to do, *by Natty*, who understood what was happening to her; perhaps better than you did, or you do right now! *And* He was also answering *her* prayer *through you!*"

"Every so often I hear versions of, 'Millicent is going to die.' I'm trying not to think about what that could mean!" She shakes her head in disbelief. "*I've never killed anyone, Henry!*"

Henry holds her hand. "Perhaps you're being prepared for whatever is to come, for what *needs* to happen. It doesn't necessarily mean you will kill her. Then again, maybe it has to be you, and these other men are to step aside?" He squeezes her hand. "No matter what happens, *or how it happens*, I think

hearing that phrase is to help you prepare and process things *as* they happen."
She nods.

"*Oh, Henry...*" she squeaks as her eyes fill with tears again, "*my babies are gone.*"
Her tears flow down her cheeks. "*What am I going to do?*" She holds the tissue
to her mouth to hold in her urge to cry.

Henry hugs her. "I think we should look into having them brought to
Newhaven for their final resting place. I can work with Maggie, Peter, and
Carlotta to get it all arranged." She nods. "We will also reach out to those
who are here, that we will coordinate for them to come to the girls' funeral if
they want to attend."

"Thank you." She softly says.

He stands up and sees Jack is closest. "Don't keep pushing these wonderful
men away when you need them the most right now."

"I just needed some space..." She takes a deep breath, then controls her
exhale.

"And that's okay! *But now...*" he switches places with Jack, "you hang on to
them and let them help you take it one day, or one step, perhaps even one
moment, at a time. *I promise* I'll always be here for you, just like Maggie and
everyone who loves you is here for you. *However,* what I think you need at
this moment, will come from these three."

Jack sits facing her. "We *are* here for you because we *want* to be here for you!
Please, lean on us and let us!" He reaches for the back of her neck and pulls
her into a hug.

"Cry, scream, yell..." David tells her.

Lawrence agrees and adds, "Like David said earlier, *get angry!* We *are* all angry,
and angry for you! Angry that this vindictive b—*woman* is going to keep coming
at you, until she comes for you and—."

"*And one of us dies!*" Bri says and sits up a bit. "But she can't come after me
yet; *she needs me.* Besides, if she goes after those I love, she tortures me, *which
is way more fun for her anyway!*" Jack hugs her closer. She sits back up, her jaw
shaking. "I knew it was a possibility she could go after Emmie and Natty, but
I was hoping that with an ocean in between, she would be more focused on

me!" She clenches her fists and exhales in frustration. "*Ugh*! The girls had plans to come to the UK this summer! Not just for the baby, but they also wanted to spend time helping out at The Mill and with The Foundation, *but now...*" She turns her head to the window.

"*Bri—.*" Lawrence tries to apologize again, but chokes up.

"Here." Jack gestures the bed as he moves, so Lawrence can sit on the bed with her.

Lawrence sits close to her and hugs her tight. He hears her hold her breath and he whispers next to her ear, "*It's okay to cry, crying can be therapeutic...*" He feels her jaw shake against his shoulder as she fights hard not to cry with his ear right there, but when she hears him tell her, "I promise, *we've got you...*" the flood gates open again, and she cries; crying so hard no sound is heard, except for when she has to inhale. He holds the back of her head as he quietly cries with her.

Watching all this makes it hard for Henry, Jack, and David to contain their own emotions. Henry wipes his eyes with his handkerchief walking to the door. He steps out of the room and tightly hugs Maggie. David turns around when he can no longer suppress his emotions. Jack is emotional, too, and walks over to David. They lean their shoulders together for support, staring out the window...

The family watches David, Jack, Bri, and Lawrence through the windows. *All* their hearts are breaking for the mother who has lost her babies.

"I can't imagine losing one child," Carlotta says, staring through the window, "*and she lost two?!*"

"I thought we would have more time before Natty..." Maggie can't bring herself to say it.

The doctors overhear that, and Dr. Wright says, "Natty was suffering in *immense* pain and would've continued suffering; getting worse that whole time, because all the pain medication she was getting wasn't enough." Dr. Reeves solemnly nods in agreement.

With that, the family is relieved Natty isn't in pain any longer. They all turn to peer into Bri's room again.

Lawrence has been whispering here and there in Bri's ear, "*I'm so sorry!*" She hadn't heard him until now.

"*What?*" She squeaks. Jack and David turn to look at them.

Lawrence sits back to look at her. "I'm *so* sorry for *all* of this."

"Lawrence, I told you," Bri cups his cheek, "*none of this is your fault!*"

"If we hadn't—if I hadn't..." He stumbles to find the right words. "I'm *not* sorry for falling in love with you, *and I'm grateful you love me*! I just wish that having you in my life didn't—."

"Lawrence, I knew when I was in my coma that choosing to come back came with a price. No, I didn't know how big the price would be, nor how deep it could go, *or will go...*" she pushes down the lump in her throat. When she can't, she just hugs him, and she feels his arms hug her firmly again. She whispers next to his ear, "*Hug me tighter.*"

He does and tucks his face into her neck and smells her perfume. He exhales, "I love you!"

"I love you, too!" She squeezes him a little tighter.

He asks, "Is there anything we can do for you?"

She pulls back. "You're doing it." She looks over at David and Jack. "Whether you're in the room with me, right outside the room, or a phone call away, having you three here for me means a lot!"

Jack walks over and sits on the other side of the bed. Lawrence kisses her forehead and gets up to let them have a moment together. Lawrence steps out of the room to try to catch his breath. Bri sits up more and gives Jack a loving look through the heartbreak on her face.

He gives her a small smile back and holds the back of her jaw. "*You* are the strongest person I know!"

She softly shakes her head. "Only because of you three..."

"We'll help you through this, Bri." He tells her. "*Whatever you need!*"

She can only whisper, "*I love you, Jack.*"

He hugs her saying, "I love *you*, Amore Mia!" He pulls back. "I'm going to leave the room so you and David can have a minute." She nods and he taps a kiss on her lips before he leaves the room.

David walks over to Bri and sits facing her. "Oh, Macushla..." He tucks some hair behind her ear on the other side of her face, then cups that cheek as he leans in and kisses her cheek closest to him; he holds his kiss there a little longer. This sweetness has always meant a lot between the two of them, making her want to cry from the love she feels from him on a normal day; *oddly*, not at this moment.

She looks at him with red eyes, "How am I supposed to move on and be happy; *have another baby, or three*, with two *huge* pieces of my heart missing?!"

"You have that answer, Macushla. As Uncle Henry said," he gives her a loving look, "it's with your *incredible* faith! It makes you *so* strong, because you have an eternal perspective! You genuinely believe the saying, 'everything happens for a reason' *so deeply*, I've been thinking a lot about that. I've been wondering *what reason* could there *possibly be* for such *senseless loss*?! All I can come up with is that Millicent can *never* hurt them again! Then I remember the look of joy on Emmie's and Natty's faces when they were reunited..." His eyes get teary with emotions, and he whispers, "*Wow!*" He gives her a faint smile. He holds his finger and thumb a little bit apart as he struggles to say, "*That had to do your heart* a little bit *of good!*"

Her eyebrows go up a little. "You're right..." Something about his statement begins to change her. She quietly thinks out loud, "*Millicent can never get to them again!*" She looks at him. "Thank you for that, My Love." He hugs her close.

Lawrence and Jack bring in a tray of food. Jack tells Bri, "The nurse asked us to bring this to you. You need to eat some food *before* you're released. He wanted us to stress *before* in case you wanted to be discharged *today*." He gives a little grin. "He told us to stress that, too."

She looks at the tray Lawrence is holding and says with sarcasm, "*Sure hope this food isn't poisoned.*"

"Sad to say, but the thought occurred to us, too." Jack admits. "But it quickly left, because she still needs you alive." Bri slightly turns up her nose with a soft grumble in agreement at that.

33

Lawrence adds, "Plus, she won't risk using poison on anyone around you, at least not yet anyway."

"Not until she *wants* me dead. Then she won't care who else dies in the process." She throws out there and the guys reluctantly agree. "We have a little bit of time before she will want that." Bri says with her hands on her abdomen. David gets the bed table and pushes it up to Bri, then Lawrence slides the tray onto it. She gives them a sweet little smile saying, "*With noble and kingly service*! How can I *not* eat?!"

"That's our girl!" Jack replies with a small handsome smile.

"We'll gladly serve our Queen anytime, *anywhere*." Lawrence slightly bows with the other two agreeing.

Jack sits at the foot of the bed. "Peter and Carlotta have gone down to the morgue to arrange for Natty and Emmie to be flown to Newhaven with the help of Gabriel." Bri nods. "James and Amy are helping the family here with their travel arrangements through Carlotta's staff. Maggie and Henry went to the funeral home to meet up with Jeff and Olivia's family. They will let them know that the girls are going to be flown to Newhaven, and they will offer all of them travel arrangements to Natty & Emmie's funeral."

Bri reaches for the phone. "I don't want Emmie or Natty moved, until after I go down to see Emmie first."

Lawrence puts his hand on hers, stopping her from picking up the phone's receiver. He gives her a compassionate look. "Bri," he takes her hand in his, "you *don't* want to see your beautiful Emmie like that!"

Bri's face is upset, and she says with a bit of anger. "*I have to see*——."

"*No, you don't!*" Lawrence firmly states. "For the same reasons you gave me about my mother's crime scene and autopsy photos! You don't want to remember either of your beautiful daughters like that! Remember them as you just saw them a little while ago; together, happy and smiling! Don't taint that, *and all the wonderful memories you have of them*, with what you will see in the morgue!"

David adds, "Remember how excited they were when they were reunited! It makes me think about how wonderful it must be on the other side, to be *that* happy!" She looks at David, giving him a teary little smile with her nod.

It isn't long after she is done eating that she is also done with her IV fluids. While the arrangements are being made for her to be discharged from the hospital, she sends a text to McMasters.

> Bri: "Will you get word to Rex Stirling that I would like to see him? Let him know will be back in a few days and the funeral for the girls will be in Newhaven; we can meet before or after."

> McMasters: "Do I tell him what this meeting is about?"

> Bri: "It can be summed up in one word: Millicent."

> McMasters: Sends a thumbs up.

The nurse comes in and takes out Bri's IV, then goes over her discharge paperwork. Bri sees the guys have her things and they follow the nurse pushing her out of the room in a wheelchair. She stares into Natty's room, now empty. There are a couple of maintenance people looking at the crackled window, baffled at what caused all of the cracks and splinters.

She asks the guys, "We're paying for a replacement window, right?"

They nod, with David replying, "Father already took care of it."

Bri stares at her hands as the go to the elevator, thinking that once the funerals are over, she will focus on taking Millicent down. She hopes to have Rex's help to do that, beginning with the name of a genius hacker she can hire to get started.

Phillip had issued a Press Release right before he and McMasters left on a private jet to fly to DC.

ROYAL PRESS RELEASE

It is with great sadness that The Royal Family issues this announcement:

Her Royal Majesty BriaLynn, The Princess Imperial's daughters, Lady Emerson and Lady Natalie, have been murdered. His Majesty King Lawrence asks that you respect The Royal Family's privacy during this difficult time.

~ *His Majesty, The King Father*

This causes a huge uproar across Newhaven, and spreads across the entire UK. It isn't a huge leap for people to connect Millicent to the tragedy, and assume it is in retaliation for The King stripping her of her position and titles for her assault on The Princess Imperial. Going after kids is a low blow, even most of the criminal underworld sees this as 'bad form.' It already caught the attention of criminal mastermind, Jonathan "Rex" Stirling.

Over the years, Rex has put together a team of geniuses in their criminal fields of expertise. He calls it, 'The Underground Secret Society,' and it is their mission to police the criminal underworld; to correct serious injustices. Millicent went straight to the top of Rex's 'End List' after what she did to Bri's daughters. He wanted to meet with Bri, to offer his organization's services, and is relieved she reaches out to him through McMasters. He wants to work together with her to bring this woman down, *once and for all.*

CHAPTER 4

Life *Must* Go On!

Bri is getting ready for Jeff and Olivia's funeral in her room at the Bradshaw's house. Carlotta had picked up a black dress for her at the local boutique Bri had used in the past. She also had seen to the men's black suits being dry cleaned and ready for today. Bri is adding her Diamond-Heart Necklace and the matching earrings.

David walks up to Bri and holds one side of her face. "We should get going." She gives him a weak smile with her nod.

She looks at Lawrence because protocol pairs them up. He gives her a loving look walking over to her. "We will start off with me escorting you, but that's as far as we will go with making sure we follow formal protocols. We will follow *your lead* the rest of the day, *alright?*" She gives a little nod and holds out her hand for his. He takes it and kisses the back of it.

David and Jack follow Lawrence and Bri out the door. The whole family leaves for the church together to pay their respects to Jeff and Olivia. They all arrive at the church and there is a crowd that has gathered to see The Royal Family, only they are not as loud as they usually are; Bri is grateful for that. The service was nice and seemed to move along, although it is surreal to Bri. She looks at the family and sees how upset they are... '*More sorrow and grief that didn't have to happen.*' She painfully thinks to herself. '*And this is all going to get SO much worse, before it gets better!*'

That evening, they are all gathering in the sitting room at the Bradshaw's house. Bri sits in her overstuffed comfy chair staring out the window with a tissue in her hand, and a folded piece of paper in her other hand. She has been mulling over what she is going to say at Emmie and Natty's funeral. She unfolds the piece of paper to take another look at what she has so far. All she has managed to come up with are bits and pieces of sentences, with an occasional full sentence.

She is half listening to the family talk about various things, until they start talking with James and Amy about their wedding. She hears them offer to postpone it.

"*No, Amy!*" Bri is *adamant.* "Natty and Emmie called this your 'true-love wedding,' and they would hate for it to be put on-hold because of them!" Bri puts her hand on her heart and says, "In honor of the girls, let's celebrate your wedding! *Please.*"

"Then we will postpone our honeymoon until after their funeral. That is *not* negotiable." Amy counters with James' support. Bri hugs Amy.

Our Deepest and Heartfelt Condolences
We Love You, Your Royal Majesty

The Newhaven News Chronicle Staff

It is with heavy hearts we announce the deaths of Her Royal Majesty The Princess Imperial's daughters, Lady Emerson and Lady Natalie. They were cruelly poisoned in their US home, along with their father and stepmother, by what we have learned to be crimson powder. Since the crimson flower is not found anywhere in The United States, their deaths are classified as homicides and under investigation.

The Royal Family and The Worthington Family are in the US capital of Washington, D.C., for the wedding of Lord James Worthington to Miss Amy Walker. Her Royal Majesty insisted the wedding continue as planned, because Lady Emerson and Lady Natalie would have wanted it that way.

The paper has had numerous inquiries into where to send cards and flowers. What we posted on the website, and we are putting in here, is our suggestion that, in lieu of flowers, donations be made to The New Beginnings Foundation in their names. Lady Emerson and Lady Natalie would volunteer with The Foundation every chance they could, even planning their US school holidays to volunteer.

Any amount is appreciated! We are only tracking the combined total of all donations, then we will make one significant donation to The Foundation in memory of these two lovely young ladies, who were taken from this world much too soon.

Your Royal Majesty, if you are reading this, your people's love and prayers go out to you and your family during this difficult time. Our deepest and *sincerest* condolences.

Bri helps Amy the day before the wedding at the hotel, while Amy and her sisters have last minute fittings, along with salon and spa appointments. Bri is grateful to keep herself busy and focus on other things, rather than thinking about how much she misses her daughters, and about what happened at the hospital. However, when she does think about them, she tries to focus on the memory of how happy they were when she last saw them.

The wedding goes *almost* seamlessly; at least nothing significant goes wrong. Bri finishes dancing with David again, when Jack comes over to dance another dance. She tells them her feet are hurting and asks Jack if he would escort her upstairs instead. Since James and Amy had already left for the evening, there was no reason she needed to stay.

David tells her, "I'll go find Herst and tell him you're going up to your suite."

"Thank you." She kisses his cheek.

Jack escorts her upstairs and notices her grimacing with each step. When they get off the elevator, he scoops her up and carries her to the door of her suite with Lawrence. She is able to use the keycard without him putting her down and they go inside. He carries her to the bedroom before he carefully puts her down. She has been staying in this room by herself, so she could cry anytime without worrying about waking up Lawrence. Jack unzips the back of her dress and helps her out of it, then tosses it on the chair.

He caresses her face as he asks, "Do you need anything else?"

"I think I can handle it from here." She gives him a small, sweet smile and hugs him. "I'm just going to go take a bath and soak for a little while. I love you, Amore Mio."

He hugs her a little tighter and says, "I love you, too, Amore Mia." He kisses the curve of her neck. "Goodnight."

After he leaves, she goes into the bathroom and draws a bath in the jacuzzi tub. She gets in and lays back, closing her eyes and taking a deep breath, relaxing for a bit.

She jumps when there is a light knock on the bathroom door, followed by Lawrence's voice asking, "May I come in, Darling?" She is startled for a moment, realizing she had dozed off.

"*Yes.*" She replies, then yawns.

When he comes in, he sees the tiredness on her face. He grabs a washcloth and sits on the edge of the tub. He puts soap on it, then washes her back. She pulls her knees up and folds her arms around them, then rests her chin on her knees and closes her eyes.

He notices she is still, and he puts his hand on her shoulder. "Let's get you into bed so you can sleep, or I'm afraid you might drown." She gives him a ghost of a smile.

He pulls the plug, then he helps her up. He hands her the towel, and she dries herself off. However, with as tired as she is, he helps her out of the tub and dries her feet off, so she doesn't slip.

"Thank you." She softly says.

He gives her a small smile back. "You're welcome, Darling."

She puts on her pajamas before walking into the bedroom. He follows at first, but then gets ahead of her to pull back the covers on the bed, so she can just crawl right in. He covers her up and kisses her forehead.

He whispers, "*Goodnight, My Queen.*"

She puts her hand on his arm and whispers, "*Would you sleep next to me tonight?*"

"*Whatever you need.*" He whispers back. "*I'll be right back.*" She barely nods before he goes to his room to change.

When he comes back to her bed and carefully crawls in next to her, so he doesn't wake her. He realizes she is *kind of awake* when he hears her barely whisper, "*I love you, Lawrence.*"

"I love you, BriaLynn." He kisses her cheek.

He snuggles with her for a while. He thinks about the other nights, when he was outside her door while she mourned her daughters. Wanting to go to her, but wanting to give her space; he knew when she wanted him there, she would ask...*and she did.* When he is sure she is *sound asleep,* he kisses her shoulder before he rolls over to his side of the bed and goes to sleep.

CHAPTER 5

It's What The Foundation is All About

The next morning, David texts Bri that he and Jack are going to go back to Newhaven a couple of days early; he has some work issues that he should really sort out in person. He also tells her that Peter and Carlotta are also going to go back with them to work on Natty and Emmie's funeral; David and Jack will help where they can. Jack and David want to give Bri some one-on-one time with Lawrence, so they are only reaching out to make sure she is okay with them leaving early.

Bri replies quickly to David and Jack, saying she loves them, and she will see them in a couple of days. She puts her phone back on the bedside table, then feels Lawrence snuggle up behind her and he lays an arm on her waist. She turns her head to the side to see him out of the corner of her eye.

She softly smiles. "Good morning, Ace."

He kisses her shoulder. "Good morning, My Queen."

She turns to face him. "I'm sorry I've been keeping to myself at night and not spending more time with you."

"You're grieving. No apology necessary." He hugs her. "I bet you and the baby are hungry." He feels her nod. He squeezes her a little more before they get up and order room service.

After they have eaten breakfast, Bri gets a call from Ken; he and Bill want to see her today. Since the hotel would be closer for them, she suggests lunch in their hotel suite before she and Lawrence go back to Henry and Maggie's that afternoon.

"Sounds good!" Ken replies. "How about noon?"

"See you then!" She says and they hang up.

Lawrence sends Bri to take her shower first, while he starts packing; there isn't much to pack since most of their things are at the Bradshaw's house. When they are dressed, and everything is all packed, Lawrence brings their luggage out and sits it next to the door of their suite.

"Is there anything you would like to do this morning?" He asks, walking over to her.

"I'm not wanting to go anywhere and draw a crowd." She tells him. "How about we snuggle in and watch that movie you've been wanting to watch?"

Lawrence sweetly smiles. "I won't argue with that!" He wraps his arms around her. "*Especially* the part where I snuggle in with you."

She smiles and hugs him, then she leads the way to the living room couch. They get comfortable and enjoy the rest of the morning watching a movie together.

Ken and Bill arrive at the suite for lunch. Lawrence and Bri greet them at the door, then they all gather around the dining room table for lunch.

Bill looks at Ken. "Did you tell her anything?"

"No, I wanted to discuss it all in person." Ken answers.

Bri can already guess, "What about Katie?"

Ken explains, "She was part of a drug bust a while back and has spent some time in jail; right now, she is in court ordered rehab. The judge remembered her and the case against her involving Jack, along with the restraining orders for you and the family."

"That didn't help her at all." Bill adds, pulling out something from the inside of his suit coat; he hands Bri a couple of photos.

One picture shows a passed-out Katie, sitting on a dirty wooden pallet in some grimy basement, or it could even be a warehouse type of a building. The next picture is a closer shot where you see Katie with drug paraphernalia by her side. She hands the photos to Lawrence so he can have a better look.

43

Bri is sad for Katie...at how low her life has gotten, and it didn't have to be this way.

Bill sees her expression. "Hard to look at?" Bri nods.

The next two pictures are from security cameras. One of them is when Katie was in jail talking with other inmates in a common are; the other picture is more recent, with Katie sitting in a group circle at a rehab center, *clearly* not participating. Bri sees the sad, pathetic woman Katie has reduced herself to because of her choices. Bri would help her get, *and stay*, clean, *if* Katie would accept Bri's help.

"She got herself mixed up with a pretty rough crowd this time. We're hoping she has hit rock bottom," Ken says, "but..."

"*But* it doesn't feel like she has." Bri finishes his sentence, with Bill and Ken shaking their heads. She tells them, "It feels more like there is still a lower level she has to sink to; *although* seeing these pictures and hearing what you're telling me, I'm not sure how much lower she can go that doesn't result in her death?" They reluctantly agree.

Bill replies, "From what we hear, she's only doing what she's being *required* to do in rehab. Her counselor asked if we'd be able to reach out to you, as her only relationship connection on her paperwork, to see if you would come for a visit."

Bri is surprised and points to herself asking, "*I'm on her forms?!*"

"As her emergency contact." Ken tells her.

"*They must have old records...*" She thinks out loud. "I knew she would list me for an emergency contact in the past, because she didn't have anyone else; but after everything that has happened between us, I don't see how she would *want* to do that now?"

"You already said it," Ken points out, "she doesn't have anyone else, other than Maggie and Henry." Bri gives him a, 'that's true,' expression. He goes on, "And she's not ready for the love and care Henry and Maggie would give her, which would include their persistence in getting her cleaned up and back on track to a healthy life!" Bri agrees.

Bill shifts a little. "Maybe seeing you would help Katie, or at least *jar her enough* that the counselor can finally get through to her, to *really* be able to help her?"

"If she is only doing the bare minimum, *that's not promising.*" Bri worries. "If she continues to blame me for everything, I can't see how I can help her? *However,* if her counselor knows all that *and* still thinks it will help..."

"She does." Ken tells her.

Bri says with a bit of reluctance, "*Well,* I guess I'll go to see her tomorrow morning."

"We'll meet you at the rehab center at say..." Ken looks at his watch, "nine o'clock?"

"That should work." Bri replies.

"Hold on!" Lawrence interrupts. "This doesn't sound like a very good idea! This woman——."

"*Can't do it alone.*" Bri gently states, laying her fingers on his arm. "She needs to know she has *some kind* of support, *or* she *will* fail! I don't want to worry about someone finding Katie dead in some gutter somewhere! *We have enough to worry about with Millicent out there!*" She states. "Besides, isn't this what The New Beginnings Foundation is all about?" He looks at her and his face softens a bit. Bri looks at Ken and Bill. "Tomorrow morning," she stands, "nine o'clock, gentlemen." They nod and stand up.

At the door, Bri hugs Ken and Bill goodbye, while Lawrence shakes their hands. Lawrence isn't thrilled about the idea of seeing Katie, but he will support Bri, *as long as he is there to protect her!*

Later that afternoon, they are at the Bradshaw's house. Bri goes downstairs after taking a nap and joins Lawrence, Phillip, Maggie, and Henry, in the living room. Phillip stayed in DC after James and Amy's wedding because Lawrence wanted Bri to discuss her vision about Millicent with him, without worrying about prying eyes, *or ears*, back home.

Bri gives Phillip a small, acknowledging smile as she sits next to him on the couch. Phillip smiles back and he gently pats her hand with an empathetic sadness on his face.

"I wish there was something I could've done to protect Emmie and Natty, as well as their dad and stepmother, from Millicent." He tells her. "*No one should die like that!*"

"I've seen the girls, Phillip," she looks at Lawrence, "*we've* seen them, and they are *truly* happy." Lawrence nods in support.

Phillip gives Bri a faint smile. "That has to be a little easier for you." She softly nods as she tears up and holds her thumb and finger about half an inch apart as if to say, '*a little.*'

Lawrence tells his father, "There *is* something I wanted to talk to you about. Well, *Bri* would need to explain, because it's regarding Millicent's past." Everyone curiously looks at Bri.

She takes a deep breath. "One of the things that can happen with my gift, besides seeing spirits and ghosts, are visions. These visions just come to me; I can't force them, nor pick what I see."

"Visions?" Phillip asks.

Bri explains, "I've been able to fully experience a few of the things Lawrence went through in his past." Lawrence looks at her apologetically, while Phillip gets a knot in his stomach thinking about what those visions of Lawrence's past could be. Bri continues, "My visions are mostly of the past, although I do get a rare flash of a future event. The latest vision I had was from Millicent's past; specifically, when she was a teenager. Of course, she doesn't know *I* know..." she glances at Lawrence, "*well, the four of us.* David and Jack also know, because they were there when I had this vision."

"I'm not sure I want to know." Phillip plainly says, shifting a bit uncomfortably on the couch.

"If you don't want to know," she pointedly looks at Lawrence, "*we will respect that.*"

Lawrence gives her his own pointed look back as he tells Phillip, "Father, you had a right to know *years* ago, *from the very beginning!*" Bri slightly glares at Lawrence.

Phillip is now intrigued about what it could be. "Alright then," he looks at Bri, "tell me."

Henry and Maggie look at each other, with Maggie saying, "Maybe we should give you three some privacy."

They go to leave, but Phillip puts up his hand. "No, no." He tells them. "*Please stay*. We're family." Maggie and Henry lightly nod and sit back down to stay.

Bri closes her eyes and takes a deep breath. "My vision was of a *beautiful* sixteen-year-old Millicent." Everyone looks at her a bit surprised. "Yes, she *was* beautiful, which only adds to the sadness of what happened to her all those years ago; *the toll it took on her on* so *many levels!*" Bri looks at Phillip. "You see, by this point the sixteen-year-old Millicent has already had *multiple* abortions in her young life that her uncle made her have." Phillip does have a sad look on his face when he hears that; Henry and Maggie do as well. "The vision I had was what happened *after* her last abortion, because that last abortion didn't go like it should have and it caused a serious problem." Phillip's eyebrows scrunch together as he rests his elbows on his knees, wondering where this is all going; Maggie, being a woman, senses where it is going, and her heart sinks a bit for young Millicent. "In this vision, the young Millicent was forced to have a hysterectomy because of that *botched* abortion."

Phillip looks down at the floor as the weight of what Bri just said sinks in. He begins to seethe with anger, "*That woman* KNEW *she couldn't have children* BEFORE *we got married?!*"

"Phillip," Bri turns on the couch to face him better and has a compassionate look for him, "*whatever you would've done differently*, you would've changed the course of *all* our lives!" He stares at her for a moment considering that. She asks, "Do you remember what Vivian said; that none of us would be together *now* had *anything* been different in the past?" He nods. "*You're grandchildren* would've been denied *their destiny!*" She puts her hand on her lower abdomen. "I thought about that when I was thinking about the choice I made when I was in a coma. I thought if I hadn't chosen to come back, Emmie and Natty would still be alive, *but*," she places her other hand on her baby bump, "*this*

47

baby, and my future children, wouldn't be born. They, *too*, would've been denied *their* destinies." She looks around at Henry, Maggie, and Lawrence, then back to Phillip. "Consider what would've happened if Millicent had your heir, *The Heir to The Throne*?! What would've happened to Lawrence, along with Seth and Abby?" Phillip thinks about everything she is saying, *especially* that last part! "I remember Vivian wrote in her journal, something like: '*Millicent would be the type of mother who would eat her own young!*'" The others softly chuckle, but none of them can dispute that! Bri assures him, "*Everything* does *happen for a reason!*"

"*I wasn't allowed to marry Vivian...*" Phillip thinks out loud. "*Perhaps Millicent not being able to have children* was *for the best...*" They wait patiently for him to wrap his mind around everything. After a couple of minutes, he stands up. "I need some air." He looks at Bri. "Would you join me for a private walk? We don't have to walk far."

She softly smiles. "Sure."

Phillip offers his hand to Bri to help her stand up and he asks Lawrence, "Son, would you mind if Bri and I talk alone outside?"

"*Not at all!*" Lawrence replies supportively. He walks to the patio door with them. "I know I *always* feel better after talking with her." Lawrence winks at Bri as he opens the door for them; Henry Maggie, and Phillip lightly laugh.

Bri gives Lawrence a little glare behind a faint smile. She points her finger at an upward angle in front of his chest and says in a slightly playful stern voice, "*Don't you try to kiss up to me after you convinced him to hear about the vision,* after *he had already said he didn't want to know!*"

"What?" Lawrence grins as he puts his hand up to his chest. "I *do* feel better after talking with you!"

She softly laughs and shakes her head as she steps outside. Phillip gives Lawrence an appreciative smile and pats his upper arm passing by him, following Bri outside. He takes a deep, relaxing breath of fresh air, then they start walking side-by-side. They slowly make their way to a walking path.

After a couple minutes, Phillip asks her, "How are you feeling?"

48

Bri reflexively lays her hand on her lower abdomen and tells him, "So far, so good...*considering...*"

"Well, if my first grandson is as strong as you and David are, there's *nothing* to worry about with this little one!" They take a few more steps, then he shares with her, "By the time Vivian was pregnant the third time with Abby, I had learned some things about her that were unique to her pregnancies; just like David, Jack, and Lawrence are learning with this pregnancy, and they will catch on to you being pregnant a little sooner each time." Bri's steps slow down and she comes to a stop; her heart sinking as she braces herself for the question that will inevitably come next.

Phillip turns to face Bri, and he asks, "Vivian was pregnant when she died, wasn't she?"

Bri closes her eyes and whispers, "*Yes.*"

Phillip sharply inhales and holds his breath. Lawrence sees that they have stopped walking, and he watches them to make sure everything is okay.

Phillip slowly exhales. "I assume she was only a few weeks along?"

Bri sadly nods. "She told me she had just found out and hadn't had a chance to tell you yet." Phillip pushes down the growing lump in his throat. "I didn't want to tell you; *I wasn't going to!*"

"I appreciate your honesty." He replies. "Seeing Vivian after all these years and being able to see her before I die, along with being reunited with my children; well, I'm feeling better than I have *since* Vivian's death!" He needs to ask, "Is there anything else I should know about?"

Bri slowly shakes her head thinking. "I don't think so...then again, I haven't read through all her journals. When Vivian said it was okay for me to give them to you, I thought I would respect your privacy with Vivian and give them to you without reading the rest of them."

Phillip softly smiles. "I appreciate that."

"I didn't want to say anything to anyone about Vivian's pregnancy, but David and Jack guessed it in front of Lawrence, and I *won't* lie to any of them."

Phillip nods in understanding. She goes on to tell him, "There is the abuse at the hands of Millicent that I will let Lawrence share with whomever he chooses to share that with. I did have a vision, of pieces of Lawrence's abuse, *although* I didn't need to feel any of that abuse to know she is a sadist and loves to torture people! However, I did gain some insight into his abuse to help me connect with him on a different level."

"*Feel?*" Phillip says with a horrified look.

"That vision was *very* real." She replies. "I was actually seeing the vision from Lawrence's point of view and experience, rather than observing the events as they unfolded."

"I knew the scars on his back were telling of the physical abuse he suffered at Millicent's hands, but it was *far worse* than that, wasn't it? It was her uncle, too?" She reluctantly nods and she hears him swear under his breath.

She reminds him, "Phillip, I told you Lawrence was going to be upset *at first* when he found out about his real mother, but then relieved once he knew the full story. *I promise you* he doesn't blame you, because he knows Millicent, and the cruelty she inflicts on others, *probably better than anyone*! He has *never* said anything but words of gratefulness that he knows the truth, *and you're in our lives.*"

"*Thank you.*" He struggles to say. He clears his throat. "Millicent has always been an anomaly to me. *I could never figure her out!*"

"Let's talk about *that* when we get back inside." Bri puts her arm around his and they start walking back.

Lawrence sees them walking towards the house and he goes over to sit back down to wait. When Phillip and Bri come inside, the two sit with Maggie, Henry, and Lawrence once again.

Maggie says with a little amazement, "I never thought I would *ever* feel bad for that *awful woman!*"

Henry replies, "I think it's that we feel bad for the young woman who never had a chance." They all agree.

Bri turns to Phillip. "*Millicent* is *an anomaly*! She grew up thinking she was in-love with her uncle in a sort of weird, twisted, 'Stockholm Syndrome' effect. I'm thinking it started as self-preservation, but keep in mind, a part of her remains that brainwashed young girl because of the abuse she endured all those formative years, *including the forced abortions*!" She sadly remembers, "I watched the light fade right out of her after her hysterectomy! I think the pain and suffering she inflicts on others is *deeply rooted* in all of that, because it caused a self-hatred she never wants to face. Instead, she projects her self-hatred onto others. While I feel empathy, *and sympathy*, for that young woman, along with the fact that Millicent was messed up at such a young age, she is a *growing* threat *right now* to those I love, as well as the innocent people who will get caught up in all this!" She takes a deep breath and exhales slowly. "Ever since meeting Millicent, I have felt like I've been on a train that is gaining momentum at 'full speed ahead,' heading to what feels like a cliff that is *somewhere* down the track, and I don't know how much time there is before that train flies right off a cliff! I do feel this will all come to a point where I will have to face Millicent; *however*, I'm hoping to bring the fight to her *before* I'm pregnant with Lawrence's heir! In Millicent's *twisted* mind, *I'm to blame* for *all* of the more recent trouble in her life, making me her focus until I'm 'neutralized' as a threat, and eventually disposed of when she no longer needs me. So, the sooner I can bring her down, the sooner our family, *and everyone else around us*, will be safe!"

"Bri," Lawrence moves to sit on the coffee table in front of her, "it's '*we*' will bring her down. *You're not doing this alone*!"

"Lawrence, I'm the only one *who can*!" She replies.

"*No, you're not*!" Lawrence tells her. "*She needs me, just as much as she needs you*!"

"True, *but* you're limited in your movements, because you're 'The King.' You need to be, *and will be*, kept safe *to run the country*!" She states. "Besides, after I have our baby, we can't stop her if she is bent on getting to me, *or our baby*!" Bri replies. "And Millicent *will* kill me after she has no more use for me, just like she killed Vivian. *She has to* in order to clear the way to take over The Monarchy, like she *desperately* wants to do!"

He looks her in the eyes with a very serious look. "*Over* my *dead body*! That woman will *never* touch our baby!"

"*You can't promise that!*" Bri tells him. "She wants to rule this country, *and have all the power that comes with it!* Where there's a will, and let's face it, *the woman is determined,* she *will* find a way!"

"If I need to, I'll hide you away in your own tower, Bri!" Lawrence tells her.

"I have long ago learned that if someone is determined to hurt, or kill, another person, they will succeed in at least a serious attempt! Millicent has lots of people and lots of money to help her succeed."

Lawrence notes, "After what she did to Natty and Emmie, she doesn't have as much support as she once had!"

"Perhaps." Bri replies.

Henry says, "Desperate people do tend to make mistakes."

"True." Bri agrees. "*But she won't make very many.*"

Maggie suggests that they let the conversation go for now and they all go into the dining room to eat dinner. They follow her and take their seats. They talk for a little bit before the subject of Katie comes up.

Lawrence is a bit agitated asking Bri, "*Why in* hell *would you want* anything *to do with that* ghastly woman *ever again?!*"

Maggie answers, "Lawrence, that's just who Bri is. She is one of the most compassionate people we know!"

Lawrence has an 'that's true' look and he gives Bri a small smile. "I'll support you going to see Katie, *but only if* I *come along!* I'd *never* forgive myself if something happened and I wasn't there! *What's worse,* Jack and David would never forgive me!"

She squeezes his hand. "*I've been expecting you to go with.*"

Lawrence is relieved and holds her hand to his heart. "Thank you."

She smiles with her nod. Henry changes the conversation, and they finish their meal on a more pleasant note.

CHAPTER 6
Caught Up in a Wicked Web

Bri is in a picky mood looking through her things in the closet. She is trying to find a shirt to go with the dark blue jeans she already has on, which are snug around her lower abdomen. She makes a mental note that she needs to go shopping for some maternity clothes. She *hates* tight clothes; it makes *everyone* look bigger than they really are. It is an optical illusion that is *not* in anyone's favor, regardless of a person's body size, or shape!

"*Finally!*" She whispers to herself when she finds a darker royal blue shirt to wear; she puts it on.

 She looks for a necklace...she picks one that has small round stones of blue, pink, and white, all set in an antique style setting, with matching earrings. Then she puts on her two-toned Cartier watch from David that she frequently wears, with a diamond to mark the hours of 12, 3, 6, and 9.

She stands in front of the full-length mirror for one last look. She softly smiles when she sees Lawrence's reflection appear in the mirror behind her. She turns around when he walks over to her.

He lovingly smiles, cupping her cheek. "I could stare into your beautiful eyes forever..." he taps a kiss to her lips, "*but* we do need to leave."

"Hnnn," she softly smiles, "I could say the same thing about your incredible blue-green eyes." He handsomely winks at her.

She goes to pick up her jacket, but Lawrence takes it and holds it open so she can easily slip it on. They grab their phones, his wallet, and her purse on their way out of the bedroom. The motorcade is waiting for them in front of the Bradshaw's home.

They drive up the driveway of the state's rehabilitation center and see a dated, but well-kept, large brick building with a freshly mowed lawn. There are flowers in the flower beds that run along the front of the building, and two big flowerpots with colorful flowers on either side of the main entrance's sliding glass doors.

Ken and Bill are waiting for them outside the main entrance. They helped The Royal Guards earlier do a security sweep, then talked with the staff and Administrator about Bri visiting Katie before Bri and Lawrence's arrival. They walk up to the SUV as it pulls up to the front doors. Bri climbs out of the SUV after Lawrence, and they greet Ken and Bill.

They all walk into the building through the main entrance and go up to the reception desk where the staff are expecting them. Bri gets a creepy feeling and looks around where she sees all kinds of people staring at them, *at her*. She pushes the creepiness out of her mind, unaware a few of Millicent's minions were lurking among the other patients and visitors.

Ken whispers to Bri, "*They're only aware of 'Duchess BriaLynn' because I wasn't sure if Katie knew about your new titles?*"

Bri whispers, "*Good thinking!*"

Lawrence tells Bri. "We will follow your lead, *to a point.*"

She is confused. "*To a point?*"

"I refuse to let anything happen to you." He replies. "*Especially with you being pregnant!*"

"Well, let's hope this visit stays friendly." Bri replies.

The Administrator comes over and walks them to Katie's room. She explains Katie's recovery to Bri along the way.

"Ms. Barnes hasn't been committed to her recovery as much as we would like to see by this point. She seems to only be going through the motions, and we're afraid that if she doesn't have support outside these walls when she is released, she could easily go right back to using again." Bri's heart is saddened, but it is the same sadness she would have for anyone in Katie's situation.

"Has she made any progress towards getting better?"

"Oh, she has improved *some* since she first came, but..." The Administrator trails off thinking of how to say the rest.

"But she has no enthusiasm to excel?" Bri helps.

The Administrator nods. "I guess that's a good way of putting it."

Bri curiously asks, "How old are your records? I'm thinking that having me as her emergency contact may be old information."

The Administrator's eyebrows come together as she opens her folder to double check. She shows Bri the paper and points asking, "Isn't this you?"

Bri's eyebrows go up; she is expecting to see 'BriaLynn Harris,' but instead she sees the updated 'BriaLynn Worthington.' She replies, "That's me."

The Administrator puts the paper back in the file saying, "Ms. Barnes wants me to tell you that she will see only you."

"*Out of the question!*" Lawrence is alarmed at the thought of Bri being alone in a room with Katie.

Bri squeezes his hand and looks at the Administrator. "*Most* of these wonderful people won't be coming into the room with me."

The Administrator nods. "Her room is right here." She motions with a little wave. "There's a waiting area right there," she points, "with a view right at her door and down both ends of the hallway." Watching her gesture all that reminds Bri of a flight attendant doing the 'in case of an emergency' how-to before take-off.

"This should work." Bri says, looking at McMasters, who agrees.

Lawrence shakes The Administrator's hand saying, "Thank you." She smiles with her nod at him and Bri, then she goes back down the hallway.

McMasters has a few guards stay in the waiting area with Ken and Bill, while the rest of The King's Guards disperse around the facility and grounds to join the other Royal Guards who had come earlier for the security sweep and to take up their positions prior to the royal arrival.

Bri turns to go into Katie's room, when Lawrence gently stops her. "*We* go in with you," he firmly says moving his finger back and forth between him and McMasters, "or *you* don't go in at all." Then he points to himself saying, "*My terms.*"

Bri takes a quick, deep breath. "Well, there's only one way to find out if she will agree to *your terms.*" She lightly teases with his accent.

He gives her a soft smile and tips his head towards Katie's room whispering, "*Cheeky.*"

She faintly smiles as she walks past him going into the room; Lawrence and McMasters follow. They see Katie sitting on the bed writing in a journal. Her bed is made with a plain thin bedspread and two pillows propped up against the headboard. Across from her bed is a little cove that has a loveseat tucked in it. In front of the loveseat is a coffee table with some old magazines on it, and an end table on each side of the loveseat. Then there is an armchair sitting perpendicular to the loveseat, facing the door. Lawrence sits on the loveseat, while McMasters takes the armchair.

Bri walks over and cordially says, "Hello, Katie."

"Bri." Katie returns the cordialness, then points with the top of her pen to Lawrence and McMasters saying with a hint of annoyance in her voice, "*I didn't approve them.*"

"It's the only way I could come, Katie." Bri politely tells her.

"Kept on a short leash nowadays, are we?" Katie asks.

"*Katie...*" Bri softly scolds her.

Katie exhales, "*Fine.*" She takes a real look at Lawrence, becoming a tad 'greener' realizing who he is, and it is heard in her snippy tone. "Why *are* you here, *Your Grace? Or is it 'Your Majesty?'*" Her eyebrow goes up. "*To gloat?*"

"Katie," Bri patiently points out, "if you really thought that's why I was coming, you wouldn't have agreed to see me."

"Then *why* are you here, Bri?" Katie asks with a touch of irritation.

"I wanted to see how you were doing and how your rehab is going." Bri answers. "Do you need anything—."

"*Nope*. I'm just *peachy* in this five-star luxury spa." Katie says with sarcasm. "I'm sure Ken and Bill have filled you in."

Bri is disappointed. "If this is how you want this to go, I'm *not* playing." She starts to turn to leave.

"*Seriously*, after everything that has happened between us, you came here?!" Katie is baffled. "You're living a dream life and yet you come to this dreary, *way off* 'Fifth Avenue' place, to visit me, *some criminal?! Why?!*"

"You're not just '*some criminal,*' Katie."

"*Why*—?!"

"*I don't know!* Alright?!" Bri shoots back at her, tossing her hands up in the air. "They said it might be helpful if I came to see you, *so here I am!*" Then she scoffs, "And this is some *dream life!* Emmie, Natty, Jeff, and Olivia have all been murdered—."

"*Murdered?!*" Katie is shocked.

Bri is puzzled. "You haven't heard?"

"We're not allowed to stay current." Katie points to the outdated magazines on the coffee table. "Those are *years* old." Katie is genuinely concerned, "*What happened?*"

"It's still under investigation, but they were poisoned." Bri tells her.

"*Poisoned?*" Katie whispers to herself looking down as her eyes get teary. She looks at Bri again and says, "*I'm so sorry.* No matter *our* history, I loved Emmie and Natty. I wanted them grow up and make better choices than I ever did!"

58

Bri takes off her jacket and lays it over the footboard of Katie's bed. Then she sits at the very end of Katie's bed.

"Aside from this nightmare," Bri takes a deep breath, exhaling slowly and moves the conversation back, "you could've been part of this life with me."

"*Not when you took Jack!*" Katie snips.

"*Jack is a grown man, capable of deciding* what *he wants, and* who *he wants, to be with!*" Bri shoots back. "Besides, we can't go back to when I *stupidly* thought we were *best friends*." Katie's eyes dart away from Bri, and she shamefully looks at the floor. "Regardless, I *do* want you to succeed in rehab, so you can rebuild a happy, *healthy* life, if that's what you want!"

Katie snorts a scoff. "It's not like I can go back to the marketing job I had!"

"Probably not, but there *are* other marketing firms out there." Bri replies.

Katie tsks. "*Who's going to hire someone with a criminal record?!*"

"Katie, you *first* need to focus on rebuilding a *solid* foundation. *Then* when you go back into the workforce, you won't start at the same level you once were, but you *can* get there again, *if* you work hard for it! *Who knows?* You could surpass that position; or end up in a position that is completely different, *and* you love even more!"

"Well, it won't be like living *your* fairytale life!" Katie snaps.

Bri is a bit annoyed. "Katie, *seriously?*"

"What Bri? You're out there living *the* life, as a duchess no less, married to a duke and have two other hot men, *a King and* my *Jack!*"

Her 'my Jack' is an irritation, but Bri pushes past it. "You never showed interest in Jack until you got bored with James. Your behavior just turned them off, *even as a friend*."

Katie rolls her eyes. "You probably helped convince Jack of that, after telling him about our past!"

"*That's just it*! I didn't tell him about our past until *after* the wedding, when they asked me about it! Jack had already made up his mind about you the first week after we all met, because of your behavior and choices! *You did it all by yourself*, but 'the icing' on it came when you showed up in Rome. *Why on* earth *did you even go to Rome? To torture yourself?*!"

Katie shrugs. "I didn't really have a plan. I needed to be there for work, then I found out you two were already there..." She trails off.

"*Oy*." Bri squeezes the bridge of her nose. "Katie, Rome was our honeymoon! When David, Jack, and I signed paperwork the day before the wedding, it made Jack and I legally bound, *essentially married*, when I married David." Katie's eyebrows furrow as she looks down at her bed and thinks about what Bri is saying. "What you don't know is what David told me later, that if Jack would've committed to being 'The Noble Consort' only on paper, Jack *never* would've married *anyone else*." Lawrence thinks about that, which he agrees with.

Katie's head pops up. "Wait. *What*?!"

"Jack wouldn't have wanted being 'The Noble Consort' looming over a marriage with another woman. If Jack would've been my Noble Consort on paper and married someone else, then God forbid something happened to David, Jack would have thirty days to dissolve his first marriage, then marry me. David would tell me all this *after* we were married, because David wanted my relationship with Jack to be for love, or *none of this* would work."

Katie hears this and looks out the window. "Why not James?"

"Besides, you and James being together at first? David saw the connection Jack and I had with each other. It's not a joke when it's been said that, had David missed his opportunity to be with me that night at The Black-Tie Party, Jack wouldn't have, *and* he probably would've convinced me to elope with him soon after!"

Katie is still looking out the window. "It's not fair that you—."

"Katie, *please* understand." Bri pleads with her. "*I know* I don't even deserve David, nor to have him love me as much as he does!" Katie looks at her a little surprised because she *does* support Bri being with David. "Then, for David to keep his promise, a promise I'm told he made in front of a few others, *including you!*"

Katie looks at the floor as she remembers, "That you would be loved more than any woman has ever been loved..."

"Well, David is a blessing, and the additional love of Jack and Lawrence are *truly* a blessing's *gifts*." Bri replies.

It is quiet for a minute, before Katie almost inaudibly says, "*I've messed everything up.*"

Bri wants to keep her guard up; in case it is a way for Katie to suck her back into the mess of her life. She isn't going to sugarcoat anything.

"Yes, you have." She states. Then she firmly tells Katie, "I'm just being honest, Katie. You can't make any *real* changes if you don't acknowledge the truth. You *need* to take responsibility for your own life *and* all *of your choices that got you to this point! No one made you do any of it!* The only way you'll ever find solid ground again is by accepting there *is* a Divine Plan for you, *including* a way for you to get back on your feet and start moving in the right direction again." Bri lifts her hands stating, "*You've already started right here with rehab!*" Katie takes a deep breath; she knows Bri is right.

Katie changes the subject. "I thought I heard somewhere that you're pregnant," Bri nods, "but with a Noble Consort, *and a king,* how——."

"David *is* the father." Bri confidently tells her.

"Wouldn't they require a DNA test——."

"*They do.*" Lawrence answers, flipping through a magazine without looking up at them. "All royals and titled nobility are *required* to have their DNA tested if they are to inherit *any* title."

Bri brings her back to their conversation saying, "Look, Katie, I can see about getting you into private rehab after you're done here, *but you will stay at the next one until* they say *you are ready to go out on your own.* We will relocate you to a new city, so you won't be tempted to hang around the same people you used drugs with. Otherwise, there is a higher chance you could relapse."

Katie rolls her eyes asking, "*And go where*? Newhaven?"

"*No.*" Lawrence firmly states, still looking at the magazine.

Katie glares at him, only he doesn't see it. "I think I like McMasters better."

"*Me, too.*" Bri flatly says, looking over her shoulder as Lawrence looks up at her to see her smirking with an eyebrow raised in sassiness. "*He's quieter.*" Lawrence and McMasters lightly chuckle to themselves, shaking their heads. Bri turns back to Katie. "*Anyway*, I've heard about a great facility in Vermont. It's a beautiful place, out in the country, with various things to do and classes to take. I will have someone look into it for you, if you're serious about *staying* clean." Katie softly nods. Bri stands up and picks up her jacket; the men stand up and stretch. She puts on her jacket telling Katie, "I really do hope and pray you get back on track, Katie."

Katie watches Bri walk towards the door and asks, "How do you know it wouldn't be a waste of money?"

Bri stops and turns to Katie. "*I don't.* And you could take advantage of this for two years. I just hope you'll use your super smart brain and take the opportunity presented before you; an opportunity that I won't offer you again, Katie. Most people who are serious about getting clean and having a fresh start would give *anything* for a chance like this. I really do hope you take advantage of this opportunity to heal yourself, *along with* all *the benefits about to come your way*!" Lawrence opens the door. "Take care of yourself, Katie."

Katie waves as they leave, thinking about what Bri has said. Katie starts to feel the guilt once again about all that she has done to Bri. It does start to creep into her heart, but the feeling starts to fade when she thinks of Bri's life of money, privilege, and luxury. She doesn't consider the loss Bri has had with Natty's and Emmie's deaths; Katie doesn't even know about Bri's physical assault in The Royal Dungeons not too long ago. Katie goes back to writing in her journal, which is required for the program she is in.

Bri talks with The Administrator at the reception desk about the private rehab center in Vermont, if Katie is genuinely interested. Bri pulls out Gabriel's card with his phone number on it, and hands it to The Administrator explaining that Gabriel will help make all those arrangements when Katie is ready. They thank The Administrator and the staff before they leave.

A few hours after Bri leaves, Katie gets another visitor. A woman walks in dressed in a black tailored skirt suit with red accents and a ruby necklace.

Katie looks this woman over. "I think you have the wrong room, Ma'am."

The woman asks with a British accent, "Are *you* Miss Katie Barnes?"

"*I am.*" Katie answers with reservation. "Who are you?"

The woman puts her nose up in the air and replies with a snobby tone, "*I am The Queen Mother.*"

"*Riiiight.*" Katie is thinking this woman is suffering from some kind of mental illness. She nicely tells her, "Why don't you have a seat," she motions to the loveseat, "and I'll go get someone to help you."

"Ms. Barnes, I'm here to see if you're willing to work with me and get some payback with Her Royal Majesty, at the same time?" She says it that way, because she hopes to push her jealousy button.

Katie raises her eyebrow in curiosity. "What do you mean?"

"How much time do you have left in this..." Millicent lifts her hands up gesturing the room, her tone revealing her revulsion, "...*place?*"

"Until March," Katie replies, "or sooner with good behavior."

"Good! Now, what *I* need you to do is to continue with your rehab, then when you're released, *I'll* bring you to the *best facility* in the UK for additional treatment." Millicent tells her. "Then you can *help me* by giving me insights into BriaLynn and her family; particularly, the people closest to her." That part had Henry and Maggie coming to mind, only gets a sick feeling about telling Millicent anything about the Bradshaw's, which is easy to work around.

"Alright then." Katie agrees, not caring what Millicent needed to know about Bri, while keeping the Bradshaw family out of it. She exhales, "I better get dressed for group."

"That's it!" Millicent says, faking her support rather perfectly. She hands Katie a cell phone. "This is only to be used for contact between you and me. No other calls can come in or go out." She looks intensely at Katie as she firmly says, *"Consequences will be deadly."*

Katie nods, but she isn't completely listening as she takes the phone; she is imagining the look on Bri's face when she is 'checkmated' so-to-speak. Katie doesn't quite grasp how dangerous Millicent is; although Millicent is impressed with Katie's reaction that she doesn't care what happens to Bri.

Katie tells Millicent, "I have to keep this phone hidden, or it could be stolen, even confiscated."

"Then I won't call you, but you need to memorize my phone number in case it does get taken away or stolen." Millicent replies and Katie nods. "Make sure you check it every now and then for any text messages, and to keep me posted on your progress; then check it more often as you get closer to being released."

"I will." Katie replies.

"I'll bid you farewell for now." Millicent turns towards the door. *"Oh!"* She turns back. "If you need *anything*, let *me* know. *I will take good care of you!"*

"That's really nice of you." Katie says.

"I know." Millicent says, with a hint of arrogance and her fake smile.

Millicent leaves; proud of herself for usurping Katie to her side. Katie gets dressed and goes to her group therapy session. She keeps her excitement suppressed about the chance to knock Bri down. *'Bri can take her private rehab in Vermont and shove it!'* Katie thinks to herself. *'Whatever this lady has planned for Bri, I want a front row seat!'* Unfortunately, Katie has *no* idea she is now caught up in a *wicked* web...nor how deadly things *will* get!

CHAPTER 7

Goodbye Isn't Forever

It is the day of the funeral and Bri is up in the bedroom she shares with David at The Worthington Manor. She stares at herself in the full-length mirror with her hands on her baby bump. She is wearing a black maternity dress today, with her Diamond-Heart Necklace set, along with her two-tone watch.

She hears the door to their quarters open, followed by several footsteps. She sees David's reflection and watches him walk over to her. He comes up behind her and puts his hands on hers that are on her baby bump. He kisses her neck, then lovingly looks at her in the mirror.

"Jack and Herst are in the other room. We've come up to see if you need anything, or if you're ready?"

"I'm as ready as I'm ever going to be." Her eyes are red and moist. She turns to him and hugs him.

He hugs her back a little tighter and kisses her head. Then he follows her out to their living room where Jack and Lawrence are waiting. She walks over to Jack and hugs him first.

"Thank you," she looks at all three of them, "for *all* of your love and support."

Jack cups her cheek. "If there is anything you need, *at any time*, make sure you tell us. *Alright?*" She nods.

Lawrence steps closer. "As we did for Jeff and Olivia's funeral, we will start off with me escorting you, but you will dictate how things go after that."

"Okay." She quietly replies and hugs him.

They all go downstairs and meet up with everyone else at The Main Entrance. Maggie and Carlotta slip small packages of tissues to all the guys to put in their pockets and to all the ladies to put in their purses. Then they all file outside to the awaiting motorcade.

Driving along the various roads and streets, they pass by many crowds that have gathered along their route, the biggest one is just outside The Main Entrance of The Newhaven Estate. The people are relatively quiet with signs of condolences. Bri sees the flowers that are weaved on the black iron gate as they open, and the motorcade drives through.

They drive past Newhaven Manor and up to the doors of The Newhaven Cathedral that is at one end of The Manor. Lawrence gets out first, then helps Bri out. The rest of the family gathers at the doors before filing inside and walking to the designated pews.

Typically, after all the guests have arrived, nobility will start the 'formal procession,' in reverse order, to their seats. Then the royals go in, working their way up the king and queen, or equivalent rulers, to make an entrance and give the people a chance to pay their respects to their rulers. Although for this family, things will be done just a bit differently, because of Seth and Bri, and their relationships with Genevieve and Lawrence.

Lawrence and Bri stand in position to enter The Cathedral after the doors close behind Prince Seth and Queen Genevieve. Bri has a thought as she stands there. *'What if Millicent is in there somewhere?'* Then she thinks to herself. *'No, Millicent is much too smart for that! She would have sent someone to set up a video feed to watch my emotional state at a safe location!'*

When the doors open, Bri holds Lawrence's hand as they walk inside. She pauses when she sees the two caskets down in front of the church. She swallows hard and Lawrence takes the arm of the hand he is holding and tucks it under his arm, then they start walking again. She is *determined* not to give Millicent the satisfaction of seeing her fall apart!

They get to the front of The Cathedral where she sits in the front row with Lawrence on one side, which is next to the aisle, and David on her other side; Jack is sitting on the other side of David. Bri is staring off at nothing in particular when the services start...it all still feels *so surreal* to her! She tunes in when Joe steps up to the podium.

> "Your Majesty, *Your Royal Majesty*, Your Graces, Sirs, Ladies, family, friends."

He clears his throat of a lump forming in it.

> "Ladies and Gentlemen, while I am honored to have been asked to give the eulogy today, it's very difficult to do so when these two beautiful young ladies were taken from us, from their wonderful mother, before they ever really lived."

He struggles and swallows hard.

> "Lady Emerson and Lady Natalie are two wonderful young women with loving and humorous personalities!"

He smiles at a memory that comes to mind, then continues.

> "While they are twins and similar in various ways, there are qualities about each of them that make them beautifully unique individuals!"

Bri smiles softly to herself and looks at the floor, thinking about her girls...back to her beautiful babies and through the years...then a bit of sadness as she thinks about the things she wishes she could have done differently as a mother, *their mother...*

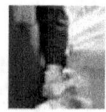 David gently lays Bri's hand in her lap and stands up, snapping her back into the moment. She realizes the funeral has ended and watches Jack go to one casket and David goes to the other. They are joined by Joe, Mitch, and Sam, along with Bri's other brothers and brother-in-laws. The pallbearers solemnly carry the caskets outside. Lawrence firmly holds Bri's hand again, tucking her arm under his as they follow right behind the caskets and pallbearers. Then they watch the caskets being carefully put inside an old-fashioned horse drawn hearse carriage.

They will be going out to the cemetery on The Newhaven Estate. The Worthington Family has their own mausoleum, which is the second largest; it is barely second to The Newhaven Family's mausoleum. While the family and close friends go out to The Worthington Mausoleum for a private service, everyone else is invited to stay for the reception in The Great Hall inside Newhaven Manor.

David, Lawrence, Bri, and Jack, walk in silence as they follow the horse drawn hearse, with the family and close friends walking behind them. Bri stares at the road as she walks and thinks about all the things the girls will never get a chance to do... When the carriage stops, so does everyone walking behind it. The pallbearers come up to the carriage and take the caskets out, then walk them to the designated places in front of The Worthington Mausoleum.

When Bri follows the caskets with Lawrence, she sees everything is set up in front of a mausoleum. She looks above the doors, and it reads: Worthington. David had just set the casket down with the other pallbearers and he sees the questioning look on her face.

David goes up to her and lovingly tells her, "It shouldn't be a surprise that our family wanted them here." He leans closer. "This way, they will always be close by and protected."

She takes his hand and holds it to her heart. Her eyes are teary as she struggles to say, "*Thank you.*"

They are guided to sit in the front row of chairs that were set up. David has Jack sit next to Bri, and Lawrence is going to have David sit on the other side of Bri only David tells Lawrence to sit there, then David sits next to him.

There is a small gust of a sharp, crisp Autumn breeze that catches Bri's breath. It wakes her up from her stare at the caskets in front of her as the caskets sit between her and The Worthington Mausoleum. She doesn't know how long she has been sitting there when Jack gently squeezes her hand, then tips his head for her to go up and stand next to The Bishop.

She quickly pulls out a folded piece of paper from her small purse, then stands up and puts her purse on her chair. She walks up and stands next to The Bishop, then faces the family, close friends, and a few trusted reporters. She takes a deep breath and exhales slowly, summoning the courage to speak.

"Thank you all for coming today." She begins. "My wonderful family planned these lovely services because I couldn't. I *couldn't* wrap my mind around having funerals for them," she looks at the caskets and her voice cracks, "*when life was about to begin for them.*" She looks at Peter, Carlotta, Maggie, and Henry. "*To my wonderful family,*" she puts her hand to her heart and squeaks to them, "*I'm incredibly grateful, and I love you more than I could ever express to you!*" She swallows hard. "I have been thinking about what to say today, but I couldn't figure out how to say what's in my h-heart...how do I say goodbye to my

69

babies?" She struggles and her jaw shakes, but she forces herself to push through, "I would write a sentence or two, here and there, then when I sat down to put all the sentences together. A poem began to form and came together..." She opens the folded paper and reads:

> "Time goes by and seasons change,
> Autumn freezes into winter,
> But it doesn't numb the pain.
>
> When the sun starts to warm,
> It melts the ice and snow,
> Dissolving winter and spring begins to show.
>
> Rain and sun nourish the plants,
> They bloom and grow throughout the summer,
> And we see flowers of every size, shape, and color.
>
> Nature announces Autumn with a vibrant color show,
> It's one last celebration of life,
> Before it all comes to a close.
>
> Now on *this* Autumn day,
> We are gathered here to say goodbye,
> Then tomorrow, we will go our separate ways,
> To carry on with our lives.
>
> Like flowers in the wind,
> You both floated into our lives for a season,
> *Only now that season has come to an end.*"

She catches her sob that starts to slip out and works to push it down, but she can't speak. Lawrence comes up and wraps an arm around her, while taking her paper and he continues.

> "How does a mother say goodbye?
> How does she let go of the pain?
> How does she look towards the future,
> When she no longer *knows the way*?"
>
> "How do I hand all of this over to you, Lord?

70

And let You show me the way?
To trust that this raw pain, won't be this raw forever?"

"Time will push our lives forward,
Whether we want it to or not.
But my love will always be with you both,
And I will forever carry you in my heart."

 Lawrence pulls Bri into a firm hug for a solid minute; she buries her face to cry so no one can see it, especially Millicent if she is somehow watching. *Everyone* is struggling with their emotions. Lawrence leads her back to their seats, and he hands her the piece of paper back, then Jack hands her a tissue. The Bishop takes a minute compose himself before he wraps up the graveside service.

After graveside service has ended, people stand up and start filing over to hug Bri on their way to the reception, back at Newhaven Manor. She hugs the last person, then notices the bystanders and crowds in the distance are also thinning out. She sits back down and stares sorrowfully at the caskets in front of her, thinking back at the various memories in her heart.

A little while later, she looks around for Lawrence, David, and Jack. She sees them standing together a short distance away. Jack sees her looking over at them and walks over to her. David and Lawrence stay where they are, they don't want Bri to feel crowded if they all come over.

In her peripheral view, Bri watches Jack as he sits down in the chair next to her. She whispers, *"I know we should go..."*

Jack lightly squeezes her hand and quietly tells her, *"Take all the time you need."* She lays her head on his shoulder, and he rests his cheek on her head.

After several minutes go by, Bri lifts her head and dries her eyes. She sees people starting to clean up and she stands up with the two white roses she has had in her hand. She walks over to the caskets and puts a rose on the top of each casket. She kisses her fingers and places those fingers on one daughter's casket; then she does the same to the other daughter's casket.

"I love you *both*," she swallows hard, "and I miss you both *so much...*" She starts to squeak again.

Teary-eyed, Bri turns to Jack and holds her hand out for him to take. He stands up, reaching out his hand to take her hand. As they walk towards Lawrence and David, she looks around again. She spots McMasters, who slightly tips his head to the side. She scans that direction until she sees a man she recognizes standing next to an angel statue that is taller than the man is, and she stops.

David and Lawrence walk over to Jack and Bri, with Lawrence asking, "Are you alright, Darling?"

Bri gives a little nod, then asks, "Will you give us a moment..." She casually tips her head towards the angel statue.

They look over and see the gentleman, but Lawrence and Jack look back at Bri confused as to who this man is; David gives Bri a nod. David recognized Rex Stirling and since he had done this sort of thing before, he tells Lawrence and Jack who he is as Bri walks over to Rex, and he is walking over to her.

Rex puts his hand to chest and says, "My sincerest *and deepest* condolences, Your Royal Majesty."

"Thank you." She replies. "Seeing as we're not in public, we don't need to be quite so formal, Rex."

He gives her a little nod. "I have had my people keeping an eye on Millicent and her people for a long time now, only today they were a bit more focused; we wanted to give you privacy, *especially from her.*" She slightly raises her eyebrow. He has a faint grin replying, "*Wi-fi connections can fail right before something is to start and by the time it would be 'fixed,' it's too late.*"

Bri gives him a faint smile. She now knows she was right to assume Millicent was wanting to watch the funeral, *to watch her*! She is relieved that didn't happen!

"Thank you for that." She explains, "I've had my guard up in case she was somehow able to watch. I didn't want her to have the satisfaction of seeing me break down."

"What Millicent did to you, *to them*," he motions the girls' caskets being carried into The Worthington Mausoleum, "is *despicable*! I know they say, 'there is no honor among thieves,' but for most of the criminal underworld, there has always been a bit of one when it comes to children, and the wives who were not involved with the criminal business. For those very few who don't have that basic honor code, we tend to police those who cross those lines ourselves." Bri nods in understanding.

"*I need your help, Rex!*" Bri says with a pleading tone that cuts to his very soul. "*Millicent is going to keep killing those I care about most, and any others who get caught up in all this. I* need *to bring this woman down as soon as I can,* before *I have Lawrence's baby,* his heir! *I can't go straight at her,* not just yet. *Otherwise, there will be* even more *casualties!*"

"Actually," he gives her a small, kind smile, "I came here to offer you my group's *services* to help you bring her down." She doesn't need to think about it, she throws her arms around his neck and hugs him. He is a bit surprised, but he hugs her back. "I will get with them, and we'll come up with a plan."

She takes a small step back. "Well, I've definitely been thinking a lot about how to bring her down...*permanently!*" Bri admits.

He raises his eyebrow in intrigue. "And just what have you come up with?"

"Well, I know I won't stoop to her level and just start killing those closest to her. *Besides*, there are only a couple of people she would care about losing, although," she thinks about it, "Millicent wouldn't care enough about them to really protect them anyway." She says. "No, Millicent's *real love* is money and power. She doesn't have any actual ruling power anymore, *not until she gets her hands on Lawrence's heir!*"

Rex reluctantly adds, "And she will kill all four of you to get His Majesty's heir, *to* have *that controlling power!* She will also kill anyone else who would interfere with that control!" Bri has a 'that's true' expression on her face.

In The United Kingdom of Provinces, an underage regnant, which is the reigning king or queen, would typically have two to three regents, or advisors, to rule with them until the child becomes of age; usually when they are twenty-five years old. *Only one* of those advisors can be a family member, yet *none of them* would take care of the child for the safety of the underage monarch. The actual care and well-being of the monarch would be placed with a nanny, or a governess. That's because when advisors get a taste of the ruling power, the child's life tends to be in grave danger with at least one of the regents, or advisors, if not all of them. The advisor, or advisors, would do whatever it takes to keep that power, even leading a coup to kill the child monarch *and the other advisors*, in order to seize The Throne. With Millicent, it would be a bit different. She would raise Lawrence's heir alone, and more cruelly than Lawrence ever was, having learned from her 'past mistakes.' She wants this child to be her legacy, to cruelly rule the country after she dies, preferably to rule in more tyrannical ways than anyone ever has!

Bri goes on to tell Rex, "The only way Millicent has power now is with money. And she needs *lots* of money to pay for that power, and for the loyalty it will take to get her into that position of power and *keep her there. That's where I want to start!* I want to attack her financially, including all her shipments, auctions, storage places, and of course, her bank accounts."

"I think going after her financially is a *brilliant* start, but I've been around long enough to know, *and you need to understand*, this is just going to keep going back and forth between you two until—."

"*Until* one of us stays down, *or dies?*" Bri finishes and he gives her a weak nod. "I've thought of that, too." She takes a deep breath. "But we cleverly, and covertly, need to start somewhere. From a covert place that she wouldn't even consider that I'm behind it, at least not at first, or until I tell her."

"Alright." He replies. "This will take some time; however, it *is* doable *with patience.*" She understands. "I'll go and present this to my team. It will require a number of my people to go in undercover and there are going to be a number of illegal things we're going to have to do just to collect our intel, not to mention what we end up doing to get into her very *inner circle.*"

Bri motions for Lawrence, David, and Jack, to come over, along with McMasters and Mitchell. When the five men join Bri and Rex, she makes the introductions, and they all shake hands.

"Gentlemen, Rex is going to help us, and I had you all come over here because Rex is going to ask his people to get involved. In order to do that, some of them will have to get embedded *deep* with Millicent's lackeys. And to do this, they are going to have to do some things that are going to be, um...let's say, *outside* of legal."

They all pick up on what she is hinting at, with Lawrence saying to Rex, "I will protect *all* who help us with whatever is needed to take this evil woman down! All I ask is that *you all* protect the innocent, *and Bri!*"

"I give you my word, Your Majesty, *to all of you*, and my word *is* my bond! We will protect her!" He offers his hand to Lawrence, and they shake on it; he shakes the others men's hands as well. "This kind of thing will require a number of my people to get embedded with her group *properly*, and *that's not done quickly!* We need to put reputations out there, so she sends her people to seek them out; she is like the rest of us and very leery of anyone who approaches her, or her people!" They all nod in understanding. "To do this right, I want to prepare you that this will all take some time, not only to get more of my people inside with her people, but they will also need to earn Millicent's trust to be the most effective for us."

"How much time are we talking about? *A year?!*" Bri panics. "Millicent could have our entire family and friends wiped out by then! *Maybe we need to rethink this?*"

"No, no." Rex waves his hand. "It'll take *about* six months," he gestures her baby bump, "which will get you through your pregnancy." Bri rests her hand on her lower abdomen. "As you know, I already have a few people on the inside who can thwart a few of her plans." She nods. "Bri, if we do this fast and hasty, we will *definitely* get good people killed, even innocent people, and that's what we *all* want to avoid!"

"True. I don't want *any* casualties, but that's not realistic. All we can do is keep that number as low as possible!" She says and Rex agrees. "Rex, I don't know how much money you want—."

"Protecting my team is all that is necessary, because taking Millicent down benefits *everyone!*" Rex tells her. "And taking her down this way means there is a greater chance she won't be getting back up!"

"Let's hope." Bri replies. She takes a couple more steps, then she remembers something. She turns to Rex again and cautiously says, "*I have one more favor...*"

"Of course! What is it?" He asks.

"Would you dig into Claude Devereaux's history for me." Rex's eyebrow shoots up; Lawrence, David, and Jack have heard his name and only know that he is pretty big in the criminal world. Mitchell and McMasters know how much more dangerous this man is compared to Rex, *or even Millicent*. Where Millicent has a reason to kill someone, even a very thin reason, Claude Devereaux doesn't need a reason. Bri explains more, "Claude Devereaux *has to be neutralized* because he is her best customer. We have to find a way to stop him, to stop the biggest flow of money into Millicent's accounts, or we're finished before we really start. *We can't have her replenishing her financial supply once we take it away!*"

Rex can't help but smile. "Your intelligence is quite remarkable!" All five men nod in agreement. "I think we just might win this war she has declared on you!" Bri gives him a bit of an eek look with her soft nod. "I'll get working on that right away as well!"

"Thank you, Rex." Bri says. "*Truly.*"

He holds her hand between his hands. "Take care of yourself, My Dear, and this baby!" He pats the top of her hand.

She gives him a teary, compassionate look because she senses he has suffered a significant loss, too. Only now isn't the time to ask him about it.

She can barely whisper with a lump in her throat, "*You're a special man, Jonathan Stirling!*"

He softly chuckles. "Don't tell anyone." She shakes her head as she mimes zipping her lips and the guys smile. "I promise I'll be in touch." Bri nods.

Rex looks at Lawrence, Jack, and David, and shakes their hands goodbye; then he respectfully shakes hands with McMasters and Mitchell. The six of them watch Rex walk towards the angel statue that he stood next to several minutes ago. Then Bri and the men walk to the two golf carts and climb in, they all head back to Newhaven Manor for the reception.

CHAPTER 8

Love & Support

A few days later, Lawrence and Bri are sitting across the table from each other on The Royal Jet; they are flying to London for the day. Bri wants to find some books to study up on The Duchy of Ashbourne and The Ashbourne Estate. She doesn't want to see it without knowing more about it, since one of her titles is 'The Duchess of Ashbourne.'

"What happens now?" She asks.

"We're going to London for the day so you to find some books on Ashbourne's history, *and* I will soak up every minute we are together, before you go back to Newhaven later this afternoon." He tells her. "Then I plan to keep myself *insanely busy* until I see you again in a couple weeks."

"Whoa! Wait a second! *A couple weeks?*! *No way!*" She shakes her head. "If I have to, I'll fly a helicopter myself to come see you *way* before that!"

He reaches across the table with his hand open; she leans forward and puts her hand in his. "Your helicopter is *almost* ready. What you and I need to do on this flight is decide if you want to use your coat of arms or your seal?" He digs some things out of his bag. "As for the *two weeks*, it's to help line us up for a longer visit with The Royal Holiday Concert and The Royal Holiday Party, and the holidays coming up."

"I understand," she sits back, "but for the record, I'm *not* thrilled at the 'two weeks before I see you' part."

"Noted. *And for the record,*" he reaches out his hand again, "I'm not thrilled either." She gives him a small smile. He spreads out the papers saying, "Let's take a look at your coat of arms and your seal to see which one you would like on your helicopter?" She leans in.

The Royal Helicopter comes around to The Royal Apartment side of The London Palace. Like she has done many times in the past, Bri looks out the window and watches as they land; however, this time is different. She sees a crowd not far from The Royal Apartment's Main Gate.

"*Lawrence*," she has a worried tone to her voice, "*what are all those people doing out there? I thought you put out a press release thanking everyone for their concern, but to——.*"

"*Darling*," he softly says, giving her a loving look, "they don't expect *anything* from you, they just want you to see that you're cared about."

Bri's eyebrows furrow as she studies him and stands up. The helicopter door opens, and Bri hears the soft noise of the crowd, only she can't make out what they are saying. Lawrence steps off the helicopter, then turns to Bri and holds his hand out for her. She takes it as she steps off. Then they start walking towards The Royal Apartment's Main Entrance.

Bri looks in the direction of the crowd and starts reading their signs...'*You're in our hearts and prayers!*'...'*Heaven has two beautiful angels*'...'*We love you!*'...And variations of '*deepest sympathy*' and '*in our thoughts and prayers.*' The urge to cry begins to swell within her chest.

She halfway waves hearing random, "We love you!" Along with, "We're so sorry for your loss, Your Royal Majesty!" There are so many, she can't hear them all.

Eventually, the outpouring love and support makes it almost impossible for her to quell her sobs, she has to turn away. Lawrence takes her hand and starts walking to The Royal's Apartment's Main Entrance. Bri waves with wet eyes and a faint smile as they walk towards The Royal Apartment.

Inside The Royal Apartment, Bri goes up the stairs; Lawrence follows her. She gets to the top of the stairs and abruptly stops. She holds her hand tightly over her mouth, to try to stop herself from crying for the millionth time since Emmie and Natty died. Only this time, when Lawrence pulls her into another hug, she loses it completely. With one arm firmly around her and the other hand holding the back of her head, she grips his waist and cries hard.

At first, she cries so hard she barely makes any noise, then it turns into sobs of mourning that echoes throughout The Apartment and parts of The Palace. The staff pause in whatever they are doing to listen, trying to figure out what it is they hear. When they realize they are hearing a mother, mourning the loss of her children, their hearts break for her and many of them have tears of their own.

It takes several minutes for her to quiet down. Lawrence is still hugging her close when she is finally able to take a deep, shaky, calming breath.

"What do you need?" He asks.

She looks at him with wet eyes and cheeks. "You're doing it." She wipes her eyes and cheeks with her hands.

He cups her cheek. "I want to do more." She shakes her head.

"No," she replies, "you want to take the pain away, but that's impossible." His eyebrows go up as he considers what she said...*and she's right.*

He thinks back and asks, "Couldn't your broken heart be healed, like the gashes on your back were healed? David, Jack, and I were able to help you heal those wounds, so couldn't we do something to heal your broken heart."

She gives him a loving look through her sad eyes. "While people have been known to die of a broken heart, mine won't get to that extent because I've seen Natty and Emmie. *However,* grief *is* a process; a process that is different for everyone, and there are *no* short cuts." She takes another deep breath, drying her cheeks and eyes with her hands again. "I need to bury myself in Ashbourne history for a while. Would I find the most information here about that, or in The Ashbourne Library; *perhaps a mixture of both*?"

"Both, but I would focus on The Royal Library." He cautions her, "Mr. Woodsley is The Majordomo at Ashbourne, and his world *revolves around* The Ashbourne Estate! *Aaand* he won't like you."

"*Great.*" She says sarcastically. "Another person who doesn't like me, 'The American Duchess,' or whatever it is they're calling me these days."

"Princess." Lawrence answers. She gives him a questioning look. "They are calling you 'The American *Princess.*'" She rolls her eyes a bit. "*Nevertheless,*" he adds, "once the staff warms up to you, *including Mr. Woodsley,* they will be loyal *to you* first, before me, Jack, or David; just as *tradition* would call for."

Lawrence had texted McMasters to come to The Royal Chambers. McMasters knocks and enters since they are expecting him. Lawrence asks McMasters about Ashbourne.

McMasters tells them, "Ashbourne Castle isn't quite ready, not all the security is in place. It shouldn't be too much longer." Lawrence and Bri nod. McMasters asks, "What did you want to go on the helicopter: Bri's coat of arms, or her seal?"

Lawrence replies, "She wants to have her seal to go on it." He looks at Bri who nods to confirm.

Bri's seal is a Triquetra with a heart going through all three loops of the Triquetra, and their monogram on it. The monogrammed Triquetra-heart is on a gold shield with a red and blue border of stretched-out Triquetras, and it's all protected by an orange and yellow phoenix.

They will take the phoenix and shield, and put it on The Royal Military shield, then place it on both sides of the helicopter, both sides of the tail, as well as underneath it, to be seen from the ground, making it: 'The Official Helicopter of The Princess Imperial.'

That afternoon, Bri works with Lawrence's Public Relations Consultant to release a statement directly from her.

ROYAL MEDIA RELEASE

HRM THE PRINCESS IMPERIAL

I would like to convey my sincerest appreciation for the outpouring of letters, notes, and emails from all of you. Your messages and prayers have brought us some consolation for the inexpressible heartbreak this has caused our family. I am personally reading every thoughtful message, so I know you will understand that I can't acknowledge everyone's thoughtfulness as quickly as I would like. Although this will take several months, I promise *each person* will be personally responded to, *by me*, for their kindness. I will do this for all messages sent to me by the end of the week.

With my sincerest love and gratitude for all of you,

Bria Lynn

The Princess Imperial, The Grand Duchess of Newhaven, and The Duchess of Ashbourne.

Late that afternoon, Lawrence walks Bri out to the awaiting helicopter to fly her back to Newhaven. They stop outside the helicopter door, and he tangles his hands in her hair.

"I'll see you when you come back for The Royal Holiday Concert and, of course, for the party that follows." He grins. "Until then, expect lots of video calls so I can keep seeing your beautiful face!"

She smiles as her eyes fill with tears. "Thank you for being there for me..." She doesn't bother to stop the tears this time from dripping down her cheeks.

"*Always!*" He wipes her tears with his thumbs. "*I love you, My Darling!* The next two weeks will be torture."

Bri looks at Lawrence with love. "I feel the same way!"

"Good thing my father and I will be busy the next two weeks!" He tells her.

"Why don't you let your father and Seth have Millicent's old office?" She suggests. "Maybe rename it like, 'The Family's Support Office.'"

"I love that!" He wraps his arms around her again.

"I love you so much, Lawrence! I already miss you!" Her eyes get teary again.

He kisses her soundly one last time before he helps her inside the helicopter and backs away. Bri sits down and buckles in. When they lift up into the air, she waves to Lawrence, and he waves back. The helicopter flies off and Lawrence walks back to The Palace.

When he walks inside the door, he sees his father waiting for him. Lawrence gives him a small smile and tells Phillip, "I hate how much *more* it hurts to see Bri go after what that woman did to Emmie, Natty, Olivia, and Jeff!"

Phillip pats his son's shoulder. "One way or another, that woman *will get* what's coming to her!" Lawrence knows he's right. "Come!" Phillip says. "Let's get you busy!" They walk to The Official Royal Offices together.

That evening, Jack is with David flying home to Newhaven in the corporate helicopter. They know Bri is already back from London and is at The Manor. David uses this time to talk to Jack about Bri.

"I want us to help Bri find her footing again. I'm taking a few days off to help her in Kingsbury, so I thought you could help her with The Mill and The Foundation. I also have a business trip to Brazil I think she might enjoy."

"I think that's a fantastic plan!" Jack replies.

"I'm glad you think so, because I think she will be ready for some quiet time at The Cottage with you." David smirks at Jack, who is lifting his eyebrow. "You may be 'the life of the party,' but you're also the closest to normal she has," he looks at him pointedly, *"which is exactly what you wanted!"* Jack nods. "And to get her through this, she will need to get back to her regular schedule, while living a more 'quiet life' for a couple of weeks." Jack agrees.

Up on the fourth floor of The Manor, Bri is pouring over the books she brought with her that she found in The Royal Library. She has everything spread out on the coffee table and couch in their main living room.

"Hello, Gorgeous!" Jack smiles wide as he and David walk over to her.

She smiles and stands up. "Hi!" She hugs them both. "I've just been devouring Ashbourne's history! *I can't wait to see this place!*" The guys chuckle.

"With Ashbourne," Jack says with a serious tone, "I have one condition."

"Really?" She raises her eyebrow in curiosity. "What's that?"

"You make The Private Apartment *yours*." He replies.

She is surprised. "*What?* That doesn't make sense. *You* are 'The Duke of Ashbourne' after all!"

"Bri, you're *always* coming to us! Whether it's to The Manor, The Cottage, or The Palace; then there's The Villa and The Château. I want Ashbourne to be the place *we* come to see *you*."

She looks at David and he happily says, "It's a *brilliant* idea!" He sits in an armchair and smirks, "We may never see you any other way, once you see Ashbourne!"

Jack gives her a loving look. "It could be the beautiful fortress you need when you want to lock yourself away from the world." She softly nods.

David points to the books and asks, "What have you learned so far about The Ashbourne Estate?"

"Oh my gosh, *a ton*!" She replies. "I want to read everything I can find on Ashbourne! Then I'm going to have to cross-reference with another significant duchy at the time that technically no longer exists. But I will tell you guys all about what I learned when I think I have it all laid out properly up here." She points to her head.

"Fair enough." Jack replies, then a yawn comes over him. "I'm exhausted. If you don't mind, I think I'm going to leave for The Cottage and go to bed a little early tonight."

David stands up. "I'll go take a quick shower and you two can have a few minutes." He says goodnight to Jack, before he goes.

Jack wraps his arms around Bri. "I love you, Amore Mia!"

"I love *you*!" She walks with him to the stairs. "Goodnight, Amore Mio."

"Goodnight." He kisses her once more before he goes down the stairs.

She goes back to the books and writes some notes in her notebook. She is deep into reading when she feels David kiss her shoulder; she jumps a little.

"Sorry, Love. I didn't mean to frighten you!" David says to her. "I thought you would've heard me walking up behind you."

"It's fine." She smiles over her shoulder at him. "I'm almost finished here."

David suggests, "How about I make us some popcorn while you wrap up, then we can watch a film, or whatever you want to watch." Her heart squeezes for this wonderful man.

She puts her pen down as she stands up. She walks around the couch to him, and he sees a bit of a playful look on her face. He curiously smiles back at her. She takes his hand and leads him to their bedroom. She turns and kisses him, taking both of his hands and pulling him with her as she walks backwards to their bed.

When the backs of her legs are against the bed, she sits down and starts to lift up his t-shirt. He puts his hands on hers to stop her for a moment.

"Are you sure?" David doesn't want her to feel pressured. "I'm okay watching something and just being next to you in bed." He cups her cheek. "*I promise.*"

"Good, because I can't promise you anything..." She lifts his t-shirt up and off, then tosses it.

He takes her hands and kisses them then leans in to kiss her. She ghosts his lips for a moment before he captures them in a heated kiss. He carefully pushes her back onto the bed.

David looks down into her eyes. "We'll take things slow and it's okay if you need to stop."

She gives him a loving look as she nods, running her hand up into his hair and pulls him into another kiss...

A few days later, Bri and Jack are working at The Textile Mill when Amy comes to visit them. Amy has been enthusiastic about Bri's foundation since the beginning and wants to talk to her about it.

"Bri, what you all are accomplishing *is amazing*! I told you that you'll be in a position to do great things, to make a *real* difference, *and you're doing it!*" She smiles excitedly.

Bri's eyebrows go up as she inhales. "There has been so much to do, *Jack has done most of the work!*"

"Oh, no!" Jack replies walking in. He goes over and gives Amy a hug. Then he gives Bri a determined look telling her, "We've been over this! *All of this* has been *your* vision, *your* project! You have been busy with so many things, only Gabriel has been keeping you extremely organized that you haven't noticed the amount of work you are actually doing!" He sits on the edge of Bri's desk. "Something I'm sure our beautiful sister-in-law is an expert at!"

Amy lightly laughs. "*I had to be!*"

"That's true!" Bri agrees.

"Bri, *I want to help!*" Amy tells her. "Like you, I want to do something meaningful with my life! I've given you my schedule and I would like to focus that time on The Foundation, *but I can help with anything additional as well!* And you know we work very well together!" She grins.

Bri softly giggles. "Amy, I think it's a *wonderful* idea!"

"*Really?!*" Amy gets excited and Bri nods encouragingly. Amy lightly claps her hands saying, "*Yay!*"

After the three of them talk a little bit more, Amy leaves with some things Bri has given her to get started. Jack walks her out, while Bri takes a phone call. When Jack comes back, he and Bri talk about what Amy proposed, along with The Wool Farm and The Mill. He sits on the edge of her desk again, and they continue talking while she collects her things to go home. He tells her how they have perfected making their wool its softest.

Jack eagerly says, "*Spring can't come soon enough!*" Bri stands and he gently pulls her to stand in front of him. He puts a hand on her hip and his other hand on top of her baby bump and smiles. "I *especially* can't wait for this little one's arrival!" He kisses her. "Let's go pick up some things from the store, excite your people who are randomly fortunate to see you in person at the supermarket, then go home and cook together!"

"Cooking with you sounds wonderful!" She replies. "But I'm not sure about going into the store.

She picks up her bag and Jack takes it to carry for her. Then they walk out of the office and make their way outside to the motorcade.

"I don't think anyone will bother you; they never really do. They usually take a quick picture and move on."

"True." She admits. "Let's see how busy they are."

That evening, Jack locks up The Cottage and turns out the lights before going upstairs. They had finished cleaning most of the kitchen after dinner when Jack sent Bri upstairs to take a hot bath. He finished the rest of the clean up.

She is soaking in their large tub when she hears taps on the door. "Come in, Amore Mio..."

He sweetly smiles as he opens the door. "Do you need anything?" He sits on the edge of the tub.

"You." She grins when she sees him trying to read her face. "Yes, *I want you*. And to be even clearer, that means I want you, *naked*, in this tub with me." She knows his next question and answers, "And *yes*, I'm sure!" She bites her lower lip.

"Then how can I refuse?" He handsomely smiles.

He stands up and takes his clothes off. She scoots forward so he can slide in behind her. He starts to massage her shoulders, and she relaxes into it.

"You had to have been a masseur in a past life, Amore Mio..." She inhales and exhales, relaxing more. She lays back against him and he hugs her close.

He says next to her ear, "*Only if you were in that past life with me.*"

She softly giggles and turns her head to tell him, "I can't imagine any life without you in it!" He hugs her close, relaxing with her.

After several minutes go by, she fully turns to face him, then passionately kisses him. She gently pulls their lips apart and he sees the love in her eyes for him. He lets her take the lead and they get out of the tub, dry off, and go into their bedroom...

Last November, The Worthington Family adopted the U.S. Thanksgiving Holiday in honor of Bri and Amy, but also because they really like the reminder of being grateful for all the blessings in their lives, including their staff! James and Amy thought it would be fun if The Worthington Family served their employees the traditional American Thanksgiving feast this year, family style, then the family spreads out among their employees sitting at the two long tables in The Great Dining Hall, and *everyone* has a blast! Bri focuses on being happy, and grateful, for who she has in her life and remembers how happy Emmie and Natty *are* on the other side.

After everyone is finished eating, Bri walks to one end of the room and stands between the two extremely long dining tables. Jack and David walk up and stand on either side of her, then the rest of the family gather around them.

"We had a lot of fun!" David gestures to the whole family. "We hope you all know how *grateful* we are for each of you, and for the dedication you give every day."

Peter adds, "From the bottom of all our hearts, we *truly* thank you!"

There are cheers with their applause, along with many of the employees expressing *their* appreciation for The Worthington Family, and their excitement of 'the wee one to come!'

In the two weeks between seeing Lawrence again, Bri is not only reading and researching Ashbourne's history, but she is also rehearsing for The Royal Holiday Concert. She spends time with David and Jack working in Edinburgh, Kingsbury at the government building, The Mill, The Manor, or The Cottage House. David had also taken her to Brazil with him on his business trip. She is starting to feel more settled, like things were getting back to *some* sort of normalcy.

CHAPTER 9

The Improved Royal Offices

Although they had numerous video calls between them, it has been two weeks since Bri was with Lawrence in person. The time has gone by both fast and slow for various reasons. Jack is flying to London with her, and he will stay for The Royal Holiday Concert and Party that night. The rest of the family will be coming in later that afternoon to attend the events that evening as well.

Jack always has a wonderful, energetic feel about him, and Bri can't help but feel more upbeat and happier being around him. He smiles his signature smile at her, and she smiles adoringly back at him.

He holds her chin with the side of his finger and his thumb. "This sweet smile of yours is one of my favorites."

Her eyebrows go up. "Why?"

He gives her a loving look. "Because of your eyes..." He cups her cheek. "Your eyes look at me with so much love, yet..." he exhales, "I don't know...there's so much more!

"*Because there is*!" She tells him. "You're love for me is so enthusiastic, I feel like I can do anything, *like I could fly*!" She hugs him tight for a minute. She pulls back. "Thank you for traveling to London with me. I feel safe with my security detail, it's just—."

"I understand, Amore Mia. Flying with you means I get more time with you! I *won't* pass that up!" He happily says. "I do want to go away with you after the holidays and while you can still comfortably travel. I'll take you anywhere in the world and shower you with gifts! All you need to do is tell me *where* you'd like to go?"

"Jack, that's sweet, but you already know the answers to *all* that!" She gives him a determined look asking, "*Where am I the happiest*?"

"You're *happy* when you're with one of us, but *happiest* with all three of us!" He answers.

"*Precisely*!" She teases with his accent. "As for taking me away somewhere, I say lock us up in The Cottage House and lose the keys and phones!"

"How about Tuscany?" He asks.

"*How about perfect*!" She smiles wide. "As long as you don't shower me with gifts! *I just want you...*" she looks him up and down, "*preferably naked.*" She bites her lower lip.

He gives her a bit of a smoldering look. "That can be arranged, Amore Mia, *but no promises on the 'no gifts.'*" He kisses her before she can protest.

The helicopter lands at The London Palace and Jack gets off first. When Bri steps off the helicopter, she takes in the image of The Royal Palace with a snowy winter backdrop and how the snow gives it a magical feel. Jack offers his arm, which she takes, and they start walking towards The Palace.

When they get inside The Palace door, Bri turns to Jack and he smirks knowing what she is going to say, so he cups her cheek and replies, "I love you *more*, Amore Mia!"

She giggles. "I do love you, Amore Mio!"

He taps a kiss to her lips before they part ways; he goes to his room in The Royal Apartment to work, while Bri winds her way to The Royal Offices. Lawrence has the door already open for her and he waves her in when he sees her. She steps inside and quietly shuts the door. He is not happy with who he is talking to, and she hears it in the tone of his voice; Although, it's *nothing* like it would have been if his mother was still running things. Bri walks over to him, taking off her jacket and laying it in a chair in front of his desk. He finishes his conversation and doesn't *quite* slam the phone down.

He turns to her and the frustration on his face disappears. He smiles, pulling her into a hug; he exhales and relaxes.

"I'm so happy to see you and have you here..." He squeezes a bit more before he steps back. He walks over to the door that goes into Millicent's old office. She watches him shut the door and is curious when he locks it. She watches him walk over to his main office door as he asks her, "Are you ready for tonight?"

She replies as he locks his main office door, "As ready as I'm going to be with all these butterflies in my stomach." She follows his eyesight to the other door that leads to a conference room; that door is already locked. "*What's going on?*" He walks up to her and takes her hand, leading her behind his desk. He sits her on his desk and kisses her. He steps in between her legs, and she breaks the kiss when she realizes what his intentions are. "*You can't be serious?!*"

He starts to feel bad. "*Too soon?*" He is genuinely concerned for her.

"No, no. I planned on romance tonight, *in our room!*"

"I don't want to push you!" He says.

"It's not that." She replies. "Just *here?!*"

He leans in and moans next to her ear, "*BriaLynn...*" she holds her breath, "don't make me say it..." he kisses down her neck; she rolls her eyes, because he's implying he is 'The King' and can do whatever he wants.

"Do you really want to risk someone seeing me in *this kind of position,*" he lifts his head and gives her a look making her add, "*even if it* is *with you, The King.*" She can't help rolling her eyes again. She looks in the direction of the office door saying, "The main hallway is *highly* trafficked!"

"It's not like I'm having some sordid affair! I'm with *My Queen...*" he gives her a mischievous grin, "*on my desk.*" She can't help but giggle, and he kisses below her ear.

"That will just give the gossips more fodder in their gossip circles, *especially* when your goal is to make me 'The Queen!'" She flourishes her hand for effect.

He kisses her neck some more. "Then they will have the proof!"

"Proof?!" She laughs, "*Of what?*" He stops and stands up straight.

He looks so deeply into her eyes; it takes her breath away. "The first time you were in here, *you* challenged me to be a better man, and ultimately a better king. *The proof* that I'm changing for the better would be that the woman who dared to challenge me, is *still* in my life; *the real force to be reckoned with!*" She goes to argue, but he adds, "*Bri*, you can be whatever force you want with me, and I'm okay with that, *as long as...*" he runs his hands up her outer thighs and rests them on her hips, "*that force* submits *to me,*" he tugs at her waist with a playful grin and raises his eyebrow, "wherever we are *and* whenever *I want!*" He ghosts her lips with his and sees her eyebrow flick up a bit with his last comment. He says against her lips, "Within reason, and it's *always* your choice."

"Thank you for that." She says. "Well..." she has a playfulness in her eyes, "being naked wouldn't show me as much of a force now, would it?" She smirks. "Besides, *you fight this force!*"

His expression becomes more smoldering, "And you fight mine! 'All's fair,' don't they say?" He gives her a determined look. "If you are *very* quiet, no one will know, *and* you'll have nothing to worry about." He kisses her fiercely, melting away any excuses she may still have...

As they straighten themselves up, he tells her, "I have a couple of surprises for you, Darling. Will you indulge me?"

She raises her eyebrow with a faint smirk saying, "I thought I just did?!"

"*Careful,* I find your cheekiness *very* sexy," he wraps his arms around her, "like right now..."

"Cheeky?! *I was merely pointing out—*." He kisses her and she moans into it, making him stop before things get heated again.

"First," he walks over to the adjacent door. "I took your advice and made this my father's and Seth's office. Abby will use it if she ever needs to cover my duties, but as you know, she prefers to be the *absolute last* resort for this job." Bri nods. He opens the door, and he follows her into the updated office.

"Two desks! That's a *great* idea!" She looks around. "Lawrence, this office is so bright and cheery, and it *feels* that way, too! You must've hired a witch doctor to come in and do some of their voodoo magic to cleanse this room!" She teases.

"Can you smell sage?" He teases back.

She giggles. "You know sage is used with that sort of thing?!"

"I haven't got the foggiest idea!" He shrugs. "I guess if I'm right, I must've heard it from somewhere."

She ponders, "I'm not entirely sure either, but I think sage might have something to do with neutralizing the air, or changing negative energy into positive energy?"

"Do you believe in that sort of thing?" He asks.

"It's not so much whether I believe in it or not, it's just that my belief and faith are placed in a much higher power. *However*, I do think there is something to it," she throws her hands up a bit, "because medicine men, shamans, Chinese medicine, and such, have been using flowers, herbs, spices, acupuncture, and so on, for hundreds, *even thousands*, of years. To use something in a way they would use it, well, I feel it should be done with at least a respectful attitude, or it most certainly wouldn't work and could potentially have its own ramifications by working against the objective."

"Like karma?" He asks and she nods.

She teases again, "If the sage doesn't work, then it may need to be cleansed by fire!" He stares in awe of her. "*Too much?*" She asks.

"*Not at all!*" He answers. "I'll even light the match!" He tells her, "I'm just in awe of you! You have *such conviction* in your faith, but you have all this respect for other people's beliefs! *You really are extraordinary!*"

"You give me entirely too much credit!" She replies.

He scrunches his eyebrows saying, "*Nnnooo...pretty sure you're not giving yourself enough credit!*"

She tsks. "I want to treat people, *and their beliefs*, the way we all should treat each other! I don't think it's right for people to *force* their beliefs on others for anything. These are the ones *so blinded* by their way of thinking, determined *their* beliefs are the only ones that matter—."

"They don't see that, *at the very least*, it makes things worse!" He adds and she nods. "They lack the intelligence to see how they might actually *be* wrong, even partially."

"It's like a toddler plugging their ears with their fingers, because they don't want to hear what the other side is saying. Neither side sees that they're *equally* 'extreme!' Plus, *no one* wants to be told what to think, what to believe, nor how to feel; and many will dig their heels in when they feel people are doing just that, then the proverbial walls go up! They will fight against it, even if that's not exactly how they feel, *just to prove they can't be told what to do, nor how to feel.* It's also why people stop listening." She adds compassionately, "*Everyone* wants to be, *and should be,* respectfully heard as long as the conversation *stays* respectful."

"Yes! *Precisely*!" Lawrence agrees. "That could be said on pretty much any issue where there are disagreements. And if we all did just that, the world wouldn't be in quite so much turmoil..."

"True!" She agrees, then brings the conversation back, "How does Seth and Phillip like their new office?"

"*So much better than my last office*!" Phillip happily answers, walking over to Bri and hugs her. "These offices are where my sons and I work together and have the relationship we should've had *years ago.*" He looks at Lawrence, then looks back to Bri. "Thanks to *you*!"

Bri is surprised. "*Thanks to me?!*"

"You helped Vivian and me get *our* family back!" He replies. Bri's eyes get slightly teary, and she hugs him again. He tells them, "Now go, you two," he waves towards the door, "spend your time together! Seth and I have this all handled!"

Lawrence smiles and takes her hand, tucking her arm under his as they walk out of The Royal Offices. They greet the various visitors and staff they pass along the way to The Royal Apartment. Once inside The Royal Apartment, they take Kahla upstairs with them, stopping outside The Royal Chambers.

Lawrence tells her, "I have some gifts for you, as my date tonight. Your dress is hanging in the closet, and McMasters had your Diamond-Heart Tiara brought down with you."

"A date?" She asks with confusion. "Isn't this for The Royal Holiday Concert tonight, and the party that follows? *I already thought we were going together?*"

"Ah, but this time we're *officially* going as 'The King and The Princess Imperial.'" He proudly tells her.

Bri holds up Kahla and asks her, "Don't you think it would be *wonderful* for The Princess Imperial to accompany His Majesty tonight!"

"*Nnnooo*," he corrects the statement, "for *His Majesty* to escort *Her Royal Majesty!*" Kahla's little tail is wagging, and she licks Bri's cheek. "I think she agrees. *But*" he takes Kahla from her, "before we get ready, Maurice said he would hang out with this little one tonight." Lawrence waves his arm out towards him.

Maurice is getting up there in years. He keeps his silver hair clean-cut, and he is in fairly good shape for his seventy-plus years and severe back pain. Although, no one would know he is in pain just by looking at him. What pain medication doesn't help with, he hides well. The staff understands that is why things are done differently with him, or by him. Lawrence doesn't want to make him retire, because his wife passed away a few years back and they never had children; Lawrence, Seth, Abby, and Gen became his family, and now Bri, Jack, and David have as well. Maurice is taking Kahla because he shouldn't be working at the party with his back the way it is, and this is the excuse Lawrence needs to get him to stay off his feet. Maurice doesn't want Kahla to be left in her carrier for the duration of the concert *and* party, if she doesn't have to be.

Bri turns and happily smiles at Maurice. "I think she's going to be spoiled more than she already is!" She giggles. "Between you and Mitchell, she's going to think she really *is* a princess!"

Maurice takes Kahla and holds her up to his face and whispers loud enough to be heard, "*Shhh*, it's still our little secret!" Kahla's little tail is wagging vigorously.

"Why do I picture the two of you on a couch watching the *telly* and sharing a bowl of popcorn?" She teases with their accent.

Maurice fakes a surprise. "*Share?!*" He grins at Bri and, with a *professional* tone he states, "A princess gets her *own* bowl and will be hand fed!" He covertly winks at Bri and Lawrence softly laughs.

Bri giggles, petting Kahla. "Thank you for taking care of her tonight for us!"

"*My pleasure, Ma'am!*" He bows to them, then pets Kahla as he walks off with her. He will gather Kahla's things, including her actual food and snacks, to take to the room near The Royal Apartment he will be staying in for the night.

Bri turns to Lawrence and sees he has a bit of a pained look. He says, "I think he is in more pain than he's confided in me."

"Maybe you could think about a way to ask him to officially move into The London Palace, or another residence close by, and retire *but* ask him to help run a charity with volunteers so he can work when he's up for it." She also suggests, "Maybe after the holidays you can talk with him about what retirement, even partial, could look like for him. Then he can still be in control of how things go, along with when and where he works?"

"Has anyone told you how bloody brilliant you are?!"

"You know," she taps her chin, "I think I has been said a time or two..." He lightly laughs as they walk into The Royal Chambers.

The rest of The Worthington Family flew to London for 'The Royal Holiday Concert' and 'The Royal Holiday Party.' Originally, Bri was to sing one song for the concert, with Lawrence accompanying her on the piano; however, since this is the 125th year, they asked her to sing a few more songs, which will unknowingly help her popularity. She had been practicing six days a week for weeks, except this week her day off is today, the day of the performance, to rest her voice before the performance. She is nervous because, even with state-of-the-art videoconferencing for the rehearsals, it's not the same as actually being there. She prays it all works out!

CHAPTER 10
The Royal Holiday Concert

That evening, in The Royal Chambers, Bri is getting ready with Genevieve and Abby. Lawrence had asked Abby and Gen to get ready with Bri and they happily agreed. They have heard Lawrence play the piano beautifully many times over the years, and they are excited to hear Lawrence and Bri perform a song together!

Genevieve excitedly tells Bri, "*I can't wait to hear you sing!*"

"*Me, too!*" Abby happily agrees. "Lawrence has been practicing and seeing to some of the details to ensure your debut goes off *splendidly!*"

"*No pressure!*" Bri says with a bit of horror, a handful of butterflies, and a splash of fright.

"You'll be *fantastic!*" Genevieve encourages her.

Bri takes a deep breath. "Let's talk about something else, *anything else.*" She points to her back and asks, "Will one of you zip me up, please?" Abby does since she is closest to Bri.

Genevieve tells her, "Bri! You.look.*breathtaking!* Lawrence is going to be one proud man, *and King*, with you on his arm!"

"He won't be able to keep his hands off you!" Abby adds.

Bri laughs as she looks at herself in the mirror. There is a knock on the door and Abby goes to answer it.

Bri hears Abby say, "Give us a minute." Abby comes back over. "Gen, are you ready?"

"I think so!" Gen answers.

"Hold up!" Bri says to both of them. "I haven't seen you two all put together...*WOW*! You two look *gorgeous*! If I didn't know Abby, I'd be jealous of her being escorted by David and Jack tonight!"

"Oh, Luv, look at it this way," Abby grins, "I'll keep them safe from the other women wanting a piece of them!"

"*Oooo*, I like that!" Bri laughs. "I'm sure with Lawrence, I'll have my hands full keeping the ladies away from him!"

They hear a throat being cleared behind them at the door. "Sorry, Brother!" Abby and Gen are going downstairs when they walk by Lawrence; Abby pauses to whisper, "*She's absolutely stunning!*"

Lawrence smiles and walks in; he stops in mid step. "*Briii*," he exhales, "you're...*Wow*! Stunning...gorgeous..." he stumbles, then just lets out an exhaled whistle with his eyebrows raised. "I can't settle on just one..."

Bri looks him up and down. "You should talk! With my hormones and *My King* looking so handsomely dashing, *we may be late!*" She looks at her watch for effect.

"I'll agree on being *Your* King!" He walks up to her explaining, "I had my eye on something from The Crown Jewels Collection, if your ruby-heart necklace set was forgotten." He smiles sweetly, opening the flat velvet box he brought with him.

'The Ruby Heart and Diamond Necklace Set' has a row of heart-shaped rubies, haloed with tiny diamonds, going all the way around the necklace. They are all the same size except the middle one in front is larger. The stud earrings have a heart-shaped ruby surrounded by tiny diamonds.

Lawrence gives her the earrings to put on, then she turns around so he can put the necklace on her. When she finishes with the earrings, she looks in the mirror to add her Diamond-Heart Tiara he had also made for her and given her not too long ago.

"Nothing like a Diamond-Heart Tiara to make a girl *feel* like royalty." She grins at his reflection in the mirror.

"Good." He replies. "Anything less would be an *epic* failure!" She lightly giggles. He hugs her from behind, putting his hands on her lower abdomen and lovingly asks, "How are you feeling with this little one?"

"Surprisingly well!" She puts her hands on his. "*And energetic!*"

He gives her a small, smoldering look. "Glad to hear it." He kisses under her ear. "Promise me you'll let me, David, or Jack, know if you need a break this evening, or call it a night early? Like you did at James and Amy's wedding."

She has a slightly confused look. "I will, but aren't you—."

"I'll be at your side *almost* the whole time; David and Jack will be with you when I'm not." He cups her cheek.

She leans in and he meets her lips in a gentle kiss. "*That's* a teeny preview of what might come your way later."

"Then we better get going," he takes her hand, "or your right..." he opens the door, "*we will be late!*" She softly laughs while walking out the door.

They go down to meet up with the others in the living room. They all go down to The Royal Concert Hall where they will split up; some of them go to form a receiving line, while the rest of the family goes to their seats.

Jack smiles. "*Gorgeous! You* are *stunning!*" He kisses her cheek.

"Thank you, Amore Mio."

David steps closer to her. "Exquisitely beautiful, Love." He kisses the inside of her wrist.

"Thank you, My Love." She smiles.

When they go to leave, Lawrence looks at Genevieve. "Shall we?"

Gen smiles and nods, still holding Seth's arm. Lawrence takes Bri's hand and tucks her arm under his, then they lead the way. Gen and Seth follow them; then Abby, who is between David and Jack. Phillip goes next, with Peter and Carlotta behind him; James and Amy are at the end.

Lawrence and Bri lead the way for those going into The Blue Room to form a receiving line. This room looks like it belongs in The Palace with its lavishness seen in all the gold, red, royal blue, and famous artwork. There is no furniture since their guests will be filing through to greet the main royals, while the rest of the family happily goes to The Royal Concert Hall to take their seats upstairs in The Royal Box, overlooking the stage.

As their guests walk in, they see Lawrence and Bri standing side by side, with the red of her dress matching his red sash that is over his tuxedo, setting them apart as *The* Royal Couple. Lawrence sees Bri shaking hands and talking with their guests, noting to himself how she already looks like a queen.

After their guests have all filed through, they have formal pictures taken of them for the press to use for The Royal Concert, and their social media releases. Then he escorts Bri to the backstage door of The Concert Hall.

He goes to leave her with McMasters *and* Mitchell, and she questions, "With The Royal Guard at every turn, is it necessary for both, Your Maj—."

He puts the side of his forefinger to her lips. "*My* Queen will *never* address me so formerly!"

"I would say this," she has a bit of an attitude gesturing The Palace, "*calls for formality!*"

He wraps an arm around her waist, holding her close. "Your defiance is noted," he leans in next to her ear to whisper, "*for later,*" he pulls back and adds, "and I *do* expect you to keep these two close by, *except* for when you're on stage."

"*See!* Right there you sound 'kingly' *and demanding!* That requires a 'Yes, Sir' with maybe a little two finger salute," she salutes, "or is it Lawrence *asking me* to keep them close?"

"*Which will you obey?*" He gives her a pointed look.

She raises her eyebrow with the word 'obey.' "If you're focusing on my *obeying*, what do you think will be my response?!" She keeps her eyes locked with his. His jaw is clenching as he studies her; his desire for her is burning red hot right now, which is *exactly* what she wants.

Thankfully, the backstage door right there pops open, and they hear, "Your Royal Majesty—*Oh!* Your Majesty, we thought you'd be here later." He bows.

Lawrence doesn't break his eye contact with Bri as he replies, "I was just escorting Her Royal Majesty back here."

No one can see him sliding his hand down to her bum and he squeezes, getting a hint of a glare from her. He raises his eyebrow and winks.

"*Splendid!*" The gentleman says. "Your Royal Majesty, we do need to warm up your vocal cords." He glances down the hall and sees The King Father. "Your Majesty, so lovely to have you with us, Sir!"

"Thank you! I wouldn't miss it!" Phillip shakes the gentleman's hand. Phillip looks at Bri. "*You are a vision!*" He looks at Lawrence. "Son, you two look like a real power couple!" He tells Bri, "I've heard you practicing over videoconference a few times with the choir. You're going to be *fantastic!*" He kisses her cheek as she thanks him.

Phillip starts walking down the hall, going to The Royal Box when Lawrence stops him, "Father, hold up! I'll walk with you." Lawrence encourages Bri, "*You've got this, Darling!*" He taps a kiss to her lips, and she smiles.

She watches him walk with his father, and their security detail for a moment, then she goes backstage to warm up her vocal cords. When she is done warming up her vocal cords, someone explains where she needs to stand for various songs. Then, while she waits for The Royal Holiday Concert to start, she tries to calm herself by picturing what The Royal Concert Hall looked like back when she and Lawrence went on a private tour of The London Palace not too long ago.

The Royal Concert Hall is majestically exquisite with a celestial mural on the ceiling, carvings to match, and scrollwork sculpted to decorate the edges of the walls and ceiling. In the center of ceiling, there is a huge domed skylight. The main floor seating is in three sections; the seating up on the second-floor balcony has seating on the sides, and straight-ahead is the special section for 'The Royal Box.' The Royal Box has more comfortable chairs in its rows. There is a hallway behind connecting The Royal Box to The Palace.

When the time comes, Bri takes her place, stage right of center. She appreciates there is a live nativity on display, and she will be singing in the dark for most of the first song; the butterflies in her stomach are making her feel nauseous. Bri hears the curtain start to go up and she takes a deep, calming breath as she hears the music begin to play. She listens for the note to begin singing...

HRM The Princess Imperial in The Royal Holiday Concert with HM The King!

By: Francis Chapman

Her Royal Majesty The Princess Imperial has stolen the show with none other than His Majesty The King himself! Her Royal Majesty toured Newhaven last year with The Grand Duke of Newhaven and The Duke of Ashbourne, where they made a stop in a local Strathbury pub and she sang karaoke. We, Newhaveners, were introduced back then to her beautiful singing voice, but now the entire United Kingdom of Provinces knows of her talent!

The first song had a live nativity scene playing out, while a woman was singing in the background with The Royal Choir. By the last verse, there was just enough light to see The Royal Choir and none other than Her Royal Majesty! They sang *so powerfully* together; they gave us goosebumps for the first time of many that evening.

Later, UK band, *Guess Affinity*, with lead singer, Matt Turner, asks her to join him in a duet, accompanied only by his guitar. She joins him on stage, then charms the audience saying, "You can't beat a man and his guitar, *unless it's The King and his piano.*" Then she slightly over exaggerates

a wink at His Majesty to everyone's amusement. The song Her Royal Majesty and Matt Turner sang together was a Christmas hymn that has to be a new favorite for many of us, at least their version of it anyway!

The evening's concert is filled with the songs of the season about sleigh rides, snowy wonderlands, and longing to be home for Christmas. The Royal Children's Choir sang 'We Wish You a Merry Christmas' beautifully. At one point, Her Royal Majesty sang, 'Have Yourself a Merry Little Christmas' and we heard the incredible wide range of Her Majesty's vocal chords!

Towards the end of the show, His Majesty walks on stage with Her Royal Majesty and there is a massive amount of cheering and applause. His Majesty sits down at the grand piano and Her Royal Majesty stands in the curve of the piano to face the audience and His Majesty. With both choirs behind her, and the full orchestra down in the orchestra pit, the last song was amazing!

After the last word and the last note of the last song is sung and played, the entire audience erupts in an enthusiastic ovation. Her Royal Majesty gestures His Majesty and the choirs. His Majesty stands and the two of them clap for the choirs and orchestra, then His Majesty claps for her and one could read his lips telling her she was 'smashing!' *She was*!

While every song was better than the last, it would be the last song of the encore that would be the most phenomenal of them all! That last song had Her Royal Majesty singing with the choir. The entire auditorium was completely silent. She sings the last verse with the choir, which is so powerful and *so moving* with their combined voices, that when the song completely ends, everyone is absolutely quiet...*until the lights come up*...then the applause and cheering explode from the audience!

This year, The Royal Holiday Concert for many of us will be remembered as '*the best one ever*!' Let's hope they do this again next year, and every year after, for a *new* royal tradition!

The end of the concert came with thunderous applause and cheers! Everyone cheers for Bri, Lawrence, the choirs, the orchestra, The Maestro, and emcee. When the curtain goes down for the last time, everyone makes their way off stage. Lawrence and Bri stop to talk with various people along the way to the backstage door.

Lawrence got ahead of her, and he is patiently waiting for Bri as she makes her way over to him. When she gets closer to him, she excitedly leaps into his arms and he happily catches her, swinging her around once.

"You *smashed* it, Darling!" He says as he spins her around. "Just like I said you would! The entire concert was a hit because of you!"

"It was a hit because of *everyone* involved, *including you*!" She is still smiling ear-to-ear. She holds his jaw and kisses him fiercely.

Since His Majesty and Her Royal Majesty are to officially enter The Royal Holiday Party last, they want to personally thank as many people as they can and wait outside the backstage door to do so. They thank them for all their hard work at making 'The Royal Holiday Concert' a *huge* success!

Suddenly, without warning, there is a loud explosion and horrified screaming echoes off the walls. The force of the blast shakes The Palace, sending shockwaves out and around a huge radius of The Palace.

CHAPTER 11

The Aftermath

Phillip, Peter, Carlotta, David, Jack, Abby, Seth, Genevieve, Amy, and James are at the doors to The Royal Grand Ballroom, to greet guests as they go inside. The last of the guests are being greeted when an explosion blasts out a large radius from inside The Ballroom. The Ballroom's wall that the family is standing in front of, flies back, pushing the family with it. It rests at an angle against an interior Palace wall. The family members that are caught in the pocket it has created between the two walls, only suffer minor scrapes and cuts. Unfortunately, Carlotta was hit with greater force from the blast, as well as being hit with more debris as she is thrown; she sustains more injuries and is knocked unconscious. Peter and Maggie tend to her, while Henry goes to check on the other family members. He is relieved to find the rest of them are in decent shape.

David and Jack go to find people who can help, such as doctors, nurses, first responders, and so on; sending the first they find to Carlotta, who fortunately happens to be a doctor. David and Jack assume Lawrence and Bri weren't in the blast, and they are being rushed out of The Palace to a safe-house location somewhere else.

When the explosion shook the entire Palace, it created various cracks in a wall near Lawrence and Bri, which caused it to become unstable. When the wall begins to crumble, Lawrence shoves Bri out of the way! She stumbles, but she manages to catch herself with the closed backstage doorknob. She turns and watches in horror as the wall collapses on top of Lawrence!

There is a terrified panic in her voice as she screams, "*LAWRENCE!*"

Before Bri has time to do anything else, a thinner marble column falls over and knocks Bri down. It catches itself on some debris, slowing it down some as it falls on her legs. Luckily, it only pins her legs down. She struggles to free her legs, but it's no use; the marble column is just too heavy.

"MITCHELL?! CAN YOU HEAR ME?!" She pauses for a response... Nothing. "MCMASTERS?!"

"*BRI!* ARE YOU HURT?" McMasters asks, making his way over to her.

"*I'm...*" she struggles to move her legs again, "*stuck...*" She exhales in frustration. "This column has my legs pinned down."

"But you can still feel them and move them?" He is almost to her.

"*Yes.*" She replies. "I can't move them much, but nothing feels broken."

He is relieved. Then he calls out, "MITCHELL?"

"Right here." Mitchell slowly stands up, then tries to walk over, only to stop; he is wobbly, and he holds his head in his hand.

McMasters had gone over to him and managed to catch him before he fell over. "You need to sit down, before you hurt yourself more."

"No." Mitchell slightly shakes his head. "Let me help you get Bri and Lawrence out of here."

McMasters tells him, "We'll need a lot more help than the two of us. She has a solid marble column pinning her legs down!"

"*Guys!* Forget about me!" Bri points in Lawrence's direction telling them, "The wall collapsed *on* Lawrence!"

She hears McMasters and Mitchell say some swear words as they rush over and call out for him. McMasters carefully moves debris out of the way, with Mitchell helping the best he can. It takes some work to find Lawrence; he isn't moving. Mitchell reaches down and feels Lawrence's neck for a pulse.

Bri hears Mitchell say, "It's weak, but he's got a pulse!"

She exhales in relief, sending up a grateful prayer in her heart. She thinks of David, Jack, and the rest of their family, along with all the guests who may have been injured in the explosion, or worse! She *prays* no one is killed!

Lawrence starts to wake up as McMasters and Mitchell work to move more debris away. Lawrence starts to move, but he winces in pain grabbing his ribcage at the sharp pain.

McMasters sees this and tells him, "Stop, Lawrence! *Don't move*! You might have some broken ribs. Are you able to breathe?" Lawrence nods. "Good." McMasters knows he would be having a tough time breathing if he had a punctured lung. "I want the paramedics to *safely* move you out of here."

"*How's Bri and the baby?*" Lawrence struggles to ask as he shifts a bit to try to ease some of his pain.

"We're fine for now." She tells him. "I'll let you know if that changes. McMasters? Mitchell? Have either of you been able to hear anything in your earpieces?" Bri asks. "Has anyone said anything about the family, those who are injured, *or what happened?!*"

"It's a bit chaotic in our ears." McMasters answers. "What we know so far is there was an explosion inside The Grand Ballroom." He has a concerned look when he says, "I had them check on the family and everyone is alright, except Carlotta." Bri gasps, and Lawrence is listening closely. "They were able to find a guest who is a doctor and is tending to her. That's all for now. We have to keep our focus here and trust she is being taken care."

"You're right." Bri admits. She watches them checking on the others close by them, and helping those they can, or making sure they stay still while they wait for the paramedics to help them.

Mitchell comes over to tell Bri, "They're trying to get those with less injuries outside, so the paramedics can more easily tend to the seriously injured." They are each helping someone walk outside, and a few others are walking with them.

Once someone outside takes the person McMasters is assisting, he gets back to Bri and Lawrence. He calls to have paramedics come directly to The King and Queen, along with arranging rescue workers to move the marble column off The Queen's legs. He hangs up and tells Mitchell, Lawrence, and Bri, "We have an ambulance coming for Lawrence, additional paramedics to help the others, and a rescue team to get this column off Bri's legs."

"Bri is seen first!" Lawrence tells them.

Bri adamantly replies, "*No, Lawrence!*"

"The baby comes first, Bri." He states.

108

"I agree! And if I thought there was anything wrong with me, or the baby, *I swear to you*, I would let us go first." She says. "I promise, Lawrence, *we're fine.* I'm not sure how, but it's just my legs that are pinned down. I'm begging you, for my sanity, and for the baby; *please* let them tend to you, in case you are internally bleeding somewhere!"

She is pleading in such a way, he can't say anything but, "*For you.*"

He hears her shakily exhale, "*Thank you.*" She looks at McMasters and waves him over. She whispers, "*I also want to be prepared that my medical needs could change, once I'm out from under this column, so you all need to be prepared for that as well.*" McMasters nods in agreement.

With all those who need rescuing, they work to get everyone with more serious injuries to the hospital first. The family agrees to meet at the hospital where they have a wing designated for them. 'The King' is one of the ones rushed to the hospital, and a rescue team works to move the column to free 'The Princess Imperial.'

It took some time, but when Bri is free, the paramedics check her out. While she and the baby seem to be okay, they play it safe. They take her to the hospital by ambulance as a precaution, so an OBGYN can look her, and the baby, over to be sure.

When Bri arrives at the hospital, she has an ultrasound, and everything looks good. Everyone is confident they are doing well, but they want her to stay overnight for observation.

"Just get me to The King, and I promise I will stay overnight!" Bri says.

The doctor smiles. "The King has been given an update on your condition, and he knows we want you to stay overnight. He has insisted we bring a bed into his room for you."

"And how is he?" She asks.

He gives her a kind look as he tells her, "The King will be fine. He has some ribs that are cracked to varying degrees of severity, but none of them actually broke. We've wrapped them and he is resting comfortably."

She gives him a small smile. "Will you please take me to him?"

"Right away, Your Royal Majesty!"

They take Bri to Lawrence's room. She walks in and sees him sitting in bed. She stands up from the wheelchair and walks over to him. When she hugs him, she doesn't realize how tight she is hugging him, he silently winces in pain. He doesn't let her see his face; he just wants to hug her!

"I'm *SO* glad it wasn't worse and you're going to be okay!"

"Me, too, Darling!" He pulls back. "I was told you and the baby are okay." He puts his hand to her lower abdomen.

"We are." She puts her hand on top of his. "I just have some bruising on my legs." She slightly lifts her gown.

He looks at it with a worried face. "That already looks awful! It's surprising *you* didn't break anything!" He watches her go around his bed to sit on the bed next to him.

She tells him, "They thoroughly checked everything with both of us, but they want me to stay overnight for observation."

He points to her bed. "And right there is where I want you to stay!"

She sweetly smiles with her nod. "Have you heard anything about David, Jack, and the family?"

He tells her, "McMasters reported that all of them have scratches, bruises, and a few cuts, but nothing serious; *except Carlotta*. She was hit with a greater force from the blast and debris, making her injuries more severe." Bri has a worried look. "That's all I know for now. McMasters is gathering more information and will report to me shortly." She nods. "I do know David and Jack are fine, and they're still at The Palace helping with those who are injured." She wipes her tears of relief and takes a deep breath.

"The number of casualties could be high." She says, it's silent for a long moment before she softly tells him, "*Innocent people were hurt because of Millicent's hatred towards me...*"

He adamantly states, *"Her day will come."*

"Just not soon enough to prevent the deaths that are to come before this is all over!" She whispers.

"Unfortunately." Lawrence sadly agrees.

Lawrence and Bri are in their room, waiting for more updates, especially about Carlotta's condition. It seems like forever before David and Jack arrive at the hospital.

David asks Bri, "Has a doctor checked you and the baby out?"

Bri puts her hands on her lower abdomen. "The baby and I are fine. There's no bleeding, nor anything to be concerned about; *however*, they want me to stay overnight for observation." David hugs her and exhales with relief. She says, "I wish Millicent would just come after me directly! UGH!" She pulls back a little. "But she won't, because she wants to enjoy the suffering that she inflicts by torturing me and hurting those around me! *No one* is safe!"

Lawrence, David, and Jack have sad looks on their faces...*she is right.* They need to stop Millicent as soon as possible, before there is no one left, but Lawrence's heir, when the dust settles. *Then there will be nothing anyone can do to protect his son, or to stop her!*

A doctor comes to inform The King, along with Jack, David, and Bri, that over the next several weeks, they do expect Carlotta to make a full recovery. The family takes turns in small groups to see Carlotta. David and Jack push Bri and Lawrence down to see her.

When Peter sees the concern on Bri's face, he reminds her, "You said it yourself; Millicent makes her own choices."

Bri nods as she looks at Carlotta. "I'm just scared to think about how many people will die before we're able to stop her!"

Peter gives her a small smile. "I believe it was said by someone on the other side that you can't stop what is meant to be. Lotti, Henry, Maggie, and I have talked about that and *none of us* want you to blame yourself if something happens to one, *or all, of us.* We know that *if* you can stop anything, you will, and that's *if* you're divinely allowed to stop it. Bri, you will stop her *when you are meant to stop her,* and not a second sooner."

Bri wipes her cheek and nods. "Thank you for that." She hugs him, then she carefully hugs Carlotta.

Carlotta weakly says her, "*We love you, Sweetie!*" She puts her hand on Bri's cheek. "*Don't you forget that!*" Bri has a soft, teary smile.

Carlotta hugs her again, then the others, before they say goodbye. They step out of the room, then James and Amy visit her next.

Over the next few days, McMasters and Mitchell investigate with The Royal Police, while The Royal Guards and The King's Guard keep the family safe. The Worthington's went back to Newhaven, Carlotta wanted to recuperate at home. Peter wasn't comfortable with that, until she agreed to have a private doctor and nurse provide around-the-clock care.

McMasters only wanted their most trusted people protecting The Estate, *and the family.* The Estate has temporarily closed to tourists. There is also increased security and cameras at the ports and aboard the ferry going back and forth to the island and mainland, as well as the airport, so The Royal Guard can watch for *any* unwelcome guests.

Bri wanted to stay at The Palace to show Millicent that she wasn't going to scare her off. She wanted all the media pictures to show Bri calmly walking around all the destruction with concern. Pictures of Bri and The King show them compassionate, yet resolute, in their support of the survivors, and the families of those who were lost.

Bri is quoted saying, "This act of terrorism will not bring this country down, but rather, it will show that this country is strong and will persevere through whatever terrorism acts are thrown at it; *especially by a traitor!*"

There were numerous questions that were asked wanting her to name *who* she thinks committed the crime. Bri doesn't even acknowledge the questions. Her comments are aimed at Millicent, and she is confident Millicent will get the message.

Tristan does show Millicent the video footage of Bri's comment on terrorism and perseverance, while calling Millicent a traitor. Millicent wickedly grins as she remembers, "Doesn't she have a charity event coming up?"

"This Spring." Tristan replies, wondering what she is thinking.

"*Perfect!*" Millicent says. "It will give us time to plan something, in between our shipments arriving for the upcoming auction." She turns to Tristan. "How are you coming on bringing those new people on board? Were you able to find the ones we talked about?"

"It's going slow, because these guys are *incredibly* nervous, *and extremely cautious!*" Tristan answers.

"It's good for us to do this before now, because Bri could send people to spy on us after this last attack." Millicent tells him. "That bomb wasn't supposed to be *that* powerful, so it should've killed *someone* close to Bri!" She exhales in frustration. "We need to be careful; she *can't* die yet! I need her to give birth to The Heir, MY *heir!*" She wonders, "Who can we target *before* Christmas?"

Tristan replies, "The problem is, Auntie, how do we attack her loved ones *without* endangering her at those same events?" He also puts out there, "Whatever you decide to do, we need to consider Bri will become more and more pregnant, and her ability to travel will decrease."

Millicent nods a little as she paces and thinks. "Well, we should do something soon, perhaps right behind this one, for better affect!"

A couple days later, McMasters is updating Lawrence, David, Jack, and Bri on the case. They had watched the security video and figured out that the bomb was on a serving cart. They don't think the bomb went off when it was supposed to, because on the video, a server moves the cart out of the way of another cart a server was pushing. It looks like he pushes it over something and the bump sets off the bomb, killing the server, and all those in close proximity to him, *instantly*. So, one would think if he knew there was a bomb on the cart, he would've been more careful with it."

Jack sees Bri staring out the window and goes over to her. "Are you alright, Amore Mia?"

"*No.*" She barely whispers, wiping the tear off her cheek. "All these people are dead, *and* more people are going to die! I know Rex said that it'll take time to set things up to bring her down, but right now, part of me just wants to drop a bomb on The Devonridge Estate when she's there and just be done with it. *Unfortunately,* that would kill more innocent people, which is what I don't want even more!" She takes a deep breath. "Plus, if she is part cockroach, she would crawl up out of the giant crater and still be a threat!" The guys snort a laugh.

Lawrence notes, "Once Rex gets everything, *and everyone,* in place, then Millicent's days *will be* numbered."

She exhales, "*Yyyep.*"

David suggests, "You may not want to stay here much longer, but your people need to see—."

"*I need to be here.*" She says. "Not only for those who survived this ordeal, but for the families of those who didn't. On top of all that, I don't want to give Millicent any reason to believe I have run away, or that I'm hiding in fear." She looks at Lawrence. "I want to tour the damage again to talk about the repairs, but I don't want any press with us. I know they will find out, but I don't want it to be, *nor feel,* staged." The guys nod in understanding.

CHAPTER 12

A Connection to Ashbourne

Lawrence, Bri, David, and Jack are touring the damage of The London Palace bombing. There are reporters in the crowd watching The King, The Princess Imperial, The Grand Duke of Newhaven, and The Duke of Ashbourne, as they walk around the damage. They also see The King Father, Phillip, with Prince Seth, Queen Genevieve, and Princess Abagail walking over to them.

One of the reporters with the crowd of onlookers is Hayes Buchanan, her harshest critic. He has a sensitive microphone that is turned up to record what he can, and it barely catches Bri saying, "*All this history...It's sickening how some of this is* completely *ruined!*" She looks at Phillip. "*I hate the thought of throwing any of it out, but there may not be a choice with some of it.*" Hayes is surprised 'The *American* Princess' cares about saving anything historic! Nevertheless, he will come up with some kind of negative spin to put on it.

It is emotional for Bri and the others as they get closer to The Royal Grand Ballroom. There isn't a lot of debris left to clean up inside, and they find themselves near a dried pool of blood. It made it that much more real to Bri...the loss of innocent people.

By the end of the tour, someone takes a picture of Bri that shows her standing amid all the debris outside. She is stoic, yet her face also shows compassion. It is the picture that goes on the front page of many media outlets, which *infuriates* Millicent when she sees it!

When everyone goes back to The Royal Apartment, the guys talk about Ashbourne Castle. She remembers being told that Mr. Woodsley isn't going to like her, and she gets nauseous. She hopes to start winning him over when she asks him questions and he can see her genuine interest in Ashbourne Castle and The Ashbourne Estate.

David goes over to her. "What are you thinking about, Love?"

She smiles sweetly. "I was just thinking I needed to look at my ancestry, because I think there is a connection to the monarch who originally had Ashbourne Castle built."

"There is!" Lawrence tells her.

115

"Is that why you gave us The Estate?" She wonders.

Lawrence walks over to her. "It's my favorite castle, so I wanted it to be in the hands of *two* of my most favorite people!" He squeezes her hand. "And if I don't make it through this with Millicent, well, I know it will still be taken care of it."

"DON'T you *dare* talk like that!" Bri snips. She points to his chest telling him, "She knows the best way to hurt me, after Natty and Emmie, would be you three!"

"I know." Lawrence says. "I'm sorry to upset you, Darling."

"For now, you're as safe as I am, because she needs *your* heir!" Her eyes get teary. "I pray *every single day* she *never* gets to any of you, or—," she sharply inhales, then squeaks, "*or* I *won't survive this*!"

Lawrence holds the back of her head. "You *will* survive this! We have this one coming," he puts a hand on her growing baby bump, "and more children need to come into our family." She softly nods.

"Let's focus on something else." Jack shifts the direction of the conversation. "Like that family tree."

Lawrence explains more for Bri, "As you know, The Royal Family Tree can be found in The Royal Library." She nods. "All the *original* family trees of each royal and noble family are kept in The Royal Archives. Those viewed in The Royal Library are actually certified copies."

"Can we go to The Royal Library right now?" She asks.

Lawrence nods. "I'll let McMasters know."

"That will give me time to go grab my notebook with all my notes!" She turns towards stairs.

David stops her. "Let me go get it for you, Love."

She sweetly smiles. "Why don't you come with me, because I'm not exactly sure where I last put it down." He nods and walks upstairs with her.

"We keep a copy of your family tree in my father's study. We can get you a copy if you'd like?" David asks.

She lovingly says, "I appreciate the offer, but knowing where I can find one if I need it later, is fine." They walk into The Royal Chambers, and she sees David looking around. "Haven't you been in here before?"

He shakes his head. "No. We were rarely here at The Palace, but Herst's childhood bedroom wasn't The Royal Chambers." She lightly giggles.

She goes over to the end table on her side of the bed. "*Ah.* Here it is!" She picks up the notebook. She looks at David and says, "Why don't you go look in the bathroom and the closet?" He gives her a questioning look. "Considering this is your first time in here, who knows when you'll have another chance?"

"Yes!" Lawrence says, as he and Jack walk in. "Let's remedy that! Jack, David, take a look around. You'll see this is pretty similar to the rooms at The Worthington Manor, especially my quarters on the fourth floor." They agree, looking around.

Jack teases, "I think the size of that bathroom is as big as my last flat was in Edinburgh!"

"Perhaps." Lawrence lightly laughs. "I do think her bedroom at Ashbourne will rival this." David and Jack agree.

When they all walk inside The Royal Library, it's massive! The staff is lined up to formally greet The King, The Princess Imperial, The Grand Duke of Newhaven, and The Duke of Ashbourne.

The Librarian is in front, and Bri learns her name is Lady Keats. She takes them over to the parchment with Bri's family tree on it that they have ready for her to view. They had all the pieces laid out on a large table, so it looked like one giant family tree.

"This is wonderful!" Bri says to Lady Keats and the staff. "Thank you!"

"Of course, Ma'am!" Lady Keats replies.

"Now, let me think..." she looks up the 'branches' of the tree, "Ashbourne Castle was built right around the time of The French Revolution in seventeen..." she thinks a moment, "seventeen eighty-nine...so ruling the UK would have been..." she looks for the dates that encompass 1789 and taps the parchment, "King Alexander III and Queen Isabel." She looks to another spot saying, "It was a different Alexander before this one that helped his son plot to combine another duchy with Ashbourne to make it one of the biggest duchies in England."

"*Wow*! You *have* done your homework!" Jack smiles.

"I have!" She grins. "I wanted to impress Mr. Woodsley!" There is laughter around her.

"I can't remember," David thinks about it, then asks, "what was the other duchy?"

"Woodsley." Bri replies. David and Jack look at each other, then look at Lawrence, who nods. Bri sweetly smiles at them. "I think The Ashbourne Estate sits mostly on what would've been The Duchy of Woodsley, well on the edge of it, barely into The Duchy of Ashbourne."

Jack tells them, "With the pride Mr. Woodsley takes with The Ashbourne Estate, it makes sense."

Bri adds, "In a very real, and very sad way, his family was cheated out of the titles for The Duchy of Woodsley."

Jack smiles adoringly. "*You're bloody brilliant!*"

Bri grins. "Did I mention *I love history*?!" The guys lightly laugh, as well as the staff. "Oh! Plus, plus, and, and, right here," she points to her family tree, "King Alexander III, who commissioned Ashbourne Castle to be built, is *my* so many great-grandfather!" She winks at Lawrence who chuckles.

"Making Ashbourne Castle *even more* special to you!" Jack states and she nods in agreement.

David says to Jack and Lawrence, "If our girl doesn't impress Mr. Woodsley with her knowledge of The Ashbourne Estate, then he has to have a heart of stone and should be sacked!" The guys agree.

They thank the staff on their way back to The Royal Apartment.

CHAPTER 13

A Tour of The Ashbourne Estate

 When the men take Bri to officially tour The Ashbourne Estate for the first time, they introduce her to the staff, beginning with Mr. Woodsley. His official title is 'The Majordomo,' and he is in charge of the staff and The Estate. He has darker brown hair that is graying on the sides and blue eyes, conducting himself as a very prim and proper gentleman in a long tail suit coat uniform. Unfortunately, he didn't *completely* hide his dislike and contempt of this undeserving American being The Duchess of Ashbourne. However, he is proud to be showing The King, The Grand Duke of Newhaven, along with The Duke of Ashbourne, his beloved estate.

When they enter The Private Apartment, Bri sees they are working on what looks like the structural renovations Jack had mentioned. She can see its potential and David silently chuckles when he hears her whisper '*wooow*' under her breath.

David grins at her, "We were right." She has a questioning look. "This castle *does* suit you." She rolls her eyes and shakes her head a bit, but she is smiling. Mr. Woodsley stops himself from scoffing out loud at the comment.

Mr. Woodsley erroneously assumes this '*American Princess*' will modernize The Royal Quarters and *completely* ruin everything! Bri tries to overlook Mr. Woodsley's dismissal of her. She even tries to win him over by asking about Ashbourne's history, not knowing he is insulted that she, *The Duchess of Ashbourne*, doesn't know its history! *A history she should know inside and out!*

Bri doesn't think anyone notices Mr. Woodsley's feelings towards her, but the men haven't missed *a thing*! Lawrence is a stickler on Bri having the outward respect her titles call for! With Mr. Woodsley being *utterly disrespectful* by avoiding any use of her titles, like 'Her Royal Majesty,' *nor having a respectful tone*, it's *all* irritating him!

Jack and Lawrence wrap up the renovation discussions with Mr. Woodsley, who is *delighted* his cherished castle is getting the funding for the updates it needs. "I'll see to it that these things are started immediately, Sir, and I'll let you know if there are any concerns."

"Structurally, yes, call me." Jack says. "As for the rest of The Castle and The Grounds," Jack watches Mr. Woodsley closely when he says, "what Her Royal Majesty wants, *is* what we'll do." He sees Mr. Woodsley squirm and adds, "I want her to make The Royal Residence *her own*."

"Yes, Your Grace." Mr. Woodsley glances at Bri, his nose slightly turns up before he catches himself and pushes down his disapproval, "I'll make note of it, Sir. Is there anything else?"

"Actually, *there is*!" Jack replies.

Bri puts her hand on Jack's arm as she slowly shakes her head. She whispers, "*Jack, I'm an outsider and Mr. Woodsley has no reason to trust me—.*"

"*Stop!*" The King's voice is commanding, and Bri jumps a little. Lawrence turns on his heel to face Mr. Woodsley. "*Her Royal Majesty* was about to excuse your behavior away, because *that's* her kindness for you; she would rather assume the best of people." He looks at her as he says, "What she needs to understand is that your attitude *isn't* an accident *and* you are *perfectly aware* of the respect her titles call for," he looks at Mr. Woodsley, "or you wouldn't be in your post as 'The Majordomo.' *And you're more than aware of what you're doing!*" Bri sees Mr. Woodsley shrink down a little. "What *you* need to understand, Mr. Woodsley, is I can't have anyone around The Princess Imperial *we* can't trust to be devoted *to her*, first and foremost, knowing it would also be a devotion *to me*, as 'The King!' Not showing her the basic courtesy of the title *I* gave her *doesn't* build trust, it's bordering on treason! It *will*, however, *require* your dismissal if you don't correct yourself *immediately*! Now, if you look at her, you'll see she is pained by her empathy for you," Mr. Woodsley glances over and he does see her face, "she doesn't want to be the reason you lose your post."

Bri closes her eyes and looks away. Mr. Woodsley sees this out of the corner of his eye, and he starts to feel remorseful for his *shameful* behavior.

Lawrence continues addressing Mr. Woodsley. "*You know this is my favorite castle and grounds.*" Mr. Woodsley nods. "I wouldn't have put this castle in The Duke of Ashbourne's hands, nor Her Royal Majesty's hands, if I thought they would ruin it in *any* way! In fact, I knew these two would make sure it gets back to its former glory!" He walks over to Bri. "Mr. Woodsley, she was asking questions about this castle because she *loves* history," he cups the back of her neck and smiles, "and she *has* studied Ashbourne's history, she was

121

hoping to engage you in a conversation about it." Mr. Woodsley starts to regret his actions towards her that much more. "Since Jack, David, *and myself,* want her to make this her '*home away from home,*' I must *r*eemphasize that I need people around her I can trust, that *we* can trust!" He motions the three of them. "This includes respecting all her guards because some of them are also former American law enforcement." He gives Mr. Woodsley a very pointed look, "Is this, in *any* way, unclear?!"

"No, Sir." Mr. Woodsley says. Then he turns to Bri. "My apologies, *Your Royal Majesty.* It *won't* happen again, Ma'am." She feels embarrassed for him, but she also feels sincerity *from* him.

She gives him a kind smile. "I don't believe it will." He gives her a small, assured nod in agreement. She breaks the tension by suggesting, "Mr. Woodsley, I would like to tell these men that I absolutely love and adore, what I discovered when I researched and studied this castle's history. I would like you to hear this with them to make sure I haven't missed anything. *Please* feel free to add, or correct me, if something is amiss." He hesitates as he nods. She gives him a kind smile. "It's okay, *I promise.* I have read a lot of books, and I could have misunderstood something I read, jumbled it up, or I could have simply forgotten something altogether!"

He tips his head down and says, "I'll be happy to assist, *if* needed."

"Wonderful!" She smiles happily, making Mr. Woodsley slightly relieved of his guilt. She turns to David, Jack, and Lawrence. "I'm not sure how much you all know, *or remember from your school days,* of the history of Ashbourne, *or The Estate?*" The guys think back to their history lessons. Bri helps them jog their memories. "King Alexander III commissioned the construction of Ashbourne Castle, and grounds, in 1790, for his beloved Queen Isabel; it was about a year after the *French* Revolution began. He chose The Duchy of Ashbourne because it's bigger, being comprised of two duchies." She looks at Mr. Woodsley. "Let's see if I have this right..." She takes a deep breath. "The Ashbourne and Woodsley duchies shared a border. The then *Prince* Andrew met The Earl of Woodsley's only child, a daughter, Lady Sophia, and he devised a plan; *with the help of his father,* King Alexander II. He wanted to marry her and be in line to inherit her family's land; but first, he had to have the law changed to make it where those lands could be passed to a daughter, if there were no *legitimate* sons to pass The Duchy to; *otherwise,* it could go to an illegitimate son. When Prince Andrew would marry Lady Sophia, his father, King Alexander II, bestowed The Duchy of Ashbourne to them and elevated his son's father-in-law to 'The Duke of Woodsley.'" She looks at David, Jack, and Lawrence. "I'm sure you know what happens next…"

Lawrence replies, "One of the *many* mysteries in our country's history is the death of The Duke of Woodsley. Was it really an accident; or was he murdered? I'm not saying coincidences don't happen, but it's doubtful he 'accidentally died,' so soon after the law was changed, *and* his daughter married The Crown Prince."

"I agree!" She replies. "The death of The Duke of Woodsley would come when he *supposedly* fell off his horse and his head hit a rock. They would try to quell speculation when they exhumed The Duke's body in 2001. Unfortunately, the medical examiner could only confirm that The Duke's neck was also broken; meaning, if he hadn't died from a broken neck, then the blunt force trauma to his head with the rock was so severe that he would've died from the hemorrhaging in the brain."

David takes it all in. He whispers to himself, *"Fascinating…"*

Bri continues, "Upon The Duke's death, his daughter, Sophia, inherits the land and titles with her husband, Prince Andrew. He immediately takes control of The Duchy of Woodsley and one of his first orders of business was to combine The Duchy of Woodsley with The Duchy of Ashbourne, to make Ashbourne one of the biggest duchies in *The United Kingdom of Provinces*. Unfortunately, when Prince Alexander becomes 'King Alexander II,' he lets his power go to his head. There is a saying that goes, 'power corrupts; and absolute power, corrupts absolutely,' King Alexander II would be no exception; sadly, his children would only become worse. Queen Sophia would give birth to William III, along with a daughter, Mary, then another son, John, in The London Palace. One morning, Queen Sophia was discovered washed up on the shores of a vacation estate up on the northeastern coast. *Rumor has it*, The King tells his men to toss her back into the sea as he sets off to marry the next available noblewoman," she looks at Lawrence, "which happens to be his cousin, Lady Anne of Devonridge."

Lawrence sarcastically replies, *"This keeps getting better and better…"*

Bri gives him an understanding look. "We can skip—."

"No, no!" He gives her a little smile. "You're doing quite well, *Darling.*" Lawrence urges her, *"Please,* continue."

123

"Well, it should come as no surprise that *Queen Anne* was as devious as King Alexander II was, probably *more* so; *if* we consider that when she gave birth to a son, Arthur, she tried to make *him* the one who succeeded King Alexander II. She used skilled manipulation, as well as playing the 'more noble blood' card. It probably would've worked if she and her son hadn't contracted The Plague during another outbreak that swept through again. This was the last major outbreak of the Bubonic Plague which first hit Europe in the fourteenth century and would have various outbreaks pop up throughout the next three centuries." She keeps going. "King Alexander II would die days before his forty seventh birthday of typhoid fever. His son, King William III, raised his son like his father raised him, *only worse*. The son he raises becomes the most hated king in England's history. King Phillip IV would be famously known as 'Phillip the Merciless.'"

Lawrence tells her, "There is a legend that there was so much more blood spilt at The Killing Wall when King Phillip ruled, that the vegetables from the garden not far from The Wall, tasted like blood."

"*Yuck!*" Bri says with an expression on her face to match. "Well, *that King Phillip* raised the first King Lawrence, who would construct a castle that was more of a tower, hence the name 'The Royal Tower,' with multiple outside walls to protect the castle from an attack. He also wanted the height to intimidate people who would dare attack him, or the country. *You know...*" she thinks out loud, "I think he was more afraid of his own people revolting and overthrowing him, than he was of any invaders from a different country. The more unstable Paris and Europe became, the more desperate his behavior; his fear and insecurities caused many to be imprisoned or executed. As kings and queens all over the world raised their children to show power and rule with a strong fist, they didn't understand that this kind of mindset only adds to the infuriation of the people. With the lower class getting poorer and poorer and living in deplorable, squalor conditions; and the middle class disappearing to create an even bigger gap between the rich and the poor, the people took their anger out on the first King Lawrence's tower. They stormed The Tower and looted it; taking whatever they could carry, then set numerous fires that would eventually come together forming one *great* big fire they would have to let burn, completely destroying The Tower. By the time The Tower was reduced to smoldering ashes, thirty-two people had died."

"He *made* his worst fear come true!" Jack says.

"*Right!*" David replies, with Lawrence and Bri agreeing.

"So, by the start of *The French Revolution*, King Lawrence's son, King Alexander III, and his wife, Queen Isabel, were ruling the country. These two understood that they needed to change things, if they were going to prevent a revolt here in the UK. With strategic moves, King Alexander wanted to quell the revolutionary cries that were starting to ripple through the UK. He freed the prisoners who were imprisoned for less serious crimes, as well as those who were imprisoned for not paying their outrageously high taxes and dismissing their debt. He would charge a flat percentage rate for each person who rented their home from The Royal Family. For those who owned their home and land, a tax rate was a bit trickier, but they did find a flat percentage rate that was affordable. His second smart move was his most *brilliant* one of all!" She teases with their accent. "Would you like to take a guess at what that might be?"

Lawrence grins. "I would only argue that whatever it is, it would be his *third* smartest move." He watches Bri as she thinks about what she missed, *even Mr. Woodsley is thinking back...* Lawrence tells her, "His first, *and most important move*, was marrying a fantastically *brilliant* woman!" Jack laughs and claps, wholeheartedly agreeing.

David adds, "She was the mastermind behind all these other brilliant moves, was she not?" He raises his eyebrow, and she gives a small giggle as she shakes her head.

"*Oh!* Let's back up a little." She remembers something. "King Alexander III's *next* smartest move, would be setting up a 'Royal Advisory Council,' where members consisted of elected people, not necessarily titled men, to represent, 'his subjects,' or the people. At that time, duchy lines were used, but later districts would be zoned, as populations grew and shifted. The Royal Advisory Council would become what is now *Parliament*." The guys nod as they remember their history lessons. She continues, "King Alexander III kept executive control, a power he *purposely*, rarely used. All monarchs since that time, keep their, 'executive control,' yet all the wise ones are careful to barely use it." Lawrence nods. "King Alexander III saved his family's monarchy rule, which, in his writings, he gives credit to his *beloved* Bel, whom he loved and respected *so* much, he *always* gave her advice a lot of consideration. It's believed the feelings were mutually shared."

"Something I think we can all relate to!" David motions the four of them and they all agree.

Bri has a thought go through her head about the amethyst heart brooch, 'The Heart of Adoration,' Jack had given her the brooch on their honeymoon. She feels deeply that King Alexander originally gave it to Queen Isabel, the woman he loved and adored.

Lawrence holds out his hand to Bri. "Shall we walk the grounds while you tell us more?"

"I'd love to!" She smiles and takes his hand. They all start walking as Bri continues. "To show his people that he would take an, '*observe and guide*,' approach with the country, King Alexander III brought 'The Royal Advisory Council' under the roof of The Palace, along with other government offices he worked closely with. They were, and are, located just down the hall from The Official Royal Offices. Then with the big undertaking he took on building a *family* castle, he was careful not to make it too extravagant to respect the people, and the taxes they paid into the treasury, thinking that is what paid for the new home. A forgotten fact is that they used a lot of their family's money to build Ashbourne." She looks at Mr. Woodsley. "How am I doing? I have read so much information, it's *impossible* for me to remember it all! Did I miss anything vital to the story?"

Mr. Woodsley is in awe of how much history she already knew of Ashbourne. He is caught off guard by her question.

He clears his throat and shakes his head. "You're doing *splendidly*, Ma'am!"

"Agreed!" Jack smiles. "Let's finish our history lesson!"

"Where was I..." she thinks about where she left off, "*Right*...King Alexander III picked the location of Ashbourne Castle to be at the center of the woods, secluded and not easily seen, unlike most castles that are built to be large, expensive, intimidating, and mostly unapproachable. The white towers were constructed at the back of The Ashbourne Gardens, detached from The Castle for discreet security, and to house The Royal Watchmen Guards; always on alert for intruders and have a 360-degree view.

"A wall was built, but at the edge of the forest and it was built with minimal trees cut to make its path. Those cut trees were also used in the construction

126

of The Castle." Bri says. "The wall is now fortified with additional security measures like razor wire, a fence with an electric current, and so on. There is a secret entrance that is uniquely protected, and it provides additional opportunities for security methods."

"If I may," Mr. Woodsley interjects, "around the top edge of the walls of the fence is a razor wire with an electrical currant that goes through it; just enough of a jolt, it wouldn't kill the average person in good health, yet they wouldn't be so quick to attempt touching it again. These types of things are done to create an area for intruders to be 'dealt with,' before ever reaching the castle. These features are blended in with the landscape, as to not ruin the beauty of the gardens, nor The Estate."

Bri asks Mr. Woodsley, "Aren't there barracks on both sides of the gate for guards to sleep in, rather than the men sleeping on the floors." He nods.

David notes, "*Sleeping on a stone floor is dedication!*" They all agree.

"The moat was constructed around The Castle, and there are only two bridges, one centered in the front and the other centered in the back. There is a myth that started long ago about a prehistoric predator living in its waters with piranhas. While common sense would say it's, '*just a rumor*,' it did instill uncertainty of what *could* be in the water to deter most intruders from trying to swim across it." They all had stopped to look at the moat.

"It does give one pause." Jack says, as he looks at it.

"It does." Bri agrees and she explains, "While moats are known to have been built for protection, they were also a status symbol of grandeur and wealth; for example, a created moat could be far more impressive than a dammed-up moat. Moats were used for aesthetic landscaping and the reflections off of them, particularly of The Castle itself, gave a greater sense of grandness. All of which, is right here." She motions the moat with her arms. "What's sad is that Queen Isabel wouldn't live to see the completion of The Castle. King Alexander III was *so* devastated by the loss of his beloved wife, he went into seclusion, leaving his son, Prince Phillip, to take over most of the responsibilities of The Crown for his father. King Alexander would live to be seventy years old, which is unusual for that time period when life expectancy wasn't past the forties. Sadly, Prince Phillip had preceded him in death. King Alexander III would officially step down several years before his own death, so his grandson, and Prince Phillip's son, Prince Henry, could reign. Come to think of it..." she thinks back, "that's all I've heard, well read, on King Henry."

"He wouldn't rule very long before he was murdered." Mr. Woodsley adds.

"*Really?*" Bri replies. "I don't recall coming across that story yet."

"It's *rumored* his wife killed him when she grew tired of him." Lawrence says and Mr. Woodsley nods.

"*Daaang!*" She replies. "I wonder if she is related to the Devonridge line?" The men lightly chuckle. "Anyway, Ashbourne Castle had been sitting vacant for quite some time, before the overseeing of The Ashbourne Estate was given to a Woodsley descendant. They oversee its upkeep as The Majordomo of The Estate." She gestures to Mr. Woodsley. "That position has been passed down in your family for quite a few generations now, hasn't it?"

Mr. Woodsley nods. "Our family has taken great pride in maintaining The Ashbourne Estate!"

Bri enthusiastically tells him, "*You should!* This place is *absolutely* beautiful!" The guys laugh and she gives them a questioning look.

Lawrence tells her, "We knew you would love this place!"

Jack adds, "Especially when The Royal Residence is finished!"

She giggles. "I think I'm actually starting to believe you three!"

Mr. Woodsley starts to think about what it could mean if, '*The Princess Imperial*,' made her official residence his beloved Ashbourne Castle...He goes further and wonders what it would mean if, '*The Queen*,' made it her official *royal* residence?!

CHAPTER 14
Fact-Finding Information

They finish their tour of The Ashbourne Estate and Bri gets the feeling there is something more to The Estate. They make their way to the back of The Castle and its extensive grounds.

Outside, Bri sees a helicopter waiting on the helipad and teases, "I could be wrong, but I believe a helipad is not historically accurate to The Estate, Your Majesty!" Mr. Woodsley finds himself smiling at her humor.

Lawrence teases back, "I consider it an improvement with the necessity of the times."

"Yes, but I was *hoping* to keep things as close to original as possible." She notes, "A helipad wouldn't be original to The Estate."

"Point taken, Darling, *however,*" he smirks, "what about the improvements to electricity and plumbing over the years?"

"Touché!" She admits. "Alright, I'll give you that." She concedes with a smile. He holds her hand as they walk to the helicopter. Bri's eyes fall on the seal on the door, then she looks at the entire helicopter. She stops. "*Wait a second... It's so...big!* Why so big?! I thought this size of a helicopter is used for the military?!"

"Military helicopters are various sizes." Jack states.

"True." She replies. "I guess I didn't think this size was for *civilian* use."

Lawrence gestures the helicopter asking her, "How do you like it?"

"Lawrence..." she is at a loss for words, "*this is incredible!*"

"I can't take credit for it; this is all David and Jack! They just told me where to sign at various times." He winks at them.

"Ah, so *that's* the secret!" She playfully smiles. "Just put a document in front of you and say, 'sign here.'" The guys chuckle.

Jack leans in closer and whispers, "*For you, being naked wouldn't hurt.*"

Lawrence hears Jack and admits, "I can't argue that!" He kisses the back of Bri's hand. They walk up to the helicopter, and he says to Jack and David, "Bri is right, *this is fantastic!* And this all looks even better than I pictured it!"

Bri gets a better look at the seal on the door. "*Two* crowns?" She shakes her head. "Lawrence, that's not appropriate——."

"Just planning ahead, Darling." He grins.

Before she can say anything else, David purposely interrupts to introduce Jack, Lawrence, and Bri to the pilots. "Everyone, this is Mrs. Caroline Coleman and her husband, Mr. Chad Coleman."

"Please, just Caroline and Chad. It's easier and quicker." Chad says to them as they all shake hands.

"I *love* that our pilots are married!" Bri happily tells them. "With all the traveling that we'll be doing, you can travel together!"

"*That's what we thought!*" Caroline smiles wide. "Our youngest of four is about to go off to college next year. While he has a girlfriend we love, he also has sports and two jobs to juggle, all while keeping his studies up! We're very proud of him, *aaand* we're also happy he's so busy, he can't spend *too* much time with his girlfriend."

Bri smiles as she agrees, "I can understand being grateful when time is filled keeping kids *out* of trouble!"

"*Right!*" Caroline laughs. "We've wanted to start our own business for quite some time, then this opportunity comes along and, well, *here we are!*"

"I'm so glad!" Bri says.

 While Caroline and Chad go over their preflight checklist, Bri looks around inside the helicopter. She sees the monogram and shield on a door and traces it with her finger; Lawrence smiles as she does. She turns and sees him staring. She smiles as she walks up to him and hugs him goodbye.

He hugs her firmly. "I love you, Bri!"

What she says next to his ear chokes him up a bit. "*I absolutely* adore *you, Ace!*" She feels him hug her a little tighter. "*And I love you deeply.*"

He keeps one arm around her, while the other hand tangles in her hair. "I'll miss you!"

She grins saying, "*I already miss you!*"

Lawrence chuckles and kisses her one last time, then says goodbye to the others before he steps off the helicopter. Once they are in the air and on their way to Newhaven, he and Mr. Woodsley make their way to the front of Ashbourne Castle where the motorcade is waiting. Lawrence pulls Mr. Woodsley aside to privately thanking him for his change of heart; *Lawrence really didn't want to fire him.*

Bri gets comfortable in her seat; she glances down and sees a larger envelope inside her bag. Curious, she pulls it out and sees a smaller envelope taped to it. She opens the small envelope and pulls out the note. It reads:

> My team says they're <u>all in</u>! They're already on various missions for you and our mutual goal. The best hacker in the world has taken the lead on what you wanted to accomplish first with the shipments and money. I will be sending the hacker to you soon!
>
> Remember, this will all take some time. I'll be in touch.
>
> ~ *R*

She opens the large envelope and pulls out what is inside. On top is a list of Millicent's shipments coming into a port near Devonridge over the next few months. Her brain starts brainstorming several ways for things 'to happen' to these shipments. She pushes those ideas aside for now, moving that page to the back to look at what else Rex has for her.

The next page is a 'fact-finding sheet' on Claude Devereaux that she had requested.

BIRTH NAME: Claude Edme Devereaux
AKA: The Curator ('Red-Listed')
DOB: October 23 (52)
SEX: Male
HAIR COLOR: Brown   EYE COLOR: Green
HEIGHT: Average   WEIGHT: Average

MARKS OR TATTOOS: Scar above his left eyebrow from when his father threw a broken bear bottle at his 11-year-old head. *** He has 3 tattoos: barbed wire around his upper arm; a skull above the barbed wire; and a dagger on his chest 'piercing' his heart with 'blood' dripping out of the wound.

MARITAL STATUS: Never been married. * Currently single.
    His last relationship was with a South American politician, Lola Hernandez, who is four years older than him. They broke up because he didn't need Lola anymore; her connections were now his connections.

CHILDREN: 1 infant from a 'hookup' (daughter 3 months old) – he killed child's mother for trying to blackmail him with the child – the child has a nanny and live elsewhere, but their whereabouts are unknown at this time.

Although Bri hates to do it, she highlights this part, because she knows this child could be the key to getting Claude Devereaux out of the way.

MAIN RESIDENCE: A French Chateau – Bardeaux, France

HOMETOWN: Bardeaux, France
    * Grew up in the poorest part of the city; now lives in the most affluent part.

PARENTS: Father Deceased; Mother still in Bardeaux

** Mother was a drug addict and prostitute; his father was his mother's pimp; she would have to have sex with whoever he told her to, and he would keep the money. However, she would secretly prostitute herself out for drugs, and money for drugs. His father rarely found out, but when he did, he would beat her; most of those times he would beat her within an inch of her life.

*** His father was mean and abusive, but worse when he was intoxicated or high on drugs.

**** It is believed his father is the first-person Claude killed when he had enough of his father's abuse.

OCCUPATION: Art Gallery Owner – with locations in Paris, London, New York, Los Angeles, and Tokyo

* They are partly legitimate businesses, but each are used as a front – these are located in port cities to be used to covertly smuggle items, and humans, around the world; disguised as shipments to and from his galleries.

**Millicent Devonridge is one of his main suppliers.

PERSONAL BUSINESS: Specializing in art, but will find *anything* for the right price (and specific clients).

FEAR: Being double-crossed

MOST SIGNIFICANT TRAIT: He is creative and smart, although he can be very ruthless *and violent* when angered! The bloodier he leaves his victim the better.

* He tends to kill on the spot; rarely sending someone to do it.

WEAKEST TRAIT: Wants what he wants no matter the cost.

GREATEST THREAT: Anyone more powerful than he is.

Bri takes that all in, contemplating how to best approach.

MISC: Aside from his father, his first victim was a 19-year-old young woman who mouthed off to his girlfriend; he walked up to her and shot her point blank in the face. He was so 'cool, calm, and collected' about it that it scared those who witnessed it. No one messed with him, or anyone who was with him, after that. After that incident, he found he liked being feared, because everyone got *out* of his way!

'That might be a reason why he and Millicent get along so well.' Bri thinks to herself.

> *Claude's childhood best friend, Gustav Cuvier, died when they were 24 years old. The cause of death was injuries sustained in a one-car accident — they were speeding.
> **His current best friend is Michael Moreno, whom he met in Colombia when he was on a multi-country visit. Michael is an MMA Fighter, and Claude enjoys going to his fights and placing a few bets; the bloodier the fight, the more Claude enjoys watching the fight.

Bri's thoughts are never far from Millicent and how to gain the upper hand with her. She assumes Millicent is always planning something, knowing it could be anything. Waiting is hard, but Bri tries not to let that stop her from living, and she refuses to hide in fear.

One way Bri copes is by figuring out how to quietly, *and strategically*, bring the woman down. One of those strategic moves will be through Millicent's shipments. A *huge* strategic move will be taking Claude Devereaux away as a source of money Millicent, once Bri cuts off Millicent's access to her bank accounts.

Bri pulls out a small notepad and starts brainstorming. She writes whatever comes to mind, regardless if it makes sense or not.

Millicent has arranged for Katie to check into the state-of-the-art luxury rehabilitation center in The Duchy of Somerherst this Spring. Millicent doesn't worry about Lawrence finding out, because he never looks at the list of visa applications that come to his desk, unless someone points out an issue. Millicent plans to pamper Katie and make her think she cares more about her well-being than Bri, while skillfully gleaning valuable information about Bri from Katie.

Tristan comes in and tells Millicent he has lined up the hitman that will be going to the US to make Millicent's next move: killing Bri's parents. Tristan tells her, "This guy's specialty is setting up hits to look like real accidents."

Millicent gets an evil smile. *"Perfect!"*

"May I ask a question, Auntie?" He asks and she nods. "Don't you *want* Bri to know you're behind her parents dying?"

"*Oh, she'll know.*" Millicent deviously smiles. She puts a hand on Tristan's cheek, "Thank you for being someone I know I can always count on, My Pet."

"*Always*, Auntie!" He says proudly. "You said you wished you were around to witness Bri finding out about her daughters' deaths, because there wasn't much in the press showing her devastation. Are you wanting to go to the US and be there as this *tragedy* unfolds for her?"

"*Yes, I would!*" Millicent gets a wicked smile. "I can't *wait* to see her and in *more pain* after the loss her daughters!"

135

CHAPTER 15

And So It Continues...

It's about a week-and-a-half before Christmas and Bri has worked all day in her office at The Worthington Corporation. She walks into David's office to ask him about a couple of questions when she sees he is on the phone. She is about to turn around and leave, but he motions for her to come in and waves over to the couch. She walks over and sits down. She watches him, studying his handsome features, then her mind starts thinking about how wonderful his heart is... David leans back in his chair and glances over at her; he sees she is staring at him, and he winks at her.

When he hangs up, he stands up and stretches, then walks over to her. "Is it the end of the day already?"

She softly laughs. "*I'm still working!*" His eyebrow goes up. "I'm working on studying *all* your handsomeness!" She stands up. "You know," she straightens his tie, "I had come in here to talk to you about something, only, I can't seem to remember what it is now."

"Funny," he wraps his arms around her, "I don't feel bad for making you forget." He hugs her. "Let's go grab your things and go home." She nods.

On the way back to her office, she lightly gasps, "Oh! *Now* I remember! I wanted to talk to you about the yearly planning for Newhaven that we've been working on for this coming year. Plus, ideas on bringing in revenue."

"My short answer is to focus on increasing tourism." He replies.

"Got it." She says. "And the long answer?"

"That we will discuss in detail, *and at length*, once we're in the helicopter."

"At length? David, you're stretched thin as it is. You literally have Mary block off our time together! How are you—."

"Love, I don't worry about Newhaven because, rumor has it, The Princess Imperial is doing a *fantastic* job!"

"Wow!" Her eyebrows go up. "That *SURE IS* a rumor!"

He chuckles. "No, it's not. *And you know it!*"

"*Mister* Worthington, our predecessors are the brilliant ones who hired outstanding people to work in those posts and *they* do it all fantastically well! I'm not fantastic, they make me *look* fantastic!"

"I'll agree with the fantastic people in their posts and making someone look good; *however*, if you weren't someone they could work for and work with, those fantastic people would go elsewhere, *and you know that as well!*" He gives her a pointed look.

She tries to hide a smile as she glares, "*Ooo...*"

He chuckles as he takes her laptop bag, then he waves his arm towards the door. She goes to walk past him, but he lightly grabs her hand to stop her.

He smiles adoringly, "I'm madly in-love with you, BriaLynn Worthington!"

He sees her face match her cheeky response, "*I do know that!*"

He chuckles, then kisses the back of her hand. "Come on, Love..."

After grabbing his computer bag, they go up to the roof and walk out to the helicopter. Bri's phone rings, and she pulls it out of her purse. She sees it's her brother and stops at the helicopter's door to answer his call.

"Hi, Aidan!" Bri greets him.

Aidan replies, "Hey, Bri. Can you talk?"

"Sure! What's up?"

He is unemotional replying, "Mom and Dad dead."

"What?" Bri is a little surprised, but also unemotional. "How?"

"They died of carbon monoxide poisoning." He tells her. Bri knows that, even though they were divorcing, her parents were still living in their house together until it sold. "Marley was to meet up with Mom

137

for something, I don't remember why, but she said when Mom didn't show up, she went to the house and found them. Dad was on the living room floor and Mom was on the bedroom floor."

"When is the funeral?" Bri asks, with David looking at her with surprise, then concern.

"We thought we would have a little service at the graveside. None of us want big or fancy, so I can let you know the date when we get it all arranged. Do you have a preference?" He asks.

"Not really. I should be able to make whatever work." Bri tells him.

"If you can't make it, Bri, don't stress over it. We understand that there are a lot of variables to consider just to get you *to* the US." He tells her.

"Thank you for that and for letting me know. Call me when you have things planned out; I'll see what I can do."

"Will do." Aidan replies and they say their goodbyes.

David has been watching her, and she isn't upset. He is relieved about that, because she doesn't need any more heartbreak. He thinks of Millicent and knows it's only a matter of time before she strikes again...perhaps this is another strike...

When Bri tells David what happened, he can't help but ask, "Do you think this is tied to Millicent at all?"

She shrugs as she answers, "I don't know. I wouldn't put *anything* past her! *However*, this seems harmless; it lacks any real bite, or sting, to it. Then again, if it was Millicent, she wouldn't necessarily know how unattached all of us kids are to our parents, so it could be her." She shrugs again. "If she *is* behind this, she'll be disappointed, *and angry*, that it won't have the effect on me she would be hoping for." David agrees with that!

Millicent has noticed her bank accounts are not quite right; the hacker Rex has helping Bri is messing with Millicent's bank accounts, to make her paranoid, just as Bri had asked. Bri wants Millicent *so nervous* that she won't take the time to think things through when Bri's next step comes: tangling up her shipments.

Millicent has been in contact with her accountant, Nico MacTavish, and he has been working feverishly trying to figure out what is going on with her accounts. Millicent wants to meet with Nico before she flies to the US and they meet at Millicent's office, in Devonridge Hall, to discuss Millicent's accounts. He is uneasy about meeting with her because he doesn't have good news, and he knows how vicious Millicent can be.

Nico is a short round man with chubby cheeks and a larger nose, which sit his too-small-for-his-face glasses. He has thinning, gray hair around a large bald area on top of his head. He has lighter brown eyes, and deep wrinkles on his face. He nervously wipes his forehead with his handkerchief.

Millicent sees him and angrily tells him, "*MR. MACTAVISH*," he jumps, "YOU BETTER KNOW WHAT'S GOING ON WITH MY MONEY!"

Nico calmly replies, "We found that there's some sort of glitch in the computer system, but it seems to only be affecting a small fraction of your money in each account. The IT specialists are working hard to fix it."

"Did you consider that *maybe* my money would be safer in a different account? *ONE THAT IS WITHOUT GLITCHES?!*" Millicent snaps.

"We don't recommend that, Ma'am!" Nico tries to explain, "The glitch—."

"*THE GLITCH WOULDN'T BE IN A* NEW *ACCOUNT, YOU TWIT!*" Millicent's anger is growing.

"Or—." Nico is cut off again.

 "*JUST TAKE THE ACCOUNT WITH THE MOST MONEY AND MOVE IT TO A NEW ONE! THEN MOVE THE REST OF MY MONEY TO MY ACCOUNT AT THE WORLD BANK!*" Millicent tells him.

Nico doesn't try to talk her out of it anymore. He just nods and pulls out some forms, while Millicent paces the floor. She doesn't want anything happening to her precious money, but it doesn't occur to her that if there is

139

a glitch inside her accounts, the glitch could travel to the new account, which is what Nico has been trying to tell her and wants to avoid for her.

"I need you to sign these," he says pointing to the signature line, "which allows me to move the account ending in 62354 into a new account and to transfer the rest of your money to you account at The World Bank."

She takes his pen out of his hand to sign the forms. "I want this done as of today!" She signs and slams the pin down on the table.

"Yes, Ma'am." Nico replies as he puts the forms away.

He closes his briefcase and bows to Millicent. Then scurries off, leaving while he still can.

The graveside funeral for Bri's parents is only a few days later. The family wants to have it before Christmas, so it will be a little easier for those who are traveling; especially Bri, who is traveling the furthest. Bri didn't want to make a big show so she asked Jack, Lawrence, and David if they would let her go to DC on her own. *None of the men liked that idea!* So, Bri tells them the other option is only one of them goes with her. She wants them to slip into DC and slip right back out the next day. It has to be David or Jack, because 'The King' would automatically make it a big deal just in security alone!

Jack has an eek look. "Hate to break it to you, Amore Mia, but you being '*The Princess Imperial*' is also going to automatically make *you* a big deal, too!"

"True." She replies. "*However*, it will be that much more with Lawrence traveling with me."

"Alright. I'll give you that." Jack acknowledges.

The three of them discuss it, and agree, David will accompany Bri to the US. The Bradshaw's want to go with them, and while Bri thinks it's very sweet, she asks them not to go. She explains that she doesn't want to draw Millicent's attention to them if they are not on her radar yet. She wants to keep The Bradshaw's as safe as she can from Millicent's wrath, which also means keeping them a bit removed from Bri, not necessarily away from The Worthington Family. They understand and want Bri and David to stay with them on their way back to Newhaven. Bri didn't see the harm in staying one

140

night before they went back home. For all Millicent knew, David is visiting his family before they go back to the UK.

David and Bri arrive at the cemetery about fifteen minutes before the services begin. Most of their motorcade parks on the street; half of those park at the entrance and the other half park at the exit, then the officers and agents spread out and around the cemetery. Their SUV, plus one other, parks close to the gravesite so Mitchell, along with other guards and law enforcement officers, can take up positions closer to the area where the service will take place; McMasters will stay next to David and Bri.

David and Bri join her family gathering at her parents' graves; they all greet each other. The last time they saw each other was at Emmie's and Natty's funeral.

Aidan pulls her aside. "We would've understood if you didn't come." He gives her a compassionate look. "How are you holding up with everything *and* being pregnant?"

"We're doing fine." She says as she puts her hand on her lower abdomen. "If there was any issue with this little one, we wouldn't have come." Aidan nods in understanding. She slightly tips her head to the crowd in the distance. "I just wish I wouldn't have brought a crowd with me."

"What crowd?" Aidan winks. He steps closer to whisper, "*Do you remember that Mom and Dad left you as the executor of their will?*" Bri's eyes go big for a few seconds as she nods, then she takes a deep breath. "*We know you didn't want the job, which of course is why mom picked you.*" He states and she rolls her eyes agreeing. "*Anyway, we want to use your time wisely while you're here, so we have their estate lawyer meeting us at my house this afternoon. If that works for you?*"

She gives him an appreciative expression. "That works."

They go back to the group and take their seats, so the service can start. She sits next to David and he holds her hand, lacing their fingers together; she squeezes his hand and gives him a loving look.

Millicent and Tristan had hired someone to sneak into the cemetery and place hidden cameras and microphones, so she could watch Bri at the graveside service from a safe location. Millicent had seen the little smile Bri gave her brother, and now David, and she is confused... '*How can she be smiling?! Why isn't she heartbroken and crying?!*' She gets frustrated as she watches Bri throughout the service and doesn't see Bri shed one tear.

By the end of the service, Millicent is fuming Bri isn't more affected by her parents' deaths. She thinks about Bri being unemotional, then considers that it may be because she is in public. '*She wasn't very emotional in public when I had her daughters killed...Maybe she's queenly material after all?!*' She angrily exhales; she has seen enough. She has Tristan put everything away, so they can leave; she has no reason to stick around.

There is a reception at Aidan's house, with David and Bri helping in the kitchen, so they don't take all the attention. After their guests leave, David and Bri have their Christmas gifts for everyone brought in since Christmas is right around the corner. Everyone opens their gifts and thank David and Bri. They finish cleaning up by the time the estate lawyer comes to go over the will with Bri and the family.

When they are nearing the end of their meeting, Bri says, "I don't want this to drag on for anyone, but with everything on my plate in the UK, would any of you object to me asking Henry, and The Bradshaw Law Firm, to represent me here in the US to help keep all this moving along for us?" Everyone is fine with that.

Bri didn't want any money, or property, so she will ask Henry to somehow revert it back to her parents' estate and have it divided out with the rest of the money and property. The estate lawyer leaves, and Bri and David say their goodbyes to the family. Then Bri and David leave for the Bradshaw's house in DC to stay the night; they will leave for Newhaven first thing in the morning.

On the way to the Bradshaw's house, David is thinking about Bri growing up in the Midwest. He asks Bri, "How is it your parents and some of your siblings are close to DC, rather than back in your hometown?"

"It's my mother's doing. She is constantly moving back and forth. There is no other place on Earth that is better than where she grew up." She rolls her eyes. "Yet, as I've said in the past, she is never settled, always restless. She is like a child with a new toy; she's happy with it until the newness wears off."

"Sssooo, she has to move to a place, then when the newness wears off and she gets bored, she moves again?" David asks.

"Basically." She replies. "What my dad wanted was never a consideration. It always had to be what my mother wanted, or you would face her wrath."

"Another piece of *your* puzzle that makes it understandable why your family isn't close."

"Yeah." Bri replies. "My mother has no problem throwing 'family is important' and 'blood is thicker than water,' but she never really understood what that meant, or she wouldn't say it." David smiles as he says it with her, "*Love* is thicker than blood!" He kisses the back of her hand.

Bri is getting ready for bed that night in her room at the Bradshaw's when her phone rings. She sees it's from a restricted number and her mind flashes to Millicent; she briefly wonders if Millicent is calling to taunt her.

She cautiously answers, "*Hello?*"

"Your Royal Majesty."

She hears familiar male voice and is relieved.

"Hi, Rex!"

"Hullo, Bri. I'm calling to let you know that I'm sending Hazel Williams to meet you at the airport there to fly back to Newhaven with you and David. She's prepared to travel with you, anywhere at any time, so you can continue to work together a bit more easily."

"That's great! *Thank you!*"

Bri is happy to take this next step, and getting that much closer to bringing down Millicent, *for good!*

"The so-called 'computer glitch' was put into motion and it was successful at being an irritant and making Millicent extremely nervous about the safety of her money. She had demanded that her money be moved right away, *and it was,* only Hazel's virus wiped out

143

virtually *all* her money." Rex says. "Unfortunately, she's going to get a surge of capital with her next auction that's not very far away if we can't stop it."

"Well, hopefully we will stop it from ever happening!" Bri replies. "But first, we need to take Claude Devereaux out of the equation beforehand, and I have an idea about that."

Rex is curious. "What is it?"

"Kidnap his child." Bri states.

Rex's mouth drops. "Really? I *never* would've thought *you* would support the kidnapping of a child!"

"The child won't be harmed at all; *not one scratch*!" She stresses. "I also want her nanny taken with the baby, so the baby will be less traumatized through this whole ordeal." Bri tells him.

He nods. "I agree with that, only we need to locate them first."

"Try Bardeaux." Bri suggests.

Rex asks in curiosity, "Do you really think he would risk hiding her in his hometown?"

She explains, "If he's taking care of his mom at all, then I would assume she would at least be in the same city, perhaps within the same area; I'm thinking it would be the same for his child."

"That's as good of a place to start than any." Rex replies.

"You know what they say," she adds, "sometimes 'the best hiding place is in plain sight.'" He softly chuckles.

There is a little bit of a longer pause before Rex has to ask, "Do you think Millicent is behind your parents' deaths?"

"I'm not sure. I wouldn't put it past her, but it could just be carbon monoxide poisoning." She says.

"That's true." He replies. "I'm not sure if I should tell you, or if you would want to know, but there *is* a hitman that was recently hired for a job in US whose specialty is making hits look like accidents. I can have someone dig deeper to find out more."

"After hearing that, I'm starting to wonder if maybe she did have something to do with it? Only, right now, I'm more interested in using your time and resources with keeping my family safe, *including the Bradshaw's.*"

"I understand." He says. "I'll be in touch." She thanks him and they say their goodbyes.

Bri goes down and joins the family for dinner. Bri talks to Henry about representing her as the executor of her parents' will, and he says he would be happy to help. They also talk about the law firm and how Joe has been increasingly taking over more, so Henry can retire any day he wants. Maggie jokes that it is a matter of when he wants to let it go. They finish their dinner and talk in the living room for a while. David and Bri go up to bed a little early that night; they have an early flight to Newhaven the next morning.

Millicent and Tristan left DC and flew home, because she didn't see a need to stick around when Bri wasn't a crying, sobbing mess. They slept on the flight and when they woke up, they were about to land at the small airport not far from The Devonridge Estate.

Millicent is still baffled. *"How is she not distraught over her parents?!"*

Tristan shrugs, "Bri has always been soft, so it *is* odd she isn't affected more by the loss of her parents. Then again, she could just be numb from everything that has happened."

Millicent gets hopeful. *"Do you think so?!"*

"It's the only thing that makes sense, *isn't it?*! But at some point, the numbness *will* wear off and she *will* feel the awful pain *you've* caused her." He deviously smiles.

Millicent is happy, almost giddy. *"Thank you for that, My Pet!"*

She ponders on all that in the car ride home. She thinks about how Bri will look when she *finally* feels *all* the pain of *all* her losses. She smiles to herself the rest of the way home.

CHAPTER 16

Hacked and Messed Up

On the plane back to Newhaven, the hacker, Hazel Williams, is with David and Bri. Hazel is a beautiful twenty-two-year-old Black woman with just a hint of 'computer nerd,' and a stunning smile! Bri really enjoys working with Hazel! She is quirky and fun; they just click! The three of them are talking about Millicent's upcoming shipments.

"We might need to focus on the next auction, since we won't have time to stop the auction right around the corner." Bri's eyes travel down a list Hazel has given her, looking at the dates.

"*Not necessarily...*" Hazel gets a mischievous grin on her face. "If some of these are still in port or, better yet, *in transit...*" She types on the keys of her laptop, then her smile gets wider. "How about we make these crates ship to a warehouse that Rex had me set up for you under the name, 'Regina I. Cameran.'" Bri gets a confused look on her face, trying to figure out where that name came from. Hazel smiles. "Regina means 'queen,' and the other letters spell 'American.'"

"*Seriously?!*" Bri snorts a little laugh. "But why 'queen' when my title is 'The Princess Imperial?'"

Hazel gives her a knowing look. "When the current Queen is calling for it, and we all can see how much The King adores you, almost *everyone* knows it's just a matter of time. *Plus,*" she smirks, "it's a taunt to an evil woman who thinks *she's* the rightful queen!" Bri gives a faint laugh. "Now, if we have these shipments sent to this warehouse, and the paperwork is messed up, lost, misplaced, and so on, she won't be able to track it down to get it back; at least not right away, some of it she wouldn't be able to get back at all, if the paperwork is lost!" Hazel tells her.

"That's great, but wouldn't that endanger innocent people in the shipping business if she retaliates..." She trails off when she reads the growing smile on Hazel's face. "*You've got that figured out!*"

"I do! *Her name* will be on *everything!*" Hazel says. Bri and David lightly laugh.

While Hazel works on her laptop, Bri and David work on their own things. After a little while, David goes and gets the three of them something to drink. He hands Hazel her glass, then gives Bri hers as he sits down next to her with his own glass.

"How are you feeling?" He asks.

She gives him a little smile. "I'm fine, I promise. Is it sad they died? *Absolutely*! If you're expecting me to fall apart, it won't happen; my relationship with my parents wasn't like that; none of us kids had relationships like that with them. If it were Henry or Maggie, let alone both of them, *I'd be a mess*!"

David agrees with that. "You know, I've wondered, and after today I'm even more curious, if you all would've had a better relationship with your dad, if your mother hadn't gotten in the way to make sure you all didn't?"

Bri nods. "Control and jealously are *definitely* two of her strong characteristics!" She thinks about that as they go back to work.

An hour or so later, Bri's eyes get heavy, so she goes and takes a nap; Hazel is napping on the couch. David wraps up a couple of things before he goes in and joins Bri; they both sleep for a while. Then they eat dinner with Hazel and get to know her more.

Their flight lands at Newhaven's airport and the motorcade takes them to The Worthington Manor. Jack and Lawrence are waiting for them when they arrive. They meet Hazel and make her feel welcome. Then ask Bri how she is holding up. She tells them the same thing she said to David; that she would be a mess if it was Henry or Maggie, or both of them.

After they talk for a bit, Bri goes up to take a shower and gets ready for bed. Jack stays over and the three men go up to the fourth floor after a billiard's game, to check on her; she is reading more on Ashbourne's history in the main living room. They talk for a few minutes, then decide to watch a movie before going to bed.

Millicent is about to have an aneurysm as her anger builds, listening to Tristan tell her about the mess with the shipments at the docks! There are multiple shipments that had arrived, only are now missing; and some that have never shown up at the port at all.

"HOW DID THIS HAPPEN?!" Millicent's anger blows.

"I've been on the phone *all morning* trying to track everything down! Some people say they received new paperwork upon their arrival, saw it was to go to a different address, then scrambled to get it to a new address for you as soon as possible. I asked what the addresses were, but they didn't have that paperwork back yet and a couple of them said they lost the paperwork! However, the one thing that is consistent is that *your name* is on everything!"

"WHAT THE—UGH!" Millicent is beside herself! "WE HAVE AN AUCTION COMING UP AND AT THIS RATE, WE'LL *BARELY* HAVE ANYTHING TO AUCTION!" She looks at the little bit of paperwork Tristan was able to gather. "It looks like we need to focus on one thing right now, and that's the 'live product' that is still coming yet." Tristan nods and they get to work restructuring the auction, as well as reorganizing *a pickup* at the docks.

Millicent's assistant, Ms. Dunn, comes in and says plainly, "Mr. MacTavish is here to see you, Ma'am. He says it's urgent."

"*Send him in!*" Millicent tells her. Ms. Dunn nods once before going out and sending in the gentleman.

About a minute later, Nico MacTavish is quickly walking into Millicent's office frantically saying, "I have *terrible* news, Ma'am!"

Millicent glares at him and says in an almost angry whisper, "*What have you done?!*" Thinking Nico forgot to transfer her money right away that same day.

"As *you* requested, *and signed the paperwork for us to do,*" Nico reminds Millicent, "we moved some of your money into another account and the rest was sent The World Bank. *However,*" he cautiously informs her, "your money was lost in the transfer, *because* of those glitches."

Millicent angrily stands up asking, "YOU *LOST* MY MONEY?!" She fumes. "GET IT BACK!"

It pains him to tell her, "*We're trying to, but we haven't been able to yet.*" He watches her narrow her glare even more. "Remember when I said we should fix the glitches *first*, because we weren't sure if those glitches would travel with the

149

money or not? Well, they *did* travel with the money, then the glitches sent the money elsewhere, *without a trace.*"

Millicent tightly furrows her eyebrows. "*How much* of my money was sent elsewhere?!"

"Just about all of it." Nico answers. "The money seems to have evaporated into thin air!"

Millicent casually picks up her letter opener and walks around desk. She starts to pace and when she walks behind Nico sitting in the chair in front of her desk, she swiftly puts her left hand over his mouth and firmly holds his head against herself, plunging the letter opener with an extra sharp tip into his neck; almost severing his artery.

"I've *never* liked being told, 'I told you so.'" She yanks out the letter opener and the wound starts spurting blood. She takes a step back and looks at Tristan as she points, saying, "Clean this mess up."

Nico is stunned and holding the side of his neck. He slides out of the chair and falls onto the floor; Millicent watches the blood begin to pool on the floor. Tristan had gone out of the room to get a couple of people to help with Nico's body and the cleanup. Millicent watches Nico dying on the floor with eager anticipation. She steps over Nico's dead body and behind her desk.

She calls the local bank and The World Bank to threaten whoever she needs to get her money back. When her threats don't work, she calls Rex; The World Bank is his bank, and he has the power to do anything! The call is unanswered and goes to voicemail, so she calls right back because Rex *has* to take *her* call! It goes to voicemail again and she leaves him a message. She slams her phone down on the desk. She looks at her hands and they are shaking. '*Odd.*' She thinks to herself, then she realizes, '*I'm Scared? Of what? Ridiculous!*' She pushes that aside, not understanding she is scared of losing all her money; being poor and destitute.

Tristan and the others finish cleaning up and bring in a new chair for the front of Millicent's desk. He takes a seat and asks, "Did the bank put your money back?"

Millicent scoffs and angrily replies, "There's no way of getting my money back because they can't trace it! They tried to tell me that they weren't liable if my money was lost, because of one of the forms I signed! I only have a tiny percentage of what should be in there!"

"Can't you call Rex Stirling!" Tristan suggests. "He owns The World Bank and has tons of connections; there has to be something he could do!"

"I tried, but it goes to voicemail!" She replies. "The man is known to have *the best* bank security, so the transfer glitch never affected his bank because the money never made it there! It sounds like from the bank that the transfer was rejected because of the glitch, but the money didn't bounce back to the original bank account." She exhales, "*THIS IS A DISASTER!*"

"Auntie, do you think Bri is behind this?" Tristan asks.

She scoffs at the ridiculousness of it. "I *doubt* she could come up with *an idea* like this on her own, *and I know* she doesn't have the computer skills to pull something this sophisticated off! She would need help, *only that kind of help would have to come from criminals*. I don't see her hiring, or becoming friends with, criminals being that she is wrapped up in the criminal justice system like she is. And *I highly doubt* too many criminals are going to want to help her out! She had better watch out for Rex Stirling! He is on every country's 'most-wanted' list!" She tells him, then goes on. "If that virus got into The World Bank's system, Rex will be out for Bri's blood! Aside from that, if we think about it, she seems to have moved past mourning her daughters' deaths and she is seemingly unfazed by her parents' deaths." Her mind goes to Bri's reaction to her parents' deaths and gets irritated saying, "Then again, she was so angry in the beginning at the deaths of her daughters, she *stabbed* your hand! *She even carved it up!*" Tristan looks down at the simple phoenix scar. "I need to keep coming at her, until she breaks!"

Tristan asks with curiosity, "Why until she breaks?"

She gives an evil smirk. "Because when she breaks, she will do *anything* I tell her to do; she won't have any fight left in her! Then, when I have MY heir, I'll kill her to get her out of my way permanently!"

151

CHAPTER 17
Winter into Spring

Christmas comes and The Worthington Family hosts The Royal Family in Newhaven. The Heathherst's enjoy Christmas together as the family they are, for the first time since Vivian's death. Bri enjoys Christmas as much as she can, even though she misses Emmie and Natty dearly. She gives them all the gift of asking their missing loved ones to join them Christmas morning. It does all of their hearts good to have their *whole* family together, even if their visit doesn't seem long enough.

Bri spends the time between the Christmas and New Year's holidays with Lawrence at The Palace. He is working away in his office one day, when he is given the list of people approved to come into the country on various visas. He doesn't usually pay much attention to this list, since he has employees monitoring this. However, being The King, he can always deny someone entry for any reason, *or no reason at all*, which is why he is given a copy. He goes to put it in his 'to be filed basket,' when his phone rings; he lays it on his desk and picks up the phone.

Lawrence is talking on the phone and mindlessly staring at the paper, when his eyes fall on the name: *Katherine Elizabeth Barnes*. He picks it up for a better look, to make sure he read it correctly. *He did.* He hurries the conversation along and after he hangs up, he picks up the page again and reads the entire line of information with it. He reads that she will be staying at Serenity Springs House in Somerherst starting March 6th. He knows Serenity Springs House is a well-known, high-end rehabilitation center for various addictions, including drugs. He doesn't recall Bri saying she was bringing Katie to the UK for additional treatment; he thought she said Connecticut or Vermont?

There is a quick knock before Bri opens the door and walks in. She sees she has startled him, and she watches him shuffle some papers around on his desk, before he lays a folder on top of them. It gives her an uncomfortable feeling, causing a 'red flag' to go up.

"Are you alright?" She asks, watching him closely. She notices his 'wheels turning' and she unknowingly takes a cautious step back. "If I didn't know better, it looks like you're trying to come up with something to say, *other* than the truth..." She sees guilt on his face and warns him, "*Please*, don't lie to me!

Even if you think it's for my own good, *don't* ever *lie to me*!" She's not mad, just firm. "I'd like to think you've never lied to me—."

"*I haven't had to*!" He quickly replies.

"Whoa! *Wrong answer*! But we'll get back to that! *First*, since you haven't *yet*, *don't*.start.now!" She looks at him with a very stern face. "It's insulting!" She goes on to explain, "The fact that you 'haven't had to' lie yet, could make me question *everything* you will *ever* tell me going forward; *we can't survive like that*! We *won't* survive like that!"

"Bri, as King there are things I *can't* tell you, unless you were 'The Queen,' for various reasons, like our nation's security. It could be seen as treason."

"And I understand that!" She replies. "I can live with an answer that goes something like, 'my position as The King, won't allow me to tell you,' *or any version of that*, as long as *that is* the truth! But, once I am 'The Queen,' there are *NO secrets*!" She gives him a pointed look and he apologetically nods. "Lies are not only insulting, big *or small*, they are *all* a toxic poison in *any* relationship, Lawrence! So *please*, *don't* poison this fantastic thing we have going here." She says moving her finger back and forth between them.

Lawrence goes over to her. "You're right." He holds her hands. "I'm sorry I even considered it. And you're *crystal clear*, My Queen."

"Thank you!" She lovingly smiles. She points to his desk asking, "What is it?"

"Now, my position as King won't allow me..." He teases with a playful grin.

She playfully slaps his shoulder. "Uh-oh!" She gives him an eek look. "I could be executed for physically assaulting 'The King!'"

He laughs. "*I* would be the one publicly drawn and quartered *if I even tried*!"

Her face scrunches up a little. "*You*?"

"The law of public opinion would call for, no, *demand*, MY execution!" He tells her.

"*That's crazy*!" She shakes her head.

He studies her for a moment and chuckles. "Bri!" He holds her upper arms and tells her, "*You're more popular than me!*"

"*Whatever.*" She rolls her eyes. "Now that Millicent isn't running things, I think you'll find that your popularity has increased *dramatically!*"

"*Because of you!*" He states, then he looks at her more seriously. "We need to go back to our original, um, *topic...*"

"Alright."

"What's Katie's full name?" He asks. She lifts her eyebrow. "Trust me just a moment longer, please."

"I'll trust you longer than that!" She states. Then answers his question, "Katherine Elizabeth Barnes." He glances down to verify the name, then hands her the list. She takes it and reads the names until her eyes find Katie's name; her face turns white. "*No!*" Bri whispers. "*This can't be...*" She looks at him and tells him, "When I called her to discuss a rehab clinic in Vermont, she said she had a better offer and hung up on me before I could ask more about it. I didn't call her back; I *refuse* to chase after her to clean up her life. Getting, *and staying*, clean has to be *her choice.* That's the basis of The New Beginnings Foundation helping anyone! They have to *want* to do it, or it won't work, and it would be a waste of resources that could help someone else who is already at that place of *wanting* to clean up and start fresh."

Lawrence points to the paper in her hand and Bri looks at it as he says, "It says she's staying at Serenity Springs House in Somerherst; *she can't afford something like that?!*" Then she whispers, "*Millicent...I might be sick.*" She puts her hand on her stomach thinking that, *as far as she knows*, the two women don't know each other. "I felt safer with Katie *anywhere* in the US—."

"Because there was at least an *entire* ocean between you two." Lawrence finishes her sentence.

"Exactly. But now..." she looks at the paper again, "to be here for an indefinite period of time?! Ugh!" She takes a deep breath. "Hopefully, being at this rehab center means she's going to make her best effort of starting over!" When she looks up from the paper, he sees the fear, mixed with sadness, in her eyes. "With Millicent a threat, I don't need any added problems with Katie—." She inhales sharply and holds her breath. "Katie helping Millicent could put Henry and Maggie in danger."

"Would she really set them up to die?" He asks.

She shrugs. "After what she did to me, *is there a line she wouldn't cross?*"

He hugs her tight. "There's no valid, or legal, reason for me to automatically deny her into the country; *however*, 'The King' can deny anyone without giving a reason."

She shakes her head. "That could send her permanently 'overboard.' Maybe she would seek Millicent out, if by chance they aren't working together?" He partially sits on his desk listening to her. "She's already on the road to a healthier lifestyle when she checks into Somerherst. If she is denied coming into the country, well, it seems cruel to deny her a chance to learn more tools *to stay clean* and to have a new place for her own fresh start. She has no one else, Lawrence." He looks at her in awe and she asks, "What's wrong?"

He shakes his head. "After *everything* she has done to you, and put you through, you still won't stop caring about her!" He reaches for her hand. "You're such an amazing woman!"

She softly shakes her head. "No, I'm not. I just refuse to be cruel and heartless." She squeezes his hand. "Her childhood wasn't as bad as yours, but it was rougher than most. I know all of her behaviors and choices stem from that. It doesn't make what she has done okay, but I *can choose* to have compassion..." She trails off.

He stares at her for a long moment, then asks her, "What aren't you saying?"

She shakes her head. "It's nothing." She goes to change the subject, but he shakes his head.

He tells her with a look, "*Please don't do that.* Being open and honest goes both ways, Darling."

"It's fine. I just know how much David and Jack loathe her, so I keep any talk about her to a minimum."

155

"That's understandable." He replies. "But you don't have to be with me. No matter what it is, I've been through more with Millicent." She gives him a 'that's true' expression. He cups her cheek for a moment. "What are you keeping to yourself?"

"Up until Katie and I met, Katie was on her own, even before her mom died. She had to raise herself, only she didn't have good role models around her to learn from. It's like there's this internal war going on, but until she becomes consciously aware of what she has been doing, she won't be able to make the positive, transformative changes she needs, to permanently change for the better on an emotional level." She has an apologetic look. "I'm not sure if that makes sense."

"Actually, it does." He sweetly smiles. "It also explains why you want to be there for her; to be a good influence on her when she finally comes around."

"At this point, I *carefully* care and hope *from a distance*." She replies.

"How can I help you? Should we make The Ashbourne Estate the fortress it was designed to be, whenever it is needed to be?"

"Lawrence," she takes a deep breath, "I need to say something to you that I said to David and McMasters back in DC before I was shot, which I'll remind them about it later, when I tell Jack and Mitchell the same thing." She rests her hands on his chest. "Right now, I need you to *really* hear me, so *please* let me say this."

"Alright, Darling." He stands up and motions towards the couch in his office and they go over to it. He has her sit on the couch, while he sits in front of her on the coffee table.

She holds his hands. "Just as they couldn't promise nothing would happen to me in DC with Antonio, *you can't promise anything like that now*! I trust you, just as I do all of them, to do everything in your power to protect me and soon our children." She puts a hand on her lower abdomen. "We came into this life knowing we were only allotted so much time to live on earth; no more, no less. That's what Emmie and Natty reminded me of." She squeezes his hand. "You *can't* stop what's meant to be; *even if what's meant to be is my death*." She sees Lawrence's uneasiness and assures him, "I *know* where my faith lies, and my faith is strong and *unwavering*!" Her conviction is so strong it sears into *his* heart. "We are human and have *finite* abilities. With the gifts

156

and powers I possess, and might possess, they have their limits. I would've rather healed Natty, but I couldn't change what is meant to be. You can't either, which is why you can't make a promise that takes *infinite* power to uphold. If anything happens, it won't be yours, David's, or Jack's fault, neither McMasters's, nor Mitchell's. I've been convinced since college that if someone wants to hurt or kill another person, they *will* find a way. More often than not, law enforcement is more *reactive* to something that is happening, or has already happened, because you can't arrest someone until a crime has been committed."

He gives her hand a little squeeze. "Thank you for not telling me to stand down."

"*Oh gosh no!*" She shakes her head. "*I don't have a death wish!* It's just important to me you all know that, if something *does* happen to me, I don't want any of you to blame yourselves, or each other; *especially*, for the rest of your lives! That's the worst kind of life sentence!" He agrees. Then she suggests, "While I'm almost positive it's referring to Katie on that piece of paper, I think we should confirm that it truly is her, then go from there."

He stands up with her. "Sounds like a good start." He stands up and he helps her up. He holds her jaw and looks her into her eyes. "One of the many reasons I love you, is because of your strength! You can take on everything thrown at you; yet, after seeing you drive a knife into Tristan's hand, I have *no doubt* you can, *and will*, do whatever needs to be done to bring Millicent down!" He gives her a soft smile. "I also love the part of your strength that allows you to let us take care of you at times."

She gives him a small smile. "I should also tell you that I feel very strongly we should have a '*NO prisoners*' mantra!"

"I'm on board with that, even if it means we have a trail lined with bodies!" He adds.

"I know part of you is joking, but we both know more people are going to die because of Millicent." Bri states. "Her silence right now could be for torment; to keep us constantly looking over our shoulders for a while, only to strike when she thinks we're least expecting it." Lawrence can't argue with any of that. She taps a kiss to Lawrence's lips. "It's getting late."

"It is." He walks over to his desk saying, "Let me grab my phone."

157

When they leave his office, he holds her hand as they walk to The Royal Apartment together. They wave to various visitors and staff along the way.

After the holidays, there were romantic getaways spaced out. They spent New Year's Eve together, then she and David left for The Chateau New Year's Day. A few weeks later, Lawrence took Bri on a romantic getaway to Hawaii for her birthday. Jack wanted Valentine's Day, so he could continue to work on his mission for her to one day *love* 'the day of love!'

When Bri and Jack return from Tuscany, they focus on getting ready for the launch of The Newhaven Wool and Textiles that is fast approaching this coming Spring. It corresponds to the first sheering of their sheep at The Newhaven Wool Farm. They are also preparing last-minute details for their charity fundraising gala, also coming this Spring.

CHAPTER 18
A Brief Moment of Happiness

They have been preparing for the baby's arrival. She has been wanting to come up with a list of names with David, but once she had the name 'Jackson Christopher Worthington' go through her mind, *that was it*. She tasks David with name ideas by their next ultrasound, which will confirm *to the doctor* they are having a boy.

David, Jack, and Lawrence are in the doctor's office with Bri for the ultrasound. The doctor confirms what they already knew; they were having a boy. The doctor points to the ultrasound screen to show them.

Jack tips his head looking at the screen. "We'll have to take your word on that, Doc! It takes a special skill to know what you're seeing on that!" Everyone in the room lightly laughs.

When the doctor and nurse step out of the room, David looks at Bri. "Love, will you *please* tell us what our son's name is?"

"David," she says, "I *swear* he never told me his name!"

"I'm not questioning that." He smiles sweetly. "I just know that you, *being his mother*, had to have a name come to you!"

"I've had one name come to mind," she looks at them, "but if any of you have any ideas——."

"*No, Love*. If this name came to you, *I* have enough faith to know that there's a reason for it!" He tells her. Jack picks up her other hand and Lawrence rests his hand on the baby.

"David, I feel bad that we never discussed names togeth——." He softly puts his fingers to her lips.

"*Stop*, Love. *Please*." David gives her a loving look. "*Tell us* and end the torture!"

"Jackson Christopher Worthington." She holds her breath and waits.

When she sees a huge smile spreading across David's face, she slowly exhales. She looks over at Jack who is beaming, and Lawrence is happily smiling as he nods.

David kisses her excitedly. "It's perfect! *Absolutely*, brilliantly *perfect!*" He looks into her eyes that are tearing up. "*I love it!*"

He looks at Jack and happily pats his shoulder, while Lawrence pats Jack's other shoulder. David steps back for Jack to have a moment with Bri.

"Wow, Amore Mia!" Jack's eyes have tears as he smiles. "*You do beat all!*"

She can only whisper, "*Now there will be a 'Jack Worthington,' Amore Mio!*"

Jack kisses her with so much love, then hugs her. "I love you."

She smiles as she wipes her eyes with her fingers. "I love you, too." He hands her a tissue before he steps aside. Bri looks at Lawrence and asks, "Are you alright, Ace?"

He is surprised. "*Yes! Fantastic!*" He enthusiastically smiles. "This is amazing! *YOU* are *amazing!*" He hugs her firmly.

David puts his hand on Lawrence's shoulder. "We're a family! Unconventional, but a family!" Bri nods, wiping her eyes again.

Jack circles his finger around. "We're here for each other and," he places a hand on the baby, "for the children of *our* family!"

David and Lawrence add their hands on top of Jack's, with Lawrence adding, "The *Four* Musketeers!" She giggles.

The four of them work most of the day. David and Lawrence work at The Manor, Lawrence is using Bri's office. Bri and Jack work from their office at The Cottage House. Bri's phone rings and smiles when she sees who it is.

"Hi, Henry!"

They chat a bit about a few things, including an update on her parents' will, the allocations in it, and probate, before Henry gets to the other reason for his call.

"Sweetie, I want to ask you something, but I want you to know it's okay to say 'no,' or tell us you need some time to think about it."

"Okay. What's on your mind?" She asks.

"Well, as you know, Joe has been taking over at the firm and doing a marvelous job! What I now have is lots and lots of free time! Maggie and I have been talking about selling the house, but we aren't sure where to live when Joe lives here in DC, Mitch is in New York, Sam is in Boston, and then there's you across the pond. We talked with the others and, since Maggie and I would like to one day be buried there, we *all* feel Maggie and I should move to Newhaven one this house sells."

Bri's mouth drops, then it quickly goes into a huge smile.

"Really?! *I LOVE that idea!*" She tells him. "It's even better that Joe, Mitch, and Sam support your move here?"

He laughs. "They love the idea of visiting more!"

Bri bursts out laughing. "I'm going to tease them that I'm hurt *I* wasn't enough!"

"Sam figured you'd say something like that and says to tell you he still hasn't received his *personal* invitation!" He laughs. "And Mitch expected his to be in gold calligraphy sent from The Palace with Her Royal Majesty's wax seal!"

Bri softly scoffs, "*He would!*" She rolls her eyes, shaking her head. "Honestly, I would love having my parents close by! I want this baby, and the ones to come, to have as many *healthy* adult relationships as possible!"

"That's one of the big reasons! We were also hoping to help you out with your New Beginnings project, *if you'll have use for us.* We'd love a chance to work with you and your wonderful foundation."

"Please let us, Sweetie!" Maggie adds from the background having come into the conversation during Henry's last comment.

"Amy has been helping with The Foundation." Bri tells them. "We've been working with a psychologist to match the right candidate with the right mentor for the program. We had all the management and employee-mentors learn the ropes and get a solid hold on their own job before we added the responsibility of a mentorship. Once this all comes together, things will get even busier between The Textile Mill and The Foundation!"

Maggie replies, "We could help you and Amy so *maybe* you could be more open to the idea of a royal coronation *sooner* rather than later."

"*Oh, wow!* Have you been secretly talking with Lawrence?" She teases. "Honestly, I'd absolutely *love* to have you help with The Foundation, and *I know* Amy will be *thrilled!*"

"If you don't mind, I'll reach out to her once we're done. I certainly don't want to step on her toes, so if she isn't for this, then we'd find something else to help you with." Maggie explains.

"I understand and appreciate that, but I'll be surprised if Amy doesn't agree to this! She has taken on not only my things, but most of Jack's so he could focus on The Wool Farm and The Mill; Jack has been busy preparing for the launch of the textiles. This also helps keep the business side of The New Beginnings Foundation separated better from The Mill and The Farm." She gets an idea. "*As for Henry*, I do have something else in mind for you, if you're willing."

"Oh really?" Henry is intrigued. "I'm all ears!"

"How about helping me with the courts and the criminal justice system in Newhaven?" Bri explains, "I've been bouncing so many things off you and Peter already, that it should be pretty easy to get you up to speed on everything. You can also help me continue restructuring the criminal justice system like we've been doing in Newhaven and maybe help brainstorm to expand it throughout the country. We'd make sure you have time to come and go to enjoy your retirement with Maggie as well."

Henry excitedly replies, "I think that's a great idea!"

They agree to nail the specifics down after Henry and Maggie sell their house and move back to Newhaven. Bri insists they take up residence at The Manor; she knows David and the family would insist on it, too! Maggie grew up with her brother Peter in The Manor and Henry, being Peter's best friend, stayed over when Peter wasn't at Henry's family's estate.

They hang up and Bri sees Jack sitting handsomely at his desk. She tells him about the phone call, and he is excited for Henry and Maggie to join them! She looks at him, biting her bottom lip with a playful look in her eyes.

He grins. "What's going on in your gorgeous mind, Amore Mia?"

She asks him, "Are we going to be alone for a while?"

He matches her playful smile. "*I'll make sure of it*."

"These hormones," she says watching him walk over to her, "are making me..." she bites her lower lip again. He leans down, putting a hand on each of her armrests and kisses her. He takes her hands and pulls her up. He leads her out of their office, through the living room, then upstairs to make sure they're not disturbed.

After they dress, Jack hugs her. He suddenly pulls back and puts his hands on her baby tummy.

"*Did I just feel...*" He excitedly asks and trails off watching Bri's tummy. He puts his hand over the place he sees pop out. "*He's kicking!*" He squats down saying, "*This is amazing!*" She smiles; she wants him to enjoy this moment. "Uncle Jack loves you, Baby Jacks!" He kisses her tummy.

"Jacks?" She isn't sure if she likes it or not.

"You don't like it?" He asks.

"I'm not sure. I *do* like that his nickname *is* started by his namesake."

When the baby is finished kicking, she asks, "Please don't say anything to David, or Lawrence, about feeling the baby kick. David hasn't felt him kick yet. I won't lie and I don't expect you to either, but if he doesn't ask…"

He lovingly smiles as he tucks a strand of hair behind her ear. "This moment is ours, Amore Mia. We could say it was 'behind bedroom doors,' because *technically* it was." His heart squeezes seeing her smile at him the way she is!

"We best get back to work, Amore Mio." She taps a kiss to his lips before they go back downstairs to their office.

They go to The Manor that evening for dinner. For dessert, David secretly requested Chef Edwin to make a cake with 'Jackson Christopher Worthington' written on it in blue icing. David expected the kitchen staff to know, but Chef Edwin kicked everyone out before he wrote anything. Then he covers the cake and brings the cake out to The Dining Room himself.

"Alright everyone, the moment of reveal!" David says as he wraps an arm around Bri's waist and has the staff join them. "With Chef Edwin's help, *and Bri's forgiveness*, I'd like to reveal the *name* of our baby!"

Bri's eyes go wide. "*Name?!*"

Chef Edwin counts, "One…two…"

Bri tries to stop Chef Edwin. "*Wait!*"

"Three!" Chef Edwin uncovers the cake.

Carlotta excitedly reads, "*Jackson Christopher Worthington!*"

"Jack!" Peter pats Jack's shoulder, "It's *bloody fantastic* he's going to be named after you!" Peter hugs him, as Carlotta hugs David. The whole family works their way around hugging all four of them.

Bri pulls David aside as she whispers with a scolding tone, "*David, I can't believe you did that!*"

David says to Bri, "I told you; I love the name and we *all* love the name!" The guys nod. "Besides, this way," he playfully tugs her waist, "it can't be

164

changed! *And...*" he takes his finger and scoops up some icing off his piece of cake, "it's officially written in icing!" Bri rolls her eyes but smiles. "*And* you heard my father! It *is* bloody fantastic!"

"I say..." she takes David's finger and pulls the icing off of it with her teeth and lips, then smirks hearing him clear his throat, "let's have some cake with that frosting!" There is chuckling around them and Bri pecks David's lips. She looks at Jack and Lawrence; they are laughing.

"Well played, Darling!" Lawrence says when she walks up to him.

"Come and have some cake!" David tells the staff. "Spread the word! This cake is for *all* of our family! If you don't want any cake, that's fine, but at least join us for a break!"

When everyone has a slice of cake who wants one, Lawrence walks back over to Bri and kisses her cheek. He looks and looks again, "Wait, no cake?"

"I had a small piece already." She replies. He feeds her his next bite, then takes a bite for himself. "Mmm, I think yours tastes *SO much better* than mine did!" He softly laughs feeding her another bite. She smiles saying, "Yep! I'm right." He winks at her.

There is a buzz of excitement and Bri smiles as she looks around at everyone. Her hands are on her baby tummy, and, for a moment, she feels like *The Grand Duchess* carrying 'The Heir of Newhaven,' the next generation in a long line of heirs in this wonderful noble family.

"*Are you feeling alright, Darling?*" Lawrence whispers as he feeds her another bite, noticing she is lost in thought.

She nods as she swallows. "Yes!" Bri quietly tells him, "I was in the moment of thinking about how I'm carrying the next '*Heir to Newhaven*'..." She looks at him and says, "Then when we're—."

"*No, Darling.*" He whispers, "*Just be in* this *moment. A wonderful and* beautiful *moment!*" She nods with a little smile. He feeds her another bite, then kisses her cheek.

The family walks around, talking with various people who have come to celebrate with the family. It is a perfect way to end the day.

CHAPTER 19
Royally Picture Perfect

The day of 'The Black & White *with a Splash of Gold* Gala' has arrived. After Bri eats her breakfast that Saturday morning, tiredness overcomes her, and she goes back upstairs to take a nap. About an hour later, David goes up to check on her and he finds her standing in front of the full-length mirror with her hands on her baby tummy. David walks up behind her and places his hands on her tummy, too, as he kisses the curve of her neck.

"How's my beautiful wife and our son doing this morning?"

"*Your son* was awake most of the night last night." She teases.

He grins. "Oh, so this is how it's going to go already? He misbehaves and he's *my* son?" He winks and she smiles as she nods, then she stares at her tummy. He sees her expression slightly fade. "*Are you alright, Love?*"

She softly smiles. "I'm excited and thrilled for our baby to come, but there are times I wish I could keep him in here forever, safe and sound...at least until Millicent is permanently out of our lives, one way or another. But mostly," she turns and hugs him, "*I can't wait* for him to come!"

He looks at her so lovingly, then squats down and kisses her belly. She runs her hands through his dark-brown hair. She smiles down at him hearing him tell the baby, "I know you'll remember how special your mum is, because there is *no one* better!"

"David, there are *a lot* of great moms out there!" She tells him.

He stands back up. "I agree, but you're the only one carrying *my* son and *the only one* I want to be the mother of *all* our children!" He hugs her.

She steps back a bit and sees he's thinking about something. "Are *you* alright, My Love?"

"I am..." he caresses her face, "forgive me. I was thinking about Ava, and what it would have been like; how it would've felt more like a duty, than love and family. *Nothing like this!* Going through all that I went through with her

167

was worth it when I have you, *this*, our life now!" He holds her hands. "I love you, Macushla! *You* truly *are the only one for me!*"

"I love you, *Mister* Worthington! It's hard to remember what my life was like before I met you and Jack; it seems like a different lifetime altogether." He chuckles in agreement. She asks, "How busy are you today?"

"I'm all yours! Did you want to go somewhere?" He asks.

"Well, are you up for some..." she has a playful look as she walks her fingers up his chest, "...naked time?"

"*Always!*" He says.

"These hormones seem to have me in overdrive!" She says a bit exasperated.

"And thaaat'sss bad...*why exactly*?" He grins.

She lightly giggles shaking her head a little. He kisses her *so* passionately; she gets lost in the kiss and *almost* forgets she is pregnant...

David spoons her in their bed, having one arm under her neck and the other arm over her with his hand on the side of her tummy. Bri feels the baby kick and places David's hand on it.

"*Is that...*" He starts to ask.

"Your son kicking?" She giggles. "*Yes!*"

"This is...*wow!*" He has tears in his eyes.

"Pretty wonderful to *feel* a miracle?!" Bri asks.

"*Incredible!*" He is in awe and doesn't move until the baby stops kicking. He moves so he can talk to the baby. "Daddy can't wait for you to come! I love you, wee one!" He kisses her tummy.

Bri runs a hand into his hair saying, "We love you, too, Daddy!"

"Thank you for loving me so much, you went on this crazy life adventure with me!" He gives her a sweet tap of a kiss, then they get up.

They spend the day relaxing and enjoying their family time with everyone. Later that afternoon, they all get ready for the Fundraising Gala that evening.

Bri is upstairs in The Worthington Manor, almost ready for the gala. She has on a short sleeve dress, with an empire-waist of white rhinestones on a gold ribbon, coming up over her growing belly. Jack had asked Lawrence to make her a black and white with gold jewelry set for the evening. Lawrence used black and white diamonds and pearls with a hint of gold accents, which are more noticeable when they sparkled.

The Fundraising Gala is held at The Kingsbury Park & Gardens, in the beautiful building they have for events to be held in. The glass ceiling makes the building seem even bigger and it has a picturesque courtyard with gardens and a wishing fountain in its center.

Inside, the tables are covered with gold tablecloths that are beautifully set with white plates, black napkins, crystal glasses, flower bouquets for center pieces. Fairy lights are strung across the ceiling for a 'starry' feel. Name cards are arranged around each table, with the family paired up and placed at random tables around the room: Jack and Bri; Lawrence and Phillip; David and Abby; Seth and Genevieve; Peter and Carlotta; James and Amy; Henry and Maggie. There is also a place for dancing and a stage where the orchestra plays.

As people arrive at the gala, people take notice that The Princess Imperial looks more like a queen; more so standing next to The King. An offhanded photo of all of them greeting their guests is taken and it is immediately posted to their social media page; it goes viral with the title: *Royally Picture Perfect*.

When all their guests have arrived and are seated, Bri walks up on stage to the microphone and welcomes everyone.

"Good evening! I'm so grateful and excited that all of you have joined us tonight for a cause that is near and dear to my heart. It isn't difficult to know what The New Beginnings Foundation's goal is: to help lift those who are in need of a fresh start, *a new beginning*. While the emphasis has been focused on people released from jail or prison, its goal is to help *anyone* in any number of ways. With your donations, we will be able to help more people get a real start at a new beginning; a healthier life for themselves and their families! Thank you all *so much* for being here, and we hope you enjoy your evening!" Everyone claps as she walks off the stage.

Once Bri is seated, dinner is served, and they enjoy wonderful food and conversations with those at their tables. After dessert, they dance and mingle, too. At the end of the evening, Jack goes up on stage and announces The Foundation had almost doubled its goal; the guests applaud and cheer. Then Jack introduces the editor of The Newhaven News Chronicle, Guss Langford. He shakes Jack's hand and bows to Bri. Then he goes to the microphone where he speaks to the guests, and specifically Bri.

"Your Royal Majesty, on behalf of your people in Newhaven and the UK, and those beyond, I'd like to express our deepest and sincerest condolences to you and your family on the loss of your precious daughters. At the time, our readers wanted to know where to send flowers and condolences. We at the newspaper had inspiration! We thought donations in your daughters' names to The New Beginnings Foundation would be a lovely way to honor Lady Emerson and Lady Natalie. We put a link on our website for people to make their donations. Well, word spread throughout the UK, and it went across the pond to the US, as well as down into Europe, and eventually around the world. A new wave of donations rippled through again at the time of The Heirloom Wool's launch, and for several days leading up to The Fundraising Gala. Tonight, we would like to present you with what has been raised thus far."

When Mr. Langford announces the total raised, there is loud clapping and cheering. Bri's hands go to her mouth as she turns her back to the guests and works to silence her cries while she faces the orchestra. Jack hugs her with tears of his own. Bri gets ahold of her emotions and turns to face Mr. Langford and the guests. She shakes his hand and steps closer to the microphone, taking a deep breath to steady herself.

"Thank you all for your love and support—."

She inhales and holds her breath to keep herself from crying. She exhales slowly to steady her nerves.

"The outpouring sympathy and love can be so overwhelming at times, like now." Her hand goes to her heart. "The compassion you've all shown means *so much*——." She squeaks.

Jack hands her a tissue, which she takes, then he wraps an arm around her. He clears his throat of the lump forming in it, then takes over talking.

"As you can see, the kindness everyone has shown means a lot to this wonderful woman." He squeezes her a little more. "Emmie and Natty were excited about The Foundation and would come to Newhaven to help any chance they could and were looking into attending college in the UK. I'd like to think they are watching all of this, and delighted The Foundation will get such an amazing donation in their honor!"

Bri smiles and nods. "Thank you *all* for the contributions to The New Beginnings Foundation! We appreciate every single one of you for your kindness and magnanimity!"

Jack takes her hand, and she squeezes it firmly; he squeezes in kind for a show of support. They wave as they walk off the stage; they join the family in talking to the tables that didn't have a pair of the family sitting with them. Their goal is for every table to have at least one interaction with the family, to thank everyone for making the evening a wonderful success!

CHAPTER 20
Another Strike

As people are about to leave, Jack, Bri, Lawrence, and David make their way to the doors, winding around the tables, to say goodnight to their guests. Bri glances over, then looks again when she sees Tristan, and now sees his large gun pointed upward. He sees her and wickedly smiles as he pulls the trigger. There are about a dozen bullets that fly up to the ceiling, shattering the huge panes of glass, causing pieces of glass to sprinkle down around the people below. The guests scream and take cover under tables, behind walls and pillars; anywhere they could!

Bri jumps when more shots ring out from multiple guns, as the shooters run around, randomly shooting, and shooting at the guests causing more screaming. Lawrence grabs Bri and takes her down with him, Jack, and David. The men shield her until some of The King's Guards can surround them to protect them. The Royal Guards are protecting the guests while trying to defuse the dangerous situation with The King's Guards. There is a fire fight going back and forth between the shooters and the guards, some of the shooters being hit, as well as a few guards and guests.

Tristan angrily shouts into their coms, *"Careful!"* He warns them, because he knows if Bri is shot, *or worse*, Millicent will kill them, and trusted people are hard to find!

Lawrence catches a glimpse of Tristan, just as Tristan yells, "DONOVAN!" The two men make a run for it and Lawrence takes off after Tristan. McMasters takes off after them, along with some of The King's Guards.

Tristan sends Donovan on with the others, while he hides behind a large bush at the edge of the gardens. He waited until he heard Lawrence's footsteps get closer before he pops out with his gun pointed at Lawrence's chest; Lawrence stops abruptly.

Tristan sneers at Lawrence telling McMasters and the others, "STAY BACK! It won't take much to *accidentally* pull this trigger!"

"Then do it!" Lawrence challenges him.

Tristan scoffs. "You don't think I will?!"

"*Not yet!* I tend to think you're smarter than that!" Lawrence glares. "You know Millicent *would kill you* if you would kill me now!"

Tristan scoffs, "*She'd never kill me!*" His arrogance has him believing, "I've got her wrapped around my finger!"

Lawrence is surprised. "*If you believe that, you're more damaged and delusional than I thought!*"

Tristan glares in hateful anger and yells, "*YOU'RE THE ONE WHO'S DELUSIONAL!*"

Lawrence is surprised. "How do you figure?!"

"YOU THINK YOU'VE GOT ALL THIS POWER!" Tristan's anger makes everyone more nervous about the gun he's pointing at Lawrence's chest. "ONCE SHE SAYS YOU'RE NOT NEEDED ANYMORE, YOU'RE DEAD!" He steps closer to Lawrence and says through gritted teeth, "*And I'M going to ENJOY doing it!*"

Lawrence turns up his nose. "You sound just like Millicent! It must be awfully difficult to live with yourself."

Tristan furrows his eyebrows together in confusion. "Not really."

"I guess you made selling your soul to the devil work for you; *for now, at least.*" Lawrence states.

"What's that saying? 'Better to be at the right hand of the devil, than in his path?'" Tristan says to Lawrence.

Lawrence shrugs. "Either way, the destination is still the same!"

Tristan gets angry at that and shoots his gun up in the air. When Lawrence and the others reflexively duck, Tristan runs away.

"DON'T!" McMasters grabs ahold of Lawrence to stop him from chasing after Tristan again. He sends Mitchell and the guards after Tristan. Lawrence struggles wanting to go with everyone else. McMasters sternly whispers, "*Live another day, Lawrence! Live for when* you *have control of the situation and can end him for good."*

Lawrence stops struggling as he thinks about that for a moment. He looks at McMasters and nods; McMasters releases his hold on Lawrence. They turn to go back inside the building to check on everyone and look for the others. When Lawrence finds them, he sees they are not seriously hurt, and they, too, are helping their injured guests.

Outside, The King's Guards are not too far behind Tristan and the other shooters. They see one of them has a pretty significant injury from the blood trail he was leaving behind. Mitchell and the guards hear a gunshot and cautiously keep going until they come across a dead body. They take a closer look and determine it is the injured shooter; the shot they just heard was Tristan getting rid of 'dead weight.'

Back inside, Bri had just checked on Amy and James. James is injured, but it doesn't look too serious. It looks like the bullet grazed his upper arm. She glances around and sees Peter laying on his back and freezes...*he isn't moving.* She rushes over to him with James and Amy following her. Bri sees Peter has been hit with a few bullets in his torso. She feels his neck to find a pulse...she doesn't feel anything. She looks around for his spirit, but she doesn't see it. She frantically feels his neck again... '*He has to be alive!*' She thinks to herself, then she feels a *faint* pulse. Suddenly she hears Carlotta's emotional cry of Peter's name and rushes over. She drops down on the other side of Peter with Henry and Maggie hurrying over to them as well.

Bri tells Carlotta, "There's a faint pulse."

David heard his mother cry out and watched her run over to Bri. He sees them kneeling down to help someone on the floor, he rightfully assumes it's his father and runs over to them. Seeing David running over to someone gets Jack's and Lawrence's attention, and they follow him.

The paramedics get to Peter before David, Lawrence, and Jack, and they begin working on him, but it's too late. Bri sees Peter's spirit leave his body.

She softly shakes her head, whispering a barely audible, "*No.*"

Peter's spirit squats down next to Carlotta, resting his hand on her shoulder trying to comfort her. She is holding his body's hand and brings it up to her face to rest her cheek to it; she quietly cries. Bri reaches for a chair to stand up, to give Carlotta some space; David helps her up.

She looks at David with teary eyes and her jaw shakes. She goes to apologize, but he shakes his head.

"Don't you *dare* give Millicent that kind of satisfaction by taking *any* of the blame!" He is angry at Millicent and the situation, not Bri. "*You* don't get to take responsibility for *anything* that woman has done, or what she will do!" She hugs him and he holds her as tight as he dared to without hurting her or the baby. David steps back and he goes to his mother. He bends over and says, "Mother, let me help you up."

Carlotta hesitates as she looks at Peter's body on the floor, then lets David help her up. She looks at Bri. "Do you see him?" Bri's red eyes fill with more tears, spilling down her cheeks, and she moves her fingers in a quick circle to let Carlotta and the family see him, too. "*Peter...*" Carlotta whispers, giving him a teary, loving look.

"No, tears, Mo Stór." Peter tells her. "We knew this could happen and we came close when you were wounded at The Royal Holiday Party."

Carlotta softly replies, "But I'm not ready to lose you!"

"I wouldn't have been ready to lose you either!" He lovingly smiles. "We've had a *wonderful* life together, and I'll be waiting for you when the time comes." He puts a hand on her cheek and her eyes close. He tells her, "Our family needs you!"

She tearfully nods. "I love you!"

"And I love you!" Peter tearfully smiles back. He looks at David, Jack, and James, "Take care of your mother." They nod.

Bri says to Peter, "*We all will!*" Carlotta hugs Bri and Amy.

The white light gets brighter and brighter until they have to look away. Carlotta takes a deep breath and works to push her feelings aside for now.

She looks at Bri with concern. "How are you and the baby? Were you hurt?" Carlotta puts her hands on Bri's tummy.

"We're both fine." Bri says, putting her hands on the top of Carlotta's hands.

Lawrence steps over to them wondering what to say, only Carlotta hugs him before he can say anything. He hugs Carlotta with a hand on the back of her head. A few minutes later, Carlotta hugs James.

McMasters pulls Lawrence aside. He explains that one of the shooters is still alive and will be taken to the hospital.

Lawrence leans in and whispers so only McMasters can hear him, "*Is this actually one of hers—.*" McMasters nods his head. "Then I want this guy executed straight away!" Lawrence orders McMasters. "We *won't* be sending him, nor any others, back to Millicent! We want to weaken her any way we can!"

McMasters agrees and he goes to carry out The King's orders. He has the shooter taken far enough away so the shot won't be loud enough to frighten anyone, then they will send the body to the morgue. McMasters will let David and Bri know, so officially The Grand Duke and Grand Duchess will send the necessary paperwork to The Medical Examiner's Office.

Maggie and Carlotta are wanting Bri to go to the hospital, but she said a paramedic had looked her over already. She is more worried about their guests and wants to make sure the ones that are hurt, are treated and taken to the hospital if they need to go. For those who are going home, she stands with the family as their guests get into their cars; even shutting their car doors.

With all their uninjured guests, or ones with minor injuries, sent home, things are winding down. David, Bri, and Jack send Carlotta to The Manor with James, Amy, Henry, and Maggie. Soon after, they send Phillip, Genevieve, Seth, and Abby to The Manor. A little while later, the motorcade pulls up to the front of The Kingsbury Pavilion for Bri, Lawrence, David, and Jack to be taken home to The Manor. All is quiet during the ride back to The Manor...

CHAPTER 21
Another Goodbye

The next morning, Jack comes into Bri's bedroom at The Manor with a newspaper and some articles. They all stayed there, with Jack and Lawrence sleeping on the couches in the living room of her quarters with David. Jack sits on the edge of the bed and hands her the articles and newspaper.

"I thought you would like to see some of the articles on the fundraiser." She hesitates to take the articles. "These went to press *before* the shooting."

She looks at the articles Jack handed her. Normally, she would've passed on reading anything about herself; however, she makes an exception with the fundraiser. She wants to know where she stands, because Lawrence wants to begin changing things soon in the UK's criminal justice system. When she finishes looking at the various articles, she hands them back. She sees he has a newspaper under his arm.

"What's that one?" She points to it with a questioning look.

"This is about the shooting." He had it tucked under his arm because he wasn't planning on showing it to her. "It says what the other headlines and articles say in the various newspapers and media outlets." He hands it to her.

She opens it up and sees the front page of The Newhaven News Chronicle in bold print: **DUKE OF NEWHAVEN IS DEAD**. She remembers the use of 'The Duke' is used for the current duke, which would be David's title, although 'grand' has been reinstated since David was coronated. The article also lists the number of casualties and injuries.

She folds the paper and tucks the other articles and newspaper inside it, then hands it all to Jack. He goes and lays it on her dresser. He sees her staring off when he walks back over to her.

"What is it?" He asks, sitting down next to her.

Bri says to him, "I keep thinking about Millicent's attack and wondering if we should've had it at a different venue! UGH!" She tsks at herself.

"Bri, we *did* seriously discuss a different venue, but we'd have to go to Edinburgh or London. If we did that, you felt, *and I agreed*, it would take away from the focus of what we are trying to do *in Newhaven!*" Jack puts his hand on top of hers. "The only thing we could've done differently would have been to cancel the gala altogether." Jack squeezes her hand. "What is it that you say, if someone is determined to hurt another person, or in this case, to hurt a bunch of people—."

"They'll find a way." She plainly finishes the statement.

Jack stands up and helps her up. He hugs her before she goes to take a shower and gets ready for the day.

The family purposely arranges for Peter's funeral to be the last. Bri wants to be at the funerals of the people who were killed the night of The Gala. She wanted to keep the arrival and departure of them as low key as possible, because they were there to pay their respects to the victims and families; not to win popularity points. The Newhaven News Chronicle caught wind of them going to the funerals, but after Bri spoke with them, they respected her wishes to keep them out of it.

On the day of Peter's funeral, the family walks from Newhaven's Parliament building where Peter's body has 'laid in state' for three days, to The Newhaven Cathedral that is on The Newhaven Estate, part of The Newhaven Manor. They are walking behind the old hearse carriage with Peter's casket inside. James and Amy are on one side of Carlotta, David and Jack are on the other; behind them are Bri and Lawrence, with Lawrence holding Bri's hand with her arm tucked under his.

They walk down the front driveway, toward The Newhaven Manor, then turn towards The Newhaven Cathedral. They come to the front of The Cathedral that is at one end of The Manor. Even though it is attached to The Manor, it still has a feeling of being separate. The *entire* estate is gorgeous and The Cathedral is no exception, with its stunning stained-glass windows, with high arches of the gothic architecture. The carriage comes to a stop and they gather next to The Cathedral's entrance.

Suddenly, it occurs to Bri and she leans in whispering to Jack, *"This is where your family lives?!"* He nods. She apologetically says, *"I'm sorry I didn't think of it when we were here before for Natty and Emmie."*

He cups her cheek and softly replies, "Your heart was heavy with the loss of Emmie and Natty. You have nothing to feel bad about. As for my family, *I'm with my family!* Loving you and you loving me, well, it makes everything I went through *completely* worth it!" He kisses her forehead and hugs her.

They patiently wait for Peter's casket to be taken out of the carriage; Lawrence has personally asked some of The King's Guards to be the pallbearers. When the casket, covered with Newhaven's flag, goes through the doors of The Cathedral, the family files inside passing their guests who are standing to bow and curtsey, down to the front of The Cathedral.

While the ceremony is restricted to invited guests, there are speakers set up outside so the crowds can listen to the services going on inside. In the rows reserved for family, Amy, James, Carlotta, David, and Jack are in the first row. Lawrence, Bri, Phillip, Abby, Genevieve, and Seth sit behind them in the second row. The Archbishop begins the services and Bri goes up to read one of Peter's favorite Bible passages.

> "'Fear thou not; for I *am* with thee: be not dismayed; for I *am* thy God: I will strengthen thee; yea, I will help thee; yea, I will uphold thee with the right hand of my righteousness.' Isaiah, chapter 41, verse 10."

After a hymn, The Archbishop has David come up to give his father's eulogy.

> "Distinguished guests, including Their Majesties, Her Royal Majesty, Their Graces, Sirs, Ladies, Prime Ministers, Members of Parliament, family, and friends: good morning to you all and thank you for being here with us today as we say goodbye to my father, and Duke of Newhaven, Peter Worthington."

> "There is a special relationship that sons can share with their fathers, and as I thought about my father over the years, I think I can speak for James and Jack as well when I say, our father is a *remarkable* role model for us! To us growing up, he was a formidable, but gentle giant. He is a great man, leading by example, while somehow making sure we never thought we have to fill *his* shoes. He wanted us to

179

continue doing the things he did right, and change, or improve on, everything else. The relationships we have with our father helped him to figure out what we are good at, then he encouraged us in those things. We wouldn't be half the men we are today, without his love, guidance, and support, *all these years*." He clears his throat.

"Our father taught us that our privileged life *wasn't* something that put us above others, but rather, it put us in a position to help people, The Duchy, and our country. To hold such a position requires integrity, deep rooted values, and family support. Our father valued a person's character *far more* than a person's title, money, placement on a family tree, or in society circles. He had a gift for being able to find something to relate to with just about anyone!" David silently swallows hard.

"Another important lesson he taught us: what it means *to serve* with integrity, honor, and a deep love for Newhaven and its people. My father loved Newhaven and all the people who live here, even those who visit our beautiful duchy. He took those same values and applied them to The Worthington Corporation. The success of The Duchy and The Corporation are a direct result of *his* dedication and love of the employees, who returned that love and support to him, making The Worthington Corporation a success all these years."

"*Now*, I cannot stand up here and speak about how great a man our father was, without mentioning the woman he loves more than anything in this world; she is the woman he gives credit to for all his accomplishments. Our mother is her own formidable force of love and brilliance, and he always said partnering up with her was the smartest thing he had ever done! Together, they accomplished many things together! They would say their greatest accomplishment would be raising three sons, who built their own successful careers, and went on to marry beautiful and brilliant women themselves. They passed the torch of Newhaven, The Corporation, and The Estates to his sons, knowing he never had to worry about their success."

"His three sons are honored to have them as parents, and to look up to as our *admirable* examples, who hope one day to pass all this down to our children."

Bri sees Peter standing at the side of the church, proudly watching his son. Then he is in front of Carlotta looking at James and Jack. He squats down and reaches out to cup Carlotta's cheek with a loving smile. She feels something and puts her fingers on that cheek.

> "Father, we're going to miss you. Through our tears and grief, we will remember the loving husband you are to our mother, the wonderful father you are to your sons and daughters-in-law, and the amazing legacy you leave with us, and all your descendants, to carry on! We love you, Father, and we will carry you in our hearts until we're all together again on the other side."

David steps away from the podium and walks down to his mother. He gives her a kiss on the cheek before he sits back down next to her. Peter wants Bri to tell David something for him.

Bri leans forward and whispers, *"David, your father wants me to thank you for the thoughtful and loving words. He also wants you to know knows you will be a wonderful father! He says you have nothing to worry about, because——."* She looks at Peter who is giving her an encouraging smile as she shakes her head with teary eyes.

"Because?" David whispers.

She can only barely whisper, *"Because you've chosen your partner well."*

"I completely agree with that!" He whispers back and winks at her.

Carlotta looks at them and lovingly whispers, *"Me, too!"* Bri puts her hand on Carlotta's shoulder and she pats her hand.

A little while later, the funeral services end and Peter's casket is taken to The Worthington Family's Mausoleum, in The Newhaven Cemetery, which is on the edge of The Estate where Emmie and Natty were taken. It's a cemetery where nobles of Newhaven, and their families, have been buried for centuries. There will be a short graveside service before Peter's body is interred there.

When that short service is over, James and Amy walk with Carlotta to one of the awaiting golf carts to go back to The Manor for the reception in The Great Hall inside Newhaven Manor. Bri stands there, with her hand on top of the casket. Lawrence and Jack watch her and they see she is frozen in place. David walks over to her, wrapping an arm around her.

She faintly says, "*We know I need to bring Millicent down; unfortunately, it won't be fast enough to stop more people from dying?*"

"Bri, one of the *many* lessons I've learned from you is '*everything* happens for a reason.'" David states. "We can try to rush things, *try* to make them happen, or *try* to make them happen *faster*; but all we do is get in the way and risk ruining the blessings we would have been given. Rex thinks you have a good plan, and he said it would take time to have people in place." He turns her to look at him. "Whatever you have planned, whatever comes next, *keep your faith*, and let it continue to guide this at whatever pace it needs to happen at; no more, no less." He holds the back of her jaw and she sees he has teary eyes when he tells her, "I *need you* to keep your faith! *Please.* I want this woman dead just as much as the next person, but it needs to fall together like it was meant to, or it could fall apart and Millicent could win!"

She can barely whisper with a lump in her throat, "*Okay.*"

They hug for a minute before Jack and Lawrence hug them in a group hug. Her stomach growls and they all lightly laugh as they wipe their eyes. They all walk to the awaiting golf cart to go back to The Manor.

Pulling up to The Newhaven Manor, Bri says staring at it, "This place *is* beautiful!"

Jack takes a deep breath and exhales to himself, "*And lonely...*"

"This place is bigger than The Ashbourne Castle, so it would be easy to get lost," she gives him a small sympathetic smile, "*or forgotten about.*" He squeezes her hand a bit.

Inside The Manor, the foyer is wide and open. The Grand Staircase is off to the left with the second-floor hallway open, backing up against the frosted walls of The Conservatory. The Great Hall is on the main floor and as they start walking int that direction, Jack stops to stare at the bottom of the stairs.

Bri asks, "Is this where she died?" She is referring to Jack's mother. He nods and watches Bri walk closer to the stairs and she stands there for a minute.

Jack asks. "Did you have a vision?"

"No." She turns back to him. "Just seeing if I can sense anything, but I don't."

"What does that mean?" He wonders.

She shrugs a little. "It could mean nothing; it could mean she has crossed over." She looks at the stairs saying, "I've never been to where someone has died and *not* sensed them, but that could simply be because I was to help them cross over. Not sensing your mother now *could mean* she has crossed over. Which means all I would need to do is call her here."

He shakes his head saying, "Not right now; *not yet.*"

"I'm not trying to push you, Amore Mio. I just think it will do you some good; *do your heart good!*"

He hugs her. "*You* do my heart good!"

They don't have the time right now to call for his mother anyway, so she leaves it be. She takes Jack's hand and they walk to The Great Hall together.

CHAPTER 22
A Royally Noble Delivery

Bri's pace has slowed down, as she prepares for the arrival of her baby. Her wonderful family has taken on the extra work until after the baby is born, and she is back to work again after her maternity leave. Bri lives by the motto: 'prepare for the worst, hope for the best!' Only now, she has 'know your enemies' going through her mind *a lot*! She never would have dreamed of ever having an enemy, but after Millicent killed Emmie and Natty, well, enemy is really the only way it *could* go. While Millicent is focused on cruel revenge, Bri, with the help of Rex Stirling, is focused on bringing Millicent down. She will use the extra time she has to make a plan so she can take this woman down, and keep her down, *permanently*.

On the night of July 3rd, Bri is restless all night; she is anxious to go into the hospital for her c-section. She had a c-section with Emmie and Natty, so she knows what to expect; however, every pregnancy is different. She is excited, but nervous, too...Millicent is out there; and now, *so is Katie!* Even though Millicent wants Lawrence's baby, she could still do something to this one for revenge; she did it so easily with Natty and Emmie, *a defenseless baby would be that much easier!*

Her nerves overwhelm her and she sits straight up in bed. She loudly whispers, "*What was I thinking?!*"

David struggles to sit up halfway and hoarsely asks, "What's wrong, Love?" He rubs his eyes.

"I had my chance with the girls, but I failed them in so many ways! Their amazingness *wasn't* because of me!" She says. David sits all the way up and turns on the light; they squint as their eyes adjust. "Their amazingness is *all* the Lord's doing, in spite of *all* my *horrible* shortcomings!" He turns to her as she says, "And now—."

"*Stop.*" He covers her mouth. "BriaLynn, you *are* amazing! You were meant to be Emmie and Natty's mum, just like you're meant to be Baby Jacks' mum!" He holds her face and lovingly smiles. "*You know this!* He was excited about coming to you, *his mum!*"

"He was excited about coming into this *family!*" Bri replies.

"No, Love," he looks at her pointedly, "*you!*" She gives him a weak smile as he wipes her tear with his thumb.

She apologizes, "I'm sorry." She rubs her hand on her very pregnant belly, "I'm just scared..." She exhales slowly.

He nods. "I know. I wish I could say you're over exaggerating, but you're not." He takes her left hand and points to the wedding band he gave her. He knowingly asks her, "Do you remember the day I gave this to you?"

"*Of course!*" She lightly laughs. "It was one of the best days of my life!"

He lightly chuckles. "The other day being your day with Lawrence?" He winks and she smiles. "Good! Now, you should also remember," he holds her hand and laces their fingers, "what I said when I did this?" A tear skips down her cheek as she nods. "Then say it..."

She chokes up a bit. "*Together.*"

He smiles as she wipes her cheeks. "I love you, Macushla! And we're also in this together with Jack and Lawrence, who are also part of our amazing family, too!"

"I love you." She takes a deep breath.

"I know!" He grins and she softly giggles. "The proof of your love, and your *incredible* amazingness, is that our son *already knows* the fantastic mother he's coming to!" He holds her cheek. "When you look at his little face in the morning, remember that! Remember how excited he was to come into this family, *to come to his mother* who has the *purest love* for him!"

She kisses his hand before she lays back down. He helps her to get as comfortable as she can, to at least rest for a few more hours before they need to get up. He snuggles in and lightly runs his fingers up and down her arm to help her relax.

Later that morning, it feels like forever when they are finally at the hospital and all checked in. They are waiting for an operating room to open back up.

They apologized that the doctor had an emergency patient, but Bri isn't upset; she gets to keep her baby in the safest place for just a little longer.

When they're ready for Bri, her doctor happily comes in and asks. "Are you ready to meet your baby, Your Royal Majesty?!"

Bri nervously smiles. "Part of me can't wait to hold him, while the other part of me doesn't want him to come out–*ever*!" She runs her hand around her belly, "He's in the safest place he can be..."

Jack goes over and sits down next to her on the bed. True to 'Charming Jack' himself, he says in his calm, soothing voice, "Bri, you *do* want this!" He puts his hand on her tummy. "You've dreamed about his little face and being able to hold this precious baby in your arms!" He holds her hand and tells her, "*You've got this*, because the three of us *have you*! Now, go with David and bring our nephew into our family! Uncle Lawrence and Uncle Jack will be anxiously waiting!" Jack stands and holds her face, kissing her tenderly, then he steps aside and goes around to hug David.

Lawrence goes up to Bri and points to Jack, "He's right! We have your back, just as we have each other's back." He grins as he leans down and kisses her. "We love you!"

She hugs him saying, "And I love you both!"

A nurse wheels Bri down to the operating room where they prepare her for her c-section. Another nurse takes David to put a gown, hat, mask, and such on him, then the nurse brings David into the operating room; they're about to start the c-section.

David sits down on the chair next to Bri and smiles at her. He sees her nervousness and runs his fingers across her cheek. She smiles up at him trying to hold her jaw from shaking.

He smiles so lovingly at her. "I love you, Mrs. Worthington."

"*I love you so much, David!*" She loudly whispers.

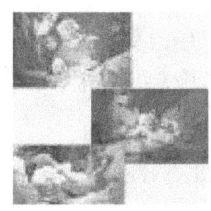 They have already started to cut and David laces their fingers together, giving her a teary smile of his own. Bri nods, taking a shaky breath, trying to calm herself. David rests their heads together.

They hear the doctor say to the room, "It's a boy!"

When they hear the baby cry, it brings tears of joy to their eyes. "He's here, David!" Her jaw shakes and she squeaks, *"He's really here!"*

"I can't believe how beautiful that sound is to hear!" David says, smiling with tears about to spill out from his eyes and she nods in agreement.

She exhales in relief when the doctor says how great everything looks. He holds the baby up over the curtain for Bri and David to see their son.

Bri cries, "David, he's beautiful!"

"He certainly is!" He looks at her and says, "He's perfect. Just like his mum!"

The doctor asks, "Dad, do you want to cut the cord?"

David puts his hand up in a stopping motion telling them, "No, no, no! I'm *not* going to be responsible for cutting our little guy's lifeline to his amazing mother!" There are some soft chuckles around them. The doctor cuts the cord, then the baby is cleaned up. A nurse goes to hand David the baby. He hesitates to take the baby saying, "His mother should hold him first."

"David, look at me." When he looks at her, she tells him, "I can't hold him yet, so *please* hold him; hold our son and let him *feel* loved..." She sweetly smiles at him.

He nervously holds his arms out for the nurse to hand him the baby. *"Oh, Bri..."* he can only whisper. He sits back down next to her again while the doctors finish closing her incision. A tear slides down his cheek as he traces a finger around his son's face. "He's *fantastic...*" he holds him up so she can see, "absolutely perfect!"

"Oh, he is!" Her tears trickle down to her temple.

The nurse turns to David. "If you want to go tell your family—."

David shakes his head. "Not until Mama holds her baby." Bri looks at him. "Don't try to talk me into going, Love. This is where I want to be right now." She sweetly smiles, feeling so much love for him she could burst.

When the doctors finish, David is asked to put the baby into a bassinet for a nurse to push down to Bri's room. "Hospital policy."

David follows close and stays out of the way as they get Bri situated in her room, then they leave to give them privacy. When they are alone, David ever so carefully picks up the baby, who grunts and squeaks in his father's arms. David brings him over and places him in his mother's arms.

He tearfully tells her, "Here's your son, Mrs. Worthington."

Bri looks at her baby in her arms and she lights up. "*Hello, my sweet boy!*" She studies him. "Oh, David! He's wonderful!" She cuddles him close. "*Absolutely brilliant!*" She grins, teasing with his accent and he laughs.

"McMasters and Mitchell are by the door, so would you mind if I go tell our family? I've texted once, but it was a really short, 'He's here!'" He runs his hand to the back of her head. "And you'll have a couple minutes alone with *your* beautiful son." She sweetly nods.

He taps a kiss to her lips before he walks to the door. When he looks back at Bri, he smiles as he sees the mother of his son looking adoringly at her baby. Watching her made him remember Henry's words during his wedding toast, '*Wait until you see her fall-in love with her babies; it's a beautiful sight.*' That's what he is seeing! He thinks to himself, '*The picture of a true mother in all her loving beauty!*' He steps out of the room and quietly closes the door.

He walks down to the private waiting room and when he sees their family, he excitedly says, "Mother and baby are doing *very* well!" There are cheers and tears of joy from their family.

Henry says to David, "We'll be down in a little bit to see Bri and the baby."

David waves for Jack and Lawrence to come with him. When David walks back into Bri's room, she lovingly smiles watching him walk in. Her smile carries over to Lawrence and Jack who are right behind him.

"You're *radiant*, Amore Mia!" Jack adoringly smiles at her.

"I think you're biased." She says.

Lawrence agrees with Jack, "*You really* are *radiant, Darling!*"

She quietly scoffs as she hands David their son to show Jack and Lawrence. "He's beautifully and wonderfully perfect!" David steps closer to them.

"That he is!" Jack agrees.

"He's so tiny!" Lawrence says, holding his little hand. David goes to put the baby into Lawrence's arms. "No. Wait. I've *never*—."

"No better time than the present!" David says, placing the baby in his arms. One look at the baby's face and Lawrence melts...

"*See!*" Jack gently holds the baby's hand. "Uncle Lawrence is a natural!"

Bri teases, "I think we just saw Uncle Lawrence melt into a puddle."

Lawrence handsomely winks at her, then he looks down at the baby again and sees his eyes are open. "Hey there little guy!" The baby gives an audible squeaky exhale.

David smiles. "*Look at how relaxed he is in his Uncle Lawrence's arms!*"

Lawrence smiles watching Jacks fall back to sleep. "He's wonderful!"

"May I?" Jack asks. "Before the others flock in here."

"*Oh!* Of course!" Lawrence carefully hands the baby to Jack.

"It's so good to have him here!" Jack runs a finger along Jacks' sweet face.

CHAPTER 23
A Whole Family Gathering

David, Lawrence, and Jack are in Bri's hospital room with Baby Jacks, when there is a knock on the door just before it opens. Bri smiles happily watching her family file into the room with them.

"I'm *so* happy you're all here with us!" She looks at everyone, but a little longer with Phillip and he gives her a small nod.

"We wouldn't miss this for the world!" Henry smiles wide and hugs her, kissing her head.

"Well, we are short a few important family members and if we can block the windows to the hallway," Bri points, "maybe we can have them join us?" James and Abby close the blinds and shut the door. When 'the coast is clear,' Bri calls for, "Peter, Emmie, Natty, and Vivian, will you come join us for a little bit?" When Bri sees them start to appear, she takes her first two fingers and circles them around in the air to allow everyone in the room to see them.

"*Everyone*," Bri gestures the baby, "meet Jackson Christopher Worthington!"

Carlotta looks at the baby, "He's *absolutely* and *wonderfully* beautiful!" She goes over and gives Bri a big hug.

"Would you like to hold him?" Jack asks.

"*I'd love to*!" Carlotta tearfully smiles at Jack as she takes the baby from him. "Oh, you sweet baby!" She kisses Baby Jacks' forehead and cuddles him close. "It feels so wonderful to hold this tiny bundle of joy..." She looks at Peter as she walks over to him.

"He *is* perfect!" Peter smiles at the sleeping baby.

Carlotta's eyes are a little red and she whispers, "*Oh, My Love...*"

He shakes his head. "This *is* a happy time, Mo Stór." He cups her cheek and she nods.

Phillip looks at Bri. "You did good, Mum! He's beautiful!" Phillip hugs her.

David comes over and sits next to Bri on her bed, kissing above her temple and hugging her. "He's beautiful like his Mama!"

She grins. "He's *handsome* like his daddy!"

Phillip takes the baby from Carlotta and looks at the baby like a proud grandpa. Vivian looks at Phillip with so much love, then she looks down at the baby.

"Oh, Bri..." Vivian looks at her. "You may not believe this, but this little blessing is a big part of the wonderful life you will have with your children!"

Bri's eyes tear up as she looks at Emmie and Natty who are nodding. "Life would be better with *all* of my children with me."

"You still have us with you, Mom!" Emmie replies.

Natty grins adding, "And now when you call, we actually come right away!" Everyone lightly laughs.

They all talk for a while before Vivian, Natty, Emmie, and Peter need to go. Peter and Carlotta step aside for a quick private moment, as do Vivian and Phillip. The others try to get information about the other side from the girls.

Emmie laughs. "We can't give you details, but we couldn't even if we tried to, because there are not words that are descriptive enough!"

Natty shakes her head. "There really isn't!"

David's curious and asks, "Where do you go when you leave?"

"Not far, but we do have work to do!" Emmie answers.

"Are you summoned back?" David curiously asks.

Natty explains, "It's more of a feeling. Spirits aren't meant to linger on earth, so after we've chosen the light and we come for a visit, we can only stay for so long, before we're 'pulled back,' in a sense, to the light."

Emmie nods in agreement. "Ghosts are stuck here and some spirits don't feel a 'pull' because they haven't chosen to go into the light yet for reasons often described as 'unfinished business.'" Everyone who is listening, nod in agreement.

Natty also tells them, "There are a few spirits who are able to put off going to Hell. We're not exactly sure how that works when justice *has to be* paid!"

Bri wonders, "Perhaps that's the point; you shouldn't know."

"*Because* you chose the light!" Henry adds and the girls think about that for a moment.

They all say their goodbyes and watch Emmie, Natty, Vivian, and Peter disappear. Phillip goes to hand the baby to David, but Bri holds her hands out doing a 'give me' gesture by making her hands open and close.

"I *need* my baby, people! I need my 'baby snuggle time' or I'll implode!" She tells them, with chuckling and soft laughter from the others. She takes her baby in her arms and gets comfortable.

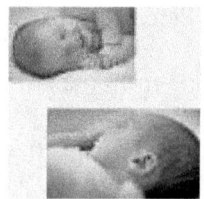 Jack smiles and points to Jacks' face, whispering, "*Look at that smile!*" He takes a picture and shows everyone the photo. "Lawrence and I are going to leave with everyone else, so you and David can have time alone with Baby Jacks." Then Jack cups her face. "I love you, Amore Mia!"

She smiles. "I love *you*, Amore Mio!" He kisses her and hugs her, before he steps away.

Lawrence comes over to Bri. "We'll be back in the morning. Jack and I will release a statement and it should satisfy the public until you're released from the hospital."

"Sounds good!" She replies.

Lawrence bends down and whispers to the baby, "Take care of your Mum and Dad!" He kisses his head, then taps a kiss to Bri's lips.

David walks everyone to the door and they all say goodbye as they leave. He closes the door behind them and walks back over to Bri.

He sits beside her on the bed. "It's hard to believe he's so tiny!" He picks up his tiny little hand.

When Jacks gets a little fussy, Bri doesn't even think about it, she just situates the baby and starts nursing him. When she notices David's surprised look she asks, "Does this bother you?"

"*Not at all!*" Her question catches him off guard. He explains, "My expression is for how you just knew what to do! Then again, you are his mum and this isn't your first baby." She smiles.

When the baby finishes, David wants to burp him. He stands up and gently pats his back. Bri kindly smiles telling him, "You can pat a little harder, Love." David is surprised and she reads his face, replying, "*No*, he won't break or crack." She puts up her right arm, "I promise." She waves him close and shows him by patting her hand on Jacks' back. "Like this." David does it just like she did and sure enough, Jacks burps.

She has him lay the baby down on the bed in front of her, then she has him hand her a diaper. "It's a good rule to change the diaper *before* feeding, so that if he has fallen asleep, he'll stay asleep without risking waking him up when changing his diaper. In fact, we can use changing his diaper to help wake him up, just enough to eat when he is on a schedule."

He watches her. "I assume there's a trick to it?"

She giggles, "There is! And an added one because he's a boy." She walks him through it, then she teaches him how to swaddle Jacks back up. She picks up the baby and snuggles with him; he falls back asleep. She tells David, "A newborn's brain is still forming which why they sleep a lot."

"*Fascinating!*" David whispers. He remembers he has something for her and slips her a silver box Lawrence brought with him and left with him. "This is from Lawrence, Jack, and me." She looks at it confused and he encourages her, "Open it!"

She brings her knees up to rest the baby on her thighs, but he takes the baby and snuggles with him. She opens the box and sees a cameo necklace with a mother and baby carved into the white stone with a dark blue background. It is all set in gold, with a long gold chain and on the back is a pin, so it could also be used as a brooch.

"David! This is beautiful!"

He cups her cheek. "I *so* deeply love you, *Macushla*!" He chokes up.

"I love you, My Love! But you didn't need to give me a gift!" She tells him.

"Just something to remember this day, the day you gave me, *and our family*, an *amazing* gift!"

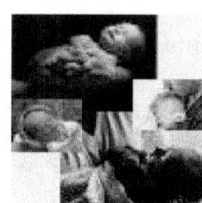 She sets the necklace down and rests her head back on the pillows. She adoringly watches David hold his son. She tells him, "It's believed there are two times a person is closest to Heaven on Earth." She points to the baby. "One of them is the birth of a baby..." David gently hugs his son and she softly smiles. "Our perfectly wonderful, made from our love, heavenly gift!"

He smiles in agreement. "*And the second?*"

She softly replies, "When someone is dying."

Before he can say anything about that, a nurse taps on the door before coming in and checking Bri's vitals. When the first nurse leaves, another nurse comes in to check on the baby.

The baby's nurse asks, "Would you like to keep the baby in the nursery tonight, Your Highness, er, Your Royal Majesty?" Bri stares at her baby, not sure what to do.

David says her name a couple times before she hears, "*Bri!*"

"Sorry." She says to him. "I don't know what to do...I want him to be here, safe, *with us*; however, I know I need my sleep. I also know the nurses can help us get him on a feeding schedule and for him to also use a bottle." She starts to get teary-eyed.

David compassionately smiles. "What if you keep him until late and then he's only in the nursery for a few hours or so; long enough for you to get a few hours of consistent sleep?" She looks down at her baby in her arms and a tear drips down her cheek. He wipes it with the back of his finger. "In order to best take care of him, we have to take care of his mum! Even if it includes extra help." He touches Jacks' soft head of brown hair.

"Only if McMasters or Mitchell stay with the baby, *at all times!*" Then she looks seriously at David with her forefinger pointed at him, "If one hair on this head is misplaced, *even just a little*, there will be—."

"*Heads that roll?*" He smirks. "I figured that already, Love!"

"You smile, but I'm serious as a heart attack, *Mister* Worthington!"

"I know, *Mrs.* Worthington." He states and kisses her head. "Let me go talk to them."

He has an idea and he steps right outside the door to talk to McMasters and Mitchell; then he calls Jack and Lawrence to see what they think. David goes back into the room and finds Bri sleeping with her head back on the pillow, while Jacks is sleeping with his cheek on her upper chest. David quietly sits and watches them sleep for a little while.

When the nurse comes in to take Bri's vitals, she wakes up. Bri sees David sitting there and realizes he was watching them sleep.

"*Please* tell me you just sat down."

"*Nnnope.*" He grins.

She faintly smiles as she rolls her eyes. "Some may find that creepy."

"What can I say? The view of the most beautiful woman in the world, snuggled with our son who is sleeping *so* peacefully in her arms...*Ah, Love*, it's a sight to behold." His accent is strong with that last sentence.

The nurse says to Bri, "That has to be the sweetest thing I've *ever* heard, Ma'am." She points to David, "I'd hang on to him."

Bri smiles adoringly at David, "I definitely plan to!" The nurse softly laughs as she leaves the room.

Jacks starts squirming, so David takes him and lays him in the bassinet and begins changing his diaper. He remembers what Bri taught him and when he wraps him back up, he hands the baby to Bri. While the baby nurses, David is surprisingly comfortable in the chair and dozes off for a little bit. Bri goes from watching Jacks to watching David. Jacks finishes and she puts him on her shoulder and burps him. He burps just loud enough to wake David who wasn't sleeping hard.

He rubs his eyes and yawns. "*You burped him?*"

"You were sleeping, and *I* didn't want to wake *you* this time and ruin *my* view."

David smiles sweetly. "I appreciate that, Love, but I really like doing it."

"I'm sorry, My Love." She apologizes.

"Don't be sorry. I just want to be a part of everything!" David replies and Bri lightly nods.

David's phone chimes with a text message notification that she knows is Lawrence. He texted a picture of the official announcement to show Bri.

 "Wow, *Prince of Newhaven!*" She looks down at Jacks and asks, "How does such a little guy have such a big title?!"

David leans over, "Tell Mum to wait until your brother is born!"

"*Says Dad,* who is so busy with The Corporation, he doesn't fully surmise the extent of the duties that come with The Duchy of Newhaven, or he would be drowning!"

"*Point taken!*" David concedes, lightly chuckling.

CHAPTER 24
Mama-Bear-Lioness

The two of them spend a long evening together with Baby Jacks, before his nurse comes for him after his eleven o'clock feeding. David tells the nurse that he wants to feed Jacks for a five or six o'clock feeding that morning.

"Of course, Your Highness! We'll have him bring him back, ready for his bottle." She replies.

Bri is nervous and she hugs Jacks close, then kisses him before she hands him to the nurse. She asks, "David, is McMasters or Mitchell out there?"

"Yes." David lovingly says, "They told me to tell you they had to flip a coin for who got baby duty." She softly giggles. "Then they agreed to take turns after that." She nods at that, then gets ready for bed.

While David is in the bathroom, Bri's nurse comes in to check on her and brings in a bed for David. When he comes back into the room, the nurse has already turned out the light; however, he is able to see Bri has fallen asleep with the light that is coming in through the windows. He crawls into bed and gets comfortable, then he watches her sleep thinking about how hard it was for her to let her baby go to the nursery tonight; so right now, she sleeps...

 At five o'clock the next morning, a *very hungry* baby comes into Bri's room being held by his Uncle Lawrence, with Uncle Jack following behind them. David hurries over to take the baby and the bottle.

Bri tells David, "He might not take the bottle right away, but stay calm and he might calm down to eat. If he gets any worse, he may need to nurse this time around."

David gently works at having Jacks take the bottle. It does take a bit, but Jacks finally starts drinking the bottle. David sits and gets comfortable, then watches his son eat. He glances over and sees Bri is watching him as he feeds the baby.

He handsomely smiles at her and says, "Hullo, Beautiful!"

197

She smiles and asks, "Do you have *any idea* how handsome and sexy you look right now feeding our sweet baby?!"

He sweetly grins, "I'll keep that in mind!" Bri giggles.

She looks over at Jack and Lawrence as she sits up. "I know you're early morning risers, but you must've gotten up even earlier, and skipped exercising, to come here this early in the morning!" She points to the loungewear they are wearing.

Jack replies, "I think we look ruggedly dashing!"

"*Oh, you do!*" She wholeheartedly agrees.

"We had a sleepover with our nephew last night!" Lawrence grins.

"A sleepover?" She looks at them, then she looks at David.

David explains, "I knew you had a hard time letting him be away from you for even a few hours, so after I talked to McMasters and Mitchell yesterday, I also called my brothers and asked if they'd be up to having a sleeping over with their nephew?"

"We were happy to!" Lawrence says, then he hugs her. Her eyes fill with tears.

Jack smiles adoringly at her, "We knew his mum needed her sleep, so the two of us, with the guidance of his nurse, took care of him. And, well, I think we did a pretty fantastic job, don't you, Herst?!"

Bri squeaks from emotions, "You both did a *wonderful* job!" She looks at all of them and whispers the best she can, "*You are all so amazing!*" She swallows hard and says squeaks, "*I don't deserve any of you...*"

Lawrence lifts her chin with his finger. "No, Darling. *I'm* the least deserving of the musketeers and yet, I'm *not* going anywhere."

Jack comes over to her. "We love you, Amore Mia. And it really is amazing how much love we have for little Jacks already!"

"*Right!*" Lawrence agrees. "*So how could we turn down a sleepover with the cutest addition to our family?!*" He smiles and cups her cheek.

She feels tingling in her lower abdomen, like her body is wanting to heal itself, but she won't let it; not yet. She would have to explain to the doctors and nurses how she healed so quickly. She decides to wait and have them help her to heal when she is released from the hospital.

The nurse comes in and sees David feeding the baby. "Way to go, Dad! You're a pro already!"

"Nah, his incredible mother is the pro!" David replies. "I'm just trying to keep up!"

The nurse smiles as she finishes writing some things down. "Well, it's clear to see she's in-love with her baby!"

Bri struggles to shift in bed to alleviate some of her pain. Jack and Lawrence see her grimace.

Jack asks, "How much pain are you in, Amore Mia?"

The nurse goes to look at the machine. "When's the last time you had your pain meds, Deary?"

"Sometime earlier, I'm not sure..." she shrugs, "it was dark out."

"Well, this says it's been *way* too long!" The nurse lightly pats the machine as she unlocks it. "We need to get some going again!"

"No!" Bri shakes her head reaching to close the door to the machine. "*Please.* I don't want morphine, nor any other strong painkiller, *especially* when I'm breastfeeding. Can I just have some ibuprofen, acetaminophen, *or whatever,* something *not* a painkiller?"

"I can check, but it may not be strong enough for the pain you're having right now." She sadly answers.

"I just need to take the edge of the pain off." Bri grimaces. "I'll manage with the rest, I promise."

199

The nurse studies her. "Alright, I'll see what I can do. I'll be back as soon as I can!" She hustles out of the room, because she knows Bri has to be in more pain than she is telling them! She just had a c-section and pain from that would be excruciating for a few *days* after without any meds.

David is worried. "Love, if you need it, take the morphine." He hands the baby to Jack to burp.

"I promise, if whatever the doctor prescribes doesn't at least take the edge off, I'll take something stronger. *Please*," she grimaces shifting in the bed again, "I want to look back at Jack's birth and remember it all clearly! *And,* with Millicent a threat, we can't afford for me to be fuzzy!"

"You can't afford to be in pain either, Darling!" Lawrence is also concerned.

She agrees as she quickly wipes a tear from her cheek. Jack walks over to her and puts her baby in her arms, hoping to distract her a little bit.

David sits next to her. "Can't we help heal you like we've done before?" Lawrence and Jack are curious about that as well.

"I've thought of that, then it occurred to me that I would have to explain how I healed so fast to the doctors and nurses." She tells them. "I'm not prepared to answer those questions."

"Good point." Jack says.

Bri looks at her sleeping baby, "He's *so* worth it!" She kisses his little fingers, then hisses in pain, handing him to David. "I can't hold him until whatever she brings me starts working." David nods and he takes the baby. "You three can help me to heal *after* I'm released." They reluctantly nod.

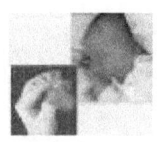 At the baby's next feeding, Jack and Lawrence sit on either side of Bri while she nurses the baby. Lawrence caresses the Jacks' tiny hand, causing him to stretch out his little fingers. Lawrence puts his finger on Jacks' palm and he reflexively grabs Lawrence's finger.

"*Wow!*" Lawrence softly says with surprise. "*He really has a grip!*"

Bri softly smiles, tracing her finger along Jacks' soft arm and cups his little head, quietly telling him, "You are *smart*, you are *strong*, you are *brave*, and you are *so* very loved..." His eyes get heavy.

When the baby finishes eating, Jack takes the baby. "I've got this wee one. Let Herst cuddle up with you, so you both can rest a while."

Bri and Lawrence make themselves comfortable and snuggle into each other. Lawrence whispers next to her ear, "You are *extraordinary!*"

She deeply inhales, then exhales saying, "*Only because of the extraordinary men who love me.*" Lawrence and Jack smile as they watch her drift off to sleep.

Later that afternoon, after the family came for a visit, Bri is in the shower and the guys talk while they wait for her. After her shower, the four of them discuss the public announcement.

Bri wonders, "Being that he's, 'The Heir to Newhaven,' does that mean there's going to be some kind of ceremony?"

"For Lawrence's heir there will be a ceremony officially naming him, 'The Crown Prince,'" David looks at the door and, in case anyone is listening, he adds, "or The Crown Princess." He clears his throat. "For us, we would just have to submit the appropriate paperwork for The King to sign making Jacks officially, 'His Royal Highness Jackson, The Prince of Newhaven and The Marquis of Newhaven.'"

"That's right!" Bri says. "I read something about that in Newhaven's history. It also talked about how Newhaven's spelling of 'Marquis,' as with other Scottish duchies, is a different spelling than—*waaait.* 'His *Royal* Highness?'"

"You're The Princess Imperial, *a royal*, so *your* children will be princes and princesses." Lawrence explains. "Little Jacks here is 'His Royal Highness Jackson, Prince of Newhaven,' but he could use, 'His Royal Highness Jackson Worthington,' for his schooling. The media will probably dub him, 'Prince Jacks' for a shorter, more frequent reference."

Bri is a little reluctant. "I'm not sure if I want it going to any of their heads when they're younger...then again, I guess we know if it does, they'll grow out of it if we work to set them straight." They smile, knowing she is referring

201

to his adult spirit. "I'm not liking 'royal' being used for them, when David is addressed as 'Your Highness' and Jack—."

"It's fine, Amore Mia." Jack tells her.

David assures her, "'The Crown Prince' will be addressed as, 'His Royal Highness,' no matter what. I'd rather have *all* our children be addressed the same way."

Jack agrees. "*Remember*, we grew up with all this."

"True." She says with a gentle expression to match. She takes a deep breath. "Alright then, don't let me get in the way of tradition." She winks and the guys chuckle.

"That's our girl!" Jack smiles with his signature smile.

NEWHAVEN NEWS CHRONICLE

The Grand Duke and Grand Duchess of Newhaven Welcome a Son!

By: Steven Richter

The Worthington's would like to announce the birth of their son, Jackson Christopher Worthington, at 11:11 am on the 4th of July.

Welcome, Your Royal Highness Jackson, Prince of Newhaven and The Marquis of Newhaven!

Bri is preparing to leave the hospital today and go home to The Worthington Manor. The baby has his checkup before he is officially released and his nurse takes him down with a Royal Guard. Bri's nurse takes out her IV, so she will be able to shower more easily. When the nurse steps out of the room, Bri pulls Jack, Lawrence, and David around her.

"Now it's time for you three to help me heal." She sweetly smiles.

They happily gather around her, relieved to finally be able to help her. She feels so much love from them, she is pleasantly surprised at how fast she heals. She hugs each of them, thanking them, before she goes in and takes her shower. David and Jack finish packing up her things, while Lawrence takes a call.

Bri isn't in the shower long, since she no longer has an IV, nor pain from her c-section incision, to slow her down. After she gets dressed, she brushes her hair, then she brushes her teeth. She is putting her hair up in a clip, when she hears a bunch of voices out in her room. She listens for a moment and they sound panicked; she gets a sinking feeling in her stomach.

She opens the bathroom door and asks, "What's going on?!"

David tries to guide her over to the bed saying, "You probably should sit down for this."

She pushes his hands away demanding, "*Tell me*!" She looks from David to Jack, then Lawrence. Then she gets a horrified look on her face realizing, "*The baby*?!"

Lawrence replies, "Bri, we're searching—."

"He was supposed to be protected, *with his own guard*!" She looks at them and she is getting angrier... "*WHAT THE HELL HAPPENED*?!"

"His guard was struck from behind and knocked out by the nurse. The nurse was paid to do it." Lawrence tells her.

"To do *what*, exactly?!" She asks through gritted teeth.

"That's just it. *We don't know*. The nurse isn't talking!" Jack replies.

"Like HELL she won't!" She tells them in a tone that gives them chills, "*Take me to her*!" The guys look at each other, which angers her more. "*NOW*!"

David tries to calm her down. "Everything is being done to find him—."

203

"*David Christopher Worthington*! EVERY SECOND COUNTS! *This woman* took OUR baby, and if she doesn't talk, we may never see him again! That sociopathic woman already killed Emmie and Natty, so she could care *even less* if Jacks dies! I *WON'T* say it a third time! *TAKE ME TO HER RIGHT NOW*!" She has a look that says she will *destroy* anyone who gets between her and her baby!

Lawrence opens the door and tells McMasters, "She wants you to take her to see this nurse."

McMasters goes to insist they stay in the room while everyone else searches, but one look at Bri's face and he doesn't argue. "*Follow me.*" Bri wastes no time and walks beside him.

McMasters takes them to a room next to the stairs. The nurse only sees McMasters walk in at first, and says with contempt, "*I'm NOT talking without my solicitor!*"

All of a sudden, there is a loud *BAM*! It's the sound of the door slamming all the way open and hitting the wall behind it. Everyone inside, and within close range of the loudness, jumps from the sound, which echoes off the walls of the room and down the hall.

Bri says in a cold, angry voice. "*You won't need one!*" The face of this twenty-four-year-old nurse goes white seeing this angry 'mama bear-lioness.' Lawrence steps inside the door, while Jack and David stand in the doorway; the three watch Bri walk over to the nurse telling the others, "*Clear the room!*"

David and Jack come into the room, as McMasters clears everyone else out. Mitchell comes jogging up and McMasters has him step inside. Lawrence, David, and Jack stand together and watch Bri.

Bri moves to stand in front of the nurse and reads her name tag. "Jennifer," the nurse has a tough look on her face, trying not to be afraid, "Millicent underestimates me, but *you*, on the other hand, are about to learn how wrong she is!" Everyone's eyebrows come together as they watch and listen to Bri.

Jennifer rolls her eyes and scoffs as she says, "*Oh, please.*"

Everyone's mouths drop open seeing Bri yank Jennifer up by the upper arm; Bri's fingertips digging into a pressure point on Jennifer's arm and she grimaces. Bri quickly takes the arm and twists it behind Jennifer's back and slams her hard, front first, against the wall, then pulls back on her hair. The guys are stunned by what they are witnessing.

"You have until the count of three to start talking! ONE!" Jennifer refuses to answer so Bri pulls her hair tighter, causing Jennifer to cry out in pain. Bri angrily says next Jennifer's ear, "*TWO!*" Still nothing. She knows three needs to be drastic and she gets an idea.

Bri yanks Jennifer away from the wall and slams her back into the chair. She steps back next to McMasters and grabs McMasters' gun. He tries to stop her, but the angry glare she gives him has him holding up his hands in a partial surrender.

Jennifer partially laughs our of scared nervousness asking, "Do you expect me to believe *you're* going to hurt me?!"

"You're a slow learner!" Lawrence tells Jennifer as he steps closer to them. "We've never seen her this way," Jennifer sees the others shake their heads, "and we're not sure *what* to expect right now?! *You did just take a baby away from his mother!*"

Bri says coldly to Lawrence, as she looks at Jennifer, "*Expect me to do whatever is necessary to get my baby back!*" Jennifer goes white when Bri places the tip of the gun to her forehead. Bri keeps the barrel firmly in place, *but* her finger *isn't* on the trigger; she really doesn't want to shoot her, but Jennifer has to believe she will.

David and Jack try to stop all this, but it's McMasters and Mitchell who stop them. If anyone is going to get answers from this woman, it would be the angry mother!

Bri angrily says in a low, bone-chilling whisper, "*THREE!*"

Jennifer blurts out, "*He's down in the basement!* H-He-Heee's in a supply closet no one uses! It's the one next to the door to the parking garage!"

McMasters turns his head. "Mitchell, take David and Jack with you, and some guards, and go check it out! The King and I will handle things here." Referring to Bri and the nurse.

David and Jack don't waste a second taking off down the hallway with Mitchell and the guards. Lawrence looks back at Bri; her adrenaline is still pumping and she is frozen where she stands. Jennifer is afraid to breath with the gun still pressed to her forehead.

Lawrence carefully walks over to Bri and softly says, "Bri..." She doesn't move. "Bri..." He softly says again, only now he lays a hand on her shoulder and runs the other hand down the length of her arm to her wrist. "If she lied, I'll gladly help to continue this, I'll even throw in various torture tactics that would get her to reveal her deepest, darkest secrets." He looks at Jennifer.

Jennifer scarcely whispers, "*I-I'm not lying.*" She swallows hard. "I was told to put him in *that* closet!"

Bri asks in disgust, "You were *paid* to leave a baby to *die?*! *What kind of monster are you?!*"

Lawrence moves his hand from Bri's shoulder down to her lower back. "Let me have the gun..." He runs his hand from her wrist down to her hand; he is relieved to see her finger isn't on the trigger. He slides the safety on before he says again, "Let me have the gun, BriaLynn."

She slowly lets go and he takes the gun into his hand, then lowers his arm to point the gun at the floor. She says to him in a very serious whisper, through gritted teeth, "*Millicent IS going down!*"

"Tell me how I can help!" Lawrence is just as serious.

She turns her head to him and firmly says with an expression to match, "*Stay out of my way!*"

She turns on her heel to leave, but he grabs her; and in one swift movement, he holds her head firmly to his chest with his hand on her other ear, then points the gun and shoots Jennifer in the chest. He feels Bri jump, then she pulls back in horror to look at Jennifer's dead body. Her spirit quickly appears, just to instantly disappear. Lawrence hands McMasters his gun back.

Lawrence puts his hands on Bri's upper arms and turns her to look at him.

"You *know* Millicent will do whatever it takes to get her hands on this woman, to learn everything she possibly could from her about this incident, *about you,* before she would kill her! *And you know she would kill her!*" Bri takes that in. "After everything that happened in this room, Millicent would no longer underestimate you!" Bri closes her eyes and holds them closed, solemnly nodding in understanding.

McMasters steps into the hallway and has a couple of the guards take Jennifer's body down to the morgue. Bri walks out of the room and down the hallway, with Lawrence beside her. They both walk to the elevators, hoping to find David and Jack with the baby.

CHAPTER 25
Aligning the Pieces

Bri is impatiently pushing the elevator button, as if pushing it numerous times will have it magically arrive on their floor. When the elevator finally dings announcing its arrival, she waits right in front of the doors. As they open, 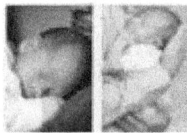 Bri's eyes fill with tears when she sees her baby. She scoops Jacks out of David's arms and holds him close, exhaling in relief; her tears spilling out of her eyes and down her cheeks. She silently prays, thanking God he wasn't harmed!

"What are we going to do about Jennifer?" David asks.

"Jennifer is in the morgue." Lawrence tells them.

"*The morgue?!*" Jack is confused. He looks at Bri. "*What happened?!*"

Before Bri can explain any of the details, Bri sees Jennifer's spirit; the guys look where she is looking. Bri circles her fingers so they can all see Jennifer.

"I'm so sorry." Jennifer explains to Bri, "You see, she told me I had to do this, or she would kill my son along with my sister who came to live with me after our mother died." Bri closes her eyes for a long moment as she realizes a son no longer has his mother. "She told me if I asked for a solicitor and kept my mouth shut, you would have no choice but to let me go."

Bri gives Jennifer a compassionate look. "Do you see the light?"

Jennifer hesitates to nod. "I don't deserve the light! A baby almost died because of me!"

"That's your guilt, but you need to listen to your heart." Bri kindly asks, "What does your heart say about the light?"

"There is love and forgiveness..." Jennifer looks in the direction of the light. "I feel the pull to go into it, but..."

"*Then go.*" Bri implores. "You don't have evil intentions, or an evil heart, and you regret your actions."

Jennifer remorsefully nods. "I hope one day you can forgive me."

Bri gets choked up and swallows hard. She tells her, "I already have, Jennifer."

Jennifer tearfully thanks Bri and waves as she steps into the light, which gets brighter and brighter until they all have to look away, with Bri instinctually shielding the bright light from the baby's eyes. When the light is gone, they all blink several times to help their eyes adjust.

Lawrence asks, "Shall we go pack up to leave?"

"*Yes!*" Bri exhales in relief.

They return to her room and Bri lays the baby on the bed to change him into his 'going home' outfit. She opens his blanket to find a note pinned to his onesie. Bri reads to herself: *I can get to anyone I want!* Bri scoffs as she crumples it and tosses it aside, then gets back to changing Jacks. When Bri has put his little outfit on him, she wraps Jacks back up in his blanket and holds him close.

David steps closer to her and she looks at him. "I seriously didn't think you were actually going to shoot Jennifer!"

She's a little irritated. "*What if I had, David?!*"

David says with a slight scolding tone, "*Bri—.*"

"NO, *DAVID*. You are *all* forgetting I'm empathic!" She motions them with a wave of her arm, "All your anger was combined with mine, but I was actually able to channel it and focus it to where I could function, rather than be a complete mess and no good to anyone, *especially for our son!* I *won't* apologize for that, *or for what happened!* Millicent *can't* win, *or we're all dead!* We're talking about the woman who killed Emmie and Natty, not to mention Jeff, Olivia, *and your father*, that's not counting the countless others she has killed over the years—."

"*That were no longer of use to her,* or *got in her way!*" David's frustration is heard. "*Just as Jennifer got in your way!*"

209

Her anger boils over. "SHE DIDN'T GET IN MY WAY, *SHE TOOK OUR SON!* AND IF YOU SERIOUSLY THOUGHT THIS ALL THROUGH, YOU WOULD HAVE CONSIDERED THAT HER DEATH WAS HUMANE, COMPARED TO WHAT MILLICENT WOULD'VE DONE TO JENNIFER AFTER SHE GOT ALL THE INFORMATION SHE WAS GOING TO GET FROM HER!" Jacks starts to fuss and she bounces as she sways with him.

David angrily whispers back, *"Is that how you're justifying killing her?! What about her family?!"*

Bri's eyebrows come together and she glares more angrily than he has ever seen her. "I feel horrible for her family and loved ones *but think David!* She was dead *the second* Millicent set her sights on using her!" That hits David and he knows she is right.

Lawrence interjects, "David, it *was* merciful; however, it was also necessary. Jennifer would've told Millicent everything she knew, including Bri's actions with her in that room, and Millicent would no longer underestimate her. *I won't apologize either, David!* You have *no idea* the depths of the pain that woman is capable of inflicting on another human being, *and we spared Jennifer!*"

"David, that woman tortures like *no one* can fathom!" Bri tells him, remembering what it felt like to *feel* Lawrence's pain in the various visions. In one vision, he is being burned with the tip of a red-hot fire poker and her skin actually burned in that same location as Lawrence's skin did in the vision!

David's memory flashes to when Bri was in all that pain, when her back was full of lacerations from being whipped. His face softens and he tells her, *"You're right."* He gives them both a reluctant look. "I don't know from experience what Millicent is capable of, but I do believe both of you when you say she tortures mercilessly." He looks at Bri with compassion. "I just remembered what she had done to your back and the pain you were in then; you even refused to take pain meds because," he cups his son's head, "you had found out we were blessed with him." He looks at her. "I'm sorry. I guess I'm still in shock watching you with Jennifer; then again, she took your cub."

She takes his hand and squeezes a bit. "I'm sorry I scared you."

David shakes his head. "I was surprised." He lovingly smiles. "Whatever it takes to save our son, *and his siblings.*" He holds her cheek. "To protect his mother!" He adds, "I knew you were a force; I just didn't know it could be a hurricane and a tornado wrapped up into one!"

"*Because of you, Jack, and Lawrence!*" She stresses.

"No, Amore Mia." Jack cuts in. "While we may have brought it out with you being an empath, you already had this strength within you!" Lawrence and David are nodding in agreement.

Bri looks at the three of them. "I feel all of your angry feelings! And we will get Millicent." She looks at her sleeping baby. "*We have to!*" She looks at David. "If this is too much for you," she looks at all three of them, "if it's too much for any of you, then I'll understand and we'll filter how much we tell you. But I meant what I said," she looks at Lawrence, "*no prisoners!*" She looks at all of them. "Millicent will continue to 'up her ante' to knock me down and to gain the upper hand! Now that I'm not pregnant anymore, I need to concentrate on going after her, to bring her down once and for all! *Before* I get pregnant again!"

"I want to help!" Jack tells her.

"Me, too!" David says.

"As I said to Lawrence, all I need right now is for you three to stay out of my way to accomplish this." They nod. "How about we take our sweet little boy home to The Manor?" They guys happily agree!

At The Manor later that afternoon, Bri reaches out to Rex Stirling and informs him of the events that happened with Baby Jacks at the hospital.

"Now that I'm not pregnant, *I will bring this woman down!*"

"Then you're going to like that we've found Claude Devereaux's child." Rex tells her. "You were right about concentrating on his hometown. His daughter is living with a nanny in a little secluded house, right outside Bardeaux."

"Good. If I want to hit Millicent hard, she can't have anyone to fall back on for financial support. The best way to do that is to take

Devereaux out of the game altogether; however, we need his child for leverage."

"There's an easier way, and quicker, too." Rex hints, but he suspects she won't agree to it, and he's right.

"*That's Millicent's way.*" Bri replies. "He has done nothing to me to justify that!"

"Then, I'll get that leverage arranged for you." He replies.

"If we take the child, we need to take the nanny, or there's a chance he will kill the nanny because his child was kidnapped in the first place. *I really don't want that!*" She tells him. "*Please* make sure nothing happens to the child, or the nanny."

"I will personally see to it." He says. "The next question is, where are we going to put them? It's one thing to stash a child; we can have them blend in somewhere, especially an infant. However, if you want the nanny brought with, then it won't be quite so easy."

"I read somewhere that there's a hidden room at Ashbourne."

"There is." He admits to her because *she is* 'The Duchess of Ashbourne' and she will be using the room soon enough working with him and his team. "It's for The Duchess of Ashbourne's personal use and if it's ever needed, it links The Castle with its own tunnel for another way out of The Castle, *and* The Estate."

Bri is intrigued, but she pushes that aside for now. "Can we use that to keep them hidden away?"

"No. That room is called 'The Secret Room' for a reason. I only admitted it to you, because you *are* The Duchess of Ashbourne. There are now *three* people who know it isn't a rumor, or legend."

"Aright then, is there a nice place, or some place we can make into a nice place, for them to stay that won't make them feel like they're prisoners?" She asks.

"There is a little flat, of sorts, for them to stay in." He replies.

"I'm hoping it's only temporary. Eventually, I would like to take them to The Worthington Inn where it would be more comfortable for them."

"Well, if no one knows this child exists, no one can go after her." Rex states and Bri agrees. "I'll get this all going as soon as possible."

"Stealth, Rex." She reminds him.

"Agreed." He says.

They wrap up their conversation and Rex says he will be in touch. He would get the remodel done within a day or two, but it would take a bit more time to arrange the kidnapping; plus, he has some unrelated business to tend to as well. Bri thanks him before they hang up. She will get with Hazel about Millicent's shipments that she continues to track, so they can start wreaking havoc on Millicent's business.

CHAPTER 26
Need to Rest Up

Weeks are going by and things are progressing with Bri's plan for Millicent. Today is Bri's and Baby Jacks' six-week doctor appointments. David had a meeting that he couldn't get out of, so Uncle Jack went with them.

The doctor is looking over her c-section incision in awe. "Your body healed fantastically well in such a short period of time!" He tells her, "I don't see why you can't physically be intimate; however, as I tell all my patients, listen to your body." Bri nods in agreement.

After the appointment, Bri goes to The Worthington Corporation for a little while. Jack takes the baby with him to his work to show him off and to do a couple of things. Jack is under the strictest promise that *no one* holds the baby, and he only comes out of his car seat when *absolutely necessary*. Jack told Bri that he wouldn't dream of letting the baby out of his sight for even a second! That made her feel better.

On the top floor of The Worthington Corporation, Bri steps off the elevator and she hears David on the phone, so she walks to her office. David heard the elevator and when no one pops their head in, he goes looking for her after he finishes his phone call. He goes into Bri's office and sees her standing at her desk listening to her voicemail messages. He goes up and hugs her from behind; she smiles.

When she finishes, she hangs up the phone, and he asks her, "How was your appointment?"

She turns to face him. "Both appointments were great!"

David looks around. "You let Jacks out of your sight?!"

"Jack wanted to show his team the baby. I agreed, as long as he *swore to me*, he would leave Jacks in the car seat to sleep, and *no one* would hold him during this visit; we would bring him by another time for that. Exposure to germs is a good thing, but not just yet. Plus," she grins, "Mitchell is stuck their side." David chuckles. "*Oh!*" She says grabbing her phone. "I snapped this while we were waiting..." she brings up a picture on her phone and shows him, "*look* at those *incredible* blue eyes!"

David takes the phone and smiles lovingly at the picture. He looks at Bri, then goes to tap a kiss to her lips, but she pulls his jaw in and passionately kisses him. He quickly pulls back and puts their foreheads together, closing his eyes to push his intense feelings down that want to ignite.

He exhales, "You have *no idea* how much I want you right now! Not being with you has been difficult, but now it's compounded with you being the mother of my son..."

"Is that raging fiery inferno inside you about to burn *super-hot!*" She asks with a knowing look.

He strains to say, "*Yyyep.*" She ghosts his lips with hers. "*Briii*, you're killing me..."

"Oh," she seductively grins, "did I forget to mention that I have the green light for some *other* activities?!" She bites her lower lip, then goes and locks the door. She walks back over to him asking, "Do we have a little time to have some fun, or——." He captures her lips in a passionate kiss...

David tangles both hands in her hair and cups her face. He looks at her with so much love saying, "I can't begin to tell you how much I love you! All that you do, all that you are, all the love you give, and now a wonderful baby, there are *no words*..." He takes her hand and places it over his heart. "*I've* fallen in-love with you *so* many more times since Jacks' birth, I've lost count!"

"I have with you, too!" She tells him. "There's something to be said about a hot, sexy man with an adorable baby!" They hear the elevator ding and figure Mary is back from lunch.

David asks, "Are you going to meet up with Jack, or are they coming here to pick you up?"

"I said I'd go there, but I can have him come..." She holds up a finger and listens. "Sounds like Jack beat us to it!" She straightens up her hair. "Do I look normal?" She asks, combing her fingers through her hair. She shakes her head and rolls her eyes when she sees him looking her up and down.

"You're as beautiful as ever!" He handsomely smiles. They walk out to Mary's desk. David hugs Jack, thanking him for going with Bri and the baby at the last minute.

Jack happily smiles. "Anytime!"

Mary takes the car seat and gushes over Jacks. "I can't believe how *adorable* he is!"

"He definitely looks like his daddy!" Bri says.

David steps over and picks Jacks up. "His mum gives me the credit when it has to be her genes that makes him *this* adorable!" He picks up the diaper bag noticing Jacks' diaper needs to be changed and goes into his office; the other go with them.

Jack tells him, "On the way over, Jacks and I discussed that we three should take his mum to lunch."

"I think we can manage lunch!" David looks at Mary to be sure.

Mary tells them, "All of you should get going, so you will have time to eat without any rush."

Bri hugs Mary. "You're wonderful! Thank you!"

"I have to earn my keep!" Mary winks with a smile.

Bri turns to David and grins, "Oh, I think it's more that David has to be *worthy* of keeping you!"

David wraps an arm around Bri, still holding the baby, and says "I *definitely* agree with that!" He smiles at Mary. "I wouldn't be successful at all with the corporation without Mary!"

Mary lightly laughs. "*Everyone* is replaceable!"

"True." David says. "However, the replacement wouldn't even compare!"

Bri smiles proudly at him. "*Fantastic answer*, My Love!"

216

The elevator dings and they step into it; Mitchell and a couple of other guards go with them. Bri waves to Mary as the elevator door closes.

David looks at Bri, "And *you*, Macushla, made me a better man..."

"I say she has made us *all* better men!" Jack adds and David agrees.

They all walk to one of Bri's favorite restaurants, it's the one she and David walked to the week Peter and Carlotta stepped down as The Duke and Duchess of Newhaven. This time, Bri is in a half-circle booth with her most favorite people in the world, except one...Lawrence; he is at a conference in Paris. Jack has the baby and David is holding Bri's hand. Jack's phone vibrates and he answers it. It sounds like he needs to fly to Rome for the day.

David whispers, "*Why don't you let Jack take you tomorrow and you can spend some time at The Villa?*"

"What about the baby?" Bri asks. "I can't leave him, nor do I want to separate you from him. I've even been having Lawrence coming here—."

"*Love*, you need a little TLC right now and I'm just suggesting an overnight trip, *nothing* more. I don't want you to feel like I'm trying to separate you either, but I want Jack to take care of you since I'm swamped." Jack hangs up the phone and David says to him, "Sounds like you need to make a trip."

"I can easily do it in a day." Jack replies.

David explains, "I was suggesting an overnight and for you to take Bri along for some TLC." He looks at Bri. "I'm sure between Grandmas, Grandpa Henry, an aunt, *and an uncle*, we can have his care covered while I'm at work!"

She has tears in her eyes. "I can't leave my baby behind, David, not yet. Please don't insist, because if you do, I'll do it for you," tears drip down her cheeks, "but I'll cry like this, *or worse*, the *entire* time!" Then she exhales in frustration at her emotions.

David holds her hand to his chest. "I'm sorry, Love. Maybe the focus should be you, Jack, *and* Jacks."

She shakes her head. "But I don't want to—."

"I'll be okay, Love. It's not even forty-eight hours." He shifts to face her more. "How can I ask you to do it, if I'm not willing to do the same?" She looks from David to Jack.

Jack smiles handsomely. "I'm *always* in when it comes to spending time with our favorite girl, and now this cute little guy!" He looks down at the baby and says to him, "More 'baby snuggle time' with you and time with Mum, how could I pass that up?!" Jacks studies his uncle.

"Looks like it's all settled!" David smiles a heart melting smile at her. *"If you're okay with it?"*

She sarcastically says, "I guess I can *tryyy* to enjoy Tuscany." She grins and winks at Jack.

Jack chuckles. "And *I* will try my *hardest* to see that you do!"

Their food comes and as they eat, they chat about Bri getting back into her regular rotations with each of them.

That evening in their bedroom, Bri asks David, "Are you sure about Tuscany? About being separated from Jacks?"

He holds her cheek. "Will it be easy? No. Is this necessary for you? *Absolutely*! Bri, *please* relax while you're there. I swear I'll miss you both like crazy, but I won't regret sending you with Jack when I'm at work. Plus, I have a feeling you're going to need to rest up before you *personally* join the mission that brings Millicent down."

She scrunches her eyebrows together. "I hadn't thought about it like that."

"I have..." he admits, "*a lot*. I know you need to do what you need to do, but can you promise me that if you can't bring McMasters, Mitchell, or even one of us, will you *at least* have Jessica with you so she can help keep you alive?"

"I hope it doesn't come to that, but if it does, I promise to have Jessica with me as much as she is able to." She lovingly smiles. "Thank you for trusting me to do what I need to do, including going after her personally."

"I'm not excited about it and I will be nervous, *especially* if you just up and leave, so will Herst and Jack, which means you need to check in *often*, or as often as possible."

She nods. "I won't just up and leave without reaching out giving a 'heads up.' I love you and I wouldn't want you to worry that something bad happened, unless it did." She hugs him and lovingly smiles. "I love you!"

"I love you." He replies. She kisses him and it turns passionate...

CHAPTER 27
Tuscan Getaway

The next morning, David is dressed and about to go to work. Bri is sitting up in bed and he walks over telling her, "Jacks has been changed, dressed, fed, burped, and is having 'snuggle time' with his grandmas and grandpa. Jack is in the living room." He tosses his thumb over his shoulder. He says leaning in, "I love you and I'll miss you. I'll be *extremely* busy, so don't worry about me. I want you to enjoy your time with Jack!"

"*I'll try.*" She teases, then says loud enough for Jack to hear, "You know how difficult it is to be around Jack!" Jack is smiling as he steps in the doorway.

David suggests, "Maybe consider that if you're getting away on the spur of the moment, it'll keep Millicent and her lackeys on their toes!"

She raises her eyebrow. "*Are you not wanting me to come back?!*"

He chuckles. "You know the answer to that." He taps a kiss to her lips. "I do need to get going. I love you, Mrs. Worthington!"

"I love you and I'll see you tomorrow afternoon." She pulls on his tie a little, so he'll lean in again for another kiss, and he does.

They say 'I love you' once more as David heads out the door. She hears Jack say he'll take good care of them and David says he has no doubt, then they say 'goodbye.' Jack comes into the bedroom with a huge, charming smile.

"Oy," Bri rolls her eyes, teasing, "you're going to be an insufferable morning person right now, aren't you?"

"*Maaaybe*...especially if you're going to be feisty this morning?" He smirks.

She looks at the clock, then back at him as she gets a sly smirk on her face, "*Maaaybe....*"

He chuckles and leans down to kiss her, grabbing hold of the covers while she is distracted. He pulls back with a mischievous smile and he yanks the covers back.

She gasps very loudly. "*Jack*, please!" She reaches for the covers. "It's cold!" She is wearing David's shirt.

"*No way!*" Jack tells her. "While this is a gorgeous sight, the only way this could be perfect is if you were naked!"

"*You would say that!*" She smiles with pursed lips.

He lightly laughs as he takes her hands and helps her out of bed. "Now," he pats her bum, "go get dressed! We have a plane to catch!"

She goes and starts getting dressed. "I thought this was supposed to be *relaxing*, not stressed with a rush!"

"*No rush!* I'm just excited to get us all to The Villa!" Jack happily tells her.

"You make it sound like we're a group." She replies.

"*We are!*" He says looking in her closet for a light jacket for her; he finds one and grabs it, along with her shoes.

Bri comes out of the bathroom and asks, "What do you mean? Is there more than us three?" She takes her shoes and jacket from him, then goes over and sits on the bed to put her shoes on.

He gives her a loving smile and says, "I agreed with both of your points at the restaurant yesterday. So last night after dinner, I pulled James and Amy aside and explained the lunch conversation. I said they'd be two on an *very* short list of who you would trust to leave the baby with as I *try* to take care of *you*. I asked if they'd be able to come out with us this morning for an overnight stay at The Villa." Bri smiles, then goes over and grabs her purse and phone. "Carlotta, Maggie, and Henry overheard us and thought it would be fun for James and Amy. Plus, the three said they will be around to take care of things here and in Kingsbury." He waves for her to go first and he follows her out of her shared quartets with David. "James and Amy are waiting for us downstairs."

"Thank you, Amore Mio." She squeezes his hand as they walk downstairs.

When Bri and Jack walk into The Sitting Room downstairs, Carlotta is getting in her last few Grandma kisses and hugs in. She sees Bri and hands the baby to Maggie so she can have another minute of snuggles.

Bri is a little sad. "I'm sorry to take him away from you guys."

Carlotta shakes her head and looks at her with motherly love. "Bri, we'll miss *all of you*, granted this baby a wee bit more," she teases as they all lightly laugh, "but enjoy this stage. You know as well as we do, this first year has *so many* firsts!" She kisses Bri's cheek and hugs her.

Maggie hugs Bri, then hands her the baby. She looks at the three grandparents and says to them, "It also helps having parents who love us so much!" Jack, Amy, and James agree!

Henry, Maggie, and Carlotta walk them all out to the helicopter. They say one last goodbye before James, Amy, Jack, and Bri, with the baby, climb inside. The flight is smooth and they play some card games, making the flight seem like it went faster.

Once they've landed, they all gather their things, and Jack picks up the empty car seat. Bri carries Jacks as they all leave the helicopter and go to the awaiting motorcade. The drive takes them past some beautiful countryside and vineyards. They turn into The Villa's driveway that is lined with trees and surrounded their vineyards.

"This is beautiful!" Amy says.

Bri smiles as she looks around, taking it all in again. "I think I love this place a little more each time we come here." Jack smiles, because it does his heart good to hear her say that.

Jack tells James and Amy, "The door is always open for you two to stay whenever you'd like!"

James looks at Amy with a smile. "We just might have to take you up on that! This place *is* beautiful!" James says. "We've been to The Chateau a couple times and it's beautifully charming in its own way, too!"

As the SUV pulls up to the front door, they see the staff have come out to greet them. James and Amy are taken to their room, while Jack and Bri go to

The Owners' Suite with the baby. A few minutes later, their bags are brought into the room for them.

Francesca asks them with a strong Italian accent, "Lord and Lady Worthington have asked to have the room closest to nursery, if possible, but still giving Your Royal Majesty and Your Grace privacy. We hope that is okay?"

"*Absolutely*! Thank you so much for accommodating them." Bri smiles.

"'Tis *no* problem!" Francesca smiles. "Is there anything else I can do for you?"

Charming Jack tells her they are fine and are just going to settle in. They will let her know if they need anything. She nods and smiles back at both of them before she leaves the room.

Jack starts to shut the door, but Bri stops him. "Did I hear 'nursery' just now?" She grins.

"*Perhaps...*" He says coyly. All she does is smile sweetly and he gives her a look asking, "Do you want to see it?"

She gets excited. "*Yes!*"

He takes Jacks out of the car seat and offers his hand to Bri. She takes it and he leads her to the nursery. "Close your eyes." She does and he slowly walks her into the room. "Alright...*open!*"

"Jack!" Bri gasps. She is turning in a circle to take it all in. "This is *wonderful!*" She stops turning and looks at him. "This has your touch written all over it!"

"I may have picked some things out a while back and had them delivered here, then recently added a few more things." He says, pulling her close with his free arm. "I wasn't sure exactly when we would visit, but I wanted to be sure we were ready to bring the baby. I did add a couple pieces earlier this morning. I think the staff had fun putting it all together for me."

"I'm sure they did!" She says, walking over to the crib.

She runs her hand across the railing, noting it's a smaller crib. She turns her head and sees the toddler bed in the corner with a little longer rail than one

223

would expect. There's an overstuffed rocking chair and ottoman with a table next to it, but the table is really a carved rocking horse, stabilized under a clear glass tabletop. Jacks will be able to use it as a rocking horse when he gets a little bigger.

There was an extra soft blanket and... "A neck pillow?!" She laughs.

Amy and James have joined them. Amy asks, "Why a neck pillow? Wouldn't you take something like this on a plane or in a car?"

"Haha," Bri sits and gets comfortable. She looks at Jack and holds out her hands for him to give her the baby. Bri replies to Amy, "Nursing releases oxytocin which makes moms want to cuddle and snuggle, bonding with our babies. It can also make a mom *very* sleepy." She smiles at the baby as she situates herself and him, while trying to stay discrete; James also turns away for her privacy.

Amy gives Bri an 'ah' expression and says, "I guess I'll have to keep that in mind in about six more months." She beams at Bri, who realizes what she is saying.

"Amy! James! Oh my gosh! Congratulations!" She says excitedly, startling Jacks. He starts fussing and Bri's voice has a sorry tone, "Shh...Mama's *so* sorry, Sweet Love." Once he is nursing again, she wipes the big tears from his sweet little face. "Amy, I'll hug you like crazy in a bit." She looks at Jack, "Jack, will you..."

"I'm on it, Amore Mia." He smiles at Bri, then wraps Amy in a big hug, congratulating her and then he hugs James, "I'm so happy to be an uncle again, Little Brother!"

"He couldn't have a better one! David and Herst are a close second, though!" James tells Bri, "I accidentally said something to Herst when he was at The Manor last and begged him to let Amy tell you. Please don't be mad."

"Oh, I'm not! *I might tease him*, but there's really nothing to be mad about; it wasn't his news to share...we're good!" She reassures him.

Jack walks with James and Amy back to their room, while Bri nurses. Then Jack goes and talks with The Head Steward, in charge of The Villa, about The Owners' Suite. There is a tower in the suite that is privately theirs with a comfortable couch to look up at the stars. They go to the suite where Jack climbs the stairs, which sort of looks like a ladder, and sees the telescope he had delivered, along with the large pillows.

The Head Steward lets Jack know, "The blankets were washed and will be added shortly."

"This all looks *fantastic!*" Jack smiles and climbs back down. Jack shakes his hand, "Thank you! Please thank the staff for helping to pull all this together!"

The Head Steward smiles, "They had fun, especially preparing for the bambino!"

Before Jack can say anything more, his phone pings a text alert. The client he was to meet in Rome has agreed to let Jack fly him out to The Villa. The driver is texting that they are about to leave the airport and will arrive in about twenty minutes.

Jack and The Head Steward go downstairs where they talk to The Chef, and they decide to have lunch out in The Courtyard. The staff busy themselves getting everything ready, while Jack takes another phone call. The staff will bend over backwards for any request, because they don't have people visit very often. It's usually only Jack and Bri, with their guests here and there.

About twenty minutes later, Jack ends his phone call, then hears footsteps behind him. Before he turns around, he hears a familiar voice, "Jack, *Daaahling!*" His stomach twists into a tight knot; *hoping* it isn't who he thinks it is as he turns around, *but it is.*

"Maddy? What are you doing here?!"

Jack hasn't seen Maddy since he broke things off with her, a few days before he first met Bri and escorted her to that first Black-Tie Party. Maddy leans in and kisses the air on both sides of Jack's face.

"I came with Edward." Maddy points to Edward who walks up beside them.

"I hope that's alright?" Edward shakes Jack's hand. "She said the two of you dated a while back. She also said you had been looking for a place buy in Italy, and she wanted to see the place you finally bought!"

"It's fine." Jack says, not wanting to hurt Edward's feelings. "It did take me a few years, but it may be that I needed the right motivation." Jack lovingly smiles wide as he sees Bri walking up to them; he wraps his arm around Bri's waist.

Maddy sees how Jack is looking at her and thinks to herself, '*Of course*, she *has to be here...*' She looks Bri over... '*Natural hair, nails,* no make-up; *disgusting.*' Maddy pastes a smile on her face as Jack introduces her to Bri, but Bri senses Maddy's insincerity under her fake smile and niceness.

"Bri, this is my client Edward Quinn and his guest, Maddy——."

"*Lady* Made*lyn* Cunningham." She daintily holds her hand out saying, "Charmed, I'm sure."

Bri raises her eyebrow at the thickness in her snobbery and glances at Maddy's flimsy hand; she doesn't know what to do with it. Maddy's smile fades when Bri doesn't shake her hand and she clears her throat as she pulls her hand back.

Bri apologizes, "I'm sorry, but I didn't know what to do with a floppy hand like that."

Maddy snips, "That's alright, *Bri.* Not everyone knows the proper way for an introduction."

"You're right, *Lady Cunningham.* Someone should've taught you the proper way to shake someone's hand, because a hand *shouldn't* be flopping around." Bri states with Jack and Edward quietly chuckling. Maddy glares at them.

Bri says, "Lady Cunningham and Mister Quinn, welcome to the picturesque villa Jack bought."

"*For you,* Amore Mia!" Jack lovingly smiles as he kisses the back of her hand.

Maddy is about to say something, but she is interrupted when someone from the kitchen staff announces lunch is served. Jack steps over to them and asks for an additional place setting for the table. They file outside and take a seat around the table. Bri purposely watches Maddy as she goes over and sits next to Edward, *then* she pats the empty chair on the other side of her for Jack to sit next to her. Jack purposely sits on the other side of Edward, then pulls the chair out for Bri to sit next him. Amy and James join them; Jack pulls out Amy's chair next to Bri. Amy takes the baby monitor from Bri and puts it between her and James before she sits down.

With everyone now sitting, Bri starts to ask, "Mr. Quinn—."

"Please, call me Edward." He tells her.

"*Edward*," Bri says, "how long has Jack been managing your accounts?"

"For quite some time! He tells me he works out of his home office most of the time now, sharing it with '*the love of his life*!'" He winks at Bri. She looks at Jack, who is looking so adoringly at her. Edward adds, "It's plain to see he has *definitely* found the love of his life!" He lifts his glass, "To love, and the good bloke who found his beauty!"

The others lift their glass, with Maddy barely lifting her, and the others say, "To love!" Maddy is silent.

"Actually," Jack says, looking at Bri, "marrying this amazing, *bloody brilliant*, and *gorgeous* woman was the smartest thing I've ever done!" Maddy scoffs, but everyone ignores her, which only irks Maddy.

When Jack and Edward are discussing Edward's sources of income, Bri has a thought come to her: '*Millicent's Tunnels*.' The Tunnels are where Millicent stores the things she is going to auction off, including the cells where she keeps people sold into human trafficking. She hears Edward ask about the baby, then is brought into the conversation as Jack squeezes her saying, "She's amazing to watch with him!"

Maddy scoffs with her nose turned up. Bri asks her, "Not fond of babies?"

"*Ew*, no!" Maddy says with disgust. "They're messy, sticky, smelly; *they're just plain gross*!"

"*Maddy*!" Edward scolds her.

"What? *It's the truth*!" Maddy defends herself.

Bri looks at Edward with a compassionate look. "It's okay. It's probably the most honest thing she has said since she arrived. Babies can certainly be all those things, but those are overshowed by the best parts!"

Maddy rolls her eyes. "Like what?"

Bri takes her phone and pulls up a photo as she replies, "Like the baby snuggles, their sweet faces, and these..." Bri shows her a picture of Jacks smiling as he sleeps. "Unless someone has ice in their veins, it's hard *not* to smile when seeing a sweet baby." Bri tips her head to Maddy who has a little smile as she looks at the picture. Maddy sees them looking at her and tsks, trying to cover her smile as she looks away. Bri expounds, "Maddy, raising children *is hard!* This first year to eighteen months can be super easy compared to all the 'terrible twos,' 'horrible threes,' and so on. The teenage years will have you thinking you are losing your mind, as they have you questioning your very sanity, with their self-centered version of their reality, and they will talk you in circles. *But.* With *all* that, there are *incredible* moments you can only experience with them throughout the stages of their childhood! Seeing this little one smile warms my heart; however, when he starts recognizing people and smiles *at* them, *at me*?! *That's* magical!" Jack drapes his arm on the back of Bri's chair and Bri casually leans into him. "*Nothing* can beat the *wonderful* moments with kids at *any* age!"

"Why is it that the people who have kids, put down those who don't want them?" Maddy asks with frustration.

"*On the contrary!*" Bri replies and Maddy's eyebrows come together. Bri explains, "I absolutely respect people who have thought it out and don't want children for any number of understandable reasons. *Parenting isn't for the faint of heart!* The last thing in the world we should want are children born to someone who doesn't want them *and worse! They keep them, punishing their children for it!* However, it's a completely different story if they put them up for adoption, which I have a *HUGE* amount of respect for *those* birth and adoptive mothers! When we're trying to raise a family, children *will* grow us up in ways we never could've dreamed of, cutting through our own childish behaviors like rudeness, meanness, callousness, and the toughest ones of all...selfishness and pride." Maddy glares at Bri, only Bri has a small, compassionate smile for her because she has unknowingly proven Bri's point a few times since her arrival.

Jack and Edward talk more business as they eat dessert, when Jacks wake up. Amy leans over whispering to Bri, "*I'll go check on him.*"

"*Are you sure?*" Bri whispers back. "*You're not done eat——.*"

"*Bri, the whole reason we agreed to come here in the first place was for the sweet baby snuggles!*" Amy teasingly scolds. They all lightly laugh, except Maddy who rolls her eyes. Amy tells James, "I'll be right back."

Bri hears Maddy say barely above a whisper, "*Jack could've done so much better!*" Jack is getting more infuriated with Maddy.

He humorlessly laughs, "*Like you?!*" She frowns, feeling a bit embarrassed. "Maddy, you have absolutely *no idea* what it takes to be *a real lady! You're clueless.* One of the many reasons I think Bri is amazing is because she is genuine...unlike you," he waves his hand towards her, "*like this!*" Jack stands up saying, "Edward, I need a break from her!" He wipes his mouth before throwing his napkin down. He holds his hand out to Bri and she stands up as she takes it; he leads her inside.

Edward looks at Maddy shaking his head. "You couldn't be more jealous, even if you were painted green!" He wipes his mouth. "What I'm curious about is whether you are jealous of *her,* or are you jealous of Jack being in-love with any woman *not* you?" He watches her body language and gets his answer: both. He rolls his eyes and asks, "Why did you even break up with him in the first place?!"

Maddy starts to say, "I want——."

"*He* broke up with Maddy." James chimes in. "Jack *always* broke things off with *every* woman he dated; that is, until Bri came into the picture. There was only one woman I've ever heard him say he would chase around the world if he had to."

Maddy scoffs, "*Bri?*"

"Bri *is* the love of his life!" James states. "At the risk of sounding as rude as you," he explains, "natural beauty is *way* more beautiful than dye jobs, manicures, pedicures, or plastic surgery; it's *all* fake, which make those women look, *and seem,* fake, because they're hiding who they truly are, even from themselves! It's sad. The men they date will eventually see that, then

229

start looking for someone who is genuine if they, themselves, are genuine; they don't want fake anymore. Bri described Jack and David as having a 'revolving door of women' and that under the hair, skin, make-up, and boobs, all those women were *basically* the same." Edward chokes on his drink of water. James turns to walk away, but stops and turns back to say to her, "The problem *isn't* that you don't believe any of this, Maddy. The problem is you don't *want* to believe it! Try, if you must, but you're wasting your time with Jack. You should move on," he tips his head towards inside. "*Jack has* and he will *never* look back!" James goes inside and upstairs to find Amy.

Maddy stews over what James has said. She is annoyed, because she knows James is right...

CHAPTER 28
Tuscan Date

When Jack had led Bri back into The Villa, he didn't say a word as they went upstairs. His strides cause her to almost jog to keep up with him, only slowing down when they reach their room. Jack shuts their door, but Bri still senses the tension. She hugs him and he wraps his arms around her; he takes a deep breath and exhales, squeezing her a little firmer.

Jack pulls back and says to her, "I'm sorry about Maddy. I had no idea she was coming—."

Bri covers his mouth, shaking her head. "You have *nothing* to be sorry for. First and foremost, I trust in your love for me. Second, I know you would've warned me, had you known."

"*Probably not.*" He says. She gets a confused look on her face and grins, "She wouldn't have come at all."

"*Ooo,* even better!" She replies. "How about a distraction?"

He raises his eyebrow. "What do you have in mind?"

She kisses him passionately and he moans. He runs his hand down to her bum and pulls her to him. He kisses her in the way that makes her knees weak, knowing she wants to play her flirting game.

He pulls their lips apart and grins. "I do believe the score is now even."

"*For now.*" She winks.

They go out and stand on the balcony for a little bit, before Jack goes back downstairs to get Edward's business over with, which will ultimately get Maddy out of the house. Bri settles in and watches a movie. Something in the movie has her thinking of Millicent and she texts Rex Stirling.

Bri: "Do you know where Millicent's tunnels are?"

Rex: "Between Devonridge Manor and Devonridge Hall. Why do you ask?"

Bri: "I'm proposing a 'cleansing of evil' so-to-speak..."

"Cleansing of evil?!" Jack asks, standing behind her and the couch; she jumps. "Sorry, Amore Mia, I didn't mean to scare you."

"It's fine." She smiles sweetly.

Rex: "Make a trip to Ashbourne Castle tomorrow, on your way back from Tuscany."

Bri was surprised, for a split-second, that he knew she was in Tuscany; but of course he would know, he is 'Rex Stirling!'

Bri: "It's a date!"

Rex: "See you then!"

Jack chuckles at her text and she puts her phone down. He hands her a note that says James and Amy have gone into a nearby village and took Baby Jacks with them. They are hoping she is okay with that and a 'P.S. *We have extra security with us!*' Bri smiles.

Jack walks around and sits next to Bri on the couch; she texts Amy.

Bri: "Thank you, my wonderful sister! If it were anyone else, I'd send out a search party!"

Amy: "Haha! James and I don't doubt you would! He's snickering saying you would have if it was just him and the baby!"

Bri: "Not if he had extra security with, or he would be escorted by the posse that I would've sent! (Adds a smiley face) I'll see you guys later!"

Since she is already texting, she texts David quickly:

Bri: "I want to let you know that we will be taking a detour; I need to go to Ashbourne Castle tomorrow for a meeting, before going home. I love you and miss you! (adds a heart)"

Then a text to Lawrence:

Bri: "We need to make a detour to Ashbourne Castle tomorrow for a meeting. If you can swing by to say 'Hello,' I'd love to see you!"

Lawrence: "You can count on it! Just let me know what time! I would love you, too, My Queen! (adds the three-finger sign language for 'I love you' hand)"

Bri: "I can't wait to see you either! I love you!"

Bri receives a text from David:

"Can I call? I don't want to wake up the baby."

Bri smiles and texts a 'thumbs up.' A few seconds later, David calls.

"Hi, Handsome!" She smiles.

"It does my heart good to hear you happy!"

She smiles. "How has your day been?"

"Exhausting. Mother called not too long ago and wants me to take the helicopter home soon so I can eat and go to bed early."

"I think that's a *great* idea!" She replies.

"You do, do you?"

"Honestly, David, you three are your own unique versions of 'superman' to me. Now with the baby, *you* have been doing so much that an early bedtime will do you a lot of good; plus, it may be the only good consequence for not having us there."

"*Ah, no, Love,*" his Scottish accent is thick, "I sleep better with you here, even if you're at The Cottage House."

"I understand that, but please make your sacrifice worth it by getting some extra sleep, *for me?*" David exhales loudly thinking. Bri asks, "Didn't you tell me that you'd do *anything* for me?"

"Wow!" David responds, "You're using *my own words* against me?!"

Bri laughs, "As you say to me, I'm using them *for you*!" There is a long pause. "David?"

"Sorry, Love, I'm texting Mother that I'll gather my things and leave the office early."

He hears Bri smile as she says, *"Thank you!"*

"I *would* do anything for you!" He reminds her, smiling to himself.

"Just like *I* would do anything for *you*!" She tells him.

"I know!" He tells her, then he says, "I need to go. I love you, Macushla!"

"I love you and we'll see you tomorrow!" Bri says, and they hang up.

Jack moves to sit across from her on the coffee table and starts to rub her feet. He gives her sexy smile as he runs his hand up her thigh; she smiles.

"Will you go out with me tonight? I already have a dress in mind for you to wear." He stares at her waiting for an answer.

"I'd love to go on a date with you! And I'm *more* than happy to let you pick out the dress," she points towards the closet, "although, I'm not sure what you'll find in there..."

Jack stands and playfully says, *"I never said anything about a dress you already have."* He goes to the door and grabs a gift-wrapped box he had brought. She smiles so lovingly at him, but as he gets closer to her, he sees, *"Tears?"*

"*Ugh*! Yes! It's all the spoiling you three do! *And* teary has been a regular visitor since my coma; *plus*, I'm becoming *more* empathic!" She takes the box he hands to her, as he sits on the coffee table in front of her again. Bri takes the lid off the box and pulls out a fitted, yet modest, sexy red dress. "Oh Jack!" She exhales. *"It's beautiful!"*

"It'll be gorgeous when you have it on!" He states.

"I hope it fits, considering I have some baby weight to lose?" She looks closely at the dress. "When should I be ready for our date?"

He looks at his watch. "Will two hours work?" She nods. He gives her a little more than a peck of a kiss on her lips before he leaves the suite.

Bri hangs the dress in the closet, then goes to get ready, taking her time. When she needs to put her dress on, she picks out a matching bra set that also matches the dress. Bri adds a soft slip, then puts on her dress. She hears a knock on the door.

"Bri? It's Amy."

"You can come in!" Bri replies. The door opens and Amy steps in. Bri turns and points to her back asking, "Would you zip me up? I pray it fits."

Amy zips it and it's only a little snug. "Breastfeeding seems to have worked fast!" She smiles as Bri turns to her. "WOW! You look H-O-T, *HOT!*" Amy grins saying, "I think I'll be keeping the baby with us tonight! It might be quieter for him." She giggles. Bri lightly snorts a laugh and shakes her head. "OH!" Amy remembers the bag she came in with and hands it to her.

"What's this?" Bri takes it.

"Jack said this was delayed and wasn't delivered until a little bit ago. He asked if I would bring the bag to you." Amy says. "How much time do you need until the big reveal?"

Bri says, "About five minutes?"

"I'll pass that along." Amy smiles and leaves to go downstairs.

In the bag, Bri finds shoes and a clutch to match. She is thinking she will need to tease Jack about not picking out jewelry, until she sees a larger box at the bottom of the bag. She opens it and finds a diamond and ruby necklace set. She finds a little card with it and reads:

'The Imperial Ruby Necklace' was made specially for My Queen. ~ L

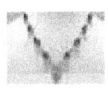 A pendant of rubies, accented by white and yellow diamonds to look like a phoenix, with diamonds attaching the phoenix to the

necklace, which looks like a crown. There are pear-shaped rubies going along to the back, with round white and yellow diamonds in between. Bri puts it on, then adds the matching earrings.

She slides on her shoes and takes one last look in the mirror. Then she gathers a few things in her clutch, including her phone, before making her way downstairs. They hear her shoes on the marble floor and gather around the bottom of the staircase. When she appears, Jack's breath catches and his hand goes to his heart. He tries to say something, but he struggles to breathe.

He manages to exhale, then says, "Once again, you've taken my breath away, Amore Mia! You're a stunning, *gorgeous* vision!" He steps up to meet her on the stairs and kisses her cheek.

"You *always* manage to look incredibly sexy in your tux! I love the red touches to match!" She smiles, biting her lower lip.

"A picture of perfection!" Amy says, holding up Jack's phone and snapping a few pictures on it.

"Amore Mio, please don't send any pics to David until the morning. We want him to sleep well and a picture or few of, *well...*" She gives him a little 'eek' look biting her lower lip.

He chuckles. "Point taken. I won't torture him tonight so he can sleep *and* I'll hold off sending them to Herst, as well."

"Good idea!" She sweetly smiles. "Thank you."

Bri steps over to James with Jacks, and she kisses her sleeping baby. They both see Jacks' smile and she kisses him again with the same result. She kisses his little fingers before she and Jack say goodbye to James and Amy. Jack places his hand on Bri's lower back for her to go out the door first, then out to the awaiting motorcade.

Inside the limo, Bri and Jack are sitting together in the back. She shifts to look at him better.

She asks, "Are you going to tell me what you have planned for us?" He studies her, trying to decide if it'll be more fun to make her wait. "*Oh, come on!* A little hint?" She bites her lower lip and grins as she gets an idea. She

236

shifts in her seat and starts kissing his neck. She whispers next to his ear, *"Maybe just one piece of your plan at a time?"* She runs her lips down his neck and she feels him shiver and he swallows hard.

"Keep this up and it won't matter, because we'll be rushing into the closet hotel!" He tells her.

She smiles against his neck and says, "Just *one* little piece..." She taps a kiss below his earlobe.

Jack can't help himself; he turns and captures her lips in a lip melting kiss. He pulls their lips apart and gives her a smoldering smirk. "Temptress..."

"And you know how dangerous that can be; *however...*" she starts to run her hand up his thigh, "I'm planning on *both of us* winning later tonight." He quickly grabs her hand.

"*Daaamn...*" he cups her face with one hand, resting their foreheads together, "I think you just won the game, Amore Mia." He works to contain himself.

"Are you okay?" She asks. "Maybe we should stop flirting until we're heading back to The Villa?"

"Bri, you're *always* gorgeous, but right now I'm trying to push aside my *favorite* memory of you!"

"What memory is that?" She wonders.

"It's from when we were on our honeymoon in Rome. You are *naked* with the diamond jewelry set we had just bought...*aaand in heels.*" He bites his lower lip and grins.

"Heels? I didn't—*aaah.*" She smiles with her nod as she realizes he *added* that part. "We can arrange that, *with your little addition,* soon enough..." He gives her a smoldering look and she clears her throat, "Let's change the subject."

Jack snuggles in with her in the back seat and tells her, "First, we're going to have a lovely dinner before we go to the *Teatro della Pergola*, a historic opera house, and we'll see an opera after we eat."

"I've never been to an opera!" She smiles, trying to cover her concern of her sensitive hearing.

"I know." He says. Bri is confused; she doesn't remember when she told him. "You *first* mentioned it the weekend we all first met." She is amazed he remembered! He hands her earplugs. "To protect your sensitive ears."

She gives him a small, knowing smile. "David reminded you."

He cups her cheek. "I told him my plans and he mentioned it."

She taps a little kiss to his lips, "Thank you." She puts the earplugs in her clutch as they pull up to the restaurant.

After dinner and the opera, they take a romantic stroll around the town square, *Piazza della Signoria*. Bri marvels at its beauty, the statues, and ancient buildings. It's dark enough that their security is bit more spread out and blending in.

When they return to The Villa, all is quiet. They hold hands as they walk upstairs and to their room. After Jack shuts and locks their door, Bri asks him to unzip her dress. She goes into the closet and hangs it up while Jack takes his jacket and cufflinks off at the dresser. As he unbuttons his shirt, Bri walks out to him in her bra set with her new jewelry still on, *and heels*.

He exhales a whistle walking up to her, throwing his shirt on the chair. He tangles his hands in her hair and pulls her into a *hot*, passionate kiss...

He sits on the edge of the bed, watching her put his shirt on. She looks at him and he winks with a smile. He holds out his hand and she takes it, smiling behind her pursed lips.

"Why do I get the odd feel you could go for another round?"

"Because I could!" His other hand goes to her bum and tugs her closer with the playfulness they enjoy with each other. He leads her up the little stairs to their private tower where he has large pillows and soft blankets on a couch, as well as a telescope for a better look at the stars.

"Are we sleeping up here tonight?" She asks with a hopeful look.

"We are if you want to, but I'll settle with at least watching the stars with you for a little while." He sits.

Bri sits down next to him. "I don't know how long my eyelids will stay open, but sleeping under this many stars seems *wonderfully* romantic, Amore Mio." He agrees.

They snuggle in and it isn't long before they're *both* asleep...

CHAPTER 29
A Slight Detour

The next morning, Bri wakes up with Jack spooning her on the couch. She mindlessly runs her fingers lightly up and down his arm that is draped over her. She jumps a little when she hears him say, "Good morning, Gorgeous!"

She smiles. "Good morning, Amore Mio." He kisses the curve of her neck. "Let me run to the bathroom quick." She gets up to go down the stair-ladder, but she freezes when she hears something...she concentrates on listening.

He asks, "What is it?"

She hears her baby crying and looks down at her chest. She says to herself, "*Well, this is embarrassing...*" Jack hears her. She turns to go down the stair-ladder and tells him, "There is a *very* upset baby that I somehow need to get to..." Jack sits up and listens carefully...then he hears Jacks.

A few minutes later, Bri hears the crying getting closer, and how upset Baby Jacks has gotten; *he is mad!* She hears Jacks in their room. She comes out and takes the baby from Jack. He is so worked up; she knows it will take time to get him to nurse.

 "Oh, sweet baby, come and tell Mama *all* about it." Bri walks over to the couch bouncing him and making the 'sssh' sound next to his ear.

It takes quite a few attempts, but when Jacks finally calms down, he starts nursing. His sobs are subsiding, but he does give a few more cries here and there before he completely relaxes in his mother's arms. Jack sits on the ottoman and caresses Jacks' head.

"You said something about being embarrassed..." He looks at her so lovingly. "*What could you possibly be embarrassed about with me?!*"

She looks at him and replies, "I heard our sweet baby crying and started leaking..." she looks at the baby again, "not exactly sexy."

"Amore Mia," she looks at him and he runs his thumb across her cheek, he tips his chin towards the baby nursing, "this is beautiful! Your body not only

240

grew a baby, but now you can feed and bond with *your* baby! Don't you *ever* feel embarrassed around me again, Amore Mia! Okay?"

Bri nods with tears. "I think you're *incredibly* amazing!" She cups his cheek and pulls him into a kiss.

He looks down and sees the baby watching him. "How about I go find some food for Mama?" Jack kisses his head, then looks at Bri.

"Proving once more how amazing *you are*!"

"It's just food." He chuckles.

"Ah, *to you*, but to our little guy you continue to be his hero!"

"Hero?!" He handsomely scoffs. "That's a bit of an exaggeration!"

"Amore Mio, who went down to get him, not to mention rescuing poor Amy and James from a *very* upset baby, and brought him to his mama?" She points to him saying, "*Hero*! Now you want to bring his mama food and ultimately feed him!" She points at him again. "*Hero*!" He lightly chuckles as he goes downstairs for their breakfast.

When Jack comes back, Bri has changed the baby around. Jack has some fruit, eggs, and a sweet roll of sorts, with a glass of milk. He sets the tray down and she smiles at him. He sits on the coffee table again so he can hand her things to eat.

"James and Amy went out for a bit and said to let them know if we needed them. I said the only plans I had was a lazy morning with the woman I love and the cutest baby in the world!" He smiles at Jacks. "I said for them to have fun and if they needed any more recommendations, to let me know!"

When Jacks finishes nursing, Jack takes him and burps him while Bri eats some more. The baby has a really good burp and a couple small ones before he 'passes out' on Jack's shoulder. Jack had brought the bassinet back into their room while Jacks nursed and put it on her side of the bed. He goes over and lays the baby in it to sleep.

Jack takes the plate and glass puts them on the tray, then takes it all downstairs. When he comes back into the room, Bri had gotten comfortable

241

in bed and it looks like she may already be sleeping. Jack carefully slides into bed next to her and wraps her in his arms facing each other. She isn't sleeping and she snuggles with him and kisses him tenderly.

They fall asleep for a while and Bri wakes as the baby stirs. She gets up and uses the restroom. She comes out and smiles seeing Jack holding Jacks.

"I thought you might have him in your arms already."

"How could I not?! He is wide awake and deep in thought, looking just like his mama!" He smiles at Jacks. "You definitely have your daddy's and grandmother's dark blue eyes, though!"

"*I know!*" She says wrapping her arms around Jack from behind and kisses his shoulder.

He kisses her hand. "Go get comfortable before I hand you this handsome boy of yours."

After the baby eats this time, Jack burps him and has Bri go get comfortable on the bed. He puts the sleeping baby in his bassinet again, before he grabs some massage oil from under the bathroom sink. He starts working his hands at massaging her feet and legs.

"Ah, Amore Mio, such masterful hands!" Her eyes are closed, soaking in the massage. "Being a masseur is definitely one of 'Sexy Jack's' *many* talents!"

"*Only* for the woman he loves!" He leans down and kisses her neck.

They are gathering their things, getting ready to leave for London. Bri's phone chimes with a text notification from Rex.

Rex: "Meeting time 5:00; begin in The Library. Come alone."

She walks over to Jack, putting Jacks into his car seat and buckles him in. "What is it?" He asks.

"You, *Your Grace*, are nosy!" She teases.

He grabs her bum and pulls her up close. "I'm protective, *Your Royal Majesty*! Now, *spill!*"

"It was Rex with a meeting time at Ashbourne." She replies.

"I'm not sure how deep you should be involved in all of this." Jack holds her face. "Let me go for you."

She shakes her head. "You can't. I'm to come alone. I'll be fine."

"Well, I'll try to support you dictating how all of this goes, but for your safety, maybe you should let Rex, and his team, do most of the heavy lifting."

"Rex would agree." She replies. "However, it's only going to get worse, *before it gets better*, because we all know Millicent wants Lawrence's baby." She reminds him. "This is going to *require* me to do *some* heavy lifting, to ultimately bring her down, and to keep her down. Which means I'm going to have to bring the fight to her!"

Jack is surprised. "You're always the first one to shy away from veng—."

"*Vengeance?!*" She snaps with her eyebrows furrowed. "If that was the case, don't you think I would've gone after her right after she killed Emmie and Natty?!" She picks up her bag. "Jack, I have to shift gears and start a more aggressive, *more strategic,* offense! That's the only way I can protect those I love, *and* protect the public!"

"I'm sorry I upset you." He has an apologetic look. "I just worry. I love you."

"I know and I love you, too." She replies. "You guys are going to have to have faith that this will all work out as it was intended to *for several reasons*. One of them being, we still have children coming into our family. I would *really* like to have all this dealt with *before* we add the next baby to our family, especially being Lawrence's baby and heir!"

"I can understand that. I also trust you're not going to do anything hasty, because everything you've done so far has been thought out and deliberate." He replies and she nods. Their suitcases have been taken out and Bri is also bringing the diaper bag with her bag, while Jack carries the baby in his car seat. James and Amy are outside waiting for them. Jack reminds them,

243

"You're still welcome to come with, but if you change your minds, I can arrange another flight for us while you two continue on to Newhaven."

The two of them look at each other and shake their heads. James tells them, "We don't have any plans and we both want to see The Ashbourne Estate!"

"*Fantastic!*" Jack smiles and Bri agrees.

They all go to the airport and settle in for their flight. Bri digs in her bag for her water and finds the jewelry box with her diamond-ruby necklace set from last night. She opens it and runs her fingers around it.

Jack watches her and tells her, "I spoke with Herst some time back about the perfect red dress I bought for you, but the ruby jewelry you have wasn't the right shade of red. He wanted me to send the dress to him for him to have inspiration and to have the right shade of red."

Bri hugs him. "Thank you for the dress *and* the entire evening last night! It was wonderful!"

He gives her a loving smile. "You're welcome, Amore Mia!" He kisses her.

Their flight is smooth and when they arrive by helicopter at The Ashbourne Estate, Bri is pleasantly surprised to see Lawrence *with David!* It does her heart good to have all three of them with her.

"*You're both here!*" She smiles wide, stepping off the helicopter.

David watches her walk up to him. "I've missed you, Mrs. Worthington!"

"I missed you, too, *Mister* Worthington!" She kisses him sweetly. David steps back and Bri turns to Lawrence. "I've missed you, too, My King!"

"And I *you*, My Queen!" Lawrence kisses her and hugs her firmly.

David takes the baby out of the car seat. "I've missed you, too!" He says holding Jacks close and kisses his forehead.

"Macushla..." he says as they all walk towards The Castle, including Mr. Woodsley, "I'm hoping you had a nice, *relaxing* time?"

244

"*I did!* It was nice that James and Amy were there so I could have Jacks close and still go out with Jack, *knowing* the baby was in *great hands!*" She looks at James and Amy. "I honestly didn't worry about him! I missed him, but I *never* gave a thought to his well-being!"

Amy and James smile, with Amy saying, "*Anytime!*"

The rest of Ashbourne's staff greet them when they come into Ashbourne Castle. Jack, Lawrence, and David take James and Amy around The Castle, while Bri sets off for The Library. The Library is on the other side of The Castle and it takes her a few minutes to find her way there.

Bri walks into The Library and pauses inside the door to take in the room that is two floors tall. The Library is beautifully made of stone and dark wood. She sees wooden bookshelves all around, with some bookshelves carved into the stone walls.

 She walks over to a window and looks out at the beautiful estate. Walking around outside, it feels like they are out in the country. However, looking out the window, she can see the beautiful city they are surrounded by!

"Your Royal Majesty."

Bri's heart freezes. She turns to see Mr. Woodsley walking up behind her. She starts to apologetically say, "I'm sorry, Mr. Woodsley but..."

He puts up his hand in a half surrender and eases the tension by saying, "I was asked to show you the way, Ma'am," she glances down and notices a flashlight in his hand, "by our *mutual friend.*" He implies. She picks up that he is referring to Rex Stirling, and nods.

He steps over to the wall and reaches under a shelf to press a button. A section of shelves releases and pops open. When he moves his hand, he points, and Bri catches the faint symbol carved into the cement. It has an underlined 'U' with two 'S' shapes, mirrored and overlapped, inside the 'U.' It's the symbol for The Underground Secret Society. It makes Bri wonder how old this 'secret society' is!

Mr. Woodsley pulls open the door and steps inside the hidden passageway. He gestures for Bri to come through the door with him, which she does, and he closes the door. Then she follows Mr. Woodsley along the passageway that leads to another passageway. They step out of this passageway, and she looks around.

"Is this 'The Secret Room' I've read about; the rumors and legends around The Ashbourne Estate?!" She asks.

"Yes, Ma'am." He replies. "The Secret Room was built for a few reasons. One reason is to hide The Royal Family in case of an attack of some sort, or it could be used as an emergency exit if it ever came to that. *The main reason* was, *and is,* for The Duchess of Ashbourne to have a place of peace and solitude from the outside world."

"*This is a wonderful room!*" Bri thoughtfully says as she continues to look around. Mr. Woodsley watches her and softly smiles.

The room has a shorter ceiling, but the windows go from the ceiling to the floor on the outside wall; from the outside, the windows seem to blend into the windows for The Library. In front of the windows sits a comfortable plush couch and matching large ottoman, across from it is an armchair, *and an overstuffed chair with its matching ottoman.* 'Interesting.' She thinks to herself. She didn't think Jack knew about this room, so he wouldn't have known to put that kind of chair in here...

"Is everything alright?" Mr. Woodsley asks.

She is curious. "An overstuffed chair is in here, but I didn't think Jack knew about this room to even to have one put in here."

"He didn't." He simply, and shyly, states. With that, Bri knows that once Mr. Woodsley found out she liked the overstuffed big chairs, *he* saw to it that one was put in here for her.

There is a large fireplace with a portrait of a family; Bri wonders if it's King Andrew and his young family at the time. Her eyes flow up to the carvings at the top of the wall, then to the serene half-daytime and half-nighttime sky mural on the ceiling, with the middle being the colors of a sunrise or sunset; a simpler light fixture is used as a half-sun and half-moon.

"Come over here to this angled wall, Your Royal Majesty." Mr. Woodsley says. Bri looks over and sees that the shorter length angled wall has three cut outs with large art pieces in each section. "This whole section of the wall will open, and you can step right into the passageway. It's a bigger opening so the family could leave quickly together if they ever needed to." He goes up to the large wooden bookshelf around the corner from the wall. He points to the bottom shelf, then tells her as he does it, "There's a wood panel on this end. Inside is a lever, pull it to release the door." There is a light popping sound and he opens the wall just enough for her to slip into the passageway. "This is where I leave you, Ma'am." Mr. Woodsley hands her the flashlight.

She holds up her phone and tells him, "I'll just use this one; I don't have a lot to carry, but thank you."

He nods. "Just follow the passageway down to the main tunnel. There's really only one way to follow them, without opening another doorway."

Bri nods in understanding and turns on her flashlight. He shuts the door, then she cautiously starts to follow the passageway.

CHAPTER 30
The Underground Secret Society

Bri slowly follows the dark passageway, which is only illuminated as far as the reach of her phone's flashlight. The passageway has the cold, damp smell one would expect in an old basement or a cave. She eventually comes to a set of stairs and goes down them, then down another dark hallway. When Bri turns to the next corner, she sees a tiny light down at the far end of this hallway.

 As she gets closer to the light, she sees an empty chair coming into view. It's sitting in the middle of a room with a light straight above it. Two gentlemen stood on either side of the chair, watching and waiting... '*For me?*' She wonders. Another man comes into view, sitting to one side. He is sitting with an ankle resting on top of his other knee and one hand on that ankle, with a gun in his other hand that is pointed at the floor.

"Sit." He sternly tells her, pointing to the chair with his gun.

Bri's eyebrow goes up as she looks at the chair, then back at the man with the gun. "No." She bravely states. "I have no weapon, *because* I don't want to harm any of you. *I'm here for your help*! In fact, some of you may already be helping me!" She crosses her arms. "So, *no*. No, I *won't* sit." She firmly states. "I don't know what this is all about, but stop wasting my time, *and yours*! I came to see Mr. Stirling at the time *he told me to be here* and to come alone! *I did*. If he's not here..." She takes a step back, about to turn on her heel, when the man in the chair stands up.

"Alright then."

Her eyebrows come together. "*What's going on?*"

"I'm sorry if I offended you, Your Royal Majesty," he slightly bows to her, "but we wanted to get a sense of who you were for ourselves. We had a fairly good idea after hearing what happened when Millicent took your baby." The man takes a couple steps closer gesturing the others around them. "*You just might have what it takes to win this!*" He puts out his hand. "Clyde Mezzanotti." He tries to read her expression, curious is she knows who he is.

"You're studying me pretty hard, Mr. Mezzanotti." She says, firmly shaking his hand.

"He's trying to figure out if you know who he is, Your Royal Majesty." She hears a familiar man's voice say.

"Does it matter who he is?" Bri asks, purposely not answering, although she is perfectly aware of who he is.

Mr. Mezzanotti faintly smiles. "Not at the moment."

Mr. Mezzanotti is known as one of the coldest of cold-blooded killers in the criminal world. Although, standing in front of him, she senses he isn't quite so 'cold.' She also senses that he wants to know he will be safe from her guards, particularly McMasters.

"Mr. Stirling," she turns and looks in the general direction where she heard the familiar voice come from, "I didn't know I was auditioning for something!"

"*Not at all!*" He steps into the light. "My associates wanted to size you up, to make sure you were up for this. *And* if they will be safe from arrest *while* they help us."

Rex Stirling stands before her in a dark suit, with a crisp white shirt, black tie, white pocket square, and a black hat, looking rather 'debonair.' The air about him is similar to Lawrence in that she senses danger with him, but the difference with Rex is *he is absolutely dangerous.* One *never* wants to cross him; let alone *no one* should *ever* double-cross him. She knows being around them, she has to make sure *none of them* see her as a threat.

Although she isn't sure how old he actually is, Rex looks like he's in his upper fifties with brown eyes and graying brown hair. She can't tell how fit he really is under his suit, but she remembers he is very agile because he was a great dancer when they danced together in the past when he was in DC, adding a certain 'charisma' to his captivating ways. It all comes together to make it *very difficult* not to like the man!

Bri turns back to the other gentleman and says with a charm of her own, "Mr. Mezzanotti, I *have* heard of you," she gently waves her arm to the others she sees in the shadows, "just as I'm sure I've heard of some of your associates. As far as I'm concerned, you checked your criminal record at the door, because I'm not here to bring any of you down; I just need your help to bring one person down: *Millicent Devonridge!*"

Rex tells the men, "Remember, gentlemen, Her Royal Majesty, along with her family, and guards, are under my protection *indefinitely.*" The men stoically nod in understanding.

Rex goes to the chair she was told to sit in and moves it back to table, then he motions for her to sit. Bri walks over and puts her phone on the table before sitting down; the others join them.

Bri explains, "I'm here because Millicent Devonridge has killed my two daughters, my father-in-law, and innocent others! I wouldn't be surprised if she was behind my parents' death, although their deaths could really have been an accident. *Regardless,* there are more deaths to come from her, and I need your help to stop her *once and for all!*"

"And that's why we're *all* here." Rex motions the others who are now sitting around the same table.

"We agree she needs to go down and stay down!" Mr. Mezzanotti adds, with the others adding supporting comments.

Rex walks over to a wall and turns on a light to reveal more of what now appears to be a rather large room. With another switch he turns on a fireplace next to Bri. He takes off his hat and hangs it on the back of his chair. He walks over to the nearby cabinets and takes out some wine glasses, then pulls out a bottle of wine from the refrigerator.

She politely tells him, "Thank you, but I don't drink alcohol."

He smiles. "I've known you don't drink then, more recently, I discovered you own a business in Tuscany," the cork pops, "that makes nonalcoholic wine and champagne." He shows her the familiar label before he pours a little into his glass. He swirls it, then tastes it. Like everyone who tries it for the first time, they are surprised at how great it tastes. "*Remarkable!* This tastes better than regular wine!" He looks at his glass. "I'm going to order more to have in my personal wine cellar. *Perhaps Her Royal Majesty will join me at some future date?* I promise you won't have to come alone."

"*Perhaps.*" Bri coyly smiles. "You know, since The Duke of Ashbourne bought The Vineyard," she takes a drink of the wine, "maybe he should come, as well as The King and The Grand Duke?"

"*Of course!*" He chuckles. "You know," he sets his glass down on the table, "I have a feeling The Duke of Ashbourne bought that vineyard *for you.*" She winks with a smile. The others lightly laugh, taking a glass from the tray Rex is bringing around to them.

"Bri, *I have a confession.*" He puts the tray down, then he scratches the back of his head walking back over to his chair next to her. "I have been following you, well, *your unique family.*"

She holds the glass close to her mouth and flicks up her eyebrow. "Should I be worried?" She takes another drink as the group chuckles.

"No, no." Rex lightly laughs. "I am interested, though, in how a woman who is wrapped up in the 'black and white' criminal justice system, can see the world in various shades of gray?"

Her eyebrows raise with her, "*Ah.*" She watches him add more to her glass. "*The law* is black and white, Mr. Stirling, but *life* is various shades of gray. Sometimes the criminal justice system can be *too harsh* with its black and white view, which can also miss the mark for 'justice' altogether; just as not being harsh enough can also miss the mark."

He stares at her in the way she is used to by others. "I'm starting to think some of the other rumors about you are also true..."

"Do I want to know?" She teases, giving him a small 'eek' look. The men softly laugh.

"One rumor says you're incredibly intelligent, *which I've already figured out is true.* There is another rumor that has me curious!"

"Oh?" She asks. "What's that?"

"That you have a *huge* amount of faith." He replies. "Which makes you, *and this*, more intriguing *because* of how involved you are in the criminal justice system."

251

She gives a kind smile. "We all have darkness within us, gentlemen," she looks around the table, "which makes us *all* various shades of gray, although some are a little closer to one than other." They all chuckle and nod. "We *all* could do evil things; however, it's our consciences, our personal moral and ethical codes, that we use to keep ourselves in check and to keep others in check."

He agrees, but adds, "You realize that involvement with us to bring Millicent down *might* require you to do things you never dreamed of doing?"

"With the recent events in my life, *I already have when Millicent had someone kidnap my baby!*" She replies.

There is a moment of silence as they consider her statement and drink from their glasses. Then Rex gets a solemn look and tells her, "I'm so truly sorry for your loss, BriaLynn. *We all are!*" He softly waves his arm, gesturing around the table. "Losing one daughter was hard enough!" He gets teary-eyed, and Bri's eyes fill with tears as she feels *his loss*.

"I get the feeling you have an idea; at least more than most parents would." She replies and sees his reply on his face. She looks around the table at the others and admits, "To be perfectly honest, I've had dreams of revenge..."

"I don't doubt that." Someone replies.

"More recently, when Baby Jacks was born, I was so protective of him, yet Millicent *still* managed to get to my son!"

Rex gives her a compassionate look. "*Everyone* has a price; you just have to find their currency." Bri has a 'that's true' expression on her face.

She points to herself. "I never knew this mama bear-lioness could throw a woman up against the wall, let alone hold a loaded gun to her head, *but I did!*" She scoffs at herself, "That's *not* me!"

Rex tells her, "Like you said, that was the protective mother in you; the 'mama-bear-lioness.' Nothing more, *nothing less*. And as we go down this road with you, I have a feeling *that* is who will be taking on Millicent in the end; to protect those you love and care about most!" The others agree. "One of the things I wanted to talk about while you were here with us, is how we're going to tell Claude Devereaux *who* kidnapped his daughter and nanny. If you

252

prefer, I can take the responsibility, but I tend to think you have a plan for that, too."

"*I do!*" She replies. "I need to meet with Claude, face-to-face, but I'm not exactly sure how to arrange that."

"I can arrange that for you, but you would need to alert your security, particularly McMasters and Mitchell, to allow him to come see you *and* to be able to freely leave." He says and she agrees. He shifts the conversation, "Bri, I think you're fully aware of how evil Millicent is and the extent of her cruelty."

"*Oh, I am!*" She says with her eyebrows raise. "*And* that there is *no* limit!" She also tells them, "I told Lawrence that Millicent needed to be brought down, and I told all three of them, *for now*, they need to stay out of my way. They have agreed to give me that space, *to a point.*"

"Good to know." He replies.

"*However*, I'll have to bring one of them, *or* either McMasters or Mitchell, so I can come and go more easily without them worrying even more about me."

Rex nods. "We understand."

"We have stopped Millicent's access to *most* of her money, and now we need to stop her from replenishing that money. Devonridge is one of the bigger duchies, so it brings in quite a bit of income when she, and her family, still had their titles. She should no longer be receiving those funds from The Duchy, so the only place she can get significant income now is by her illegal auctions, and I'm focusing on stopping that flow from every direction."

"Bri, I'm curious," he studies her to see how much she will open up to him, "why do you want to do this to His Majesty's mother?"

"Millicent is NOT Lawrence's mother!" Bri sees his stunned expression, along with the same reaction from the others; they weren't expecting that answer!. She opens up the photo album on her phone and shows Rex one of pictures of the ancestral tree from The Royal Library. "*Vivian*," she tells him, "King Phillip's Royal Consort, is the mother of Lawrence, Seth, *and* Abagail?! *It's even recorded that way*?!" She hears various whispers of surprise.

Rex whispers in awe. "*I didn't see that coming!*"

"*No one did!* Least of all Lawrence and his siblings." Bri replies. "Millicent killed *everyone* who knew the truth, *except* The King Father, but swore him to secrecy by threatening to kill Abby and Seth."

"*How did* you *find out?!*" Rex innocently asks.

"Let's just say I discovered the truth in something I was reading." Bri says.

He softly chuckles. "Alright, but whenever you're ready, I'd love to hear more details on that!" The others agree.

"That could be what we can discuss over that wine or champagne, when this is all over!" She raises her glass to them and takes a drink.

He raises his back. "*You're on!*" The others raise their glasses and take another drink.

She sets her glass down. "I'm so grateful to you," then she motions the others, "*and everyone involved* for using their," she uses air quotes, "'evil powers' for good, to help us!" She hears them chuckle.

"Well, our group and resources are exactly what it's going to take!" He replies and she nods in agreement. "It's taken a while to put this group together, but these are some of the world's finest men, *and criminals*; *we* still have a *basic* moral compass." She smiles at them. "Those at this table have contacts far and wide. And in the smaller group we put together just for you, there is already the hacker who has been helping you." Bri nods. He goes on, "I also have someone who is part my private investigator and part *business manager*, we'll say, that has been working on this; along with the people integrating into Millicent's world. There are also a few grifters, thieves, arsonists, bomb makers, and so on, who have offered to help, *to help you*, with anything that might come up." Her eyebrows are as high as they'll go, listening to all that.

"We'll *definitely* need the bomb maker for destroying her tunnels, *after* we clean them out! And the PI part of the PI-business manager combo would be useful to help me 'know my enemy' as much as possible!" She says.

"Words to live by!" Rex slightly grins. "However, I think you already know your enemy better than any information a PI could give you at this point."

"*Possibly.*" Bri looks around at everyone saying, "You all have to have a price in mind for financial compensation?"

"Bri, I know, *you know*, my fees are not free and given your intelligence, you've already considered how valuable having an ally with your connections would be to us." He watches her shift uncomfortably. "Please, hear me out."

"*Okay.*" She quietly replies.

"I also know you're not comfortable with wiping out all of our past sins. Besides," he waves his hand around motioning the others, "we don't think it's fair to ask that of you in *any* situation!" He sees her relax. "What *is* fair is what you've already agreed to do; protecting those who are helping you with this goal. What we also need from you, *what we ask of you*, is that you protect the integrity of our group."

"*Meaning?*" She innocently asks.

"Our motto is: *Justice restored!*" He states pointing to the phrase painted at the top of the glass wall that separates the room they are all in, from whatever is on the other side of it. "We can't help those who have been seriously wronged, if The Underground becomes compromised."

"I haven't talked about any of this outside of Lawrence, Jack, David, McMasters, and Mitchell. I doubt they've said anything outside of the six of us, because 'secret' is pretty straightforward; *however*, I will make sure." He hands her a card. She takes it and sees the symbol for The Underground Secret Society. She flips it over and furrows her eyebrows; it's blank. She asks, "What do I do with this?"

Rex knowingly smiles and pulls out a pen with a UV light on the opposite end. He twists that end and shines the light on the back of the card to reveal a phone number.

"Just in case you don't have one these UV lights lying around." He hands her the pen.

"Thank you." She takes it and tucks the card and pen into her back pocket.

"That number is for the date and time of our next meetings. You call the number and type in the code 1676. The recorded message will give you a date and time for our next meeting here."

"Does correcting injustices require kill—. *No*. You know what?" She puts her hand up in a stopping motion telling him, "*Don't* answer that. I have to be careful on what I *knowingly* protect."

"I understand your hesitation. All you need to do is *never* admit to knowing about us and protect those who specifically help you." He says to her.

"*Done*." She replies.

"Alright." He stands up. "We're working *for you*, Your Royal Majesty, towards *our* common goal!" The others nod.

"Thank you." She sweetly smiles. "I appreciate you working *with* me." Everyone smiles and softly laughs. She stands and so do the others. She asks looking at the glass wall, "Does the group usually meet down here?"

He nods. "*The Underground Secret Society* first united back in 1676," she catches the date is also the code to use with the phone number, "but during World War II it fell apart, and by the Cold War it had completely dismantled. In *1996*, I met other people who were using their 'evil powers,'" he grins, "for good, but the law was after them for one reason or another. I started pulling them together so we could fight for worthy causes and, of course, so we could keep us all one step ahead of the law. Since the technology boom and adding hackers to the team, they've helped *tremendously* keeping us *a few* steps ahead!" He watches her carefully when he says, "They assassinate those in power who rule with an iron fist, who cause the deaths of many, or cause hardships for purposes that violate the basic human rights of innocent civilians."

"I understand things like that happen, because people are trying to protect the 'greater good.'" She replies. "In a way, those so-called-leaders, brought it upon themselves."

"True." He agrees.

"I only caution that *sometimes*, those who take over after an assassination can be *far worse* than the one assassinated!" She notes.

"There is truth to that." One of the men replies. "We do try to consider that, which is why we've left certain ones alone until that part of the problem is somehow resolved."

"Come." Rex says. "I'll walk you back."

She shakes the gentlemen's hands and thanks them for any assistance they've provided *and will provide*! Then she starts to walk back the way she came, with Rex walking along beside her.

CHAPTER 31
The Kidnapped Baby & Nanny

Rex and Bri walk beside each other down the long, now dimly lit, corridor. With each step, Bri contemplates whether to ask Rex about his daughter.

Eventually, she summons the courage to start to ask, "How old was your daughter when she..."

He quietly answers, "*Twelve.*"

"Do you mind my asking how she died?" She asks.

As he takes in her question, only their footsteps could be heard softly echoing off the stone walls. "They used her to get to me. I did *everything* they asked, and they *still* slit her throat right in front of me..."

Bri deflates a little. "*Like I'm doing with Claude Devereaux's child; using her to get him to do what I want him to do.*"

"I can see why you might make that connection; *however*, you have no intention of hurting his daughter, *and* you're focused on doing it the least traumatizing way possible for her. So it's *not* the same thing; *not even close.*" He walks them past the stairs she came down saying, "There isn't much out there on how your daughters died."

"They were poisoned..." she swallows to push the lump down that is starting to form, "*by crimson powder.*"

Rex stops in mid stride and his face goes white. "I...*Bri*, I knew someone was planning a hit with crimson powder. I did think it was odd because there are other things more readily available in the US, but I had it smuggled in..." He looks like he might actually be sick.

"Thank you for your honesty." She gives him a kind, understanding look. "If you had known more details, even simply that *any* child would've been hurt with it, would you have tried to stop it?"

His face matches his quick response, "*Hell, yes!*"

"Then that's all that matters." She tells him.

"Thank you for that." He has an appreciative expression. They take several steps in silence before Rex says to her, "You know...our daughters would be about the same age." She looks over and sees his eyes are moist.

They continue to talk about what her girls, and his daughter, were like as they walk along. Eventually, a huge metal door starts to come into view. They stop in front of it; Rex knocks and they hear a faint, muffled voice; the words are in audible. Then the door opens.

"This is another reason I wanted to walk with you..." He says as he motions for her to step inside first.

Bri sees a bright, cheery room with a tiny kitchen in one corner; a crib in the other; then a bed with a couch at the foot of it and an entertainment center across from it. A woman holding a baby stares at Bri, taking in *who* Bri is.

Bri gives her a kind smile. "Do you speak English?" Bri asks and the nanny nods. "By your reaction, you know who I am?" The nanny nods again. "What's your name?"

The nanny stumbles trying to push aside her confusion, looking between Rex and Bri. "Rrro-Rosalee." Then she tips her head towards the infant. "She is Elise."

"Beautiful names." Bri smiles. "May I call you Rosalee?" Rosalee nods. "Rosalee, I can understand that you're scared, because you and Elise were kidnapped." Rosalee nods. Bri explains further, "These people know I don't want either of you harmed." Bri assures her. "The two of you will be taken care of and, if you cooperate during this time, we can discuss what I can do for you after." Rosalee's eyebrows come together, so Bri tells her, "For example, if you feel going back to work for Mr. Devereaux puts your life in danger, we will give you a new life, even with new identities, *anywhere* in the world you want to live."

"With my mama and sister?!" She asks. "Here, or US?!"

"*Absolutely*!" Bri states. "Even if you just want to move somewhere to start a new life, think about where and we can discuss those details later." Rosalee nods. Bri gets serious saying, "I'm only going to say this once, because I don't have the time to play games and you need to know that if you cross me, it will be the *only* time. What I'm going to do is too important, and I *won't* risk my children's lives with a second chance for anyone!"

Rosalee shakes her head. "I stay down here as long as you like, if it means my mama and sister will be safe!"

Bri wonders, "Are your mama and sister in trouble?"

"They will be, if Mr. Devereaux blames me!" Rosalee tells Bri.

Bri turns to Rex, but before she can ask, he looks at his phone to find a number saying, "We'll bring them here *straight away*!"

"Thank you." Bri says to Rex, then asks Rosalee, "If there is anything you need, please, make a list?" Bri points to a pad of paper and a pen on the counter.

Rex tells Bri, "*I'll* personally see to their comfort, Your Royal Majesty. We need to protect you!" Bri nods in understanding. He adds, "We need to get you back to the others."

She walks over to Rosalee. "It was nice meeting you." She pats the baby's back and Elise smiles at Bri. She smiles back saying, "Take care of yourself and this sweet girl. Rex will see to it that your mama and sister join you soon."

Rosalee smiles and says to both of them, "Tank you!"

They wave goodbye and Bri follows Rex out. They talk about their daughters a little bit more as they walk, going back to climb those stairs they walked past earlier.

They approach the door to The Secret Room. "*Odd...*" She stares at the door that is ajar. "I thought we closed this all the way when I left?"

"Mr. Woodsley is anticipating your arrival." Rex tells her as they stop. "I'll keep you posted on our progress and just let me know of any move you make beforehand, so you don't unknowingly walk into something, nor my people."

"Sounds good." She says. "I'll let McMasters and Mitchell know that as well." To his pleasant surprise, she hugs him. "Thank you for all your help!" She is feeling the support she needs in order to do what needs to be done to bring Millicent down.

He hugs her back. "I'll see you soon, BriaLynn."

He holds the door open for her and they say goodbye as they wave. He shuts the door and she hears the clicking sound of the door latching once again. She checks that everything on the shelves is where it's supposed to be; she is also looking for dust out of curiosity...there isn't even a speck! She thinks to herself, '*Impressive, Mister Woodsley...veeery impressive.*' She goes to the door that connects to the passageway to The Library. She opens it and is a little startled to find Mr. Woodsley inside the passageway, he was coming back for her.

He slightly bows his head. "Your Royal Majesty. I trust it all went well with our mutual friend?"

"It did." She replies.

He shuts the door, then leads her back to The Library. When they get to the door he says, "In the future, whenever you come back from The UG and I'm not here, you can check this room for people over here." He shows her a concealed peephole, "This has a great angle for the main aisles of concern. I normally don't allow people in here without your approval; it will always be off limits to all if I know you will be needing privacy to go through the passageway. The Secret Room is for 'The Duchess of Ashbourne,'" he politely gestures her, "and that means only you, me, and Mr. Stirling know about it. I won't mention anything to The Duke of Ashbourne about its location, *unless you specifically tell me to disclose it.*"

"Thank you." Bri gives him a polite little smile. "Maybe The Duke of Ashbourne should know, when the time is right."

"Very well." He acknowledges. "My friend, *Jonathan*, and I have been friends for many years. He sneaks, er, *visits* The Castle every now and then," he winks and she faintly giggles, "to have tea and catch up. I *may have* confided in him about an American-Duchess I *erroneously* wasn't fond of." He has a regretful look. "My friend laughed and said maybe I should give this American-Duchess a chance before I rush to judgement. *Sadly,* I didn't take his advice."

She smiles. "I knew I liked that man."

He softly laughs. "Well, for what it's worth, he respects you a great deal and that isn't easy to get from him."

She shakes her head with her eyebrows raised. "*Nooo, it's not!*"

Bri and Mr. Woodsley walk over to the door of The Library. They step out and Mr. Woodsley shuts off the lights and closes the door. As they walk down the hall, she looks at the paintings and artwork they pass by.

Mr. Woodsley tells her, "I'm to take you to join the family out on the grounds where your helicopter will take everyone up to Newhaven."

"Sounds good." She replies. They make their way through The Castle and she asks, "How are the renovations coming along?"

"The kitchen should be finished next week, and the work on the rooms of The Private Residence just needs your approval for the interior design. His Grace should have them in his email."

"*Perfect!*" Bri smiles wide. "We'll get right on that when we get back!" She is relieved it feels like they are working together. "Mister Woodsley," she sees movement in the corner of her eye and glances at McMasters coming their way, "I'm a preserver of history. I'm supportive of you wanting to save as much of the original castle as possible. Hire the skilled people to restore and reinforce what needs to be, as long as they make it as seamless as possible." She is proud of herself when she sees Mister Woodsley a bit gobsmacked.

"Let me know if there is anything else I can do for you, Your Royal Majesty." Mr. Woodsley bows before he walks away.

McMasters is standing next to her and waits for Mr. Woodsley to get further away before he asks, "How did it go?"

"I think it went very well. *Oh!*" She holds up her finger taking out the pen and business card from her back pocket. She looks around to make sure they are alone; she sees Jack, David, and Lawrence walking up to join them. She lights up the number and calls it. She enters the code 1676 when prompted, then listens for the next date and time. "I need to be back here in two days, for an eight o'clock meeting that night."

"Have you considered Stirling may double-cross you?" McMasters asks. The guys' ears perk up, curious about her answer.

She gives him a faint smirk. "Are you asking if I *know*, know him?" He nods. "I'm very aware he is called, *The Menagerie*, because he has his hand in all types of businesses with all kinds of people at his disposal. He's a sociopath with a small range of morals that can be turned off at any moment to accomplish what he wants done, to benefit himself. How am I doing?"

McMasters chuckles, "Not bad, not bad..."

"Even with that, Rex respects honesty, even if it's brutal." Bri adds. "I can't explain it, but I trust him. He had a lot to lose approaching me and offering his group to help me," she looks at Lawrence, "*to help us*," she looks at everyone, "*all of us*! All he asks in return is for us to protect his people who help us with this common cause; and for me, even all of you, to deny knowing the existence of The Underground Secret Society, and *anyone's* connection to the group." They all nod. "And after today, I guess I trust him more, because we have a rare bond..." She goes quiet, thinking about it.

"What kind of bond, Darling?" Lawrence asks.

"He says there may not be much for 'honor among thieves,' but most criminals will agree children are off limits. Which, on some level, seems of little comfort when we think of the children who are left orphans..." The whole mood of their distrust shifts to more of a 'cautionary trust' when she tells them that. She looks at Lawrence. "*We have to protect all of those who help us—.*"

"I meant what I said to Rex, *and* I'll support you in whatever you promised him, because," he holds her upper arms, "I trust *you* without question."

She tells him, "He knew I would've already figured out that my value to him would be because of my connections, which would be worth *more* than money. *He also knew* I wouldn't be comfortable with that, nor if he were to ask for all his past sins to be pardoned." The guys relax a little more. "He is good with our agreement of protecting those who are helping us bring Millicent down."

"Well, then," David says, "let's get to Newhaven, so we can get you back here in a couple days."

"*Just so we're clear*, I'm going alone again. *They need to trust me; I need* them *to trust me!*" Bri says.

Jack is surprised. "Isn't that what you just did, *and proved?!*"

"Well, yes. *However,*" she watches James, Amy, and Jacks, getting into the helicopter, "I did tell him that as this all gets going, I will have *one* of you five with me. After this next meeting, I'll have one of you with me." She looks at McMasters. "I know you've been after this guy for quite some time when you worked for the FBI, and I'm sure Mitchell isn't too fond of him either;" Mitchell shakes his head, "but right now, I need to know from both of you, that you can put all that aside, because *nothing* matters more right now, than bringing this woman down!"

"Before Emmie and Natty, I might have had an issue." McMasters replies.

"Agreed. It's easier to support you making a deal with someone who isn't *pure* evil and seems to operate with some kind of a small moral code." Mitchell replies with McMasters nodding.

"I appreciate your honesty," Bri says to him, "because it would make sense for you to go with me, since you're with me the most."

Mitchell holds out his fist. "Whatever you need!" She fist-bumps him with a nod and a small, thankful smile.

Everyone else gets settled in the helicopter, except Bri. She and Lawrence stay back to say their goodbyes.

He cups her cheek. "I'll see you in a couple days."

"*Can't wait!*" She smiles sweetly.

They say, 'I love you' and he kisses her as he wraps his arms around her in a hug. He helps her into the helicopter and shuts the door. He waves to everyone before he walks back to The Castle, then makes his way to the front of The Castle where his motorcade is waiting to take him back to The Palace.

At The Manor later that evening, Henry, Maggie, and Carlotta greet them all at the door. Bri giggles as Maggie takes the baby.

"Why do I get the feeling if we left again, you'd never notice, as long as we left the baby here?" Maggie scoffs into a laugh and everyone follows her into The Dining Room, where they discuss the trip to Tuscany while they eat.

After dinner, Amy feeds the baby with the others joining her in The Sitting Room; James and Jack go to The Billiards Room to play a game. They ask David if he wants to join them, but he politely declines; he has a different idea for the evening.

David looks at Bri. "Since it's a beautiful night, how about a walk in the gardens?" He kisses her hand.

Bri softly smiles at him. "I'd love to!"

David and Bri walk out to the gardens. David talks about how swamped he has been for two days, but getting extra sleep did help! They stop on the bridge and talk some more.

He turns to her, partially leaning on the railing. "I'm sorry."

Surprised and confused, she asks, "For what?"

"For doing all the talking!" He grins.

"You know I love listening to you and your voice, My Love..."

She taps a tender kiss to his lips. He hugs her firmly and kisses. Bri tucks her arms inside his suit coat and around his waist, while he slides his hand down to her bum.

She mischievously looks at him. "The things going through *my mind...*" she bites her lower lip.

"*Me, too.*" He kisses her again and they *carefully* make out a little more. "If we keep this up, we'll end up naked *right here!*"

"I'm not complaining, but what's gotten into you?" She grins and they start walking back.

"*You!*" He answers and she slightly rolls her eyes as she smiles. He tells her, "*Always* you, Macushla!" She smiles adoringly at him.

They walk to The Manor and up to their floor holding hands with their fingers laced. David gets a text from Jack as they get to their floor. Bri hears David's breath catch as he looks at his phone.

He looks at her and playfully grins. He hands her his phone and scoops her up, then takes her to their bedroom.

She tells him, "Jack was going to send these to you last night, but I told him not to because with any luck, you were already asleep."

"It *definitely* would've been hard to fall back asleep!" He admits.

"He agreed not to torture you, or Lawrence, and waited to send them."

"And now I can appreciate these pictures more with you here..." He lays her on the bed.

They put loungewear on and go down to The Sitting Room. Henry hands David the baby and David smiles at his son.

"Hi, Jacks!" David holds eye contact with Jacks.

"I'm glad he's back to accepting bottles!" Amy mentions, with James agreeing. "He was *very* mad this morning! We couldn't calm him and we were *so* relieved Jack came to get him to bring him to you!"

"It broke our hearts to have him so upset, *and so worked up,* that he wasn't going to eat. Poor little guy..." James says.

Bri sympathetically smiles. "It took a few minutes to calm him down enough to nurse."

"We're so sorry, Bri!" Amy says to her.

"*You couldn't have predicted that!* I also know you, and you would've tried everything short of buying him off!" Bri tells Amy and they all laugh.

266

"We both were able to relax when he had finally quieted down with you." James says and Amy nods.

Carlotta notes, "Your nervousness might've added to his being upset." Bri reluctantly agrees.

"What do you mean?" James is curious.

Bri answers, "It's a conundrum because he was upset and he could sense how anxious and tense you two felt, *adding* to his frustration. *Yet*, the more he cried, the more stressed you two got, as would anyone, *me included!*"

Carlotta agrees. "In those situations, like the one you had with Jacks, it's best for someone else to come in who is 'fresh.'" She gestures to Jack and Bri.

Maggie adds, "It could also be that he was tired of bottles and just wanted to snuggle with his mama."

"Once he was nursing, he did stop a couple times to cry a little," she looks at Jacks, "to get it *all* out of his system before he was *completely* content."

Jack teases, "*OR* he was giving his mum a little more of a sad tale to get extra attention from her."

Bri giggles. "*Possibly!*"

Jack grins. "I don't blame him! I would, too, but I'd probably make a bigger show of it!"

"Ah, so more of a baby than a baby?!" She winks and he chuckles.

"Well, he wanted his mama!" James looks lovingly at Amy, cupping her cheek. "As it should be!"

Maggie catches their sweet exchange and smiles excitedly, "Are you two going to have a baby?!"

Amy smiles as James says, "She's a few months along!" Carlotta squeals and goes over to congratulate them, then Maggie and Henry go over.

David sees Bri's reaction and whispers, "*You knew?!*" He discreetly tips his head towards Amy and James.

Bri teases with a cheeky grin whispering, "*Whatever do you mean?*" He quietly laughs and kisses her cheek. Once Maggie and Carlotta back away, Bri goes up and hugs them, congratulating them again.

David happily tells them, "I'm so excited for you both!" He looks down at Jacks, "It's hard to believe the love, joy, excitement, with a dash of terrified that comes over you."

"Terrified?" James asks.

"When I found out Bri was pregnant, I was *ecstatic*, but I was surprised to feel a little terrified, too. The terrified feeling was brief, but it came when I realized I was going to be a father, responsible for raising a little human to be a positive influence on those around him, and the world, *and* raise him to be the next heir." David smiles at James and Amy. "I bet watching Amy with Jacks has made you see how incredible she is, and it helps make any terrified feelings go away, *because* she's incredible!" David winks at Amy.

James wraps his arms around Amy. "She's *absolutely* amazing!" He kisses her cheek and Bri smiles, grateful her friend, *her sister*, is adoringly loved by the man *she* loves and adores!

"Bri, how is Ashbourne's renovations coming along?" Carlotta asks, taking the baby from David for some snuggle time.

"Would it be blasphemous to compare Paris and France with Tuscany and Italy, or even The Château with The Villa?" Bri teases. "They're both *fantastic* places!" She teases.

They all talk about Italy and France, but also about Ashbourne Castle and other things. When Bri takes the baby upstairs, Jack and David come with them, so they can have some quality time together. They get Jacks ready for bed, then settle in and watch a movie together.

CHAPTER 32
The Underground's Preparation

In the two days until the next meeting of The Underground Secret Society, Rex Stirling made it his mission to correct a *huge* injustice against the death of two innocent teens that he unknowingly supplied the poison that killed them. He found the hitman responsible and used his execution to send a message that the killing of children will *not* be tolerated! He also wants to make the more powerful criminals nervous about having anything to do with Millicent, or her 'business.' Then he sends Millicent a present.

When Millicent receives the package, she sees it's from Rex and gets excited. She has several thoughts going through her mind about what could be inside: is it a priceless piece of art, or jewelry... Her mind is swirling as she sits the box on the table right there in the foyer of Devonridge Hall; the house her family has been living in for quite some time.

She opens the package like a teenager would, with excited anticipation. She quickly removes all the tissue paper and exhales, deflating in disappointment. She is eye-to-eye with the head of the hitman she had hired to kill BriaLynn's daughters.

Unphased at the grotesqueness of it, she hands Tristan the piece of tissue paper she is holding; saying in a dull tone as she waves her other hand towards the opened box, "Get rid of this of rubbish."

Curious, Tristan looks in the box and is disgusted by what he sees. He quickly closes the box and carries the box outside. He hands it to the first person he sees, Donovan, and tells him to get rid of it.

Millicent went to her office to tend to the things she needs, in order to get ready for the next auction. She needs *everything* lined up, so she can bring in the revenue she *desperately* needs. There are 'particular items' to meet specific requests. All of them will need to be carefully brought into the port.

Bri is back at Ashbourne Castle early that afternoon and it is almost time for the next meeting of The Underground Secret Society. She is walking through the same secret passageway corridors she had taken a couple days ago. She walks a little more confidently since she has already done this.

She gets to the end, walking into the large room that was divided by a glass wall, only this time she can see the room on the other side of the glass wall. There are two large glass double doors in the center that are now open. Inside the room, one wall is covered with large screen televisions on the top half with a row of computers on long tables below them with people at those stations. There are screens on the adjacent wall showing stock markets from around the world and world satellite maps with things being tracked, but she doesn't know what. Rex walks over to her and interrupts her observations of the room.

"Your Royal Majesty!" Rex beams holding out his hands for hers and she puts her hands in his.

Bri smiles. "Please, it's just Bri when we're in private." She looks at those with him, "That goes for everyone." They smile in acknowledgment.

"BriaLynn, let me introduce you to someone who has already been helping you in a big way." Rex gestures to, "This is Vincent Cooper, my private investigator and business manager I told you about." Bri shakes his hand. Hazel comes over and Rex says, "Here is the best hacker in the world, WebKingMaster,."

"She has been living up to her reputation!" Bri happily tells them. "And I love the hacker name and how it makes people assume it's a man behind it!"

Hazel grins. *"My thoughts exactly!* I'm glad to be helping end this evil woman's reign of terror!" She says with disdain for Millicent.

"Everyone here," Rex gestures the room, "is helping behind the scenes in one way or another!"

"This is all so fantastic!" Bri tells Rex. "I knew you were busy getting everything together, but this is...*WOW!"*

"And last, but not least, is a personal trainer to train you in the martial arts." He puts a hand on the woman's upper back. "Meet Li Chang." Rex explains, "Li and I chatted, and we thought that if you didn't know self-defense, you probably should, as a *necessary* precaution."

"I think that's a great idea!" Bri shakes Li's hand. "Thank you!" She tells everyone, "Thank you all!"

Rex also mentions, "Coop will know who to contact as things go along and he'll have inside information with my lead guy inside Millicent's circle who has carefully and steadily spent this time working his way into Millicent's tight inner circle." Bri's eyebrows go up as she wonders how he managed that! Rex sees her expression.

"Well, he must be good, or he would dead." Bri states with everyone nodding. She gets the conversation back on track saying, "Maybe we can videoconference from Newhaven for our next meeting and we can all stay in the loop?"

"I think we can pull that off." Rex says, looking at Hazel who agrees.

"It will be easy to say Li is my personal trainer after having a baby. We can have Hazel disguised as IT for The Newhaven Heirloom Wool Farm and Textile Mill, along with The New Beginnings Foundation. As for Mr. Cooper..." she thinks.

"Please, call me 'Coop.'" He says.

She smiles. "Well, *Coop*, if you're willing to trust McMasters and Mitchell, they could work you into their fold somewhere which might work the best for everyone since you will have a connection to Rex's top inside guy." They sit down at the same table that she sat at a couple days earlier. "Sometimes the best hiding places are in plain sight. If I have McMasters keep you close to him and Mitchell, it may be better so you're at the center of a lot of things with them, and you can be a connection with the group Rex has on the inside. *Plus*, he would be able to help *when* something happens to me." They all look at her and she states, "It's inevitable."

"*Unfortunately.*" Rex reluctantly agrees.

Cooper tells her, "Well, we are tracking her and her people's movements, as well as their acquisitions and shipments for her upcoming auctions."

Bri comments, "These meetings will need to be added to my schedule if I'm to have the time blocked off to attend them. We should come up with a group name, like 'Think Tank,' or whatever, so no one would really question it."

"That's a good idea." Rex says. "People will assume you're meeting with a 'Think Tank' because of your work."

"If we're in agreement, let's just put a group of our phone numbers in our contacts under 'Think Tank.' We can touch base in a week, give or take?" She turns to Li, "If you come to Newhaven, there's a gym at The Manor and a small one at The Cottage House, plus a gym at The Palace and now one here at Ashbourne, so you can travel around with me and we can start training right away!"

"I can definitely do that!" Li smiles.

"Wonderful! If you can give me your address, I can have McMasters send for you in a couple of days to give you time to pack without being in a rush?" Li writes her address down and hands it to Bri.

They wrap up the meeting and Rex wants her to walk with him, out the back way so she knows every way into The Castle. They walk down a not-too-long corridor that ends in the woods on the edge of The Estate where there is a car waiting for him. He opens the back door for her and she slides in, then he gets in.

As the car pulls away and down a service road, he tells her, "Claude Devereaux will be paying you a visit this evening yet."

Bri's eyebrows go up and she takes a deep breath. "Is this the preverbal 'lion's den,' or 'directly into the fire,' *maybe both*?"

"Well, he isn't as invested as a 'mama bear-lioness.'" He states. "All he knows is that you have information about the kidnapping."

"Where will this meeting take place?" She asks.

"I told him Ashbourne Castle is expecting Her Royal Majesty this evening." He sees her nervousness. "I made it clear that if he hurts you, I will make it my personal mission to destroy him and he will be forced to live the remainder of his days, reduced to living under a bridge somewhere."

Bri gives him a faint 'eek' look, then looks at her phone. "I need to send a quick text to McMasters."

"He and I have already been in contact about that." Rex replies and she nods.

They pull into the driveway of Ashbourne Castle and right up to the front doors. Mitchell opens the back door and Bri gets out; she turns back to Rex.

He kindly smiles. "Channel that 'force of nature' you can be and stand your ground with him. He will respect that more than anything else." He tips his head in a 'hello' to Mitchell, who returns one back to Rex.

"*Oh*! Do you think you could get me floor plans, or pictures, *something* of this Devonridge Manor?" She asks.

"I could. Is this part of your 'getting to know your enemy?'" He asks and she nods. "Then I think it would also be a good idea to sneak you over there." He sees the confused look on her face. "Devonridge Manor is falling apart. There is another large house called 'Devonridge Hall,' on the other side of The Estate, where Millicent and her family actually live; I'll get you those floor plans as well."

"That makes sense." She recalls, "I've read that a lot of these old estates have a manor house, but then various other houses scattered around an estate's property."

"I've been meaning to get out there with Cooper, to see if there still is a 'back door,' of sorts, to get into The Tunnels." He tells her. "Let me see what I can put together before you go back to Newhaven. Do you have anything scheduled in the next few days that you can't get out of?"

"I don't think so." She glances through her calendar on her phone to be sure. "If you plan it, I'll make it work!"

"Fantastic! I'll be in touch." He waves and they say goodbye.

She turns to go inside with Mitchell, as Rex's car pulls away. McMasters stepping outside the doors to meet up with them. Bri tells them about the meeting, then explains, "I have someone who will personally train me in self-defense and in martial arts, who will need picked up in a couple days to stay at The Manor for a while and travel with us." She hands him the address.

"Great idea!" McMasters says, agreeing with Rex's idea. He tucks the address in his pocket as he walks up the stairs and into The Castle with them.

CHAPTER 33
Claude Devereaux

Inside Ashbourne Castle, Mr. Woodsley has been anxiously waiting for The Princess Imperial's return. When she walks in, he bows as he greets her, "Your Royal Majesty."

"Mr. Woodsley." She acknowledges him, then asks, "Would you take me to 'The Royal Offices,' or whatever it's called here? I'm expecting a visitor."

"Follow me, Your Royal Majesty." He leads her down the hall, not far from the main doors; McMasters has Mitchell go with them.

They walk up to the door of the office, and he has her walk in first. She wasn't sure if Claude Devereaux would be there, but then again, Mr. Woodsley would have warned her.

"Your Royal Majesty, this is 'The Office of The Duchess of Ashbourne,' but now it's," he gestures the plaque next to the door, "The Office of The Princess Imperial, The Grand Duchess of Newhaven, *and* The Duchess of Ashbourne." Bri sweetly smiles as she walks into the room.

The Office of The Princess Imperial isn't as lavish as The Official Royal Offices at The Palace, which is fine with her. However, there are a few things here and there to give it a royal feel. There are only two large, priceless paintings on the walls: one that is on the wall opposite the desk and the other painting is on the wall perpendicular to the desk, which across from the two sets of tall balcony doors. Behind the desk is a large mirror above a fireplace, flanked by built in bookshelves full of books on each side of it. There is a deep brown leather couch that sits between the two sets of balcony doors. There is a smaller desk sitting in the corner across from the main desk and straight across from the office door.

Bri notices the desk is being used and Mr. Woodsley sees her looking at the desk. "My apologies that I haven't moved my desk yet. I will see to it right away, Your Royal Majesty."

"It's fine, Mr. Woodsley. I don't mind if you use this office while I'm not here." Bri tells him.

Mr. Woodsley gives her an appreciative look. "Thank you, Ma'am."

The large desk has carvings of the Ashbourne 'A' on the two front corners. There are two cushioned chairs in front of the desk, with the desk chair having a softer leather and it is extremely comfortable when she sits in it. She sees the desk is varnished and very shiny with a thick layer of glass to protect the top of the desk.

"Is there anything you need, Ma'am?" Mr. Woodsley asks. "Like certain pens or notepads? Anything?"

"This is great! Thank you!" She replies. "If I think of anything, I'll let you know."

"I'll show Mr. Devereaux to your office when he arrives." He states, then sees himself out. Bri figured Mr. Woodsley knew who was coming, but he just confirmed it.

Bri is deep into her work when Mr. Woodsley knocks twice. There is a pause before he opens the door and enters with Mr. Devereaux; Mitchell stays close to the door. Bri stands when she sees Claude enter with Mr. Woodsley.

Claude says with a bit of forced cordialness, "*Your Royal Majesty.*"

"Mr. Devereaux," Bri gestures the chairs in front of her desk, "please, have a seat."

"I'll stand, thank you." He plainly replies. He turns his head and looks at the floor as he watches Mr. Woodsley leave, shutting the door behind him in his peripheral view. He turns back to Bri, "Let's cut the niceties and talk about what you know about my kidnapped daughter and her nanny."

"*I* have your daughter and nanny, Mr. Devereaux." She tells him and watches his eyes narrow in anger and his jaw starts clenching.

He struggles to keep his voice calm, "If you were *anyone* else, I'd kill you right where you stand."

Bri rolls her eyes a bit and plainly states, "I'm sure you would." His eyebrow goes up. "Now," she lowers herself into her chair, "can we stop with the posturing?" She gestures to the chair again. "If you were to kill me now, it wouldn't gain you anything, other than an enemy, or several, who would make it *their mission* to kill *you*."

"Then *what* do you want?" He snips, *but* he does sit down in the chair across from her.

"It's simple." She tells him and he studies her. "Stay out of my way when it comes to Millicent." Then she makes it clear, "Do *not* buy anything from her. Do *not* invest in anything with her. Do *not* give her any money for *any* reason. In short, stay out of anything, *and everything*, that involves her."

"Or you'll what? *You'll kill my daughter*?!" He asks with disgust.

"*Oh, don't be ridiculous!*" She scoffs, catching him off guard. "I could *never* hurt a child." She sees his face start to soften.

Then his eyebrows come together as it occurs to him, "Pardon me for saying, Ma'am, but you're not very good at negotiating something like this."

"The life of any child is not up for negotiation where I'm concerned, Mr. Devereaux. I have *no* intentions of hurting *any* child, no matter who their parents are. *I'm not a monster!*" She replies and he shakes his head a bit in agreement. "I have your daughter *just* for your attention *and* for you to have an excuse, *if you need one*, to give Millicent when you have to tell her 'no' for *everything* she asks of you. We both know she doesn't take any kind of rejection well, but she *might* understand if your daughter has been kidnapped, even if she won't really care what happens to her." She adds, "*However*, you *can't* tell her *I* have your child."

"And if I do help her, or get in your way?" He asks.

"Simple." Bri leans forward giving him a stone-cold, serious look saying, "I'll take you down *before* her." He studies her seriousness. She also tells him, "I prefer Millicent continuing to underestimate me; although, I don't want you to. Millicent already killed my daughters and my father-in-law; *and* she kidnapped my son after he was born. The nurse who helped with that was dead before she left the hospital." He is surprised by that. He watches her stand up. "While I *refuse* to hurt a child, Mr. Devereaux, trust me when I say

277

this: I *won't* think twice to kill you myself the very first time you get in my way." Claude feels the chills go down his spine. Bri tells him, "Millicent *needs* to go down, and that time is *fast* approaching. The question for you, Mr. Devereaux, is," she places her hands on the table to lean towards him again, "do you want to go down with her, or would you rather enjoy being in a world without her in it; perhaps improving your own businesses?"

He leans back as he continues to study her, crossing his leg with his ankle resting on the other knee. "Rex warned me about you." Her eyebrow raises. "He said you were one of the most intelligent women he has ever met! He also said a determined mother protecting her children has the strength of ten armies." He looks her up and down as she stands up straight again. He says, "I tend to agree; you seem to be a force all your own!" He takes a deep a breath and sits up straight. "If you promise to continue to take care of my daughter, I'll stay out of your way. I'll even promise not to distract you with trying to get her back." She is a little surprised. He gives her a small faint smile. "I keep my daughter separated from me, so she can't be used against me. Her being with you, Your Royal Majesty, only makes her safer from *my* enemies."

"That's sad." Bri quietly says.

"I can see why you would think that being as fierce of a protector of children as you are." He replies. "Look at it this way, who would ever think you, of all people, would kidnap a child, let alone kidnap *my* child?"

"*True.*" She admits.

He stands up. "Will you promise me something?"

"It depends." Bri honestly answers.

He gives her an understanding look. "Promise me when Millicent goes down, she won't be going to jail to wait for her execution. Basically, so some twit, or group of idiots, won't be able to break her out beforehand."

"I don't plan on her getting to a jail cell at all." She tells him.

He nods and holds his hand out. "It's a deal, Your Royal Majesty."

She shakes his hand. "Then I have your word you will leave them alone if I were to move them to a more *comfortable* residence?" He understands she is hinting at one of her residences.

"Like I said, she is safest with you, because no one would ever fathom *you* have *my* daughter." She lightly nods. He goes to turn to leave, but stops. "If you need anything, for Elise and her nanny, or taking Millicent down, *anything at all*, please don't hesitate to reach out. Rex can find me but," he pulls out a card with a phone number, "but this is my personal number."

"Thank you." She takes the card, and he watches her slide it into the pocket of her skirt.

They go to the door and he opens it. He sees Mitchell, but it doesn't faze him since he knows he is able to leave. He turns back to Bri. "I'm not familiar with how fertility stuff works, but rumor has it, Millicent is looking for buyers of what I'm guessing are your eggs." Bri's mouth drops, while Mitchell keeps a poker face. "If she is at this point, it probably means she already has a place medically set-up to take them from you. My guess is that place would be in, or near, The Tunnels, since they are referred to in their code within her circle as 'Knox.'" He reads Bri's questioning look and explains, "She likes to think The Tunnels are locked up and secured, virtually impenetrable, like the American 'Fort Knox.' *They're not*. However, it will take someone on the inside to help navigate the security."

"Thank you for the warning." She tells him and he nods.

Bri keeps to herself that removing a woman's eggs for fertility reasons isn't as easy as going in and taking them out. She walks Claude out, with Mitchell right behind them.

Claude bows to her this time. "Your Royal Majesty." Then they say goodbye. He turns and walks out of the front door where his car is waiting for him.

When Claude is in his car, Mitchell says with disappointment, "It's hard to let him leave, knowing the good people he's responsible for killing, and *how* he killed them."

"Thank you for doing it anyway." Bri turns to him with an appreciative look.

He shakes his head. "I get it. I'm just not comfortable about it."

"If it helps, he's not being pardoned for his past crimes, nor is Mr. Stirling and the others." Bri tells him.

"It does." He politely replies.

"Good. Now," she brings up her phone to text Rex what she tells Mitchell, "I want to arrange James and Amy to come down and get to know Elise, so they can eventually take her, along with the nanny and her family, up to Newhaven to live more comfortably."

"*Seriously?*" Mitchell is alarmed.

"There's one thing he is that Millicent could *never* be?" Mitchell furrows his eyebrows as he considers what that could be. She says, "A parent. He is concerned for his daughter's safety, and he knows she is actually safer *with me*, because almost no one knows of Elise and those who do wouldn't think to look for her with us."

"I'll give him that." He says, as they walk back to her office so she can pack up her things to leave.

On the way over to The Palace, Rex texts back that he will make arrangements to have James and Amy brought in, but she should prepare them that they will be blindfolded. Bri says she will discuss it with them, then she will get back with him.

280

CHAPTER 34
A Promise to Keep

At The Palace, Lawrence is waiting for Bri in The Royal Chambers where they can talk privately. He is on the couch playing with Jacks, who is smiling at him. Bri barely gets inside the room when Jacks gets fussy. Bri walks over and sits next to them, then she lovingly smiles at Jacks as she takes him. Lawrence waits for her to get comfortable feeding Jacks before he asks her any questions.

"How did it go?" He asks.

"Funny," she grins, "I was about to ask you the same thing."

"*He*," Lawrence leans in and caresses Jacks' arm with his fingers, "was *such* a happy baby. The only time he fussed was when he saw his mum."

Bri looks at Jacks. "I like hearing my sweet baby was a happy boy while I was gone!" Jacks pauses nursing long enough to smile at her, then starts nursing again. She looks at Lawrence and kisses him. "I have a 'Think Tank' and I also have a personal trainer who will be picked up in couple days to stay with us for a while."

"Personal trainer?" He asks.

"Rex thought it would be a good idea for me to learn some self-defense, and some martial arts, to have a way to possibly protect myself, should the need arise." Bri replies.

"I love the idea, but I thought with your power though..." Lawrence starts to think out loud.

"I'm still learning how it works, and to what extent, because timing is an issue when someone has to make a choice *first*, *before* I can use my power to counteract it. Training with Li means I might be able to buy me some time, until I figure something out."

"How much does Stirling know?" He asks.

"About my power?" She asks for clarification and he nods. "Nothing. I was tempted to when we talked about the death of his own daughter, but I couldn't and when that happens——."

"The Spirit is keeping you from saying anything." Lawrence finishes her sentence, remembering her saying something about that before.

"Right. I was thinking that maybe after all this is done, I can thank him by bringing his daughter's spirit to him?"

"I'd think *that* would be an *ultimate* thank you!" He tenderly smiles at her.

They snuggle in and enjoy just being together for a little bit. When Jacks finishes eating, Lawrence burps him and changes his diaper before rocking him back to sleep. He is about to put the baby in the bassinet when Bri comes over; she gently kisses the baby's head. After Lawrence lays him down, she wraps her arms around him and he hugs her back.

She smiles. "It's almost time for us to start trying. Are you ready?"

He turns to cup her cheek with one hand, "Is it too soon? I mean," he looks at Jacks, "he just got here, then to add another right away..."

"Lawrence, it will still be ten months, at the earliest, before we would have another baby, assuming I would get pregnant right away." She says.

"We can wait a bit yet." He looks back at Jacks.

"But we need to start trying in October." She replies.

He steps back from her and frowns. "If I had something like that—like we need to fulfill a contract, *you'd*——?!" He stops himself from getting louder and waking Jacks.

The gravity of what she said hits her, and she is horrified. "Lawrence——."

"*Don't.*" He puts his hand up in a stopping motion. "Let's just go to bed." He turns and walks around to his side of the bed, turning out his light and the room goes dark.

Bri stands there, feeling awful...she isn't sure how to explain it without making it worse. She watches Jacks sleep for some time and when she hears the steady breathing of Lawrence sleeping, she goes and tries to sleep on the couch, but she can't.

After Bri feeds Jacks in the middle of the night, she lays back down on the couch and is able to doze off. When she wakes up again, Lawrence is down at the gym. She asks McMasters to have the helicopter ready for Newhaven, but Lawrence already told him not to take her home a day early if she asked.

"Fine. Take me to Ashbourne." Bri tells McMasters.

"No." Lawrence says, walking up behind her.

McMasters turns and walks away. Lawrence motions for Bri to walk back into The Royal Chambers and he follows her.

He barely gets the door shut when Bri blurts out, "I'm sorry I hurt your feelings. I know it seems heartless to say, but I made a promise to the people that after Jacks was born and I was healthy, our two years would start! That time is now and you know I don't make promises I don't intend to keep!"

His didn't expect his heart to squeeze and *he* feels bad. "I'm sorry I didn't think about *why* you might have felt the way you did. Now I wish there wasn't a contract with any date."

"Oh, I don't know," she gets closer to him, "all these contracts weaved us all together." She gets a faint playful look on her face. "How about we forget the word 'contract' and enjoy our time together?"

He gets a smoldering look, "I accept your challenge, My Queen..."

Lying in bed together, Lawrence holds her close and asks, "Tell me about your meetings you had yesterday."

"What meetings?" She teases.

"*Brrriii...*" he lifts her chin. "I agreed to not get in your way, but I meant what I said when I want to be by your side. I supported you going to these meetings by yourself, but I draw the line at you keeping me out of the loop."

"I'm only teasing, Ace." She replies. "I want you all to know so you can navigate accordingly. In fact, Rex knows I'll be keeping the three of you, McMasters, and Mitchell in the loop. Besides, how can you help cover for their not-so-legal ways of helping us, if you're kept in the dark?"

"*True.*" He says.

She continues, "I wanted to be up front and I don't want to lie to them, because they *are* helping us; we all need to count on each other. Plus, people say Rex is ruthless and heartless, but I don't think that's *entirely* the case."

"I tend to agree; however, I *am* curious as to why you think that?" He asks.

She shrugs a bit. "Just a feeling."

"Promise me you'll be careful and you'll at least consider anything McMasters, or Mitchell, tell you." He pleads.

"Ace, I'll consider what any of you say to me, *as long as* you trust me if I have to do something differently."

"Deal." He listens to her explain the meeting. He suggests, "When you meet for this 'Think-Tank,' I want to be a part of those, too, to hear about what's going on, and maybe help bounce some ideas around as well."

"I planned on that, too. I expect you three, with McMasters and Mitchell, to be a part of it all, because it saves me having to relay it all back to any of you, and it would be difficult to remember everything that is discussed."

"Sounds good." He then asks, "Now, about Claude Devereaux?"

"Are you asking if I have another enemy to worry about?" She gives him a look and he nods. "No. I don't. *In fact*, he offered his help if we needed it."

He stares in amazement. "How do you do it?!"

"What do you mean?"

"How do you win people over so easily?" He asks.

"Well, Millicent would be proof that *isn't* always the case; even Katie." She notes. "Plus, there are people in DC who weren't won over by me. However, with Mr. Devereaux, I told him his daughter is safe; I just need him to stay out of everything that involved Millicent; to say 'no' to anything she asks. He can use that his daughter has been kidnapped for an excuse."

Lawrence is curious. "What does he think will happen if he doesn't?"

"Nothing. His daughter will be safe either way." She watches his eyebrow raise and she giggles. "He said the same thing you're thinking! And I said that I wasn't a monster, I could *never* hurt a child! And he respected that."

"Probably more so than the threat." Lawrence replies.

"Probably." She tells him. "He said that he wouldn't even distract us by trying to get her back, because, in the end, she is safer with us. I've talked with James and Amy about coming down to London and getting to know Elise; they can stay at Ashbourne while they do. I want Elise to be comfortable with them, eventually all of us, and have her stay at The Manor as part of the family. They agreed to Rex's terms, which is that they have to be blindfolded to keep the location a secret."

He has a caring look. "Have you thought about when this is all over and we have to give Elise back?"

"It has crossed my mind, and I've talked to Amy about it. We both know it will be difficult, but it's a lot better for her than being stuck inside some room all day, every day." Bri looks down at Jacks.

"Absolutely!" Lawrence agrees. "I think this is all *fantastic*! Now..." he gives her a mischievous grin, "let's practice some more..." She giggles, then kisses him fiercely.

CHAPTER 35
An Unexpected Trip

The following week, The Princess Imperial is back in London for a State Dinner at The Palace with King Lawrence. David and Jack stayed back in Newhaven with the baby for the night, but they will go to London in the morning. Bri was reluctant to go to London without Jacks, but she knows it's healthy for both of them. It's also good for David and Jack to have bonding time with the baby without her there.

Bri is wearing a white dress with The Sapphire-Heart Necklace Lawrence made with the matching earrings. The blue of the sapphires matched the blue sashes she and Lawrence are wearing, and she has on The Diamond-Heart Tiara for the finishing touch.

He watches her walk down the stairs. "You are breathtaking as always, *My* Queen!" He takes her hands and holds them out for a better look.

"*You* are somehow more incredibly handsome than ever!" She winks and he chuckles. "I think we'll be a showstopper, My Handsome King!"

"*You already are!*" He kisses the back of her hand as she lovingly smiles at him.

They meet up with Phillip, Abby, Seth, and Genevieve, and they all walk to The State Dinner together. They arrive where The Royal Photographer has set up; Bri and Lawrence pose for a picture together. Then Phillip asks for a picture with all of them together.

The King and Queen are seated as protocol calls for, at each end of a very long table. Bri is seated to Lawrence's right, at The King's request, and he has Ambassador Lombardi next to Bri, with Callista seated next to her husband. Across from Bri is an Arabian Sultan, and the wife he brought with him is next to him; she is *very* quiet. It is almost impossible to carry on a conversation with her, yet Callista is doing wonderfully with her.

As everyone finishes dessert, there is an orchestra that begins to play. The Ambassador stands and asks Bri to dance. Bri smiles as she stands, glancing at Lawrence and he gives her a slight nod. He knows it would be rude for her to refuse, and he is getting better at accepting their agreement; that she will only dance with people she knows. It helps that he knows the history of her friendship with the Ambassador.

Out on the dance floor, Bri and the Ambassador waltz. Lawrence has asked Callista to dance, and they are out on the dance floor together. Bri and the Ambassador are conversing and he offers his condolences for Emmie and Natty; they also talk about his 'new life' with Callista, along with their twins, a boy and a girl.

After the waltz, Lawrence asks Bri, "May I have this dance, Darling?"

"I can't refuse My King!" She grins as she takes his hand.

He pulls her close, wrapping an arm around her waist and holding her other hand close to his heart. "You're so beautiful, My Queen! And everything you're wearing only highlights that beauty..." He sweetly kisses her.

She says with her hot breath on his ear, "I'm hoping this part of our evening is almost over..." he pulls back and he sees her playful look as she tells him, "the things going through my mind..."

He replies, "I'm tempted to take you to a private room very few people actually know about."

"I'd love to see it!" She bites her lower lip.

He shakes his head. "You wouldn't want to go there," he reluctantly says, "I've taken other women back there."

She leans in and whispers, "*Lawrence, it's okay so long as I'm the only one you take back there now.*" She feels him hug her a little closer.

"I'll take you there to show you, but you look too exquisite to do anything in a room that—."

"If you're uncomfortable, we can skip it *this time.*" She offers and he is relieved. "*However,*" she adds, "I want you to take me there some time, so we can work through whatever has you feeling uncomfortable with that room."

He shakes his head. "It's more like I've outgrown it."

She sweetly smiles. "I can understand that, but what if we updated it and made it ours?"

"*That* sounds like a *much* better idea!" He tells her.

The song ends and they walk off the dance floor. The Duke and Duchess of Wellington are the first people Bri and Lawrence come to and they talk with them for a bit.

"Your Royal Majesty, would you honor an old man with a twirl or two on the dance floor." Duke Wellington happily asks.

She is about to refuse him because they have no history, but Lawrence asks, "Duchess, would you do *me* the honor of this dance?" He asks The Duchess, who gets a happy smile across her face and accepts.

Bri smiles and looks at Lawrence, who gives her the slightest of nods. Bri loops her arm in The Duke's arm, and they walk out to the dance floor. When the dance ends, the four of them join a small group for a discussion. More and more people have started to notice how well Bri compliments Lawrence, the way a queen would for a king. She shined, but she doesn't outshine him; she strengthens him.

It's customary for The King and Queen to leave right before the last dance. Lawrence thanks everyone for coming, then he purposely walks over to Bri and they leave as the last dance begins; so does Gen and Seth.

Lawrence and Bri made their way to The Royal Apartment. Up in The Royal Chambers, they get ready for bed. Bri sits at her vanity table and takes off her jewelry. She stares at her tiara, in a tired, exhausted gaze; she jumps a little when Lawrence comes up and kisses her cheek.

"Sorry, Darling." Lawrence softly says to her.

She takes a deep breath and says on her exhale, "I'm just tired and staring off into space."

He holds out his hand. "Let's get you to bed then."

She puts her hand in his with a playful grin and stands up. "Don't you mean, 'Let's get *us* to bed?!'"

He reaches down and scoops her up. He walks over to their bed and he gently lays her down...

The next morning, Bri's phone chimes. Jack texted a picture showing David and Jacks getting into the helicopter in front of him.

> Bri: "Good morning! Can't wait to see my baby! Er, the three of you very soon! (adds a winking face and a kiss)"

"Everything alright?" Lawrence asks.

She needs to go to the bathroom. "Here!" She tosses her phone to him. "I'll be right back." He sits up and looks at the picture.

He walks into the bathroom. "We're all meeting at Ashbourne Castle when they get to London to see how your restorations are coming along!"

"I'm *super* excited about them! I *really* want to impress Mr. Woodsley!" She tells him.

He chuckles. "Didn't you both say there was a 'clean slate?'"

"Yeah, but some of these British men can be *pretty tough* to crack!" She teases.

He grins. "It's easier when it's done by a beautiful woman."

"IF that's their preference!" She notes.

"Touché!" Lawrence concedes and she lightly giggles.

They have gotten dressed for the day. "Okay, Ace, take me to my baby!"

He softly laughs and takes her hand. They make their way outside where The Royal Helicopter is waiting for them. They board the helicopter and make the short flight to The Ashbourne Estate, arriving before the others. Bri walks the grounds with Lawrence while they wait. When they hear another helicopter, they rightfully assume it's the one carrying Jack, David, and Jacks.

Lawrence and Bri walk over as The Helicopter as it lands. When the doors open, she hears Jacks crying. David climbs out first and Jack hands him the baby. Bri quickly kisses David, then Jack.

She sees Jacks' sad little face. "Oh, Love..." she takes him, "*come here!*" She kisses his sweet face, then holds him to comfort him.

"What's wrong, Buddy?" Lawrence asks looking at Jacks' incredibly sad little face. Jacks' lower lip sticks out as far as it'll go, his cheeks are wet, and huge tears sit at the bottom of his eyes. "That's a heartbreaker look!"

Bri snuggles Jacks a little more and hears him take a deep shaky breath as he relaxes. They start walking towards The Castle.

"He saw his mama walking towards us and that was it!" David tells her.

"Well, I'm glad he wasn't like this the whole trip!" She says. "*That would've been miserable for everyone!*" Bri and Lawrence greet the pilots, Chad and Caroline, getting off the helicopter.

As they all walk towards The Castle, Mr. Woodsley and the staff greet them when they first walk in. Mr. Woodsley has a car waiting for Chad and Caroline; he has someone take them to it.

Lawrence is able to get Jacks to come to him and they snuggle with his soft blanket. Mr. Woodsley takes them on a tour, showing them the work that has been completed and discussing what is in process, along with what projects are coming next.

Mr. Woodsley asks, "Your Royal Majesty, in your research so far, have you come across the castle's monogram and seal?"

"I have! And I've seen it around. The one I see most is the lion's head on a bronze shield, or the 'A' in various places." She replies.

 "Most royals dress up their residence's monogram to make it more personal to them." Mr. Woodsley explains. "Since this is to be your official London residence, personalizing for 'Her Royal Majesty' would be a nice touch." She picks up on a faint bit of excitement from him.

David leans in and whispers, *"Keep in mind what you already know about elevating a name, house, or family."*

Bri turns to Mr. Woodsley. "I need you to believe me when I say that I love Ashbourne! However, I won't consider this castle mine, but the citizens of Ashbourne and of what would've been The Duchy of Woodsley." She sees The King smile a little. "I also understand that when a situation calls for an elevation of some kind, it's tradition for a person, *and a family*, to benefit from it. So, if you can come up with something that elevates while keeping with the simplicity of the feel of Ashbourne Castle, then I would love to see it! Things that are permanently part of The Castle, are to be maintained *as they are*, to be *kept as is*."

"If you'll permit me," Mr. Woodsley pulls out a paper, "this is what His Grace and I were thinking about. We thought this could go on the main front doors and back doors." He hands it to her.

 She glances at Jack, who has a slight grin on his face as she takes the paper from Mr. Woodsley. She sees the same monogram, with the gold lions, Lawrence has used for various things.

"I think it's a start, but it doesn't feel quite right." She says.

Mr. Woodsley moves closer to her as he picks up his tablet and makes some quick taps and movements, then hands her his tablet asking, "How about something like one of these?"

 She flips through and says, "Now this one could work..." It's the double-phoenix on a bronze shield and a gold crown on top, with Ashbourne on the bottom ribbon.

Mr. Woodsley starts to say, "We can change the one above the gate—."

"Wait." She stops him to clarify, "Is it permanently attached to the gate?" He nods and she thinks back... "I don't recall that one at the moment."

291

Mr. Woodsley takes his tablet and brings up a picture of it. He hands it to her saying, "It could use an update."

Bri takes the tablet and looks at it closely. "Oh..."

 She stares at two gold lions holding a shield. There is a beehive on top of a knight's head gear that is on top of a gold crown that sits on the shield. All of which holds meaning, but what moves her the most is the winged lion *on* the shield, bowing under the weight of the great responsibility of The Crown.

"What are you thinking?" Lawrence asks.

"I like the symbolism of this and I don't think we should change it. There *is* a great weight that comes from the responsibility of The Crown, even a dukedom, and it should be respected by everyone, *including* The Monarchy and those who serve The King." She hands the tablet back to Mr. Woodsley, who is impressed by her once again. "Please don't change that one. As for the new one you created, let's put the new ones in a few places around The Castle, while keeping the simplicity of Ashbourne Castle, which was the whole point of its original construction." Mr. Woodsley nods in understanding and agreement.

Jacks gets fussy and the guys get their things together so they can go. They say their goodbyes to Mr. Woodsley as they walk out the front door.

Mr. Woodsley says to Bri. "It'll be a pleasure to see you again, Your Royal Majesty." He bows and kisses the back of her hand.

She smiles back. "Thank you, Mr. Woodsley! I look forward to my next visit, *and to the time where we can stay longer!*"

CHAPTER 36
Keeping Everyone Safe

At The Palace and inside The Royal Apartment, McMasters and Mitchell sit down with Bri and the guys. McMasters, Mitchell, and The Royal Guard have been working hard to keep Bri, and the family, safe.

"Bri, we need to start doing things more strictly." McMasters emphasizes, "You canNOT go anywhere by yourself!"

"I understand," she replies, "and so does Rex. I've already prepared them that you all will insist one of you come with me. Aside from that, you've agreed to work with the private investigator and business manager, Vincint Cooper, He will be a connection to Rex, when the need arises, as well as having the inside scoop inside Millicent's camp." McMasters nods. "I need you all to know that if I have to go with Rex, or the team, on a moment's notice, trust that I'm not alone; Rex wouldn't hear of it either."

"Good to know." McMasters admits.

"Bri, any one of us would go with you!" David says.

"You're The Grand Duke of Newhaven, Jack's The Duke of Ashbourne, and Lawrence is *The King!*" She hands the baby to him. "*All three of you* need to pull back and protect the duchies and the UK, but most of all..." she shakily adds, "*my ssson!*" She blinks back the tears that start to form in her eyes.

"I agree with all that, except one thing." Jack says. Bri thinks about what she said and shakes her head in an 'I don't know.' Jack holds her cheeks, "Me!"

"No, I'm—."

"*Bri!*" He tells her, "The Duchy of Ashbourne isn't the same caliber as Newhaven. *I'm the obvious answer!* I can go with you *aaand* I've already had martial arts training!"

"Darling, he's onto something, from the standpoint that the *same* person should be going with you all the time. He would know more by just being there every time and have a faster response to handling something." Lawrence says, with David agreeing.

"I'm not thrilled about *any of you* coming with me! However, McMasters and Mitchell would have the training! *None of you* are considering what would happen, if this woman got her hands on the person who is with me, except Lawrence!" She says, looking at Lawrence, "Imagine the torture she could inflict on them, then multiply that, *the pain*, by an infinite number!" She looks at all of them. "Not one of you can truly picture the extent of that, *except Lawrence!*"

David has been studying her. "What *aren't* you saying?"

"What do you mean?" She asks.

David says, "Bri, you're planning something!"

Bri is surprised, "*I'm not* planning *to do anything!*"

"Then what is it? *Out with it!*" David says in his authoritative voice.

"*David Christopher Worthington*, I'm not a child!"

"*You're my wife*, who basically said she can't promise not to disappear, because she is thinking of *our* safety! *But WE need to know!*"

"It's just a feeling, David! *I don't know much more than that!*" She tells him.

Jack lightly chuckles at the thought that occurs to him, "I think you're one of very few people who could have the power of ruling the world, and still let people govern themselves!"

"*Of course I think they should govern themselves, so do all of you!*" She says.

McMasters discusses The Worthington Family's security, as a whole and individually. He suggests for Mitchell and himself to reach out to a few more people that he and Mitchell know, and trust, within UK' law enforcement and military about coming to work for The Royal Guard, particularly putting together 'The Queen's Guard.'

"*Brilliant idea!*" Jack says.

David is quick to tell him, "Feel free to hire *anyone* we can trust," he rubs Jacks' back, "and for our little guy here."

"*For this little guy*," McMasters explains, "I've already arranged for Ms. Valerie Evans to be *his* personal guard. She is trained as a member of the special forces and the top of her class." He looks at Bri, "Think of Ms. Evans as an extra set of arms. She'll be the one carrying Jacks in public when you all need your hands free, like to greet those who come out to see you."

"*Those* are Lawrence's fans!" Bri says.

Everyone laughs and Lawrence tells her, "Then you're not really listening!"

"Oh?" She asks.

"*Darling*, we've been over this! It's not my name they're shouting the most!" Lawrence says with a dimpled smile.

"I tend to hear plenty of fans shouting, *even screaming, for your attention*," then she points to herself, "not mine."

McMasters chuckles a bit. "Seriously, though, Ms. Evans is onboard to be his personal guard and her personality should fit right in."

"I think I like her already," Bri tells them, "*especially* if she helps me give you *all* a hard time!"

"I'll arrange for you two to meet when she has completed her training for The Royal Guard." McMasters tells her.

"Great!" She smiles wide.

There isn't much left to talk about and they wrap up. David walks them to the door and they all wave before he shuts the door behind them. Jack had slipped down to the kitchen to get Jacks a bottle. When he comes back, he hands Lawrence the bottle so he can feed Jacks.

Bri's phone chimes with a text from Rex:

Rex: "Cooper and I want to pick you up as soon as possible."

Bri: "Jack will be with me, or, if you prefer, I can have McMasters or Mitchell instead? I'll let you pick."

Rex: "The Duke of Ashbourne will be fine. See you in ten minutes."

Bri explains Rex's texts to everyone. Bri hugs David and Lawrence, then kisses her baby. "I'm not sure what time we'll be back."

"Don't worry about that," David says, "just be safe." She nods.

Bri and Jack leave The Royal Apartment to go down to wait for Rex. McMasters arranges for Rex's car to be allowed to come up to The Royal Apartment's main door. When Rex's car pulls up, Jack has Bri climb in first and he follows. McMasters waves to Rex before he shuts the door and pats the top of the car twice for the driver to know he can leave.

CHAPTER 37
The Devonridge Manor

Inside Rex's car, Bri greets Rex and Cooper, then introduces Jack to Cooper. The men shake hands, respectfully greeting each other.

Cooper explains to them, "I'm sorry to be so abrupt with this, but when Rex told me that you wanted to see Devonridge Manor, I happened to know this was a great night to do it, because Millicent is staying a couple days near the port where she gets many of her shipments. She would be taking most of her people with her, so there will be less around here at this time. Since her shipments have been *out of sorts*," he winks at Bri, "she is *personally* receiving a small shipment. It's nothing that will give her the income anywhere close to what she has already lost; only a fraction of what she needs. Oh!" Cooper hands Bri a larger envelope. "Devereaux said that he told you he would get these for you."

Bri opens it and pulls out the floor plan of Devonridge Manor, as well as a map of The Tunnels, or 'Knox,' as Millicent would like to think of them. "The Tunnels are a bunch of small tunnels along a main tunnel."

"It's mainly one long tunnel. Parts of the 'branches' have collapsed over time." Rex replies. He also tells her, "I'm not sure how much you know, but Millicent grew up in Devonridge Manor, along with her older brother and sister; they were all raised by their uncle when they were orphaned."

Bri quietly states, "The Duke of Devonridge."

Rex nods. "His reputation was, well..." He hesitates.

"There are various words that are coming to mind that gradually get worse, like: conceited, egotistical, mean, horrible, *ghastly*, disgusting, horrific..." she trails off when she sees them giving her perplexed looks; they didn't know how she would know. She tells them, "*Looong story*." Then it occurs to her, "Let's just say *extremely vile!*"

"Well, that's probably the *most* accurate description." Rex says.

"The place is nicknamed '*Devil's* Ridge' because of the rumors of the depravity that went on there." Coop throws in. "Given all that, I'd say the rumors are more *true*, than not." Bri doesn't say anything, so he continues, "Some of the gossip circles say The Duke was spending his money on the 'evils of the world,' and neglected the care of The Manor."

She shifts the conversation a bit. "Are we using the cover of darkness so we aren't seen?"

Rex tells her, "The Manor has been uninhabitable for quite some time. We most likely wouldn't run into another soul during the day, especially with Millicent out of town; but we want to protect you, so going at night helps us do that."

"I appreciate that." Bri says.

Jack looks at Cooper and Rex saying, "*All of us appreciate that.*" They both nod.

The four of them discuss Millicent's financials as they ride in the car. Rex tells them, "Millicent is once again receiving income from The Duchy of Devonridge. We can only assume she has threatened, and/or bribed, someone to restart those payments again."

"I'll discuss that with Lawrence right away! We need to get those stopped again!" Bri says. "Even if it means firing someone to block her access; *she cannot have access to any significant amount of money!*" They all agree.

 They pull up to the old manor and climb out of the car. With a full moon, Bri can see the sad state that the dilapidated old manor is in. It reminds her of a picture one would see of a haunted house for Halloween, or even a location for a horror movie.

Everyone is handed a heavy-duty flashlight, then they make their way up the sidewalk to the front door. One of the front doors creaks open and they step inside; Bri gets an eerie chill. She looks around at the awful state of such a huge manor, slowly being reduced to a pile of rubble. She shines her light on the floor and sees dust collecting on the footsteps of whoever was here last. Considering the footsteps have almost disappeared, it has been a while since anyone has been here.

They stop in the middle of The Foyer and she asks, "Is it safe for us to split up and cover more ground?"

"If you're extremely careful, the floors could give way at any moment." Coop warns. "Why don't you and Jack stay in this section, while Rex and I search the other side? We're going to look for an entrance to The Tunnels and if there's still a viable entrance to The Tunnels from this place, it's going to be on that side," he waves his arm in that direction, "through the basement."

Bri and Jack turn and start going the opposite way. Jack shines a light and sees the floors are uneven, or they have huge holes in them. "Stay on the outer edges here." He motions with the light.

Everything has been mostly cleared out, but they can't get too far on the main floor with the caved-in sections of the floor that have completely rotted through. They shine their light up on the ceiling that is still intact and decide to go upstairs.

There isn't much upstairs either. The secret doors they do find lead to the room next door. The couple of possible secret hiding places are full of dust. However, one room they walk into is darker, because of the dark mahogany wood and a dark shade of green on the walls.

Standing in the center of the room, she feels like she is being watched again. She concentrates...then she senses The Duke.

"I feel you lurking..." Bri looks around for him.

"*Okay*," Jack whispers, "*I'm actually feeling chills.*"

"Show yourself, *Devonridge!*" She asserts.

The Duke of Devonridge appears in front of the door. Bri swoops her fingers around so Jack can also see The Duke.

"*Come here to steal like common thieves, have you?!*" The Duke sneers.

"Steal what?" She gestures the room. "There is *nothing* in this sad place to steal! Kind of resembles your legacy; *not worth remembering!*"

Jack barely whispers, "*Daaamn.*"

The Duke is angry. "THAT'S RICH, COMING FROM A NOBODY LIKE YOU, *AND YOUR CASTOFF!*"

Jack isn't fazed and plainly replies, "*Anyone* who is a decent human being is already better than you."

The Duke glares at Jack, but before he can respond, Bri asks The Duke, "Why *are* you here?"

"*You didn't banish me from this place!*" He retorts.

"No, I didn't. But if you're as rude as you were that day at The Palace, I'll banish you to Hell, or *far* worse, *for Lawrence!*" Bri glares.

He circles Jack. "Why didn't Lawrence come?"

She rolls her eyes, but Jack answers, "He wasn't interested."

"You're lying." The Duke states. "He's afraid to face me——."

"*Oh, please!*" Bri rolls her eyes. "Afraid of a piece of garbage like you?! *Not a chance!* If you were still alive, he'd personally drive the dagger through your hollow heart to kill you! *Oh, wait!*" She flicks her eyebrow. "*He already did that!*" She sees his eyes glare with his angry expression and she adds, "Guess he isn't scared to face you after all!"

Jack keeps a neutral face as he watches The Duke's odd behavior while he and Bri are going back and forth. It seems like The Duke is trying to keep them away from a certain area...trying to keep their attention away from something...*but what?*

"I prefer to spend my time here." The Duke walks towards the other side of the room, where there is a step down into the other part; he is hoping they follow him. "My best memories are here with Milly..." he thinks about that time with her, "we would——."

"*Stop!*" Bri's hand makes a 'stop' gesture and she has an appalled look on her face. "You *don't* need to go into any disgusting details, you sick and twisted Bas——." She stops herself.

"Well, well, *well!* Showing unladylike behavior is *unbecoming* of a royal, don't you think." He glares with another sneer.

"I never claimed to be *your kind* of royal! A stuck-up, pretentious, self-righteous, sanctimonious evil twit!" Bri is exasperated. "Even in death *you still* don't get it, *do you?*"

Jack sees a floorboard move when Bri steps on the edge of it. He takes the couple steps over to it and squats down.

"Hold this!" He says, handing Bri his flashlight.

"*GET OUT OF THERE!*" The Duke snaps.

Jack has a grin on his face and is even *more* determined to see under the piece of floorboard, knowing how upset The Duke is right now! He pushes on the edge of the board Bri had stood on and lifts it up a bit, then he uses his fingers to lift up the board completely.

Bri squats down next to him asking, "What's in there?"

"There are two buttons, one labeled 'LAB' and the other 'FUN.'" Jack replies.

"Lab?" Bri looks at The Duke. "Is this the secret lab I've read about in The Devonridge Manor's history?"

"*No one* is allowed in my lab! In fact, *no one* has been able to find it to this day!" The Duke proudly says, puffing out his chest.

There is a click and a panel in the wall pops open. "Looks like it's been found." Jack states. There is another click and a connecting door pops open.

Jack stands and dusts himself off. "I thought we could take a look at both!" He grins. "Let's start with 'FUN' and go from there!"

"*Jack!*" She whispers, putting her hand to his chest to stop him from going to that secret room hidden door. "This room isn't even close to the type of 'fun' you think could be there! His idea of 'fun' is sick and demented." She tips her head to The Duke and tells him, "Someone like him finds 'fun' in torture, pain, blood..." Jack's face is horrified, then disgusted. Bri goes to the door and shuts it. "I've seen visions of Lawrence's abuse, and what little I have seen of it, well, I don't want to see any room like that in person, up close and personal!"

The Duke gets an evil smile. "Even without Milly being Lawrence's mother, Lawrence is *still* kin to us! That *same blood* is in his veins!" He is trying to get under her skin. "Our time together when he was a young teen gave him a taste, *a thirst*, for it!"

Bri humorlessly laughs, "All you did was make him hate you more! Or have you forgotten something?" She glances down at his chest.

The Duke glares at her and struggles through his frustrated anger to demand, "*Stay out of my lab! I don't want you claiming credit for any of* my *work!*" He sticks his nose up in a 'humph.'

"If we aren't going to look in *that* room," Jack points to the 'FUN' door, "I'm not sure we should know what all his experiments entailed..." He puts the floorboard back and dusts away the extra footprints, fingerprints, and smudges in the dust around the floorboard.

"I *am* curious about this lab!" She walks over to the part of the wall that Jack had popped open.

"*NO!*" The Duke is red, seething with anger. "*I FORBID IT!*"

Bri rolls her eyes and says to Jack as she opens up the panel, "My suspicion is that The Duke was somewhat a different person when he was in his lab?"

Jack is surprised. "*How do you figure?!*"

"Well, from what I've been able to put together, it seems The Duke," she waves her hand towards him, "might've been a brilliant scientist, as well as a professor at the prominent university not far from here."

Jack exhales a scoff. "*Brilliant?*"

The Duke's face is red. "Why you smug little bas–."

"BEFORE you dismiss that little fact, Amore Mio," Bri purposely interrupts The Duke, "if we consider how protective he is with this lab," she tips her head, "he was probably serious about his work and what he was working on." The Duke's mouth falls open a bit.

"I'll take that under advisement!" Jack handsomely smiles at Bri and she softly giggles. She turns and is about to go inside the passageway, but Jack stops her. "Let me go first, Amore Mia, in case it isn't safe."

"Are you scared of answering to David and Lawrence if I got hurt and went home with a bandage?" She teases.

"*Yes!*" He states. "*But I'm scared of answering to Jacks more!*" He playfully swats her bum as he passes by her, and he hears her giggle, a sound he always loves to hear.

Jack shines the light down the passageway and sees that it's a narrow stairway down. She closes the door behind them and follows Jack down. Inside the lab, she walks around the room that has bookshelves covering one of the outside walls. In front of those is a couch and two chairs, with a coffee table and two end tables. There's a floor lamp near one of the chairs. A desk is on the other outside wall, facing the reading area. The rest of the room is the lab with two large lab tables with the wall behind it *full* of every possible ingredient imaginable!

The Duke appears. "I heard the others say they were coming to find you! Do you think you could keep this lab to yourselves?" Jack and Bri look at each other and nod.

They quickly head upstairs and get back inside the bedroom, with Jack shutting the door. Bri looks down the hall and doesn't see anyone. When she looks back at Jack, she happens to see a few books on top of a bookshelf, hidden. She only notices them because of the angle and a reflection of light off a piece of metal on the spine of one of the books.

Bri walks over and goes to grab them, only she wasn't tall enough to reach them. Jack comes up beside her and gets them for her. They wipe the dust off the books, and he slips them inside his pullover jacket so they don't have to carry them. They might need their hands free to help them get out of this run-down place that threatens to fall apart before they leave!

They step into the hallway and no one is there. Bri glances into the next room. "Let's see if there's anything in here. It feels like it could be The Duchess of

Devonridge's room, whenever the last one would've lived here?" Jack follows her inside.

The room is empty and they focus on finding secret passageways and hiding places, including the floorboards. They find a bigger compartment under one of the floorboards and pull out a decent-sized green velvet bag that has a golden 'D' in calligraphy on it. They open it and find various jewelry boxes with the same 'D' on them as well, along with some loose pieces of jewelry at the bottom of the bag.

"Are these the missing jewels that belong to The Duchy of Devonridge?" Bri asks, looking at a couple pieces.

"That would be my guess!" Jack replies. "We should bring them with us and show Herst, he might know; or Nigel," The Royal Jeweler, "will know."

Bri puts the jewelry back in the bag while Jack puts the floorboard back and shifts the dusts around to make it blend in, so it wouldn't give anything away that there is a secret hiding place, let alone that someone has found it. They meet up with Rex and Cooper coming down the hallway.

They all make their way out of The Manor, passing The Library and Bri gasps in sadness. She walks inside and is sick at the state of The Library.

"*A caved in ceiling and all these books...*" she glances around, "*there are so many...ruined!*" She picks up various books and looks at them closely. She whispers more to herself, "*Some of these are rare and priceless!*" She holds up one book and says, "This is heartbreaking! *A first edition!*" She gestures around. "How many first editions and rare books are in here?! Can any of them be saved?! *It's appalling!* I would rather someone had stolen all these to sell into private collections; at least they would've been taken care of and appreciated all this time!"

They make their way to their car, and when they are on their way back to London, Bri sends a text to David, Lawrence, McMasters, and Mitchell, that they were on their way back to The Palace. Then the four of them talk about the journals Jack and Bri found. Coop said he could help read them, but they both thought it would be better for one person to get the full picture. Bri doesn't offer for them to read the journals after she is done with them, just in case there are things in there about Lawrence, or even things *no one* should read about between The Duke and Millicent. She promises to tell them anything that would help their mission. Jack wonders why Bri doesn't say anything about the lab, but he'll ask her about that in private.

When they arrive at The Royal Apartment's Main Entrance, they thank Rex and Coop and say goodnight. When they walk into The Apartment, Lawrence and David are in the living room waiting for them. Jack, Bri, McMasters, and Mitchell join David and Lawrence to discuss what happened.

"Honestly, guys, it was rather uneventful." Bri says.

"Our only *real* concern was not breaking our necks in a place that was literally falling apart and falling in on itself." Jack tells them. "Oh! I did get to see The Duke of Devonridge!" McMasters and Mitchell have bewildered looks on their faces, until they remember Bri's gift.

"What did *he* want?" Lawrence asks with a hint of irritation.

"He was trying to keep us away from a floorboard hiding two buttons that unlocked secret doors." Jack tells them. "Bri pointed out that the button labeled 'FUN,' was *not* a normal person's idea of fun, and it probably had everything to do with pain and torture."

Bri does a full body shake at the thought of it. "We didn't say anything about those switches, or the rooms, to Rex and Coop, nor these..." She shows Lawrence the jewelry.

Before she can ask, Lawrence confirms, "The Devonridge Jewels?!"

David looks at them, too. "Blimey! They really *are* still around! Millicent was always irritated they could never find these and blamed her sister!" He passes the jewels around. "Where *did* you find them?!"

Jack answers, "Under the floorboards in a bedroom Bri think's was The Duchess of Devonridge's room." Jack turns to Bri. "I understand why you're reading the diaries, and so do they, but what I'm curious about is why didn't you say anything about the switches, or the jewelry?"

"The quick answer? They're criminals. A longer answer? If there's anything to come out of this lab, I want to be fair in how it gets handled. I trust Rex would, even Coop, but we are working with *other* criminals and the temptation may be too great for others."

"As you say," David smiles sweetly, "fair enough."

When Bri yawns, they all decide to turn in for the night and could talk more in the morning. They all say goodnight. Bri takes Jacks upstairs to nurse in The Royal Chambers, and Lawrence isn't far behind.

When Jacks has finished nursing, Bri goes to shower while Lawrence burps him. When she comes back into the bedroom, she sees Lawrence staring out at the city lights. She comes up behind him and wraps her arms around him. He holds her hands against his chest.

"I'm amazed at how full my heart is of love for you." He turns to face her. "I never knew I could love someone so much, *so deeply*..." he holds her jaw, "then there's Jacks! How can such a tiny baby have such a giant hold on my heart, too!"

"Love is amazing in so many ways, Ace! It's associated with the heart, because *no one* can physically live without a heart; and no one," she squeezes his hands, "can *happily* live without love."

"I wasn't really living without you; without your love." He kisses her hands.

"Love fills us, moves us, inspires us, even lifts us to new heights...without it, we *barely* exist..." She tells him. "True, adoring love, has us worried about someone else's happiness over our own; true adoring love is the purest love and it's the safest love..." she smiles playfully, "where one can feel safe enough to give themselves completely to the relationship." She playfully bites her lower lip and smiles.

He gives her a playful look, leaning in and growling a moan, then he kisses her. He steps back and says, "Stay." He untucks his shirt and takes it off.

"*Gladly*!" She smiles. "I *love* this view!"

He lifts her up and she wraps her legs around him. He takes her over and lays her down crossways on the bed, then he walks around to the other side. He kisses her upside down as he pulls her arms above her head, then runs the backs of his fingers down them. She gasps a little and exhales shakily. He kisses her chin and down her neck.

She whispers, "*Let's start trying tonight?*"

Lawrence looks at her upside down for a moment as that comment registers in his brain. "Are you sure?"

"Yes! It took over a year with Jacks. I wasn't tracking anything, just letting things happen without...um, *restrictions*, shall we say."

"I'll repeat what I've said before," he gives her a smoldering look, "I deny you *nothing*, My Queen." He lightly taps her chin with his finger. "*Especially* when you're smiling like that at me." She runs her hand into his hair, to the back of his head and pulls him into a kiss.

He takes a finger, sliding the hair out of her face and tucking it behind her ear. "I love you, BriaLynn!" Then he rests his forehead to hers, "*Will you become my queen...*" He whispers.

"I thought I already agreed?!" She taps a kiss to his lips, then gets up to go into the bathroom, putting his shirt on along the way. When she crawls back into bed, she grins as she straddles him and asks, "Now, what were we talking about again?!"

"You don't play fair!" He says back.

"Ah, but I *am* playing fair!" She smirks. "*You're* just lucky I don't care you're The King!"

"Oh really?" His eyebrow goes up. "How do you figure?"

"Because it's *my* choice and not because 'The King' *pressured* me into it."

He studies her for a moment and kisses her again. They say, 'I love you' and 'Goodnight' before getting comfortable and going to sleep.

CHAPTER 38
The Château

The next morning, Lawrence comes back from his morning workout to find Bri nursing Jacks in her overstuffed chair. She sees him and smiles sweetly at him as he walks over to her. He kisses her and points towards the bathroom, letting her know he is going to go take a shower; she nods.

When Lawrence comes out of the bathroom after his shower, he finds Bri putting the finishing touches on her outfit. He watches her zipping up tall black boots to complement her super soft, ivory-white, light sweater dress. She looks and looks again when she sees him staring.

"Something you like?" She winks.

He walks over to her with a smoldering look. He wraps his arms around her, and he kisses her passionately.

She feels his hands appreciating her curves as he says, "*Somehow* you're even *sexier* in this *whole* outfit!"

He kisses her as he walks backwards with her to their bed. He sits and pulls her closer. She ghosts his lips seductively, as he rests his hands on her hips...

Bri kisses him soundly, before she gets up and gets ready again. "You know, if you keep smiling at me like that, I may never leave!"

He pats her bum on his way over to get her the perfect necklace for her outfit; he has a secret stash in one of his dresser drawers. He walks over to her saying, "This will match your outfit splendidly!" He puts it on her. "Now, you can't look at this until you're back at The Worthington Manor." He steps in front of her. "Promise me."

She smiles lovingly. "*Don't you want to see my reaction?!*"

"*I already know what it will be!*"

"Me, too!" She grins. "*But still...*"

"Bri," Lawrence holds her face, "you'll *love* it."

She sweetly smiles. "When did you make it?"

"*Years* ago!" He tells her.

"You didn't make it thinking of me?!" She teases and her mouth drops open as her hand goes to her heart. "I'm hurt. *Really hurt.*"

He softly laughs. "Every single piece I give you has been made with love *for you*, even before I met you."

"oooOOOooo, *good answer, Ace!*" She kisses him. "That has to be one of the sweetest things you've ever said to me, and you say a lot of sweet things!"

He grins. "I love you, My Queen!"

"I know." She gives him a cheesy grin and he chuckles. She wraps her arms around his neck. "I love *you*, Ace!"

He smirks. "I know." He hugs her and lifts her feet off the floor.

She giggles. "Good! *Don't you forget it!*" She taps another quick kiss to his lips before they go downstairs.

Bri notices the same reaction to her outfit on Jack and David, as she did on Lawrence. They all eat breakfast together before Lawrence walks with them all to the helicopter; he is holding Jacks along the way. He says his goodbyes to David and Jack, then Jacks.

He kisses his little cheek, then tells him, "Be good for Mum, Dad, and Uncle Jack!" Jacks smiles at his uncle. Lawrence hands Jack the baby, then turns to Bri. "I'll see you in about a week."

"*You will!*" She smiles. "I love you, Ace!"

"I love you, My Queen!" He says, kissing her fiercely.

She gets on the helicopter, and he shuts the door before stepping back to a safe distance. He waves as they lift into the air and when they are flying off in the distance, he turns and goes inside The Palace to bury himself in work.

David squeezes Bri's hand. "Ready for our getaway, Beautiful?"

She smiles. "I am!"

He smiles. "Me, too..." He kisses her hand. "I thought we could leave later today, or early in the morn—."

"A big NO to *'early in the morning,'* because *early* to you, well, *to all three of you,* is *insanely* early!"

He chuckles. "Alright, Love, this afternoon it is! One other thing. Jack and I wanted to see about leaving Baby Jacks with him?"

Jack sees her face and sees her nervousness about leaving her baby behind. "This way you can horseback ride, make appearances in town, and not worry about his safety. We all know that when the time is right, you'll be going straight for Millicent and, if we're honest, this will be the fight of your life, *and our lives!*" Bri eyebrows go up taking that in. "*You will need every ounce of wit you've got!*"

Bri looks down at her sweet baby. "But you want me to leave my baby?"

Jack leans forward. "Bri, it's just a couple of days—."

"*AND a couple of nights!*" Her tears are showing.

"What if I promise to stay home the entire time, showing him your picture, and rarely putting him down?" Jack asks. "Come on, Amore Mia, he loves his Uncle Jack, *and* you know I'll have Grandmas and Grandpa checking in with us *often*, along with Uncle James and Aunt Amy with Elise!"

She wipes her tears that escaped her eyes. "Promise me you *both* will be waiting when we come home?"

"I *swear!*" He holds up his right hand.

She looks at Jacks as she says, "*Promise me you'll send pictures!*"

"It'll be a rarity, but yes, I'll send them to David, though." Jack says, bracing for her response that comes.

"What?! Why?! *And why rare?!*" She is *almost* angry.

"Because you'll miss him *more*," he tucks some hair behind her ear, "and I don't want to do that to you, or David."

"I can understand that Jack, but please know it'll do my heart good to see him being so well taken care of," she cups his cheek, and he kisses her palm, "and maybe a little more spoiled by his Uncle Jack and the family." He smiles and nods a little. She hugs him tight with her free arm. "Thank you!" She kisses him. "*Now, change the subject before I change my mind!*"

The helicopter lands on top of The Worthington Corporation. Bri carries Jacks inside and down the stairs with David and Jack behind them.

Mary comes around the corner. "So good to see you, Bri! *And this little guy!*" Jacks has a smile for her.

"It's good to see you, too!" Bri smiles.

Jack comes up to them and smiles at Mary, "Good morning, Mary, Luv!" He kisses her cheek.

Mary lightly laughs, being charmed by Jack and replies, "Good morning, Your Grace!"

Jack winks at her, then turns to Bri. "Paul is downstairs to take me over to Watchtower for a little bit, there are a few things I need to quickly do." He rubs Jacks' back.

David had come up behind Bri. "I need to duck into the conference room for a minute." He tosses his thumb over his shoulder. "Love you, Jacks!" He kisses Jacks' head, then he walks over to the conference room.

"You're putting David to work already?" Bri teases. David smiles as he opens the door and walks in.

Mary tells her, "Just for a minute or two. The meeting is wrapping up and David likes to say 'hullo' to everyone."

311

Bri looks at Jack and sees his face. She knows he wants to get going and needs to take Jacks with him. Bri kisses Jacks head and says her goodbyes to him and Jack at the elevator. She watches them get into the elevator and the doors start to close. Just then, the conference room door opens, and Bri sees David wave her over. She walks over to him and he places a hand on her lower back as she walks into the conference room.

"Gentlemen," David says, "this is my beautiful wife, BriaLynn, The Princess Imperial."

Bri sweetly smiles saying, "*Mrs. Worthington* is shorter." There is soft laughter from those in the room.

One of them steps closer. "The pleasure is all ours, Your Royal Majesty." He shakes her hand.

Bri greets everyone before she and David walk the visitors to the elevator. When everyone is in the elevator, the door closes, David turns to Mary and tells her, "Why don't you go home early and take the next couple days off."

She hesitates, but he insists that anything pressing can be done on the phone or laptop; she can't argue with that. She packs up while David goes to his office, and Bri goes down to hers to work for awhile.

Before Mary leaves, she pops her head into Bri's office. "Have fun at The Château!"

"Thank you!" Bri happily smiles. "I'll try to keep his attention away from business, so you don't have to open your laptop!"

Mary lightly laughs. "That's *usually* not a problem whenever he's with you."

"Glad to hear it!" Bri smiles.

"My problem with not being here when he is away, is I can get caught up on things the I've put aside as 'less pressing.'" Mary adds.

"I can see that!" Bri replies. "Well, look at it this way: there will be another time you can play 'catch up,' so enjoy your time off!"

Mary laughs. "*Good point!*"

They say goodbye, then Mary goes back to her desk to grab her things and leave. Bri sifts through her mail and listens to her new voicemails. She returns a few emails, then she finishes a chunk of items on her to-do list, all before it's time to go. She gathers her things again and walks down to David's office.

She sets her bags down right inside his office door, then quietly shuts the door. She walks up behind him as he talks on his cell phone; he smiles, turning around to hug her with his free arm.

"Mrs. Worthington." He says, ending his call and wrapping his other arm around her. He kisses her and his hand slides down to her bum.

He goes to lift her dress, but she grabs his hands. "*Oh, no*, Mister *Worthington. WE are* not *doing this here, when* you *are taking us to The Château!*"

He rests his forehead against hers. "*Briiii...*" he exhales, "it's been *extremely* difficult to keep my hands to myself with you in this dress..." He steps back, holding her hands out to look her over again. He exhales a soft whistle saying, "*WOW!*" He gives her a smoldering look.

"You know? I heard that earlier today..." She grins.

"Oh, really?" He turns her to sit her on the edge of his desk.

"NnnnHnnn...even a request to wear this outfit again." She stares at him.

"Doesn't surprise me, *Sexy Vixen!*" He leans in to kiss her, but she places a finger on his lips.

"*Paaatience, My Love!*" She gets down and steps away from his desk. "It'll be worth the wait." She crosses her heart. "*I promise!*"

"Always is!" He smiles. She looks over her shoulder and winks.

At The Château, David had the meeting of her 'Think Tank' there, with the help of Rex and Hazel. David, Mitchell, Cooper, and Hazel are at The Château with them, while McMasters, Lawrence, Rex, and Jack are on a video call from The Cottage House and Ashbourne Castle's Library. Rex's 'inside guy' is on as well, only by telephone, so they can talk things out from all the angles they can.

When they get on the subject of The Duke of Devonridge's journals, she tells them, "I won't get into detail about the journals, although some details I skimmed through, even a few I've passed over completely because of the content..." She has a slight shiver. "What I've discovered so far is that since Millicent was five years old, she witnessed some *horrible* crimes that would be *extremely* difficult for *an adult* to process after seeing it! It makes my heart sad for that little girl who didn't have *a soul* to protect *her*!" There is a silence that falls over them as they picture a five-year-old little girl witnessing horrible crimes. "I've learned that the *main* tunnel runs all the way from The Devonridge Manor, to Devonridge Hall. The Tunnel is lined with shorter tunnels and rooms holding the things for upcoming auctions, as well as cells to hold people prisoner." She opens one journal and pulls out a folded piece of paper. "The tunnels are all laid out on this map." It's the map Claude Devereaux gave her, but she doesn't tell them that. "The journals also talk about the *prisoners* they've kept down there, where they would torture in various painful, and very murderous, ways, and all this they have been doing *for decades*. They've also had their hand in human trafficking before it was called 'human trafficking.' Those prisoners were kept in starvation states, so they would be too weak to even try to escape."

She goes to fold up the map again, but David takes it for a closer look. "These are simpler than I had imagined..." he leans closer, "it looks like their design is also for stability. If it's constructed like they could be, they could withstand a bomb going off a short distance away!"

"That's exactly why they are constructed that way!" Rex's inside man replies to them.

Bri goes on. "Between the ages of twelve and fourteen, a lot more happened in Millicent's life. Her sister was pregnant and was given an ultimatum, *after* The Duke killed her boyfriend: either get rid of the baby, or leave. Her sister chose to leave. Not long after the baby was born, her sister was forced to watch her uncle kill her baby anyway." Everyone gasps. "His reasoning in the journal was to teach her a lesson."

"Now we know where Millicent gets her ideas of 'lessons' from!" Lawrence offhandedly throws that in there.

"But what kind *of lesson?!"* Jack asks. "It doesn't make sense..."

"You're trying to rationalize something that's irrational." Bri states. Jack and the others agree. "The reasoning his gave for this situation is he would only allow legitimate children to be born into The Devonridge Family. However, *before that*, he *refused* to let Millicent's sister, Marjorie, marry her boyfriend."

Hazel realizes, "So he *forced* her to have the baby out of wedlock!"

Bri nods. "But The Duke doesn't see it that way. There is *nothing* about him that seems very rational, unless it's scientifically based. One can't even describe him as 'eccentric,' because it would be an *insult* to those who are harmlessly eccentric!"

"So, in a way, we can think of it as that baby was spared a difficult existence." Cooper puts out there.

"Perhaps." Bri considers that a moment, then moves on. "Millicent's brother started taking on a more active role in their 'family business.' This frees up The Duke's time and even though he was already grooming her in various ways, by the age of twelve, Millicent's uncle was sexually abusing her. I'm not sure how many abortions she would have altogether; however, in his journals, The Duke made her have the abortions telling her it was better *for her.*" She rolls her eyes. "We *all* know it was to hide what he was doing *to* Millicent." The others nod, absorbing her point of what happened to Millicent at the time. Bri purposely doesn't say anything about Millicent's hysterectomy. Bri has Hazel discuss what she has found.

Hazel explains, "Millicent's local account balances were lost in our 'computer glitch' and we gained control of her funds at The World Bank. We recently learned she is getting payments from The Duchy of Devonridge once again. After our last meeting, I went in and reworked those payments so that once they go to deposit into her account, then that deposit, and any subsequent ones, disappear. So she can see the money deposited and disappear." She gets a nervous look on her face. "Millicent may start to suspect Bri and retaliate."

Bri says to her, "Hazel, Millicent may suspect me, but I doubt she will for too much consideration . She has been, *and hopefully still is*, underestimating me. *However*, this next step, collapsing her tunnels, should have her at least seriously considering me, or at least someone close to me." She explains, "It will take *a lot* of people for the work it will take to clear *everything*, and *everyone*, out of them *before* we collapse the tunnels. The people she is holding hostage

315

are obviously *the* most important! It would also be nice to preserve any priceless artifacts, or works of art, *anything* of value, that could be in there; *I don't want to destroy any of them...*" The others nod in understanding. "Then, I want us to take that momentum, and knock her completely down; otherwise, she will come straight for me, taking down everyone in between!"

"Seriously?!" Hazel asks.

It's Rex who replies,, "*She will see it as not having a choice, to maintain dominance..*"

"And once I have Lawrence's heir, she won't stop until she has our baby, even killing the four of us first to do it!"

They start making plans to bring in reinforcements, first to scope out the entire estate, then make a plan. Cooper tells Bri, "I'll get with Rex, after the meeting, to discuss who we should bring in." He asks McMasters, "Would you like to be a part of that conversation?"

McMasters is pleasantly surprised. "I would! And I would like Mitchell to be a part of it, too." Coop and Rex nod.

"Sounds good." Bri replies. "Hazel, I want to have a cyber plan ready to implement at the same time we collapse those tunnels. Anyone involved with Millicent will have a computer virus that tangles up every cent of their money with the tightest knots; if it's easier, just freeze the money!"

"Got it!" Hazel replies.

Bri talks to the others, "We need to have any animals she may have 'collected,' taken home to their native lands. We can work with those local wildlife experts. Everything else can go to a warehouse Mr. Stirling owns to be sorted and returned to their *rightful* owners. That will infuriate those who stole it, *or* those who bought it on the Black Market; *no one* will be getting compensation for any of it. Then, I want The Tunnels rigged to blow up. Afterwards, we'll douse *everything* in gasoline, The Hall included, then stand *way back* and watch the evilness burn to the ground! Of course, all of that will make Millicent laser focused on me!"

"*That's what I'm afraid of!*" David tells her.

316

"I understand that, David," she gives him a compassionate, loving look, "but having her focused on me, means she won't be thinking things through so thoroughly, and she will make mistakes. *Hopefully*, ones we can use to our advantage!"

"She has a point." Rex says. "If Millicent is seeing red, and focuses on Bri for revenge, *she* will be *vulnerable* to making mistakes. If she does get her hands on Bri, those mistakes could help Bri escape; *or help us find her!*" He says to Hazel and Cooper, "We have *maybe* two weeks before her next auction."

The meeting wraps up and they make an appointment for their next 'Think Tank.' Then everyone says their goodbyes as the leave. After everyone has left, David and Bri go back to spending time together there at The Château.

CHAPTER 39
Unforeseen Change of Plans

A couple days later, David and Bri are getting back to The Château from an evening out. When they get out of their car, an SUV comes up the drive. David takes a protective stance standing in front of Bri.

"They wouldn't have let the car through at the entrance if the person, or people, weren't safe." Bri notes. "When Bri recognizes the passenger, she puts her hand on David's arm, she whispers, *"It's Rex."* She steps around David, walking up to Rex getting out of the SUV. She asks, "What do we owe the honor?"

Rex has a concerned look. "I wish I could say this was just a social visit..." He kisses her cheek, then shakes David's hand.

"Let's go upstairs." David extends his arm towards The Château's front door and he follows Rex and Bri inside.

They go upstairs to The Owner's Suite where Mitchell has it checked for bugs and other surveillance devices before they begin discussing anything; Cooper and Hazel are also called into this important meeting.

Rex explains, "Millicent is preparing for her next auction with various artwork and artifacts, as well as tanks, armored trucks, and military aircraft. These things are kept at a warehouse in a secret location within The Duchy of Devonridge. We now know where that warehouse is, and we will incorporate accordingly into your demolishing mission." He shifts in his chair. "I asked Cooper to follow any leads that come from our intel."

"There is one lead Rex had me looking into and I just found out they're going to send out a shipment of children and young adults *tonight*." Cooper informs them. He moves his finger between him and Hazel saying, "We've also pinpointed where they're being sent."

Hazel sadly nods. *"All of them* will have a *horrible existence* if they get to this place; *we need to stop this right away!"*

"What we have going for us," Rex says, "is what Bri said at our last meeting: Millicent is desperate for funds. What we also have going for us is her desperation; her hurriedness to get money. If we intercept now, we can take advantage of the rush, and, hopefully, save these kids. However," he gets a grieved look on his face when he says, "we won't have the other attacks ready to go, in order to do it all at the same time. *Plus*, we need to consider that your safety could be in worse danger if we do help these kids."

"Thank you for being concerned with my well-being, but honestly, I've been in danger this whole time. Only that will change to 'mortal danger' after I have Lawrence's baby. I just have to *keep* her underestimating me. She believes she is smarter, more cunning, more fill-in-the-blank, than everyone. She can't fathom I might be able to outsmart her; she won't want to believe I'm behind any of this. She'll think it's a criminal rival of hers, before she'll ever think it was me!" Bri freezes.

David reaches for her hand. "Bri?" He squeezes her hand a bit.

"I just remembered something." She replies. "Before Mr. Devereaux left Ashbourne that night, he said he heard Millicent was looking for buyers for my eggs and that she was preparing a place to be ablet to take them from me. What I didn't tell him, but I'm telling you all, is that getting a woman's eggs isn't as easy as someone might think. They can't just go in and take them out! *There's a process to it*. That process includes timing on precise days of a woman's cycle during the month." She explains. "What worries me is if I happen to be early in a pregnancy whenever she decides to this; *that process would jeopardize a pregnancy!*"

Rex suggests, "Then maybe we should wait with this rescue. If we wait, we will have time to plan; a plan to get her, before she tries to take your eggs."

Bri has an overwhelming need to say, "*No!*" All of them look at her and she sees Jessica appearing out of the corner of her eye. "Sorry. I just *feel strongly* that we need to save these people *now!*" She lovingly smiles at David. "Remember," she squeezes his hand, "*my faith is strong.*" He nods and clears his throat.

Rex considers that statement...her faith, and the courage of her faith...he finds it, *and her*, more fascinating... Rex brings himself back to the conversation. They discuss how the operation will come together.

319

That evening, Bri lives up to the promise she made David. It started with a romantic bubble bath, massages for both of them, and ended perfectly.

She lays her head on his chest. He hugs her and smiles. "You definitely delivered on your promise, Macushla."

She lifts her head and smiles. "I love you," her eyes fill with a little bit of tears, "more than I could ever put into words."

"I feel the exact same way!" He lovingly smiles and she kisses him.

She kisses his chest, before laying her head back down and snuggling in. Time seems to stop and they enjoy just being together.

With only a few unforeseen, not-quite-minor problems, the rescue mission was a success. The 'cargo' was loaded on one of Rex's unmarked ships and taken to a nearby port. He decided to do it that way, when he heard Bri say at some point, something like 'sometimes the best hiding places are in plain sight.' They got everyone out of their cramped quarters and sent them home.

Thankfully, Millicent is still clueless about Bri's involvement; however, she does start to wonder if Rex Stirling is behind it, because of the organization it took on short notice. She would consider Claude Devereaux, only he has issues of his own; something about a kidnapped family member.

Now, Millicent has to focus on moving up her timeline for Bri and her eggs, because she is running out of options for money. She needs to finalize a couple of things first, like twisting the arm a little harder on a top specialist in the field.

Back in Newhaven, Lawrence calls Bri early one morning about several huge crates that were delivered to The Royal Residence's main gate for 'Her Royal Majesty The Princess Imperial.'

> "Security isn't wanting to let them inside; in case it's some sort of 'Trojan Horse' set up." He says. "There's a note they brought to me, addressed to you. Do you mind if I open it?"

"*Please*! I'm nervous, too! I'd hate for that 'Trojan Horse' to be some sort of bomb!" She says. "Although, it could be anything if Millicent sent it!"

"It's nicer handwriting than hers." He comments as he opens the envelope. "It reads: '*Now these books will no longer be destroyed by the elements, and they can be in a collection to be admired and appreciated.*'"

"Remember when I told you that we found The Library inside The Devonridge Manor in ruins? With its rare and priceless books being destroyed by the elements?! So many books of rarity and various early editions that were falling apart...*it made me sick*!"

"*These* are *those*?!" He is surprised.

"*They must be*!" She replies.

"I'll let them know what should be in the crates and if it is them, I'll have the crates sent up to you straight away. Then you can decide what you'd like to do with them; keep them there, split them up, or auction them off for The Foundation. No matter what you decide, they'll be taken care of no matter where they end up!"

"*Brilliant* idea!" She teases with his accent and he lightly laughs. They talk for a little longer before they say their goodbyes.

Later that morning, Bri and Jack go up to The Manor for breakfast. She tells everyone about the shipment of books and that Lawrence is sending them to The Worthington Manor for her to figure out what to do with all of them.

Bri tells them, "Lawrence had a clever idea of auctioning some of them off for The Foundation." She looks at Maggie, Henry, and Carlotta, who also like the idea. "Maybe you guys can take a look and if we need to, hire specialists so we can catalog everything and see what we actually have. Then take that list and figure out which ones we will donate, sell, or auction off?"

"That sounds like a *wonderful* idea!" Maggie says and the others agree. Henry and Carlotta offer to help. Maggie asks, "Should we wait for Amy?"

Bri shakes her head, then tells them, "For this first part, I don't think she'll mind you all going through them to get them cataloged and seeing to their care. She should have a say in what to actually do with them."

Everyone continues to pass the baby around as they eat breakfast. Lawrence had the books delivered to The Worthington Manor before anyone leaves for work. They all gather in The Great Hall around the crates of books, as Mitchell and one of the staff open the lids. They are amazed at the books they pull out of the boxes!

"These are *extraordinary*!" Henry holds up four books. "I've looked for this set for ages, but I could never find them!"

"Set them aside for your collection." Bri tells him. "We can talk about them once we know what we have." He smiles and nods. She says to the rest, "The same goes for all of you, including staff," she waves her arm towards them, "if any of you find something, set it aside with your name on a piece of paper inside it and we can talk about it once we have everything cataloged." She also wants to the staff to know, "I'm more interested that these books have a good home, than I am in the value of them when it comes to our wonderful family *and extended family*!" The staff excitedly thank her before anxiously taking the books out of the crates.

Carlotta looks at a rare, *easily* one of the earliest editions of The Holy Bible. It is already in an airtight display box that seems fully intact, not even a crack.

"*Incredible*!" She says in disbelief, examining the case. "*This should be in a museum!*"

"When you're cataloging them, write a note as to which ones you think should be donated to a museum, even which museum if you have an idea as to which museum would be better equipped at preserving the books in worst shape; giving extra TLC to those that *desperately* need it." They all agree. She pulls Maggie and Carlotta aside and whispers so only they can hear her, "*Make sure to note if any of the staff have an interest in something that they may not feel comfortable making it official by putting their name inside it. I would really love to send some of these home with them!*" The ladies think that's a wonderful idea!

Bri, David, Jack, and the baby say their goodbyes to everyone, before going out to the helicopter. They drop David off at the office before heading to Ashbourne. They can work on their normal work, but there are some renovations that need their attention. Most of the renovations have been going rather well, considering the mishaps they have had here and there. They are walking through the now *completed* Royal Residence, including the bedrooms, and Bri is *thrilled* with the work!

"Mister Woodsley, this is *perfect*!" She smiles. "It's *exactly* like I pictured it would be! *I love it*!" It makes him proud and happy that she feels that way!

The living room has beautiful furniture that is arranged to flow with the space opposite the living room that has a grand piano tucked into it for Lawrence. There is a simpleness to the décor, like the whole castle, but there are highlights in the details that give it a little something more to make it more regal, because it *is* a royal castle.

 Her bedroom is structurally similar to The Royal Chambers in The Palace, with columns for bedposts, a silk wall above the headboard and a gold crest: '*The Triquetra Heart Monogram.*'

Jack smiles. "Do you like it?"

"I do!" She looks at him, still smiling.

He studies her. "What is it?"

"It's just..." She takes a deep breath and exhales with her eyebrows raised. "There are days it all hits me; *this is my life*!" He lovingly smiles at her and cups her cheek. All of a sudden, she yawns really hard. "My apologies!" She clears her throat. "Mister Woodsley," she looks at him, "*you've outdone yourself*! I don't know how to thank you for such a wonderful job?!"

"Your Royal—."

"*Please*, call me Bri, when we're not in public, *I insist.*"

He gives her a little smile with his nod. "*BriaLynn*, I know I wasn't welcoming in the beginning, and I sincerely regret that. I could simply say this is my job, and while that's true, I wanted to make sure everything was perfect for you, *The Duchess of Ashbourne.*"

Bri genuinely smiles and says, "Thank you!"

Jacks makes it known he is getting hungry and Bri's attention goes back to him. Mister Woodsley excuses himself and Jack walks him out. When Jack comes back, he sits with Bri on the couch. He smiles at Jacks who is watching him as he nurses and reaches for his Uncle Jack with his little hand. Jack holds his hand and leans in to kiss it a few times.

Bri lays her head on his shoulder and he shifts to get comfortable. "This is a priceless moment, Amore Mia..."

She yawns again. "Sorry." She lifts up her head. "I love you, Amore Mio." She kisses him sweetly and smiles.

"I love you!" He replies and she yawns hard again.

She lays her head back down and rests her eyes. They both are wondering if she is pregnant again, but they don't say anything. When Jacks is finished eating, Jack burps him and lays him down in the small crib that is in her bedroom. He goes back to Bri and picks her up, then carries her to her bedroom and lays her on the bed.

"Is it just me," her eyes open, "or is this mattress *super comfy*?"

He whispers, "*Very. It's like a memory foam mattress, but better!*"

She whispers with playfulness, "*Let's break it in...*" She looks up at him, biting her lower lip. He passionately kisses her...

CHAPTER 40
Beautifully Different Intimacies

Bri, Jack, and the baby are going to The Palace for Bri to spend time with Lawrence. She also has to practice for The Christmas Holiday Concert. Jack is with her to stay with the baby while she practices. They go to Lawrence's office to surprise him.

Lawrence has a huge smile spread across his face when he sees her walk in. "Hi, Beautiful!" He says, then adds, "And Brother!" He hugs Jack before he hugs and kiss Bri. Jacks reaches for him and Lawrence happily takes him. "I think you're getting cuter and cuter every time I see you!" Jacks smiles wide.

Phillip and Seth walk in and walk over. Phillip sees Jacks. "Look at him smiling! You look a lot like your daddy!" Jacks gives him a big smile and leans over for Phillip to hold him. "How could I *not* hold such a happy baby?"

Seth hugs Bri and Jack, too. He smiles at his father holding Jacks. "You *are* a happy boy!" Jacks smiles and Seth takes him.

Phillip goes over and hugs Bri. "So good to see you, My Dear." He hugs Jack. "Good to see you, too!"

"Same here!" Jack replies as they pat each other's back.

Bri interrupts. "We didn't mean to bring everything to a halt. I just wanted to say 'Hi' and let Lawrence know we were here, before we went to The Apartment to settle in." She goes to take the baby who is back with Lawrence, but he pulls back.

"Hold up!" Lawrence says. "I'll go with you."

"I want to warm up a bit for this evening's concert." She says.

"We'll drop you off." Lawrence offers.

They say goodbye to Phillip and Seth, then make their way to The Royal Concert Hall. The reconstruction and renovations of The Royal Concert Hall and The Royal Ballroom were recently finished, just in time for The Royal Holiday Concert and Party this year, a year later. There are always lots of eyes on them, but with The King carrying Baby Jacks, who is smiling a lot at everyone, are *definitely* more people who stop in the hallways to stare!

Even with the bombing last year, The Royal Holiday Concert was sold out again this year! There are added security measures, *and guards*; but even with all that, the concert is a bigger hit this year. It was a lot of fun, as well as exhausting. Bri tends to be a 'night owl,' only tonight, she tires out earlier. David and Lawrence think it's just the craziness of the holidays; Jack thinks that is part of it, yet he is still wondering if she might be pregnant.

The Royal Family and The Worthington's spend the holidays at Ashbourne Castle this year. They enjoy a special, magical Christmas that comes with having little Jacks and Elise around. The staff, *especially* Mr. Woodsley believe it or not, *love every minute of it!* He had an extra bounce in his step making sure everything *was* perfect for the family, and that the children's gifts had lots of ribbons and bows!

Bri looks around and watches the kids, listening to their laughing and happy squeals. She takes it all in, realizing the guys were right; it *is* a castle she loves, and it's become her favorite.

It's New Year's Day and the whole family is at The London Palace for Lawrence's surprise for Bri, which he has been planning for weeks! His surprise? The Royal Coronation for *his* beloved queen, with the help of his father, siblings, Gen, as well as David, Jack, and the entire Worthington Family! He needed their help to keep it a secret from her. Luckily for everyone, Bri usually goes with the flow and never really bothers reading much of the various media outlets on gossip and social circles. They just made sure not to draw her attention to any of them, even removing any parts that mention The Royal Coronation. Which, leading up to that day, has them removing all the newspapers from wherever they are, be it The Manor, The Cottage House, The Palace, or Ashbourne Castle.

That morning, Lawrence has already come back to bed after his workout and shower that morning. He only goes back to bed when she is there; Jack and David are the same way. Bri snuggles into him and rests her head on his chest. She starts tracing the grooves of his muscles on top of his t-shirt.

He closes his eyes. "I'm not sure why, but that's relaxing."

She looks up at him. "Good morning, My Handsome King!"

"Good morning, My *Exquisitely* Beautiful Queen!"

She giggles. *"That was a mouthful!"*

He gets a playful look and rolls her over, kissing her passionately...

Lawrence pulls her to him saying, "Come here, My Darling." She snuggles into his chest and they lay in silence for a few minutes before he says, "I love you." She lifts her head and he caresses her cheek adding, "I love you more and more every day, and I'm not sure how that's even possible?!"

Her eyes are a little teary and she sweetly chokes up saying, *"I love you so much!"* She kisses him tenderly.

He glances and looks again. He sees her neck is light pink. "Did I hurt you?!" He shifts to see her neck better.

"No, Ace. *I* put your hand there. And these tears," she points to her eyes, "are the visible sign that my love is actually *overflowing* for you!" She wipes her cheeks. "I can't begin to express how beautifully different intimacy is with all three of you!"

He chuckles. *"You* are very much the reason intimacy is so beautiful..." He taps a kiss on her lips.

"Lawrence, I'm going to tread lightly because of my 'behind bedroom doors' rule. When we do that, er, this," she points to her neck, "well, Jack and David," she stumbles trying to be respectful...

He smiles sweetly. "This is *our thing?"*

"Well...yes." She answers. "I want us to reclaim sex for you; to bond in the *loving* way it's intended to be! Putting your hand on my neck is a way for me to show you that I trust you *completely*. We both know you could hurt me; *I trust you never would!"*

"At the risk of crossing a line," he replies, "and I will respect it if you don't want to answer..." she nods and he asks, "how would you describe your intimacy in each relationship? Let's say you can only use one word to help us keep it within the boundary."

She thinks about it. "David and I had a magnetic bond from the beginning, something that pulls us to each other. The passion within him I've described as a 'fiery inferno' when lit, but it's *always* smoldering inside him. David keeps it tightly contained until...well...he says it can only be lit with me."

"Take that for what it means, Darling. 'Only with you' means he has had offers that he gives no real thought to." He tells her.

She is a bit surprised by that for a moment. She hasn't thought about it before; then again, she thinks to herself, '*Of course he has had offers! All three of them would!*'

Lawrence sees her thinking about that. He tells her, "Bri, I don't think you've considered *why* I get annoyed when other men's hands are on you?"

Her eyebrows come together in confusion. She innocently asks, "You mean it's not jealousy."

"*Partly.*" He truthfully answers. "*You're* 'The Princess Imperial,' *and* directly connected to The Crown. You're also 'The Grand Duchess of Newhaven' running a very prominent duchy, not to mention 'The Duchess of Ashbourne,' and soon 'The Queen!' *That's considerable power for you under all that beauty!*"

She rolls her eyes a little. "There's a difference between having someone's ear for consideration, versus power."

"Granted, you'd have to have one of us sign off on *officially* changing, or enacting, something; however, what have I told you?" She scrunches her eyebrows and slightly shakes her head. He grins, "*There's* nothing *I'd deny you!*"

"Well, yes, *but* I also know if I were to exercise that in manipulation, or had some lover on the side, *that* wouldn't be true. *And it shouldn't!*" She states.

"*I know* you wouldn't do anything of the sort." He holds her face. "Which is *why* I deny you nothing!"

She snorts a little laugh. "I wouldn't have the time, *or the energy*, for a lover on the side!" She taps a kiss to his lips. "Because I know you would deny me nothing, it's why I wouldn't have been comfortable if Rex wanted to keep me in his pocket! I was relieved he already considered that and how I wouldn't be comfortable with that either."

Lawrence nods, then asks, "What about Jack?"

"Well, let's see...Jack and I also had a connection from the beginning! He is *always* fun and so full of life, it's only natural we have a lot of fun together! His love and passion for me are right there!"

"So David's word is 'inferno' and Jack's word is 'fun.'" Lawrence notes.

"Well, let's hyphenate and say 'sexy-fun' for Jack."

Lawrence laughs, "*That sounds right!*"

"As for you and me, Ace, that one is easy! Our word is '*intense.*'"

"I think I can agree with that! But go on..." He gives her a smoldering look.

"We have this 'intense passion' that's *always* there, making us," she gestures the two of them with her finger going back and forth, "*easily* frustrated when we have to keep it all contained."

"Making it *extremely intense* when we no longer have to keep it contained!" He gently touches her neck.

"This love is growing stronger *with* our intense passion, Lawrence!" She takes a deep breath. "You, David, and Jack, are 'alpha males' in your own ways, but this vulnerability and surrendering intimacy between us is something I only have with you; *it's something I only want with you!* Just like what I have with David and Jack, I only want with each of them. I trust you'll never do this," she points to her neck again, "in a malicious way."

He shakes his head. "*Never!*"

She holds his jaw and looks into his eyes. "I feel this is a time we'll look back on and see it as one of our defining moments for us as a couple...*if* we keep trusting each other." She kisses his heart. "I truly and *deeply* love you!"

He holds her tight. "I am a king who is *nothing* without his queen!"

"I can't offer much, Ace. I can only give you all the love and adoration I have in my heart for you." She says with a loving smile.

"*That's all I want!*" He replies and she kisses him fiercely. Then Lawrence says with seriousness, "No matter what comes, no matter what Millicent throws at us, *never* doubt that I love you!"

"*As long as you never doubt my love for you!*" She replies resting their foreheads together. She clears her throat and states, "Enough of all that mushy-love stuff." She winks and he lightly chuckles, knowing she loves that stuff.

They hear the baby and Lawrence gets up. He walks over to the crib and Jacks smiles wide at his Uncle Lawrence.

"I just love how happy you are!" He happily smiles back as he picks him up. "I'm happiest too when I'm with your mama!" He takes him over to the changing table. "Let's freshen you up a bit."

Lawrence lays Jacks down on the changing table and talks to him while he changes his diaper. When Lawrence is finished, he picks Jacks up and kisses his head on his way over to Bri. She smiles wide at Jacks, who is already happily smiling at her.

"Good morning, Sweet Love!"

Bri snuggles in and feeds Jacks while she and Lawrence talk. When Jacks finishes nursing, Lawrence burps him. Bri uses the restroom and when she comes out of the bathroom, she sees something sparkle out of the corner of her eye. She turns on the closet light and steps inside.

"*Lawrence!*" She gasps. "*Where did you find this?!*"

He and Jacks walk into the closet. "Do you like it?"

"*Oh, Lawrence,*" she replies, barely above a whisper, "*this is beautiful!*" She looks closer at the fabric. "It looks like they used *real* gold thread!" She looks at Lawrence and reads his face. "This *is* real gold thread?! *Why?!*"

Lawrence smirks. "*That dress is going to make history!*"

She rolls her eyes. "*Be serious!*"

"Oh, Darling, you're about to find out just how serious I am!" He grins, then looks at the time. "We do need to get ready, though."

She exhales a light laugh asking, "*For what?!*"

"We have somewhere to be in a couple of hours." He replies.

"In formal attire?!" She asks. "*On New Year's Day?!*"

"Yes. *Now, no more questions!* I'm going to take Jacks to his dad and Uncle Jack." He smiles.

"Alright, but *only* because I love the dress!" She teases.

He grabs her bum with his free hand and pulls her close. "*Liar.*"

"Okay, okay, *because I love you, too!*" She holds his cheeks and kisses him, then she kisses Jacks' cheek several times in a row to get him to happily squeal.

Lawrence smirks. "*Better.*" He and Jacks leave the room, while Bri goes to take a shower.

CHAPTER 41
The Royal Coronation

In The Royal Chambers, Bri is almost ready to go to whatever Lawrence has planned for her. He zips up her dress, then kisses her neck.

"I have jewelry for you, too."

She giggles, shaking her head. "*Of course you do!*"

He raises his eyebrow. "*Just* close your eyes, Cheeky!" She matches his raised eyebrow. He states, "I *could* play the 'I'm The King' card."

"Isn't that what this is?" She motions to herself moving her hands up and down. "*Besides*, you *think* that card works on me..." She teases.

He lightly chuckles. "*Well*, this isn't anything I've made this time and these are on loan. I felt something from The Crown Jewels Collection would be more appropriate." He has her put the earrings on, then turns her away from the mirror while he puts the necklace on her. "Now, close your eyes." He gently moves her in front of the full-length mirror and admires her for a moment before stepping out of the reflection. He stands where he can watch her reaction. "*Open!*" She opens her eyes and stares...he steps behind her and smiles. "Call me crazy, but I was *kiiind* of hoping for more of a reaction," he grins, "preferably telling me how incredible I am, *or something along those lines...*" She turns around and kisses him fiercely. "*That works!*" He smiles with his dimples and she kisses him again.

 She pulls their lips apart, "You *are* incredible and so is this," she steps back and points to herself, "the dress, jewelry—*all of it*!" She turns different angles in the mirror. The dress is cream colored with rhinestone sequins around the upper chest and through the long sleeves; gold thread was used to make the swirls around the bottom six inches of the dress. She looks at him in the mirror. "It feels like you're trying to make me look like a qu..." Her eyes go a bit wide as she trails off, staring at herself in disbelief.

"Like what, Bri?" He has a knowing smirk on his face as he steps closer to her, then lifts her chin. "You can say it." She shakes her head with a little bit of teary eyes. "Then I'll say it! You look *exactly* like I wanted! Like a queen. *My Queen*! Soon enough, *The Queen*!" He kisses her with so much love, she can't even think, so she didn't catch everything he said. He looks at her and says, "I hope *you know* I love you deeply."

She nods. "More importantly," she can only whisper, "*I feel it*." She clears her throat. "When do we need to leave?"

He looks at his watch. "They'll wait for the guest of honor if you need another minute."

"Sounds like they've waited for you before." She gives him a faint, playful smile.

"*I'm not the guest of honor this time.*" He winks.

"In that case, I *hate* being late!" She says, quickly gathering her things to put in her small purse.

"You can't take anything with you right now." He tells her, taking her things and putting them on the dresser.

She is confused. "*That's new.*"

He smiles a dimpled smile. "Trust me," he grabs their coats, "and just come along with me." He leads her by the hand.

They get to the main door of The Royal Apartment side of The Palace. Lawrence holds open a gold-colored cloak that matches Bri's dress.

"Well, Ace, I have deduced we're leaving The Palace." She smirks and he smiles as he leads her outside. "Carriages?" She looks around. Lawrence helps her up into the first carriage and he climbs in after her. "What's going on, Lawrence? *Spill.*" The carriage starts to pull away.

"I have worked hard on this surprise, as well as *the whole family*, so I'm *not* ruining it." Lawrence says, caressing her cheek. "Please don't ask me to."

"Well," she smiles sweetly, "when you put it that way..."

He takes her hand. "Thank you!" He kisses the back of her hand.

It takes a few seconds, but Bri starts to hear cheering. She looks around and smiles. "Your fan club is out in full force today, *Your Majesty*, in spite of how freezing it is outside!"

"All these *wonderful people* are here for you, Darling!" Lawrence replies.

They both wave and smile at the people who have gathered along their short route. The carriage pulls up to the front of The Parliament Building. The cheering gets louder as they get out of the carriage. They walk up to the front door and Bri looks over her shoulder at the excited crowd.

She nervously asks him, "*What's going on?*"

"Let's go inside." He gestures towards the door.

"All these people are out in the freezing cold, like there's some kind of royal event—." She puts it all together and inhales a gasp. "Lawrence Alexander Heathherst," she scolds in disbelief, "*this is a coronation?!*"

"You said *last* New Year's was too soon and thought we should wait for the first little addition to our family to come. Having him in our family has truly been a joy, and now that we're trying, well, I don't want to put this off any longer. I took my time planning this and pulled it all together *with* our family's help!" He gestures to those who have gathered outside. "They *all* know you're here to be crowned queen, *and* they know Genevieve has been planning this *all along!*"

"It's just, *well*...this is a *huge*—." She inhales sharply, holding her breath.

He takes her hands. "*Please*," he looks at her with so much love, "do this *because* you love me *and it's time...*"

She takes a deep breath and exhales slowly. "*Alright.*"

He happily smiles. "*Really?*"

She flicks up her eyebrow. "Do you want me to answer that differently?" McMasters quietly laughs and opens the door for them; they step inside.

334

Red coronation robes are put on The King and Princess Imperial. Then someone gives Bri 'The King's Coronation Crown' and he kneels down on one knee in front of her.

"Your Majesty..." she smiles, then places the crown on his head.

In their robes, they walk into the main room on the ground floor in The Parliament Building. The ceremony, conducted by The Prime Minister, isn't long. Bri vows to support The King and the weight of The Crown; there are also vows weaved in, accounting for her marriage with The Grand Duke of Newhaven and her Noble Consort, The Duke of Ashbourne. Because of her bloodline and being The Queen, bylaws stipulate she is to have a 'Royal Consort.' For a brief moment, Bri's heart stops. Then it's read that The King name's The Grand Duke of Newhaven as her Royal Consort. That move makes Jacks 'The Heir to The Throne,' until The Queen gives birth to The King's biological child. *'He not only planned everything,'* she thinks to herself, *'he thought of everything, too!'*

Bri is gently guided to where needs to stand and The Prime Minister asks her to kneel before The King. Only right before she kneels, Lawrence holds her upper arms to stop her for a moment.

He says to her, but for all to hear, *"This* will be the *only* time The Queen will ever kneel to The King, because a *true* king *always* kneels before *his* queen."

Bri gives him a small smile and kneels before King Lawrence. He carefully puts 'The Queen's Coronation Crown' on her head, then helps her stand back up. Then they are formally announced:

> "Members of Parliament: The King and Queen of The United Kingdom of Provinces, Their Majesties King Lawrence and Queen BriaLynn."

There is a lot of applauding and cheers, even cheers can be heard coming from outside! Bri stares towards the windows and listens in awe.

Lawrence looks in the same direction and leans in whispering, *"All that is for you, My Queen!"* He takes a finger and pulls her chin to him. He smirks saying, *"Long live The Queen!"* He kisses her, then steps back. He waves for David and Jack to come over and have a moment with her.

David kneels down, "*Your Majesty.*" He stands back up and kisses her cheek.

Jack steps over and also kneels before her. "*Your Majesty.*" Then he stands back up and kisses her cheek.

She smiles with a little glare. "You both knew and somehow made sure I didn't find out?!"

David smiles. "It's not hard when you already don't read much for the media and society pages."

"I don't have much confidence in getting *only* facts," she replies, "*especially* when one of our interns mentioned they can't use *any* news media as a source for their papers! If universities won't allow news media to be a source for students to reference for *factual* information, then why on *Earth* do we even listen to them as authorities in anything at all?!"

"A fantastic question *all* intelligent people should ask!" Jack agrees.

They pose for official pictures, with their crown and robes, then with only crowns. After they're done, Genevieve helps Bri take the heavy crown off and takes it to Nigel, who is patiently waiting to switch it out with The Diamond-Heart Tiara. Nigel will take both Coronation Crowns back to The Palace with his own Royal Guards. Abby helps Bri with The Diamond-Heart Tiara, then Bri asks for a personal, separate picture to be taken with David, Jack, and Lawrence; then all four of them with Jacks for a complete family photo. Even though they are missing a few *very important* members of their family, they gather everyone for a family photo.

Bri turns to Gen. "I don't know what to say. You've been *such* a great friend to me." She reaches for Gen's hand, then she reaches for Abby's hand. "*You* both *have been*! You two, along with Amy, have blessed my life with more genuine friendship and sisterhood," she can barely whisper through her emotions, "*than I've* ever *had*!"

Gen smiles a teary smile. "We feel the same way!" Abby agrees.

The three of them grab Amy and hug each other in a group hug. They hand out tissues to each other and carefully dry their eyes and cheeks.

Bri asks Lawrence, "What's next?"

"We all have a luncheon with Parliament, diplomats, and The Royal Court at *Her Majesty*'s Royal Residence, Ashbourne Castle, in The Great Dining Hall. Then we will rest for a few hours before The Coronation Ball back at The London Palace in The Royal Grand Ballroom."

"Does that mean another carriage ride where you parade me through the streets on our way to Ashbourne?" She teases.

"What kind of king would I be," he puts his hand up to his chest, "if *I* denied your *adoring fans* their first chance to see *their* Queen?!" She giggles, rolling her eyes and shaking her head.

She looks over and sees Jacks in his car seat, sitting on a large table. She walks over to him, with Lawrence, David, and Jack gathering around them.

"Hi, my sweet boy! You look SO *handsome*! You should do a cover of GQ with your daddy and uncles!" Jacks smiles wide. "Should we go have some lunch?!" He's excited because she is excited. "Then let's get going!"

Bri steps back and Lawrence lays her gold cloak on her shoulders. Henry, Maggie, and Carlotta take Jacks, with James and Amy taking Elise, out the back way, while Phillip, Seth, Gen, and Abby go out front to the awaiting carriages ahead of Lawrence and Bri.

When The King and Queen walk outside, Lawrence holds Bri close for pictures to be taken. Lawrence helps her up into the carriage and he follows; both of them waving to the crowds of happy people cheering, '*Long live The King and Queen!*'

Bri gets teary-eyed as she feels all the excitement around her. "Lawrence...I'm lost for words, *it's overwhelming*."

"These are a representation of *almost* everyone in our country! You're more loved than you give yourself credit for, Darling!"

"Oh, I think you're blinded by the proverbial 'rose colored glasses.'" She teases him.

"No, *I'm* seeing perfectly, but *you're* glasses are *way* too dark!" He teases back.

337

"They're out here on a cold winter's day, so *please* tell me they have access to hot chocolate, tea, apple cider, *something hot* to keep them warm?!" She asks.

He lightly chuckles. "I figured you would worry about them being cold, so I made sure places that sell hot drinks would be prepared to sell more today, *and* they would be allowed to set up stands along the route today."

"That *does* make me feel better!" She smiles sweetly at him.

They wave to people on both sides of the carriage. The energy and excitement of the people makes the cold trip to Ashbourne Castle go by a little faster.

CHAPTER 42

A Royal Reception

The Great Dining Hall inside Ashbourne Castle is decorated like a page right out of a fairytale book! There are lots of red and gold, crystal, and fresh flowers. However, there are not a lot of extra dishes, or pyramids of food, like they would at The Palace. They purposely wanted to keep in line with the simplicity of Ashbourne Castle, and their new Queen's preferences.

The guests included the world's royalty, nobility, and elites. Among them, there are tons of expensive jewelry with formal attire and tiaras, not to mention suits with medals and sashes, even a few military uniforms.

"Lawrence, this is amazing!" She tells him. "You and Mr. Woodsley have outdone yourselves!"

"It does my heart good knowing you like it!" He replies. "*Mr. Woodsley* has seen to *every* detail of this reception!" He walks them to the podium.

> "Ladies and gentlemen, if you all will forgive me, I'm changing the protocol today. The Queen will sit next me and The King Father will be sitting opposite me."

He leads the way to the table. He purposely has David sitting next to her, with Jack and Abby sitting across from Bri and David. Seth and Genevieve are at the other end with Phillip; Carlotta is sitting across from them, with Henry and Maggie next to her.

After lunch, Lawrence and Bri say goodbye to their guests as they leave The Great Dining Hall. She gets a chill; she feels like she is being watched. She looks around and just sees friendly faces. She scolds herself, '*Millicent is too smart to be here herself!*' What she doesn't know is Millicent did have a couple of people sneak in after the last sweep of bugs The Royal Guards conducted. They planted a few cameras around The Great Dining Hall; they didn't dare plant more than that or they could have been caught!

Later, they meet up with their family at The Royal Apartment. When they walk into The Apartment, she sees Amy and James with Jacks and Elise. "Thank you so much, you two!" Jacks wants to go to his mama. She takes him and asks, "Does he need feeding?" Jacks starts fussing and trying to move her dress. "I guess so!"

She goes upstairs with Lawrence following her. Inside The Royal Chambers, Bri asks Lawrence to unzip her. He does and helps her take her dress off. Jacks is about to start crying, then she gets him nursing. She asks Lawrence to help take the tiara off.

She gets comfortable on the couch while Lawrence takes off some of his layers. He joins them on the couch, grabbing Jacks' soft blanket and covering him with it; he puts another blanket on Bri.

She smiles at Lawrence. "Th—." She yawns hard. "Sorry. *Thank you* for the blanket." She smiles at Jacks as he holds his blanket to his cheek.

"I'll watch and make sure Jacks is okay while you rest." He tells her so she will close her eyes.

Jack and David text that they are outside the door and Lawrence has them come in. They quietly chat and watch over Bri and the baby while she rests. She wakes long enough to change sides with him and smiles at Jack and David. When Jacks is done nursing, David takes him to burp while Bri rests a little longer. Later, they get ready for The Royal Coronation Ball. Abby and Gen have come to help Bri. Lawrence, Jack, and David, are down the hall getting ready.

Bri looks at Genevieve, "This doesn't feel right."

"*Bri*, this *is* what Seth and I have wanted *all along*!" She assures Bri. "To be in *supportive* roles."

"From Queen to Duchess?" Bri asks.

"*You're* rightful place is with Lawrence, *as Queen*! And soon, as the mother of *his* heir! As it should be!" She says. "And *I* will start our family with Seth!"

"And I'm *really* excited for the two of you starting your family!" Bri hugs her.

 Bri steps into a beautiful, deep red short-sleeve dress with a sweetheart neckline, velvet bodice with a gold rhinestone belt design. The bottom half of her ballgown is dark red satin over white satin with the edge of the dark red satin having the same gold rhinestone design as the waist. Lawrence has her 'Ruby Heart Necklace Set' for her to wear with The Diamond-Heart Tiara.

Genevieve excitedly tells her, "*You* look like 'The Queen of Hearts,' *Your Majesty*! But I think I'm going to start calling you, 'Queen Bee.'" She winks.

Bri giggles. "Yellow isn't a color I can pull off like I can black."

"Bees make life beautiful and they seek out the beauty around them!" Gen says to her.

"*That's perfect*! Our Bri *certainly* does that!" Abby agrees. She turns Bri to see her own image in the mirror. "*You're stunning!*"

From the doorway they hear, "You *definitely* look like 'The Queen!'" The ladies turn to see David standing in the doorway with Jack.

"*The Queen of OUR Hearts!*" Jack lovingly smiles.

Gen lightly laughs. "Abby and I will meet you all at The Grand Staircase with Lawrence." Bri nods.

Jack walks over to Bri first. "Bri, *you're breathtakingly stunning!* And you *do* look like 'The Queen of Hearts!' A role you're perfect for *because* of your amazing heart!" He taps his finger over her heart.

"I just want to continue our work for Newhaven, as well as The Textile Mill, The Foundation, Ashbourne, and now *the whole country.* But with a baby and trying to get pregnant, I feel like I'm trying to hold up a gigantic bolder in the middle of all that quicksand we talked about not too long ago!"

"That's why we're here, Love." David says. "Yes, you'll be working with Lawrence, but he's hoping your focus will continue being the criminal justice system, and take what we've been doing in Newhaven, and apply it, *or something similar*, to the whole country; something Uncle Henry is also helping with." He reassures her, "Bri, we can hire a nanny and Gabriel has already incorporated the duties of queen with you, so it's not the huge adjustment you're scared of because *you've already been doing it*! Uncle Henry along with Mother, Aunt Maggie, James and Amy, not to mention Abby, Genevieve, Seth, *and Phillip* will continue to be there for us." David smiles. "We meant what we have said, we've got you're back *and each other's backs*!"

"Just trust in that, *in us*, Amore Mia!" Jack says. He kisses her firmly. "I love you, *Your Majesty*!"

"I love you, *Your Grace*!" She smirks and kisses him again before he heads downstairs to wait for them.

David lovingly smiles. "It's mind boggling to think how it been almost three years since we met, and somehow our lives have already grown into something so extraordinary," he holds her hands, "all because a lost man found *the love of his life* in an amazing, feisty, sassy, and sometimes cheeky, American." He cups her cheek. "I have always been *thrilled* to call you my wife and I *always will*. You've never let this family down and you never will, because you have already lifted this family emotionally, lovingly, and yes, socially, too, but that's a side effect." She snorts a laugh. David takes her hand and leads her to the window to show her the people outside. "Look at them." He cracks the curtain. "They see an American woman who embraced a centuries-old tradition and *magnified* it! They see how great our King is, because he is partnered with a *brilliantly* intelligent, and *loving*, woman!"

She smiles sweetly with tears in her eyes and whispers, "*You'll* always *have my heart*!" She kisses him and he deepens it. "You realize if my heart is this incredible, your heart is more...even Jack's and Lawrence's. You all love me, yes; but you love each other as close brothers and support each other as such, *and* your relationships with me! *Your hearts* are more incredible than mine because, as I've pointed out before, I wouldn't stand for any of you to be with another woman!"

"If you were with anyone outside of the three of us, we wouldn't stand for it either!" He replies.

"Very true." She kisses him once more before she freshens up her make up and applies lipstick.

David holds out his hand and asks, "Shall we, My Enchanting Queen?"

Bri softly laughs and takes his hand. "*To you*, I'm Mrs. Worthington." He laces their fingers.

"You're *always* Mrs. Worthington, only now," he grins, "I'm married to *The Queen*." He kisses the back of the hand he is holding. She smiles, shaking her head as they leave to meet up with the family.

David doesn't lead her down the stairs. He leads her down the hallway to The Public Drawing Room. When Lawrence sees Bri walk into the room, he freezes and stares at her as she walks over to him. Jack pats Lawrence's shoulder to snap him out of it. Bri is smiling as she walks up to him.

He smiles adoringly at her. "You are more of a vision than I've tried to picture about this moment a hundred times!" He holds one cheek and kisses the other. He holds her cloak open. "We're going to step out onto the balcony." She turns for him to lay the cloak on her shoulders.

The family files out onto The Royal Balcony and the crowd cheers. It gets even louder when they see King Lawrence step out in front and the crowd roars when Queen BriaLynn joins him by his side. The entire family waves to the crowd with Phillip standing on the other side of Lawrence and Genevieve standing on the other side of Bri with Seth on the other side of Gen. Then David and Jack, holding Jacks, are behind Lawrence and Bri with the rest of the family around them.

Jacks is nervous with all the cheering. Everyone tries to distract him from wanting to go to his mama but when he starts crying, Bri takes him. Pictures are taken of this and used in various media outlets with a title: 'The First Public Picture of The Royal *Family*!' Under the picture the caption reads: 'Their Majesties King Lawrence and Queen BriaLynn, who is holding The Prince of Newhaven, next to them are His Highness The Grand Duke of Newhaven, and His Grace The Duke of Ashbourne.'

In all the photos, Lawrence is smiling hugely and hasn't taken his eyes off Bri. He is *ecstatic* he *finally* has *His* Queen officially beside him!

CHAPTER 43

A Royal Coronation Ball

The Coronation Ball kicks off when King Lawrence and Queen BriaLynn are introduced as they walk into The Royal Grand Ballroom. The King dances with The Queen for the first dance and continues through the next one.

Bri teases, "If I didn't know better, *Your Majesty*, I might think you are fending off anyone else who would *dare* dance with me."

"Unless they're Jack, David, or family," he holds her closer, "*I am.*" He says with a commanding voice.

"Ooo, *careful*. I need to dance with certain people, don't I? To show 'good sportsmanship' so-to-speak?" Bri innocently asks.

"No. *You don't.*" He states, then looks lovingly into her eyes. "Now that your 'The Queen,' you *are* to be *extremely* picky." He kisses her tenderly and there are some 'awes' around them.

"I'll do my best, but feel free to cut in and rescue me *anytime*!" She taps another kiss to his lips.

A little while later, Lawrence finds Bri mingling with The Earl of Willoughby. He joins the group's conversation for a few minutes, before he walks with her up on the stage.

"Ladies and gentlemen. Thank you so much for joining us to celebrate Queen BriaLynn's coronation." He wraps an arm around her waist and says to her, "I'm *eternally* grateful to you for bringing me into *your* family." There are 'awes' and Bri's eyes tear up. "You're the most incredible and loving mother I've ever seen! Baby Jacks has hit the jackpot having you as his mother," Bri wipes her tears before they fall, "as will our other children who join our family!" He looks at Carlotta, Maggie, Henry, and his own father, Phillip saying, "And there's *no doubt* our children will always be surrounded with love having our amazing family around them helping them grow up."

"That's for sure!" Bri adds looking at Carlotta, Maggie, Henry, and Phillip with lots of love of her own for them!

Lawrence looks back at Bri. "From the bottom of my heart, thank you! I love you, BriaLynn, and I look forward to our *many* years together!"

"I love you!" She lovingly smiles, with teary eyes.

He takes two champagne flutes and hands her one. He whispers, "*Your favorite.*" She smiles as she takes the glass.

Lawrence raises his glass to Gen, "To The Duchess of Brexton, *you're a wonderful person!* We've been blessed to have you in our family! To The Duke of Brexton, I'm grateful to you, Brother, for your support all these years. I wish you both all the love and happiness you deserve!" He lifts his glass a little higher and says, "To The Duke and Duchess of Brexton!"

"To The Duke and Duchess Brexton!" The guests collectively say and everyone takes a drink from their champagne flutes.

"To Queen BriaLynn, the queen of *my* heart!"

"Long live The Queen!" The guests collectively say.

He takes her out to the dance floor for another dance before David and Jack dance with her again. Afterwards, she is mingling with Lawrence when she slightly turns to take a glass of champagne from a tray, then sees Richard McCleary. Her stomach turns, seeing the smirk on his face but she manages to hide it.

"*Your Majesty.*" Richard sneers.

"Is there something you need, or do you think can we skip all this unpleasantness and go our separate ways?" She asks.

Lawrence hears this and turns to see who she is talking to, wanting to protect her. His whole demeanor changes when he sees Richard, and he takes a protective stance between him and Bri.

345

"Oh, my date just wanted to say 'hullo.'" He says with a smug look as he points just behind Bri; she braces herself knowing there is only one person this could be...

They turn to see Katie walking up to them with an arrogant smile of her own and she stands next to Richard. They both turn to see the look on Bri's face, only it's disappointing. While Lawrence's face shows annoyance, Bri's face is emotionless; she had figured as much.

Bri reads Katie's disappointed face at Bri's lack of reaction and Bri tells her, "Honestly, Katie, if you're happy, *that's all that matters*, because life is *too short* to be miserable." Bri gives her a weak smile and walks to the next group before Katie has a chance to say anything back.

Lawrence whispers in her ear, "*That doesn't bother you?*"

Bri smiles shaking hands with the guests they pass by, but she whispers back, "*Oddly, no.*"

He studies her for a moment. "*You're serious?!*"

"*I am. If she's happy, maybe she won't be so focused on me.*" She stops and looks at him. "Lawrence, we knew Katie has been in a treatment facility in Somerherst. If it's with Millicent's help, we also know Millicent would be getting something from Katie."

He holds her cheek. "You never cease to amaze me."

She shakes her head. "I've been preparing for the things to come the best I can. I'm at the point where I feel more like, 'Bring it on! Let's get this over with already, so we can move on with our lives!" He nods a little and they go to the next group of people.

A little while later, Bri catches Jack looking her way and she covertly mouths, '*Save me.*' She needed a break from all the pretentiousness. When charming Jack smoothly steps in and asks her to dance, Lawrence smiles and winks at her with a dimpled smile.

Walking out to the dance floor, Bri tells Jack, "Thank you for rescuing me, Amore Mio. I was about to do something drastic, if I had to listen to anymore snobbery!" She exhales.

346

"Wow, *that* bad." He replies.

"Not all of them. It's the few that are so pompous, it's hard to stomach listening to them! It's all so draining trying to navigate through a conversation that always circles them." She says.

"You know I'll take any reason, or no reason, to be with you, Amore Mia." He grins and she watches him do a double-take.

"McCleary?" She asks.

"Yes, but you don't want to know with who." He says.

"Katie." She says. He gives her a questioning look. "They came over to Lawrence and me a little while ago, hoping for a reaction from me, but I didn't have one." She shrugs a little.

"Seriously?"

She nods. "Let's just enjoy our dance."

"Agreed." He holds her closer.

David cuts in for the next dance. He dances with her for a few minutes before he brings up Katie. She says the same thing she told Jack and he mentions, "Have you considered she might be working *with* Millicent?"

She nods, then thinks for a moment. "Maybe Katie and Richard are meant to be a distraction, but since I didn't have any reaction maybe they have to regroup?"

"*Possibly*..." David considers what she said.

"Then again," she considers, "she could be ramping up to something."

"Let's not think about them anymore right at this moment. Let's just enjoy this dance." He pulls back and taps a little kiss to her lips, then he rests their cheeks together.

The rest of the evening, all four of them avoided Katie and Richard. At the end of the evening, The King and Queen leave before the last dance; Jack and David aren't too far behind them. They all say goodnight in the upstairs hallway of The Royal Apartment and go to their bedrooms.

In The Royal Chambers, Lawrence and Bri get ready for bed. Bri has taken her jewelry off and is staring through the vanity in front of her. Lawrence walks over to her as he untucks his shirt.

"Are you alright, Darling?" Lawrence kisses her neck as he unzips her dress for her.

"What? *Oh.*" She gives him a weak smile standing up. "I'm just tired." She takes off her dress and Lawrence tosses it in the chair next to them.

He gives her a smoldering look. "My Queen..." He pulls her into a kiss and she moans into it.

She slowly pulls their lips apart and he sees the playfulness mixed in with the tiredness. She bites her lower lip as she unbuttons his shirt. He tries to help and she lightly slaps his hands away.

"This part is for me to enjoy, Ace!" She sees he goes to argue, because he wants the control. "Isn't this my night?" She smiles behind pursed-lips and raises her eyebrow. In order for her to freely give him control, he yanks his shirt open, popping all the buttons off. She inhales deeply and exhales, "*Damn that's sexy!*"

He gives her a determined look as he captures her lips in another passionate kiss, walking backwards with her to their bed. He sits and gently pulls her to straddle him. He just stares at her beautiful face, soaking it all in...

"*My Queen...*" He whispers. He tangles his hands in her hair and she ghosts his lips as he says, "*I finally feel like——.*"

"*That you got what you wanted?*" She whispers against his lips with a little smirk.

He flips her onto the bed and straddles her as he pins her arms above her head. He looks down into her eyes with a loving playfulness.

"I finally feel like I'm on my way to becoming 'The King' I want to be, to be 'The King,' *you deserve!*" He kisses her firmly until she moans again. He sits back up, taking his tie that is draped around his neck and holds it, waiting for her to give him her wrists.

She raises her eyebrow and sasses a bit, "Aren't you going to *demand me* to give you my wrists?"

"If I demand it, then you're not *freely* submitting to me." Lawrence tells her. "That's *the only way* to have *complete* control."

"And you think I'll just give you that control? *Just like that?*" She asks.

"Forcing someone's submission is 'the coward's way.' However, if I work to seduce you, to earn your trust, then when you *freely* submit yourself to me..." he hovers over her and lightly brushes her lips with his, "that's the *ultimate* act of submission!" He sits back up.

"A true *king* who's devoted to *his* queen." She gives him her wrists. "How can I resist?" He winks at her as he ties her wrists...

When Lawrence moves his hand away from her neck, he unties her wrists as he lovingly kisses her neck. "There's nothing I'd deny you..." He grins as he moves to her feet and begins massaging one of them. She smiles as she gets comfortable with her head on her pillow. She relaxes into it and when he gets to her other foot, she is drifting off to sleep. When Lawrence realizes she is falling asleep, he carefully covers her up.

She barely wakes and softly says, "*I love you, Lawrence.*"

"*I love you, BriaLynn!*" He kisses her cheek.

He goes into the bathroom and when he comes back out, he carefully crawls into bed to go to sleep. *Life is perfect...*

CHAPTER 44
The Time Has Come

Lawrence and Bri saw David, Jack, and the baby off, along with Kahla, yesterday morning. Jack and David wanted Lawrence and Bri to spend their last day together. This morning, Bri is preparing to fly back to Newhaven. Unfortunately, Jack has a last-minute appointment in Edinburgh, so he isn't able to fly back to London to fly home to Newhaven with her.

Bri is in The Royal Chambers packing the last of her things. Lawrence comes in carrying a tray of breakfast for them.

She lightly laughs. "Wow! What do I owe the honor of being served by His Majesty this morning?!"

Lawrence sets the tray down. "I live to serve The Queen, *Your Majesty*." He wraps his arms around her and looks at her so lovingly. "You're looking *exceptionally* beautiful this morning."

"I think that comes from you being biased, *and* that you might be missing me already." She smiles.

"While I can't argue that; you're *still* exceptionally beautiful."

"Just keeping up with *My* Handsome King!" She winks and looks at the tray. "This all looks good and *smells* wonderful!" He smiles and takes the tray to the table where they sit and talk.

"How much trouble was Katie last night?" He asks.

She shakes her head and shrugs. "I ignored her all evening. I was busy either talking with our guests, or dancing with the *very* handsome men in my life."

"Do you *really* think Katie would work with Millicent?" He is worried about the possibility.

"At this point, *anything* is possible and I *refuse* to underestimate Millicent!" She replies and he agrees. "It *is* odd that, if she is working with Millicent, Millicent hasn't gone after Henry or Maggie; nor Amy, and not to mention anyone else close to me for that matter." She takes a bite thinking...then she offhandedly says, "Millicent has been quiet, *too* quiet...like this is the calm before the storm and we should be bracing ourselves. She has to be getting ready for *something!*"

After breakfast, Lawrence walks Bri outside to her helicopter. He gets a text from Phillip that says his dad needs to see him right away about an urgent matter. Phillip didn't say more than that, because he doesn't want to ruin Lawrence and Bri saying goodbye to each other and getting Bri up in the air. Lawrence explains the text before he hugs and kisses her goodbye. He leaves Bri at the helicopter door when he turns around and rushes back to The Palace. Bri climbs into the helicopter and hears a familiar text notification sound. She puts her things down and sits down. She pulls up Jack's text message and reads:

> Jack: "If you wait an hour I will fly down there and fly back with you. We've just wrapped up here."

> Bri: "I would have, but I'm already in the helicopter. Besides, I'm tired and I'll probably nap most of the way anyway. I'll see you soon! I love you!"

> Jack: "I'll be there when you land. Love you, too!"

She sends a thumbs up, then makes herself comfortable while she waits for her pilots, the Coleman's, to board the helicopter. She puts her feet up and closes her eyes...she dozes off...

She wakes up a little bit to the feeling of them lifting up into the air. She wakes up all the way when she gets an eerie feeling...She goes to look at the time on her phone, only it isn't on the table. She looks around for it, but it's nowhere... '*Odd.*' She thinks to herself. '*Where did I put it?*' She gets nervous when she remembers putting it on the table next to her, after she had finished texting Jack.

She quickly stands up and goes to the front section where McMasters or Mitchell will sit with another Royal Guard or two...*no one is there*. She tries not to panic when she realizes she is in *serious trouble*...

After seeing Bri to her helicopter, Lawrence had rushed inside. When he comes around the last corner on his way to The Royal Offices, his father is frantically coming down the hall towards him!

"*We can't find Abby, Seth, OR Genevieve!*" Phillip tells his son.

"What?! *Since when?!*" Lawrence is in shock for a second, but it quickly fades. "*Millicent!*"

Phillip nods. "That occurred to me, too! You saw Bri off, right?!"

"I was walking with her out to the helicopter when you texted." He replies.

Phillip is relieved. "Thank goodness she is safely in the air, *safe for a little while at least!* We need to make sure to have extra security in place when she lands!" Lawrence agrees.

They hear running footsteps getting closer. They turn and see McMasters rounding the corner and running up to them. They figure he has news for them, until it hits Lawrence: *he should be* on *the helicopter with Bri!* His heart sinks anticipating what McMasters says next.

"Bri's helicopter was hijacked and she is being taken to *only God knows where!*" He tells them.

Earlier, while McMasters was leading the search for Abby, Seth, and Genevieve, Mitchell and The Royal Guards, now The Queen's Guards, who were going to Newhaven, were outside The Palace preparing to leave. They had watched Lawrence walk with Bri out to her helicopter. The two said their goodbyes, then Bri boarded the helicopter and Lawrence rushed back inside The Palace.

They didn't see two of Millicent's men, also pilots, board Bri's helicopter while she was napping. When the men saw Bri sleeping, they quietly hurried to get the helicopter airborne. One of them goes into the cockpit, while the other Bri's phone and tablet, then tosses them outside the helicopter before he shuts the helicopter's door.

Bri stirs when she feels the helicopter lift up, but it will take a minute for her to wake up more. The man by the door sees her guards below with their guns drawn, only they couldn't shoot at the helicopter, because they would be risking Bri's safety. This guy sees no one is going to shoot at the helicopter and he goes to join his partner in the cockpit.

When Mitchell and The Royal Guards heard the helicopter start, they looked to see what was going on. They look around and they see her pilots, Chad and Caroline Coleman, staring helplessly at the helicopter with confused looks. Mitchell and the guards spring into action: they had a security breach! With their guns drawn, they get as close to the lifting helicopter as they dared to, but *no one* shoots at it; they couldn't risk shooting at the helicopter and hit Bri in any number of shots.

Mitchell's heart sinks. He knew this day was coming; *they all knew this day was coming*, even Bri. It was only a matter of time and not the time has come...

"*What the hell happened?!*" McMasters asks through the coms, running to the security room. "Ramsey?!" McMasters wants to see what the cameras picked up. Ramsey brings up the footage around the helipad, while Mitchell tells McMasters what little he knows so far.

"We watched her board the helicopter like she has done *so* many times in the past, and with her safely onboard, we put more focus on Seth, Genevieve, and Abby."

McMasters tells him, "The cameras show two men slipped onboard." Mitchell kicks himself. "I'm having Ramsey send this footage to The Royal Police to have them run their facial recognition software and whatever else they can do to help!"

"Good! And send it to Rex, who will send it to his people." Mitchell says.

McMasters tells Mitchell, "We knew this day was coming, so now we need everyone to get to their posts! You need to call David and Jack; I'll break the news to The King. Tell them not to call her phone, in case it draws attention to it, if by chance they somehow missed that detail. She'll reach out if she can."

After Lawrence, Jack, and David have been informed, McMasters calls Gabriel to set up a secure conference call with them, along with Rex and Coop. He asks him to stay on the line and work with Hazel to ensure the integrity and security of the call.

"Gentlemen," McMasters starts, "Gabriel and Hazel have set us up on a secured line and I have asked them to stay on the call with us to keep this call secure."

"Fine. What's going on?!" David cuts to the chase.

"Bri's helicopter was hijacked while we were all focused on the search for Abby, Seth, and Genevieve who went missing last night." McMasters says.

"Missing?!" Jack asks.

McMasters replies, "They were last seen before the last dance of the evening. Abby left a little while after Genevieve and Seth."

"We think they were taken as a distraction." Mitchell adds.

"Well, it worked." Phillip says disappointedly. Everyone nods in agreement.

"Right now, we need to focus on rescuing *all* of them." McMasters tells them. "Jack and David, how fast can you get down to London?"

David replies, "We'll leave straight away!"

"David," Jack says, "we'll pick you up in Edinburgh on the way to London!"

"I'll be ready. Oh, see if Henry will come to The Palace with us. It'd be nice for Phillip to have him there and I'll call James about having Amy, Maggie, and Mother moved to The Inn with Jacks and Elise."

McMasters tells them, "I have a text here from The Royal Police. They are working on facial recognition from the security footage and they also tracked her phone. They said the kidnappers tossed it off the helicopter, because the signal is pinging at The Palace, on or near the helipad."

"They've been preparing for quite some time to be able to pull something this big off!" Lawrence states.

"I agree with Herst!" Jack says.

"Why now?" Phillip asks. "*Why not wait until Millicent* knows *Bri is pregnant?*"

354

Mitchell shakes his head a bit. "That's what concerns us as well!" McMasters nods in agreement.

David remembers the conversation he had with Bri and Rex at The Chateau. "*Her eggs...*" He whispers. He sees everyone looking at him, so clears his throat and tells them, "Bri found out that Millicent has been wanting to get her hands on Bri's eggs! Only she wasn't worried about it." David answers. "She said it wasn't as easy as just going in and taking them."

"Which means," McMasters thinks out loud, "we have some time. How much, I don't know; we should look into that. Hazel, would you research that kind of a procedure for us?"

"I'm on it!" Hazel tells him.

Lawrence looks at Rex and McMasters. "Do we have Devonridge Hall under surveillance?" Rex nods.

McMasters replies, "Rex has had it under surveillance for quite some time."

"Let McMasters and Rex gather what they can, and we will continue this conversation when we're all together in London." David suggests and they all agree with him.

Henry is more than willing to go to London with Jack and David, as well as Hazel and Cooper. Most of The Royal Guards who are already there in Newhaven will stay there to guard The Worthington Estate and protect the rest of the family who are staying at The Inn.

CHAPTER 45
Counter Measures

The helicopter starts to descend and Bri looks out the window to see where they were landing, only it's somewhat foggy. Then again, she doesn't think she would know where they were if they were landing on a clear day. Logically, it would stand to reason that they are landing on The Devonridge Estate. As the helicopter is about to set down, the cockpit door opens and a man points a gun at her.

After the helicopter shuts off, both men come out of the cockpit; Bri doesn't recognize either of them. The first man opens the helicopter door and the other one motions with his gun for her to follow the first man out. Bri complies since she can't use her powers to compel them to do something, without knowing more.

 It seems to be foggier in some places where she can barely see a couple feet in front of her at times. Eventually, they begin walking up a narrow stony path, to a back door she can only see about five or six feet around it. She wonders if this is Devonridge Hall... They go inside an old basement of sorts and into the center of the house that is open to the floors above, with a symmetrical circle in the center. She looks up through the floors above her and sees a stained glass domed skylight.

They start climbing the stairs that go up along the wall. On the first floor she sees chipped paint covering the walls that once seemed a turquoise blue type of color, with dark wood beams and pillars. The stairs can be seen above and below through the open center of the floor. She follows behind one man, walking along very creaky wood floors and the place begins to have a familiar feel...then it hits her: '*We're* inside *The Devonridge Manor*!'

There are a lot of hallways, twists and turns. Bri is thinking they are purposely doing it this way to confuse her; *it works*! They come to a doorway, one of the men opens it and the three of them go through it. She sees a long corridor with doors and openings on both sides and she has another thought: '*We're in The Tunnels*!' The first door is opened and she is lightly pushed inside. Bri sees a bed, a toilet, and a sink, giving it all a jail cell feel. She turns to see the huge steel door shut, and she hears it lock.

The helicopter carrying Jack, David, Henry, Hazel, and Cooper, lands at The Ashbourne Estate. It was a quiet flight as they all absorb Abby, Genevieve, and Seth are also missing, as well as Bri. They try not to let their minds think about the horrible trouble all four of them are in!

Lawrence, Mitchell, and Mr. Woodsley are waiting for them outside as they land. Lawrence hugs Jack, David, and Henry, then shakes hands with Hazel, Cooper, and McMasters. They all walk to Ashbourne Castle and Mitchell goes to apologize to everyone.

David shakes his head. "No apologies. *We all knew* this was coming, *especially Bri*; it was only a matter of when. Let's just focus on finding her." He pats Mitchell's shoulder with Mitchell giving him an appreciative look.

Lawrence says, "Henry, Mr. Woodsley here will see that you get to The Palace where my father is waiting for your arrival." He turns to Mr. Woodsley and tells him, "I trust you'll take care of the man who is Bri's father in *every* way."

Mr. Woodsley's eyebrows go up a little. "I'll *personally* see to it, Sir!"

"I know you will." Lawrence says, shaking Mr. Woodsley's hand; Mr. Woodsley slightly bows.

The rest of them make their way through The Castle and outside The Main doors where there is an SUV waiting. They all climb inside with Cooper getting into the driver's seat so he can take them to the back entrance of The Underground Secret Society Headquarters. He carefully watches to make sure they are not being followed, taking an indirect route to be *absolutely* sure.

They turn on the long, barely used, back road until they come to Rex's parked car. They all get out of the SUV and see Rex waiting for them. There are quick introductions and Rex shakes all their hands. He gestures to the door that is open for them, but McMasters pulls back when he sees Rex is a bit nervous to let him and Mitchell inside. This location would bring Rex, and his organization down, *including his allies*.

McMasters says to Mitchell in front of Rex, "You *never* saw this place."

Mitchell says with seriousness, "*What place?*" Rex nods in appreciation and they go inside.

Rex has everyone sit around the conference table and tells them, "We don't know much at the moment. Some of the people I have working on the inside are trying to add some cameras, while covertly gathering information; I'll know more a little later." Rex says. "We *must* be careful. If Millicent finds out about any one of my people, or *suspects* anyone as a spy, she'll kill them on the spot. If she finds out we're closing in, she could strike out in any *number* of ways, like killing everyone working for her and starting over; *she's done that a few times before. And,* if she feels all hope is lost with her plans with Bri, she *will* kill her."

Lawrence is alarmed. "*What do you suggest we do?!*"

"We start by making her think we're looking in the wrong places." He replies and he sees them think about that. He suggests, "Jack is the only one who has been traveling with her and I suggest he continue to be the one who travels with us; my team knows him and already trust him."

Jack doesn't hesitate. "*Absolutely!*" David and Lawrence are in full support!

"David," Rex addresses him next, "I hoped you would stay here at Ashbourne. I need someone down here to be 'on point,' so-to-speak, while I meet with various contacts to get more information about Millicent's plans."

"Anything you need!" David asks.

Rex adds, "I don't expect anything to happen, but if anything does happen to me, Mr. Woodsley will know the procedures in that event, and he will notify all those who would need to be notified."

"I can help—." Lawrence starts to say. "*Right.*" He realizes. "I have to be the public face."

"Right." Rex replies. "Gentlemen, I'm not trying to be frustrating, I'm just trying to reduce the danger of people dying, especially the four we are *desperately* trying to find *and rescue!*" The guys say they understand. Rex gives them an empathetic look. "What you need to do now is the hardest. I need you to be patient *and wait.* We are working fast, because we know how dangerous Millicent is, but we need to do it as safe as possible, *for everyone!*"

They follow him into the bigger room. They look at all the monitors showing the surveillance they have all over the world. Hazel brings up the cameras they have around The Devonridge Estate.

"We have been trying to get more cameras up, but it's harder than someone might think. We have to put them in particular places so they aren't found by Millicent's people, so some of them are really tiny." Rex tries to give them some hope. "I have more people mixed in with hers than *ever* before, because we were getting ready for what Bri wanted to do: to rescue everyone held hostage; clean everything out of the prison cells; and blow up the tunnels. At the same time, Hazel is going to launch a cyberattack on Millicent's emails, phone, and website, so that anyone visiting her website would be embedding viruses to infect all her associates' computers and phones, all of their electronics!" He tells them. "We were working on that when we got the news of the shipment of children and young adults. We could rescue them, *or* complete the tasks for the cyberattack, but we couldn't do both at the same time that time around. She chose saving the young people and children."

"And she would choose them again!" Lawrence says, and the others agree.

"We still put everything in place, because we wanted to time the cyberattack and bombing at the same time for next week." Rex says. "I had my people putting the finishing touches on that, only they've shifted into gathering intel. As soon as I know anything more, you will know as well." The guys tell him they appreciate that.

Bri has been sitting on the bed in her cell, or pacing. She is sitting down when two other men come in and take her to the opposite end of the main tunnel. There is a wooden door with a frosted window in the top half that one of them opens and they go inside. It is a small room with two chairs to the left, right by the door. There is a small window with a counter and a door next to it. The door opens and a male nurse has the two men bring her back.

Bri looks around as she walks down a narrower hallway and notices a lab in one room, then an exam room. She is pushed into the third room that Bri quickly assesses is some sort of an operating room.

Bri hears a recognizable voice say, "Strap her down, boys! She isn't leaving until I have *everything* I need." Bri doesn't need to look to know it's Millicent.

Bri tries to fight being strapped down to a table, but the men are too strong for her. She does give them quite the struggle, because the men are breathing heavy by the time they have secured her in all the restraints. Bri watches the nurse as he sets up to put in an IV. Millicent walks over to Bri, followed by a woman in a white coat over scrubs, which she rightfully assumes is a doctor. Bri's eyelids are getting heavy; she tries to fight this, too, but it's pointless. She uses her last conscious moments to pray Millicent *doesn't get what she wants*...

When Bri is regaining consciousness again, she overhears Millicent getting angry at the doctor over something Millicent isn't happy about. Bri lays there, as still as she can, and focuses on listening.

She hears Millicent angrily ask, "*What do you mean?!*"

"I'm sorry, Ma'am. There's a process using the course of her monthly cycle *just to prepare* her eggs to harvest. It's biology and no other way around it, Ma'am." The doctor takes a little deeper breath when she sees Millicent take half a step back. "Besides, had I done anything right now, it could've put her current pregnancy at risk!" Bri's heart catches that. "At least now, with this pregnancy, you're ahead of schedule."

Millicent scowls as she thinks about not getting the money from Bri's eggs she desperately needs. She exhales and asks with irritation, "How far along is she?!"

"Without a full examination and asking her some questions, I'm guessing eight, *maybe* twelve, weeks." She tells her.

"Why didn't we know about this sooner?!" She asks.

"Her OB/GYN is keeping her information on a computer that *isn't* online so it can't be hacked." One of the guys tells her.

"If it's on a computer, it *can be* hacked. I just need to find a better hacker! I need to get my hands on this 'webmaster king' and get him working for me!" Millicent says. Bri smiles to herself knowing Hazel is working with her...

Bri slowly moves her head and Millicent catches this. "*It's about time!*" Millicent snaps. Bri is blinking her eyes open so she can focus. Millicent tells the two men, "There's a change of plans! Take her back to her holding cell until I make arrangements for other *accommodations*."

Millicent puts her phone up to her ear walking out of the room. The men release Bri's arms, hands, and legs from the straps, then one of them goes to carry her, but the doctor says it would be better if they help Bri to walk. What the doctor doesn't tell them is that walking could help Bri regain her strength quicker, so if there is an opportunity to escape between now and whenever, she might have a chance!

Back at The Underground, David, Lawrence, and Jack wait as Hazel and Rory bring up the new video feed after one of Rex's people inconspicuously placed a very teeny tiny camera in a hole within the old block wall outside Bri's cell and inside her cell just above the small window with bars. They see some movement and everyone watches as Bri is being helped walking as she goes back into her cell.

Lawrence asks, "What happened to her?"

Rex is on speaker phone and answers Lawrence's question, "My guys say she was with a doctor in an exam room. She was given something to knock her out, but that's all he knows at the moment."

David angrily states, "*Millicent must've tried to get her eggs!*"

"What *will* Millicent do if she does get them?" Someone in the room innocently throws out there. "Wouldn't Millicent need a surrogate?"

"Yes." Rex replies. "And knowing Millicent, she would have a surrogate already lined up to carry a baby."

David is horrified at the thought, "It could be Katie!" Lawrence and Jack are also horrified at that!

Lawrence adds, "She could sell the rest of the eggs to other monarchies *and make a fortune*! She would kill Bri, because she will have no more use for her, as well as the three of us, once her surrogate is pregnant." Lawrence looks at David. "Then she would be able to reposition herself within The Monarchy! *Hell! She'll* become *The Monarchy again*! We *can't* let that happen!" They all shake their heads.

"What if she's already pregnant?" Jack asks. "Wouldn't whatever process it takes to get her eggs endanger a pregnancy?"

Lawrence is alarmed. "We have been trying, so there is always that possibility!" David is also nervous and concerned.

Rex tries to put them at ease a bit telling them, "If she has hired a good doctor, and knowing Millicent she has hired one of the best fertility doctors in the world, I would think that would be the first thing they would check for." The guys agree.

Hazel continues to work behind the scenes trying to help them figure out what Millicent is planning and what her next move is. Lawrence, David, and Jack are glued to the screens, watching and waiting...

Bri lays on the bed and focuses on the voices she hears in the corridor...'*Ugh!*' She exhales; she can't make out what any of them are saying, and the voices fade away.

When it's quiet, she assumes Millicent could be watching from a hidden camera, so she whispers as quietly as she can, *"Jessica, I need to see you please."* Jessica appears before her. Bri has a worried look as she covertly whispers, *"Is there any way I can escape?"*

"You won't be able to yet." Jessica replies.

The door to her cell opens and different men come in. One man puts a pillowcase over her head and grabs her upper arm telling her, "Let's go!" He pushes her out the door.

They lead her down the hall and have her wait. There is a group of people by the outside door, some with hoods, and there are some white vans right outside. It's dark out, so some of Millicent's people put night vision goggles on and cut the lights outside. They want to apply counter measures in case there are hidden spies in the woods, drones above them or satellites hacked watching their location.

Outside, each van is backed up to the door and loaded up with those who have hoods on. They do this five times to prevent anyone on the outside from seeing what they are doing, or where they are going. David and Lawrence are watching the screens until the lights outside The Tunnels are turned off. They glance at the blank screen and start watching it again when the headlights on the vans pop on. Then they watch the vans' lights file off the screen. From the screen, they didn't know all five vans would be going to separate locations.

Millicent purposely told people *only* what they needed to know, *nothing more.* Rex's men have to be careful not to be detected, so they have to limit any questions they would ask. Hazel and Rory work to locate these vans on satellite, while Rex has five of his people catch up to the vans and follow them to wherever they go.

CHAPTER 46
"New" Accommodations

With a hood still over her head, two men lead Bri back through The Tunnels. They get her right inside The Manor where there is a narrow, spiral staircase they climb; she thinks the steps are made of stone. At the top of these stairs, they take her hood off because the floor has holes in some places and is falling apart in other places; she needs to see to safely navigate around these things. They warn her where they can, where to walk to avoid the weaker places they know about.

Eventually, they come to the room they are to bring her to and push her inside. She trips a bit, but she catches herself. The men quickly leave, locking the door behind them. The lighting is dim with only a lamp on, so she finds a light switch and flips it on. She blinks several times for her eyes to adjust to the light. The room has been swept, dusted, and scrubbed down. New mattresses have been brought in with fresh, new bedding on it; along with an overstuffed chair and ottoman. '*Odd.*' She thinks to herself. '*How would she know about the chair—Katie.*' She rolls her eyes thinking to herself; this confirms Katie *is* working with Millicent. '*But why would Katie bother to tell her about a specific chair? Better question: why would Millicent even bother with it? Then again, Millicent could think that if I was more comfortable, 'her heir' would be, too?*' Bri exhales, shaking her head; it only has to make sense to Millicent.

When she sees books on a bookshelf and movies to watch, she starts to wonder how long Katie has been working for Millicent? She remembers the last time she sat and talked with Katie, and how Bri *had* hoped she *finally* had gotten through to her; that Katie was starting to come around. Then, when it came time to make arrangements for her to go to a private facility, Katie said she no longer needed Bri's help. '*Millicent must've gotten to her by then...But then why hasn't Millicent gone after Henry or Maggie, not to mention Joe, Sam, or Mitch?*' She wonders. '*Surely Katie would've told her that's the family that means the most to me, outside of my in-laws? Then again, Katie loves the Bradshaw's, too...*' Bri shakes her head; she can't think about that right now. She looks around to take it all in, hoping *something* will spark an idea of how to escape.

There is an archway and a step down into a small section. '*This feels familiar...*' She thinks to herself. It's when she sees another two-shelf bookcase it registers; she is in The Duke of Devonridge's room! She thinks to herself, '*Well, this should get interesting when he finds out* I'm *staying in his room!*' To one side of the bookshelves, there is a small table with two chairs, sitting in front of the window right there.

Bri goes over and sits in the overstuffed chair where she calls for Jessica. When Jessica appears, Bri asks, "What have you found out? Is Millicent trying to get her hands on my eggs?"

"Millicent *was* going to have the doctor remove some of your eggs, but the doctor couldn't. As you know, it isn't that simple; however, you're already pregnant." Jessica tells her.

"I heard them talking as I was waking up. The doctor must've followed procedures to check for that first, or it could've caused me to miscarry." She looks at Jessica. "Is this pregnancy meant to come to term? Is this the young man I've seen in spirit?"

Jessica kindly smiles. "Yes."

"Knowing a spirit is in perfect form, it wouldn't show any abnormalities that would be on, *or in*, a mortal body." Her eyes get a little teary. "Do you know *for sure* I wasn't *given* anything that could hurt this baby?" She puts her hand on her lower abdomen. "That this baby will be healthy?"

Jessica kindly smiles and says to ease her mind, "You will have a healthy baby and raise him to be the next 'King of The United Kingdom of Provinces.'"

"Thank you." Bri says, then exhales slowly to relax her nerves.

There is a knock on the door, before it's unlocked. Bri isn't surprised to see Katie and watches her put a bag with fruit and various snacks on the bed on her way over to talk to Bri.

Katie explains, "I'm to tell you that while this door will be locked, should you try to escape, the floors beyond this one are unstable in a lot of places, so you may want to think twice about trying anything." Katie continues talking, but Bri isn't paying much attention. She looks back out the window at the blackness of the night, with stars peaking between the pockets of clouds in the sky. She thinks of how worried Lawrence, Jack, and David must be...

"*Damnit*, Bri! *Aren't you listening*?!" Katie snaps.

"No, Katie." Bri honestly replies. "My mind is a bit preoccupied." She turns to Katie, emotionless. "What is it that you need to say to me?"

"*Nothing*." Katie grumbles. She looks at the doctor who is standing just inside the door. "I'll be back in twenty minutes for you." Katie stomps to the door and leaves, locking the doctor in with Bri.

Bri looks at the doctor who gives Bri a little smile, but Bri doesn't return it; she sits down. The doctor walks over to Bri, "I swear I didn't choose this, Your Majesty! She threatened to kill my husband and children if I didn't do this for her. *I even prayed you were pregnant!*"

Bri is confused. "*Why?*"

The doctor nervously clears her throat. "It's the only thing that could have prevented me from harvesting your eggs, and, *hopefully*, keep my family safe. Since you hadn't announced a pregnancy, she assumed you weren't. I insisted on a pregnancy test to be *absolutely sure*; telling her you could be so early in a pregnancy that you wouldn't have known yet. She relented and I was able to test your blood *and prayed*. I was so relieved and sending up a silent, thankful prayer, or few, that the result came back positive!" She squats down beside the chair. "Your Majesty, you have *no* reason to trust me, but I *swear* to you, *on the lives of my own family*, I'll put you and your baby's safety above *everything and everyone else*."

Bri gives her a compassionate look. "Thank you, Doctor. Let's hope it doesn't come to that."

"Then I will die doing the right thing!" She states. "*Now*, my name is Doctor Sheila Blackwell." They shake hands.

Bri and Dr. Blackwell discuss medical information. She gives her the very minimum, but she does tell her she has had c-sections. She said she will prepare the operating room when the time gets closer. Although, she is hoping Bri is rescued *long* before that; Bri is hoping for the same thing! Katie comes back and they wrap up; Bri walks the doctor to the door. Katie hands Bri her dinner tray and she quietly says 'thank you' as she takes the tray from Katie. She goes over to the small table by the window.

"Would you see if Millicent would be able to get me a breast pump?" Bri asks. "I'm not sure what to do with the milk yet."

Katie points to the walk-in closet. "There's one in there with a small freezer. Sara Kemp should be able to smuggle the milk into The Palace." Katie sees the surprised look on Bri's face. The look is hearing 'Sara Kemp,' only Katie misinterprets the look on Bri's face and says, "Millicent isn't the monster you think she is, and neither am I."

"I never would've checked in on you last Fall to see how you were doing, and how things were going for you, if I thought you were a monster like Millicent." Bri tells her.

Katie is a little taken aback by that, she isn't sure what to say so she doesn't say anything more. She and the doctor leave and Jessica joins Bri at the small table while she eats.

"How do I get out of this?" Bri asks her.

"Bri, you *are* going to get out of this place," she motions the room with her hands, "but it's going to take a bit of time, because there is something you need to do first in 'The Secret Lab.'"

"What could *I* do in The Secret Lab?" Bri asks. "I'm not a scientist."

"As you already figured, regardless of how vile The Duke was, *and is*, he did make some fantastic discoveries!" Jessica tells her. "We will need to wait until it's a night when they won't feel they need to check on you, so you will be alone until morning."

Bri asks before she takes her next bite of food, "How are David, Jack, Lawrence, and the family doing?!"

"They are all worried, but they're working on a plan." Jessica tells her. "*Patience* will work to *everyone's* advantage." She tells Bri a little bit about what's happening with them while she eats.

CHAPTER 47
The Secret Lab

Reports are making their way to The Underground Headquarters as Rex's men catch up to Millicent's vans. The first report tells of the man in the first van yanking a hooded person out of the back of the van, then he pushes them to their knees and shoots them in the back of the head. His head snaps in the direction of running footsteps the man hears and he takes off down the block. The footsteps are of one of Rex's people now giving chase. Millicent's guy turns a corner, a minute later a car speeds past Rex's guy.

Rex's guy goes back to the dead hooded person. They remove the hood and they see it isn't Bri, Seth, Abby, or Genevieve! One-by-one, all of the hooded persons' fates are ending the same way...

"I sure wish that vile woman would get bored with killing people!" Jack asks. David agrees.

Lawrence tells them, "It's easy to kill as many as she does, because she doesn't have a conscience."

They go back to the footage of when all the vans leave...it takes several minutes, but they barely make out an SUV leaving The Tunnels, then The Estate. Their hearts sink, because *if* that one had Bri in it, that van could be anywhere right now!

"HOW THE HELL DID WE MISS THAT?!" Lawrence exhales in anger, throwing his glass and smashing it into the fireplace.

McMasters had been in contact with his CIA, FBI, MI-6, and Interpol connections. Everyone believes Millicent did not take Bri out of the country and they believe she is being kept somewhere in The Duchy of Devonridge; their educated guess would be The Devonridge Estate. Unfortunately, The Estate includes several houses, along with The Tunnels.

"Keep in mind, any rescue attempt *will trigger Millicent* to move Bri somewhere else." Rex frustratingly says. "*Somehow*, she found out about the attempt MI-6 made to rescue Abby, Genevieve, and Seth." He remembers his last conversation with his guy inside Millicent's circle. "Donovan said he isn't going to tell any of our people about our plans until it's time, then there's less of a chance of Millicent planning anything ahead!"

It takes several nights before everyone is comfortable that Bri won't try to escape. A little while after Katie has taken Bri's dinner tray away, Bri calls for Jessica.

"Am I alone the rest of the night so I can go to this lab?"

"Yes." Jessica answers.

Bri goes to the place where the switch to the lab is hidden. She lifts up the floorboard and pushes the button.

"Bring a bottle of water with you." Jessica says as she points to one. "You'll need it."

Bri puts the board back and grabs a bottle of water. Then she walks over to the wall where the door panel is ajar and opens it. She steps inside and closes the door behind her. There is no lighting, but with Jessica's light she is able to lead the way down to the lab. Jessica's light is perfect, because it was bright, but only Bri can see it!

Inside the lab, Bri half expected The Duke of Devonridge to appear and start yelling at her to get out of his lab. Then again, the more Bri thinks about it, being in Jessica's light, *Jessica's light* might be what *is* keeping The Duke away...

Bri walks over to the lab tables. On the wall behind them is a *huge* array of various chemicals, flowers, herbs, anything and everything conceivable one would need for any kind of experiment. A large section labeled 'POISONS' catches her eye. She pulls an old dusty journal off the shelf next to them and randomly opens it to...*How to Make Someone Sick*. It talks about how Silver Ash, Pneoxin Milk, and Furine, if administered in small doses, any one of them will make someone sick; doubling the dosage would make someone deathly *sick*, but it wouldn't necessarily kill them. Anything more than that would kill them; however, it would change the taste of the food or drink too much and the victim would taste the poison and most likely wouldn't consume a lethal dose.

369

Jessica points out a book for Bri to look at titled: *'Crimson Powder.'* Bri opens it and flips through its pages. It contains all the information and discoveries The Duke learned over the years, even all the failed recipes to create a cure.

Bri gasps, *"Jessica..."* She stares at a page, "Did you know he actually *created* an 'antitoxin' and a vaccine for crimson powder poisoning?! *But why doesn't it work better?*" She wonders, then reads further and understands. "He put a watered-down version out there! *That's why it never works!*" She reads a bit more. "It looks like he came up with the vaccine to make one's body immune to the poison, but..." she flips the page, then flips the last few which are blank pages, "wait. *That's it?* Then what?"

"He was looking into testing it out on a couple of people." Jessica replies. "But he never got far with it."

That doesn't seem like a problem for them when they take, *or kidnap,* whatever or whoever they want!" Bri states. "He could've mass produced it and earned a ton of money!" Then it occurs to her. *"He didn't want it mass produced!* It was his 'go to poison' just like it is for Millicent!" Bri's eyebrows come together as she wonders, "Did he vaccinate her to protect her?!"

Jessica shakes her head. "He was torn. He wanted to make sure it was safe for her, yet at the same time, he never wanted to wipe out the effects of the poison with anyone, even her." She gets Bri back to the task at hand. "Now, the reason I had you come down here is for this vaccine specifically, which can be made right here; you just need fresh water," Jessica gestures the bottle of water Bri has in her hand, "and the recipe." Bri looks down at the book.

"You can't be serious!" Bri says in disbelief. *"I'm not a scientist!"*

"You don't have to be! Follow the directions *exactly*, and I'll help you!" Jessica says, then answers her next questions, "Yes, you'll have enough time, and no, no one will know because no one even knows how to get down here."

"Why didn't they just look for the lab by looking in all the outside windows?" Bri asks.

"The lab needed to be protected from others until this precise time." Jessica answers. "After your time here, it won't matter anymore who finds it." Bri nods in understanding and gets to work on the vaccine.

It takes a couple of hours, but Bri has made the vaccine and she fills a vial. Jessica tells her, "Drink it, Bri." Bri looks at her as she places a hand on her lower abdomen. Jessica gives her a reassuring look. *"Trust me."*

That's all Jessica has to say and Bri tosses the vial of antitoxin in her mouth. It tastes horrid, but she forces herself to swallow it down in one gulp...she does a full body shake.

Bri asks Jessica, "How fast will it work?"

"It will work when you need it to!" Jessica replies. Bri gives her a bit of a confused look. Jessica adds, "That's all I can say."

Bri refills the vial and is able to fill another one, plus a partial. She cleans up her mess and puts everything back. She sees another journal and adds it to what she is going to bring up to the bedroom with her, but she'll keep it all right inside the passageway door. Then she can pull things out to look through and read when she's alone, while keeping it all safe from Millicent.

Bri is about to leave with a stack of things she has gathered, when she sees the desk and wonders if there is some sort of bag she can use. She comes around from behind the lab table and walks over the desk; something on a bookshelf catches her eye. She picks it up and sees it's a small drawstring bag she can maybe use for the vials. She looks around some more and finds a leather messenger bag on a bottom shelf. She pulls it off shelf and a small  wooden box falls onto the floor. She goes to pick it up and sees an old pocket watch had started to fall out. She picks it up with the box and notices another familiar symbol etched into it: a snake wrapped around what looks like a flame. She is about to put the pocket watch back inside the box when she gets an idea. She looks at Jessica, and she nods at Bri.

Bri briefly closes her eyes and quietly says, "*Lord, help me...*"

 She goes back over the lab tables. First, she puts her stack of reading materials inside the messenger bag. Then she carefully wraps each corked vial in a paper towel to protect them from easily breaking, securing each one with a rubber band. Next, she grabs a small plastic bag and a pair of gloves. She puts the gloves on, along with the goggles and a face mask again. She opens the pocket watch and carefully puts a tiny amount of crimson powder on the face of the watch. She

closes it and shakes it to spread the powder. She holds it by the end of the chain and drops the watch portion into the powder to dust the outside of it. Then she carefully puts the watch and chain into the small plastic bag, then dumps out the extra powder before she closes it up. She puts everything away again and cleans up the counter once more. She uses her left hand to start carefully taking the gloves off, then throws them away. Then she thoroughly washes her hands before putting on another set of gloves and puts the bagged pocket watch into the drawstring bag; she ties it up. She carefully takes those gloves off and thoroughly washes her hands again, before taking the mask and goggles off. She puts the drawstring bag into an outer pocket of the messenger bag. She takes the messenger bag up the stairs and sets it all right by the door, inside the passageway.

Bri goes into her room and gets ready for bed. She grabs a small snack from the bag Katie brought her earlier to refill what Bri may have already eaten from the last bag she had brought. As Bri eats her snack, she thinks about her escape and the snacks she started collecting, just in case she has to hide somewhere for any length of time. When she crawls into bed, she is surprised she feels hopeful...

Rex has told the family that they know Bri is being held at The Devonridge Manor. They all think they might have a better chance of rescuing her, if Jack is the only one that goes in to do it. Rex has Jack brought to the border of The Duchy of Devonridge and dropped off not far from The Devonridge Estate. Jack will hike the rest of the way to the edge of The Estate to meet up with Rex's lead guy, Donovan. He will get Jack through Millicent's high voltage fence she has around the entire estate, then explains how to get back across once he has Bri with him.

CHAPTER 48
Stopping Leaks

Bri has been learning the routines of those coming in and out of her room. Lately it has been mostly Lady Sara Kemp, although Bri isn't sure why this changed. She has also been watching out the windows and noting how often they patrol, which is a long time in between rounds. She has also been tracking the moon and it seems to be getting fuller, which will help her escape one night, *if* she escapes soon.

She has been reading and going through all the things she has collected, learning quite a bit each time she goes through them. She has been back to the lab and looking through more books and papers. She has been talking with Jessica about escaping, and now that Bri has a rather good feeling for the comings and goings of people, she needs to figure out how she will actually escape and where she will go.

Bri has a good sense of direction, and she has been studying at an old map of The Duchy of Devonridge that she also found in the lab. Jessica tells her the landscape is vaguely the same, but she will help Bri navigate around when the time comes. Bri's eyes are getting heavy, so she gathers everything up and puts it all inside the passageway door.

She goes to the overstuffed chair and rests her eyes for a little while. A knock on the door wakes her and Sara comes in with a tray of food. Bri rubs her eyes as she walks over to the table where Sara put the tray.

Sara tries to comfort Bri. "This won't be forever."

Bri sits and lays the napkin in her lap. She tiredly replies, "Sara, when this is over, and if it all goes Millicent's way, I'll be dead."

"No, you won't." Sara makes a shooing gesture with one hand.

Bri's eyebrow goes up at Sara's naivety. "What do you think is going to happen once Millicent has my baby?" Her hand is on her lower abdomen. "She *will* kill me, because she will have no more use for me. What *you* need to think about, *Ms. Kemp*, is that if she is going to kill me when she's done with me, what do you think she'll do to you, *to anyone*, when they are no longer useful to her?" There is a long silence as Sara takes that in.

Bri sees Katie is at the doorway. She is also contemplating what Bri said to Sara. When she sees Bri looking at her, she quickly tries to brush it off.

"Don't be so overly dramatic, Bri!" Katie says.

Bri asks Katie, "What do you think she'll do when she no longer needs you working for her?"

"I'm *not* working *for* her." Katie corrects her. "I'm going to be part of her family. Millicent says she'll give Richard and me a duchy when she is running things again."

Bri says with sincerity, "I meant what I said earlier, if you're happy, that's all that matters."

"*Oh, I am!*" Katie replies.

Sara leaves with Katie, locking the door behind them. Bri eats and walks around the perimeter of the large rooms for exercise. In the beginning, Katie had come numerous times to see what she was doing, making sure Bri wasn't trying to escape. But now, Bri can walk without interruptions...she sometimes pictures wearing grooves into the wood floor with all the loops she makes. She does some yoga and Pilates to try to keep herself in some kind of shape, and ready for whatever comes.

Rex, Lawrence, and David have noticed Lady Sara Kemp coming and going from Devonridge Hall with Katie. Since Sara also works at The Palace, Rex has tasked Lawrence to meet with this woman to see if she will smuggle a phone into Bri. Because of his loving, fatherly nature, Lawrence asks Henry to help in hopes it will help Sara to side with them.

McMasters gives Lawrence a secure phone, fully charged, along with a charging cord. All noises are silenced, Hazel has added specific numbers and called to make sure the service is working, then the phone is turned off again. All that is left is for it to be slipped to Bri with the charging cord.

Lawrence arranged a meeting with Sara Kemp, having her bring him and Henry breakfast to his office in The Royal Apartment. They ask her to have a seat in a chair at the table. They can see how nervous she is, hesitating as to whether she should sit down; she is shaking like a leaf. Both Henry and Lawrence have compassion for this young woman who is still so very naïve.

Lawrence kindly says, "Please," he motions the chair, "sit and hear us out."

When she sits, Henry shifts in his seat to face her better. She starts to nervously fidget and looks from Henry to Lawrence.

Henry says in his fatherly, comforting tone, "We need your help, My Dear."

Lawrence shifts towards Sara. "I'm going to cut to the chase. I have it on good authority you're working for Millicent." She starts to shake her head and is about to deny it, but Lawrence says in his kingly voice, but with a kind tone. *"Please, don't lie to me.* All I'm asking is for you to slip these to her." He slides the phone with the cord wrapped around it towards her. He remembers what Bri said she offered Claude Devereaux's nanny and makes a similar offer. "If you give these to her, I will grant you immunity and give you a new identity with a whole new life *anywhere* in the world you want to go."

All Sara wants to do is get out of there as fast as she can. She is feeling guilty for 'helping' Millicent, as Millicent framed it, to get back her family. She remembers what Bri said to her about Millicent getting rid of people she no longer has a use for, and once Millicent gets what she wants, The Throne, Sara now realizes she won't be useful anymore after that and she is terrified.

She doesn't say anything, she just grabs the phone and charging cord, shoving them into her pocket under the apron she has on as she scurries out of the room. Lawrence and Henry nervously look at each other, trying to be hopeful Sara will give the phone and charging cord to Bri.

"Why else would she take them if it isn't to give them to Bri?" Lawrence asks. Henry shrugs with his nervous look. Lawrence thinks out loud, "Of course Bri would come up with all sorts of reasons to be cautious about any calls coming from that phone..."

"Then we make sure we are, too!" Henry replies. "Ask her something only she would know if she does call." Lawrence agrees and he makes a note to pass that along to the others.

Everyone is hoping Bri will have the phone and charger in a few days or so. They didn't know that Sara kept losing her nerve to slip Bri the phone and charger, but when she got another surge of courage to do it that particular night, she is determined to go it and get it over with.

That evening, Sara brings Bri's dinner tray up and carefully puts it on the table. Sara is walking back to the door when suddenly Millicent bursts into the bedroom and Sara jumps. Bri walks over to them and sees Millicent is *coldly angry*. She sees Katie is with her, hugging a tablet close to her chest. Bri is trying to think back to what Millicent could possibly be upset with her about, because there is *no way* Millicent could know about The Secret Lab, not after all this time!

"*Lady Kemp!*" Millicent says through gritted teeth. Bri's head snaps to look at Sara; confused as to what Millicent could be upset with her about... Sara shrinks back with a step and has a terrified look on her face. Millicent's eyebrows are tightly furrowed in anger. "Sources tell me you recently met with The King." Millicent watches Bri's reaction closely and determines with Bri's surprised look that Sara hasn't told Bri anything about the meeting.

"I didn't say *anything!*" Sara desperately says. "*I swear!*"

"*You know how to find Bri!*" Millicent angrily states. "*And now I have to move Bri tomorrow!*" Bri's heart stops...she can't be moved; she has to escape *tonight!*

"I *swear* I didn't say anything!" Sara pleas.

"I believe you." Millicent says walking up to Sara with a fake smile on her face. She puts her hands on Sara's upper arms. "You see child, the reason I'm able to do so much without people finding out about any of my plans all these years, is for a few reasons." She starts to walk behind Sara; Bri senses it's like a predator circling its prey. "You see, when a potential for a leak arises, *no matter how small*, I *always* put a stop to it straight away."

Sara thinks Millicent is referring to having to move Bri to be sure no one tries to rescue her; Bri is suspicious Millicent is up to something. However, in one quick movement Millicent grabs Sara's head with one hand and cuts Sara's throat with the other hand. Millicent makes sure to cut 'ear-to-ear' to cut through both arteries for the most damage. Bri gasps as her hands lightly slap over her mouth.

With tears filling Bri's eyes, she shakes her head, 'no.' Sara's facial expression is seared into Bri's memory: Sara stands there, frozen in shock and disbelief, her hands grasping her throat; the blood pushes out between her fingers. Sara loses consciousness and collapses to floor; her blood is now spurting everywhere. Bri rushes over to her, but there's *nothing* anyone can do! Sara will bleed out in less than a minute; Bri holds Sara's bloody hand...

"*Donovan!*" Millicent yells. He quickly comes in, stopping mid-step when he sees Sara and all the blood. "Clean this mess up for me!"

"Yes, Ma'am." He replies.

He grabs Bri's arm and assertively pulls her up. He isn't rough, but he isn't gentle either. Bri sees Sara's spirit and steps back a little, giving Sara a sad, sympathetic look. Donovan picks up Sara's body and takes it out of the room. Bri stares at the trail of blood drops going out of the room.

Millicent takes a deep breath and smiles; happy she stopped a leak. She turns to Bri and Katie. "No one has thought to look at an old, rundown manor, Bri." She smirks, but so does Bri, *in her mind*...if Millicent only knew Bri had been here once before with Rex, Jack, and Cooper, *in this very room*...

"You're going through all this, killing people, and for what? *My baby?!*" Bri asks with a bit of disbelief.

Millicent laughs at the ridiculousness of that statement. "I'm going through all this for *my* heir, *my* legacy! *MY baby*! Who knew an American would have thicker royal blood than centuries of a royal family?! But this," she gestures Bri's abdomen, "will have thicker, purer royal blood than any of us!"

"Your plan doesn't make sense." Bri thinks out loud. "You would have to kill everyone, more people this time than when you wanted everyone to think you were the mother of Lawrence, Seth, and Abby! Only this time, it will be *impossible* for you to do all that!"

Millicent gets a smug look on her face as she snatches the tablet from Katie's hands. "It's already begun..." She replies and pulls up a video on the tablet and presses play. She turns it for Bri to watch and she watches Bri's reaction with eager anticipation. This time Bri has to have a reaction!

Bri sees three people down on their knees, then their faces are focused and clear: Seth, Abby, and Genevieve. Bri goes to look away, *knowing* what's coming, but she can't; she's frozen. When each shot is taken, Bri gets more and more nauseous. She grabs a trash bin and throws up, but she *refuses* to cry in front of Millicent. That horrifying video will be on instant replay in Bri's mind for a *long time* to come.

Bri glances at Katie and sees she is horrified, too. Bri is relieved Katie didn't know about that, and her expression tells Bri that Katie has a crack in her resolve and commitment to what Millicent is doing. Bri quickly tries to think of what to ask Millicent, which will continue to chip away and gnaw at Katie.

"I've known for some time you've been plotting my death at one point or another. What I can't seem to understand is how you can order the death of Emmy and Natty, of innocent children, even the kidnapping of my newborn son that could've led to his death?!" Katie is more horrified and shocked; she didn't know Millicent was behind Emmy and Natty's deaths either, or that Bri's baby was also kidnapped!

Donovan comes back with a couple of others to clean up the blood on the floor. Bri nervously steps back and out of the way. Millicent is satisfied that Bri won't be getting close with anyone. Sara was a weakness that could've been very costly, but she is happy that it is no longer a problem.

Millicent turns and walks out, sternly telling Katie, "Come!"

Katie is still processing what she learned about Emmie and Natty, snapping out of it enough to follow Millicent and they leave. Bri stands there, staring at Sara's blood that has soaked into the wood and won't easily be washed out.

All she can think is, '*Why?*' and '*This was senseless!*'

CHAPTER 49
Navigating Around Millicent's Ego

When Donovan and the others had finished cleaning up the mess, they gather everything and leave the room. Bri is standing in the same place she had been before Millicent and Katie left, but after she hears the sound of the door locking, she walks over to the table with her dinner on it and Sara's spirit follows her over. Bri looks at the tray and lifts up the cloche dome revealing the dinner plate. She doesn't want to eat, but she forces herself to try to eat for the baby. She takes her fork and as she pushes the fork through a bite of food, she notices the plate is a little wobbly. She puts the fork down and lifts the side of the plate to find a cloth folded around something.

Bri carefully pulls it out and sets the edge of the plate back down. She unwraps the cloth to find a phone with its charging cord.

Sarah tells her, "It was the only way I could think of that could make the tray as flat as possible."

"*Oh, Sara,*" Bri whispers, then looks at her with teary eyes, "*this is what you risked your life for?! I'm so sorry.*"

Sara gives her an understanding look. "Unfortunately, I was foolish to think Millicent wouldn't kill me. I thought I was just being helpful in assisting her with various tasks. I can tell you from this side that I understand what happened. *I chose this.*"

"To die?!" Bri asks with a touch of disbelief.

"I chose to connect you with your loved ones." Sara points to the phone. "That will help start your rescue; a rescue that will save the rightful queen, *you*, Queen BriaLynn." She sees Bri's nervousness. "This has already started uniting the country with you, and it will only solidify when this is all over!" Sara is about to leave, then adds, "Millicent thought I would sympathize with you, if I hadn't already....*she was right*. Which meant she had to put a stop to it, *to me...*"

Jessica appears and quickly tells Bri, "Hide the phone and cord in the passageway with your things right now! Millicent is on her way back and will search your room for anything that isn't supposed to be here. I'll go with Sara, but I'll come back. Just stay calm and everything will be fine."

Bri nods wrapping the cloth around the phone and cord again as she stands up. She waves to Sara who waves back before she disappears with Jessica. Bri quickly opens the passageway and then puts the phone and cord inside. Bri remembers she needs to walk her rounds to keep her routine and do what little walking she can. She is fighting back the tears as the deaths of *all four people* are on instant replay in her head...

Bri is lost in her thoughts, walking around the room, when Millicent and Katie come back with Donovan. Millicent studies Bri to see if she is acting any differently. She looks around, having Donovan and Katie check between her mattresses and under the bed, as well as around the room, while she looks in a few secret places that Bri could have found, to use them to conceal whatever Sara might have brought her.

"What are we looking for?" Katie asks.

Millicent is annoyed. "*Anything!*" She holds back name calling with Katie, she needs Katie to believe she has Katie's well-being at heart. "*You'll know it when you see it!*"

To calm Millicent down a bit, Bri plays to her ego. "Queen Mother, may I ask you something?" Bri goes to stare out the window.

"*You may.*" Millicent answers.

Millicent is always delighted to hear herself referred to as 'Queen' in any positive way, only to hear Bri say it gives Millicent more satisfaction; it feels like she is winning. However, she remains stoic on the outside.

"What was this room?" Bri already knows, but she is hoping Millicent might reminisce and relax a little.

Millicent is skeptical, her eyes narrow. "*Why do you ask?*"

"You'll probably think I'm crazy—."

"*I already do.*" Millicent smugly says with her nose slightly up in the air.

Bri chooses her words specifically, "Well, I envision The Manor being a very *magnificent* building when it was in its prime." Her response catches Millicent by surprise. "There's a beauty that has faded with time, but if one looks closely, *it's still there...*" She takes a small, deep breath and shrugs a little. "It's just something I think about to fill my time with, I guess..."

"This Manor was beautiful *and magnificent*! This," Millicent motions the room, "was my uncle's quarters." She squashes any nostalgic feelings saying to Bri with a chill in her voice, "Fitting, *don't you think*?" Purposely, Bri continues to stare out the window as she nods in agreement. Millicent lightly clears her throat. "Goodnight."

Bri respectfully replies, "Goodnight, Ma'am."

Nothing more is said and Bri listens to the footsteps going towards the door to the room. She hears the door open and close, then it's locked. She notices she doesn't hear footsteps on the other side of the door going down the hall. She figures they're listening to see if Bri will possibly retrieve something that Sara may have left. Millicent sends Katie back into the room under the guise to help Bri put her bedding back on the bed; Millicent goes to check on the preparations to move Bri out of The Manor tomorrow.

Katie asks Bri, "Why don't you ask me many questions?"

Bri shrugs a little, then says matter-of-factly, "She really does believe no one will question the whole slew of deaths that will have to come if she is to rule in place of Lawrence's heir."

Katie is quiet; deep down she really doesn't want to lose her only friend, but she works hard not to think about it. She knows Millicent is trying to be her new friend, but Katie can sense something is missing...Bri sees Katie's worried face.

Katie quickly tries to cover it with a faint smile and asks, "*All set?*"

Bri uses her worried state to ask, "Why did you join up with Millicent? You were doing so well! You were going to go up to Vermont to finish rehab, so you could have both feet on solid ground and be in control of your life again...then, all of a sudden, you gave all that control to Millicent..."

"I didn't give her any control!" Katie tells her. "I wanted to prove that even someone who gets everything they want, can't *always* be happy."

"You *do* remember Emmie and Natty were killed, don't you? By Millicent, no less?!" Bri replies. "Their deaths were NOT what I wanted! And I don't think you wanted that either!"

Katie shakes her head. "*Of course not!*"

"Then *how on earth* could you think that I deserved more than what you put me through with your boyfriend way back when, and now, *far worse than what you did directly to me back then*, are Emmie's and Natty's deaths?!" Bri shifts a bit. "Regardless, even with everything that you've done to me and are doing to me, I *still* want you to be happy!"

"*I know!*" Katie lightly scoffs. "*And for the life of me, I don't know why?!*"

Bri doesn't tell Katie that if she were genuinely happy, she wouldn't be so focused on bringing misery to anyone, let alone her. "Why haven't you told her about Henry and Maggie?"

Katie's eyes closed for an extra moment. "She had already killed your parents and I didn't want anything to happen to Henry or Maggie. *I still don't!* I love them too, you know!" Bri nods as she keeps a stoic face about her confirming Millicent killed her parents. Katie exhales. "She already knew that if anything happened to David, Jack, or Lawrence, you would be devastated. She hasn't done anything to them yet, because they are too heavily guarded. Right now, she is frustrated you weren't more upset with all these deaths." Katie's eyebrows come together. "*Why weren't you?*"

"I knew Millicent was waiting for me to fall apart." Bri says. "I knew she was either watching my every move, or she wanted to see front page photos, perhaps both. I refused to give that to her!" Bri changes the subject, so she doesn't accidentally tell Katie any more than that. "I do have a different question. As I get further along in my pregnancy, what if I need someone? Like an emergency?"

"I'll let you know what Millicent says tomorrow." Katie replies. Then she mindlessly tells her. "She wanted to put cameras in here, but it was insanely priced because of the state of this place. She wants to carefully dismantle the entire Manor and preserve as much as she can to supply the rebuilding of

Devonridge Manor with all the original materials she can salvage for it. Plus, she is hoping that it will help her find her uncle's old lab no one can seem to find. She thinks he knew of a few more ways to torture people without actually killing them." The list of poisons that can make people sick and not kill them, comes to Bri's mind.

There is a loud sound of glass breaking. Bri and Katie look at each other with confused faces. Bri watches Katie walk over to the window. Katie opens it to see if she can see anything; Bri comes up beside her.

"What happened?" Katie asks one of Millicent's guards below.

"Just a dead tree hitting a windowpane. It's fine." He says.

They hear grunting as the two guys pull it away from the wall; they are oblivious to Jack hiding in a dark crevice of The Manor. They take the tree limb and toss it into a ditch for now. The men brush themselves off before they start their patrol again.

Katie is satisfied with the answer and closes the window; it has gotten chillier in the room. Katie sees Bri shivering as she wraps a blanket around herself.

Katie asks Bri, "Would you like me to start a fire?"

Bri gives her a small, appreciative smile. "That would be great! Thank you!"

"No problem." Katie says and builds a fire in the fireplace. Bri could build one, but she wants company a little longer, even if it is Katie. She isn't in a position to be picky about who that company may be...

"Thanks for checking into the glass breaking! I don't need to dream of ghosts in this place!" Bri says with a faint smile.

Katie nods with a small smile, then stokes the fire to get it good and crackling, before she leaves for the night. Bri thanks her again and Katie gives her a tiny wave before she closes the door. Bri goes and sits on the overstuffed chair and stares into the fireplace for a while. She has been thinking of ways to escape, only now she needs to figure out a way to escape *tonight!*

Lawrence is at The Underground Secret Society Headquarters with David and Rex's people. They are still hoping Sara got a chance to slip the phone and charger to Bri. David pours them a drink as they watch the various screens and wait. Hazel has been watching for a signal from Bri's phone on her laptop.

When the phone finally turns on, Hazel leaps out of her chair sending her chair flying as she excitedly says, *"She's turned it on! I got a signal!"*

CHAPTER 50
The Rescue

Jack hiked at a fast pace for a good distance, just to get to the new high-voltage fence that surrounds The Devonridge Estate. Rex's inside guy, Donovan, met him at the agreed location so he could get Jack inside. Jack tucks behind bush next to a tree to wait. It isn't long before he hears someone, then he partially sees them approaching.

Jack sees his phone screen light up with a message from Donovan.

Donovan: "I'm here."

Jack steps out from behind the tree and bush. He whispers loudly, *"Over here!"*

Donovan waves him over, *"Come down this way, Mate."*

Jack jogs to catch up to him as Donovan puts in a code from a piece of paper. It opens up a narrow panel and Jack is able to step through to the inside with Donovan.

"Are there a lot of these checkpoints?" Jack asks.

"Take this!" Donovan quickly shoves the paper at Jack's chest. *"Don't lose it!"* Jack puts it in his pocket as Donovan closes the gate in time for the fence to reset. Donovan explains, "Every fifteen minutes of an hour, the fence resets. Hazel set it up that way, but you only have a 45-second window; those places are also noted on that paper. Don't lose it! You saw the light flicker," Jack nods, "do NOT touch the fence after that happens, or you will have the jolt of your life! If something like that happens, it will stop a healthy man's heart!" He tells him, "I can take you a little further to help you gain a little bit of time."

"Fantastic!" Jack says.

He follows Donovan back to his SUV and climbs in; Donovan checks in with Millicent's guards like he normally does with perimeter checks. Donovan drops Jack off near a faint trail and tells him how to get to The Manor without being seen. He also tells him to stop at the edge of the tree line to get a feel for things, particularly the routine of the two men patrolling; there is a bit of time in between each pass by. If he times it, he'll know roughly how much time he has from one passing until the next.

"The side of The Manor you will be facing when you get over there is the side you need. She's being kept in The Duke's old quarters. If she has a fire in the fireplace, you will be able to see the glow of the fire from the upper floor windows." Donovan explains, *then he warns,* "*You need to get to her tonight!* Millicent plans on moving her tomorrow after she found out Lady Kemp met with The King."

Jack is shocked. "*But my understanding is she didn't say a word!*"

"Millicent will *always* assume someone spilled everything they know, then take countermeasures!" Donovan tells him.

Jack doesn't catch the hidden meaning, because he is too focused on rescuing Bri. He thanks Donovan and shakes his hand. He gets out of the SUV and puts his backpack back on. Then he turns on his flashlight and disappears into the woods, promptly finding the faint path Donovan told him about. He carefully used the flashlight to scan the trail in front of him to navigate larger rocks, holes, dips, and crevices. Jack makes decent time to the tree line where he hides behind a tree and pulls out his night vision binoculars to watch for Millicent's guards. He figures he will make his way up to The Manor after they pass by him the second or third time, depending on how long it takes in between their walks around The Manor.

It takes a bit longer for the two men to pass by on their patrol the third time around. However, once the men pass by him, Jack quickly makes his way over to that side of The Manor. He sees gentle, flickering light through a couple of windows, as well as a partial shadow at times. He gets right up to The Manor and carefully checks around *both* corners for any guards, just to be sure they didn't double-back for something, or others coming. He looks at his watch to get an idea for the time that is left.

First, he looks for a place to hide and finds a dark crevice of The Manor he can slip into in case he needs to hide. Jack looks up at the windows with light, then his eyes drop down to the darkened windows underneath. He says to himself, '*If they're keeping her in The Duke's room, then these dark windows below are the lab and I can get to her that way?*'

Jack hurries to climb up and see if any of those windows are unlocked, but they're locked up tight. He does see a latch to open one and gets the idea to break the one windowpane, only he hesitates and thinks to himself, *If one pane is broken and a guard comes by, how would a single windowpane be logically broken on its own? No, I can't break one pane, or it would look suspicious. However, if something were to break the window naturally, like a branch or tree limb, well, that would be easier to dismiss!*

He looks around in the full-moon lit landscape, when a tree catches his eye. Specifically, a broken, dangling tree limb catches his eye. He knows by its size it will take a great deal of strength! He takes off his backpack and tosses it into the dark crevice he found a few minutes ago. He looks around both sides of The Manor again to be sure the coast is still clear. He goes over and climbs the tree to get a better look. It's rotting and he thinks he can jump on it to loosen it up. He thinks about how he will get down in case someone hears it and comes running to check out the noise. He takes a moment to formulate a plan.

He grabs hold of the large branch above him, then looks up at the night sky and whispers, *"If there's a better way, I'm all ears; otherwise, help me accomplish this."*

He holds the branch above him tighter and bounces a couple times, then jumps once when the limb crashes down top first. As it lands below him, Jack quickly climbs down. He hears more creaking and looks up. What he hasn't counted on is the bigger limb that it was attached to, comes crashing down, breaking a random window; *the crashing is loud!* Jack jogs several steps before hearing the guards' footsteps and Jack gets to the crevice he spotted earlier and all but dives into it, just as the guards come into view! He stills himself, waiting to hear something, but he doesn't hear anything at first.

Jack hears Katie ask the guards, "What happened?"

The guard replies, "Just a dead tree hitting a windowpane. It's fine." He says.

As Jack waits for the men to move the bigger tree limb, he starts to think about what to do next, *after* the guards to leave. They can't leave fast enough, but even though he doesn't like Katie in the room with Bri, he still has to wait for her to leave, before he can get to her.

After Katie leaves Bri's room again, Bri walks her circles as she brushes her teeth. She sticks to her routine, just in case anyone is paying attention to her movements. She starts to formulate a plan: she will escape out a window in The Secret Lab. She will make her way around to The Tunnels, or to whichever vehicle she comes to first that has keys in it!

After enough time has gone by, she tiptoes to the passageway door to retrieve the phone. She crawls into bed and turns it on under her blankets. For the first time since she was abducted, Bri is connecting to the outside world. She feels a surge of fresh hope come over her, because *she knows* Hazel will capture her signal, if they don't already know where she is!

Bri finds the group text that Hazel had set up after she programmed the necessary phone numbers into the phone. Even though she trusts this phone is secure, she is still nervous that somehow someone would know she had a phone, and they would come back for it! Her heart is pounding so hard and so loud, she is shaking.

> Bri texts the main group: "Is anybody out there?"

> Everyone in the group texts: "Yes!"

> She texts quickly: "I'm at Devonridge Manor, in her uncle's room."

> Lawrence: "I really hope this is you, Darling, but we need to be sure! Tell me something only we would know!"

There's a long minute wait as Bri tries to think of something...

> Bri: "Inferno; sexy-fun; intense."

> Lawrence: "It's you!"

> David: "Yep, it's you!"

David looks at Lawrence and they nod to each other. Bri told him and Jack of her conversation with Lawrence; about a word that would describe the intimacy for each of them.

> Bri: "I have to escape tonight! Millicent is planning on moving me somewhere else tomorrow."

Jack: "I'm outside right now. The breaking glass you heard was me and I'll be in as soon as I can; her security guys are moving the large limb out of the way."

Bri has tears of relief skipping down her cheeks.

Bri: "I can open a window for you!"

Rex sees their texts.

Rex: "Hang tight, Jack. I'm going to get some guys to help you out!"

It takes a little time to coordinate, but Rex's men have taken out all of Millicent's men over at The Manor, except one. Jack heard this in his earpiece. He also hears they are watching The Hall; in case someone finds out something and tips off Millicent that something is going down.

Donovan tells him, "Jack, go in now!"

"Copy that!" Jack says.

Jack sends a text to Bri to open the window. She gets out of the bed and whispers, "*Jessica, I need your light!*" Jessica appears. "*Thank you!*" Jessica smiles and leads the way down to The Lab once more.

She sees Jack and opens the window closest to him. As fit as he is, he is able to climb up without much difficulty. He shuts the window as Bri circles her two fingers, so he can see Jessica and her light.

"I have her, everyone!" Jack tells those on coms with him. He winces as people cheer and clap in his ear. "Come here, Amore Mia." He hugs her tight.

She hugs him back just as tight, with more tears going down her cheeks. "*I cannot begin to tell you how good it is to see you, Amore Mio!*"

"I feel the same way, Amore Mia!" He squeezes a little more.

Rex: "We left the one guard who is currently sleeping in a chair by the stairs on the main floor. He usually sleeps until his alarm goes

389

off, which is about a half-hour before the shift change. We'll keep an eye on him in case that changes, but we want to keep him there in case Millicent calls him. We may have to regroup."

Jack sends a thumbs up, then hugs Bri again and kisses her. "Mmm, minty fresh!" He holds her face. "Are you alright?"

"Yes." She replies and unknowingly rests her hand on her small baby bump.

He glances down at this innocent movement and smiles. He covers his microphone and tells her, "*I wondered!*" She scrunches her eyebrows together. "You were yawning a lot, *hard* yawns. I remembered the same thing happened when you were pregnant with Jacks."

She wipes a tear and exhales adamantly, "She will NOT get her hands on this baby, Jack!"

He holds the back of her jaw. "*No,* she won't!"

"Should we get going?" She says and goes up the passageway stairs to grab her things. She stops at the door and yawns so hard, her body shakes.

Jack says into the coms, "Guys, *she's exhausted.* I think she should get a little nap in, or this might not go smoothly."

Jack hears Donovan in his earpiece, "I think she could get a few hours of sleep. It will take us a bit of time to get The Tunnels cleaned out and rigged up to be demolished like she wanted. Just be ready to leave at a moment's notice, in case something unplanned comes up!" Donovan knows Bri is pregnant, as does Rex. They both want to give Bri the chance to give the news to her family.

"We will be!" Jack replies.

They set a time and place to meet up. He relays the message to Bri as she crawls into bed. She had already packed up her things, and some of her snacks like extra crackers, dried fruit, pretzels, cookies, anything in packaging that would keep. She had it all in the messenger bag. She felt like she was forgetting something, then remembered: her phone! She quickly grabs them and puts them into the messenger bag with everything else. Then she crawls back into bed again and they get comfortable.

Bri says to him, "Even though we aren't out of the woods yet, I do feel safer with you here."

Jack's heart is relieved. He holds her in his arms; he never wants to let go of her again. Meanwhile, David and Lawrence use this time to get up to Devonridge.

CHAPTER 51
An Opportunity Taken

It's 2:00 in the morning when Rex's people gather at the edge of the woods. It's a time when most of Millicent's people would be gone for the night, and everyone in The Hall would most likely be asleep. There are a number of people Rex and Coop have organized to be there to help rescue those being held in the cells, along with the exotic animals; plus, they want to get all the priceless artifacts out of there as well. It all comes together and flows well with some 'snags' here and there.

They have loaded a few semis, along with some trucks with trailers, as well as moving vans. Then they send all those vehicles out, using The Manor's back entrance where Hazel has taken the fence offline, and the gate opened.

Rex sees Bri and Jack walking up to them. "Happy to see you, *Your Majesty!*" He hugs Bri, then shakes Jack's hand. "I hear you made it to the fence in record time!"

Jack looks at Bri and lovingly smiles. "It helps to have the right motivation!"

"Thank you for the assist with the rescue," Bri says to Rex and gestures around, "and thank you for all of this!"

Rex explains, "My people have gotten everything *and everyone* out." He gestures to the caravan of semis, trucks, and vans that are leaving. "My guys are finishing up rigging the last bit of explosives so everything will be set to go off at the same time." She nods. He adds, "Lawrence and David are almost here. They can't fly to Devonridge, because she has spies everywhere, including the airport."

With everything emptied and all the explosives set up to go off at the same time, everyone moves back to the escape vehicles and they take cover. Bri puts her messenger bag inside the hole of a tree that is right there to protect it from the blast. She goes back over to Jack and Rex; they are talking to Grayson who has just joined them. They wait to hear from Rex's men after they've done their final check. Luckily, they don't have to wait long.

Hazel tells the group on coms, "Tunnel is given an 'all clear!'"

"STOP RIGHT THERE!" A woman's voice commands.

All their heads snap to see Millicent standing there with Tristan, who has his gun pointed at Grayson's chest. Donovan is jogging up to them. Rex wanted him to keep his work schedule and stay close to Devonridge Hall, so he could be there when the explosion happens and can be part of the small group Millicent would keep with her. Just before Donovan's arrival at Devonridge Hall, word has gotten to Millicent that there was something going on at The Tunnels, and they go out to see what was going on. Millicent has Tristan text Donovan to tell him what was going on.

Donovan comes up to Millicent, as she holds her hand out to Rex thinking he has the detonator. "*Give it to me!*"

Rex sees Grayson shift out of the corner of his eye. Grayson is covertly handing Bri the detonator phone. She feels something nudge her hands and carefully takes it. She casually looks down and sees it's a phone. Millicent goes into a rant about how stupid Rex is for helping Bri to destroy The Tunnels! How she can't believe he would steal from her, *of all people*, with their history!

While Millicent is ranting, Grayson whispers to Bri, "Press send twice."

Millicent gets in Rex's face and sneers, "*I'll destroy you!*"

Rex knows she wants him to argue with her, but he has no desire to right now. With all eyes on Rex and Millicent, Bri ever so slowly glances down and double-taps her thumb on the green button. About two seconds later, several explosions are going off with everyone reflexively ducking, then taking cover. Millicent watches in horror as her precious Tunnels are destroyed right before her eyes and collapsing within itself.

"NO!" Millicent gasps in surprised horror.

Millicent's family comes running out from The Hall to see what happened. Millicent is confused and looks at Rex; she doesn't understand how it Rex did it?! She had Rex and Grayson in her view the whole time...'*They must've had them on a timer...*' Millicent takes Tristan's gun and turns to Rex and Grayson, seething with fury, when her eyes catch a glimpse of the flip-phone in Bri's hand. Millicent's face goes from shock to incensed.

"*You did this?!*" Millicent asks. "*How?*" Bri doesn't deny it. Millicent glares and coldly tells Bri, "*I'll kill you for this!*" That causes Rex and his people to raise their guns in defense of Bri, which causes Millicent's people to raise their guns and point them at Rex's people.

"Calm down everyone." Bri says, then she looks at Millicent. "She won't shoot me! *Not yet anyways.*"

"Try me!" Millicent sneers, trying to cover her bluff.

"No, Millicent!" Bri confidently glares back. "Try *me!*"

Suddenly, Bri punches Millicent harder than she had punched Katie. Millicent is knocked back into her men. David and Lawrence had arrived as the last of the explosions went off and are now running up them. While Millicent is disoriented, Bri feels the need to run and she quickly turns on her heel and takes off; Millicent sees Bri running away and follows her before The Royal Guards can stop her. Jack sees Bri running away, with Millicent going after her. Some of Millicent's people manage to break free from The Royal Guards and take off after them.

Bri runs into The Manor, making her way to the main level. Once she is on the main level, she hears footsteps. She is looking around for a place to hide, when she feels a hand go over her mouth and her scream is muffled as she is pulled into a room.

"*Amore Mia, it's me!*" Jacks whispers. Feeling her exhale in relief, he lets go of her mouth.

He goes to the door and checks to see if it's clear; it is. He waves for her to 'come on.' She follows him as they quietly, and carefully, walk along the edge of the hallway.

She whispers, "*Are you following the breadcrumbs you left from our first visit to this place? How do you know where you're going?!*"

Jack smiles, "I studied the floor plan...aaand I *maaay* have a little bit of a photographic memory."

Bri inhales and whispers out loud, *"Gasp!"* She smiles and touches her chest. "How did I *not* know this?!" She teases, but she is also serious about how she missed that?!

Jack chuckles some more. "How is it possible that you can have such a sense of humor at a time like this?!" David and Lawrence are smiling, too, as they listen to them on the coms.

"I'm *choosing* to laugh in this moment, because you're with me and in a way, so are David and Lawrence. I'm also scolding myself and wondering why in the world I ran back *in here?!* This place has to be even more unstable after those explosions!"

They come to the open place that has a symmetrical circle in the middle of the floor. Above it is the beautiful domed, stained-glass skylight. The door straight across from them bursts open.

"Millicent!" Bri whispers in surprise.

The people listening through earwigs faintly hear her. *They all scramble to The Manor to help them!* Millicent is with Tristan and Donovan, and Katie walks up behind them.

"GRAB HER AND SHOOT HIM!" Millicent commands.

Bri stands in front of Jack. "LIKE *HELL* YOU WILL!"

There are a bunch of people filing in behind Jack and Bri, as well as behind Millicent and Katie. The popping and cracking of the floorboards has them all freezing. When the sounds get louder and louder, they all look around at each other's feet. Suddenly, the whole floor gives way, taking everyone with it to the lower level. Every single one of them loses their balance as the main level floor crashes down onto the floor below.

There is a thick fog of dust hanging over all of those who fell with the floor, down to the basement level. The dust is so thick, it blackens out the early morning light. Everyone is frozen in place, unable to open their eyes and trying not to choke on the dust they can't help but inhale. Bri thinks to pull the neck part of her shirt, up over her nose, to use to filter out some of the dust; she takes shallow breaths. She keeps her eyes closed, only peaking here and there, until she is able to see.

Eventually, Bri is able to make out a gun that isn't far away. She looks around, unable to see anyone, so they are probably unable to see her; she reaches over and grabs the gun. She slowly starts to stand up, working to keep a steady balance on the boards beneath her that wabble with her movements. When she is fully standing, she holds the gun at her side, pointing it down and partially concealed behind her leg.

Bri waits until she is able to make out who the shadows are of those closest to her. When she is able to see Jack, he is holding his head; he hit it hard on something when they landed. She carefully makes her way over to him and helps him stand. He hugs her, then they wait for more dust to clear out.

David, Lawrence, McMasters, and The King's Guards, are also waiting for the dust to settle before coming inside through a large hole in one of the exterior walls of The Manor. They watch and listen, because they need to quickly determine where Bri and Jack are at so they can get to them!

Inside, Bri is now able to see Millicent, as well as Katie, Tristan, and Donovan. Donovan is pointing his gun at Bri and Jack, only his finger isn't on the trigger; Tristan is looking for his gun. Bri sees Donovan's gun; they see Bri has a gun pointed right at Millicent.

Millicent dismissively scoffs with an expression to match, "*You won't shoot me. You don't have it in you!*"

Bri exhales a light burst of a humorless laugh replying, "*Don't I?!*" She glares. "Perhaps *before* you killed Emmie and Natty that might have been the case!"

"*Even with that,*" Millicent retorts, still underestimating Bri, "you *still* don't have it in you." Then her demeanor shifts; she has a devilish, knowing look, talking in such a way that Bri realizes Lawrence is behind her, "You, *of all people*, should know of the bond between a mother and child!"

Bri can't hold back her loathing. "*I only know of a loving bond, not the sick and twisted version you're talking about!*" She adds, "However, there is *nothing* stronger, not even a family bond of bloodlines, that can truly bond people together like *real* love!"

"Oh, come now, Bri." Millicent dismissively replies. "A bond is still strong when it's between a parent and a child, because it's formed so early! You know that no matter how many times Lawrence has failed me, *deep down* he wants *nothing more* than to please me, and to make me proud of him. Like right now!" She looks at Lawrence. "Son, take the gun from her and we will start over. We will work together to create an even *more* powerful legacy for you, for *our* heir!"

Bri feels Lawrence step right up behind her. He places his hand on top of hers holding the gun; he puts his other hand on her shoulder, lightly pressing his thumb where he intimately 'marks her' as his.

"BriaLynn." He says, pushing a little more with his thumb. He adds a determined look telling her to, "*Give.me.the.gun.*" Still looking at Millicent, her eyebrows come together. He commands, "*Now!*" She jumps a bit, yet she *strongly* feels she needs to trust him; she releases her grip and lets him take it.

Millicent watches this and is excited she still has a hold on Lawrence. "*Good!* Now, get rid of him." She points to Jack.

"NO!" Bri stumbles on the debris to get in front of Jack.

"*CAREFUL!*" Millicent yells at her, scared that if Bri falls again, she could hurt the baby.

"*What's your plan here, Millicent?!*" Bri asks with a hint of annoyance.

Millicent tells Bri, "If you really want to save him," she points to Jack, "come with me *right now!*" She looks at Lawrence, "You should come, too, so we can work on a plan for *our* future!" Bri looks at Jack for a moment, then looks back to Millicent and nods.

Jack loudly whispers, "*No!*" He holds her upper arm to stop her from leaving. "*Sacrifice me! I'm ready!*"

Bri's head snaps to look at Jack and angrily tells him, "*Well, I'M NOT, ready to lose YOU!*"

Lawrence helps Bri as they make their way across the debris. Millicent watches Bri pass by her, then, in one swift movement she snatches the gun from Lawrence and fires the gun.

Bri gasps and screams, "*NNNOOO!*" She looks at Jack, only she sees David fall in her peripheral view. She, Lawrence, and Jack, go to rush over to him, but a huge, muscular guy gets in Bri and Lawrence's way; Bri turns her head and glares at Millicent.

Millicent says with an evil grin, "*I never said* anything *about not shooting him!*" She waves her arm towards the exterior wall that has caved in. "*This way!*"

Angry, Bri goes to step around this big guy in front of her, but Millicent tells the big guy, "*Bring her!*" Millicent then looks at Lawrence and Katie, "*Let's go!*" Lawrence knows the best place for him is to stay with Bri; Jack is helping David, along with Mitchell.

The big, muscular guy tries to turn her around, but Bri won't go. She is worried when she doesn't see David move, and his whole chest is covered in *so* much blood!

She *hysterically* screams, "*FIGHT, DAVID!*" Millicent's bigger guy picks her up and throws her over his shoulder. She screams at David, "*YOU DON'T GET TO DIE ON ME, DAVID! DO YOU HERE ME?!*" When she sees David's spirit appear, it's wispy like Natty's spirit had been with her body when she in a coma in the hospital. Bri starts panicking! "*NNNOOO!*" She yells, "*FIIIGHT, DAVID! DON'T LEAVE ME, PLEEEASE!*"

Bri collapses on the big guy's shoulder, sobbing uncontrollably. The big guy holding her has to stop, so he doesn't drop her. Lawrence goes over to them.

"I've got her." He scoops her up.

She wraps her arms around his neck and sobs, "*Oh God, please, don't let him die...*" Both of them having just seen David collapse from a gunshot wound, has Lawrence silently crying with her.

Outside, more of Millicent's people join them. They shoot at McMasters and The Royal Guards, along with Rex and his guys, to keep them back. With Bri and Lawrence close to Millicent, there are no clean shots to be made; each one is a risk to Lawrence, Bri, and her unborn baby! Tristan opens the back door of an SUV for Lawrence to put Bri inside.

Millicent turns to Lawrence. *"Now you!"* Lawrence slightly nods before he climbs in next. Millicent turns to Katie and says with almost a normal tone, "Will you get into the next car and go to Richard's until I send for you?" Katie nods: she is a little relieved. Millicent climbs in and Tristan shuts her door. Since Donovan is in the driver's seat, Tristan climbs into the front passenger seat.

McMasters, Rex, and their people catch up to the vehicles as they speed away. Bri sits in a stunned, emotional state; her lower jaw shaking as she stares out the window, tears running down her cheeks. Millicent turns to see how upset Bri is, with what had just happened.

"Finally, an emotional reaction!" Millicent says. "I was starting to think you had a harder heart *than me!"* Millicent stares at Bri, waiting for her response, but Bri doesn't react; she's not really listening.

All Bri can do is think to herself, *'I'm not going home until Millicent goes down!'*

To Millicent, it might look like Bri has a bit of a hardened heart; however, in reality, Bri is scared for David and is silently praying that the price she has to pay for coming back from her coma, doesn't include his death on top of all the others. She thinks to herself, *'Please, let David live!'*

McMasters, Rex, and some of his people go back to The Devonridge Manor to tend to the injured until paramedics arrive. The Royal Guards fan out, interviewing Millicent's people left behind. Rex lets them do this to keep themselves busy, but also because he knows Donovan is driving the vehicle Millicent is in, along with Bri and Lawrence. They will know where they ended up soon enough.

David was hit in the chest and severely bleeding. *No one* wanted to *think about it,* let alone *say it!* The odds of him dying are increasing with every drop of blood he is losing...

"Stay with me, Brother!" Jack is applying as much pressure as he can. *"You can't die!* Bri would *never* recover from losing you! *None of us will!"*

David weakly responds, struggling to stay conscious, *"She'd have you and Herst..."*

399

"*We could* never *replace you*!" Jack quickly changes the subject, so David can't argue. "Is it just me, or is Herst one *hell* of an actor?!"

David nods. "I think he saw an opportunity to be in a position that he might somehow gain the upper hand with Millicent, and he took it. *Let's hope it works!*"

"Right! *And*" Jack notes, "at least Bri won't be alone with that woman again!" David agrees, right before he loses consciousness.

When the paramedics get there, they tend to David first, then have him airlifted to a trauma center in London. Rex arranges for Jack and the rest of the family in Newhaven, to get down to London to be there for David.

CHAPTER 52
Change of Plans

As the vehicles drive along various roads, Bri is quietly staring out the window at the rain drenched landscape and villages they drive through. Lawrence sees her jaw shaking and in the light of a passing car, he sees her cheeks are wet with tears; he is also emotional but pushing down what he can to keep Millicent calm.

Bri is silently praying she doesn't lose David, then she feels a sensation, like a calming blanket, flowing down from the top of her head and wrapping around her body. There is a peace that comes over her and she feels: '*David will be okay; keep focused on your task at hand and take Millicent down, the time is near.*'

They pull into an old little gas station, or petrol station as they call it here. Lawrence listens to Millicent talking to Tristan. She tells him that they are going to the place where her mother grew up. Millicent gets out of the car to make a call. Lawrence notices that when Millicent walks away from the car, everyone else wanders around and he is left alone with Bri.

Bri sees Lawrence in the corner of her eye looking around. She looks at him with the saddest eyes and his heart breaks more for her.

He turns to hold her upper arms. "Do you see his spirit with us?"

She whispers, "*B-before...*" Lawrence's heart twists. She adds, "*But his spirit was tethered like Natty's...*"

"*Then he's* not *dead!*" He tightens his hold a bit on her upper shoulders. "*Bri!* We have to hang on to that! We both know that he would come straight away to see you if he is—, well, *all three of us would!*" He looks around again, still holding her upper arms. "We don't have much time." He looks at her. "*This is our chance to escape!* Whatever you do, *keep running!* It's raining and it will be difficult enough to keep up a good pace, so *don't look back* until we're far away from here! *Got it?*" She nods. They get closer to the door and he reaches around her and opens the door. He loudly whispers, "*Go!*"

Bri quickly gets out and takes off running. The rain makes the ground sloppy, and with the rumblings of thunder and the rain, she can only hear her loud footsteps crashing down on the ground.

She runs for a few minutes, before she calls out, "Jessica! *We need you!*" She sees Jessica and through her heavy breathing asks, "Where can we safely hide?" Bri sees a large tree and stops to catch her breath for a moment, bracing herself behind a large tree.

"You're safe here for a bit." Jessica says.

Bri turns to see Lawrence coming, *only he isn't there!* She carefully looks around either side of the tree for Lawrence...*all she hears is the rain...*

She has a worried look. "*Where is he?!*"

"He twisted his ankle in a hole and Millicent's men are helping him back to their car." She answers. "The others are looking for you, but they won't come this far. However, we need to keep you moving to stay warm on the way to somewhere dryer." She senses Bri's next question and replies, "No, there's nothing you can do, except get recaptured. That can't happen! Lawrence will be alright, because his plan will work." Bri sadly nods in understanding and lets Jessica guide her to where she needs to go.

Millicent's men came back with her to find Lawrence and Bri were gone! With the rain pouring down, they couldn't tell which direction they went.

Millicent exhales in anger. "*YOU IDIOTS!* THEY WERE LEFT ALONE?!"

"We thought The King was watching her!" One says in reply.

"If I didn't need you, I'd shoot you right here!" She angrily tells him and he takes a step back. She shouts, "*FIND THEM!*"

They jump, then split up and search the immediate area. They find Lawrence on the ground with a badly sprained ankle.

"He's over here!"

He thinks quickly and carelessly waves his arm in a direction saying, "*Hurry!* She went that way!" He looks at Millicent coming up to them. "She tried to make a run for it and I almost had her until my foot went into that stupid hole!" He says in honest frustration towards the hole.

He hopes his lie, supported by a touch of truth, helps her believe him, and she does. The men come back, soaked and empty handed.

"She won't get too far tonight." Millicent says and has them help Lawrence to the SUVs.

They open the back of the one SUV to look at a paper map. They were trying to see if there is a place nearby Bri might go to if she stumbled upon it. They find a few possibilities to check out.

"Remember, I only want Bri alive!" She angrily tells them. "Kill whoever she's with, whoever is helping her; leave *no* witnesses!" She looks at Lawrence. "Where's your phone?" Lawrence pats his pockets to find it, then pulls it out. She sees it is turned off as she takes it from him. "Do we need to make a special stop for your ankle?"

He knows she is testing him. He tells her, "I'm fine. I'll wrap it up later. Let's just get to Bri before anything happens to the baby!" She gives him a 'once over' to check his sincerity, then gives him a slight nod with approval. She tells her men to help Lawrence into the back seat. She takes a hammer and smashes Lawrence's phone to be sure Rex, nor any others, won't find them. She tosses the phone and hammer into the back of the SUV. Donovan hides a teeny tiny silent tracker for Hazel to pick up its signal, then shuts the back hatch and goes up to the driver's seat.

They drive to the various locations they thought Bri might be and look around. They kept coming up empty and Millicent is getting more and more desperate to find Bri. The rain has let up, so she has Donovan pull over so she could pace and think...She not only needs that baby to regain her power, but to also ensure that power in such a way that she would *never* lose power again. Her plan? To be named regnant, because her *orphaned* 'Heir' would be a minor, then change the law for her to be the only advisor and rule the country until she dies. She is so close to her goal; she couldn't lose Bri and that baby! *NOT NOW!* She angrily exhales. She stops pacing as it occurs to her: *there is already an heir!* She gets excited! '*This will actually work better! I could get established within The Monarchy, then when my heir comes, I will groom that one to be more ruthless than any other ruler in UK history!*' She makes a quick phone call to Richard McCleary before getting back in the car; she has a very important job for him to do. She tells him to take a few people with him to help him accomplish his mission, including Katie.

403

"Slight change in plans, Boys!" Millicent says. "*Get in the car!*"

Jessica and Bri are walking around for quite some time, with Jessica having Bri wait under large trees when it rains so the leave protect her from most of the rain. Then Jessica continues to guide Bri through the woods and when it starts raining again, this time she has her duck inside the ruins of an old church that has a corner where part of a roof will keep her dry.

There is a dusty, vinyl chair with no legs for Bri to sit on and wait. "Where am I?" Bri asks, moving the chair to a flatter part of the floor, then sits down.

"You're on the edge of The Duchy Devonridge, not far from The Devonridge Estate." Jessica answers.

She is surprised. "*I'm back? Why?!*"

Jessica stares out at the rain. "Millicent has changed her plans. She just remembered there is already an 'Heir to The Throne' that she hadn't considered before," Jessica gestures Bri's baby bump, "until this one is born."

Bri makes the connection and her heart sinks. "A plan that involves Jacks..."

"Yes, and to use him to assume the throne, *after* Lawrence abdicates." Jessica explains, "If Lawrence abdicates, The Monarchy will pass to baby Jacks and Millicent would name herself as *his* temporary regnant."

"Because I'll be dead." Bri offhandedly adds.

"Then she'll be right where she wants to be by the time this baby is born, because she thinks she will have Lawrence right there with her to help solidify her legitimacy." She points to Bri's baby bump again and warns, "She plans on raising Lawrence's heir the way she had tried with Lawrence. She thinks she will get there this time, because she will start years earlier than she had with Lawrence."

"Will she succeed in kidnapping Jacks?" Bri asks and Jessica hesitates. Bri pleas with her, "*Please*, just tell me."

Jessica's eyes get sad. "She already has."

"*Whaaat?*" Bri whispers in shock. "*How?!*"

"With Henry going back and forth between London and Kingsbury, along with Carlotta and James at the hospital with David," Jessica tells her, "it left Jacks and Elise at The Inn with Maggie and Amy." Bri sees Jessica's face sadden.

Bri shakes her head in disbelief as tears fill her eyes. She can only whisper, "*Who died...*"

"Maggie." Jessica sadly replies. Bri is frozen as she listens to Jessica tell her, "Amy lost her pregnancy when she was pushed down the stairs trying to stop Jacks from being kidnapped. This was after every guard and staff member that got in their way was killed."

Bri starts crying, mourning for the loss of the mother of heart. Her crying turns to sobs thinking about Emmie, Natty, Peter, Seth, Abby, Genevieve, and poor Sara. Now Maggie *and* Amy's baby are added to that count; not to mention the however many guards and staff who were also killed! Jessica lets her cry, hoping it helps her get to the place she needs to get to emotionally, to do what she needs to do when she comes face-to-face with Millicent...

After some time has passed, Jessica has Bri moving again. Here and there, Jessica would have Bri hide, so she wouldn't be seen by anyone. Walking gets her blood flowing to keep her warm and by the time the sun is setting, they are walking up to an empty little cottage.

"Jessica, does anyone live here?"

"Only seasonally." Jessica replies. "The owners were here not too long ago to check on things. You have electricity and water, along with wood for a fire, and there is some food in the pantry."

Once Bri has a fire going, she goes to take a quick shower. While her clothes dry next to the fire, she is wrapped in a blanket and drinking a cup of cocoa.

Jessica appears again and they talk for a bit. She tells Bri, "Millicent has tasked Katie with taking care of Jacks, but when Millicent is privately with him, she is actually nice and good to him."

Bri's eyebrows come together as she thinks how odd and out of character that is, until she realizes, "She *is* changing tactics! Her plan must be to bond with him as a baby, so he will be easier to mold to be cruel and ruthless later on!" Bri asks Jessica, "What about those who have recently died? How are Maggie, Seth, Gen, and Abby doing over there?"

Jessica gives her a small smile. "First of all, Abby survived!"

Bri is teary-eyed. "*Really?!*"

Jessica assures her, "She will make a *full* recovery!"

Bri tips her head upwards and whispers, "*Thank you!*" She looks at Jessica. "I have already felt The Spirit and know that David will recover." Jessica nods. Bri asks, "How is he doing?"

"He lost a lot of blood, but he fights to stay alive," Jessica lightly smiles, "he fights for you! As for the ones on this side, you should already have a good idea of how they're doing emotionally." Bri nods, taking a deep breath.

She gives Jessica a weak smile. "Thank you." Jessica nods a bit.

She stares at the fire thinking, and those thoughts make their way to thinking about Jacks. Her arms begin to physically ache to hold her baby...

"Bri, you need to sleep." Jessica says. "*Really* sleep."

Bri shakes her head. "What if Millicent's guys show up?"

"Tonight, *none of them* will be out in the rain! However, if it makes you feel better, I'll stay but I can only stay until you fall asleep." Jessica offers.

Bri gives her an appreciative look. "I appreciate that."

Millicent has Lawrence recuperating in a larger bedroom at Devonridge's *Castle*. This so-called castle is not located in The Duchy of Devonridge. It's barely inside The Duchy of Brexton, on an island of sorts, surrounded by marshy waters, with a long bridge to get out onto the island. Millicent loves this more secluded location and has no plans to leave anytime soon.

Lawrence's room is across the hall from Katie's room, who has been taking care of Jacks. Lawrence doesn't know Baby Jacks is there; he just hears a baby crying. It starts to sound familiar to him the closer the sound gets to his door. Then there is a quick 'tap-tap' before the door flies open and Katie frantically comes in holding a crying baby.

"*Help me!*" She says. "I can't get him to stop crying!" She exhales in frustration. "*He won't take his bottle!*"

Lawrence isn't sure what he can do until he sees, "*Jacks?!*" He looks at Katie in surprise, concealing his anger Jacks was kidnapped. Jacks is bent over, desperately reaching for his Uncle Lawrence.

Lawrence takes Jacks into his arms and hugs him firmly. Jacks hugs his Uncle Lawrence tight and lays his head down on Lawrence's shoulder. He starts to quiet down the safer he feels. Lawrence takes the bottle from Katie and after a little bit, Jacks is comfortable sitting in Lawrence's lap and takes his bottle, holding it himself. As he drinks, he takes a few shaky breaths, relaxing with his uncle. He watches Katie close, scrunching his eyebrows when she sits down on the edge of the foot of the bed. Katie takes a deep breath of her own, watching Jacks.

She sees Lawrence looking at her for answers and shrugs. "I don't know much. She wanted Jacks because I guess he's already 'The Heir to The Throne.' And with David in the hospital, and almost everyone else down in London, that left Maggie and Amy alone with Jacks..." Katie goes quiet thinking about Maggie.

He sees her face. "She had them killed, didn't she?"

He sees the answer on Katie's face, then she sadly answers, "Maggie...they didn't have to..." her eyebrows furrow, "but Millicent *ordered* them to. One of the guys had secretly put something into Jacks' bottle to make him sleep. Then, after Maggie put him down in his crib, they snuck him out without a peep. *They didn't have to shoot her!*" She quickly wipes her cheeks and looks down at the floor.

Lawrence can see she is really bothered by Maggie's death. It occurs to him and he whispers, "*You haven't said anything to Millicent about Bri's relationship with Henry and Maggie?!*"

Katie shakes her head, still staring at the floor. "She didn't really consider Amy, nor ask about her relationship with Bri, or she probably would have had them both killed."

"*That's pretty much a guarantee.*" Lawrence gives her a reluctant look and shifts the conversation a bit. "There's no need to traumatize Jacks anymore by making him go with you tonight when you're still a stranger. If you stay here," he gestures the other side of the large bed, "we can help him get used to you, so if Millicent insists that he stay only with you, it will be easier on him."

She nods, thanking him and goes to the other side of the bed. She crawls in and lays down. She thinks out loud, "*Who knew a crying baby could wear out an adult so quickly?!*"

"He's in a strange place, with unfamiliar people, and he misses his mum." Lawrence tells her.

Katie looks at Jacks. "It feels like we're torturing innocent baby."

"*Let's hope this is as bad as it gets for him.*" Lawrence says.

CHAPTER 53
The Time Has Come...

The next morning, Bri wakes up at dawn. She folds her blanket and straightens up a bit. She finishes putting her silverware away and Jessica comes back.

She closes the drawer asking Jessica, "Where's my son?"

"At Devonridge Castle." Jessica replies. Bri's eyebrow goes up and Jessica says, "It's about the same size as The Worthington Inn."

Bri nods taking that in. "How do I get there?"

"I know you want to go in there, scoop him up, and get him as far away from Millicent as you can; *but you can't do that!*"

"His safety is my first priority!" Bri firmly tells her.

"If she was going to hurt him, I would agree." Jessica replies. "Right now, you need to focus on bringing Millicent down once and for all, *for everyone*! It's time." Bri hears once again what she has heard before, that Millicent is going to die. Jessica turns to look at something Bri can't see and nods. She looks back at Bri and tells her, "I have to go for now."

"You can't!" Bri says. "I need your help!"

"*You can do this*!" Jessica tells her. "The end *is* near."

"I'm not sure if I should be relieved, or worried." Bri replies.

Jessica gives her a little smile and explains, "Wait until dark to go to make your way to Devonridge Castle."

"How do I get there?" Bri asks.

"You won't have to worry about the directions." Jessica replies. Bri takes that to mean that Jessica will come back to help her with that. When Jessica starts to disappear, they wave and say goodbye.

The rest of the day Bri rests and thinks about what Jessica told her and the directions on how to get to Devonridge Castle. When evening comes, she goes around the cottage to make sure she puts everything back the way she found it. She writes a thank-you note to the owners and sticks it to the fridge with a magnet. She stares at it for a moment thinking she will need to come back and properly thank them sometime. She turns and jumps, finding herself face-to-face with an intruder.

The man gruffly says, "We've been looking for you, Your Majesty!" Then he lunges for her.

Bri is able to give him a good fight with jabs and kicks. However, she doesn't know there is a second man until comes up behind her and wraps one arm around her, while his other hand tries to hold a cloth with chloroform on it, over her mouth. She struggles with him and he drops the cloth. The first guy picks it up and goes to hold it over her mouth.

She pleas with them, "*Please*, don't hurt my baby!" They both freeze, and the man holding the cloth pulls his hand back. "We don't know what those fumes could do to my baby and while the thought of Millicent getting her hands on my baby makes me sick, I don't want anything to happen to my baby!"

"Millicent doesn't want anything happening to this baby either and *she* told us to use the chloroform?" He lifts his hand and the cloth. He sees how worried she is and uses it to negotiate. "Look. If you cooperate and come with us, we won't use the chloroform." She closes her eyes and nods. "Do we have your word?"

"I will follow whoever to your car!" She waves her arm in the direction of the front door. She doesn't want to give them her word, because if an opportunity to escape presents itself, she *is* going to take it! She tells them, "Let's get this over with." They get to the door and she stops. "Can we put the fire out and lock the doors?" They look at the fire, then back at her. She puts her right hand up and says, "I promise I *will* leave with you. I just want to make sure this cottage doesn't burn down, or get robbed, because I stayed here for a bit."

They nod and the one who was walking behind her goes to the back door and locks it, while the other one puts out the fire. On the way out, they lock the front door behind them. The door to the back seat is opened up for her and she slides in, then Millicent's men climb in the front seats. Before they leave, they text Millicent that they have Bri, but they will be delayed coming back. They need to take care of the body of a busybody witness who told them about a squatter in a cottage. They will bury her in the woods near Devonridge Castle.

"Why did that woman have to tell us about someone stayin' there?!" The man says in an Irish accent, shoving the cloth and bottle of chloroform into the glovebox as they back out of the driveway.

The other man agrees. "Let's get this over with..."

They both just watch the road and Bri looks out the window at the passing scenery she could see in the dark. They come to the woods and pull off the road onto a dirt trail road.

When they stop, the passenger opens his door and he tells Bri, "Wait here."

The men go to the back and open the hatch. They grab shovels and walk in front of the SUV to dig a hole using the headlights for light. She watches them start digging a hole and thinks of the woman they killed. She turns to peak and inhales a quiet gasp when she sees the woman's eyes are open, seeming to be staring at her. She looks to make sure the men are still digging, before she leans over to check for the woman's pulse, just to be sure she is dead...the woman feels cool to the touch, so Bri closes her eyes. She glances down and sees a large hunting knife.

She hears someone say, "I'll get the lady, you check on The Qu, *er,* our passenger."

Bri snatches up the knife and sits back down in the seat. The very back opens first and one of the men pulls out the dead woman, then her back door opens as the guy with the dead woman over his shoulder walks up the other side of the SUV and goes to the grave they just dug.

"We're almost done, Your Majesty." He says as he pulls his phone out of his pocket.

He texts someone where they are, and that they will be leaving shortly. While he texts, Bri is trying to think of a way to get out of this situation. She knows it's now or never. With one guy in front of the SUV, and this guy's attention on his phone, Bri wraps her hand around the handle of the knife...she turns and swiftly plunges the knife into the side of his neck and yanks it out, getting blood spray on her face, neck and torso. Bri is frozen at what she has done; the guy is also stunned, frozen for a moment before he grabs his neck, now desperate to hold his blood in.

The other man yells, "*Come on, Jones!*" Jones stumbles back and the other man sees him. "Get over here!" He looks and looks again, "*Jones?* What's wrong?" He watches Jones holding his neck and stumbling towards him. When Jones gets into the light of the headlights, he sees the redness of the blood flooding out between Jones' fingers! He drops the shovel and goes over to him, halfway catching Jones and guides him down to the ground. "How did this hap——." He becomes furious.

The man runs to the SUV with his gun drawn and points it into the backseat, but she's gone! He looks down the road the way they came, but she is nowhere to be seen! He swears under his breath.

Bri had seen the other guy rush over to his friend. When their backs were turned as the one guy helped this Jones to the ground, she ran right inside the woods and hid behind a wide tree. She watches the other guy rush to the SUV, then he looks around for her. When he comes back towards the SUV, she moves to completely hide behind the tree she is next to.

A minute later, she carefully looks over where Jones is at, looking for the other man to be tending to Jones, but he isn't. She goes to look for him from the other side of the tree, only he pops out in front of her. She gasps loudly being startled!

"*Hullo, Your Majesty...*" The man says pointing his gun at her. She tightens her grip on the handle of the knife, knowing a knife won't help her against a gun, unless he is closer. She is trying to think of something to get her out of this. He angrily tells her "You *said* you would come with us so we could deliver you to Millicent!"

"I said that I would follow you to the car." Bri reminds him. "That's all I said. I *specifically* made no other promises."

Bri jumps with a loud shot! Both of them are surprised, and she is waiting to feel the pain of the bullet...she is confused when she sees the guy in front of her drop to his knees. When he collapses on his side, she is horrified to see one of Millicent's right-hand men standing behind him, smoke wafting up and away from him and his gun. She can't seem to form a thought, let alone a sentence.

"Are you hurt, Br–, *Your Majesty*?" Donovan asks.

He checks for a pulse on the man in front of her; he's dead. Donovan picks him up and carries him over his shoulder to where the dead woman is and sets the guy down. Then he goes to Jones and adds him to the other two.

While Donovan is moving bodies, Bri takes off down the driveway. She runs past the SUV she was in and follows the tire tracks until she comes to the SUV Donovan had driven there. She quickly checks to see if it is locked; it's not. She feels the ignition and the keys are still in it! She climbs in and turns it on.

When she sees Donovan coming, yelling something she can't hear, she goes to put the SUV in reverse, then think about four-wheel drive. She sees the SUV is already in four-wheel drive, so she shifts into reverse and slams down the accelerator! She drives the short drive backwards to the main road, so she doesn't see Donovan double back for the other SUV.

Bri thinks quickly to recall the way they came, to try to figure out how to get to this Devonridge Castle. She gets on the main road and straightens out the SUV. She turns off the four-wheel drive, yanks it into 'drive,' and squeals the tires as she floors the accelerator down again going in the direction they were heading before they turned off this road.

Bri is about to call out for Jessica, when she sees she is approaching a set of security gates. She is surprised to see the gates open for her! '*Hhhow?*' She briefly wonders, then is just grateful the gates opened! Bri looks around for a guard tower, *or someone*, as she passes through the gates and drives over a bridge...nothing, *no one*.

Bri parks the SUV over with the other cars. It's when she lets go of the steering wheel, she realizes how hard she was gripping it! She looks at her hands, opening and closing them to stretch them out a few seconds before she gets out. She ducks down to keep out of sight and listens for footsteps, cars, voices, anything that could be close. When she doesn't hear anything, she carefully looks around to figure out what to do next...then she sees another SUV coming up to the gates and ducks back down. She knows it has to be Donovan and she knows it's now or never. She has to get inside while she has an element of surprise, before Donovan tells Millicent what happened in the woods!

CHAPTER 54
Solid Oak Doors Won't Stop Her

Bri is at the front doors of Devonridge Castle. These doors are made of solid oak and are virtually impenetrable. She starts thinking about everything Millicent has done, *and will do*, to her and loved ones; all those she has killed! She gets a powerful surge of emotions that she instinctually channels, so that in one swift movement she throws her hands up and causes an invisible energy force to *explode* the solid oak doors apart!

The explosion causes the mini castle to shake as if there was an earthquake, while pieces of wood of every size and shape fly everywhere! The various pieces fly all around Bri, yet they miss her completely with that same energy field protecting her.

After all the wood pieces have landed, Bri walks through the cloud of dust, right through the now *open* front doorway. She goes inside as Millicent's people are coming towards the few stairs in front of her. She doesn't even process what she is doing as she puts up one hand, then the other hand, having her energy forcing Millicent's people out of her way, while she climbs up the stairs and into the large, open foyer of this place.

The foyer is round and two floors tall, with various archways going into hallways, or framing doors. There is a wide, open stone staircase going up with a ninety-degree turn and the rest of the stairs are against the wall going up to the second floor. Bri is immediately surrounded by Millicent's men; she doesn't do anything about them yet.

"Get The Courtyard ready!" Millicent tells Richard from the middle landing of the stairs. Richard, who had just come in from The Courtyard to see what was going on, turns and goes back out to The Courtyard. Millicent looks at Katie, holding Jacks, "Take him upstairs!"

Bri sees something from the corner of her eye. She turns to see Donovan coming in the front entrance; Bri nervously shifts. Millicent is watching her as she descends the rest of the stairs.

"Well, well, well." Millicent stops at the bottoms of the stairs, less than six feet from Bri. She is able to see Bri's face, neck, and torso, are covered in a dried brown spray. "What have *you* been up to?"

Bri doesn't play along. She firmly tells her, "I came for *my* baby!"

Millicent scoffs. "What makes you think I have *your* baby?"

Bri gives her a cold look and says, "*I will kill every person who gets in my way!*"

Millicent's eyebrows furrow again. "Empty threats—."

"They are *not* empty." Bri tells her.

"Oh, please!" Millicent rolls her eyes. "Do you really think anyone is going to believe you will kill someone?!"

Bri flicks her eyebrow with her glare. "*I already have!*"

"Then you're awfully *smug* for being a killer." Millicent replies, then her eyes narrow as she studies Bri. "*If you have, then it hasn't hit you yet.*" Millicent smirks. "*It will.*" She steps closer to Bri. "And when it does," she evilly smiles, "you'll have to live with that guilt *for whatever is left for the rest of your life!*"

Bri glares back at Millicent and sternly tells her, "*I have no regrets! And I would do it a million times over to protect* MY *family!*" She points to herself.

Millicent angrily says through gritted teeth, "Why you little—." She raises her hand, about to strike Bri, when someone comes up behind Bri.

"*Allow me, Mother!*" Bri hears Lawrence's voice and Millicent is happy to see Bri's sickened expression; Bri has to will herself not to vomit.

Millicent nods to Lawrence with a proud look. "*By all means,* Son!" She waves her arm towards Bri, almost salivating. Lawrence grabs Bri and pushes her up against the closest wall, which is the stone wall of the stairs. He holds her there with his hand to her throat.

"Didn't see that coming, did you?!" Katie happily smiles walking down the stairs; she is savoring the moment. "You've *finally* lost, Bri! I believe this is where we could say, '*checkmate!*'"

"This isn't *even close* to being over yet." Bri snips.

416

"*Watch your tone!*" Lawrence growls.

She looks at Lawrence with her eyebrows furrowed together, glaring in anger and betrayal. With his eye only she can see, he subtly winks at her, catching her off guard for a split-second. Then she winks back the same way he did, to let him know she understands. For Lawrence and Bri, Lawrence having his hand on Bri's neck is an intimate move between them. He uses this move at this time to let her know he *is* on *her* side.

To keep up the appearance, Bri loudly and angrily whispers, "*You Bas—.*"

He quickly covers her mouth. "It's a shame you couldn't be more respectful. Mother might have found a use for you, once you have my heir."

Bri pretends to fight his grip by trying to push his hand away from her neck and struggling to say, "Lawrence, *you're better than this!*"

"Nnnooo, *I'm really not!*" He replies. "I'm tired of trying to pretend to be something I'm not with you; tired of rebelling against Mother!"

"You can let go of her, *for now.*" Millicent tells Lawrence, and he lets go of Bri's neck.

Bri rubs her neck to make it look like Lawrence was holding it tight, causing it to redden more, while the others think her neck is sore. As everyone is focused on Millicent and Bri, Lawrence looks around and gets nods from various men around the room; some are Rex's men and the others have been convinced to join their side of this 'war.'

Millicent looks at Bri. "*I* have a very special surprise for you."

In a matter-of-fact tone, Lawrence says, "You know...this *is* rather *boring...*"

"I couldn't agree more!" Millicent anxiously says, "*Let's take this out to The Courtyard.*"

"I don't think you understand," Lawrence steps protectively in front of Bri, "this whole *charade* is over."

Millicent furrows her eyebrows and enunciates, "Wha*t*?" She gets *furious* and they watch it build. She looks like she could actually exhale fire out her mouth, nose, and ears. "*YOU MISERABLE...*" she goes into a rant that he ignores. Then she yells, "GUARDS!" Millicent angrily command. "*SEIZE THEM OF BOTH!*"

"If anyone is going to be seized, it'll be you and your minions!" Lawrence tells her.

"*Your guards won't get here in time!*" Millicent glares at Lawrence.

"*Look closer...*" Lawrence gestures around the room with his arms. "Their weapons have never really been pointed directly at us." They look around again. Lawrence humorlessly laughs as he gestures the room, "Do you know what it took for them to come over to *our* side?!"

"You would think their own loved ones' lives would have been enough to stay..." she notes as she looks around trying to memorize who turned against her, "but to pick you—."

"*Oh, don't be ridiculous!* They didn't choose me either!" Lawrence motions Bri with his hand saying, "They chose Bri; they chose The Queen." Millicent glares. Lawrence humorlessly laughs as he tells her, "All those years of you telling me how much of a failure I was because I didn't have my people scared of me; that I didn't have their allegiance if they didn't fear me. Having been called every foul name in the book and then some; being blamed for *your mistakes and stupidity* because I wasn't mean, or cruel, or hateful, like those before me; all it proves is that *you're* incompetent! *You're* inept at *everything* you have *ever done!* Bri is *none of those things* and has won the hearts of the people; their allegiance, *and true devotion*, are a credit to the loving woman she is *at heart!*" He gives Bri a loving smile, then looks back to Millicent. "*You're the failure, Millicent!*" He sees a hint of embarrassment on her face and he adds, "But deep down *you knew that already!* You have tried to make up for it through me, *but you keep getting it wrong!*" He is dumbfounded and asks, "*How can you be so dense?!*" Millicent tightens her hands into fists and she is angry.

Katie lashes out. "How can that *miserable* bi—."

"*Actually*, I'm *not* miserable," Bri purposely interrupts Katie, who is coldly glaring at her, "but if you don't give me my baby back, *I'll make you miserable!*" Katie scoffs and Tristan moves to stand next to her. Bri tells Katie, "I've tried to get you to come back around, to *choose* a better life for yourself, but time

418

and time again you choose *the absolute worst* option." She comes back around. "Making the demise of your life—."

"'The demise of *my* life?!'" Katie exhales a laugh. "*And how do you think* you'll *accomplish that?*" She assumes Millicent will protect her.

"*You're doing that all on your own!*" Lawrence replies.

Bri nods and adds, "Which makes your life sad, *miserable*, without true, adoring love."

Katie quickly punches Bri in the cheek before anyone can stop her, causing Bri to stumble back a bit, but Lawrence catches her. Bri's hand reflexively goes up to hold her cheek.

"*I owed you that!*" Katie loathes.

"You'll only get one." Bri states. When Bri straightens back up, Katie launches herself at Bri, only Bri is ready and swiftly steps aside, getting out of Katie's way. Bri tsks, "Katie, Katie, *Katie.* You don't charge at someone like some raging bull; I'm not a matador!"

Tristan steps in front of Katie telling her, "*I've got this!*" He puts his fists up, but he is looking at Lawrence to fight.

Lawrence's eyebrow goes up. He tells Tristan, "I'd think *you* would know better..." He gently pulls Bri back. "I want you to stay behind me, Darling."

"Alright..." Bri tells Lawrence stepping back to give them more room. "If Tristan insists, *by all means*, unleash what you've been holding back, Ace!"

Lawrence stays alert as Tristan jabs at him and misses. Tristan begins swinging and kicking; Lawrence manages to block and dodge Tristan's moves. Lawrence is *knowingly* causing Tristan to tire himself out; just as Bri was having Katie do.

Tristan is getting frustrated and very annoyed. "All you're doing is dodging!" Tristan's irritation is getting the better of him. "You're more pathetic than anyone thought, *you coward!*"

While everyone else is watching Lawrence and Tristan, Millicent slips out to The Courtyard to make sure everything is ready. Bri looks around at everyone watching The King take on Tristan; many are excited for Tristan to be knocked down.

"Is that the best you've got?!" Lawrence gestures Tristan saying, "You're tired and out of breath. You might as well give up now and stop embarrassing yourself!"

Tristan sneers. "*I've got you on the defensive!*"

"If that's what you think, then you aren't a very good opponent!" Lawrence tells him.

Tristan exhales a scoff. "Just the thing an arrogant bas——."

"*Actually*," Lawrence smirks, "the best *offensive* strategy, any sparring partner worth his salt would know, is one would want their opponent to tire themselves out! *This way*, they wouldn't have much energy left to defend themselves against an assault."

Now it's Lawrence's turn, and he pounces! Strike after strike, blow after blow, Tristan tires out completely and he isn't able to effectively block, or duck, Lawrence's moves. When Tristan is bent over and trying to catch his breath, Katie is frustrated that Bri might win *again*! She turns and goes straight to Bri. She takes a swing at Bri, but Bri sees it and ducks; Katie misses her. There are blocked punches that frustrate Katie and she lunges for Bri again, only she doesn't know that Bri has practiced a move like this numerous times with her personal trainer, Li. Bri snatches Katie's arm and quickly turns herself to use her back, to flip Katie over; she slams Katie down hard onto the floor.

It happens so fast, Katie lays there, *stunned*. Tristan quickly helps her up, then pushes her out of the way so he can focus on Lawrence again.

"Where did you learn to do that, Bri?!" Katies brushes herself off.

"Mostly from my personal trainer! I also had a bodyguard and a Duke who would spar with me. Even a time or two with a Grand Duke," Bri tips her head towards Lawrence, "and a King." Bri explains, "You see, we all wanted me to be as prepared as I could be for defending myself, *and* to be prepared for what The King and I ultimately agreed upon."

"And what was that?" Tristan asks, pausing for a moment.

Bri has a determined face when she answers, "NO *prisoners!*"

"And I couldn't agree more!" Lawrence adds.

Tristan's eyebrows come together looking from Bri to Lawrence, thinking about what that means. Before he could figure it out, Lawrence kicks his leg out, so the toe of his shoe comes up under Tristan's chin, sending his head back. Then Lawrence delivers his final blow with a turn kick, nailing Tristan with his foot square in his chest; the sound of ribs breaking couldn't be missed. Lawrence's move sends Tristan flying backwards, straight into a knight's armor. The armor is holding a shorter battle axe that shakes before it drops and slices right into the top of Tristan's head. Most of those watching instinctually close their eyes and look away, right before it becomes a gruesome sight.

Katie is terrified by what she has just witnessed and makes a run for The Courtyard. Katie is desperate to get to safety with Millicent and her protection. Lawrence stays with Bri; he isn't about to split up again!

Bri briefly sees Tristan's spirit looking around, not sure what was going on, before other black orbs come for him. She doesn't want to watch, so she closes her eyes and turns her head away, hearing Tristan screaming as the orbs tear his spirit apart, before dragging the pieces down to what she assumes is a specific place in Hell. Lawrence hugs her knowing she is probably watching something happening with Tristan's spirit.

Grayson has been in the background and he walks over to Tristan's corpse to carefully close Tristan's eyes. He turns to the others still in the foyer with them and sends their people out front with Millicent's people still devoted to her. He gives them an order to shoot *anyone* who tries to escape. Grayson will take a few of them out to The Courtyard with him to help if they can.

Grayson turns back to Lawrence and Bri for a moment. He lifts a strap up and over his head saying, "I saw you put this inside a tree trunk before we blew up The Tunnels. I made sure to grab it for you before we left. I've kept it safe." He hands her a familiar leather messenger bag and Bri is pleasantly surprised! "No one else has touched it; nor has anyone looked inside it, not even me!"

Bri gives him an appreciative look as she takes it. "Thank you. Will you do me a favor?"

"*Anything!*" He replies.

"Would you to keep protecting this for me." She starts to hand it back to him, then stops. "I need..."

She opens the bag and takes out the pouch she put inside it. Then she closes the messenger bag back up and hands Grayson the bag again. He glances down at her hand as he takes the bag and puts the strap across his chest again. Grayson is curious about what she is holding, but he respectfully doesn't ask her about it. Bri puts the pouch in her back pocket.

Bri turns to Lawrence. "No matter what happens, *trust me.*" His eyebrows come together. "Please. *You have to trust me!*"

"*I do!*" He blurts out.

"Good. Let's go!" She hustles outside to The Courtyard, with Lawrence right behind her.

CHAPTER 55
Checkmate

Bri and Lawrence run out into The Courtyard and up to where everyone has gathered in a semi-circle, about twenty feet away from Millicent and her people. Bri peaks through a couple of people and silently gasps to herself when she sees McMasters, Phillip, Henry, Jack, and Claude Devereaux on their knees, with their hands tied behind their backs, and lined up in front of everyone. Lawrence looks between a couple of people and sees what Bri sees; he swears under his breath.

Bri hears Millicent say with disgust, "*You* got weak, *Phillip*! And Lawrence always was weak! But he got worse after that horrible woman came into our lives! Although," she thinks out loud, "he has become a better liar..." Millicent catches sight of Bri, "*And here's our little Queen slag now!*"

A path opens up as people turn to look at Bri. She walks up to the front of the gathered crowd. Millicent motions to someone by snapping her fingers, then points to Bri. A scrawny, nervous man comes over to Bri and shoves something into her hand, then hurries back over to where he was standing.

Bri looks down at her hand and sees a syringe with a cap on it. She holds it up to look at and notices it doesn't have a needle. Her eyebrows furrow as she looks at Millicent, bracing herself for whatever this woman has planned.

Millicent has an evil smile saying, "*You* get to pick which one of these men," she points with her hand to McMasters, Phillip, Henry, Jack, and Claude, "gets to drink *that*." She points to the syringe Bri is holding.

Bri looks at the syringe with clear liquid asking, "*What is it?*"

"*I'm* so *glad you asked!*" Millicent replies with a fake smile. "I thought you should know how easy it is to poison someone with crimson powder!"

Bri shakes her head saying, "*Absolutely not!*" Even though the liquid is clear, Bri knows a piece the size of a granular of sand could kill a person. Millicent could have added more than that, but not enough to change the color to any shade of pink.

Millicent motions the men with a revolver. "You *will* pick someone, or *I* will shoot one of them!"

Bri defiantly tells her. "*No. I won't.*"

 Millicent can see how this is going to go, so she changes tactics a bit. She empties out the bullets in her revolver, then puts only *one* bullet back in and spins the cylinder. Bri watches Millicent as she points the gun at Claude's head again.

"CHOOSE!" Millicent demands.

"No." Bri calmly replies.

Claude closes his eyes right before Millicent pulls the trigger and they hear a 'click' sound. It all goes super quiet...Claude opens his eyes and exhales in relief. The other men were all nervous for him and now slowly exhale knowing there is more to come.

"It's not difficult, BriaLynn!"

"*I* won't *choose!*" Bri snaps.

"Choose me!" Henry says, trying to help Bri. "It's okay! I'll get to be with Maggie again!"

Bri's eyes fill with tears and she shakes her head. An eager face comes over Millicent as she quickly pulls the trigger; everyone jumps a little with the sound of another click.

Phillip tells Bri, "*CHOOSE ME!*"

Millicent walks over to Phillip and is about to point at his head, when Bri states, "*This is a waste of time.*"

They look at Bri, then hear the sound of a third click. Everyone's head snaps to look at Millicent and Phillip.

Jack angrily shouts, "*BLOODY HELL!*"

The tension builds as the chances of the next chamber having the bullet in it increases. Suddenly, Bri remembers something! Jack sees the look on her face as she looks at the syringe in her hand. His eyebrows furrow, causing Lawrence to look at Bri, and sees her looking at the syringe. Millicent looks over at Bri just as she shoves the syringe into her mouth, plunges the liquid in, and swallows.

"*NNNOOO!*" Everyone who saw her yells in horror.

Lawrence rushes over to Bri as she puts up her hand to stop him. Everyone is horrified, *terrified*, even heartbroken and angry that Bri chose to end her own life! Lawrence and Jack are *puzzled* and look at each other with questioning looks; their minds spinning with disbelief.

Bri feels bad at how terrified Lawrence, Jack, and the others must be, but she *just* remembered Jessica telling her that the vaccine, or antitoxin, she took in the lab, would work when she needed it to; *and* right now *she needed it to work!* Bri tosses the empty syringe over to Millicent and she watches the syringe slide across the ground, coming to a rest a couple feet away.

Millicent says in a cold, angry voice, "YOU *STUPID* GIRL! DO YOU HAVE ANY IDEA WHAT YOU HAVE DONE?!" Millicent now starts *fuming*. "*THAT WASN'T A CHOICE!*" She points her gun at McMasters.

"STOP!" Bri tells Millicent in a commanding voice that makes everyone freeze. "YOU WILL *NOT* SHOOT HIM!" Millicent scoffs with a glare and boldly *tries* to pull the trigger, but she can't. She is confused and looks at Bri with frustration as Bri emphasizes to her, "You told me to choose, *and.I.did!*"

Millicent lowers her gun shouting, "*YOU IDIOT!* DIDN'T YOU LEARN *ANYTHING* ABOUT CRIMSON POWDER WHEN YOUR DAUGHTERS DIED?!"

"Oh, come now, Millicent. Call it what it was: murder." Bri states.

Millicent passes over her comment. "YOU'VE NOT ONLY KILLED YOURSELF," she gestures Bri's abdomen, "YOU HAVE JUST KILLED *MY* HEIR?!"

"NO! This is *MY* baby!" Bri puts her hand on her lower abdomen. "And you will *NEVER* get your hands on him!"

Lawrence keeps his mouth from falling open. He doesn't know why he didn't catch that she is pregnant before now?! *'Wait...'* He recalls her saying to trust her, and he said he would! Even though he has *no idea* how she will get out of this, he trusts she will; however, his nerves have had enough. He takes a gun from the person standing next to him and aims it at Millicent as he walks straight over to her.

He says through gritted teeth, *"This has to end NOW!"*

"LAWRENCE, *DON'T!*" Bri says to him.

"SERIOUSLY?!" Lawrence angrily asks her. "AFTER *EVERYTHING* THIS WOMAN HAS DONE," he glares at Millicent, "AFTER ALL THOSE SHE HURT, TORTURED, *AND KILLED*?! YOU *KNOW* SHE DESERVES TO DIE FOR HER CRIMES!"

They are all surprised to hear Bri say, *"Yes. She does!* BUT NOT BY YOU!" She goes over to him. "Lawrence, *look at me.*" He looks at her and he sees the loving look in her eyes for him. She explains, "Doing it this way is *vengeance.* This," she points to him and Millicent, "is another defining moment for you!" He gives her a confused look. "You can be *'Her* King' and pull the trigger, which is *exactly* the behavior she wants you to have! *Or* you can be 'The King' *you* want to be and offer her something she has *never* freely given another soul." Everyone, including Millicent, looks at Bri with their eyebrows scrunched together trying to figure out what that could be...

Lawrence asks, *"And just what would that be?"*

"Mercy." Bri replies.

Everyone is speechless, except Lawrence. He is upset. *"Mercy?!"*

Bri steps a little closer and leans into whisper, *"If you think about it, it's actually the* perfect *vengeance!"*

Lawrence considers that a moment...he starts to nod as he understands what she means and lowers the gun. She looks at him in such a loving way that he knows she is proud of him for choosing to be 'The King' *he* wants to be.

He whispers, "*For the record, the only king I want to be is* your *king.*" She winks at him. Then her facial expression returns to stoic as she turns back to Millicent.

Millicent asks in disbelief, "*How can you be so calm? SO* stupid?! *SO careless?!*" She looks at Bri with genuine confusion asking, "How could *you* be so willing to kill your baby?!"

"There is a bit of information you, *and the others*, don't know yet." Bri replies. Lawrence, Jack, Heny, and the others perk up.

Millicent snips, "*And what is that?*"

"I'm *not* going to die." Bri states.

"Oh, good!" Lawrence exhales in relief. "You *didn't* take the poison!"

Millicent's eyebrows furrow. "*I* mixed the poison and *I* put it in the syringe myself! Unless you dumped it out, you *definitely* drank poison!"

"*I don't doubt that*, and I did!" Bri replies. "I also don't doubt that, had anyone else taken the poison, they would already be dead from your more than lethal dose of crimson powder."

Millicent raises her eyebrow with a knowing expression. "Which can only mean you *didn't* take the poison!"

"Oh, no, I took it!" Bri points to the syringe.

"*THEN WHAT ARE YOU BLOODY GETTING AT?!*" Millicent yells in exasperation.

Bri explains, "When you held me prisoner at Devonridge Manor, particularly in your uncle's room, I went to your uncle's secret lab and found his recipe for a crimson powder vaccine, or antitoxin; I'm not sure which one it would be classified as."

Millicent is angry. "You lie! "*No one* knew where his lab was! We've been looking *for decades* with no luck!"

Bri nods. "So I've heard. As much as I *despise* your uncle for what he did to Lawrence *and you.*" Millicent is surprised by that. "*Yes, you as well.*" She goes on, "I do have to admit, there was an 'evil genius' to him, and what he was able to create in his lab that would've benefited humanity; the 'evil' being he kept it all to himself."

Millicent is skeptical. "You want *me* to believe that *you* found his lab; when it makes *more sense* that you found a journal, since you were kept in his room."

"You had that room all cleared out and thoroughly cleaned. Remember? Besides, do you really think he would carelessly leave a journal *like that* in his room?!" Bri asks. Millicent relaxes her facial expression a bit, thinking about what Bri is saying. "*However,* I did find a few of his journals in his lab, along with books that had various recipes in them, along with his notes about those recipes, and the experiments he conducted! I have to say it was rather educational."

Millicent rolls her eyes. "Then where is my uncle's lab?"

Bri looks around saying, "I won't answer that out in the open, with so many people around." Millicent does appreciate that, only she doesn't show it. Bri senses, 'It's time.' She tells Millicent, "I did find something that might interest you..." She pulls the pouch out of her back pocket and lightly tosses it to Millicent, hoping she would reflexively catch it...she does.

Millicent's eyebrows come together saying to herself, "*This looks familiar...*" She opens it and pulls out the watch inside.

"The pocket watch looks like it has sentimental value." Bri says.

Bri sees The Duke's spirit appear. He watches Millicent take the pocket watch out of the small plastic bag. Bri thought she might hesitate when she sees the plastic bag, but she is focused on the pocket watch. Everyone watches Millicent go over to the small wrought iron table and sits down in a chair. She sets the revolver on the table and looks at the pocket watch more closely. The Duke looks over her shoulder to see what is in her hands.

Millicent wets the tip of her thumb in her mouth to wipe the dust off the insignia on the front of the watch. She says with nostalgia, "*This was my father's pocket watch; it was his father's...*" She opens it.

The Duke's say in annoyance, "*It should've been mine from the beginning!*"

Millicent looks at the thick dust coating the inside of the watch. She glances at her fingers and looks again when she sees red. She gasps and shoots up out of the chair! Her eyes dart over to Bri with a terrified look on her face. Then she looks at her hands, specifically to a fresh cut she has on her forefinger, not to mention wetting her thumb in her mouth a moment ago.

Bri looks from Millicent to Lawrence, then Jack and the others. "Crimson powder." Bri looks at Katie. "I believe in a game of chess, *this* is where I would say," Bri looks back at Millicent, "check*mate*." Millicent gets angry and rattles off a whole slew of vulgar, hateful language.

The Duke of Devonridge walks over to Bri with a knowing grin. "What a sly, little cunning one *you* turned out to be!"

Jack looks at Katie and tells her, "That *is* a 'checkmate,' because there is *no* possible way for Millicent to escape her fate."

Katie is confused. "Then how can it be that Bri isn't going to die, if she drank the poison in the syringe?!"

"*SHE GOT HER HANDS ON THE VACCINE, YOU TWIT!*" Millicent angrily lashes out at Katie.

"*Not exactly.*" Bri starts to say.

"*YOU FOUND MY JOURNALS*?!" The Duke is furious; his face is red.

"That's the part in my story I haven't gotten to yet." Bri replies. "But first," she looks at Mitchell, "let's get these men to their feet and untied, shall we?" Mitchell and a few others help the men stand up, then untie their hands.

CHAPTER 56
The Reckoning

Bri hugs everyone, except she shakes Mr. Deveraux's hand. She notices someone else joining them out in The Courtyard, then Millicent sees him.

Surprised and angry, Millicent says, "*Rex?*! I thought you just helped destroy The Tunnels to help yourself to my inventory!" She is stunned, almost sounding hurt, "*Why?*!"

"You've always been volatile, Millicent, but you were getting out of control! And you crossed *a huge line* killing two kids!" He tells her.

"*YOU SMUGGLED THE POISON OVER FOR ME!*" She angrily shoots back at him.

"*I DIDN'T KNOW YOU WERE INTENDING TO KILL INNOCENT CHILDREN WITH IT!*" He angrily replies. "*AND I CERTAINLY DIDN'T KNOW WHO THE CHILDREN WERE YOU WERE GOING AFTER!*"

"THEY WEREN'T INNOCENT! AND THEY WERE HER POTENTIAL *HEIRS* TO MY *THRONE*! THEY WERE POSSIBLE CONNECTIONS TO THE THRONE THAT I COULDN'T HAVE!" Millicent's fury is clear. "*IT WAS BUSINESS!* I WOULD THINK YOU, OF ALL PEOPLE, WOULD UNDERSTAND THAT!"

"*RUBBISH!*" Rex's anger matches hers. "*YOU JUSTIFIED IT AS BUSINESS, BUT IT WAS PERSONAL! AND WHEN YOU BROKE OUR CODE, YOU NEEDED TO BE STOPPED!*"

"*PUT DOWN, YOU MEAN!*" Millicent implies being poisoned as she holds up her dusty red fingertips.

"Whatever *Her Majesty* wanted," Rex tips his head towards Bri, "I supported, along with my people!" He gestures around and Millicent is dumbfounded looking at all those who were a part of it; that she thought were dedicated to her, *especially Donovan*! Her eyes narrow to glare at Donovan, but they flick back to Rex when he states, "Queen BriaLynn *IS* the rightful queen!"

Millicent looks at Bri. "How were you able to vaccinate yourself against crimson powder poisoning?"

"You see, when I found The Duke's recipe for a crimson powder vaccine, I followed his recipe and made it." She looks at Lawrence and Jack when she says, "Then I had what we'll say was a *sixth sense* to drink some." Lawrence and Jack nod, understanding that Jessica told her to take the vaccine, helping them to relax. "I decided to trust your uncle's *evil-genius* and vaccine, *along* with my '*sixth sense*,' and took the poison you wanted me to give one of these men. I'm just grateful it did its job!"

Millicent says with disgust, "Everyone thinks you're this sweet, kind, innocent person, when it turns out you're just as devious as the rest of us!"

"Oh! *More so!*" Bri replies. "*I had to be!* I've been around people like you for *way* too many years." Referring to her previous job in Washington, D.C.

"*Like me?*" Millicent dismally asks.

"In my *un*professional opinion, you're part sociopathic, part psychopathic, with a generous serving of narcissism." Bri explains, "Your hatred and belief of superiority towards me, caused you to *continually* underestimate me, which I used to my advantage! *I didn't want you to know what I was capable of, because I didn't want you to up the stakes that were already too high!*" She continues, "You see, Millicent, I knew this was some sort of game to you, and you assumed I didn't know how to play! However, just because I don't *want* to play your game, doesn't mean I don't know *how* to play you game! And if I play *any* game, you can bet," she gives Millicent a determined look, "*I will play to win!*" Bri waves her arm in Katie direction saying, "Katie should've been able to tell you that. I mean," Bri turns to look at Katie, "that's why you two teamed up together, to try to beat me, right?" Katie glances at Henry and sees he is looking at her with sadness and disappointment. Katie's heart starts to give in to the heavy feeling of shame and remorse.

Millicent goes to angrily say something but grabs her gun off the table, points it at Lawrence and pulls the trigger of the revolver. This time, the bullet flies out of the barrel, flying through the air straight at Lawrence's chest! Bri gasps out loud. Phillip tries to push Lawrence out of the way, but the bullet hits Lawrence in his left shoulder area.

Bri's face shows the anger that matches her voice, "*I command you to put the gun down NOW, and NEVER pick it up again!*" Millicent is confused when she automatically puts the gun down. "I command you to sit down!" Then she sends Mitchell and McMasters to call the UKs version of 9-1-1, which is 9-9-9, and secure the castle.

The Royal Guard, particularly The King's Guard, already secured the bridge and took control of the small island. The police and emergency personnel are getting close. McMasters has someone go out to send the paramedics into The Courtyard for The King as *soon* as they arrive!

Jack and Mitchell go to help Lawrence up, but he shakes his head. "It's just my shoulder!"

"You need a doctor, Son." Phillip tells him, but he knows what he'll say next, because he would do the same thing.

"I'm not leaving without Bri, Jack, and Jacks!" Lawrence states.

Bri looks at Lawrence with teary eyes. "Lawrence, you're bleeding pretty heavily, you may need surgery. *Please*, let them get started, so we don't risk you bleeding to death."

Phillip suggests, "Henry and Jack will stay here with Bri, while I'll go with you, and we will keep everyone updated."

Lawrence looks at Bri. "I hate leaving you in case you need me."

Bri gives him an understanding look. "I know. And your protest *is* noted." She winks and he starts to softly laugh, but grimaces with the pain. She tells him, "I love you!"

Lawrence struggles to say, "*I love you, too!*"

Phillip and some of The King's Guards take Lawrence out to meet up with the ambulance. Bri's attention goes back to Millicent. She is bent over and grimacing in pain with her arms wrapped in front of her; she is holding her breath until the pain subsides.

Millicent asks Bri, "*Isn't there something you can do?*! Anything from my uncle's journals that can help me? You can't just let me die!"

"Fitting, don't you think?" Bri asks and Millicent furrows her eyebrows. "You're experiencing what my daughters, their dad, and stepmom felt, *what Vivian felt...*" Millicent thinks about that. Bri goes on, "The difference with Vivian is that not only was she all alone and scared, but, being a mother, she was worried for her children and even feeling helpless for her unborn baby..." Millicent's eyes snap to Bri and Bri tells her, "She had just found out she was pregnant, but never had a chance to tell Phillip." Bri's emotions surface as Vivian's autopsy photos come to mind. She clears her throat. "You don't need an audience," Bri looks at McMasters and Rex and tips her head to the exit; they nod and start clearing everyone out.

Millicent cringes in pain, but manages to sneer at Bri, "Sweet and kind 'Queen Bri' poisoned me, *knowing* what it does to a person!"

"I guess we can call this '*poetic justice.*'" Bri replies.

Millicent continues to struggle with the growing pain. "*Aren't you all about* 'second chances' *and what not?*"

Bri's eyebrows slowly go up and she calmly replies, "Oh, I think we're *looong* past that after you set out to kill my family!"

"Why were you never bothered by the deaths of you parents?" Millicent has to know. "*Not one tear!*"

"Well, I figured there was a possibility that you did kill them; *I* didn't put *anything* past *you.*" Bri admits, "It's sad they died, and sadder that it wasn't natural causes, or an accident. Katie should've been able to tell you why I wasn't as upset as a person would be at the loss of their parents."

Millicent looks at Katie and Katie shrugs saying, "I didn't know you had them killed until after the fact." Katie looks at Bri and she gets the feeling Katie protected Henry and Maggie from Millicent.

Bri gestures to Jack as she speaks to Katie, "If you want to make up for *a fraction* of *everything you've ever* done, tell Jack where he can find my son."

Millicent was starting to have some nice one-on-one time with Jacks, and it did something she hadn't intended...a sweet baby got to her heart. She tells Jack how to get to the nursery. Bri thanks her as the paramedics come into The Courtyard to treat her.

Bri looks at Rex and McMasters. "We all should step back and give a dying person some room to be treated."

"Or..." Rex pulls out his gun, "we can end it quickly."

Bri shakes her head. "That *won't* be happening." She feels very strongly and states, "We *won't* deny justice it's payment!" Bri looks over at Millicent. "Besides, we still have a bit more to discuss before this is all over., *don't we?*"

CHAPTER 57
Forgiveness and Mercy

McMasters sends the last people out of The Courtyard with Claude, Katie, and Richard being three of them. This leaves only Henry, McMasters, Rex, and Mitchell in The Courtyard with Bri and Millicent. Jack is inside the castle rescuing Jacks.

Rex watches Claude leave, and has to ask Millicent, "Why Claude?!"

Millicent replies, "He wouldn't help me when I asked him to, and *no one* says 'no' to me, well, *except you.*" Her eyebrows come together and she asks, "Did you have something to do with Claude not wanting to help me?! He tried to tell me his child was kidnapped," she rolls her eyes, "but we all know he doesn't have any children!"

"*I* had Claude's *daughter* kidnapped." Bri tells her.

Millicent looks from Rex to Bri with a doubtful look, "*You?!*" She scoffs. "You expect *me* to believe you'd hurt any child?!"

"*Don't be ridiculous!*" Bri tells her. "I simply told him to stay out of my way when it came to you; that he wasn't to help you at all, in *any* way whatsoever!"

"Or you would do *what* to this child?" She curiously asks.

"Or *nothing.*" Bri states. "I told him I wouldn't hurt his child either way."

"Well, you're not very good at threats." Millicent states.

"You know, Mr. Devereaux basically told me the same thing; and so did a couple of other people. *Nevertheless, I refuse* to hurt children." Bri states. "I did, however, tell him that if he got in my way, I'd bring him down with you." She raises her eyebrow. "*That* was the greater threat?" Millicent thought she had a point, but she kept that to herself. Bri takes a deep breath. "As I said, I knew you were underestimating me and I wanted to keep it that way. That's why the nurse you hired to take Jacks was executed on the spot." Bri stands in front of her again. "I couldn't have you finding out that I had slammed her against the wall, or held a loaded gun to her head, in order to get her to tell me where my baby was!" Katie's mouth drops a bit. Millicent studies Bri

435

for her truthfulness. "*Before all that, I* arranged for your bank accounts to have a glitch," Millicent's eyes go wide, "then later drained, with the help of the best hacker in the world!" Millicent gives Rex an angry look; he doesn't care. "A whole team was put together to rescue the people, animals, and the priceless artifacts in your tunnels, while it was all rigged to come down." Bri looks at Rex with gratitude. "I couldn't have pulled this off without him, or any of his people, *and* his connections!"

"Yes, you could have, Your Majesty! You were *that* determined." Rex replies.

"Perhaps." She looks at Millicent again. "I will do, *whatever it takes*, to save and protect my family, as well as anyone else who would've gotten wrapped up in any of this!" Bri has a hand on her lower abdomen and watches Millicent's face have a touch of sadness. Bri is reminded of a young Millicent in her vision. She gives Millicent a look with such kindness that it seems to unnerve her. "It's sad that your anger isn't directed where it should be."

Millicent scoffs, "*Where might that be?*"

"At your uncle, The Duke of Devonridge." Bri answers.

Millicent is stunned a second, then upset. "*Did you find a diary of mine at The Manor and read it?!*"

Bri softly shakes her head. "No. I had a vision." Rex is intrigued.

"*Whaaat?*" Millicent's mouth had fallen open. She stumbles with her words, "Hh*how? Wwwhen?*"

Bri eyes get teary, "I had a vision of a *beautiful* sixteen-year-old young woman in one of the saddest situations any *woman* could ever imagine! She had to have a hysterectomy, because something went wrong with her latest abortion. *All* of her abortions were done *to her*; that young woman never had a choice."

Millicent shakes her head a little, trying to stop that memory from coming to the surface. She whispers, "*That day still haunts me...*"

"*I don't doubt that!*" Bri quietly, but firmly, replies. "It's a day that would haunt *any* woman!"

Millicent stares at the floor, thinking... "It felt like I died that day..." She looks at Bri, then her tummy; a twinge of envy causes her to lash out. *"But my uncle took care of me, because he loved me when* no one else *cared about me!"*

Bri is still looking at her with kindness and compassion, while firmly telling her, *"That's what he* needed *you to believe!"* Millicent's head goes back a little. "Yet, you *also* had to believe that in order to survive, while deep down you knew the truth!" She emphasizes, *"Everything* your uncle did was to make *his life* better; *you were secondary.* Watching you in that vision, *I saw you physically change!* I believe you when you said it felt like you died that day. I saw it in your eyes! *That* was the significant 'turning point' in your life!" Bri sees Vivian appear, but to everyone else it looks like Bri is staring off in the distance. Bri looks at Millicent again and those who are listening are surprised to hear, perhaps Millicent more so, when Bri tells Millicent, "That 'turning point' was the moment you *let* your soul darken. You didn't want to feel the loss of what happened, you couldn't let yourself be angry with your uncle, or life would *somehow* get worse for you. So, you shut down, and over time, you used evil acts more and more to *'get them before they get you.'* Perhaps, you thought it has been less painful that way, only you have made it *more* painful for yourself in the end—."

"My Uncle made it possible for me to be The Queen, to make up for it all..."

"Did it?" Bri asks. *"Be honest with yourself!* Could anything really make up for all the abortions he forced you to have; for *never* being able to have another baby as a result of it all? Not to mention all the horrific things he did to you as a teenager, *as a child!"* She sees Millicent thinking and she continues, "He had you believing you owed him everything for raising you; that *he* made you 'The Queen.' Only what he did was negotiate for you to become 'The Queen,' so *he* could ultimately *control* The Monarchy, *because he* controlled *you!"*

"That's absurd!" Millicent scoffs, then gasps in pain, folding down onto her lap again.

Bri starts to wonder if she should help Millicent with her pain and suffering, but Vivian shakes her head and tells her, "You won't be allowed to help her like you helped Natty!"

"SEE!" Millicent angrily says, "YOU *CAN* HELP ME! HOW DID YOU HELP THIS, THIS NATTY PERSON?!"

Bri plainly replies, "You know, it doesn't even surprise me you wouldn't know my daughters' names. *Wait.*" Bri's eyebrow goes up. "*You heard that?*"

Millicent gives Bri a puzzled look and struggles to say through her pain, "Of course, I did, you TWIT!"

Bri looks around at the others and sees their confusion. She looks back at Millicent and tells her, "That was Jessica talking about Natty..."

"Jessica?" Millicent looks around wondering, "Who's that?"

"She's my spirit guide."

Millicent's head snaps to look at Bri again; so do the others. Her attention is brought to another spirit is now appearing...

"Is that...*Vivian?*" Millicent asks in disbelief. "*How can that be?*"

Bri softly replies, "Because you're dying, Millicent, and the veil between mortality and the spirit world is thinning for you." Everyone around them gets chills. Millicent goes to respond, but she collapses to the floor. Bri looks around at those who are still there. "If you don't want to see a spirit, please leave right now." No one does. Bri makes Jessica and Vivian visible for everyone to see by quickly circling her two fingers around in the air.

"Bri," Vivian walks over to her, "your heart isn't letting you see the bigger picture. Take a step back for a moment and think about this from a spiritual, *an eternal,* perspective..."

Bri looks from Vivian to Millicent's body on the floor, and thinks out loud, "It's better for her to suffer what she can *now*, before she dies..." Millicent's spirit appears, still tethered to her body like Natty's spirit was. Millicent hears Bri say, "Millicent's uncle wasn't sorry for anything when he died!" Bri looks at Millicent and apologetically says, "He *still* isn't sorry!" Bri wants Millicent to realize why she needs to separate herself from her uncle, or she will be entangled with him for *all* eternity. "What's your uncle's *full* name?"

"Clive Benedict Devonridge." Millicent replies.

There is something fitting about that, but Bri pushes past that thought. "Clive Benedict Devonridge, I *command you* to come here!" It's quiet and she looks around, and so do the others. "I know you're here; I can feel you lurking! *You can't ignore me!*" She walks around and feels his irritation. "*Aaahhh*, you don't like me using your full name?" She asks, still looking around; she works to push his buttons, "Were the little boys relentless with you in school?" Bri senses the answer. "I see, your nickname was more fitting because of the traitor you were even back then, *Benedict Arnold!*" The Duke appears ranting with a slur of swear words right to her face. Bri isn't bothered by this and interrupts with, "It's interesting that it took something like that for you to join us." Bri moves her fingers around so the others can also see The Duke's, as well as Millicent's, spirits. He glares viscously at Bri, but she tips her head towards Millicent telling him, "Don't you care that Millicent is dying—."

"*BECAUSE YOU POISONED HER!*" The Duke yells at Bri.

Henry comes up to Bri and stands protectively of her. Peter appears and after Bri makes him visible to the others, he joins Henry protecting Bri.

Henry tells The Duke. "You WILL speak to her more respectfully, or I will ask Bri to send you to the worst part of Hell there is!" It occurs to Bri that The Duke, Phillip, Peter, *and Henry*, all have a past together, being they were raised noble and royal!

The Duke scoffs. "*She can't—.*"

"*STOP IT!*" Millicent angrily says. She is finally allowing herself to feel all the emotions she has pushed down all these years to survive her abuser, then to live with herself. She finally directs that anger at the source: *her uncle.* "All the horrible, despicable, *ghastly* things *you* did to me; you were to protect me from people like that, *not be one!*"

He tries to calm her down like he had done in the past. "Milly, you're just upset—."

"*You're damn right I'm upset!* I should've killed you myself for the horrible things *you* did to me! Or after any of the abortions you forced me to have, before you *destroyed* my chances of ever having a baby of my own! *YOU MURDERED THAT PART OF ME!*" She gasps out loud.

Her spirit retracts and is bent over from the pain. It's hard for those around her to watch. Her spirit disappears towards her body and all is quiet. The others look around at each other, then look at Bri for more answers.

Bri starts to understand more. "There is an internal, a spiritual, struggle going on with her and she has a few things to do. One of them is to decide on whether she will break free from her uncle, one-and-for-all." It doesn't take long before they know her answer; Millicent is dead and her spirit appears before them.

"Milly!" The Duke excitedly says, "*We're finally together again!*"

"*NO,*" she looks at him with disgust, "we're *NOT!*"

"*But I waited all this time for you!*" He actually sounds hurt.

Bri scoffs. "You were waiting for her to avoid being sent to Hell by yourself, you mean!"

"*How would you know?*" He snaps at Bri. "If I were to belong in Hell, wouldn't I have been sent down there already?"

Bri considers that for a moment, until she feels the answer. "Not until Millicent had the chance to decide, *for herself,* if she wanted to continue to be tied to you. If she had, *she* would be doomed to your fate."

"I'm done with you!" He tells Bri. "Milly—."

"You're scared..." Bri watches him closely and thinks.

"*Don't be ridiculous! There's nothing to be scared of!*" He replies rather unconvincingly. He turns to Millicent. "Milly, let's GO!"

Millicent pulls back and firmly tells him, "No!"

"What is it you're so scared of?" Bri asks as she studies him.

"Nothing, you mindless slag!" He sneers.

Bri begins to feel an answer. "You promised to bring Millicent's spirit down with you, in exchange for a 'lighter sentence,' so-to-speak."

"*You don't know what you're talking about!*" The Duke snaps.

"Oh, *but I do!*" She replies. "You need Millicent, because she will pay for *your* crimes," then she says with amazement, "and you think you won't be sent to Hell at all!"

The Duke reaches for Millicent tell her, "Come!"

Millicent is incensed with anger. "LEAVE ME ALONE!" The Duke is shocked and dumbfounded. She glares and says with a loathing tone to match, "*I hhhAAAtte you!* I *NEVER* want to see you again!"

The Duke says in the calm tone he has used with her many times in the past, "I'll come back when you've calmed down a bit."

"*Don't bother!*" She snips.

Something about that strikes a nerve with Bri. She doesn't want him to force 'his agenda' on her, like he has done to her so many times in the past, especially with something that has such eternal significance! She looks at Jessica and projects a thought, '*His control over her can't be forced to continue on the other side, can it?*' Jessica shakes her head. Bri feels what she is to do next.

The Duke has a red face as angrily tells Bri, "*You won't always be around, and when you're not,* then *she will be reasonable about coming with me!*"

She flicks up her eyebrow asking, "Wanna bet?"

"And just what do you think you can do..." The Duke starts to say, then tapers off when it occurs to him what she *can* do; he begins to tremble in fear.

Bri feels a strength to firmly say, "Clive Benedict Devonridge, I command *justice* to stake its claim upon you, to take you to whatever Hell you've been avoiding all these years, and to go *without Millicent!*"

Sheer terror comes over The Duke and everyone watches dark orbs come up from the ground and surround him. He screams in agony as they rip apart his spirit and take those pieces down beneath the surface of the ground." Everyone is in shock by what they just witnessed. Before they have time to process all that, the ground opens up for Millicent; only it's in front of her, not under her, like Bri has seen before.

Millicent stares at it, asking, "What's going on?"

Bri thinks out loud, "It seems you have a choice." When Millicent looks at her, Bri receives the full message. She looks at Jessica and Vivian and they nod in confirmation. Bri tells Millicent, "Justice won't be denied, *it can't*. There is a price that has to be paid. However, you can *choose* to go down and serve your sentence, while learning and growing; or justice will take you and it will be for an eternity."

"Does that mean she gets a shorter sentence of sorts?!" Jack asks with anger, walking up to them with a sleeping baby in his arms.

"No." Bri surprises herself at how quickly she answers. "Think of it as her sentence, after the aggravating and mitigating circumstances have been taken into consideration. Her penalty, or sentence, doesn't have to be for an eternity. I don't have all the answers. What I am grateful for is that God, the Father of all of us, is in charge. And while we know He and the Lord *are merciful*, personally I *never* want to see God's wrath directed at me, *nor anyone else*! We need to trust that His verdicts *are* fair, and one day when we are on the other side, we will understand everything."

Vivian says to Jack, "As you know, there is an order to everything and we all have choices. *This* is Millicent's choice."

Millicent tells them, "I *never* felt I had any choices with my uncle! I've felt my uncle's influence running my life *even after he was dead*, stupidly trying to make *him* proud!" She stares at the hole. "But now...now I see what I've done to Lawrence, and so many others, is unforgiveable..."

"He has a lot of anger to process, but after today, he will be able to work through it and let go of the anger and bitterness." Bri replies. "I already forgive you, because I don't want to hang on to the bitterness and hatred that I was feeling towards you and your uncle." Bri waits for Millicent to respond, only to everyone's surprise, they watch her jump into the hole. Then whole closes up just as fast, and all that is left is stunned silence...

CHAPTER 58
Who Pays the Price of Justice?

Henry, McMasters, Mitchell, Rex, Jack, and Bri, are all staring at the floor where Millicent had just jumped into a hole that appeared for her. Bri takes a deep breath and turns to Jack with her sleeping baby in his arms.

Jack takes a step closer to hug her with one arm, but Bri steps back shaking her head. "I might have some of the crimson powder on me."

"You don't." Jessica assures her. "It's also perfectly safe for you to hold Jacks if you'd like."

Bri looks down at herself. "I want to clean up first before that happens." She smiles lovingly at Jack.

Bri hugs Peter. "Thank you."

Peter is surprised. *"For what?"*

"For raising such remarkable men, and for your friendship with Henry!" She looks at Henry. "I'll hug you in a little bit." She motions between the two of them with her finger saying, "I'll give you two a couple of minutes."

She goes back over to Jack and sees Jacks is waking up; her eyes get teary as a wave of love comes over her. She goes to rub his back, but he leans away and starts to cry, holding onto his Uncle Jack.

Henry says to Bri, "I don't think he recognizes you with all that..." His eyes go wide for a second, truly taking in what *is* on her face and neck.

Bri gets teary-eyed. "It's blood of the man I stabbed in the neck out in the woods, Henry."

He hugs her. "We can talk about that a little later. Right now, let Grandpa take Jacks out front."

Jacks goes to his Grandpa Henry, then Henry and Peter say their goodbyes for now. Bri and Jack watch Henry and Jacks leave through the gate.

Rex comes over. "I have my car out front to take you to the airport where your helicopter will take all of you to London. I'll have my car brought closer to the gate for you to avoid the crowd of onlookers in the distance."

She gives an appreciative smile. "Thank you, but I need to walk out of here."

Rex starts to say, "Bri——."

"After everything we have been through, after losing all those we have lost, after all those who have been hurt, they need to see it wasn't in vain. We defeated her and now I *need* to walk out of here, for all of them! Yes, looking like this, so they know we all fought and it wasn't an easy battle!"

"If we walk out of here, you'll go straight to the hospital?" Jack asks and she agrees. "Lawrence has already been taken to The Royal Hospital in London, where David and Abby are also at."

"That's good." She says with relief.

Rex tells Bri, "I'm going to regroup with my people and help McMasters with anything he might need."

Rex walks with them just outside of the gate. He looks down and sees Jack's outstretched hand; Rex shakes his hand.

"'Thank you' *isn't close* to the gratitude our family feels for what you and your people did for Bri, *and all of us*." Jack tells him. Rex nods, he is choked up.

Bri tells Rex, "I need to see Grayson; he's holding my bag for me."

"*You need it now?*" Jack asks.

She gives him an apologetic nod. "There are some snacks in it."

"Ah." Jack replies.

Rex looks around. "Grayson!" He waves him over.

Grayson is already taking the messenger bag off as he walks up to Bri and gives it to her. She smiles and thanks him as she takes it.

She looks at Rex. "We'll meet up soon?" He nods.

Jack takes the bag as Bri gets into the back of Rex's car, then Jack climbs in next to her. "Be careful." She warns Jack about the messenger bag. "There are some *breakable* things in it."

He carefully holds it in his lap while he pulls out some crackers for her to snack on. She tries to stay calm, but she gets more and more anxious the closer they get to the airport.

Jack gives her a loving look. "David can't wait to see you either."

Bri looks hopeful. "He's awake?!"

"I hope so!" He replies. "Even if he isn't, his heart will know!"

She gets teary-eyed and inhales deeply, holding her breath for a moment. "Any time I think about him or Lawrence, my mind flashes to each memory of when they were shot..." Tears start to run down her cheeks.

Jack hands her a tissue out of her bag and holds her hand. "We will get you to them as soon as you are checked out by a doctor and cleaned up. *Then* we can replace the memories of them being shot with *much* better ones!" She nods as she shakily exhales and rests her head on his shoulder; he kisses her head, then takes a deep relaxing breath himself. Millicent was done.

On the helicopter, Bri remembers the helicopter has a change of clothes for everyone on it. She goes and takes a shower. She scrubs the blood off of her skin until it is red and raw. She keeps replaying the stabbing in her mind...She is about to get out and inhales deeply, only when she exhales, she is overcome with her emotions and starts to sob uncontrollably. She tries hard to stop, but she can't.

Jack had been patiently waiting for her in the bedroom. When he hears her crying, he comes into the bathroom. He calmly shuts the water off and wraps a towel around her and hugs her firmly.

He whispers, "*Let it out, Amore Mia.*" He kisses the side of her head. "*It's over...it's finally over.*" She cries for several minutes and he holds her.

When she is quiet, he helps out of the shower and dries off. They go out into the bedroom so she can get dressed. She takes another deep, shaky breath; only she is still emotionally drained. She looks at the door thinking about Jacks and how she couldn't take him rejecting her again. She looks at Jack; he lovingly looks at her and cups her cheek.

"Let's take care of you for the remainder of this flight." Jack suggests. He holds her cheeks. "Make no mistake: the next time Jacks sees you, he will know *exactly* who you are: *his beautiful mother!*" She hugs him.

She crawls onto the bed and Jack joins her. They snuggle together to watch a movie. Bri's eyelids are heavy and she falls asleep for the remainder of their flight to London.

CHAPTER 59
The Morgue

The Queen's Motorcade pulls up to the front of The Royal Hospital. Before they open the back door, they can hear the loud crowd waiting for them. Jack gets out first, then he helps Bri out. They notice lots of flashes of light coming from the crowd that is behind barricades McMasters had put in place with Royal Guards standing with those barricades to keep people from crossing them. McMasters also has Royal Guards protecting the entrance to the hospital in anticipation of Bri's arrival. There are various questions being asked, but Jack and Bri only wave as they let Mitchell usher them inside.

On the top floor, they already have Abby in her own private suite in The Royal Wing. They moved David into The King's Suite, at The King's request, before Lawrence went into surgery. Lawrence will also recover in The King's Suite once he is out of surgery; this will make it easier on Bri to be with both of them.

They have an exam room set up for Bri, and for her unborn baby, to be checked out. She walks in and sees an ultrasound machine in her room. She sits on the exam table and Jack stands beside her. There is a knock before a doctor and nurse come into the room. The doctor examines Bri and wants to run some tests; the nurse draws some blood. Then the doctor checks on the baby with the ultrasound machine.

Afterwards, The Queen is told His Majesty is still in surgery and The Grand Duke is still sleeping after a dose of painkillers earlier. Bri asks to speak with their doctors; it's only one.

The doctor meets them outside The King's Suite. She gives him a small smile before asking, "How are they?"

"His Majesty is still in surgery. He has a shoulder wound where the bullet went all the way through, and we're hopeful he will make a full recovery; however, we will need to watch for blood clots."

Bri nods. "And The Grand Duke?"

"His Highness has been healing *quite* nicely!" The doctor smiles. "He had a lot of damage from the bullet hitting him in the chest, it barely missed his heart." Bri's mind flashes to when she saw David, lying on top of all that debris after he was shot. She also remembers there was a lot of blood! The doctor tells her, "I think he will somehow heal faster now that you're here, safe and sound."

The nurse nods. "He has been so very worried about you this whole time, Your Majesty!"

"Thank you." Bri gives them a small smile. "May I see The Grand Duke?"

"He's still sleeping from the anesthesia." He replies.

Bri turns to Jack just as he is getting a text. He tells Bri, "Jacks is sleeping." He shows her the picture Henry took of Jacks sleeping in a hospital crib. She tearfully smiles and quickly wipes her cheek. "Tell Henry we'll let Jacks sleep as peacefully as he looks." Jack nods.

As Bri waits for Jack to type his text, she gets an idea. After he sends the text, she says, "I should use this time to go down to the morgue."

"What?" Jack is a little surprised. "*Why?!*"

Bri explains, "I want to go to the morgue before Lawrence, *or even Phillip*, are asked to identify *any* bodies." Jack nods in understanding of what she wants to do and why.

Jack and Bri are inside the elevator with McMasters and a few guards. On their way down to the morgue in the basement, she looks at Jack with teary eyes and he firmly holds her hand. The elevator doors open and they step out into the dimly lit hallway. They walk down the hallway and the light gets a little brighter in the empty waiting area of a reception area. Bri's nose picks up the faint smell of death as they walk up to the reception desk.

When the receptionist looks up, she is a bit awestruck seeing 'The Queen' in front of her. She collects herself and asks Her Majesty what she can do for her; Bri tells her. The receptionist calls the medical examiner's office and speaks to Dr. Charles Finley. Dr. Finley has the receptionist escort them down to a viewing window. The window they come to is a large rectangular window that has the curtain closed on the other side. Dr. Finley steps into the hallway to speak with them.

"Your Majesty." Dr. Finley bows. "My condolences to you and your family."

Bri swallows hard and softly replies, "*Thank you.*"

She tells him she is there to identify Their Royal Highnesses The Duke and Duchess of Brexton's bodies before Lawrence or Phillip are asked to do it. He has them come inside; Jack's phone rings as he follows Bri into the room. It's David and he takes the call.

> David asks, "Where are you two?"
>
> "Believe it or not, The Morgue." Jack answers.
>
> "Why did she go down to the morgue?!"
>
> Jack replies, "She wants to identify bodies before Herst or Phillip are asked to do it."

Dr. Finley says, "I'm going to close this big curtain until we're ready for you to see them." He motions the chairs behind them. "Please feel free to sit while you wait." Bri gives him a faint smile with her little nod and watches him close the curtain; she doesn't sit down.

Bri turns to Jack. "You don't have to do this with me. I can compartmentalize better than the average person. It's okay for you to wait outside."

He runs his hand around to the back of her neck. "I *refuse* to let you do this alone!"

> "*Me, too!*" David firmly says.

Jack points to his phone. "David agrees." Bri faintly nods once.

"Will you put me on speaker so I can be there the best I can?" David asks and Jack does that.

Before Bri can respond, they hear gurneys rolling up to the curtain. Several seconds later, Dr. Finley slowly opens the curtain to reveal the two gurneys with a sheet covered body on each one. Dr. Finley explains that the autopsies were completed, then he watched the video of the killings, which verified his

449

findings. Bri is staring through the gurneys as she listens to him, and wonders how he got a copy of the video Millicent made her watch?

Bri notes, "They were executed, shot in the forehead."

Dr. Finley is a bit surprised, yet calmly replies, "That's correct, Your Majesty." He sees she is staring at the gurneys as he tells her, "We will carefully pull back the sheet to only show you their face, but we can't hide everything."

"I know." She quietly replies. "That's why I wanted to do this without Lawrence, or his father. They don't need to see them this way." David hears this and it takes a moment before he realizes that Bri is also protecting Phillip and Herst from seeing Seth's and Genevieve's bullet wounds.

The first sheet is pulled back. Bri's eyes fill with tears seeing Seth and having various memories flowing through her mind. Then she remembers the video of their deaths and closes her eyes, holding them shut for a few seconds, trying hard to push down the rage building inside her towards Millicent.

"Are you alright, Your Majesty?" Dr. Finley asks.

"*Yes.*" Bri barely whispers, opening her eyes and clearing her throat. Jack goes to put his arm around her and she shakes her head. "Not yet." He gives her a faint smile of understanding.

Dr. Finley says to her, "I have to officially ask—."

"This is His Royal Highness Seth, The Duke of Brexton and His Majesty King Lawrence's brother." She calmly states.

"Thank you." Dr. Finley looks at his assistant and the sheet goes back over Seth's face.

They take the few steps over to the next gurney with David still listening on speaker phone. The assistant pulls the sheet back.

Dr. Finley quickly covers the face back up as he whispers to his assistant, "*This is the wrong one!*"

"It's alright doctor." Bri tells him. "*That* is Lady Sara Kemp." The others look at each other. Bri stares at Sara and tells Dr. Finley what he already knows.

450

"Millicent slit her throat ear-to-ear and I believe Millicent cut through both arteries..." Her eyes shut and a tear escapes, running down her cheek; she quickly wipes it away.

Dr. Finely looks at her with sadness and quietly says, "She severed the first artery and *almost* the second." Both Jack and David are sick for Bri, for all that she has gone through.

They move on to the next one the assistant had gone to bring over. The assistant pulls the sheet back and Bri whispers to herself, "*Oh, Genevieve...*" Bri swallows hard. "Queen Gen—." Bri clears her throat and stands up straight to regain her composure. "Her Royal Highness Genevieve, The Duchess of Brexton." Bri looks at her friend remembering when they were getting ready for The Royal Coronation Ball with Abby...she watches the sheet go back over Gen's face, then the assistant pushes the gurneys over to the refrigerators. Bri whispers to Dr. Finley, "*Can I have a minute?*"

"Of course, Your Majesty." Dr. Finley bows, then shoos his assistant out entirely before he goes into his office and shuts the door to give them privacy, yet close by in case they need him. Jack steps behind her and puts his arms around her, resting his cheek against hers.

Jack's voice is a whisper, "*After everything you've been through, you came down here so Herst didn't have to do this, nor Phillip! You never cease to amaze me!*"

She gives him a confused look. "*I had to!*" She steps back a little to turn and look at him better. "No one else could do this for Lawrence *and* be able to compartmentalize these images so they don't have nightmares later!"

He looks at her lovingly. "I'm just admiring this incredible woman in front of me, who is stronger than *anyone* I've ever known!"

She shakes her head, fighting not to cry. "*Lawrence is the amazing one in this!* He has been through so much unspeakable and horrific things; most of us couldn't begin to fathom!" Her anger towards Millicent builds. "*That woman did SO much to him, and to top it all off, she still killed Seth and Gen, and she tried to kill Abby, too!*" Her hands are in fists. "And poor Sara was so meek and harmless, *so shy*, and she was killed because of what we *all* saw in her; *vulnerability*—UGH!" She exhales in frustration, gripping her fists even tighter. "To walk up to someone with a fake smile and fake concern then slit their throat?! All those she killed were disposed of as if they didn't matter?!

451

They didn't deserve that! *No one does!*" Bri stops pacing and goes eerily silent...her anger turning to rage. Jack's eyebrow goes up when he sees this. She turns and looks at the refrigerator doors, but there are no names on them, only numbers. "*Doctor!*"

"What's wrong?" Jack asks.

"Jack, you should leave!" Bri tells him. "*I* have some unfinished business to take care of!" Dr. Finley comes rushing over and she asks him, "*Which one she in?!*" Dr. Finley and Jack watch her go over to the doors. "*Everyone* was brought here, right?! Which means *she* has to be here!" She starts opening them... "Empty. Empty. Emp—Oh! Nope. And you are...Alice Mae. Well, rest in peace—er, go into the light if your spirit is around." She opens the next door. "Constance, forgive me. Please go into the light..." A couple more doors and "*Ah ha!*" She pauses and looks towards the men. "Jack, it's your last chance to leave while you still can!" He doesn't move and shakes his head. "*Alright...*" She shrugs and turns back to the open door. She sees the feet under the protective plastic that is wrapped around the body. "Here is the woman who has caused so much pain to countless people her *entire* life!"

She goes to pull the drawer out and Dr. Finley panics, "*STOP!*" He quickly goes over to her. "She's been poisoned with crimson powder!"

"*I know.*" Bri states. "I'm responsible for her getting the poison on her hands." Dr. Finley looks at Jack, who nods. She moves the plastic to look at the toe card, then she removes it before Dr. Finly can stop her. She starts looking around. "Pen? Pen...pen...ah-ha!" She takes one from a cup of miscellaneous pens and markers on a small table nearby.

"*Bri...*" Jack cautiously says, although he isn't sure what to say.

"What do you think?" She looks at them plainly. "Should we change this to a more *believable* name for her?! How does 'Evil Bitch From Hell' sound? *Or* should we use a shorter one like, 'Satan's Spawn,' instead?!"

Jack's charming nature tries to diffuse the situation. "*Depends.* But if I were Herst, I don't think I'd want to have Satan, nor his spawn, as a relative!"

She points the top of her pen at him saying, "*Good point!*" She starts writing and saying, "'*Evil Bitch From Hell*' it is!"

Jack leans in quietly ask Dr. Finley, *"This won't get you into any trouble, will it?"*

Dr. Finley shakes his head and whispers back, *"If she went through as much as it seems she has, and a lot more, this may be a good release of emotions for her."* He shrugs. *"We can let this play out. A toe tag is easily replaced. Besides,"* he gives Jack a little smile, *"who's going to complain about something that never happened?"*

Jack has an appreciative expression and whispers, *"Thank you."* He nods.

Bri proofreads the name on the card. "There! We corrected a *gross* error!" She goes over to put the 'corrected' toe tag on Millicent's toe, but asks, "Doctor, have you done what you needed to with *this*?" She motions Millicent's body.

Dr. Finley comes over and hands her a mask. "I'll help you with anything you need, *but first*, I need you to hear me out." She turns to face him. "Let *me* do whatever you want, but we need to protect everyone in this room especially," he gestures her tummy, "your wee one?!"

"Although I'm protected against crimson powder poisoning," she places a hand on her tummy, "isn't it dangerous when you open up a body?"

"It is." He answers. "Although, that much more with the crimson powder poisoning. I am intrigued why you think you're protected against crimson powder, but we can discuss that at a different time." He continues, pointing at Millicent's body, "Now, I haven't autopsied her yet, but since we know she died of crimson powder poisoning, we've kept her wrapped to protect those who would come into contact with her body from the danger of the crimson powder. *However*, I will do whatever you need to help you." He gives her a fatherly look that reminds her of Henry...then Maggie comes to mind...

Bri stares at the plastic wrapped body in silence. She can barely make out Millicent's face, but Millicent's expression seems softer than the rigid one she usually had on her face. Bri's eyes go down the length of the plastic until she sees strange marks on her lower thighs. She points. "Are those what I think they are? Did she do them to herself?"

"She could have..." He replies, trying to look through the plastic from a couple of different angles.

Jack looks over Bri's shoulder asking, "Do you think she cut herself?"

Bri replies, "It would make sense; she needed to be in control of *something*, when her life felt so out of control; a release of bottled-up, suppressed, emotions..."

Bri's heart sinks and there is silence for a moment. Jack and Dr. Finley wait for her to say something.

"Bri? Are you alright?" Jack asks.

She quietly replies, "Please don't hate me if I decide to pity her again."

"I could *never* hate you, Amore Mia." He says.

"I see she is a poor, pathetic creature, who never really knew what love was; never truly felt it. She was trying to survive life with her uncle, then surviving life without him doing what she learned how to do *from him*..." Bri steps back and looks at Dr. Finley. "Please put her back."

"Yes, Ma'am." Dr. Finley is relieved to put Millicent's body back.

She watches him push the body back into the refrigerator. "It's worse she wasted her life, wasted relationships, and accomplished *absolutely nothing* with her life." Bri comes out of her 'state' and looks at Dr. Finley and Jack. She hands Dr. Finley the toe tag with teary eyes and says to both, "*I'm sorry...*"

Jack pulls her into a hug. "It's okay."

"I know it's all over; I just wasn't expecting it to be so difficult to process some of these feelings after what seemed like closer, like justice..." She says.

"You don't have to apologize, Amore Mia." Jack taps her heart. "It's proof of your *fantastic heart*! You were so angry with this woman, *and you have every right to be*, but when the opportunity came to take some sort of retaliation, you veered right into pity for a woman who, some would argue, deserves the pity *the very least*!"

She gives him a loving smile. "The ones who deserve pity the least, more than likely needs it the most."

Jack nods. "Point taken." Dr. Finely agrees.

She exhales a bit of frustration at herself. "Here I was, telling Lawrence that he had a choice between vengeance or mercy, then I'm faced with the same thing and I chose veng——."

"*But you didn't!*" Jack tells her.

"I did!" She replies. "I chose pity *after* I began with vengeance..."

Jack tries not to chuckle, but it slips out here and there when he says, "I *highly doubt* changing a toe tag to read, '*Evil Bitch from Hell,*' constitutes *revenge!*"

Her eyebrows come together. "*Are you actually laughing?!*"

"*Only at the name.*" He answers. "She *is* someone we should pity and I'm proud of you for not going the route of vengeance, even if no one would blame you for doing so!"

She reluctantly says, "*And yet,* I started to."

"After what that woman has done, *this wasn't anything!*" Jack waves his arm towards the refrigerator with Millicent's body in it.

"I guess we'll have to agree to disagree, Amore Mio." Bri goes over to Dr. Finley. "Thank you for helping me with everything," she tips her head towards the refrigerator doors, "and whatever this was."

"I'm sorry, Your Majesty, but I have absolutely *no idea* what you're talking about." He winks and she lightly smiles appreciatively.

"Then thanks for nothing." She faintly smiles.

Dr. Finley walks them down to the elevators where they say goodbye to Dr. Finley. When they step inside and the doors close, Bri says to Jack, "*I need to see David, Lawrence, and hold my baby!*"

"Then let's get you to them!" Jack hugs her.

CHAPTER 60
A Bright Spot During a Bleak Time

Jacks is up from his nap and Henry and Carlotta take him for a walk to give Bri some time with David, and Lawrence when he is out of surgery. Jack goes to meet up with Henry, Carlotta, and Jacks, after he sends Bri up to The King's Suite with McMasters. They would all come to The King's Suite in a little while.

Bri walks to The King's Suite with McMasters, stopping in front of the door. She looks at McMasters with teary eyes and can only whisper, *"There are no words for you, Mitchell, Rex and the whole team. I'm SO sorry you were personally dragged into it!"* She hugs him and he returns it.

"Just doing my job." He replies.

She pulls back with a small grin and states in an accent, "That's a load of *rubbish!*" He lightly laughs. "Seriously though," she takes a small step back and holds his hand, "you went above and beyond, and I will be *forever* grateful for you!"

He clears his throat, then tips his head towards the door. *"Go on.* Enough with the mushy stuff." He squeezes her hand a bit.

She lightly laughs and turns to the door. She knocks once before she opens the door and walks in.

"There you are, Macushla!"

"Oh, David..." Her hands go up to her mouth, taking in David's condition as she walks over to him.

He holds out a hand for her. "Come here, Love." She hesitates, not wanting to hurt him. "It looks worse that what it is."

She shakes her head. *"Don't lie to me.* Remember, I've been where you are."

"Then you also know how good it feels to have you here with me." He gives her a little grin. "Besides, my wound wasn't *nearly* as bad as yours was!"

"I doubt that!" She carefully lays down next to him and silently cries; grateful to still have David, Lawrence, and Jack with her! She takes a deep breath. "Every time I thought of you; I'd have the last time I saw you playing through my mind. How your spirit was out of your body! Lawrence said that if you had died, you would've found me; *that all three of you would!*"

"Yes," he leans back and looks at her, "we would find you!" He thinks for a moment. "I'm starting to remember pieces...were Millicent's guys forcing you to leave with them?"

"Yes."

His eyes get a little teary. "The frightened, terrified sound of your voice...I hope to *never* hear that in your voice *ever again*! I'm sorry you had to go through that, on top of *everything else* you had to do!"

"*Me, too!*" She goes to hug him, then suddenly yawns hard. David lovingly smiles with a knowing look.

"Has the doctor confirmed you're pregnant?" He grins.

She raises her eyebrow. "Well, I guess you have been updated on everything."

He lovingly smiles. "I had my suspicions since before you were abducted, Love. My guess is that David and Herst have also caught on."

"Well, before the doctor did any 'egg collecting' for Millicent, she did a pregnancy test. The doctor would later tell me she was hoping I was pregnant, because she felt that would be the only way Millicent would accept not harvesting my eggs."

David excitedly smiles asking, "So we *are* having another baby?!" She smiles and he tearfully says, "*That's wonderful news!*" He rests their foreheads together and she closes her eyes to soak in the feelings of love between them.

The door to the room opens with Henry, Carlotta, and Jack, walking in; Jack is carrying Jacks. Jacks watches his Uncle Jack shut the door. Bri goes over to hug Henry and Carlotta.

"It's so good to have you back, Sweetie!" Carlotta hugs her tight.

"It's good to be back!" Bri happily replies. Jacks' head snaps in her direction and he stares at the back of her head.

"Henry and I are going to visit with Abby and Phillip to give you three, and a baby, some time together." Carlotta says and hugs Bri again.

"Come join us when you can." Henry tells Bri. She goes to tell him she is sorry about Maggie, only he shakes his head and hugs her. "*You have* nothing *to apologize for!*"

She asks, "Will you tell Abby I'll be down to see her soon?"

"Of course!" Henry replies. Then he and Carlotta leave the room.

When Jacks sees Bri's *clean* face, he starts to cry, and he reaches for her. Bri starts to cry, too, as she takes him in her arms.

"Come here, my sweet, *sweet* boy." She holds him close, silently crying. Henry and Carlotta pause at the window to watch. They get teary eyed, too, when they watch Jacks bury his face in his mother's neck. Bri holds the back of Jacks' head saying, "Oh, Love, I missed you, too!"

They stay like that for a little bit before Bri sits in the recliner with him. Soon he moves, pulling her shirt, wanting to nurse. She wasn't sure if she could, it's been a little while since she has even pumped, but she will let him try.

She helps him get comfortable and nurse. They stare at each other, and he pats her face. He missed his mama, and every so often he would stop nursing to cry a little, bringing new meaning to 'happy tears.' He doesn't nurse long and finishes with a bit of frustration. Jack quickly makes up a bottle and hands it to him. He lays in his mama's arms again, tipping his head back to watch her as she talks with his dad and uncles.

"Mother said he would cry so much when he saw your picture, they had to turn them around. So if you see any that are still like that, well..." David tells her, smiling lovingly at his wife holding their son, "you know why."

She nods, then smiles looking at Jacks' beautiful dark blue eyes. "I missed you like crazy!" Jacks smiles wide. "*Yes, I did!*" He pats her face again, happily drinking his bottle. "It made it easier knowing Jacks was surrounded by those who love him the most," she swallows hard, "and that if it came down to it, he would be okay growing up without me!"

"*No! He wouldn't.*" Jack tells her.

David adds, "Our son knew his mum wasn't there, and he would cry at *any* picture of you he would see! No, Jacks would *not* be okay growing up without you!" David is emotional in his voice, "*He'd survive* because he would have to, *because he's YOUR son!*"

Bri stands and has Jacks sit on the bed; Jack watches him while Bri hugs David tight. David hugs her back, taking a deep breath as he does. Jacks stands and is concerned about his mama; he opens his arms wanting her to pick him up. She does and kisses his cheek several times in a row, and he pushes his cheek into her lips, loving his kisses.

She asks them, "How is Henry doing?"

"Joe, Sam, Mitch, and their families, are staying at The Manor. I think having them here helped a lot." David wants to know, "How did it all end?"

"Can we put that on hold for a *little* longer? Just long enough to go see Abby?" Bri asks. David and Jack nod. "I want to go down to the gift shop before going to Abby's room." She goes over to David, "We will be back in a little while. I love you." She kisses him.

Jack opens the door for Bri, who is carrying Jacks, and they go down to the gift shop. They walk inside and Bri says in amazement, "This has to be the biggest hospital gift shop I've ever seen!"

"What are you looking for?" Jack asks.

Bri shakes her head a little as she looks around. "I'm hoping I'll know it, when I see it..."

The Manager comes over. "We can make something for you as well, Your Majesty." Bri thanks him and continues to look around.

A beehive catches Bri's eye. She picks up a vase of pink roses to see the beehive better; it's a blank card. Jack sees she has tears in her eyes. Her hand goes to her mouth and she struggles to fight back her tears. The vase has a lightly etched honeycomb look, with a line of bees flying upward wrapping around the height of the vase. One of the ladies working there hands her a tissue; Bri thanks her as she takes the tissue.

Jack hands the bouquet to The Manager. "We'll take this one."

"What if it hurts Abby to remem—?" She inhales sharply and holds her breath. Jacks is concerned and watches his mum closely. "*She called me—.*"

"Queen Bee." Jack says, remembering he and David were standing at the door before The Coronation Ball and overheard Genevieve. "And she also said she was going to start calling you '*Queen Bee.*'"

"Awe, that's lovely." One of the ladies replies and Bri gives her a teary smile.

Bri writes a note on the back of the beehive card that says:

> "*You said bees make life beautiful because they seek out beauty around them. I've found lots of beauty with you in my life, my wonderful sister! I can't begin to express the gratitude in my heart to still have you in our lives!*"

She asks them to make a couple more vases of flowers to go with the one she found. They get everything together and Jack arranges to pay for it all. Then they go up to Abby's room.

Bri is still carrying Jacks as she and Jack get closer to Abby's room. Sam, Mitch, and Joe, with their families heard Bri is at the hospital and they are waiting outside Abby's room to see her. She tearfully smiles when she sees everyone. Joe rushes over to Bri and hugs her. He whispers, "*Thank you, God!*" Mitch and Sam join them; Jacks hangs on tight to his mama.

Henry is inside Abby's room when he hears their voices, and he comes out to join them. Bri hugs him again, as tight as she can with only one arm and Jacks lays his head against Henry. Bri pulls back and looks at Henry.

She starts to apologize to everyone, "I'm so sorry about—."

"*No, Sweetie.*" Henry gives her a fatherly look. "We all know you're *not* to blame." She sees everyone shaking their head from the corner of her eyes. "We also know, *as you do,* that we are all *here* for a certain amount of time; no more, no less."

Her tears start to run down her cheeks and her jaw shakes. Jacks lays his head on her shoulder; she hugs him closer.

"Mama's okay, Buddy." Bri tells him.

"*Yes, she* will *be.*" Henry puts his hand on her cheek. "You know *why* we're here, and that life isn't over at death! We all know we will see Maggie again!" He holds the back of her head. "Have you?"

She shakes her head. "But she may not have been allowed to see me. I'm not sure how it works; I don't see anyone regularly, except Jessica."

"I'm sure there's a reason for that as well." He hugs her again. "Go in and see Abby; she's anxious to see you!"

Bri and Jacks go into Abby's room where Phillip and Carlotta are visiting. Phillip goes over to Bri and hugs her. "It's good to have you back!" She gives him a little smile. "I'm so proud of you and how you handled all that!"

Her eyebrows go up. "Even when she was wanting me to choose one of you to die?!"

"*Especially then!*" He replies. "For the record, I would have been fine with you choosing me, just like Henry was, because I would've been reunited with Vivian!"

She looks over at Abby and is amazed! Abby's head is bandaged up, but she is sitting up and talking, as if nothing happened to her.

"*I'm so happy to see your smiling face!*" Bri hugs her friend. "*Seeing the three of you being shot——.*" Bri gets a little choked up.

Carlotta and Phillip are horrified! They both ask, "*You saw it?!*"

"Millicent recorded it and showed me the video to hurt me more. And this was *right after* she killed Lady Sara Kemp." Bri replies.

461

Abby sadly tells her, "We figured when we were kidnapped that it was the end for us, it was only a matter of time. When it happened, well, *after* it happened, I was surprised to wake up here!"

"You're survival is a *huge* bright spot during a very bleak time! I'm so incredibly grateful for that!" Bri sits on the bed and stands Jacks up between her and Abby. "What do the doctors say about you?"

"They expect me make a *full* recovery!" Abby says, smiling wide at Jacks who smiles back. "*And I'm grateful for that!* Otherwise, I would've missed watching my nephew and his siblings grow up!"

"*We're all grateful for that!*" Bri says, trying not to cry.

"I'm just confused as to why she waited to do anything?" Abby tells her. "Seth and Gen were starting a new chapter in their life! And I've been doing charity work...none of us were a threat."

"Not *directly*." Bri states.

"What do you mean?" Abby asks.

Bri explains, "She was getting rid of *anyone* who could have *any* claim to The Crown, no matter how remote that claim could be, including Emmie and Natty."

"She was barely alive when they found her," Jack tells Bri, "tossed onto a wood pile with Seth and Gen."

Bri gets teary eyed again and hugs Abby. "Abby, I...*there was nothing I could do!*"

"Bri, you weren't even there!" Abby replies. Bri gives her an appreciative look. Abby holds her hands out for Jacks. "Can Aunt Abby have a hug?" He looks at Bri, not wanting her to leave again. Bri encourages him and he does hug Abby, but he keeps an eye on his mama before he goes right back to Bri.

They all talk with Abby for a while and arrange a rotating schedule for her, David, and Lawrence, to not be alone. They will rotate between all of them, until doctors at the hospital feel comfortable transferring their care over to a medical staff the family hires.

CHAPTER 61
Not God

The nurse comes to Abby's room looking for Bri. Lawerence is out of surgery and the doctor is available to talk. Phillip goes with Jack, Bri, and Jacks, to talk to the doctor. When they arrive outside Lawrence's room, the doctor steps over to them.

The doctor bows saying, "Your Majesties and Your Grace." He tells them that the surgery went well and Lawrence's prognosis looks great! "His Majesty has been asking for you."

"Thank you, Doctor." She shakes his hand, then the doctor shakes Phillip's and Jack's hands before he walks away.

Jack tells Bri taking Jacks before he has a chance to protest beforehand, "We'll give you a few minutes by yourselves."

"Thanks." She says.

Jack and Phillip watch Bri go into Lawrence and David's room. Jacks isn't happy watching his mama walk away; he starts to lightly whine. They are able to distract him with a movie on a tablet.

Lawrence is reclined in bed waiting for her. She walks straight over and hugs him with teary eyes.

"I'm so happy you're going to be okay!" She says.

"Me, too, Darling." He hugs her and exhales. She sits up and glances over, but she doesn't see David. "They said David would be back shortly."

She sits on his bed next to him. "With you, Abby, and David making full recoveries. I'm so relieved the number of losses didn't go up by any one of you, nor by all three of you!"

"*So am I!*" He squeezes her hand saying, "I think we have something important we need to discuss, Darling."

"Oh?" She asks.

"Something along the lines that you might be pregnant?" He grins.

Her mouth drops open, realizing how he found out. "Lawrence," she shakes her head, "I wish you could've found out differently."

"Oh, Darling," he kisses the back of her hand, "this is *great* news, no matter how I found out!"

She kisses him tenderly. "You probably had your suspicions at the same time I did, even Jack and David did, too. With the holiday concert and, well..." she trails off and clears her throat. "I found out I was pregnant when the doctor checked for pregnancy before she did anything to help Millicent harvest my eggs." She holds his jaw and smiles telling him, "*Your son* is about to join our family!" He leans in and kisses her firmly.

He leans back a bit. "Are you both okay?" He asks. "Have you been checked out by an OBGYN? I mean, after the vaccine and then taking the poison, well, then again, if it didn't work you wouldn't be here, but—."

She kisses him. "We have been checked out, and I also asked Gabriel to make an appointment with our doctor."

"Good." He gives her a small smile. He changes the subject a bit. "Have you seen Abby yet?"

"*I have!*" Bri smiles. "I couldn't believe she was sitting up and talking. If it wasn't for the bandaged head, you wouldn't know anything happened at all!"

"But it did." He states.

"Yes, it did." She holds her eyes closed as the images come into her thoughts.

He looks at her with confusion. "You saw them get shot, *yet you didn't do anything?!*" Bri's eyebrow goes up. "Seriously! You have this gift, *this incredible gift*, yet Seth and Gen were wiped out, *and Abby came close!*"

"*First of all*, I need you to *really think* for a moment. *Think* about what *you do* know about me! *Look at me, Lawrence Alexander Heathherst!*" He does. "Do you honestly think that if I was there, I wouldn't have tried something, *anything?!*"

His eyebrows scrunch together as he catches, "*If?*"

"Millicent showed me *a video!*" She snips at him standing up, then explains, "I saw them executed and *by the grace of God* Abby *did* survive! I keep replaying the *video* of all three of them on their knees, shot, then collapsing over to the ground!" She doesn't realize she is crying. "*I have no idea when it happened—I still don't!*" She sits right in front of him again. "*Second,* and this is the most important point, *so listen closely!*" She points to his chest as she states, "I'm.*not.*God! What I *can do* is a gift, *but there are limits.* If I could go back in time and change an outcome like that, don't you think I'd go back *months* ago to what happened to Emmy, Nat—." She sobs.

He pulls her into a hug. He sweetly says, "*You're right.* I'm sorry..."

She hugs him tighter as she whispers, "*As you say to me, 'let it out.'*" He holds her more firmly and cries into her shoulder.

"I spent *my whole life* protecting them, but in the end, it didn't matter! When she was ready to kill them, she did!" He takes a deep breath. "I guess, deep down, I did know that." He looks at her and softly says tells her, "I'm sorry. I *do know* you would've done something if you could!"

"You're grieving, Lawrence." She gives him a sympathetic smile. "You're angry Seth and Gen died, *and Abby came close.* I am, too!"

"Thank you for being so understanding, Darling, but it's not okay. After all you've been through, then I accuse—ugh!" He exhales more frustration. "You were in danger, *pregnant,* took poison to *protect everyone,* and you *still* managed to overcome, *and beat,* Millicent!" He shakes his head in disbelief. "And on top of all that you've been through," he tells her, "*I* should be here for *you;* not blaming you! I'm so sorry, My Darling!" He holds her close.

"Well, I *am* going to need at least one of you when all of this hits me again as I process everything. If what's coming resembles the breakdown I had downstairs, I hate to think what could happen!"

Lawrence is confused. "Downstairs?"

"Let's just say Jack and Dr. Finley, the medical examiner, got a preview of what a 'crazy breakdown' could be for me. Although, Dr. Finley officially says, 'It never happened.'"

"The medical examiner?" He asks.

She shakes her head. "I want all of us together before we talk about much more. I don't want to keep repeating myself, nor forget to tell one of you about something. I'm hoping to tell the most important people everything, while it's still all fresh in my head."

He holds her hand. "Please believe me when I say, '*I swear* I'm here for you!' I may find a punching bag we can *all* use!" He says and she lightly giggles, which is what he wanted. He holds her cheek with a soft smile. "I love you!"

"I love you!" She taps a little kiss to his lips.

She texts Jack about coming down when David is brought back to Lawrence's room. He texts back that they are on their way.

David is back in The King's Suite and Jack comes in holding Jacks. Jacks sees his mama and reaches for her; Bri smiles and takes him. He is so happy she is holding him; he rests his head on her shoulder. She sits in the recliner and snuggles with him and his soft blanket.

David smiles at them, then starts the conversation with, "What happened to Millicent? Better yet, start at what happened since you were abducted?"

Jack looks at her. "Maybe you should tell him," he gestures Lawrence and himself, "our hearts are still recovering."

"*Recovering?*" David questions. "Recovering from what?"

"They didn't know beforehand that when I was being held in The Devonridge Manor, I spent some time in The Duke of Devonridge's Secret Lab." She explains.

"'Evil genius' is how she described him." Jack chimes in. David's eyebrow goes up.

"*He was!*" She defensively states. "The man created *an actual cure*, an antitoxin, or a vaccine ; *whatever you would call it*, for crimson powder poisoning!"

David is surprised. "*Seriously?!*"

Bri nods. "Jessica helped me in the lab and we made the recipe. I filled a vial and she had me drink it. She said it would protect me when I needed it to."

"*And it did!*" Lawrence says with relief.

"*Wait a second...*" David has a worried look, "that makes it sound like you were poisoned, which doesn't make sense since Millicent needed you to have Lawrence's heir?"

"Hang on! Don't get ahead of me!" She says.

"Sorry, Love."

She goes on to explain, "I refilled that vial, filled another, and a partial. The messenger bag..." she looks around trying not to panic saying, "*where is it...*"

"I had Mitchell keep it safe." Jack tells her. She is relieved, then a flash of stabbing Jones in the neck goes through her mind and she closes her eyes to try to push it out...

"*Bri?*" Jack asks.

"Sorry." She shakes her head, then gets back to what they were discussing.

"Don't move on if it's part of what happened." David tells her.

"It's not what comes next." She replies. The three shrug. "Well, after David was shot, and Millicent took me and Lawrence away, Lawrence would see an opportunity for us to escape. At that time, we took off running, only when I stopped at a large tree a ways out, Lawrence wasn't behind me. Jessica said he twisted his ankle pretty bad in a hole." Lawrence nods. "Jessica led me to a cabin where two of Millicent's men would find me the next day. They had to bury the woman who pointed them my direction. They went into the woods, right outside the Devonridge Castle, to bury her body." She looks at Jacks sleeping whispering, "*I killed one of them there...*" Bri works to push her emotions down... "I would've been brought to Millicent if one of her other men hadn't shown up and killed this other guy first! I got out of there as fast as I could and straight to Devonridge Castle, straight to Millicent!"

Lawrence is curious. "How *did* you break through those doors? Dynamite?"

"I'm not exactly sure." She shakes her head. "I just took all my emotions and wanting to rescue Jacks, tired of all the people being hurt and killed because of me and this woman," she looks at her free hand, "then I somehow channeled the energy through my hands and the doors just...*blew open.*"

"*Daaamn...*" David whispers, picturing wooden doors exploding it in his mind. Those kinds of wooden doors were usually made of solid oak, or wood that was hard, to make it the most difficult for enemies to breach.

"I would've loved to have seen that!" Jack adds.

"It definitely sounded like an explosion!" Lawrence tells them. "Millicent was already preparing for your arrival and trying to put her plan into place, but that kind of threw her off balance a bit."

"*Good!*" Bri replies.

Lawrence looks at Jack. "I didn't know she had kidnapped you, *or the others,* or we would've been working on a rescue!"

Jack shakes his head saying, "Herst, I knew you didn't know, *because* we weren't rescued!" Lawrence gives him a small nod.

Bri continues, "I made my way inside and found myself being surrounded by Millicent's people. When Lawrence came up behind me at one point," she gives him an apologetic look, "my heart sank and I was sick."

He gives her a look. "*Because you doubted.*"

Her eyes tear up a little. "*I'm sorry.*" She exhales with frustration. "Ugh! I feel like every time I turn around, I'm apologizing for something."

"*It's okay.*" Lawrence assures her. "I think with everything going on, it's understandable."

She admits, "Although, I *quickly* had *no doubt.*" Referring to when he pinned her to the wall.

He gives her a small, knowing smile. "That was the reason why I did it, to make sure *you knew* I was on *your* side."

She tells Jack and David, "When Millicent realizes almost all of the people that surrounded us were no longer working for her, *that* was priceless!"

David looks at Lawrence. "How did you manage that?!"

"Easy!" Lawrence grins at Bri as he replies, "They chose to side with their Queen!" Bri rolls her eyes.

"Fantastic choice!" David lightly laughs. "Then what happened?"

"Eventually, I found myself fighting Tristan." Lawrence takes a deep breath.

Bri tells them, "The end came when Lawrence delivered a kick right into Tristan's chest that sent him back, straight into a suit of armor behind him." David has a surprised look on his face, which turns to a disgusted look as he pictures when she says, "The short battle-ax fell *into* his head."

Jack tells Lawrence, "I don't feel bad for the traitor! However, part of me wishes he would've suffered a wee bit more before he died."

Bri looks at him with an understanding look. "I get that, but if you think about it, he suffered *his whole life* being manipulated and used by Millicent, right up to his horrific end." The guys agree with that.

Bri tells David about The Courtyard. "Millicent has someone put a syringe of clear liquid in my hand. Then I was told the liquid was poisoned with crimson powder. She had McMasters, Phillip, Henry, Jack, and Claude Devereaux on their knees, and lined up next to each other. Millicent wanted me to pick one of them to be poisoned. *I refused.*"

David's eyebrows go up. "That couldn't have gone over well?"

Jack shakes his head. "*It didn't!* Millicent emptied her revolver of bullets, then puts one bullet back in it to play a round of 'Russian Roulette.'" He looks at Bri and Lawrence, "For the record, I *never* want to play *any version* of that again!" He closes his eyes and shudders at the memory. "Every click of the trigger got harder and harder to take!"

Bri holds her hand out for his. He sweetly smiles as he goes over to her and takes it. She tells him, "I'm so sorry you all were tortured with that, but there was *no way* I could choose anyone else! And we all know she would've killed the rest of you at some point." They all agree with that as well.

David's eyebrows come together thinking about all that. *"That means you were running out of options..."*

She reluctantly nods. "I was. *I only wish I had thought about the vaccine sooner!* It would've been less torturous for everyone than hearing the clicking sound of the gun! It came to me that by drinking the poison myself, it would also throw her off her game plan, because she never would've even considered I might do something like that. Unfortunately, it made her *more* volatile, because she had *nothing* to lose..."

"Wait a second!" David is a bit terrified. *"You drank the poison?!"*

"Jessica said the vaccine would work when I needed it to!" She replies. "What would you have me do?! *Who* would you have picked?!" Jacks startles a bit and she rocks him.

"You're right, Love." David gives her an apologetic look. "You were *all* in an *impossible* situation." David asks, "So what happened to Millicent?"

"Believe it or not, she actually died of crimson powder poisoning." Jack replies.

David is surprised. *"Seriously?!"* The others nod. "You'd think she would've been high alert with that stuff!"

"With *anyone* else, she would've been!" Lawrence looks at her saying, "Bri was right. Millicent *did* underestimate her. She didn't think Bri was capable of hurting anyone, not even her. Plus, she assumed since Bri is pregnant, she would stay as far away from that stuff as possible!"

"How did you do it?!" David is curious.

"In The Secret Lab, I found an old pocket watch, a family heirloom, that I very carefully dusted with crimson powder, then dropped it into a plastic baggie, then put the baggie in a small pouch bag. Later, at Devonridge Castle, I took the pouch out of the messenger bag and put it in my back pocket before going out to The Courtyard. Then, when the time was right, I casually started talking about The Secret Lab and what I found. When she wanted to see it, I tossed her the bag, assuming she would reflexively catch it; she did. She opened it and nostalgically took out the pocket watch. The lighting out there wasn't great, so she held it closer to her face to get a closer look. Having it that close to her face would've had her inhaling some of those deadly particles. Regardless, the powder did get on her fingers and all of that was the beginning of the end for her."

Jack asks Lawrence, "Where did those who were arrested end up?"

Lawrence looks at Bri as he replies to Jack, "Even though Bri and I agreed there would be no prisoners, we arrested Millicent's people, including those who were secretly Rex's men to protect their identities." He adds, "I think after helping Millicent with her own death, *and* her uncle, it would've been too hard on your heart to even hear any other executions."

Bri's eyebrows go up as she nods and exhales, "*Probably...*" He gives her a soft compassionate look.

Lawrence explains to David how Bri helped Millicent. Then he goes on to tell Bri, "Since The Royal Dungeons are still being renovated because of the damage made by the bombing, the prisoners were taken to the dungeons at Newhaven Manor. I sent them there, rather than Ashbourne Castle, to keep the press at bay and away from the, uh, 'USS,' we'll say." Bri nods, knowing he means 'The Underground Secret Society.' "Since everyone was arrested together, Rex is aware they are at Newhaven Manor and has gotten word to them that it's only for a few days and they will be compensated separately, from me, for that additional time."

"Compensated from us," she looks around, "as a family."

"Agreed." All three of them say.

Bri takes a slow, deep breath. "I guess I know where I'm going tomorrow."

Lawrence is hesitant. "Bri, you don't have to be there."

Bri gives him a slight smile. "I know, but not only do I want to see this all the way through; I also feel like I need to be there to ensure Rex's men are released without any problems. Plus, I want to personally thank them for everything they've done for us!"

"We can understand that." David says. "We just don't want you out of our sight right now. *Above all*, it doesn't feel right that you should go by yourself."

Jack lovingly looks at her. "I'll go with her!" He smiles down at Jacks. "We'll bring Jacks with us so he doesn't have to separate from his mum just yet."

Bri shakes her head. "I love that you're willing to do this with me, but I don't want you to feel like you have to face your childhood home on top of everything we've *all* just been through!"

He goes up to her and holds her face. "*I love you more* because you're worried about me, but it isn't necessary." He starts to smirk as he reminds her, "As I've said, I've jumped off a waterfall with you, *I've offered to jump into a volcano!* So *this* will be a piece of cake!"

She rolls her eyes. "This could be like pulling a pin that's in an emotional grenade, Jack. It's *not* the same thing."

"Fine. I *want* to do this with you and who knows," he shrugs, "maybe we can take a look around, if we have time."

"*That would be brilliant!*" She lightly teases.

"No promises." Jack adds.

She gives a small nod. "And that's okay, too."

Bri puts Jacks in the playpen that is in the corner of the room with two cots next to it. Bri rubs his back until he is fully asleep again. Then they get ready for bed. Bri says goodnight to David and Lawrence before going to the cot closest to Jacks. She says goodnight to Jack, then lays down on the cot. It may not be the most comfortable bed, but she is in the same room with Jack, Lawrence, David, and her baby. With Millicent no longer a threat, she is the most relaxed she has been in *a long* time, and she sleeps hard for the first time in a long time...

CHAPTER 62
Jacks & His Uncle Lawrence

The next morning, Bri wakes to hearing a repeating, "Maaammmaaa." She smiles and rolls over to find Jacks sitting in the playpen next to her. He smiles wide when he sees her smiling at him. When she sits up, Jacks pulls himself up using the side of the playpen.

Bri stands up and he reaches for her. She lovingly picks him up and whispers, "*Good morning, My Love!*" He excitedly smiles and she hugs him. "Should we get you a bottle?" She walks over to his bag.

The nurse comes in and sees Bri with Jacks; she takes over making the bottle, while Bri and Jacks watch. The nurse goes to hand the bottle to Bri, but Jacks grabs it and starts drinking it; they quietly laugh. Bri thanks her for her help, then walks over to the reclining chair to snuggle with him. She looks around and sees Lawrence and David are sitting up in bed; Jack is walking out of the bathroom. Bri is about to sit in the recliner when Jacks is reaching his hand out to his Uncle Lawrence.

Bri smiles. "What's this all about?"

Lawrence lovingly smiles at Jacks as Bri walks over him. He takes Jacks and explains as they get comfortable, "I didn't know ahead of time that Millicent was going to kidnap him. I found out when I heard a crying baby one night, and the more I heard it, the more familiar it sounded. It's only when Katie comes into my room needing help with the crying baby, that I see it's Jacks! She almost drops him because he bends so far over, desperately trying to get to me. It was heartbreaking and heartwarming all at the same time! I had Katie stay in the room with me in case Millicent would insist Katie take care of Jacks on her own, I wanted to help *him* get used to her." He states. "Nothing more! I swear."

She gives him an understanding smile. "*Thank you* for helping him, so it would be less traumatizing for him." She looks around. "Did we wake you all a little bit ago?"

"I think we all woke to the same cuteness you did, with a little boy wanting his mama." David grins, and the others agree.

Bri holds her hands out to Jacks. "Should we go snuggle in the recliner while you drink your bottle?" Jacks looks at both of them, clearly torn at what he wants to do.

Lawrence scoots over a bit and pats the bed so she can sit next to them. "I'm glad he remembers our snuggle time!" He kisses the top of Jacks head. "That was the only bright spot to those days!"

Bri watches them with a smile on her face. "I'm *so* happy he had you!"

"I'm so glad he bonded with Herst, and *not* Katie, *or Millicent!*" David says.

Lawrence looks at Jacks. "While I'm sorry he was kidnapped, but he did my heart good!" He says to Bri, "It felt like I was still connected to you." She nods and squeezes his hand.

"He does look content with his Uncle Lawrence." David wonders, "Maybe Jacks will be alright if you and Jack go to Newhaven by yourselves this morning." Bri looks from David to Jack with an uneasy expression.

Jack suggests, "Why don't you think about it while we're getting ready to go? I'll text the grandparents quick to see where they are and what their plans are for the day."

"Alright." Bri replies.

Bri has gotten ready next door. When she comes back to Lawrence and David's room, she finds Carlotta and Henry are there. Carlotta comes over and hugs Bri in a mother's hug, then Henry hugs her.

Bri looks over at Lawrence and Jacks. Jacks is watching a movie on a tablet but he does smile at his mama before going back to watching the movie. Bri is still nervous about leaving Jacks.

David gives Bri an understanding look. "Why don't you step outside the door and if he cries, give us time to try to get him distracted. If it takes too long, I'll have you come back in and we can quickly get him ready to go with you." Bri looks at Jacks and softly nods.

Standing in the hall, Jack and Bri listen at the door. Jacks wasn't happy to watch them leave, but it doesn't take long before he does go back to his movie. When it's quiet, Bri and Jack leave with their detail to go out to the helipad, where they will fly to Newhaven.

Jack and Bri are standing, looking out a window from The Official Office of The Grand Duke of Newhaven. They are watching the prisoners being loaded into vans to go to the airport where they will be flown to London and held at a maximum-security facility until preparations for their executions are complete. Bri looks away when Katie and Richard are brought out.

When the vans pull away and go down the driveway, Rex's men are released and brought up to Bri and Jack. Bri looks at the men who were just released and the men who have come to pick them up. Her eyebrow goes up seeing Donavan among them.

Bri says to everyone, "There aren't enough words to express our gratitude for *all* your help! From the bottom of my heart, along with Jack, David, and Lawrence, thank you *so much* for helping us save our family, the country," she puts her hand on her lower abdomen, "and the country's future."

Jack adds, "I've been told by His Majesty that if any of you find you are in a bind for anything you've done to help us bring down Millicent, please call this number," he hands each of them Gabriel's business card, "and Gabriel will spring into action to fix it." They have Gabriel being the contact, because he was in the middle of everything and would know what to do quicker than anyone else.

Bri and Jack walk them outside where they shake their hands and say goodbye, then they watch as their SUVs drive away. Jack and Bri walk back inside and see Rex, Donovan, and Claude walking towards them. She addresses Claude first.

Bri takes a step forward and kindly smiles. *"Mister Devereaux."*

"Your Majesty." He gives her a friendly smile back.

"Thank *you* for trying to stay out of my way, and I'm so sorry you *still* got caught up in it." She says.

"We knew she could retaliate; that's why you gave me the excuse of saying my daughter was kidnapped." He replies and she nods. "Thank you for taking care of Elise, and her nanny." He lightly clears his throat and shifts a little in nervousness. "Now *I* need to ask *you* for a favor."

Bri is confused. *"I'm not sure what I can do?"*

He pulls out folded sheets of paper from the inside pocket of his suit coat and hands them to her. "Would you raise Elise as your own?" Bri's mouth drops open a bit as she takes the papers.

Bri opens the papers up and takes a look... *"You're giving me full guardianship?"* She looks at the next page. "This is to petition the court for adoption?" She looks at him. "I'm honored, but are you sure this is what you want to do?"

"I don't think there is any doubt with any of us here," he gestures himself, Jack, Donovan, and Rex, as well as McMasters and Mitchell, "that there's no safer place for her to be, and loved as one of the family, than with all of you." The guys agree. *"However,"* Claude goes on, "if this is too much to ask, I left the petition open, so you'll be able to find her a family. My only stipulation with any adoption is that *no one* ever knows I'm her father; not even Elise when she gets older."

Bri shakes her head. "I can't promise that." She explains, "Every child wants to know where they came from and if we adopt her into our family, *I won't lie to her.* Although, if she's adopted by a different family, it would be easier to keep that secret."

"I trust you to do what's right by her in *any* situation, while keeping her safe." Claude replies.

"Thank you." She says. "I will need to talk this over with Jack, David, and Lawrence, as well as the rest of the family."

"Whatever you decide, Your Majesty, I trust it will be the right decision." Claude reassures her. "I know this is what's best for her, to keep her safe from my enemies, and I know you won't use her against me."

"Absolutely not!" Bri quickly states.

"Proving my point." Claude appreciatively smiles.

He shakes their hands, thanking them before he leaves. He gets into the car they have for him, while Jack puts the papers from Claude Devereaux in the inside pocket of his suitcoat. They all watch the car drive down the driveway.

"*Mister Donovan...*" She gives him a smile behind pursed lips and a fake glare. "I wouldn't be standing here if it wasn't for you being in the woods at the right time. *Thank you* for playing your part *so* perfectly! I *never* suspected you were working for anyone but Millicent! You, my friend, deserve an award!" She hugs him. "Thank you for being a significant piece in saving me, my babies, and my family!"

"I never thought I would say this to anyone other than Rex," he looks at her, "it was an honor to serve you, Your Majesty! And, with Rex's permission," he bows to her, "I will serve you *whenever* you need me!"

Rex nods. "*Absolutely.* Even if he's busy, we can still discuss it. I'll have Hazel put certain phone numbers into Her Majesty's new phone." Bri's eyebrow goes up and he lightly chuckles. "The only person I will happily step aside so my people can help them, would be for you and your family. Protecting all of you will always be a priority, although since Millicent is no longer a threat," he looks at Donovan, "we anticipate other threats to be easily dealt with before they become a bigger problem." Donovan agrees.

Bri gets teary eyed looking at Rex. "*Where do I begin to thank you?*"

Rex softly scoffs. "There's no need for that. Let's call this 'goodbye *for now.*' If you need anything, big or small, call me."

She grins with her teary eyes. "We still have a bottle of wine to share," she glances at Jack, "in Tuscany."

Rex laughs. "I didn't forget!"

Jack happily adds, "*We can definitely arrange that!*"

"Maybe the four of us can get together with you," she motions to Donovan, "and whoever of the team you invite to join us?"

"*That sounds wonderful!*" Rex replies.

"Thanks again." She hugs him. "One day, you *will be* part of my history and biography!"

Rex chuckles. "It should probably start after I die! Better yet, after you die of old age! Then a few sentences of that part of the story can be crammed into your *very* lengthy obituary!"

She smiles. "*Perhaps.*" She threads her arm around his and starts walking to the door. "I'm hoping that we all die of old age, so we have decades yet."

"I can get behind that!" Jack adds. "I think we are all overdue for some time to get back to a sense of normal!"

They chuckle as they step outside. They say their goodbyes, then Jack and Bri watch Rex and Donovan go drive down the driveway.

CHAPTER 63
A Tour of Newhaven Manor

Outside Newhaven Manor, Jack takes Bri's hand and they walk back inside after they had said goodbye to Rex and Donovan. Bri looks around asking, "Is anyone here?"

"Are you asking if my family is here?" Jack smirks and she nods. "My stepmother is usually traveling and it was verified she would be at this time, prior to bringing any prisoners to the dungeons. Lawrence sent my dad and brother to The Royal Hotel & Spa in London to stay for a week; all expenses paid. From what I hear, they are enjoying *all* the perks they can think of." He rolls his eyes.

Bri's eyebrows go up, "I bet!" She turns to him. "Since they're not returning anytime soon, do you think you could give me a little tour?" She asks. "The Newhaven Trust takes care of this entire property and I was going to ask Gabriel about arranging a tour, so we could take more current pictures of the various pieces of artwork, paintings, and so on, to put with the itemized list of everything that is in this place, *buuut...*"

"*Buuut*, you want a sneak peek?" He grins.

"*I do*! Is that alright?"

"Well, usually The Duchess, *or The Grand Duchess*, of Newhaven would be living here as her primary residence and would have a pretty good idea of what was within the walls of Newhaven Manor." He explains, "Regardless, a duke and duchess would definitely keep track of a duchy's assets that *they* are responsible for! Now, with you being 'The Grand Duchess of Newhaven,' I would think you should have an official tour of Newhaven Manor every year, since The Worthington Family has been entrusted with it for centuries! I believe your predecessor had annual visits, if not more. It's a way to be sure that everything is being maintained, and all is accounted for. As for a brief tour," he starts walking with her again, "I don't think there's anything wrong with 'a preview' of sorts for The Queen, *and* The Grand Duchess."

They walk over to The Main Staircase where she feels a heaviness of sorts. She closes her eyes, to try to feel something, *anything*, about what that heaviness would be...

Jack's eyebrows come together. "What is it?"

 She has a confused look on her face. *"I'm not sure..."* She softly shakes her head. "I can't put my finger on it." She looks up the stairs as she stands back. "Can we see your room?" He holds out his hand for hers and they walk up the stairs.

She stares up at the enormous skylight. "This is a *beautiful* place!"

"A beautiful prison is more like it..." Jack says more to himself.

She squeezes his hand a little. "We don't have to do this, if it's going to be too uncomfortable for you."

He stops and faces her. "If you were *anyone* else, I wouldn't."

She sweetly smiles. "Thank you." They continue walking.

He tells her, "There are some beautiful pieces of art here that would rival some of the ones in The Palace, perhaps even the more well-known museums. I'll show you a couple of them, after I take you to see my room."

"I'd like that!" She replies.

They turn down the hallway that goes to Jack's childhood room. His room is at the very end of this hall. They come to the door and Bri turns the nob, then walks inside. She is half expecting it to be full of dust, only the cleaning has been kept up with because there is barely a speck dust anywhere.

He smirks at her saying, "Seems wrong, even at my age now, to have a girl in my room."

Bri laughs. "I think I'd feel the same way about my childhood bedroom!" She looks around and sadly says, "There's nothing in here that says this was even *your* room..." She has a pained face. *"Please tell me he didn't just throw everything of yours away?!"*

"No, but after my mother died, I took more and more of my things over to The Worthington's." He replies.

"That makes sense!" She says.

She walks around the dark wooden floors covered with a large rug. A padded wood chest sits at the foot of his bed to be sat on and used for storage. There were bedside tables on either side of the canopied, four post bed with curtains at each post with tan, blues, green, and reds in the curtain's design; a dark–blue bedspread covers the bed itself. There is a dresser on the opposite wall and a desk against a wall that is perpendicular to the bed.

 There is a framed photo Bri sees and she picks it up for a closer look. "Is this your mother..."

Jack looks over her shoulder. "It is." He takes the photo from her to look at it closer. "I'm surprised my father left *this* here..."

She looks at him lovingly. "*Anyone* could guess that is your mother!" He nods. His mother does seem faintly familiar somehow...maybe she has one of the ones she has seen regularly; then again, why wouldn't she say something to Bri? She tries to force herself, but nothing...it could be anyone...

He gives her a sweet smile, then points to the gentleman next to her. "That's Uncle Max."

She smiles. "Your mother's special someone?"

He nods. "This is from the last trip my brother and I had with her. We're on a Mediterranean beach and yet it's one of the last, more solid memories I still have of her..."

He sets the picture down, only Bri picks it back up to take with them. She will quietly put the picture among their other pictures at The Cottage House.

 She opens the wooden chest at the end of his bed. "Well, at least you had *some* toys here for whenever you were back home for whatever reason." She sees a small pile of pictures and picks up the one on top. '*Reñiato?*' She reads to herself and thinks about The Ambassador and his

 wife. She sees a postcard under the picture. It has a wax seal. She looks closer to see what it is...she can barely make out there is a shield pressed into the wax, but she will need a magnifying glass to see what is on the shield for more information about the family it represents.

It doesn't take long to look around and she puts the few things she has in her hands in her bag. He sees her do this and gives her a small smile.

"For whenever you want to look at them to just remember, or if you want talk..." She gives him a little smile.

He nods, then asks, "Shall we go see some artwork?"

"*Let's!*" She starts walking to the door and he follows.

They walk side by side, making a couple of turns before they stop. He looks at a wall that has a faded outline of something framed that *was* there.

"It used to be here, but this was years ago. It's probably down in The Gallery where most of the paintings and artwork are on display." They start walking again. "Over the years, the staff moves the artwork around to give spaces a new look, or whatever."

They go down to The Gallery, which is a large room that has artwork all over its walls. "*Wow!*" Bri whispers.

His eyebrows furrow together as he takes in the room. "Something's not right." He carefully looks around. "It seems like there aren't as many pieces in here as there should be..."

"Didn't you say that they move things around?" She asks and he nods. "Maybe they have more pieces spread throughout The Manor?"

"*Possibly.*" He doubtfully says. "Let me see if any of the other ones I want to show you are in here..." He carefully looks around.

He walks the entire room, *twice*, before he meets back up with her. She asks, "Did you find any?"

He shakes his head. "They could be anywhere in this place!"

"True." She says looking up and around. "We need to get going. I'll ask Gabriel to arrange another time for us come back and take a full inventory with pictures, maybe even bring someone who can assess their condition."

"Sounds like a great plan! I'll try to make sure my calendar is cleared for whenever that happens." He says as they leave the room. "There are a lot of great pieces in this place that I would love for you to see! We should ask David and Lawrence to join us as well!"

"You know they will!" She replies. "First, though" she says with her finger up, "there's something we all need to discuss right away." His eyebrow raises and she sweetly smiles, "Claude Devereaux's request?"

He grins as he cups her cheek. *"Is there anything to discuss?"*

"I think it's good for everyone to have a say, including the whole..." She trails off thinking.

"Bri?" Jack asks.

She looks at him and nods with a faint smile. *"I have an idea!"* She talks as she pulls out her phone, "I'm going to text James and Amy to see if they can come back to London with us; Claude's request is something we all should discuss as a family."

Amy returns Bri's text right away; they are already at the hospital. Bri sends her a 'thumbs up.' Then she sends another text.

> Bri to McMasters: "Would you find out what you can on Jack's mother and her death? I have no information, other than she died from a fall down The Main Staircase in The Newhaven Manor."
>
> McMasters: "I have it."
>
> Bri: "Of course you do. (smile emoji) Please keep this between you and me for now. I'll let Jack know when the time is right."
>
> McMasters: "Will do!"

The whole family is gathered in Lawrence and David's room. Elise is on Lawrence's bed with Jacks, both playing with various toys. Both Jacks and Elise see Bri and want her to hold them.

She stands them up on the bed and hugs them both at the same time. "This is a wonderful welcome!"

Lawrence asks what the others want to know. "What is so important we need to discuss it right away?"

"Claude Devereaux has a request of us." She replies.

"What kind of a request?" David asks, suspicious of Claude.

"Nothing sinister, *I can assure you.*" Jack answers as he hands David the papers Claude left with them.

"That's good." Lawrence relaxes as David opens up the papers.

Bri sees his eyebrows come together and she explains to everyone, "Mr. Devereaux asked if we would adopt Elise; *however,* he understood if we couldn't, and asks that we find her a good home."

David is taking all this in and thinks out loud, "*Sssooo...*Elise was taken from her home, lived in a small flat somewhere with her nanny and the nanny's family, then has been living with us, only if we don't adopt her into our family, she will have to get used to *another* place and people?!" He shakes his head. "I know she's a year old and kids are resilient, but that seems so unfair. It also makes me wonder if it could have some lasting effects on her."

"I agree." Lawrence replies. "When we consider those facts, it doesn't feel right to send her away to another family." He looks at Bri. "I support doing this, only with me being The King—."

David shakes his head. "You couldn't Herst." David interrupts and Bri's eyebrows come together. "It would have to be me, or Jack, who would adopt her with Bri."

"*Orrr...*" Bri has Lawrence take Jacks and she takes Elise over at Amy; her eyes are teary at the thought of Elise leaving. "Amy, I had a thought come to me, which is why I texted you. I feel Elise may have already found *her* mama."

485

"*Oh, Bri,*" Amy starts to cry telling her, "*she has been such a gift to our hearts after we lost our baby!*" Elise hears Amy's emotional voice and has a worried look. Amy takes her and hugs her close.

"Amy, I'd like to have *all* our family's input, because I'd like to think we, as a family, will adopt her as one of our own, only her mom and dad will officially be you and James." Bri looks at everyone. "*If* you all agree?" They all happily agree. "Mr. Devereaux left the custody petition open so we could find a different family to adopt her if we didn't want to raise her. I think James and Amy will raise her to grow up into the beautiful woman she is meant to be, without the dark cloud of her biological father hanging over her." She looks at Jack and Lawrence. "Do you know of a better family than The Worthington Family to do just that?" She sees them smile softly as they shake their heads. "I wouldn't do this if I thought Mr. Devereaux would interfere. He wants us to keep her biological father a secret to make sure Elise could grow up happy and healthy." She looks at Amy. "You know me, I think lying to her would be a *huge* mistake."

Amy nods and adds, "We can tell her something like her biological dad wanted to protect her and he gave her up to keep her safe; to allow her to grow up happy."

"Perfect!" Bri smiles.

David watches Elise and asks, "Mother, Uncle Henry, Phillip, would you three mind having another grandchild?"

Phillip grins, "*She already is!*" Carlotta and Henry *wholeheartedly* agree!

Bri happily smiles. "Well, then, I think we can have all this ironed out tonight and we will file all the paperwork right away!" James and Amy tearfully hug Elise, relieved to keep her in their family.

CHAPTER 64
An Imperfectly Perfect Great Idea

Lawrence's arm is in a sling when he is technically released from the hospital, even though he stays there with David and Abby. They all continue their rotations to make sure David and Abby aren't alone very much. Right now, the family is at the hospital, gathered in Lawrence and David's room. Bri is in the recliner with Jacks as he drinks his bottle. She watches Jacks, all content and happy again, like nothing happened. Her mind goes to when Millicent spoke about a child's bond to their mother.

David sees her staring off. "What is it, Love?" He asks.

"I was just thinking..." She closes her eyes as she turns her head to the window, and she opens her eyes again.

Lawrence pulls a chair over to sit next to her. "Talk to us, Darling."

"It's hard to process. Millicent raised you and you thought she was your mother for almost your *entire* life! Then, after the floor collapsed, when she talked about a child's bond with their mother, *she was right*. There *is* a mother-child bond that in some situations is *mind boggling*! It makes you wonder how adult children can still be sucked in with an unhealthy parent. *At the same time*, it's only natural for someone to seek their mother's approval, even when real love seems nonexistent..." She exhales out loud. "Then, the morgue, I started changing her name on her toe tag to—." She bites her lips inside her mouth to stop herself and to stay calm.

Lawrence holds her hand. "Let me be *very* clear. She and I *never* bonded, because there was *no* love from her, real or anything else, and I *never* developed it for her. So how could there be any kind of a bond? The only thing I felt was a desire to keep her content, so she would be less dangerous; *to protect Seth and Abby.*"

"*And they* still *paid the price!*" She struggles to say calmly.

"Whoa. Hold on." He squeezes her hand. "Let me finish with Millicent." She lightly nods. He says, "All I feel with that woman's death is relief *no one* will *ever* suffer at her hand, or do her bidding, *ever again*! And that you, and our family, are safe from her! We *never* have to worry about her lurking around and wondering when she'll strike, *or how...*" he puts his hand on Jacks, "to keep *all our loved ones* safe from her, along with *all* our people! *That's* what matters the most!"

"So, a *small* funeral for Millicent then?" She faintly smirks with her finger and thumb barely open.

"I prefer a celebration!" Lawrence smirks adding, "*After* we toss her into a lava pit!"

She has Genevieve come to mind and wonders, "Where would a queen be buried normally?"

"Well, normally she would 'Lie in State' at The Parliament Building, then The Throne Room in The Palace. The funeral would be inside The London Abbey, then a small service in the vault under the church." He studies her a moment and adds, "We're *not* doing that kind of a funeral for that wo——."

"*No!* No, no. *Not her!*" She shakes her head. "I was thinking for Genevieve."

His face goes from surprised to sad. "We can't. It's an expense justified only for The Queen, or The Queen Mother."

"How much is one?" She asks.

His eyebrows come together. "I couldn't begin to guess how many millions it would be."

"Would you please find out? Or I'll forfeit anything that would be for me!" She pleas. He sees she wants to do right by her sister-in-law, and predecessor. She squeezes his hand and looks at him with so much love. "I know what I'm asking and I remember you saying you'd deny me nothing, so please understand I ask you this with all my heart, *and* because of my friendship with her..." Her emotions sneak up on her and she takes a deep breath. "We can release that 'The Royal Family is personally paying for The Royal Highnesses' Funeral,' or however it would be worded. She was a loved queen, then duchess, and I doubt anyone with a heart will stand against it, *especially* if it's *privately* paid for! I want her and Seth..." she struggles to say and swallows hard, "to be laid to rest *together*." She wipes her eyes with her hand and looks at him with a hint of a smirk. "Do this for me and I'll find a volcano for you to hold the other funeral *celebration*!" She kisses his hand. "You know, Mount Vesuvius isn't too far from Tuscany."

Lawrence lightly chuckles. "I'll start looking into a royal funeral for them straight away!"

She has tears of gratitude. "*Thank you*!" She kisses him sweetly. "I love you." She looks at David and the others. "Look around everyone! This is our family," she looks down at Jacks, who is sleeping, "*this* is love!" They all smile. Bri looks at Amy and James, he is holding Elise while she drinks her bottle.

Amy sees Bri's face and Amy tells her, "I meant what I said about this sweet little girl! She has been *such* a blessing to our hearts." James agrees. "I only wish we could've stopped them from taking Jacks."

"Are you able to try again when you're ready?" Bri asks.

Amy nods. "The doctor wants me to wait a little longer, which is fine, because James and I want to enjoy her in our family for a little while anyways."

Bri replies understandingly, "You'll know when the time is right." Amy nods and wipes the tear skipping down her cheek. Bri adds, "I love you; you know that, right?"

Amy goes over and carefully hugs Bri, so she doesn't wake Jacks. "I do and I love you, too!"

Bri glances over and looks again at a newspaper on the table right here; a picture of Katie caught her eye. She has no feelings about it, other than she thinks it's sad that this is what Katie's life has finally come to, and this is where it all ends. Amy takes Jacks so he and Elise can go to Ashbourne with them; Carlotta, Phillip, and Henry, leave with them.

When it's just Lawrence, Jack, David, and Bri, she says to them, "I wanted to get your opinions on something." They all listen. "After seeing Millicent go to the lengths she did to make a handful of rooms into a hospital setting, I feel like I want to have this baby *in* Ashbourne Castle, but *only if* we can find people to secretly convert a room into an operating room and another into a recovery room." She looks at Lawrence. "It's not The Palace, but—."

489

"But it's in a home a king long ago built for *his* beloved queen; and currently The Queen is adored by The King!" Lawrence holds her cheek. "I think it's a *fantastic* idea, if David and Jack are onboard!"

"*Are you kidding*?!" Jack smiles wide. "'The Heir to The Throne' born in London, *and in Ashbourne Castle*? It's an imperfectly perfect great idea!"

"I agree with them!" David smiles. "It's a *bloody fantastic* idea!"

When they tell the rest of the family, they are excited at the thought of 'The Heir to The Throne' being born *in* Ashbourne Castle. Carlotta tells Bri, "When we get closer to your third trimester, I say we slowly reduce your workload to have you there, in case this wee one wants to come early."

Phillip nods and adds, "We can let the public know The Heir will be born *in London* and everyone will assume The Royal Hospital, because that is where a birth would typically be within The Royal Family. We will also have the hospital prepare for a birth, in the event that something unforeseen happens."

Bri takes a deep cleansing breath. "I do like to live by 'prepare for the worst, hope for the best,' and that would cover it."

A few days later, Bri and Gabriel meet with Mr. Woodsley at Ashbourne Castle. Bri wants them to work together with Bri's doctor in Newhaven to secretly prepare an operating room and a recovery room of sorts for her and the baby, preparing for every possibility they can think of. All the equipment will be donated to The Newhaven Hospital once the baby is here, and they are 'released' from the hospital.

Mr. Woodsley will make sure all the furniture is carefully removed from the two rooms they use in The Private Residence. He will use Rex's help and various secret passageways for deliveries of unmarked crates and unmarked boxes. The doctor will pick two trusted nurses to help him and Mr. Woodsley to set everything up and be ready for the big day.

At The Palace, The Royal Family and The Worthington's are getting ready for A Royal Press Conference. Bri walks into the living room of The Royal Apartment and sees Jack.

Jack smiles adoringly walking over to her. "Gorgeous as ever, Amore Mia!"

She shakes her head, but she is also smiling. "You'd say that if I were wearing a potato sack!"

"Of course! *Because it would be true!*" He gives her his signature smile.

She has her Diamond-Heart necklace set on from Lawerence, as well as her diamond watch from Jack. "Is it too much jewelry?" She asks.

"Bri, as 'The Queen,' you should have more." Jack cups her cheek. "For today, it's the perfect amount."

She hugs him. "I love you, Amore Mio!"

"I love you!" He says, then taps a little kiss to her lips.

Lawrence walks over them and he asks Bri, "Are you ready, Darling?"

She takes a deep breath. "As ready as I'm going to be..." She takes his arm and they all walk into The Royal Press Room. The room is filled with press, all the chairs are full and there are people standing along the sides and at the back of the room. Phillip and Jack, along with Carlotta holding Jacks, Henry, James, and Amy holding Elise, are behind Lawrence and Bri.

> Lawrence puts his hand up to quiet everyone. "Thank you, Ladies and Gentlemen. First, I would like to express my appreciation to all of you for respecting our family during these *incredibly* difficult weeks and months in our lives. Her Royal Highness Princess Abigail and His Highness The Grand Duke of Newhaven are recovering quite nicely and will make full recoveries. As soon as doctors feel comfortable, they will be released into the hands of a private medical staff to finish their recoveries at home.
>
> We are planning a special Royal Funeral for Their Royal Highnesses The Duke and Duchess of Brexton. While we know this isn't protocol, it's the best way we can think of to honor them."

Lawrence lowers his head to get a hold of his emotions. Bri steps closer to help him.

> "We're hoping that, even though it isn't protocol, you will support us in honoring two *wonderful* people who will be dearly missed by so many."

Lawrence clears his throat and reads from the notecard he has prepared:

> "The Royal Funeral for The Duke and Duchess of Brexton will begin with them 'Lying in State' at The London Palace on Friday, Saturday, and Sunday. Then Monday morning there will be a procession to The London Abbey for the funeral service, with a private service to follow."

Lots of hands go up and various questions are blurted out. Lawrence points, "Kris, from The Royal Magazine."

"Thank you, Your Majesties. I think most, *if not everyone here*, are in full support of a Royal Funeral to honor our former queen. Rumor has it, this will be *privately* paid for. Is that correct?"

Lawrence replies, "That is correct." He points to someone else.

"Thank you, Your Majesty. Juniper Magazine. There are a lot of rumors flying around how Millicent Devonridge died, would you please put those rumors to rest by telling us how she did die?"

"All I'm prepared to say is that Millicent Devonridge died of crimson powder poisoning." Lawrence states.

"Will you release something about how all that went down in the near future?" Another person asks. "If even a fraction of the rumors are true, it would be an incredible story to share with us!"

Lawrence looks at Bri. "We aren't prepared to answer those questions yet." Bri faintly shakes her head.

A different reporter interrupts with, *"How is Prince Jacks adjusting after his abduction, Your Majesty?"*

Bri replies, "Considering all that has happened, he's resilient like all kids," she turns to look at him, "and adjusting faster than we expected."

He holds his arms out to her and she takes him. He hugs her with a big smile, laying his head on her shoulder. One hand pats his Uncle Lawrence's shoulder to many 'awes' around the room and tons of camera flashes. Lawrence smiles at Jacks and Jacks reaches for him, which there are more 'awes' when The King takes him into his arms.

Lawrence points to another reporter who asks, "We see there's another child in the family. Who is she?"

They *are* prepared to answer this, or they wouldn't have the kids with them. Lawrence smiles at Elise, then turns back as Bri replies, "She came into our lives when she needed a family and we happily discovered," Bri looks at Amy, "we needed her!" The family happily smiles.

"Will you be adopting her then?" Someone asks.

Bri smiles. "Lord and Lady Worthington are adopting her and, as you can see, this sweet girl already loves her mommy and daddy. She will be a part of our *whole* family and we *all* love her *dearly*!" She gestures to the whole family, even Phillip, The King Father, is nodding.

They answer a few more questions before they end the press conference. The family poses for a few photos before leaving The Royal Press Room.

CHAPTER 65
A Royal Funeral

The Royal Funeral for Seth and Genevieve is today in London. McMasters put Mitchell in charge of The King's Guard and protecting The Royal Family. He and the rest of The Royal Guard have been working long hours the last few days putting additional security in place for when The Royal Family goes out into the public and they are completely exposed. It will add difficulty to protecting them, but their most lethal foe is already dead; most people are going to be there to pay their respects and will be respectful. McMasters asks Rex to keep an ear out for any possible threats. Thankfully, all is quiet.

Bri is wearing a black, straight-neck midi wrap dress with a black hat and black shoes. She has on her diamond earrings that David gave her on their honeymoon, then she puts on her gold diamond watch David also gave her, along with her wedding rings. There is a light, double-tap, knock on the door.

"Come in." Bri says, looking at herself in the full-length mirror.

Jack smiles as he walks into The Royal Chambers. He sees Lawrence walking out of the closet and hugs him. Then he walks over to Bri and hugs her.

Jack takes half a step back and shows her a small velvet box. He explains, "I was on an online auction for a client, and I stumbled upon this. I showed this to David," he looks over, "and Herst," Lawrence nods, "as well as Abby, who wants me to tell you, and I quote, *'It's perfect!'*" Jack opens the box.

"A bee!" Bri gasps, then her eyes moisten taking in the white, yellow, and black diamonds and gems, all put together in the shape of a bee, all set in yellow gold.

 "A *'Queen Bee*,'" he points to the tiny gold crown, "and Abby also said to tell you that you can't go wrong with wearing yellow, when it's yellow gold *and* yellow diamonds?" Bri lightly smiles and nods with her tears.

Bri pins it to her left shoulder telling Jack and Lawrence, "When Gen said she would call me 'Queen Bee,' I joked that I couldn't pull off wearing yellow." She wipes her tears with the tissue Lawrence hands her.

She hugs Jack. "Thank you, Amore Mio. It's beautiful."

Jack squeezes her a little tighter. "I love you, Amore Mia." He steps back. "I'll go down and wait with the others." He looks at Lawrence. "Take your time, alright?" Jack pats his shoulder.

Lawrence has teary eyes. "Thank you, Brother." Jack nods. Bri and Lawrence watch Jack leave.

She turns to Lawrence, it has been getting more emotional for him as the funeral has gotten closer, and asks, "How are you holding up?"

He quietly answers, "Minute by minute..."

She adds his crest pin to his tie; the only thing telling anyone he's The King. No sash, no formal attire today. Just a brother mourning the loss of two people dear to him.

"*You* need to talk to *me*, Ace." His eyebrows slightly come together. She lovingly adds, "*Please.*"

"There's not much I can put into words..." He exhales some frustration. "I'm hurt and bloody *angry*! I mean, they *finally* get the life they wanted, *but never got the chance to live it*! He'll never have a family with the woman *he* loves! Then there's Jacks and this baby..." he rests his hand on her baby bump, "and another to come after this one..." He exhales. "I also feel like I never really got to thank Seth or Gen for being so wonderful and supportive—."

"*Yes*, you did!" She tells him. "Not only had you flat out said it, but you also said it *every time* you considered their feelings in various scenarios! You *never* forced her to be intimate with you, *and* you even made Seth *her* Royal Consort! *Everything* you did for them told them how much you cared about them and their relationship!"

He kisses her softly but firmly, wrapping his free arm around her waist. "Sometimes I forget how perceptive you are."

"Well, it's only natural for you to love her as your family. You three, and Abby, grew up together, went through 'issues' with your parents together, particularly Millicent, and the intimacy of non-intimacy...*I hope that makes sense.*" He slightly smiles and nods. "Lawrence, I'd be worried if you didn't love her as an important part of your family!"

He kisses her again. "*Thank you.*"

Her eyebrows come together. "For what?"

"*For being you!*" He replies. She rolls her eyes. He faintly laughs. "Thank you for loving me, because that isn't always so easy." She smiles knowingly. He rests their foreheads together. "We need to get going. Do you have everything?"

"I think so." She says as they walk towards the door.

They go downstairs to meet up with their family in The Royal Apartment's living room. The King's Guard escorts the family to the entrance where the horse drawn carriages are waiting under the carriage porch. The grandest carriage is red with *lots* of gold accents; old carriage lights on the outside four posts are on; and a gold roof with various decorations carved on the edges. The horses pulling it are jet black and shiny, reminding Bri of Artemis. At Bri's request, this carriage is to remain empty with only the tiara *Queen* Genevieve wore regularly, and the only one The Duchess of Brexton wore, rests on a pillow on the seat. Next to the tiara is Seth's military sword and white gloves. Their caskets are in the hearse carriage being pulled by more black horses.

Lawrence helps Bri up into the second carriage, then Lawrence climbs in, followed by Phillip; the next carriage will have Jack, Henry, and Carlotta in it. James and Amy are staying at Ashbourne Castle with Jacks and Elise. The carriage with the caskets pulls away from The Palace first, with the other three carriages following it in succession.

The carriages wind through the city, making their way to The London Abbey. They come to a stop and Lawrence gets out first, then helps Bri. Phillip gets out next and they stand outside for a few moments as the family gathers together. The King Father leads all the royals and nobles inside. Lawrence and Bri will wait for everyone to be seated before they go inside.

The Abbey is adorned with stained glass windows, carvings in the ceilings, marbled floors, and all the details that make old churches and cathedrals beautifully similar, yet unique. When The King and Queen enter The Abbey, the main doors close behind them. Lawrence is holding her hand, with her arm tucked under his arm.

The King and Queen enter the cathedral and everyone is standing. When The King and Queen walk past them, they bow or curtsy. Once The King and Queen are seated up front, everyone sits down. The funeral of The Duke and Duchess of Brexton begins.

When it's time for Lawrence to give the eulogy, he takes a deep breath before going up to the podium...

> "To those of you who could attend, including Their Majesties, Their Royal Highnesses, Their Highnesses, Their Graces, Sirs, Ladies, Gentlemen, Prime Ministers, Members of Parliament, delegates, family, and friends: Thank you for being here with us as we say goodbye to Seth and Genevieve Heathherst, The Duke and Duchess of Brexton."

> "I remember a day at boarding school when Seth had to pull me aside to tell me about this beautiful girl he had met; he *knew* he was going to marry her one day!"

Lawrence smiles at the memory.

> "From that moment on, whenever he saw her, or talked about her, he couldn't stop smiling! Even if they were upset with each other, or arguing, *they* were still happy. Unfortunately, there was a roadblock and the only way I could make things right for them at the time was to make Seth, Genevieve's Royal Consort, and to encourage them to continue with their relationship. They would encourage me to find love. When I found a *very* special woman, both of them were excited for me, *and for us.*"

He looks lovingly at Bri.

> "Genevieve was then on a mission. She wanted to put *everything* together as it should've been in the first place! She was quite the dynamic force and she was successful!"

He swallows hard.

"The things Seth, Abby, and I went through in our childhood, strengthened our bond with each other; then, when Genevieve came into our lives, she was an added strength the three of us needed. I will be forever grateful to their example of what enduring love is!"

Bri sees Seth and Genevieve's spirits standing off to the side watching Lawrence. Genevieve looks at Bri with a big smile. Genevieve projects her thoughts, 'We understand what mother said about how everything makes perfect sense on this side! It beautifully does!'

"...They would want us to keep moving forward, and we will do that for them. We love you, Seth and Genevieve. You will be missed and forever in our hearts."

Lawrence steps down and goes back to his seat next to Bri. She holds his hand, and he squeezes it, then rubs his thumb back and forth across the soft skin on her hand.

After the public funeral, both caskets are taken to the cemetery outside, specifically to The Heathherst Mausoleum. Typically, royals are taken down to The Royal Tombs. Lawrence felt that would be a lot to ask for, when there is shuffling that has to happen for any royal to be buried down there. The most recently deceased are interred on the first level, older ones are rotated downward to the level below. The oldest one is cremated, then put into a rectangular box that is slid into a permanent space in a room, on the main floor of The Abbey.

Lawrence and Phillip asked Bri, Jack, Carlotta, and Henry to come to the private service in The Heathherst Family Mausoleum. They all file outside and make their way to the mausoleum. Inside, The Archbishop says a few words and when he is finished, he steps out for the family to have some privacy.

Bri tearfully smiles at Seth and Gen when she sees them appear. "It's *SO* good to see you two!"

Everyone looks where Bri is looking. She looks at the others and circles her fingers for them to see Seth and Gen. Phillip and Lawrence are finding it difficult not to cry.

Lawrence struggles to say, "I'm sorry I couldn't protect you!"

Seth shakes his head. *"You did for as long as you could!"*

Gen tells him, "Don't you dare feel guilty for anything! You were *always* supportive and there for us!" Seth agrees.

Phillip steps over to them and he gets choked up. Seth shakes his head. "Father, *please* don't blame yourself anymore. Being on this side, we understand things more fully than we ever did before."

Bri looks at Jack, Carlotta, and Henry, "Why don't we let them have a few minutes." She tells Lawrence and Phillip, "Take all the time you need. *No rush.*" They nod.

She walks out with Jack, Carlotta, and Henry. They go back into The Abbey and wait in the room that is right inside the back door. Henry hugs Bri in a warm, fatherly hug. Then they all sit down and wait patiently for the others. Time passes by in peaceful silence.

Lawrence finished first and walks in the door. Bri stands up and hugs him, then they sit down to wait for his dad. He rests his arm behind her and puts his head against hers.

Lawrence softly snorts through his tears. "Seth reminded me that he had said you were the smartest decision I ever made, and not to screw it up!"

She lightly giggles. "I knew I liked that man!" They all softly chuckle.

Phillip comes in and Bri hugs him. "How are you holding up?"

"Better after seeing them. *Thank you!*"

"They appeared on their own." She tells him.

"Without your help, we couldn't have seen them, not really having a chance to say goodbye." He gives her an appreciative look. He looks down at her baby bump. "When the truth came out about Vivian, I promised to do right by them, only now I'll never have the chance with Seth."

Bri squeezes his hand. "*You did!* And his death doesn't lessen that! Just keep doing the right things now and enjoy being the best grandpa you can be to *all* your grandchildren!" He smiles at her. "Remember how happy Vivian was in the light?" He tearfully nods. "Seth and Gen are just as happy now!" He smiles as he thinks about that.

Then his eyebrows come together. "Wait. Was this the first time you saw them after they died?"

She nods. "There could be a number of reasons why I didn't see them before today." She remembers something. "Being at The Devonridge Manor, it could've been that The Duke somehow blocked their light; like too much darkness, or something."

Phillip hugs her. "I'm sorry you had to go through everything you did, and I'm *so* grateful you and my two grandsons are safe and sound. Plus, we already have another grandchild added to make it instantly sweeter."

Lawrence takes Bri's hand, and they walk to the front of The Abbey where the carriages are waiting. When they step outside, they see signs and comments of sympathy. They wave in a few directions before they climb into the carriages. Their ride back to The Palace doesn't seem quite as long this time. They go back to The Palace, to The Royal Great Hall for the reception.

That evening, Carlotta and Henry are at the hospital for the night to stay with Abby and David, respectively, for the night. James and Amy are in the living room at The Royal Residence at Ashbourne Castle with Lawrence, Jack, and Bri. The kids are in the nursery, sleeping for the night. Bri, Jack, and Lawrence start talking about getting into their routine again.

Bri looks at Lawrence. "I've never been comfortable leaving you behind when I go back to Newhaven, *sssooo*, I have an idea..."

Lawrence's eyebrow goes up. "*I'm intrigued!*"

"Why don't you come and stay at The Worthington Manor when I'm at The Cottage?" She suggests. "This way, you'll see Jacks and the baby more than the three-*ish* days when we're together; plus, you'll be able to make sure Elise still sees her Uncle Lawrence. Then we can fly back to London and have our time together." She suggests. "We're going to need a nanny to help this all

500

work out better and by the third baby, we'll probably need a second nanny to keep it flowing as smoothly as possible."

"The details can be worked out, but I think it's a great idea!" Lawrence tells her, with Jack agreeing.

They all watch a movie together and have popcorn. They start a second movie, only Bri keeps yawning and decides to go to bed; Lawrence goes with her. She tells everyone goodnight before pulling Jack aside.

"I love you!" Bri hugs Jack. "Goodnight, Amore Mio!"

He smiles. "I love you, too!" He kisses her. "Goodnight, Amore Mia!" He steps over and gives Lawrence a brotherly hug.

Bri takes Lawrence's hand and they walk to The Royal Bed Chamber. She starts to get ready for bed when she sees Lawrence sitting on the couch staring at the dark fireplace. She walks over and sits on the coffee table in front of him.

"Lawrence...what can I do?" She quietly asks.

He looks up at her, then pulls her to straddle him. He hugs her for a while, before he begins to softly cry at the loss of his brother and a dear friend...

He calms himself and says with a hint of frustration, "In the end, Millicent still got to them, *and Gen!*"

He dries his eyes with his hands, then stares at her sitting on his lap. He tucks some hair behind her ear and pulls her in for a kiss that he deepens. She pulls back to look into his eyes; she feels he just wants to forget...he wants to connect with her. She starts unbuttoning his shirt while he continues to kiss her passionately...

He tangles his hands in her hair and looks at her with so much love; she holds her breath. He kisses her firmly once more.

He whispers, "*Let's go to bed.*" She nods and leads the way.

When they're in bed, he spoons her so he can rest a hand on her baby bump.

"Goodnight, My King."

He smiles. "Goodnight, My Queen."

He kisses the curve of her neck and holds her a little more snuggly. He finds himself relaxing, finally coming down off the emotional rollercoaster he has been on for far too long.

CHAPTER 66
Missing Pieces

The next morning, Bri is down in her office at Ashbourne Castle working away. There is a knock on the door and the door opens.

Bri is surprised to see and smiles, "*Gabriel!*" She is expecting Mr. Woodsley, since she is at Ashbourne Castle.

"I caught an earlier flight as soon as I could this morning. I didn't want to try to do this over the phone or text, nor by email." He tells her.

"Great." She says with a sarcastic tone, putting her pen down. "That leads me to think that something bad has happened."

"*Thaaat* might be an understatement." Gabriel replies.

He lays out the inventory sheets and pictures of Newhaven Manor for her to see. Her eyes fall on the word 'MISSING' in red ink flowing down the sheet, and through all the other pages.

"It looks like there are *more* missing on these sheets than there are still in inventory!" Bri says. "I think I'm going to be sick..." She puts her hand on her stomach. "Do we know what happened?" She asks. "A theft? A flood? I'll even accept a raging, strategic fire!"

"If it was a burglary or a theft, you, and The Worthington Family, would've heard about it." He replies.

"True." She rolls her eyes and turns up her nose. "That means Jack's father, or brother, likely sold these pieces..." He nods. "Have we checked the basement, or an unused house, shack, or barn on the property?"

"Not yet." Gabriel says. "I wasn't sure how you would want to handle it, since we slipped in when the place was empty, with The Earl and his son still in London?"

"Maybe arrange a day and a time where I can bring a full inventory list to The Earl, then we see what they can resurrect." She throws out there.

Gabriel asks, "What happens if he doesn't have them anymore?"

"Well, we do need to prepare that he *won't* be able to get them all back, because he won't have the funds to do so." Bri reluctantly states. "*Unless* he goes to Jack for the money..." She takes a deep breath. She doesn't want Jack to have to deal with this man yet. "Please bring The Earl to me with me right away!"

"Yes, Ma'am." He bows before he leaves her office to arrange that.

Bri is carefully looking through the inventory sheets they have on The Newhaven Collection; the section for The Library alone is extensive! She reads through some of the titles of the books and wonders if these titles can be replaced with the books Rex saved from the library that was falling apart at The Devonridge Manor.

> Bri to Amy: "Will you take a look at the missing titles of books under 'The Library' section of these inventory sheets for The Newhaven Collection, to see if any of those same titles can be found in what was sent to us from The Devonridge Library? I'm hoping we might be able to replace some of them..."
>
> Amy: "Sure! I'll get right on it!"
>
> Bri: "Thank you!"

A little while later it's time for lunch and Bri's stomach growls. She stands up and there is a knock on her office door, then Mr. Woodsley walks in with Reginald, The Earl of Newhaven, also Jack's father; Bri is expecting him. Reginald walks towards her; he doesn't wait for Mr. Woodsley to announce his arrival.

He demands to know, "WHAT'S THE MEANING OF THIS?! YOU HAVE YOUR THUGS COME INTO THE RESTAURANT AND DRAG ME AWAY LIKE SOME CRIMINAL!"

Bri's eyebrow goes up and says with a serious look, "Aren't you?"

He is caught off guard with her response, then stutters, "WH-OF C-COURSE NOT!" Then he gets angry at the accusation. "HOW DARE—."

"No!" She purposely interrupts and leans one her desk saying, "How.*dare*.you!" His mouth drops. "*First,* did no one teach you the *proper* way to address, or talk, to a queen?!"

He snorts in disgust. "*You're* no *queen.*"

Mr. Woodsley gets angry, but Bri discreetly puts her hand up in a stopping gesture. Bri looks at Reginald and points to a chair in front of her desk. "Sit down and listen!" He is defiant, folding his arms...until she gives him a look that makes him sit. "Since I'm married to David Worthington, who is The Grand Duke of Newhaven; *that* makes *me* The Grand Duchess of Newhaven! The Worthington Family is responsible for The Newhaven Collection and *all* its contents." Bri continues, "*Now,* being that you're my father-in-law—." He scoffs and rolls his eyes. "Fine. If you prefer, this conversation will continue contentiously: *Mister Carlisle*—."

"*You* will address me as 'Sir!'" He angrily corrects her. "That's the respect of *my* title!"

"Do you really want to correct me on what's proper when *you* are disrespecting 'The Queen' standing before you?!" She tells him and he glares at her. "As far as I'm concerned, you *are* a criminal! *You stole* directly from the people of Newhaven, and I demand to know what happened to the missing inventory of The Newhaven Collection!"

He takes a defensive position. "What happens in my family's house is *none* of your concern!" Jack had walked up to the office door where Lawrence was already listening with Mitchell and McMasters; he listens with them.

"*Correction,*" she says with a bit of anger in her voice, "the *entire* estate belongs to The Grand Duke of Newhaven, and other than your bit of personal belongings, *everything else* belongs to The Newhaven Estate! The Carlisle Family is *allowed* to stay there with His Highness' permission, which can be *revoked* at any moment." She reminds him.

"Then why isn't *he* here?" He sneers. "*I should be dealing with him!*"

"Why should he be here?" She retorts. "Do you need an audience for your misconduct and thievery?!"

"*Of course not!*" He snaps. "But if all that stuff is important, then shouldn't The Grand Duke be here?! If he doesn't think it's important enough to be here, then I'm leaving!"

"If I invited The Grand Duke into this conversation that would make this *even more* official, which could make this all get legally *really* ugly, *really* fast. Of course, *with your attitude towards me*, David might've had you hauled away in chains to the nearest dungeon!" Reginald glares. She continues, "*Everything* that is missing is roughly worth ten million; probably considerably more. Will you be able to get any of these missing pieces back?"

"No." He quickly states, folding his arms again.

He doesn't think there is anything she can do about it, especially if there isn't any money to get them back. Plus, he doesn't think David would allow her to throw him in jail, or sanction him, because of Jack.

"I'm going to need more than that, or you're going to force me to have you thrown into The Royal Dungeon!"

"I *can't* get anything back."

"You sold them?" She asks, just to be clear.

"Some of them." He says. "The others The Queen M—er, Millicent Devonridge wanted pieces to sell. Something about losing some of her money in a computer glitch, or virus?" He shrugs not knowing, or caring, what happened, only Bri knew exactly what had happened; so did the guys listening in. "Most of that inventory list," he points to her desk, "is what she took from Newhaven Manor's extensive collection. The fact that it came from Newhaven and would hurt you, was a bonus for her."

"Then *you* have a problem, don't you?" She states.

"No. *I* don't." He starts to stand.

"*Sit. Down.*" She says very sternly. He is about to ignore her, but he thinks twice when he sees her face. "*YOU* have the problem of finding *every.single.piece.on.this.list*, or *YOU* are responsible for paying The Estate back for its value. *That's where the ten million comes in.*" She sees him squirm and knows he is paying attention, *taking her seriously*. "I don't care to hear what excuse you try to come up with. *You* are being held responsible for *every* missing item, because you chose to continue living there, which includes taking care of The Estate! For some time now, The Newhaven Trust has been taking care of The Newhaven Estate and had a list of The Newhaven Collection. It looks like we should've been keeping better track of things lately. Well," she sits down, "we can't change that, but we can keep better track going forward."

"*I would have* no idea *who bought what from Millicent!*" He snaps.

"Then I suggest you better get busy locating them! I will be discussing a deadline with The Grand Duke for returning the pieces, or we will be forced to publicly bring you up on charges, along with assessing fines and penalties." She glances at the door, and it looks like it isn't closed all the way. She assumes Jack and Lawrence are outside the door and hopes they will take the hint when she tells Reginald, "My office will be in touch. You can see yourself out, Mister Carlisle. Good day."

The men on the other side of the door heard her and disappeared out of sight. Mr. Woodsley comes over to Reginald when he sees him in the hallway outside Bri's office and walks him to The Main Entrance. Mitchell goes with them to make sure Reginald gets into the car and leaves, which he does in a bit of a huff. Bri is sitting at her desk when Lawrence and Jack walk into her office; she looks and looks again.

Her face has a pained expression when she asks Jack, "You were listening with Lawrence, weren't you?"

"I was." He replies. "I only listened so I would know if I needed to come in and protect you from him, but you didn't need any help! You handled him *brilliantly!*" He smiles wide.

"Well, it helps that I loathe the man for how he treated you and *still* treats you!" She replies. "Anyway, I want to reach out to Rex with this inventory list to see if he is able to track down any of these pieces for us. I just pray he is able to locate a lot of these, or all this history could be gone forever."

507

CHAPTER 67
Falling Apart

David has been released from the hospital and into the care of a private medical team to finish recuperating in Newhaven. David is already on the helicoptor with a nurse, Jack is getting into the helicoptor with Jacks.

Lawrence is walking towards the helicoptor with Bri holding her hand. "I'll be up in a few days, when you're at The Cottage House with Jack."

"*Great!*" Bri stops and looks at him. "Lawrence, whenever you need me to, I'll call for Gen, Seth, even Vivian."

He feels the end of a curl in her hair, loving the softness of it. "I know, Darling." He holds her cheek a moment. "The time in the mausoleum helped greatly, and I'm grateful for that!"

He starts walking with her again, rubbing his thumb across the softness of her hand. At the helicoptor door, they stop and face each other.

Bri holds both of his hands and tells him, "As you said to me, we *all* grieve differently and there is nothing wrong with how you need to do it." She gives his hands a little squeeze. "Grieve on your terms, *unless you're going to lose yourself in your grief,*" he knows she means like his father did when his mother was killed, "then I *will* step in."

"*Good.*" He gives her a small, appreciative smile. "Because that would also mean I would lose you to a degree, and losing you in *any* degree, would be far worse than death itself!"

Her eyes fill with tears. "That has to be the sweetest, *and the sappiest thing,* I've ever heard!" She wipes the tears before they spill out of her eyes with one of her hands.

"A combination I happen to know you love!" He kisses her hand as she nods.

She chokes up as she hugs him, "*I love you!*"

He hugs her firmly, with a hand going to the back of her head. "I love you more than I ever thought I could!"

They say goodbye and he kisses her once more. She gets onboard and he closes the door before walking back to a safe distance and watches them leave. Bri waves to Lawrence from the window as they lift up into the air; he waves back. When they start flying off towards Newhaven, Lawrence starts walking back to The Palace. She watches him until she can't see him anymore.

She continues to stare out the window as they fly. David is sitting next to her and takes her hand; she looks at him and gives him a small smile. She sees Jack sitting on the floor playing with Jacks. She goes back to looking out the window...she starts to think about everything that has happened.

When they are over Newhaven, and getting close to The Manor, David gives her hand a little squeeze. When she looks at him, he sees she needs to talk. He starts simply, "How are you, Love?"

She gives him a look to go with her, "I should be asking *you* that!"

"Alright." He shifts to look at her better, "*I feel grateful every.single.day you're still here with us!*"

She sweetly smiles. "Me, too. And I'm even *more* grateful *you* are still with us!"

"Well, it would take a lot more than a little bullet to keep me from you!" He winks. She smiles with pursed lips, shaking her head.

They look over at Jack helping Jacks snuggle in his soft blanket while he drinks his bottle. She rests her hand on her baby bump and thinks about how much time she lost with Jacks. She thinks about how much change there is in just the first year, so she is also grateful that the time she missed with him wasn't more than it was!

They land and she stands up to stretch. She looks over at Jack, standing up carefully so he doesn't wake Jacks. He looks at her and handsomely smiles as he studies her face. He looks at David who nods, understanding Jack's unspoken expression; she needs to talk things out.

Since David wasn't there when everything happened, he thinks it may be better is she talks with Jack first. "Why don't we leave Jacks at The Manor with me and his grandparents, so you and Jack can talk some things through?" She shakes her head.

Jack suggests, "Let me take Jacks to The Cottage House and the two of you can have some time to yourselves. We'll be back in time for dinner."

Bri shakes her head. "I don't want to be away from any of you. It's hard enough not having Lawrence here and trying to heal after everything that has happened."

David and Jack know she is struggling with something and they want to help; only, they are not exactly sure how to do that. They go inside The Manor through the back door and find Carlotta and Henry there to greet them in The Sitting Room. When David and Jack see Henry, they are relieved; they know Henry will pick up on whatever is bothering Bri.

Henry hugs Bri, then looks at her. He sees she is struggling not to cry. He gives her a concerned, fatherly look; it pierces into her and cracks her resolve.

She starts to cry. "Oh, Henry..." She hugs him again.

"*Sweetie...*" He chokes up, hugging her back.

Carlotta, David, and Jack back away, so Henry can talk to her. Jack sits in the comfier armchair with Jacks while he sleeps.

Henry tries to comfort Bri, "It isn't as bad as you think—."

"*Henry,*" she shakes her head, "you can't get worse than *killing someone*! And I'm responsible for *two deaths*!" She exhales, taking a step back. "*I don't know how to process that*! How *do I* come to terms with it?! How do I come to terms with killing a guy in the woods and, *if I had the opportunity*, I might've killed the other, only Donovan did it for me!" She turns and starts to pace. "Then there's Millicent—."

"Uncle Henry," David cuts in, "we came the closest to losing her—."

Henry puts his hand on David's shoulder. With a small, fatherly smile he points to Bri saying, "*This time she was prepared to fight back*!"

Bri scoffs. "Yes, I fought back; but only after Emmie, Natty, Peter, Maggie, Amy's baby, Seth, Genevieve; not to mention all the others over the years!"

"*Bri! You didn't* murder *anyone!*" Henry tells her.

"Didn't I?!" She looks at him with red and wet eyes.

He gives her a compassionate look. "Do you remember what we discussed when you said you kept hearing, 'Millicent needs to die,' or something along those lines?" He sees her thinking and keeps going, "I suggested that maybe it was to prepare you for what needed to happen, *however it needed to happen?*" She nods. He puts his hands on her upper arms and states, "Perhaps, you also kept hearing that phrase to help you in a moment like this, right now." Her eyebrows come together, so he further explains, "*Bri*, perhaps The Spirit has been preparing you *to help you* come to terms with this." He asks her, "Have you spoken with Jessica since Millicent's demise?"

She shakes her head. "No."

"Will you call her here so we can *all* help you?" Henry asks. "*Please.*"

"Jessica, would you come see me, well, *us?*"

In a few seconds, Jessica appears. Her white dress seems to always glow with such a bright white, yet it doesn't hurt one's eyes to look at her like it would with the sun. Bri takes her two fingers and circles them around so everyone can see Jessica. They all greet each other.

Henry puts his hand on Bri's upper arm talking to Jessica. "She is carrying a heavy burden."

"*I* stabbed that guy in the neck when he wasn't expecting it! *I* covered that pocket watch in the deadly powder *for* Millicent!" Bri wipes her cheeks with a tissue.

Jessica gives her a compassionate look. "Bri, what would've happened had those two men in the woods lived?"

Bri has frustration in her voice saying, "*They would've brought me to Millicent, which is where I wanted to go! Which means they didn't have to die!*"

"Millicent was *prepared* to have you *brought* to her." Jessica explains, "She was caught off guard with you bursting your way in. Then, when *her plan* was to force you to choose one of her prisoners to be given the poison." She motions towards, "Jack, Henry, and McMasters, being part of that line up. You knocked her completely off balance when *you* took the poison, because she never thought *you* would ever do something like that!"

"It's not like I chose to take the poison right away!" She states. "They might have PTSD from the clicking sound of a pulled trigger on an empty chamber!" Jack shakes a bit at the memory.

"*Did you* have *to take the poison*?!" David asks. "Couldn't you have just dumped it out?"

Jessica shakes her head. "Millicent was already volatile; had Bri just dumped it out, she would've killed *all* of them in a rage." She waves her arm towards Jack, Henry, and McMasters.

Bri thinks a moment. "I had to consume the crimson powder so she wouldn't know what to do."

Henry considers that and says, "It sounds like her mind was spinning because just like that," he snaps his fingers, "all her plans for The Throne were going to die with you, *or so she thought*."

Jessica has Bri sit on the couch with her and tells her, "Millicent's death wasn't as premeditated as you want to blame yourself for."

Bri squeaks, "*How can you say that*?! *I* put the poison in the pocket watch. *I* tossed the pouch to her so she would catch it! *I* told her about the engraving inside pocket watch to get her to open it, *knowing* she wouldn't suspect anything sinister with the watch, *because* she underestimated me!"

Jessica stresses to her, "*Bri*, it was something you brought with you, *in case* you needed to use it."

Henry sits in front of Bri on the coffee table. He holds her hand and notes, "I'm wondering if you're blaming yourself, because you're not sure how you should feel."

"What do you mean?" She asks.

"After *everything* Katie has done, you haven't given up on her, *not completely*, because you've *always* had hope that at some point in her life, she would gain the maturity and understanding she needed to change her life *for good*. Sometimes it takes hitting rock bottom to do that."

"You can't get any more 'rock bottom' than where she's at now, *but it doesn't matter*. She is going to be executed and what's worse, *I don't care if she is?!*" Her eyes tear up.

Henry points to her tears with a kind look. "Those tears say *you do care*, Sweetie. Maybe it's that you don't want to care, because caring would mean it's one more death you're going to have to face?" She cries into her hands and he hugs her the best he can. They let her cry for a minute.

Henry hands her a fresh tissue and she squeaks, "*Thank you*."

Henry feels he needs to ask her, "What happened in the woods?"

Bri takes a deep breath and tells him the whole story; with all the details she can remember... Everyone listens supportively as Bri told them what happened; she wipes her tears with a tissue.

Henry lovingly smiles. "Sweetie, your faith *is* strong! Yes, you feel guilty, because their lives have ended," Bri nods, "but, Sweetie, above all other reasons, you were protecting Jacks and *this* baby!" He points to her baby bump and she rests her hand on it. "I think it would be good for you, along with our entire family, *me included*, to have some counseling to process everything that has happened!" Everyone agrees.

Henry pulls out his phone and he looks up the phone number for a retired psychologist he knows who might be able to travel to them, or with them, for their appointments. He'll see about getting everyone lined up with their first appointments and then they can each schedule future appointments on their own from there.

Jessica says to Bri, "Work through your feelings with love and patience; not only for others, but for yourself as well."

Bri gives her a small smile. "Thank you." Jessica nods. They all say goodbye to her and she fades away. Bri stands. "I'm going to go lie down for a little while." She goes over and kisses Jacks' head, then she cups Jack's cheek a moment. She turns and starts to walk past David, but he gently grabs her forearm. He goes to hug her, but she steps back shaking her head. "Not yet."

They all watch her walk out of the room and down the hall. Carlotta walks up to David. "You know, she has said in different situations, that when no one could hug her, it's because——."

"*She'll fall apart...*" David finishes her sentence and she nods.

Henry says to David, "Help her to fall apart, then all three of you will be able to help her put herself back together; she will be even *stronger* for it."

Carlotta agrees. "She may need to scream, stomp, or throw things, but let her; *things* are replaceable and The Manor is structurally sound; it can take it."

David gives his mom a hug. He hugs Henry, thanking him for his help, as well. Jack is about to get up when David tells him, "I think she'll understand if you don't want to move him again."

Jack looks at Jacks and smiles. "I don't think there is much that will wake him. She can be as loud as she needs to be, I don't think it will wake him up."

David uses the elevator to go up to the fourth floor. He steps off the elevator and walks into their main living room; all is quiet. He goes into their quarters and finds Bri standing at the patio doors staring outside. She looks over and sees him walking over to her as he puts his finger to his lips in a 'shh' gesture. He leads her to the bedroom and helps her change into more comfortable clothes, then he quickly changes into some leisure wear of his own.

When he walks up to her again, she steps back shaking her head. "Don't. I don't want——." He puts his fingers to her lips.

He walks her over to the full-length mirror and he wraps his arms around her from behind, placing his hands on her baby bump. He very quietly tells her, "*You* are safe. *This baby* is safe. *Jacks* is safe, *peacefully* sleeping in his Uncle Jack's arms downstairs. You don't have to be strong for anyone right now. I wasn't with you to face Millicent, *so let me be here for you now.*" He kisses her shoulder. "You are loved *dearly.* You know Jacks loves his mum, and he has loved you since before he was even conceived; the same goes for this little one!" He feels her tense up, and he sees her jaw shake in the mirror. Her eyes turn red and fill with tears. He turns her to face him and quickly wraps his arms around her in a hug before she can protest. "You're here, *safe* in my arms, Macushla." When she feels him hug her firmer, she can't hold it in

514

anymore and she cries. He holds the back of her head and her cries get louder; she holds him tighter. *"Let it out, My Love."* He whispers next to her ear.

He stands there, holding her for a long time, eventually she cries herself out. He holds her in silence, gently swaying with her as he holds her. She takes a deep breath and pulls back to wipe her cheeks with her hands. He steps over and grabs a couple of tissues for her.

David looks at his watch. "If you need Jack, I can have him come up, or if you need Lawrence, we can get him to fly up here, or we can videoconference with him for you?"

She shakes her head. "Jacks is sleeping and I don't want to disturb that." She takes a deep breath. "Lawrence feels guilty enough that Millicent caused all these problems; then with his brother and Gen gone, almost losing Abby, not to mention he feels responsible for Sara Kemp's death, he doesn't need to take me," she motions herself, "and this mess on."

"I can understand that's how you feel; however, you *are* aware there are similarities between Jack, Herst, and I, and this," he moves his finger back and forth between them, "would be one of them. Herst needs to talk this through with you, Love."

"We have." Bri tells him.

"But has he heard how your feeling, *and* what you're dealing with?" He asks.

She shrugs. "Everything is all blurred together right now."

He holds the back of her jaw. "Don't shut him out thinking you're protecting him; you're inadvertently hurting him by not confiding in him. He needs to relate to you and make that connection. Alright?" She nods a little.

Jack texts that Jacks is awake. He also says James and Amy are there with Elise for some play time. David tells Bri, and she says she could use twice the baby time. David replies to the text, then he and Bri go back downstairs.

515

CHAPTER 68
Not a Typical Favor

A few days later, Lawrence flew to Newhaven. Jack and David have breakfast set up on the fourth floor for the four of them, and Jacks, to have breakfast together. They send Lawrence in to wake Bri up.

He kisses her cheek, then sits next to her as she wakes up. "Good morning, My Darling." Lawrence smiles.

She smiles back. "Good morning, My King."

"Jack, David, Jacks, and I would like to have breakfast with you this morning, if you're hungry." He says.

David comes in holding Jacks, with Jack right behind them. Jacks reaches for his mama and Bri sits up to take him. Jacks points to the vase on her side of the bed.

Bri smiles. "*Those* are rainbow roses!"

David teases, "Jack and I *assumed* red roses are your fav—."

"*They are!*" She is quick to reassure them.

"Really?" Jack grins. "Then how come all the gardeners, at all the estates and properties, seem to think it's rainbow roses."

She looks confused. "I'm not sure...When I'm with Lawrence, I like the kaleidoscope, or rainbow, roses; the real ones, *not dyed.*" She smiles. "When I'm with the two of you, red, pink, white, peach," she shrugs, "*all* the colors are my favorite!" She kisses Jacks' cheek.

"Well, the rainbow ones are *definitely* you! You bring lots of color to our lives!" David smiles at her.

She lightly laughs, shaking her head. "You're laying it on pretty thick this morning!" David laughs, as well as Lawrence and Jack.

She gets up and throws some leisurewear on, then they all go out to the table with their breakfast on it. She puts Jacks in his high-chair and sits down next to him. She puts the napkin in her lap and sees the newspaper the staff left on the table for whomever wanted to read it; there is an article about Millicent. That's all she cares to read and starts cutting up her eggs. It does get her thinking about Katie.

She asks Lawrence, "Has Katie been executed yet?"

"The end of this coming week." He replies.

"I have a huge favor to ask." She takes a bite.

"*No way!*" He about drops his knife and fork on his plate. "There is *no way in Hell* I'm going to back down!" Lawrence says standing up. "*Don't you dare ask me to!*"

Bri's eyebrows come together trying to figure out what he means. "Back down from what? *Her execution?!*"

"That woman was working side-by-side with the woman you, yourself, renamed 'Evil Bitch From Hell! *What would you have me do?!*" He asks exasperated, throwing up his hands as he walks to the door; Jacks is fussing, he isn't sure what is going on.

She calls after him, "Lawrence! Wait!" But he keeps walking. "I wasn't going to talk you out of it!" She pauses and waits, hoping he heard her…He stops, and she quietly exhales. He turns around and stands in the doorway. "I *swear.*" She puts up her right hand. "My apologies if my tone was misplaced. It's a little surprising when the US allows for appeal after appeal while the person sits on death row for *many years;* some of those prisoners dying of natural causes before their execution is ever scheduled!" Bri watches him walk back over to the table.

"I'm sorry." He says apologetically. "It's just that you wanted a favor and with your loving heart I thought you were going to ask me to stop her execution." He sits next to her again.

"I was only going to ask to see her…maybe give her a chance to show some remorse, to find some kind of peace before she dies. However, I don't want her to know ahead of time that I'm coming to see her." She says. "She may refuse to see me and turn away her only chance before it's all over."

"That means the prison couldn't know and it would be a 'drop by visit.' You'll need to use your charm to smooth it over, because you didn't give them a chance to make everything perfect for 'The Queen's visit.'" Lawrence informs her. "We'll need to do it soon, with her execution eminent."

She squeezes his hand. "I'm not sure if bringing any of you is a good idea."

"That's the only way I'll agree to this." Lawrence says. "I'm playing the 'I'm The King' card, Bri, *because* I love you *and* you *are* The Queen. She has hurt you *way* too much, so you're *not* going in there by yourself."

"Ssssooo, if 'The Queen' shows up unexpectedly, they could turn me away?" She asks.

"Only if I were to specifically call The Governor and tell her not to allow you access." Lawrence replies. "I don't want to do that. However, *if you love me*, you *won't* go by yourself."

"Okay." She notes, "For the record, I wasn't planning on going alone." His eyebrow raises. "I planned on taking at least McMasters or Mitchell with me." Jack and David chuckle.

Lawrence lightly laughs, shaking his head. "Thank you."

She asks all three of them, "Does anyone *want* to go with me?"

David and Jack actually want to go, having known Katie a bit. They do hope she uses Bri's chance to find some closure and peace in this life before it ends. Millicent did. One of the many things Lawrence loves about *His Queen*, as do David and Jack, is her compassion and kindness. After all she went through, she still wants to visit Katie in prison and help her make amends in this life before it's too late...not many people would do that.

It's the night before they are going to see Katie. Bri is with Lawrence in The Royal Chambers, and he is waiting for Bri to come to bed. He is sitting on her side of the bed, staring off at nothing in particular. Bri crawls on the bed from the other side, to come up behind him and hug him. She kisses his shoulder then rests her chin on it.

"What's on your mind, Handsome?" She asks.

He exhales. "I love you, Bri...and the thought of almost losing you, and our baby, not to mention losing all the people we did, makes me want to kill Katie myself for ever helping Millicent." He shifts on the bed to face her more. "I wish I didn't feel that way—."

"I know." She taps a little kiss to his lips. "No judgements, Lawrence. *Alright?*" He nods. "That was the most difficult time of *all* our lives." She sits more comfortably.

He tells her, "After McMasters conferenced Jack, David, and I, to tell us you were kidnapped, all I could hear were your words that if someone really wants to hurt another person, they'll find a way...days would go by and news seemed to trickle in, because it wasn't fast enough; we weren't rescuing you fast enough." Lawrence smiles a little remembering, "Jack said we needed to channel you, channeling a criminal." She snorts a little laugh.

She squeezes his hand. "The phone was a *huge* relief, because I felt connected to the outside world! Then hugging Jack felt like a physical connection to all three of you..." Her eyes are a little teary.

"Then Sara didn't die for nothing..." He looks at her. "When was Sara killed? How did it come about?"

"Lawrence..." She shakes her head.

"*I sent her to her death!*" He snaps. "*I deserve to know!*"

"You didn't send her to her death! You sent her to smuggle a phone, *a lifeline*, into me!" She tells him.

He stands up and scoffs, "Oh, come on, BriaLynn! Stop protecting me, damnit! We both know I knew how dangerous it would be for her, and how naïve Sara was about Millicent! Any way you word it, *I'm* responsible for her death!"

He sees her raise her eyebrow with a bit of annoyance and he knows he is pushing it with her. She remembers what David had told her about Lawrence needing her to help him process everything. When she realizes she won't dissuade him, she changes her approach a bit.

"*Before I tell you*, I first want you to know her spirit lingered with me until I was alone, and we could speak. She is at peace, Lawrence. *I swear to you*, she wasn't angry with you at all!"

"Or you could be just saying that!" He snips.

"When have you ever known me to make a promise, *or swear to something*, I don't mean?!" She pushes back. "I just wouldn't have said that part at all! Now, cut this attitude out, *or you can leave and find another room to sleep in!*" She watches him pull back a little, taking all that in. She continues, "She also said what others have said being on that side of the veil; that she understands, and *everything* happened like it was supposed to happen."

"I appreciate you telling me that, *I do*." Lawrence's tone is more respectful. "And I'm sorry for my rudeness. I just want you to open up to me; I need you to." He implores her. "*Please*, talk to me. *I need to know what happened*. I can't explain why, other than it's for closure..."

"Can I ask you to promise me something?"

His eyebrows come together cautiously replying, "*Sure...*"

"Promise me that after I tell you this, it won't stop you from making a decision that could very likely result in someone's death." She watches him look at the bed as he considers what she is saying, then he shakes his head.

He honestly tells her, "Bri, I *can't* promise that!" He looks at her. "*Of course it will affect the next decision I make; it could affect every decision I* ever *make like that!* I shouldn't have asked her to do it, *because* she was so naïve. She didn't really know what I was asking her to do, *not the risk she truly was taking*. If I would've asked someone like Donovan to smuggle the phone in, he isn't naïve and *fully aware* of what Millicent would've done if she found out!"

She leans forward and puts her hand on his. "*Sometimes*, being a great leader means sending someone somewhere *knowing* that person won't survive, in order to save everyone else the leader needs to protect."

He looks at her. "Maybe knowing what happened could help me process it all and to be more certain there wasn't any other way, like using a 'Donovan,' if I have to make a decision like that again." She gives him a little smile with her nod.

She sits up straighter and takes a deep breath. "Sara had brought my dinner that night and she barely gets the tray on the table, when Millicent comes storming into the room. I thought Millicent was upset with me, *until she focused in on Sara.* She knew about Sara's meeting with you. She swore she didn't say anything to you about me, or where I was."

Lawrence shakes his head. "*She didn't!* Then again, I was just so focused on getting that phone to you, I may not have heard her..."

"You had Henry with you, didn't you?" She asks and he nods. "Then one of you would've made sure she had a chance to tell you, if she was going to say anything." Bri says.

"I did remember your promise to Devereaux's nanny, so I promised Sara the same immunity, with a new identity anywhere in the world. Unfortunately, she took the phone without saying a word. Henry and I didn't know if that was an agreement, or, well," he throws up his hands a little, "we just didn't know what it meant. For all we knew, she could've given it to Millicent to score points with her, which is why when you texted from it, we needed to be sure it was you texting us..."

"Lawrence, the phone *wasn't* the issue!"

He has a surprised look. "What do you mean?!"

"*Millicent didn't know about the actual phone!*" Bri tells him. "She knew about her meeting with you and figured she *could've* smuggled *something* in for me, but that was the extent of it! The problem was her being seen as a weak link." She explains further, "Millicent used Sara's meekness to her advantage; a link to know what was going on inside The Palace, but when you met with Sara, her meekness was then Millicent's weakness. *Millicent couldn't have that, and she flat out said it that night!* And she is right! From a criminal perspective, you don't want weak links inside your group to undermine whatever you're trying to accomplish."

"True. *Or infiltrate your people.*" He adds, thinking of Donovan and Rex's other people.

"*Exactly.* That's why Millicent was stunned to see Donovan, someone she let into her inner circle." She takes another deep breath. "Millicent walked over to Sara, saying something about how Millicent has lasted for as long as she has, because even the mere whisper of a weakness, Millicent gets rid of it."

"Like Sara."

She nods. "You can see where this was going, but Sara couldn't. Perhaps that was for the best, because it happened so fast; Sara didn't have time to think about what was coming. Millicent grabbed hold of Sara's head with one hand and braced Sara's head against her chest; while she raised her other hand, exposing the knife, and in one quick, *forceful* movement she cut Sara's neck from 'ear-to-ear.' I say that it happened fast, and yet, it also seemed like it was all in slow motion. For a split second, Sara didn't know what had happened; but then there was so much blood that it was obvious! Sara's hands couldn't contain all the blood with her hands, *it was going everywhere.* With the amount she was bleeding out, I figured both arteries were severed. The medical examiner said one artery was completely severed and the second one was *almost* severed" Bri keeps how terrified Sara was to herself.

Lawrence gives her hand a little squeeze. "*Please, keep going.*" He struggled not to sound emotional.

"Like I said, it was happening super-fast *and* in slow motion. It only took thirty seconds, give or take, before Sara lost consciousness and collapsed to the floor. I went over to her, but there wasn't anything I could do. It would've been hard to save her with one artery being severed *in* an operating room, *but not two.* She would bleed out in less than a minute. Millicent would call Donovan into the room to have him take care of 'the clean up.' While Donovan cleaned up, she made a point to tell me that no one has thought to look in the rundown Manor for me. Honestly, Lawrence, keeping me there, was smart on her part; most people would overlook it. Knowing about Donovan now, it wasn't long before Rex knew where I was."

Lawrence nods, then gives her a little grin. "Jack didn't overlook it!" Bri has a faint, questioning smile. "He mentioned it and the very next day we got word that you were there." He then asks, "What I don't understand is *why* she would switch her focus to Jacks, when she was so hung up on *our* child?"

"She was looking for a way to gain power as fast as she could, *until* she got her hands on our baby!" She lays her hands on her baby bump. "This one has more royal blood than she did, or any of her own children would've had! Even Jacks! So Jacks was 'good enough for now' to gain power. Afterwards, she would've killed Jacks, then focused on raising our baby worse than she ever raised you, Seth, or Abby."

"Where was Katie throughout all this? Did she watch Sara die?!" He asks.

"She was there, but she was just as surprised as Sara and I were!" Bri answers. "Katie was also naïve and oblivious to the depths Millicent would go. She didn't know Millicent was responsible for Natty and Emmie's deaths until I mentioned it that same night. Anyway, Katie was in the background standing by the door. But I think when Millicent killed Sara, Katie was stunned at what she had witnessed."

"Do you think she would've left Millicent if she could?" He asks.

Bri considers that question out loud. "She needed to process Millicent was responsible for Natty and Emmie's deaths; two girls she did love and watched them grow up. I think she would've wanted to leave, especially with Maggie's death added to it all, *but where would she go?* Where could she hide that Millicent wouldn't find her, and kill her, because she had kept Katie close, so Katie probably knew more than most?" Bri shakes her head. "She would've thought that she needed to bury her head down in the sand and force herself not to think about it. She would've had to disassociate with what was going on around her, to focus on life with maybe Richard McCleary."

"I know she was sad that Maggie died. She even said to me that Millicent didn't have to kill her." Bri's eyes get red and teary. He has an apologetic look. "I'm sorry. I shouldn't have said that."

She shakes her head. "I'm just relieved Katie didn't set Maggie up to be killed!"

"So, if Katie was in the background the night Sara was killed, why did Millicent even bring her there in the first place?" He asks. "To torment you?"

"She had Katie holding the tablet Millicent would show me the video—."

"A video of—*Oh!*" He realizes, "Millicent showed you the video of Seth, Gen, and Abby being shot, right after killing Sara in front of you?!" She nods as she closes her eyes and wipes her cheeks with her hands. She keeps her eyes closed, trying to stop the instant replay. "*Tell me...*" He whispers.

She doesn't even try to convince him otherwise, but she keeps it simple. "She had three people down on their knees and when the camera zoomed in, I saw it was Seth, Gen, *and Abby*." She struggles not to cry as she tells him, "*I wanted to look away, but I couldn't. I was wishing*, hoping, *that what I felt was going to come next*, wouldn't; *but it did.* One by one, *Millicent* shot each one. After watching it, I threw up in the trash bin. I couldn't help that, but I *refused* to cry in front of that woman!"

She looks at Lawrence, sitting on the edge of the bed, staring at the floor. She goes over and stands in front of him to hug him. He hugs her close, then kisses her baby tummy before he lets go.

He asks, "Then what happened?"

"When Sara's spirit left her body, she stayed with me until we could talk." She sits next to him and holds his hand. "Millicent and Katie would leave and I went over to the dinner Sara brought. I took my fork and when I was getting a bite on my fork, I noticed the plate was wobbly. I looked under it and saw that Sara had put a phone and its cord as flat as she could under the plate. Then the cloche she used was a bit bigger that went completely over the plate and rested on the tray." She wipes the tear trickling down her cheek as she tells him, "I told Sara I was sorry. That's when she said she understood that this was how it was always meant to be."

His eyes are red. "*I love you with every fiber of my being!*"

"And I have so much love for you, I could burst!" She leans in and he meets her lips for a little kiss. They rest their heads together.

"Bri," Lawrence says quietly, "part of me wants to be there for you tomorrow, but I can't seem to bring myself to go."

"Remember, I said *no judgements.*" Bri reminds him. He kisses her temple.

They get ready for bed and crawl in. They snuggle for a little while before they go to sleep on their own sides of the bed.

CHAPTER 69
HM's Condemned Row

<hr>

Bri didn't sleep very well that night. She must have slept some, because when she gets up to take a shower, Lawrence isn't back from exercising. She stands in the hot water, lost in thought, and jumps when she feels Lawrence's arms wrap around her.

"I'm sorry, My Darling. I didn't mean to scare you."

"Usually, I can tell when the bathroom door opens, but this time it was like '*poof*,' here you are!" She turns around in his arms.

"I wanted to hug you for a few more minutes, before we get ready to go our separate ways for a few days." He tells her.

"I'm happy you did!" She hugs him tight, tapping a kiss to his neck.

He relaxes into their hug and they hug a bit longer before she gets out. As she gets ready, she really doesn't say much; she is lost in thought. When they're both dressed, Lawrence sees Bri putting on a more casual watch.

"That's probably the better choice, considering you're going to visit a prison." He smiles a bit and she softly laughs.

There are light taps on the door; Lawrence goes to see who it is. It's Mr. Langford, Maurice's backup as Majordomo, only she can't think of his official title.

She overhears Mr. Langford saying, "Your Majesty, The Grand Duke of Newhaven and The Duke of Ashbourne are waiting downstairs for Her Majesty."

"Thank you, Mr. Langford." Lawrence says. He leaves the door open when he walks back to Bri. "For what it's worth, the little time I spent with Katie, she doesn't seem evil just...*lost* and maybe so green with jealousy, the green only looks black."

She gives him an appreciative smile. "Thank you for that."

He lifts her chin, "I love you, My Queen."

"I love *you*, Ace." She sweetly smiles. He firmly kisses her.

"Are you ready?" He asks.

She exhales, "*I think so.*"

She looks around as she gets her small purse and puts her phone inside it. Lawrence takes her hand as they walk down to the living room where David and Jack are waiting. Lawrence walks the three of them out to the awaiting motorcade. Gabriel is waiting next to their SUV and will give them an update on their way to the prison.

Lawrence tells her, "I've asked David and Jack to call me so I can listen in."

She nods as a few tears sneak out. "I miss you already!"

"I miss you, too, but I'll see you in a few days." He smiles and kisses her.

Bri climbs into the SUV as Lawrence says his goodbyes to David and Jack. He shakes Gabriel's hand and pats his shoulder. Lawrence watches them leave before going back into The Palace and down to The Royal Offices to work, keeping himself busy for a while.

On their way to Blackforth Women's Correctional Facility, Gabriel explains that no one knows of her arrival until today. "At this time, McMasters is letting the prison know. He'll join you at a side entrance, as they usher you in; I'll stay with the motorcade."

It isn't long before they pull up to the prison, taking the employee entrance route. They are brought into the prison through the staff door where McMasters is waiting with The Governor, the same as a warden in a US prison.

McMasters makes the introduction. "Your Majesty, this is Ms. Evelyn Camshaw, The Governor of Blackforth Women's Prison."

Bri puts out her hand to shake. "It's nice to meet you, Ms. Camshaw. Or should I call you 'Governor?'" Bri's kind smile starts to put everyone at ease.

The Governor reaches out her hand to shake The Queen's hand and curtseys. "Your Majesty. Welcome to our facility. You may address me as Evelyn, or Ms. Camshaw, or Governor."

"While I love the name 'Evelyn,' I'll address you as 'Governor' since you are in charge of this facility and I want to keep things professional and respectful." Bri tells her and Ms. Camshaw gives a slight nod. Bri looks around. "If we can stop the flow of news of my arrival for just a little bit longer," she looks at the staff, "there's someone I'd like to see. I promise we will stay a little longer and chat with as many as we can before we would need to leave."

The Governor looks around. "I think that would be quite lovely, Your Majesty!" The staff agree. The Governor looks at Bri saying, "Mr. McMasters said you wanted to see Ms. Katherine Barnes."

"Yes. I don't want Katie to know I'm here, nor that I'm here to see her, until I'm walking into her cell. Would you be able to find someone to quietly take me there?" Bri asks.

"I will personally take you there. Will The Grand Duke and The Duke be joining you?" She asks. "We don't have a waiting area fit for nobility, let alone royalty, Ma'am."

Bri shakes her head a little. "The four of *us*," adding McMasters into the count, "will go, but The Grand Duke and The Duke will give us about a five-minute head start. Then they'll come to the cell, but they'll wait outside. I don't want Katie to feel overwhelmed." The guys agree.

"Alright then." The Governor says. Someone whispers Katie's cell number to the Governor. She escorts Bri and McMasters, along with a couple of taller guards to help block Bri's identity through the prison. The Governor asks Bri, "Would you like to go the long way on the way back to see the facility?"

"I'd love to." Bri genuinely replies and The Governor is delighted at the chance to show The Queen the facility.

They walk through a staff corridor, then various hallways, before coming to a gated door that curves out. Above the gate is an incredibly old, chipped, and faded sign that catches Bri's eyes: *HM's Condemned Row*. It was written in black with a red border. A guard comes and opens the metal door that creaks as it opens. They all step into an office area of sorts and wait for everyone to filter in, before they continue along in their journey.

They walk out of the office and into what you'd expect a prison to be, but this part of the prison has an eerie feel to it. The Governor kindly asks Bri, "Is this your first time in a prison, Ma'am?"

"Death Row." Bri says. The Governor gives her an 'ah' look. "This has me thinking of the inside of a naval ship." She keeps the eeriness to herself.

"I can see that." The Governor replies. "The ships can have an unnerving feeling like this part of the prison has." Bri considers the eeriness ships may have, although she has never been on one.

There is a steel staircase right in front of them, concrete walls, steel doors, a net in the middle so no one can jump, or be pushed, to their death from the upper floors. They climb the stairs, then pass by door after door of steel with three thin vertically rectangular windows, two of them about six inches apart, above the handle. The other one is centered for passing a tray and other things through the middle of the door.

They come to Katie's cell door and Ms. Camshaw unlocks it. McMasters puts himself between Bri and the cell first to check things out. He walks in as Katie watches the man's reflection in the window in front of her. She is sitting at a small table in front of a small window. She turns around to see who it is, recognizing McMasters just as she sees Bri stepping around McMasters. Katie's eyes close and she turns back to look out the window. McMasters stands crossways in the door, his back against the frame. He doesn't want Bri *locked* in the cell with Katie. If she were to try anything, she would have him, two prison guards, and soon David, Jack, and those guards, to deal with.

"What are you doing here, Bri?" Katie asks, staring out the window. Bri sits on Katie's perfectly made bed as Katie watches her reflection. "You don't belong here." Bri senses Katie is too embarrassed to face her. "You can't save me, Bri."

"*I know.*" Bri quietly replies, watching Katie looking down at the desk. "We can only save ourselves."

There is a long silence before Katie breaks it. "I've had a lot of time to think about how I ended up here...*ugh*!" She exhales. "I was clean and I should've been thinking clearly, but..." She takes a deep breath. "I've made so many mistakes! There were *so* many times I could've made different choices..." She lifts her eyes to stare out the window again. "Had I *appreciated* our friendship, *and you*..." she shakes her head at herself.

"Your life *definitely* would've been different!" Bri says with a compassion that hits Katie for the first time in a long time. She just nods and Bri sees her reflection as she quickly wipes her cheek.

Bri doesn't hear David or Jack approach the cell, nor does she see McMasters giving them a 'shhh' gesture, as David holds the phone with Lawrence on speaker so he can also listen to what is going on.

Katie continues talking. "You hear people talk about wishing they could go back in time and change all these things; but I would be fine with changing *just one thing*..." There is a light, humorless little laugh at herself. "I've messed up so many times that there are a number of places I could go back to and make *one change* that would change everything for the better! *Then again,* knowing me, *would I really make the right choice?* More likely I would screw things up worse and hurt you again? *God forbid your baby*!" Katie silently cries. After a couple minutes Katie says, "You needn't be worried. I wouldn't let any lawyers petition The King."

"Petition The King? For what...*Oh*!" It dawns on Bri. "For a 'stay of execution,' or whatever they call it here." Bri studies Katie's reflection and notices, "You've resigned yourself to your fate..."

"For the most part." Katie replies. "It makes it easier."

"I suppose..." Bri comments, reaching into her pocket for one of the packages of tissues that she thought she would need for herself. She hands one to Katie, who thanks her as she takes it. "Lawrence, Seth, and Abby are kind, loving, generous; although Lawrence is more resolute——."

"*He has to be*!" Katie states. Lawrence is surprised by her answer and listens more closely as she continues. "Even with this, Bri." Katie refers to her and her execution. "People *need* to know that a crime against The Crown, *against you*, is punishable by death," she looks from Bri out the window again, "as it should be..."

530

"Katie—."

"There's nothing here for you, Bri. I sided with evil over friendship *once again*..." She looks at Bri. "There's *nothing* that can change that, nor undo what has been done!"

"But it doesn't mean eternal damnation, Katie." Bri tells her.

"Doesn't it!" Katie replies.

"That's for the truly evil! *You're not!*" Bri states. "I saw your reaction to finding out Millicent was responsible for Emmie's and Natty's deaths. You were even wavering in your loyalty to her when you saw that execution video, *and* you were freaked out by what she did to poor Sara in front of us!"

"*That was* ice *cold!*" Katie whispers with a hint of disbelief.

"*It was!* And before all that, you were trying to convince yourself she wasn't going to kill me." Bri says.

In a barely audible whisper, she hears Katie say, "*I could've helped you escape!*" She scoffs at herself. "*Instead, I kept hold of the fantasy that she painted for me.*"

"Katie, you did side with evil. However, you're not pure evil, nor do you have to 'burn in hell for all eternity' for anything you have done." Bri tells her.

Katie looks at her, bewildered. "*Of course I do!*"

"No. You don't!" Bri has been cool, calm, and collected until now. Now she's firm. "Life is all about choices, but so it is on the other side! You choose whether you want accept forgiveness or not, Katie, but you don't get to choose whether you *are* forgiven. The Atonement, however, stretches wider and deeper than any finite thinking human can possibly comprehend. Will you have a price to pay? Yes, but you don't deserve Millicent's fate any more than she deserved her uncle's fate! *Please*, if our friendship ever meant anything, *promise me* you'll go into the light and let the light dictate your justice?" Katie's quiet, so Bri adds, "*Katherine Elizabeth Barnes!*"

Teary-eyed, Katie looks at Bri and weakly says, "*I promise.*"

531

Bri stands up to leave and Katie asks, "Are you here by yourself? Well, relatively by yourself?"

"Lawrence wouldn't have allowed me to come alone. David, Jack, and I are on our way to Newhaven and I had them wait outside." She gestures outside the door.

Katie goes quiet as she thinks. "Bri, I know I have no right to ask you this, and maybe you can't anyway because you're actually The Queen—." She holds her breath so she won't cry, and to summon the courage to make her request...

David, Jack, and Lawrence prepare for Katie to ask Bri to spare her life. David and Jack move to stand in the doorway with McMasters to be closer to help Bri navigate her request, if needed.

"Would you consider coming that day? I know I've hurt you the most and I completely understand if you don't want to...it's just, well, it'd be nice to have a friendly face be the last one I see." To Bri's surprise, Katie hugs her and struggles to say, *"Promise me you'll at least think about it?"*

Bri gives a faint, *"I promise I'll think about it."* She hugs Katie back for the last time. Then she steps back. "I really do wish things worked out differently."

Katie nods. "I know."

Bri gives a little wave as she turns to leave. Katie watches her walk out the door and her door closes. She goes back and sits down at her desk. However, instead of staring outside, Katie breaks down and cries hard...

Bri stands outside Katie's door and hears her start to cry. David and Jack go to hug her and she backs up, whispering, *"I have to walk through here looking strong and confident, like 'The Queen' needs to be."*

Jack holds her shoulders from behind and whispers next to her ear, "You've got this, Amore Mia." She gives him a faint, appreciative smile.

As The Governor walks up to them, David holds his hand out to Bri and she takes it; he interlaces their fingers, giving her hand a little squeeze. The Governor gives them a tour around the facility; it is a good distraction for Bri for a little while.

CHAPTER 70
Blackforth Women's Prison

David, Bri, Jack, and their security, along with prison guards and Ms. Camshaw, The Governor, walk around Blackforth Women's Correctional Facility for a while. They are about to pass one cell, when Bri sees a bassinet sitting on the bed. Curious, she stops in front of the cell.

A skin-and-bones young woman with stringy, reddish-purple shoulder-length hair that has yellow and orange streaks in it, looks over and sees Bri. She immediately stands up and gets defensive with her.

"*What are* you *staring at, Lady*?!" She snaps walking over to the cell door. Bri doesn't look away, but she sees people are about to intervene. She covertly gives McMasters and the others a 'stop' gesture. The woman adds, "Just keep your uppity nose in your own business!"

"*I was going to relate to*——."

"*You can't possibly relate to* anything *about me*!" The woman snaps.

"I was going to relate to you *as a mother*," the woman's head moves back a bit, "and wanting the best for our babies." The woman sees Bri's hand resting on her baby bump and backs down a little. "May I?" Bri gestures inside. The woman cautiously nods backing up and looking her up and down.

Ms. Camshaw has the door opened and Bri thanks them. She is about to step inside the cell, when one prison guard insists on being inside the room with them. McMasters stays in the doorway.

Bri walks in and talks as if it were just the two mothers. "How long do you have left in here?" She peers into the bassinet.

"About six weeks." The woman answers.

Bri smiles at the baby girl, who smiles back. "She's *three* months?"

"Um, yeah, er, almost four months." The woman replies.

534

"May I hold her?" Bri asks and the woman nods. "What's her name?" She asks as she picks up the baby.

"Margot. It means pearl."

Bri says to the woman as she looks at Margot, "That's a *beautiful* name for a *beautiful* baby!" Margot smiles wider. Bri looks at the woman and asks, "And your name?"

The woman puts her nose up a bit as she replies, "They call me Watchdog..." Bri raises her eyebrow and they see the woman's hardness soften a bit and she tells Bri, "Ruby Blanchard."

Bri smiles sweetly at her. "Your name makes me think of a Proverbs verse. I think it's in the third chapter..." 'Watchdog' would've stopped Bri from reciting it, but there is something about Bri that has Ruby *wanting* to hear it. Bri looks back down at the baby. "The verse goes something like, '*She is more precious than rubies and all things thou canst desire are not to be compared unto her.*'" Bri sees Ruby relax a bit more. "And this little one's name reminds me of 'The Kingdom of God' being compared to a priceless pearl' and this sweet baby should be treated as the precious pearl she is, to be given her best chance at wonderful life!"

Ruby starts to get defensive. "So you know The Bible and you've come to *save my soul*, have you? You're a bit late lady!"

"Oh, no, *I* can't save your soul!" Bri quickly replies, which surprises Ruby. "The only person who can save your soul is you, *through Christ*." Bri smiles kindly and talks softly. "I'm not a clergy, nor a biblical scholar. I'm an avid reader and have various things come to my mind at random times. I'm sorry if I offended—."

"*Nah.* Don't worry about it." Ruby tells her. "Say," she looks hard at Bri, "you look *real* familiar, but your accent...*American?*"

"Oh, my apologies! Where are my manners? Yes, I moved here from the US. For now, *while we're in here*," Bri motions the cell, "it's just Bri." Bri offers her hand to shake.

"Nice to meet you." Ruby says with a hint of hesitation, but she does shake Bri's hand in return.

"Ruby—. May I call you Ruby?"

"Please!" Ruby quickly replies. "I don't like that Ms. Blanchard stuff!" She turns up her nose. "It makes me feel like my mum, or my grandmother, are here." Her body shakes a bit.

"Ruby, could I ask you some personal questions about prison in general?"

"Sure!" Ruby replies, then pulls back when she glances at Ms. Camshaw. "Well, the best I can..."

Bri assures her, "These are not probing questions to try to get you to talk badly about the facility." She holds up her right hand and says looking at Ruby and Ms. Camshaw, "I promise!" Ms. Camshaw gives her a slight nod.

"Unfortunately, I don't have the time today, but I really want to talk with you some more. I feel you would be a great resource for me because I have a sneaking suspicion, you will tell me the unvarnished truth on pretty much anything." Bri winks.

Ruby chuckles a little. "Yeah, that's probably true!" The others are lightly laughing, too.

"I can only promise I'll be back in about a month, before you're released, to talk with you some more; perhaps sooner, if my assistant can work some magic with my schedule." Bri explains and Ruby nods. "When I leave here, you'll figure out why I look familiar, but I need you to promise me that when we discuss your views on various things, you'll be candid with me. I need you to be honest with me, and I can promise I'll be honest with you."

"I promise." Ruby agrees.

"I do need to get going." Bri reaches out her hand. "Thank you so much for your time and I really do look forward to seeing you again."

"Likewise." Ruby says and shakes Bri's hand again, only she holds it a little longer to challenge Bri's promise. "Prove your honesty! *Who are you?*" She respectfully lets Bri's hand go.

Bri looks at Margot still sleeping and lays her in her bassinet. She steps back and turns back to Ruby. "*Formally*, people refer to me as 'The Queen.'"

Ruby's mouth drops, then she swears under her breath. "My apologizes, Your—."

"Nnnope!" Bri purposely interrupts. "I haven't left yet, so it's still Bri." Bri winks with a mischievous little smile.

This is the moment Ruby knows she really likes this woman! They wave at each other before Bri steps out of Ruby's cell and everyone leaves.

Bri asks Ms. Camshaw, "How many mothers are able to have their babies with them?"

"Currently, only three." Ms. Camshaw tells her. "We have a pregnant inmate who'll be delivering any day now, then we will have four."

"How long are they able to keep the baby with them at the prison?"

"We feel it's good for the babies, *and the mothers*, if they're able to spend these first few months with them." Ms. Camshaw explains, trying to convince The Queen it's a good program. "We've had a reduction in the recidivism of these mothers—."

"Governor," Bri respectfully interrupts, "that was just an informational question. I'm not here to judge the operation of this prison. Even if I were to come back for an official tour, it would be to gather information to improve things across the board for prisons in general. We can also discuss what we can help you with for improvements." She sees Ms. Camshaw relax. "I think having the babies with their mothers for even several weeks, would be a great start to both the babies and the mothers, but I'm wondering if the first year would be better?" Ms. Camshaw agrees. "That is something I would like to talk about more in the near future, to see if maybe it should go on a list of programs to offer women in prison across the country." Bri gets an idea for the four mothers already here. She puts up her finger and asks, "One moment, please."

> Bri quickly texts Gabriel: "Would you have four soft blankets like Jacks' delivered to the prison as soon as possible; preferably before lunch is over?"

Gabriel: Sends a 'thumbs up.'

Bri and Ms. Camshaw, along with David, Jack, McMasters, and the guards, wrap up their tour with Ms. Camshaw. Jack had set up lunch to be delivered to the prison, with Gabriel's help, and everyone is excited to join The Queen, The Grand Duke, and The Duke, for their lunch break.

During this time, Gabriel personally delivers the blankets she requested and he is asked to stay and join them for the rest of the lunch break. Bri signs three of the four cards:

'*A gift for your sweet baby.* ~ HM Queen BriaLynn'

For the woman who is still pregnant, she asks if that baby blanket be given at the birth of her baby. Ms. Camshaw says she will see to it; Bri thanks her.

For Ruby's card, Bri writes a bit more of a message. Then she, Gabriel, Ms. Camshaw, and a female guard, folded up the four blankets and put them into gift bags with the small cards partially tucked into the folds of the blanket. Gabriel and the female guard delivered the gifts to the mothers.

Gabriel personally delivers Ruby her gift. Ruby is confused until Gabriel says, "From Her Majesty The Queen."

Ruby smiles thinking of her new friend. "Thank you." She takes the gift.

Gabriel sees Ruby sit down on the bed next to the bassinet, before he leaves with the guard. When Ruby pulls out the blanket from the gift bag, the card falls to the floor. She feels the softness of the baby blanket, then picks up the card and opens it. It reads:

> "*I hope Margot enjoys snuggle-time as much as Jacks does with his blanket! During those snuggle-times, I want you to think about this: Enjoy this baby time, and these tender moments! Forget where you are and be in the moment with them, because those moments will be gone all too soon! Be patient with yourself. We want our children to grow into their own persons, and we want them to be better than we ever were; yet, somehow, they will also be the very best of us we will give to the world!*

I think you have something very special in you, Ruby-gem, and I look forward to talking with you again very soon! ~ Bri"

Ruby has a faint smile on her face as she puts the card back in its envelope. No one has ever said she was special, and here a stranger is telling her she thinks she has something special...She looks at Margot and puts the soft blanket in the bassinet with her. She hears the baby take a deep, relaxing breath, and Ruby smiles at how content she is.

Margot looks at the card in her hand, then goes and sits at her desk table. If it were anyone else, she probably would've torn up the card and threw it away, perhaps even flushing the pieces down the toilet. However, this time she tucks the card inside her journal, in the pocket inside the front cover. She opens up the journal and writes today's date at the top. She begins the entry with: "*I had a surprise visitor today, and if it would've happened to anyone else, I would've thought they were delusional.*"

David, Jack, and Bri thank The Governor and her staff for a wonderful tour and a lovely lunch. Then they are all escorted to the employee entrance where they shake hands and say goodbye for now. They climb into the SUV and leave the prison gates, meeting up with the rest of their motorcade just down the road. They make their way to Bri's helicopter that is waiting nearby to fly them to Newhaven.

CHAPTER 71
A Difficult Decision to Make

They land in Newhaven, on the helipad at The Worthington Estate. The flight was pretty quiet as Bri thought about what happened at the prison. She insists David and Jack go to work; she needed more time to process...to think about Katie's request. Only she doesn't want to think about it anymore right now, so she tries to focus on work.

The Newhaven Wool and Textile Mill are doing *very* well. The product is priced to be affordable for the average middle-class person, and sales have been consistently going up. Jack has been busy running the everyday operations, while Amy and Maggie were doing an amazing job, and now Amy continues that wonderful work.

As The Grand Duchess of Newhaven, Bri has been wanting to travel to all the districts again and meet with the sheriffs who are the judges of lesser crimes, and the territorial law enforcement offices, to discuss their thoughts and concerns on how things are going. She wants to do this before she gets 'too pregnant.' Gabriel will arrange all of that for her.

Since she can't even focus on what to work on, Bri decides to go for a walk. She soon finds herself inside The Stables, waiting for Artemis to come inside when he senses she is there. Luckily, she doesn't have to wait long. He is always gentle with her, but he seems to know she is pregnant and is extra sweet with her.

"Would you like one of us to get him ready for you to ride, Your Majesty?" Bri hears someone walking up behind her ask.

Bri smiles at Artemis. "What do you think, Handsome? Should we stretch your legs a bit?" He nods.

While Bri helps brush Artemis out, a couple of the staff help her. They put a horse blanket on him, then his saddle, and Bri puts his bridle on him. She leads him just outside the back doors of the stables. Artemis kneels for Bri to climb on and he carefully stands back up with her. When he feels her give him a little kick he starts walking fast and increases his speed until he is running so fast, she feels like she is flying through the air! She tips her head up, towards the sun, and soaks in the light. She doesn't worry about where

540

Artemis is going; he usually takes her to the same place he has taken her to since their first ride together.

Bri doesn't realize it's getting dark, until the sun has set. She turns Artemis around and they make their way back to the stables at a gallop. She sees David standing at the back doors of The Stables with his phone up to his ear, then he hangs up.

When they are close to The Stables, Artemis slows down. Artemis kneeled down and she easily slides right off.

Bri apologizes to David, "I'm sorry if I worried you! I didn't mean to be out there this long."

"Well, when we didn't find you at any of the typical places, and found your phone in your office, I wondered if this is where you ended up. The staff said you had been gone awhile, even for you." He places his hand on her back and takes Artemis' reins; they walk Artemis inside.

Before she leaves, she turns to Artemis and puts her forehead to his. "Thank you for the ride, Handsome..." She looks at him, "Be good, alright?" She kisses his nose.

Bri steps back and lets the staff take care of Artemis. She turns to David and takes his hand; he laces their fingers together. They walk back to The Manor and David restrains himself from asking any questions. At the dinner table, Bri braces herself for questions that never come.

After dinner, she realizes neither David, nor Jack, said anything about Katie's request. Jack and David felt it is Bri's place to tell them. That night, Bri is ready for bed and comes out into the living room of her quarters with David and sees David and Jack are patiently waiting for her.

"I didn't know you were staying over Amore Mio." She goes and sits in her overstuffed chair.

"I may still head home, but David and I wanted to see how you're doing and if you want to talk." Jack replies. "Herst got your texts earlier this afternoon that you are still taking in the conversation, but he wants to talk, too. Maybe we can do a videoconference call with him?"

She shrugs. "You guys were there, and Lawrence was listening on the phone, there's not a lot for me to say."

David holds up his phone, ready with Lawrence's number. "I'm going to videocall him and have him join us..." She has a faint bit of reluctance as she nods. David quickly brings Lawrence into the conversation.

She asks, "When did you guys get outside the cell door?"

"When she was regretting any number of times she could've made a different choice that would've changed the course of her life." David answers.

"I ponder on that, and what Lawrence said to me; that he didn't think she was evil, just so green with envy the color *looked* black..."

"That's true." David says. "Now, I love Amy and I wouldn't change her being our sister-in-law; I merely point out Katie could've been married to James right now, had she not been jealous that Jack also had feelings for you!"

"You're right." Bri says. "I guess I was only allowed to have one man show interest in me and love me. All the other men were to only want her."

There is a long silence between them before Lawrence says, "Alright, I'll bring up the elephant in the room—."

"*No.*" Bri cuts him off. "I'm not ready. Go to bed everyone!"

"Bri—." Jack tries.

"No! Now drop this, or Jack will be staying here and *I'll* go The Cottage House *alone.*" She folds her arms, *trying* to look mad. While David and Jack see she is upset, and Lawrence can hear it, the three of them know she is scared; she just hasn't recognized it in herself yet.

"Alright, we'll call it a night, Darling." Lawrence says to keep it all peaceful for her. "I love you and try to get some sleep."

"*I'm sorry, Lawrence...*" She barely whispers, but he does hear her.

"No, *I'm sorry*. We're pushing you and if you need time, we need to respect that." He says with regret in his tone.

"Thank you." She says. "I love you, Lawrence. Goodnight."

"I love you, too. Goodnight and goodnight, Brothers." He says to them. They say it back and David ends the video–call.

David says to Bri, "I'm sorry, too, Love."

"So am I, Amore Mia." Jack adds.

"Thank you and I love you both, too. I'm really tired and I hope sleeping on it helps." She tells them. David goes and gets ready for bed, while Bri and Jack have a moment. "I love you, Amore Mio!"

"I love you, Amore Mia!" He kisses her sweetly. "Goodnight." Jack hugs her firmly before he leaves for The Cottage.

The three guys are worried for her, because Katie's execution date will be here quicker than Bri may be ready for. They may need to talk to Henry, to have his help in figuring out a way to help her get ready, *if that is even possible...*

The next couple of days, the guys text each other that they will wait until Lawrence is at The Manor before they try talking to Bri again, unless she initiates a conversation beforehand. She doesn't. Bri keeps herself busy and travels to the various districts on the island and talks with the sheriffs who are the judges for the less serious offenses. It is important for her to have this feedback to know how to best move forward.

The day Lawrence is scheduled to arrive, he asks them if they would have a little later lunch and they agree. That morning, Bri and Jack went out to The Newhaven Textile Mill and The Newhaven Housing Complex. They meet with The Mill's senior staff and discuss how production is going. Bri feels a new sample and she is amazed at how soft it is!

"Mr. McPherson, you *all* have outdone yourselves! *This has to be the softest one yet!*" She feels it with her fingers.

He happily says, "Thank you, Your Majesty!" He hands her a roughly wrapped package and points to all the employees looking up as they look down from the catwalk above. She smiles and takes the package. "We wanted you to once again have the very first product *your* mill produced this season. Think of it as a tradition!"

"*Our* Mill," she motions everyone, "Mr. McPherson." She winks at him with a smile and he smiles back. She opens the package to find her tartan colors in a scarf and it's *astonishingly* soft. "*This is absolutely wonderful, everyone!*"

He laughs. "We accidentally added less oil of one, and more of another. We were about to scrap it and start over, but His Grace thought we should let it finish and see what happens. Well, it actually turned out to be a much better product!!"

"A happy accident!" Jack adds.

Bri laughs. "Thank you all for this! *And* helping to make this business a *tremendous success* for Newhaven!" There is cheering with their applause. "You're all amazing people!" She drapes the scarf to hang on her neck.

When they finish there, they meet with the local police who run The Newhaven Housing Complex. They are preparing to hire more staff when the second stage is completed. The building is huge and work has been done in stages. The first stage is the structural stage and funded by The Royal Historical Society. All historical buildings in the UK are structurally taken care of by The Royal Historical Society.

After they wrap up there, they get into the car and the motorcade takes them to The Manor to have lunch with everyone, including Lawrence. Inside The Manor, Jack helps her take off her coat.

"I know I've said this before, but it needs to be said again," he tells her, "you keep getting more and more incredibly brilliant, and gorgeously beautiful!"

"Funny. I don't feel like it." She replies. He kisses her sweetly. She is about to take a step towards The Dining Room, but she hesitates...

"What's wrong?" Jack asks.

She turns her head to the side and asks, "You three, and the family, are going to ambush me about Katie, aren't you?" She looks at the floor, waiting for his response.

"I wouldn't call it ambush, Bri. We just want to help you with this."

She quietly, but sternly asks, "*How?* What could any of you say, or do, to make this easier?!"

"Not easier, but maybe a *little* bearable, so you won't regret whatever your decision is." He replies.

"*How?*"

"Can you honestly say you would regret going?" He asks, then he hears her hold her breath.

Lawrence and David walk out of The Dining Room and over to where Bri and Jack are. Bri hugs and kisses them.

"Everything alright?" Lawrence asks, cupping her face.

Jack answers. "She asked if we were going to ambush her about Katie when she went into The Dining Room."

"I'm sorry if that's what it feels like, Darling." Lawrence says.

"We're all sorry, Love." David adds. "It's just, well, there isn't a lot of time left and we just want to help."

They see the tears in her eyes and she quickly wipes them away. When she walks into The Dining Room, they leave it alone for now to have a nice lunch.

After lunch, Lawrence walks with Jack and Bri through The Sitting Room to the back door. Lawrence turns to Bri. "Thank you for suggesting I spend some time here, in between our time together."

"You're welcome." She smiles. "*Aaand* I feel more content having all three of you with me on The Estate, too."

He smiles as he pulls her in for a kiss. They wave as she and Jack leave through the back door to go over to The Cottage House.

CHAPTER 72
Decision Time

On the morning of Katie's execution day, which will be that night, Bri chooses to wear black all day, even though she decided not to go to the execution. She just couldn't bear watching another person die. Talking with Henry about how she felt, she would scold herself for being selfish, because she had 'insider information' that could help Katie leave this world with a bit of peace. She did it for Millicent, so why not Katie?

That evening, Bri and Lawrence are on their way to London in The Royal Helicopter. Lawrence leaves Bri to her thoughts, knowing she is thinking about Katie's execution. When the helicopter descends to land, Bri looks out the window and sees they are not landing at The Palace, nor Ashbourne Castle. She looks around, but see doesn't see anything to help her figure out their location.

She looks at Lawrence with her eyebrows furrowed. *"Where are we?"*

Lawrence shifts to face her better. "Darling, we didn't want to push you, or make you feel more torn than you already were—."

Bri shakes her head and tears flow, as she realizes where he brought her. "I c-can't. I can't watch someone, especially someone who I once thought was my best *fffri*—." She starts to cry. *"Please*, don't make me do this!" She sounds desperate when she adds, *"Don't make me watch another person die!"*

He hugs her close. "This isn't to *make* you watch her execution!"

"It's not?" She squeaks. *"Then what's this for?!"*

He gives her a compassionate look. "We thought you might want to talk with her one last time." He holds her cheek. "Regardless of everything she has done, she *does* seem remorseful."

She nods, thinking about that. "She was resigned to her fate. I am, too," she shakes her head, *"but not to witness her execution!"*

547

"How about we start with just going in to see her? I think Katie would appreciate that." He wipes her tears with his thumbs and she reluctantly nods. After handing her a tissue, he gets out of the helicopter. He turns to her and holds his hand out to her asking, "Shall we?" She takes his hand and she steps off the helicopter.

Bri looks, then looks again. "*Henry?*"

He has a fatherly look on his face. "We all thought it might be a good idea if I joined you, and maybe *we* could help Katie find some peace tonight?"

"Thank you for coming with me!" She hugs him tight.

549